The author is a senior scholar of Peterhouse and graduated from Cambridge University with a first class degree in English. He went on to study law, specialising in commercial litigation, and applied his creative skills in legal practice for his many grateful clients prior to taking up fiction. His cases are in the law books and on the syllabus. He is now Senior Partner Litigation for worldwide law firm Ince.

He lives in London and Cadaqués in Spanish Catalonia.

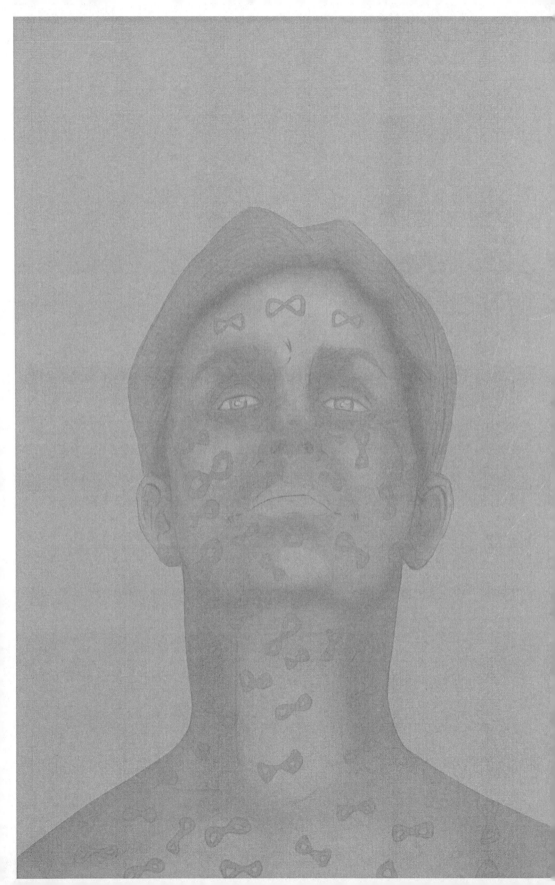

INFINITI

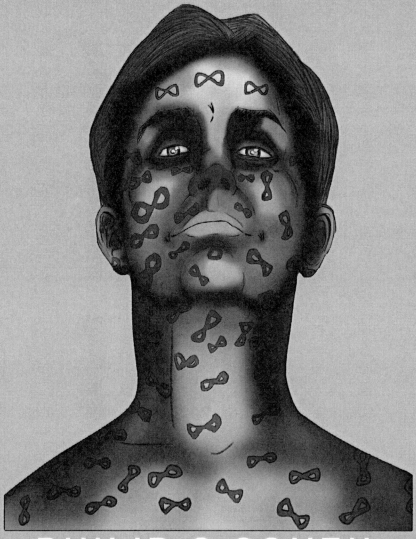

PHILIP G COHEN

AUSTIN MACAULEY PUBLISHERS™
LONDON • CAMBRIDGE • NEW YORK • SHARJAH

Copyright © Philip G Cohen 2022

A CIP catalogue record for this title is available from the British Library.

ISBN 9781398443167 (Paperback)
ISBN 9781398443174 (Hardback)
ISBN 9781398443198 (ePub e-book)
ISBN 9781398443181 (Audiobook)

www.austinmacauley.com

First Published 2022
Austin Macauley Publishers Ltd®
1 Canada Square
Canary Wharf
London
E14 5AA

To Letitia.

Thanks to my editors, Jack Pine and Justine Cohen.
If I'd had longer, it would have been shorter.
Thanks to Amy Rose Tyler for creating the Flicker Book.

Table of Contents

I saw Eternity the other night
Like a great ring of pure and endless light
All calm, as it was bright;
And round beneath it Time, in hours,
days, years
Driven by the spheres,
Like a vast shadow moved, in which
the world
And all her train were hurled.

The World, by Henry Vaughan

BOOK ONE
THE SPINNING BALLERINA

The Imprisoned Ballerina – 1959

The first girl I fell in love with was 1½" tall.

The year is 1959. In those days, it was just becoming fashionable to have your own supply of booze in the house, instead of going out to the pub. So you made a small temple in your home to the demon alcohol. In much the same way as the Trojans welcomed the Horse. In the corner of our lounge, my dad had a piece of furniture known as the bar, clad in oxblood leather with upholstered buttons sewn on it, where we were not allowed.

And on the horseshoe-shaped bar, there were many ornamental bottles. It was a way of domesticating the feral beast. One tamed alcohol by enclosing it within transparent containers of all shapes and sizes. My father had a pair of glass duelling pistols charged with honey-hued rum; a clear crystal skull of diaphanous vodka; a semi-pellucid Bolskummel elephant who dispensed gin from his trunk; a mango-sized transparent strawberry replete with unknown red liquid, resembling a giant haemorrhoid bleeding out on the counter.

There was stuff that was viscous; stuff with a meniscus; but pride of place, the apple of my eye, the object of my nascent eroticism, was the Bols Ballerina. A clockwork mechanism in the base of the bell-shaped bottle contained a music box. To the strains of *The Blue Danube*, the tiny red-headed dancer in her white tutu and gold halter top, pirouetted with one arm to her side, the other aloft, and she opened and shut her legs tapering into their minute satin-shod feet in a manner I found inexplicably suggestive.

She is the prisoner. But I am the one that is captivated.

On the label around the base of the bottle, it said *Bols Liqueur*, and there was an image of a censorious-looking old man in a red hat, like Santa Claus, but adversely judgmental.

To this day, if I hear the strains of *The Blue Danube*, I get a hard-on.

She spins within an upended glass, trapped beneath the specific gravity of some golden liqueur, on the stage of her clockwork mechanism, and she dances for my pleasure under the weight of countless atmospheres. She is a captive. She is a specimen. She is collectable.

No matter how well you tame the demon alcohol, how closely you confine it in pretty containers, how firmly you screw in the lid or hammer down the stopper, sooner or later, the bung has to come out.

I tried to free her by removing the cork and drinking the foul tasting liquid until I puked up. But she remained imprisoned beneath the glass that was somehow fused to the infernal clockwork mechanism beneath it. All the time, mocking my efforts with that infantile Viennese waltz music.

It was an absurd idea: to imagine that the only way I could dispose of it was to conceal it inside myself by consuming it. The conceit of the all-consuming passion that destroys its subject and its object together.

The story I have to tell you is another such outpouring. I scratch my skin and the characters fall off. I scoop them up in printer's galleys, rearrange them and offer them up for your delectation. The spontaneous expulsion of this infestation of letters that is in occupation of my cranium. Like a colony.

When my dad came home, he beat the daylights out of me.

I think I must be the only person in the world who has ever drunk the disgusting contents of the Bols Ballerina bottle.

You're probably wondering what my mum was doing all this time. She was dancing inside the bottle.

The Silver Bell

When I was little, growing up in Stonegate, Yorkshire, I used to be sick a lot and off school. My mum looked after me with Lucozade and mashed up bananas in milk with cinnamon and sometimes poor Knight's Fritters. She had a little sterling silver bell with numbers in square frames at the bottom that I know now to be a hallmark. The bell was a tiny ballerina. The waist of the bell was the ballerina's dress; the headstock of the bell was the ballerina's head and the crown was the ballerina's torso.

Her satin-shod feet were the clappers. My mum left the silver bell by my bedside so that when I needed her, I would tinkle the little bell, and she would come running up the stairs with my medicine or my food, or to read me a story before I fell asleep. And often the story was *Peter Pan*, and I thought of the silver bell as my Tinkerbell, and I found her enchanting and stole glimpses up her skirt at her silver legs before I rang for my mum.

Sometimes, instead of *Peter Pan*, my mum would recite a poem to me, but I didn't know what it was called or who it was by. But she would light a nightlight, place the little silver ballerina bell on my bedside table in case I needed her in the night, and stroke my forehead as she read it to me:

The sun descending in the west
The evening star does shine
The birds are silent in their nest
And I must seek for mine
The moon like a flower
In heaven's high bower
With silent delight
Sits and smiles on the night...

One night I was feeling really sick. I rang my bell and I rang it again and again and again, but no-one came. That was how I learned I didn't have a mum anymore.

Brooke Bond Tea - 1960

Because my dad was out at work travelling all week, I was pretty much brought up by my nan. I have my own egg cup with Peter Rabbit, and I have my own striped tea mug. My nan pours me a shot of piping hot Brooke Bond PG Tips Tea out of a proper tea pot with a silver strainer into my daily ration of milk; none of those tea bags that she says the vulgar people use. She calls it "milk and a dash", meaning it is 90% milk with a dash of sweetened tea.

After she has stirred it with the teaspoon, there are always bubbles on the top, spinning in the cyclone, and she calls them "money". She says "You're very rich today. You've got money in your cup! There's two and sixpence in your mug!" or "It's a good day for you. There's a florin in your tea!" That way each day seemed to start with great promise, and I associate things that rotate or spin with auguries of good fortune.

Then she upends the strainer on a plate and says she can tell my fortune from the random shapes the tea leaves form. She says she must have some gypsy blood in her. She predicts that I am going to go to Oxford and Cambridge and will make something of myself. I like the randomness of the tea leaves. But regular shapes, like stripy pyjamas or Venetian blinds, or wildlife programmes with zebras, make me feel queer.

Brooke Bond PG Tips was advertised and drunk by chimpanzees and if you were very lucky you would be taken to the zoo in Regents Park and see them doing it in real life. Guy the gorilla lives in London Zoo. But in Barcelona zoo, they have an albino gorilla named Snowflake.

I can't drink the stuff fast enough, because I am collecting the Brooke Bond tea cards. The first set I go for is British Wildlife, then Bird Portraits, next Fish of the Deep, followed by Tropical Birds and Wildlife in Danger. But my favourite (until I became addicted to superhero comics) is the collection of British Butterflies.

My nan gives me the sticker book and started me off by gluing down the first one with *Lepages*. *Lepages* is a foul smelling adhesive made out of melted down horse's hooves and pig's trotters, and to get the glue out, you have to turn the bottle upside down and bend back the rubber top until the pink slit in its lip parts and begins to ooze clear sticky resin onto the tea card. All too often, the slit doesn't open, because it has gone and stuck itself together. Then you have to peel off the dried gum Arabic with your fingernail and have another go.

I must fill up the book with British Butterflies. My favourite is the tortoiseshell butterfly. In my head it is somehow associated with the fragile girl in the bottle, but I won't know why for another fifteen years. I am single-minded of purpose. That's all I know, that I have to fill up the book. My earliest interaction with other children is swapping the cards to complete the series. This is also my first exposure to trading. That is how you make like-minded friends, of both sexes. Filling up the book transcended gender and class.

Reading books came later and turned my life upside down, because when I am presented with a book, my first instinct is to start filling it up, not read it.

I like swapping.

Flags of the World was not Brooke Bond tea cards. Flags of the World were in bubble-gum. At one point I had all of the flags in the entire world. But the world is a big place. Like a microbe, it keeps splitting and dividing, and more countries spring up and old ones cease to appear, or they change their flags. My collection of the Flags of the World is just a snapshot taken on a particular day when I filled up the sticker book, whereas most of the animals and the fish are still around, even if some of them are only now to be found in captivity. Like Snowflake.

Later on, there was Nine Flags. But Nine Flags was aftershave. Flags have had a significance in my life.

Then there was the Out Into Space series with Brooke Bond, and that kept me going until I became a Stan Lee groupie.

But the one card that eluded me was the *Scorpaena scrofa*, the large-scaled scorpionfish. I knew its name, because there was one empty space in my sticker book with the strapline, *Scorpaena scrofa*, beneath. Despite interaction with other kids and swapping and trading, I never managed to get the scorpion fish, which in France they call the *rascasse*.

That solitary absence rendered the rest of my Fish of the Deep sticker book worthless. There was an empty black hole where the scorpionfish should have been. All of the other parallel grids of the scrapbook looked meaningless whilst the empty, hollow dug-out eye socket of the space where the *Scorpaena scrofa* was supposed to be stuck, mocked me.

We have a huge illustrated Bible in embossed leather sealed with a padlock. The purpose of the padlock is unclear. Is it to keep fools away from this knowledge, or to fool people that the contents are more valuable than in fact they are? When you open it up, there is a page of *dramatis personae* where all the generations of the family through whose hands the book has passed, have entered their names and addresses in their best handwriting, as though it was a Visitor's Book and not a Holy Bible at all.

My nan read me a chapter every night and showed me the corresponding picture, and my favourite was the illustration of Jacob's Dream and the *Stairway to Heaven*; when he takes a stone for his pillow and sees the angels ascending and descending the ladder to God. Because of its sheer impossibility, it is an image that has stayed with me all my life. Often, when I close my eyes, I find myself there. In all my years, I've never read the Bible to myself, only looked at the pictures.

Maybe that's all the Holy Bible really is. A Visitor's Book. You come and you go in this life, and some of us seek to live on by writing down our comments. Maybe that's what I am doing now.

I remember my nan reciting to me the nursery rhyme, *Hickory-dickory dock, the Mouse ran up the clock*. She used it as a kind of countdown until I was fast asleep, and as she whispered it in my ear, she would stroke my forehead and then give my hair a final rustle before she slipped out of my room.

When I am sick, she puts her cool hand on my brow to take my temperature: "You're burning up in there, Nick," she would say. "You're all on fire!"

My nan gives me an empty cotton bobbin. I thread it with a rubber band and attach a matchstick to either end. Then I wind the rubber band round and round with one of the matchsticks until it won't go round any more, and set it on the floor. Off the spinning cylinder scurries like a little locomotive mouse. Who would have dreamt you could assemble a mechanical toy from such basic ingredients?

When the button comes off my shorts, nan produces another cotton bobbin from her sewing kit, but this time wound around with silky thread. Taking a needle in her hand, she says: "Nick, stick your label out!" Out pops my little tongue, and she offers the end of the cotton to it as though it were a firework's touch paper. Then she sharpens the moistened fibre between finger and thumb until it is sufficiently refined to pass through the eye of her needle.

As we get into the Christmas holidays, my nan takes me to the West

End where we view the lights in Regent Street and Oxford Street and the Christmas windows. In those days, there was no question of us ever aspiring to afford any of the things in the windows: they were for looking at; philanthropic artistic displays provided by the store owner: scenes from the Nutcracker, or Grimms, or the Bible.

Preparing for Christmas, from about October we start saving up all the coloured foil tops from the milk bottles. Then we pierce holes in their middles and poke thread through with a needle. We hang them up over the paraffin heater and watch them spinning, spinning and casting their shimmering metallic shadows on the walls. And they make a sound, like the singing of angels, as they revolve. The memory of oscillating light that thrills me and gives me a headache at the same time; the smell of the paraffin heater.

Nan has a recording of the King's College choir from Cambridge and she loves to put it on the gramophone, but only from Christmas Eve through to twelfth night. I pick up her record. It's in a brown paper bag with a round hole cut in the middle through which you can read the label. It says: *Miserere Mei Deus*. Have mercy on me, oh my God; remove my transgressions. The album art on the sleeve is a photograph of the vaulting arches of King's College Chapel with the choristers with their O-shaped open mouths gathered in the foreground in their red and white surplices.

On Boxing Day, we dismantle the decorations and count them up to see if we have enough to buy a guide dog for the blind.

One Boxing Day, we went to the Chiswick Empire to see the pantomime of *Peter Pan*. Tinkerbell reminded me of my little ballerina, and when we had to clap if we believed in fairies, I clapped and clapped until I had pins and needles in my hands, and together in a collaborative act, we brought her back to life.

A Visit to the Doctor - 1961

1961 was a special year. Because whatever you did to it, it was the same. You could write it upside down or back to front, but it was still 1961. I feel I need symmetry and consistency in my life, so this endless loop of 1961 seemed like a whole year full of promise to me. The discipline of circularity. Infinite promise. The strapline on my Beano magazine had 1961 written both ways up the same. The newspaperman brought the Beano every week, and I glanced at the cover.

But on my walk back from school, I took a one and a half mile detour to Putney where the newsagent sold AC/DC and Marvel Comics. I wrapped them inside the covers of the Beano, as my father regarded pulp fiction as "disgusting crap that was used as ballast on the steamers from the United States of America if the ship's cargo didn't bring it down to the Plimsoll line."

Apparently, they would just keep filling the boat up with pulp fiction until it sat properly in the sea. If they didn't put the right amount of comics in, the boat would topple over sideways. In that sense, superhero comics were a great leveller.

The Rainy Day Book for Boys had lots of terrific things in it. It had pages of optical illusions, such as two parallel lines that looked of different lengths but were really equal. All you had to do was stare at them for long enough and they became the same, as though there were two things happening here: the first thing was what you saw when you had your first casual glance at the lines; the second thing only revealed itself after you had stared harder and longer. They were both true and valid, a double time scheme.

Also, in *The Rainy Day Book* was a line drawing of a bird and parallel to that, a cage; and if you stared at it hard enough, it went fuzzy and the bird seemed to leave the page and end up in the cage. But I wanted to get the bird out of the cage. Like the ballerina.

Mind you, before this happened, for me, the whole room was spinning, because you had to stare at the bird and the birdcage with such intensity it gave you a head ache. It was like when the telly first started broadcasting; they recommended you took a break after 30 minutes, because no proper studies had been carried out, and they thought it might give you migraines, or cataracts. Or epilepsy.

The Rainy Day Book for Boys also gave you the recipe for invisible ink. Obviously many boys wanted to be able to communicate in encrypted format, not necessarily with girls, as we were still too young; but with other members of our secret gangs, giving instructions, meeting places, rendezvous. You had to melt sugar and lemon juice in water, suck it up into your fountain pen and write it on the paper.

The recipient had to heat the paper. If he managed not to set fire to it, he would catch a brief glimpse of the invisible ink as the dissolved sugar caramelised in brown typeface. If you get caught, you must eat your instructions. As they are written in sugar on rice paper, this is not too unpleasant. Certainly much better than the Jacobs Cream Cracker Cramming Competition. But we will come to that later.

My dad was always having to buy me new fountain pens as they got gunked up with sugar, resembling what we were doing to our bodies eating the stuff.

Later on, I learned that proper secret agents become diabetic and write their messages in wee. But if I got caught, I wouldn't want to swallow that.

These days, no-one even knows how to write a letter; no-one has a fountain pen. No-one would dream of mixing wee and invisible ink or heating up the notepaper to reveal its secrets. There simply isn't enough time. But where did the time all go? What did we do to it? There used to be enough time, but I cannot remember when this poverty set in.

Time and the bell have buried the day.

The Rainy Day Book for Boys also showed me how to build my first pinhole camera from a shoe box. The most difficult part was getting my hands on a shoe box. My dad wouldn't buy me a decent pair of shoes until my feet stopped growing because shoes were expensive. I wanted a pair of suede desert boots, but that was out of the question. When he took me to the Clark's shoe shop, there were posters with the two *Start Rite kids* beginning their long journey down an infinite road towards the point where the parallel lines meet.

They wore red hats. The man in the shop made you stand in a contraption like a jukebox and peer down at green X-Rays of the bones in your feet which enabled him to prescribe you precisely the correct fitting sandal whilst exposing your toes to highly carcinogenic levels of fluoroscopy. Alternatively, he could just have measured your feet with a tape measure, but we were suckers for any kind of gadget in those days. X-Rays existed only in superhero comics where their forces were marshalled by evil geniuses, and in the Clark's shoe shop, which shared its name with Superman's alter ego.

I went through all of this to get my hands on the shoe box. I managed to take a few snaps with it, but then my dad took the box away, because he had to fill it with tins of corned beef and lychees and sardines for me to take to school on Harvest Day. On Harvest Day, everyone took their offerings in to the teacher and without exception, the unit of measurement for containing the offerings was the shoe box, and we would ruffle up some crêpe paper to make the boxes more artistic so that the manky tins of Spam or sardines and Shipham's fish paste were displayed to best advantage.

On ITV, the Shipham's advert features a prawn dancing to the tune of *The Blue Danube* and singing *Shipham's-for-tea, for-tea, for-tea.*

I would have been happy wearing plimsolls, but my dad said that would give me flat feet. He didn't like plimsolls or Plimsoll Lines, and seemed to live in fear that we were all going to get called up to the army again and be sent home for flat feet.

Better than *The Rainy Day Book for Boys* was the *Tuck-a-Bed-Tales*. Each of its 365 pages corresponded to a day of the year in consecutive order, so that, when you opened it up and smoothed down the first page, that was January 1st, and written on that page was the story that you should read your child at bedtime on January 1st, and on the next page was the story for January 2nd; and every story was unique and beautiful, and some had seasonal content so that, as you progressed through the year in bed time stories, the seasons were moving with you:—little touches like the snow coming in the wintertime stories, the calving, the lambs, the flowers in the spring: everything had its place and was in order.

When it was bedtime, I didn't throw tantrums or beg to stay up late. I wanted to go to bed, because I wanted to know the story. I wanted to hear my mum read me that night's tale. I wanted to fall asleep and continue the narrative within my dreams. Before I outgrew books in favour of comics, the most important book in my life was the *Tuck-a-Bed Tales*. Looking forward to bed time got me through the day, and the days became weeks, and the weeks months, until, looking forward to my Tuck-a-Bed-Tales, I completely outgrew them.

I loved the old bookshops of Stonegate.

After my mum passed away, my dad wouldn't read me the *Tuck-a-Bed Tales*. He said I was too old for them, but if I wanted to read them so badly, I could read them to myself. But that wasn't the same. The whole point of them was that wasn't the same. So that was when I started sneaking out, stealing money from where he emptied his trouser pockets on the bedside table before he put his pants in the Corby, and buying comics with the loose change filched from his trousers. Superhero comics. Comics that consisted almost entirely of illustrations.

She died on a Saturday. I always looked forward to Saturdays, but this was a break in the normal order of my days. She never read me the story for that Saturday. But, somehow or other, I will celebrate it. Saturday. Saturn's day from mythology. I will find the words to write it all down.

I have a red light beside my bed. I like the red glow. I take to reading my bootleg superhero comics by the red light in my bedroom when I am supposed to be asleep.

When break is over, the teacher comes to the back door leading to the playground, stands in the doorway at the top of the stairs and rings her bell. I feel profoundly sad; sad not just because playtime is over and we have to go back to work. No; the sadness is more consuming than that. It's to do with the finality of the bell. I prefer the road in the *Start Rite Kids*, because it goes on forever, parallel lines that never meet: a journey with no clear destination; a walk into the endless unknown.

The shoe box was my first camera. I have John Bull to thank for my second camera. In Hamley's toyshop window in Regent Street, I spotted the John Bull Printing Outfit. The box featured an image of Mr John Bull himself. He was black-booted with yellow socks rolled over their tops, white riding breeches, red waistcoat and blue tails capped by a black top hat as though he was on his way to the theatre. He was hiding a riding crop behind his back. He thinks I can't see it, but I can.

By his left boot was an annoyed-looking bulldog. Man and dog adorned the yellow background of a big box with a red and blue border, and the clunky lettering said**: JOHN BULL PRINTING OUTFIT, Manufactured in the British Isles**, and the kits had numbers from 6 to 18, although I didn't know what the numbers meant and thought they were for ages.

I had no clue why John Bull was making printing presses in the British Isles. The company manufactured rubber tyres. But the letterpress letters and numbers were made of grey rubber, so perhaps Mr Bull had found a use for the spare bits of rubber when his tyres didn't work out how he would have liked. He was manufacturing printing presses from offcuts of car tyres.

Christmas 1961, I finally became the proud owner of a John Bull Printing Outfit Made in the British Isles, after dropping copious hints in the approach to the festive season. Unfortunately, my nan's resources only stretched to a No 6, and it turned out that the number didn't signify the age group for the children for whom each model was intended. The number 6 meant there weren't enough rubber letters included. There was a full alphabet, and there were numbers, 1-10, and some punctuation marks even.

But you couldn't save up and buy more characters. The only way you could get additional letters was if you bought a bigger printing press, and that's what the bigger numbers going up to 18 meant. Bigger numbers meant more letters. A hard lesson for a young lad to learn. The law of the market. Acquiring a No 18 was out of the question.

The tiny rubber letters are back to front. Using the fiddly pair of tweezers in the box, you take the characters out of the bag and insert them between the lines in the grid of your printing galley, always the wrong way round, because it's like mirror-writing. The letters are very tricky to handle, and as soon as you've dipped in the bag and trapped a letter in the tiny tweezers, the letter pops out of its grip and bounces off into obscure places and down the backs of things, so that you have fewer letters than ever.

I wish John Bull had been a plumber instead of a tyre manufacturer, because then maybe he would have had left-over lead from his pipes and the lead characters would be like a real printing press and wouldn't bounce away. If you dropped them, you would be able to find them again with a magnet.

When you have finally managed to assemble your letters in your galley, you have to prise the lid off the little tin of India ink, dip your roller in and roll the ink evenly onto the rubber letters in the galley before sandwiching a slip of paper in and closing the printing press.

The first printing commission I gave myself was to print my Thank You cards for the Christmas presents with my John Bull printing press. However, this presented challenges as there weren't enough characters to compose a coherent note. It would be good if I could make labels with **THIS BOOK BELONGS TO NICK JOBS**. But there aren't enough letters for that. Next, still going right to left and back to front, I typeset **NICK JOBS**, which will have to do. You only got uppercase with the No 6, so everything was in capital letters. I stamped this imprimatur onto the squares of paper provided, and then reached for my *Lepages* and stuck the labels in the fronts of my books.

By the time I'd gotten to this stage, which was about halfway through Boxing Day, I'd pretty well exhausted the possibilities of my John Bull printing press. The tin of ink had dried up and most of the rubber letters had pinged off into the wilderness. This was an early lesson in frustration and how things don't always turn out alright, even if you've been longing for them. But I still had a good red, blue and yellow box, so I nailed a hole in it, and thus was born my second pin-hole camera. I graduated from printing letters to printing pictures. After all, one picture, as they say, is worth a thousand words.

It wasn't until I got my weekend job that I was able to save up enough money to buy myself a second-hand Kodak Brownie. And from that day, by day, I was photographer, Peter Parker. But in my head, at night, I was the Amazing Spiderman. In addition to reading Marvel superhero comics, I buy *Amateur Photographer* once a month, because there are always artistic shots of girls with their tops off known as Life Studies.

I probably studied them more devoutly than anything on the syllabus at school. Marching into WH Smiths and asking for a copy of *Amateur Photographer* is less embarrassing than creeping in furtively and asking for a copy of *Health & Efficiency*. Strange title for a girlie book; sounds more like it should be a Ministry. The Ministry of Health & Efficiency. W H Smith also sells records that you can listen to in the acoustic booths before you buy.

If my dad had known I was spending the money from his trousers on superhero comics and *Amateur Photographer*, he would have beat the smithereens out of me again. But one day, instead of beating the daylights out of me, he took me to the doctor's. He told the doctor about all the weird things I said and did, despite my performance at school being generally good.

There was an absence of specific symptoms, just a number of examples my dad wanted to unburden himself of; but he didn't know what they were examples of, which is why he took me to the doctor. "He doesn't measure up," was all he kept saying. "It doesn't make sense." Then the doctor asked my father to leave as he wanted to speak with me alone, which I thought was pretty grown up.

The doctor asked me if I'd like something to drink. "Milk and a dash, please," I said. The doctor didn't know what I was talking about, probably reinforcing my dad's opinion that I was a few slices short of a loaf, so he gave me some Robinson's orange barley instead.

When he called my dad back in, the doctor said: "His brain is good, but its wiring is bad. You'll find that from time to time he short circuits. You shouldn't punish him. It's neurological. He is mildly epileptic. The species is known as photosynthetic epilepsy. It's exacerbated by many of the things we encounter in modern life: straight edges, parallel lines; that sort of thing. Young Nick prefers softer, rounded objects. Maybe you should consider moving to the country. In ancient times what he's got was thought a gift. I could put him on medication for the rest of his life. But as I say, it's mild, and he should be able to control it. I've given him some mental exercises to do if he feels it coming on."

The doctor says I am a bit weedy for my age and I should drink Bovril to build me up. This makes it more difficult for me to complete my collection of tea cards; but I had pretty well moved on from tea cards and graduated to furtive sessions with Wonder Woman comics under the red light. Sometimes, if my nan is running short on the housekeeping, she substitutes a crumbled Oxo cube for the Bovril.

The Bovril advertisement shows a row of oxen, happily seated in what looks like a lady's hairdressers shop with their heads in big hairdryers and their legs crossed and their arms akimbo; because they are strapped to the chairs whilst they are electrocuted in the head. The man in the white coat is about to throw the switch, and the strapline says *Bovril by Electrocution*. The advertiser is seeking to sell the product by the humane way in which its ingredients are slaughtered. I preferred the Brooke Bond chimpanzees.

Sometimes, when the ballerina is dancing and the sunlight hits her bottle at the right angle, she sheds glittering reflections all around the room, and the light dances in amongst all the other coloured bottles of mysterious liquids. Then, it's as if, when she spins, the whole room spins with her, and my head is spinning too, until it fizzes and pops, and I find I've passed out again. But I like the sensation. I like the dancing lights, and the strange places I go to when I'm blacked out.

The cities I build in my head become more populated each time; their inhabitants more real, walking straight out of the pages of my head. The narrative is consecutive, so that each time I visit the city, I find I am resuming the story from where I left off last time. It's like I can step in and out of another world where other things are happening to me.

My dad didn't punish me anymore. Nor did we ever talk about my shaming condition again until the day I was due to leave for University. Then he held me by the wrist with bone-crushing force and with the energy remaining in him rasped out: "You have transgressed for the last time! Don't you ever try and have children or they'll be the same as you. Your name in the front of the big family Bible is the last name that will ever be written in there!"

When I won a scholarship to Cambridge, he was astonished that I had achieved this despite my disability. As his last words to me had been such a syntactical mishmash, it was appropriate I went up to read English.

BOOK TWO
THE SPINNING ROOM

A Grand Entrance - 1972

It's my first dinner at Peterhouse, Cambridge. All the other Cambridge colleges are qualified by the epithet, *College*, save for Peterhouse; because it was the first. When it was founded in 1372, there were no other colleges, so it was just named Peterhouse. The House of St Peter. I am staring at the image of the crossed keys on my dinner plate, the symbol of St Peter. If I was to have a symbol that defined me, it would have to be crossed wires. In my brain. A direct short between the headphones.

We kept term by dining in the Great Hall under the William Morris hangings. There were two sittings, one at 18.30 that was self-service and could be attended in jeans, and another at 20.00 where one was served by flunkies. You could still wear jeans, but you had to wear your gown on top, which made sense, because the waiters who provided the silver service had not entirely perfected their art.

Fearing that no-one might befriend me, I'd bought a local paper to keep me company. I pulled it out of my back pocket and unrolled it. The headline, above a photo of King's College chapel, said: **ANOTHER CHOIR BOY MISSING**. I scanned the photo of the lad gone astray and read on to learn that he was the tenth minor who had disappeared from the choir of King's College Chapel in the space of ten months. There was an interview with the choir master, some words of commiseration from the Dean, and an Inspector from the Cambridge constabulary confessed they had no leads but were concerned the boys were being trafficked into the sex trade. It seemed the juveniles were just evaporating.

I hadn't made any friends yet. I was pressed against the wall in the middle of the bench, the position most difficult for the waiters to reach. But I hadn't gone through all my life calling other people *Sir* to forfeit the chance to be called *Sir* myself by men twice my age as they ladled soup onto my gown, so I had opted for the 20.00 sitting.

A stout lad whose name I subsequently learned was Spud Mullins, sporting outsized spectacles and a Steppenwolf T-shirt under his gown, was seated to my left. The space to my right was empty, and I presumed would remain conspicuously so to my embarrassment, as no-one could get in now that I was landlocked on the wall side of the bench. There was a fluted tumbler beside my hand for water and a smaller glass, presumably for wine. I poured some water into my tumbler for something to do with my hands whilst waiting for the food to arrive, and then became aware of a ghostly presence from within the water jug. The candelabra had projected the appearance of a gowned figure in the liquid, the phenomenon known in theatrical circles as Pepper's Ghost.

I looked up to see what was casting this eerie reflection, or if it was my crossed wires shorting the neurons in my head again. I was astonished by the incongruity: a tall figure was standing on the venerable table, regardless of both the antiquity of this item of furniture, the food, drink and flaming firebrands placed thereon, as well as basic rules of hygiene. He sported bellbottomed bottle green denim trousers, the type called loons where the fly was replaced by a buttoned square flap of material like sailors wore.

He was dressed in a green velvet smoking jacket beneath his gown with a red and white spotted snuff handkerchief spilling from its monogrammed top pocket, the monogram indicating that his initials were SS, emblazoned upon the background of some spurious heraldic badge; and he had a dashing cravat around his neck, something I had only ever seen in old Terry Thomas and David Niven films.

I believe in the movies, cravats were generally worn by cads, although, looking back on this manuscript so many years after I started writing it, I am buggered if I can even remember what a cad was. I think it was something that one ineffectual twit called another to impress an unworthy woman before losing a fight over her in a situation where she didn't deign to go to bed with either the winner or the loser afterwards. So a cad was the height of pointlessness, and cravats are what such creatures wore.

But I am getting ahead of myself.

We all had long hair in those days, but it was generally just our short hair grown longer, an ungoverned, unshaped mop. The monogrammed visitor standing on the table had long black hair, but professionally dressed. From the front, a Shaolin goatee embellished his chin. At the back, his hair was shaped into a Chinese queue. He had a hand-rolled cigarette stashed behind his right ear. In his bell-bottomed trousers, he was dancing between the dangerous cutlery and the fragile plates strewn the length of the table, with precise balletic movements so as to negotiate the many obstacles in his path, his gown swishing behind him and miraculously not catching any of the lit candelabra planted on the tabletop.

At first, he reminded me a bit of Disney's *Zorro* on Saturday night TV starring Guy Williams. Then, glancing from the macrocosm of the man to the microcosm he cast in the water jug, he reminded me of my ballerina in the Bols bottle. The memory of many night-time paralyses brought on a tick in my temple. It was the malware in my head I mentioned earlier. The flickering candles were not doing my condition a lot of good, but nothing I figured a Marlboro Red couldn't sort out after.

Fresh out of the buttery, he was brandishing a bottle of red wine in one hand and white in the other, and he was headed for the one empty space, next to me.

He stepped down from the table onto the bench. He was wearing velvet monogrammed slippers featuring two diminutive versions of the same initials and coat of arms that were displayed on his jacket pocket. Having placed both velvet shod feet on the bench beside me, he then turned around 180 degrees, resembling a tightrope walker steadying himself with the two bottles, until he was facing the table with his back to the wall; he then slid down the wall and onto the bench next to me.

Looking over my shoulder at the headline, he said: "To paraphrase Wilde, to lose one choirboy may be regarded as a misfortune; to lose ten looks like choirlessness."

I rolled up the newspaper in embarrassment and stuffed it under my gown.

"Why drink water when you can drink wine?" He continued. Not waiting for an answer to that question, he proceeded to his next question. "Red or white?"

I said I would be delighted to toast him with a glass of red. "If you're going to toast me, dear boy," he said as he charged my glass. "I had better introduce myself: Sydney Syzygy."

I wanted to introduce myself, but I froze. My eyes raised upwards, and that twitch, almost imperceptible, ticked lightly upon my left eye.

"Ah!" Sighed my infinitely observant new friend, brandishing his bottles and then pointing to the large water glass beside the smaller wine glass on the table: "Grand or petit mal?"

The motion of moving sideways to fill my glass caused him to jostle Spud Mullins on his other side. Spud was offended, probably more because the wine wasn't raining down on him than for any other reason, so he complained: "No need to push!"

Sydney regarded Spud's Steppenwolf T-shirt and without a moment's hesitation said "*God damn the pusher man!*"

Hearing the lyrics of Hoyt Axton, Spud's saturninity, softened and he held out his right hand. Sydney wouldn't take it: "No, no, man," he said, "Glass. Every Good Boy Deserves Favour."

I was unclear whether he was referring to the title of the 7th Moody Blues album released that year, or to the mnemonic for the treble clef.

Spud proffered his glass and it was filled. "Are you of a musical disposition then?" Spud ventured.

"I am of a mnemonic disposition," replied Sydney. "Good Boys Do Fine Always."

I didn't get the joke about the pusher man, but I was still striving to manage all the blood emptying from the left hand chambers of my brain to the right. I had immediately visualised the EGBDF as a musical notation and the parallel staves were aggravating my condition.

Planting the white wine on the table so as to free up the fingers of one of his long and musician-like hands, he beamed: "Sydney Syzygy," and pumped his other compatriot by the palm, whilst replenishing the glass he had emptied in one gulp.

"Spud Mullins," said the other, clinking glasses with him. "May I see what we are drinking?"

Syzygy seemed to pause for a moment. Five seconds that seemed like twenty seconds, whilst his brain visibly computed that the information that the man was imparting was no more than his name. Or perhaps he was surprised that one would wish to introduce oneself by a nickname, least of all one so unflattering.

Sydney shoved the bottle of white in Spud's direction for him to peer at whilst not relinquishing his firm grip on the red.

Syzygy, in an act of generosity, had offered Spud Mullins a glass of his wine, and Mullins seemed to be in the process of checking out if it was decent stuff before accepting it. Although I no more knew Sydney than Mullins did, I could see us both coming to the same conclusion, namely that Mullins' ungracious request was the consequence of social ineptitude, not ingratitude. Sydney twisted the label around for Mullins' further consideration.

Guy rolls out of a pub and onto the street swigging brake fluid.
Man goes up to him and says. "You shouldn't drink that stuff. It will kill you."
Guy replies: "I can stop anytime."

I could tell that Sydney found it exceedingly strange that anyone in his right mind should be given the opportunity to make a new start in life at Cambridge, freed from one's mum and one's dad and all the paraphernalia of pet names that one had accumulated at nursery school, primary school and secondary school, but voluntarily choose to carry with him the spent baggage of his previous existence in the form of so unflattering a soubriquet. Why would anyone want to name himself after a potato, for God's sake?

Spud grasped the bottle of white and tried to read the label in the candlelight. In an affectation I later came to understand and love, he pushed his big spectacles up so that they were parked on his eyebrows, the better to study what was written on the bottle. I thought it curious that one who was clearly, judging from the size of his spectacles, in need of corrective lenses, should remove them as soon as he wanted to read.

As if to provide further assistance, our new friend, Spud Mullins, glanced away from the label and to Sydney on his right and added: "I'm from London and I'm reading engineering."

"I'm from London, and I'm reading engineering," repeated Sydney. "Sounds like the beginning of University Challenge. Well, Mr Mullins, here's your reward." And, completely ignoring Spud's pretentious attempts to justify his thirst for alcohol by first emoting on the label, Sydney left Spud contemplating the bottle of white, whilst splashing an indiscriminate shot of red into Spud's glass.

Mullins felt obliged to make a show of rolling the red around his fleshy gob before swallowing it, although, to tell the truth, he would have been just as happy drinking Domestos as long as it got him pissed. Wanting to say something sophisticated, after he had thoroughly rinsed his gums, Spud said: "Ah, the French for wine; the Germans for sausages!" And he swigged again.

"Well then," said Sydney, "Do you think that we should find ourselves some Germans and play "hide the sausage" with them?"

"No, no," spluttered Spud. "I was just referring to their…their…" and despairing of finding the correct German word, he resorted to the French: "Cuisine."

"Prolonged occupation," explained Sydney, "Has the most pronounced effects on a region's culinary development. Just look at what the Moors brought to the Spanish kitchen. Imagine how dreary mealtimes would be if the Hun had won the War. No more pasta and pizzas. No more *foi gras,* or *jamon bellota.* We'd all be eating sausages and sauerkraut."

Turning back to my side, I had mastered the tick. There would be no fit, but I had better take it easy with the wine. "Nick Jobs," I presented my right hand for shaking whilst raising the left, the one with the glass, to toast him.

"And where would you hail from, Mr Jobs?" asked Sydney.

"Stonegate in Yorkshire," I replied.

"Ah, home of the little red printer's Devil."

"You know him?" I queried.

"I know every little Devil in Europe!" exclaimed Sydney. Then he added, "Intimately."

"What are you reading, Sydney?" I asked.

He rinsed the red wine around his palette, swallowed and wiped his mouth on his snuff handkerchief before replying: "The dark arts, dear boy. The dark arts."

Sydney sloshed more wine and then toasted the two of us:

"A warm welcome both to Peterhouse!" he said.

It was the beginning of a lifetime's jealousy.

Litter

After supper, as I was exiting through the porter's gate into the dark Cambridge night, the Head Porter grasped me by the arm, stopping me short.

"Are you sure that's a good idea, sir?"

"What on earth are you talking about?" I asked him, shaking my arm free.

"The missing boys," he said in a conspiratorial whisper.

"Well, I didn't take them!" I exclaimed. The Head Porter lacked authority. That is what had caused him to lay his hands on me. His voice alone would have been insufficient.

He was referring to the latest chapter in the saga I had glanced at in the local paper before dinner. It seemed that choir boys from King's College chapel choir were disappearing at the rate of about one a month. The authorities didn't have any leads. No bodies had turned up. The fear was that they were being traded by European paedophiles, who swapped them as I used to swap bubble-gum cards.

"Can't be too careful, sir." The Head Porter informed me.

"I'm far too old to be of interest!" I announced as I made my way through the gate, determined to sample Cambridge's Green King in as many pubs as possible before time was called. I strode out onto the streets with a warm feeling in my stomach. Some of it was my dinner. Some of it was being called Sir by a man three times my age.

And, talk of the devil, after I'd left the Cricketers, I was ambling back across Parkers Piece when I stumbled upon two choir boys sharing an illicit smoke at Reality Checkpoint. They looked incongruous, decked out as they were in their red and white surplices, white shirts, black ties, but smoking a fag. Neither one could have been any older than twelve. I still had the local newspaper in my back pocket.

"That won't do your voices any good!" I quipped.

The one who had carriage of the fag stubbed it out guiltily, although there was more than half of it still to smoke. I realised that what had compelled them to stub it out was the air of authority I was projecting, especially as I was still wearing my gown from dinner. It appeared that I had that commodity that the Head Porter lacked: authority—the power to enforce obedience and have others look up to me and call me Sir.

The one who had stubbed out the cigarette was wearing winklepicker shoes protruding from the hem of his vestments.

"I didn't mean anything," I said, feeling bad that I had interrupted their enjoyment. "Go on! Have one of mine." I extended my packet of Guards in their direction. They ran away as fast as their little feet could carry them. They had obviously been told not to talk to any strange men. Good advice.

Am I a strange man? I wondered to myself. After due consideration, I was obliged to admit that the answer was probably in the affirmative.

I continued my post-prandial perambulation of Cambridge nightlife, still early enough to dive into a few bars but late enough to break the law. But one law it was difficult to break was the licensing law, and by 11.00 pm, at which point I had strayed as far as Midsummer Common, all the bars were closed, so I began drifting back towards my set at Peterhouse, cursing my lack of planning in having failed to lay down any bottles for such a time of need.

After taking my sojourn at three public houses and after sharing Sydney Syzygy's wine at dinner, I guess that in the great Periodic Table of Alertness, I was not at my most Lert. The rooftops of Cambridge's venerable architecture seemed more active than an anthill. I could sense sensation out of the corner of my eye; but each time I looked directly up in the direction of movement, it froze, as though one was playing a game of grandmother's footsteps with nocturnal steeplejacks or masked ninjas.

The streets of Cambridge are not friendly to walkers. At every turn an unlit cyclist seemed intent on spinning me arse over apex, and I was beset by the premonition that I would imminently be sent tumbling into a ditch.

Then, rounding the corner into Trumpington Street, I was indeed knocked into the gutter, but not by any vehicular apparatus. I was upended by some huge, black, pelted animal. And knocked into Hobson's gutter. So, although the night was dry, my cuffs and the hems of my jeans were moistened by Cambridge's unique conduit.

The dark animal came to a halt. Was it possible, I wondered, for a brute beast to feel remorse at having pitched me into the gutter? I had recovered my posture sufficiently to be genuflecting, and looking up in the gas backlighting, I watched as a curtain in the dark shape was pulled aside. It reminded me of the empty black hole where the scorpionfish should have been in my sticker book. But the swished-back curtain revealed an unglazed window opening.

The animal must have been wounded, judging from the hole opening up in its side. An overpowering aroma of patchouli with a high note of marijuana exhaled through the aperture; but the smell of the weed was tempered by some surgical, antiseptic odour that belonged in an embalmers. Perhaps the beast was pickled in formaldehyde. Perhaps it had been wounded beforehand, and someone had attempted to attend to its wounds with antiseptic, and the brute had simply crashed into me in its death throes.

But then a head poked out the window, inspecting the damage to my person. The visage was wreathed in curls of cannabis smoke, the leading edges of which were rendered more yellow by the gaslight. It looked as though his face was on fire, with flame that lights but does not consume. The tip of his shaolin goatee glowed with the molten incandescence of a hot poker. I sensed some recognition in those hooded eyes, but I was as yet unable to recognise anything myself, because of the density of the smoke particles, and also a mild concussion from my fall, not aided by the quantities of the demon alcohol I had consumed. Then the head spoke.

"Link boys! Set her down!" he barked. "Set her the fuck down!"

The soft beast seemed to lower itself into a crouching position, closer to my height. I realised that the beast with the window hole in its side was suspended between two long wooden poles carried by four porters. I couldn't get the thought out of my head that this was a dead animal in a box. Maybe it was being carried off to the vet in a stretcher.

"Howdah!" the voice said. Then: "Fuck it! So difficult to get decent pallbearers, Nick! These fucking chair boys don't know how to take a corner!" My brain was confusing the chair boys with the missing choir boys. But these boys were the same age as me. I tried to put everything in order in my head.

Sydney tugged his cravat loose with such determination one would have thought it intended to strangle him. "Look at that cunt! His torch isn't even aflame. Howdah! Shadwell! Light that fucking taper! You can't go careering around the streets of Cambridge at night with your lights out. No wonder the fucking porters keep crashing into things!"

Then under his breath for my benefit: "Imbecile!"

The torchboy called Shadwell was attempting to strike a match, but he couldn't get a proper grip on it. Match after match slipped from his grasp and fizzled out in Hobson's gutter.

"They're my Calypso's Lost Boys," the cussing head added. "Oh, dark, dark, dark! They all go into the fucking dark. Hey you in there! Lyca. Show yourself!"

And then I saw there was an auburn-haired female in the dark recess of the window beside him. Unsteadily, I rose to the level of the opening and its overpowering aroma. It dawned on me that I had just been run over by a sedan chair. The red-headed woman in the palanquin seemed concerned at my situation, but unable to see.

Nonetheless, the most exquisite arm, attached to a naked shoulder, extended from the window, with a smouldering joint in its hand, as though indicating a left turn for the litter. I hesitated; but then I saw in side elevation, the swell of her naked breast beyond the arm, and I was overcome with acceptance.

For my first time, I took the proffered joint, and sucked on it as though she had offered me her nipple, after which the cuts and bruises I had sustained numbed themselves into oblivion, and my mind began making the connections, so that I came to comprehend that it was the sedan chair that was the litter and the howdah. It was mere wordplay.

"Are you alright, Nick?" he asked.

I took a long last drag on the doobie and pushed my arm back towards the window hole, where the girl with the boob repossessed her bong.

"Yes, it's nothing," I lied, the alcohol and Mary Jane doing the talking.

"Hoopsa boy-a-boy! Hoopsa!" he cried. The curtain was abruptly snapped shut. The four porters lifted up their poles and off dashed the dashing Sydney Syzygy in the direction of the Fen Causeway.

What on earth was Sydney Syzygy doing traversing the streets of Cambridge in a smoke-filled sedan chair drawn by four porters and two link-boys just after midnight? And who was the naked woman in there beside him?

I wondered if my imagination had drifted off into another century or another continent or both.

When I awoke later that morning, staring at the dark, crumbling patch of pusillanimous plaster on my ceiling, I concluded I must have been dreaming. But when I got up to shave, my shoulder was black and blue from my fall. It is sometimes so difficult for me to distinguish between reality and the realms of my imagination.

The Blind Girl

From the moment I first clapped eyes on her stowed away in the back of the sedan chair, I have never seen her with her eyes open. Is this an affectation, or is it real? How can I possibly ask so indelicate a question? I have to bide my time and find out the hard way. By subtle trial and error. By the insidious inquisition of others that passes for concern. No wonder the Russians came to Cambridge in search of promising students for espionage. People have been radicalising one another here since the Tudors; but it was all so innocent in those days.

Calypso Sitzclarence. She has a family tree that goes back to the Tudors. She is like a fragile doll, sightless and slight of build. Sydney calls her his Pocket Venus. She has this neat way of folding both her legs back underneath her when she sits down. She has to be double-jointed.

When Sydney is reading from his beloved Aleister Crowley's Magick Without Tears, he addresses Calypso as his *Jewel of the Night* and *Oh, Continuous One of the Heavens*, and *Infinite*. I have seen him bend her as if she were the puzzle he is seeking to resolve. She must be triple-jointed. He twists and revolves her limbs as though she were some diabolical Italianate lock he has to unpick, and then all the secrets of the universe will at last be his.

Sometimes Sydney refers to her by her name, Calypso. Sometimes he calls her by the pet name, Lyca.

"But how do you get from Calypso to Lyca?" I ask him. "Why Lyca?"

"Because I like her!" smiles Sydney. "Don't you? I would have thought that you of all people, our aspiring photographer, would approve of the name. Finest cameras that ever graced the top of a tripod. And built by fully accredited members of the Master Race. Their founder was Ernst Leitz. He took the first three letters of his surname, LEI, and the first two letters of Camera, CA, to come up with Leica. Even at the turn of the century the family had very progressive labour policies in their factory. Did you know that Ernst Leitz helped hundreds if not thousands of Jews escape Hitler's Germany by putting them on his books as employees and seconding them to non-existent overseas offices?"

"I didn't."

"That's probably what they've done with those mislaid choir boys from Kings," he mused. "I'll bet they're all padlocked to workstations, turning out bootleg trainers in some fucking factory in the arse of beyond. But Leitz' boys, they were the original Lost Boys. It came to be called *the Leica Freedom Train*, and nobody knew a thing about it until after his death. No self-respecting Jewish photographer would work with any other make of camera."

The only Freedom Train I can think of is the song by Cat Stevens.

Referring to the satanically inverted *mezuzah* on his door post, I asked: "Sydney, if you feel so strongly about your Jewish roots, why don't you put that thing on your door lintel the right way up?"

"Nick, you don't have to be a believer to be a worshipper. Without the likes of Leitz, people like me wouldn't even exist."

I think Sydney is a bit of a control freak. First there are the things he does with Calypso. He controls others by donations of alcohol and substances. I haven't worked out yet how he gets those four imbeciles to carry him around in the chair. Maybe they are guilt-ridden *Kristallnacht* descendants, the locomotives for his own Freedom Train. And is he really able to summon the devil?

Sydney keeps getting up and going across to his Lyca, shaking his head as though he had forgotten something the last time. He rearranges her limbs, doll-like. If she hadn't folded herself into an impossible enough position before, he bends her to the next level. Uncomplainingly, she accepts it. One would think that all her arms and legs must have gone to sleep, as closed as her eyes. But then she just gets up and walks across the room as fit as a butcher's dog. She picks up a record sleeve, goes back to her yoga position, and starts rolling a joint on the sleeve. When Sydney has me take photos of her, I think of her as my pixilated pretzel.

The pixilation is the more pronounced because she has lovely freckles that give a softness to her complexion. A Spanish artist might describe her as *La piguellada,* meaning "the freckled one". I just think it sounds better in Spanish.

Talking of Spanish artists, Sydney extracts a huge Taschen edition of the collected works of Salvador Dali and rifles through the pages until he comes to *Slave Market with the Disappearing Bust of Voltaire.*

"There you go!" He says to me, spreading the book open at that image and prodding the page with his forefinger. It's a coffee table book big enough to be a coffee table in its own right.

"Where do I go?" I ask.

"Slave Market with the Disappearing Bust of Voltaire!" says he. "Lyca, Oh Countenance Divine! My little art historian, tell us about it, if you please."

"Painted in 1940," she begins, "one of Sydney's favourite Dali double images, second only to *The Hallucinogenic Toreador*. If you focus on the centre of the painting, you can see a bust of Voltaire; but if you let your eyes un-focus, so that they're just taking in the generality of the canvas, you see the bust is in fact composed of a series of people. When you change from seeing the bust to seeing the individual human components forming the bust, it's what we call a Gestalt switch."

"My point," Sydney takes up, "is that the lost King's College choir boys are in fact hiding in plain sight, just like the individuals forming the bust of Voltaire in the painting. Can you see them? Voltaire's eyes and cheeks are composed of two choir boys. See the white collar ruffs around their necks?"

I focus and unfocus, waiting for the *Gestalt switch* to transport me, and then suddenly the two choir boys spring out of the page as if to tell me how stupid I've been not seeing them when they were there all along. They were standing there arms akimbo waiting to be found. The double image. Two for the price of one.

"Are they choir boys?" I enquire. "They look more like clergymen."

"Or even nuns," offers Calypso.

"Choir boys, clergymen, nuns. What's the fucking difference?" asks Sydney. "My point is that these absent choristers have in fact never left the chapel. They have somehow been incorporated into it. All we need is a long enough ladder to get up into those gargoyles and roof bosses, and I believe you will find them immortalised in the fabric of the building. You know about the Cambridge Cragsmen? The nocturnal steeplejacks whose passion it is to surmount noble architecture by night."

"The Cambridge night climbers," says Lyca.

"I think they have something to do with the disappearance of the choir boys," confides Sydney. "I think the night climbers have swept them up into the chapel roof and integrated them into the architecture."

"He talks such shit!" pronounces Calypso. "But it's such a delight to listen!"

As well as calling her Lyca, Sydney also introduces Calypso to others as *The Countenance Divine*. And it is true. She does have a lovely face, but I have historically looked upon the eyes as the gateway to the soul, and her eyes are always closed. What secrets is she guarding in there?

The idea of her Infiniteness appeals to me. Her fragility excites me. Her flexibility is reassuring: one could bend her into God knows what shape without breaking her. One could get away with it.

The problem is, I already know her too well.

You know how it is when you are introduced to someone at a dinner party when there are many others present. At that juncture, not appreciating this may be a kindling relationship, one nods politely, without hearing or remembering the name, or guessing that it may become important at some time in the future.

Let us say that after one has met this hypothetical person on several further occasions, so that one could say one is almost on close terms, one cannot go back and say, *But I am so sorry, I didn't catch your name? Or What did you say you do? Or Where did you say you came from?*

One should really have gotten all of that business out of the way at the outset. But at the beginning, I had no idea how passionately I wished to become acquainted with Calypso Sitzclarence. So I didn't take it all in at the beginning. I was caught sleeping on my watch. And now I am trying to build on something that has inadequate foundations. By osmosis, I have absorbed lots of peripheral detail about her; but I don't have a good grounding in her basics.

The beginning, the beginning.

I do not remember when I first noticed about Calypso's eyes. The fact is that she moved around her environment with such self-assurance and grace, it never dawned on me. There came a time when I realised that I had never seen them opened. The endless parties, night after night, but the format was generally the same: red or white wine, cheese and baguettes by candlelight. If a male was throwing the party, there would be a huge chunk of cheddar on a wooden block stabbed in the back by a knife. If a woman was throwing the party, each different cheese would have a toothpick flag stuck in it informing you of the name of the cheese.

Holy jism of the Redeemer! I knew the name of every *fromage* in the lexicon of cheese from Abbaye de Belloc and Afuega'l Pito to Za'atar Burrata and Zanetti Grana Padano, whether made from the milk of cows, goats, bats, reindeers, buffalos, camels, impecunious human wet maids, or yak; but I didn't know what had happened to Lyca's eyes.

More accomplished males had been seducing the girls at these Cambridge wine and cheese symposia; but here was I, reduced to striking up acquaintances with the cheeses. You can say what you like about my relationship with cheese, but we are on first name terms.

It was the problem with the wiring again. On paper, what I was doing seemed alright; but whilst it had associations with alright, in fact, it was not alright. I was attaching myself to the metaphor in preference to the reality the metaphor was supposed to quicken.

So I had met this Lyca on at least nine or ten occasions before it became apparent to me that she had never once opened her eyes. But she nonetheless processed visual data.

And in that situation, what is one supposed to do? Does one go up to her and say, *Forgive me for asking, but are you blind?* Or would it be better to go up to her boyfriend, the dashing Sydney Syzygy, *Excuse my bluntness, old chap, but is your girlfriend sightless?* Somehow, she had already become too well known so that one could not regress into the banality of small talk, or admit to having left an issue as significant as that, unaddressed for so long.

I have a conceit, a little fantasy that I go up to Sydney and ask:
Sydney, what's the first thing you look for in a woman?
And he answers:
A white stick.
Let us suppose she indeed had a white stick. I fantasise that I grab it off her. Pointing at her with the stick, I say:
I see a malingering, deceitful narcissist at the end of my stick.
Without missing a beat, she replies:
Which end?
Or should one achieve one's objective by brute force; suggest she was merely a malingerer: If you really are blind, would you mind telling me why you aren't wearing dark glasses like Stevie Wonder?

I don't know what she's reading at Cambridge, or how she manages to read it. It's a closed book to me.

I'll let you into a little secret. Within an hour of meeting her for the first time, I found that I was missing her. There, I've said it.

The Scientist

Whereas Sydney's rooms are all about ornamentation and plumage, Spud Mullins' rooms are all about functionality.

Spud Mullins, reading engineering at Peterhouse. By day, he used engineering to seek to solve the problems of the world, but left to his own devices, he wanted to solve the mystery by which in June 1958, someone managed to plant an Austin 7 motor vehicle onto the roof of the University Senate House. The perpetrator of the prank did not reveal his method until its 50th anniversary when he gave an interview to the Daily Telegraph aged 72.

In a sense, Spud's defining characteristic is his outsized spectacles. But as if they were not noteworthy enough in their own right, the curious thing is that they spend more time off than on Spud's nose. If you give him something important to read, the first thing he does is remove his glasses to see it better. If he is emotionally involved in his subject, he removes his eyewear and gesticulates wildly with them as though he were conducting an orchestra and his spectacles were the baton.

You could be forgiven for thinking that his specs are a stage prop used for emphasis and not needed to correct his vision at all, or are the antennae through which he receives instructions from a higher order. Probably from Sydney. Yes, knowing Sydney, that is the most likely explanation. Dashing Sydney, ever the control freak, has Spud under his thumb.

I am paying Spud a visit by invitation, and I have But Surely in tow with me. His real name is Burt Sully, but Ingram renamed him for reasons that are self-evident. Behind his back, Ingram also calls Burt, other things. This shows Ingram's hairy heel. To his face, he has coined an affectionate soubriquet for Burt, but behind his back he has a nasty one. And me, Nick Jobs. Does he have a nickname for Nick that everyone knows about except Nick? It is only by getting to know your nicknames that you find out what your mates really think of you.

Various projects in various states of construction or deconstruction are strewn about the space. It's hard to tell if he is engaged in the process of making things or destroying them, and in this respect, he has something of the Demiurge about him. Was the Big Bang an act of Creation, or a Destruction that went horribly wrong? Are we all inhabiting a post-Sodom and Gomorrah universe that God didn't quite finish laying waste to? Let's suppose that after Man's First Disobedience, He'd had enough.

He spent 6 days dismantling the Universe, then on the 7th, His wife said *Come back to bed, Dear*, and He never got around to finishing the job off. But one day He will. If we don't do it for Him first ourselves. Maybe it's like one of those cook-ahead meals, where you take all of the ingredients out of a packet and just finish them off in the oven yourself. We're washed up on the shores of a postlapsarian universe and it's our job to complete its dismantling. A death of a thousand cuts. Every day some new dismemberment. The Big Bang comes at the end, not the beginning.

There are Airfix models of WW1 fighter planes and old cars, but each with wings or tail-fins or fuselages missing. There are tiny tins of pigment and lacquer with their lids prised off, such as an elf might purchase to paint the toadstool he called home. The smell of turpentine initiates an olfactory voyage of which the terminus is a jar in which a collection of paintbrushes are crowded, each one standing bolt upright as though they had been lured here for a haircut but got stuffed into a Kilner instead. There are tubes of glue squeezed in the middle. There are transfers waiting to be stuck to the wings of a model Messerschmitt. I see he even has a bottle of Lepages.

Altruistically, he has protected the wood of his table with the local paper, the Cambridge Times, even though the table is not his own, but only rented. I see another story about the dwindling population of King's College choir boys. The paper has taken to publishing the names of all the missing juveniles as though they were engravings on a head stone. The paper is obviously expecting another one to go missing soon, or they would not have gone to so much trouble over the artwork for the template. They plan to keep covering this story until the last choir boy has evaporated. *Bare ruin'd choirs*.

The other smell in the room is from his soldering iron. Spud is engaged upon a project of making his own model car out of wood and Meccano. When Burt goes to pick it up and open the bonnet, he is visibly astonished to see that Spud has made a working internal combustion engine, but sized for a fairy. Separately, on his bench, he has also fashioned a miniature sash window, perfectly double-glazed, scaled to fit a dolls' house. I pick it up and peer through its frame into the magic world of Spud Mullins that is phantasmagorical even if you aren't stoned. It reminds me of when my nan (God rest her soul) used to take me up to the West End to look at the Christmas store windows. There is something modest in Spud's ambitions.

If I was a mad scientist, I would want to build a large Hadron collider straight off, but Spud seems content to start with more humble beginnings; first to understand how everything works and then build bigger.

"You know that Frank Whittle was an undergraduate at this very college not so long ago?" he says.

"Who's Frank Whittle?" I ask.

Spud flips his large spectacles to the top of his forehead and looks at me in disbelief. "How can someone have applied to Peterhouse and not know who Frank Whittle is?" he asks rhetorically.

"I didn't apply to Peterhouse," I explain. "I applied to King's, but Peterhouse snaffled me with an offer of a scholarship to read English."

"But surely, you wouldn't want to go to King's to read English," says Burt. "King's is for economists, like Keynes."

"I applied to King's because I liked the architecture and thought it would be a nice place to hang out for three years," I inform them.

"But surely..." begins Burt Sully, pointing in the direction of the newspaper article about the choir boys. "If you had been successful in your endeavour, you might be another name on that tombstone."

"I'm too old for a tombstone!" I explain. "Generation that dies before we grow old."

For a moment, Spud looks down whilst rolling his eyes up and peering at me over the tops of his large specs. Then he resumes his work. I didn't think there was anything peculiar in someone wishing to affiliate himself to a particular college because he liked the architecture and wanted to inhabit it. At this stage, I hadn't been introduced to Seth Godil, whose sole reason for coming to Cambridge (so he mendaciously informed me) was that he wanted to climb its buildings at night. But I'm getting things out of order again.

"Frank Whittle invented the jet engine. He read engineering at Peterhouse in the thirties, just as I am doing."

"But surely..." says Burt, "He was a fighter pilot. Spitfires and all that. I read it in the Eagle."

"True," observes Spud. "He didn't come to Cambridge until after he had broken the world flying record at 281 mph, although it was never formally awarded to him because of his dangerous flying."

"So you want to model yourself on him," says Burt, "Whereas Sydney wants to model himself on Aleister Crowley."

I feel that I am being cast as the straight man in this conversation, having to frame the same question over and again: "Who's Aleister Crowley?" I ask.

"He was also a Cambridge Undergraduate," says Spud without looking up from his work. "He wrote *The Book of the Law* and other stuff. He was a Satanist, and spent all his time at Cambridge and after trying to invoke the devil through sorcery, drugs and aberrant sexual practices."

We seem to be back in the land of Sodom and Gomorrah already. Perhaps that's what happened to Lyca's eyes. "And what became of Aleister Crowley?" I enquire.

"Apparently, with a group of acolytes, he succeeded in summoning the god Pan in an attic in Paris, generally referred to as *The Paris Incident*. When the god appeared, one of those who had participated in the ceremony died on the spot; another was struck blind; another was struck dumb. Crowley was reduced to a gibbering idiot and spent the rest of his days institutionalised."

"Strange role model for Sydney to pick," noted Burt, "and a strange experiment that he is attempting to replicate."

"There are lots of strange things about Sydney," said Mullins. "He's a very controlling personality. I think all this black magic stuff is just an excuse to get everybody mullahed and then make them do silly things, that you, more sillily, record on camera for him. So he's controlling you as well as everyone else."

"And what's wrong with that?" asks Sully.

Spud has four William Blake prints Blu-tacked to his walls. Blu-tack is an early example of corrupt practices within the corridors of Cambridge. Of course, the first thing an incoming undergraduate wants to do is personalise his set by sticking a poster of Barbarella onto the wall; but the prominent rules say that you are only allowed to use Blu-tack.

Without that rule, Blu-tack would be another struggling adhesive, like Lepages, instead of the multi-billion pound industry it is. I look at the four Blake prints and feel inadequate, in fact quadruply inadequate, because I am supposed to be producing a dissertation on Blake, but I don't have any Blake prints on my walls. Spud isn't even reading English. He shows me up. One poster is the painting of Newton with his compasses. The other is the frontispiece from *Europe: a Prophecy*, where the Ancient of Days is dividing the horrible night with his compasses.

As Spud is rarely to be seen without a set of compasses in the breast pocket of his short sleeve white shirt, these two prints make perfect sense. But the third is Blake's watercolour of Jacob's Dream, with the angels ascending and descending a kind of ethereal whorl that looks as if someone in the House of God has taken a mandolin slicer to a potato skin and unwound it to earth. It takes me back to my big family Bible where mine is the last name, and I wonder whatever became of it.

The fourth is the frontispiece from *The Book of Urizen* where the blind author with a white beard holds one book open with his foot, whilst writing two more books ambidextrously.

"I don't get it," I say, looking at the print of Jacob's Dream.

Spud raises one eyebrow from what he is doing, and shoots me that look again over the tops of his spectacle frames. He peers first at me, then at the print. Then he pushes his glasses back up to the top of his greasy nose with his index finger and looks at me again.

"I mean, I get the other posters," I ramble on, "Because they are scientific or creative in their overtones and you are a scientist. But I don't get this one, unless you are religious."

"I'm an atheist," Spud informs me. "Most scientists are."

"Well then?" I splutter.

"Do you think it has to be the case," asks Spud, "That one is not allowed to appreciate or display any art unless it corresponds to the subject one happens to be reading at university? How boring life would be!"

"Stupid of me!" I say. "Don't know why I come out with some of this crap!"

Kindly saving me from my own embarrassment, Spud adds: "But Jacob's Dream is scientific, or it is in my mind anyway."

"But surely—" begins Burt.

"It's in the grouping of the angels," explains Spud. "Have you noticed how they're all in sets? It brings to my mind the theory of the German mathematician, Georg Cantor. He developed a mathematical theory that demonstrated how one infinity could be larger than another. He was ridiculed at the time. But it's accepted now. He's almost mainstream. If you're reading mathematics at a high enough level, he's on the syllabus."

"But surely," persevered Burt, "Cantor and his theories came about a hundred years later than Blake."

"That's what's so interesting," says Spud. "Isn't that the whole point about Blake? That he was a visionary prophet? An artist can depict things without necessarily understanding them. Some artists paint what they see in their studio or in a landscape. Blake painted what he saw inside his own head. Sometimes it takes another pair of eyes decades later correctly to interpret what someone else has committed to canvas. I believe it's what you English scholars call a double time scheme."

It is evening, and Spud's room is illuminated by candles. I don't know if this was because he didn't want to put another sixpence in the meter, or because he thought it looked cool. The reflection of the flickering wicks glows in his outsized spectacles as though the interior of his head is on fire.

Flame on!

It occurs to me that Spud is the only person any of us know who does anything remotely useful in Cambridge.

There is a fishing rod, dismantled and leaning against the wall behind the entrance door, and he has tied his own flies, glistening, bejewelled works of art in miniature, disposed on his work table. They have burnished wings as though he has lacquered them. There is a glass display case with pinned butterflies, and, next to the jar of upended paintbrushes in the turps, there are two further large jars containing wriggling worms placed too close for my taste to the half-eaten sandwich and unopened bag of Smiths crisps beside them.

All the paintbrushes packed together upright back to back remind me of an assembly of meerkats, *rere regardant*. I am trying to think what the collective noun for a bunch of meerkats is. I could ask; after all, that's why people come to Cambridge University: so they can mix with other wise guys and find stuff out; but there is an intermediary step to finding stuff out which is called revealing one's own stupidity.

I have already exposed enough of my ignorance of Aleister Crowley,

Frank Whittle and indeed the subject of my own chosen dissertation, William Blake. I am sure that I can get by for the rest of the evening without knowing what the collective noun for a lot of meerkats is.

As it is hard to ignore the two jars of worms, I feel I had better say something about them right away and get that part of our meeting out of the way. I don't want to get off on the wrong foot and make the same mistake I had made with Calypso.

"Bait?" I ask, nodding my head in the general direction of the fishing rod and foul maggots. As soon as I say this, I become self-conscious of my inadequate voice, wondering if the listeners in the room assume I have simply swallowed the appellation, Burt.

Spud heads in the direction of the maggots, and for a moment I think he is going to offer me one; but I see he is simply reaching for the bag of Smiths crisps.

He tears open the crisps packet and pokes his digits around inside it, probing for the little blue bag of salt within. "The ones in the jar on the left are," he informs me. "As for the ones in the jar on the right, I am conducting something of an experiment with them."

In my head, I try to lay it out as though I am setting a crossword puzzle and the clue is *collective noun for meerkats*. I see the crossword. I visualise the clues. The uniformity of it all is hurting my cranium. Then I hear that fucking Cat Stevens lyric playing in my head again. I am wounded by the predictability.

Having located the blue bag, he holds it up for brief scrutiny, before unwinding it and emptying its contents into the packet of crisps, which he proceeds to shake, vigorously enough to distribute the salt, but carefully enough not to fracture the crisps.

I peer closer into the right hand jar. It contains 20 or 30 maggots and the remaining shreds of a plastic bag full of holes. I am at a loss to understand what experiment one performs with a jar of maggots and a motheaten supermarket bag.

Then it comes to me: a colony. Meerkats, bats and lepers group in colonies. I can't prevent my face from lighting up. Spud misinterprets this as a flicker of interest at his maggot jar. The candles are burnishing his big spectacles. It's like staring a furnace in the face.

"Wax moths," Spud says. "Or *Galleria mellonella* to give them their proper name. Their saliva seems to contain some enzyme that enables them to make plastic disappear. A plastic bag from the supermarket takes between 100 and 400 years to biodegrade. But these guys can eat one in a few hours. If I can figure out how they do it, that will be the end of landfill; no more crapulous disfigurements to our planet; no more oceans full of fish choking to death on plastic and nylon. This is a very important experiment."

It's comforting to know there is someone more socially inept than oneself. Here was I, getting on first name terms with cheeses; but surely that is a step up from maggots.

I have come across demagogues talking this sort of horseshit before, but when Spud talks about these things, they seem to come to life with his modest enthusiasm, and I want to believe in him. If I was not a poor student, if he had asked me to get my cheque book out and sign up for shares in his maggot farm, I would have done so on the spot without hesitation. I feel I can almost hear their tiny jaws munching away at the plastic bag. In my head, I am beginning a reverie starring a superhero who can deliver the suffering earth from the tyranny of plastic. I am just imagining this hero, known as Wax Moth, asking *What is the half-life of a plastic bag?* when I am aware that Spud has moved on to another subject.

"When they have finished the bag and have nothing else to eat," he burbles on, "they will eat one another cannibalistically, each successive maggot becoming fatter and more succulent, until only one giant maggot is left. Then what will happen? Do you think it will go into its chrysalis stage and emerge as a moth the size of a vampire bat?

"Or shall I put it on the end of my fishing line and feed it to a fish, and will that fish over many hundreds of thousands of years evolve so that its enzymes can consume the nylon fishing lines and plastic bags that at present are killing his forebears? Or will the fish end up being eaten by one of us and will our ancestors then develop a taste for plastic bags? Would we be a higher life form if we were able to evolve so as to clean up after ourselves more efficiently?"

"But surely," begins Burt, "If we like eating plastic bags, we will have no more use for plastic bags to carry food back from the supermarket."

"Correct," says Spud. "We would only go to the supermarket to buy more plastic bags."

"But surely—" begins Burt.

"No if's, Burt; no buts," says Spud. "We wouldn't need half of the earth devoted to agriculture and the production of food. We would just need a gigantic factory churning out plastic bags."

"Maybe in different flavours?" offers Burt. "Like those chocolate and strawberry-coated condoms."

"What do you know about condoms, Burt?" asks Spud. "I thought you were a good Catholic boy."

That's where all the King's College choir boys have gone, I think to myself. They have gone to work in the great big plastic bag factory.

Above Spud's desk, some of those old sepia photos are blu-tacked to the wallpaper. They feature an Austin 7 motor vehicle which, defying both logic and science, is on the roof of the Cambridge Senate House. They don't appear to have been touched-up. They are proper photographs of something that must have happened here in this very City.

"But surely," says Burt, "you are just offering us glimpses into a world where we all eat our own shit."

"Well," says Spud, removing his huge spectacles for emphasis and resting them on the top of his head, "isn't that better than eating Ingram's shit?"

The Lawyer

Ingram can also wax lyrical upon the theme of shit. One morning, as we are walking by Fen Court, he says to me, "Life is shit, Nick."

I am mildly surprised that Ingram should express such a sentiment, because Ingram comes from a world of advantage and sound health. He has no idea what real shit is, so I correct him.

"Ingram," I say, "life's a shit sandwich. But the more bread you've got, the less you taste the shit."

Then Ingram gives me a straight look, prises out his skinny pencil from the spine of his Letts diary and says, "Do you mind awfully if I make a note of that?" He pronounces it orfully like an Eton and Harrow rent boy.

"Be my guest!" I say. After all, the copyright wasn't mine. Just some shit I read on the door of the Birdwood.

Ingram Frazier, barrister in the making, is the only person I know who doesn't wear jeans. Today he is wearing a pin striped City suit. The regularity of the stripes is already giving me a headache. Ingram believes Calypso has gouged her own eyes out. Out, vile jelly! But I think he is a bit of a misogynist. It having become impossible to ask her directly or her closest friend, one is reduced to having to imbibe rumours pedalled by the likes of Ingram.

Ingram: *She's a self-harmer.*

Me: *Really? I've never noticed any marks on her body—and there's usually plenty on display.*

Ingram: *Not on her body. It's what she puts into her body. Her body should be a temple.*

Me: *I think it is, but she worships different gods from you and me.*

This Ingram doesn't really fit in with the rest of us. Whereas we are pretty well full-time dyed-in-the-wool libertines, he just likes to hang out with libertines in the evenings after he has been to his law lectures during the day, because he finds us edgy. And uncommonly he doesn't lust after Calypso. I think he is a closet homosexual. He draws on the spliffs, but I don't think he inhales them.

We humour Ingram and take him along for the ride, because there are always uses in having a trained lawyer with his faculties about him should the Proctor come knocking on your door. When your shit gets distorted, Ingram can sometimes see things how they really are, and by explaining, expiate the self-summoned spirits in your head.

In an enlightened age, he would have been sacrificed to the gods if the harvest failed. He wants to fit in with you whilst still looking down on you. If he is invited to a party, he buys a pack of Sobranie Cocktails and offers them around, as if anyone apart from Ingram would want to be seen dead with a pink cigarette hanging from his lips. Either Sobranie or those vile menthol St Moritz with the gold rings that he likes to pose with.

To Ingram, we're all just material. He likes to hang out with the in crowd so that he can study us and thereby take the piss out of us more authoritatively when hanging out with the people he really likes to hang with. Whoever they may be, apart from himself.

We all buy Marvel comics. Ingram doesn't, but will read your Marvel comics when he comes to your set, like a chiseller who doesn't ever buy cigarettes but always bums other people's. But if you ask him what he is doing, he drops the rag and then makes condescending remarks about it. He calls them *Penny Dreadfuls*. He is fascinated and disgusted by them in equal proportions. He would prefer not to have to deal with them; but because they are important to the rest of us, he keeps returning to them; like a dog to its vomit.

"Penny Dreadfuls!" he exclaims. "Why don't you lot grow up?"

"But I don't want them to grow up," cries Calypso. "They're my Lost Boys."

Herodotus tells the story of the soldier who fought in the ancient Greek Battle of Marathon. Most of his comrades didn't come back to camp that night. He knew he didn't want to see the disfigured corpses of his dead friends. But he also knew he had to. So, as the dawn began to illuminate the unspeakable horrors of last night's battlefield, he ran out, and he looked from one set of friend's mangled limbs to the next, and then he screamed: *There you are, eyes! Have you had your fill? Have you seen enough?* And then he plucked them out, blinded himself.

It's all a matter of perception.

Herodotus, they call him the Father of History. They also call him the Father of Lies. That antique purveyor of Fake News.

As the years pass, Ingram comes first to understand this vomit, and next, to purvey it. He is headed for politics. He is destined for the highest office.

"But don't you see the harm they're doing?" He asks me. "There's a whole generation of boys growing into manhood who've been brought up on reading this crap. Not just in England but throughout the western world. Have you ever looked at the advertisements in these Penny Dreadfuls? They're for Daisy Air Rifles, handguns, Bowie knives, crossbows, or bodybuilding aids that are supposed to make you look like a superhero, but don't.

"We are incubating an age of frustration and rage when the immature kids who read these things finally realise that they're never going to fly or crawl up walls or have a six pack like the Mighty Thor. And where are they going to go next? I'll tell you. To the knives, to the air rifles and the crossbows. Mark my words, within the next ten years you won't be able to walk the capital's streets safely; we'll be having kids stabbing each other at school if I don't do something about it. We'll see armed mobs in the corridors of Washington. If I get to be Prime Minister, I'll ban these rags."

"But, Ingram," I protest, "you'll never be elected on a ticket of censorship. Everything's headed in the other direction."

"Then how am I going to change things?" he asks me.

"You've got to go about it a different way. Don't ban the books. No-one ever made it big by banning books. Ban the crossbows, knives and rifles. And give them a hero for the people. Show them that it can come true. Give them someone aspirational that they can look up to and emulate."

Not Superman; not Batman; not Spiderman.

GentleMan.

In those days, everyone smoked all of the time. Everywhere. All of the actors in the films smoked. And all of the actresses. On the stage all of the players smoked for want of anything else to do with their hands. Even if they were acting Shakespeare in period costume. Most of the stage properties were ashtrays. If you read a James Bond novel by Ian Fleming, 50% of the book was plot, 25% was about the girl's tits, and the other 25% consisted of descriptions of how Bond smoked his cigarettes. We all practiced smoking in front of the mirror in the belief that if we could just get that right, the women would follow.

Ingram is bubbling over with resentment. "How come," he begins, "cigarettes in every country in the world are sold in denominations of 20? In England, we have 12 pence to the pound and we reckon in dozens, or if we want to be really awkward, a baker's dozen, which is 13. How did we allow a situation to come about where we accepted the decimalisation of cigarettes? This is how it all started. How the rot set in. With Yanks coming back from the war, offering cigarettes in packs of twenty to the men, and nylons to the women."

Ingram's dad is a member of the clergy. Ingram is here on some sort of a grant for those failed offspring of members of the cloth who were incapable of performing their vow of chastity. What would Ingram's dad say if he knew his son was an extra in Sydney's cast of myrmidons seeking to summon the god Pan? I would dare say that he would be gravely disappointed.

I'd never seen Calypso with her eyes open. At first, I thought this a pretentious affectation. It is alright to have your eyes closed when you are asleep, when you are coming, maybe when you are listening to certain types of music. But not all the time.

Dear Agony Aunt,
Q: Is it best to kiss a girl with your eyes open or your eyes shut?
A: It is best to kiss a girl with your mouth.

She has high cheekbones and red hair, real red hair; in those days young girls didn't dye their hair, and elderly women only rinsed it, usually blue. God knows why they chose blue. I think it must be from the AC comics where the hero's black hair was always inked in as steely blue, the same colour as the villain's gun barrels. And Lyca had that translucent complexion with a light smattering of freckles that genuine redheads are often blessed with; skin that will continue to look great if she lives to be 70. It's as though her skin is one of my photographic prints that I've blown up and blown up until it's nothing but grain.

Until I encountered Calypso, when I thought about my ideal women, I thought about whether they had nice tits or arses. I had never thought about their skin before, even though the skin was the gift wrapping enclosing all the other nice bits. If someone had asked me to describe Lyca, the first thing I'd have said about her is that she had the most beautiful skin. And then I'd have said that she never opens her eyes.

She doesn't shave her armpits. I find something indescribably sexy about this Calypso. But I don't know what it is, because she doesn't conform to any of the preconceptions the media have sold me about what should give me a hard-on. Everything about her is counter-intuitive. She's the closest a straight guy can get to being gay.

A lot of people say nasty things about Ingram behind his back, about how he is a closet queer without the courage of his convictions. But, as I come to assimilate my feelings for Calypso, none of this seems to matter anymore. Calypso does not correspond to any of the criteria my upbringing and my education have taught me I should find attractive; but, maybe for that very reason, I find her unspeakably sexy. But it also makes me think, if the apple could fall this far from the tree, how easy would it be to radicalise me into being a homo? How can I be open to all of the emotions that Calypso suggests, but closed to so many others?

For a start there's the hairy armpits, as though red tongues of flame are licking her down; then the fact that she is boyish; she has no tits to speak of; she is positively scrawny, but the upside of that is that, even when she crosses her legs, there's a Renaissance Golden Ratio at the top that she cannot close even if she wants to. She could shut her legs firmly; but she wouldn't be able to keep you out. She is involved in a hopeless struggle against her own physiognomy that is indiscriminately inviting you in.

The high cheekbones. The artist's fingers so long and articulate you can imagine them wrapped around your dick trying to coax music from it. The cut glass accent that she uses when she pronounces utter profanities from that long mouth the lips of which barely part. All the contrasts tumbling one upon the other; and the combination of her and Sydney; it is just too much. One goes into sensory overload and the metronomes start clicking in my head.

She's older than the rest of us, but I couldn't say how much older. *Old enough to know better, but still young enough to enjoy it.*

Her auburn hair is shoulder length. She is wiry and tough, but when her face is in repose, the lower lip sometimes quivers with an uncertain vulnerability that makes me want to protect her. The first time I was invited back to Sydney's rooms, there she was *in situ*. There was so much other paraphernalia in the room, but I noticed none of it. Fuck me! There was a sedan chair in the room, but I didn't see it the first time, because there was just too much to take in all at once.

On the first visit, all I noticed was Calypso. She had folded herself into a completely impossible yoga position on the floor. Every limb seemed to be counter-rotated; I'm not even sure if her head was on the right way around, and I am not positive that any part of her was actually touching the ground.

She seemed to be levitating just above it. It was as though I had stumbled into a masturbatory game where a girl had been playing cat's cradles with her own arms and legs. And, logically, now that I remember it, Steely Dan's Pretzel Logic was playing on the stereo. There was so much of her stuff there and in Sydney's bathroom up the stairs, it was obvious she was living there. When Sydney introduced her, he said, *This is Calypso. She's does Calligraphy and History of Art at Girton.*

What he was really saying to me was that, if I wanted to be as smart as him, I needed to get myself a girlfriend from Girton. Then I could have tampons and the pill brazenly displayed in my male bathroom, and I could get laid every night and race around the streets of Cambridge in a sepulchral sedan chair drawn by pall-bearing sycophants and lycanthropal link-boys.

But I didn't have a girlfriend from Girton. I had Olumidé.

Then Sydney tosses his big leonine locks in her direction and says: "She only had Curly Auburn Hair 'Til Old Age." I know this is a mnemonic for the Sin Cos Tangent of a triangle, but I don't remember the details. Useful fucking mnemonic then!

Only the dashing Sydney would have the *chutzpah* to date a girl "doing" Calligraphy and History of Art at Girton. And what was she *doing* with them? Why didn't he say *reading or studying*? I wouldn't even know how to begin a conversation with such a person. For those of us reading English, it was so easy to shine simply by having a memory, so that if somebody said Is *that the time?* One would look at one's watch and say that Time's winged chariot was hurrying near. Or if someone asked you to pass a spoon, you would say that you had measured out your life in coffee spoons. The fact is that you were regarded as a social success and also passed exams if you could remember a few lines.

But life isn't a memory test. It's a credibility test.

I had no conception of what memory really entailed until Seth Godil drifted into our collective unconscious. I am coming to that. Sorry. My canvas is so large, I am jumping around all over the place.

But Sydney can communicate with anybody. He has the gift of cutting through the routine and unimportant and getting straight to the heart of things, specific, but couched in sufficient generalities for what he is saying to have wider applications, so that more people can join in. He is inclusive. He would be just as happy chatting away to Einstein or Rasputin as he would be asking the bloke seated beside him on the bench outside the Magistrates Court what he was in for.

He has that ability that great writers and great artists have: to take something that we are all familiar with, something extremely local, and extend it into a truth of universal application.

I know what she reminds me of. It's Sir John Millais' painting of *The Blind Girl.*

Then Burt Sully tells me that this Calypso Sitzclarence is 39th in line for the throne. And my friend, Sydney Syzygy, is fucking this member of the aristocracy. He is fucking someone who is so posh, she shouldn't even have a fanny. But this Calypso, she exudes sex. She overflows like the fountain, whereas my Olumidé contains like a cistern. Calypso: fucking her must be like fucking Fibonacci's sequence.

"She's so bendy," whispers Burt to me. "Do you think she can lick her own snatch?"

"What a thought!" I say. "Can you suck your own cock, Burt?"

"This is the problem," confides Burt, pointing at his paunch. "That's the obstacle I would have to surmount."

"Well, if the mountain won't come to Mohammed," I say, "you'll just have to grow a longer lunchbox."

My Olumidé is a bit of a prick tease.

I'd walked straight up to her in Trumpington Street. She was wearing a full length white Afghan coat and I'd never seen anything like her before.

"Can I take your portrait?" I asked, inclining my head slightly in the direction of the Nikon hung around my neck. Nowadays, you'd be told to fuck off, or called a creep or a perv. But at the time we're talking of being a photographer was still thought of as an exotic profession. I took 4 shots: 2 portraits, one from the front, and one half front, and two full length right there in the main road.

"I'm living just over there," I said, "At 4 St Peter's Terrace. Can you come by tomorrow evening and we'll see if they've come out. My name's over the door: NICK JOBS.

"Okay," was all she said. At first I couldn't quite place the accent.

Getting the shots to print out right was the devil's own job. I couldn't seem to release the lovely features in her face from the paper. Because her skin was so dark, her face kept coming out as a featureless blob, and then the white of the Afghan coat was contrasting the face darker still. But I wasn't having it. I was determined to make the portraits appear as she had appeared to me. I held down the stops on the face until the sharp, high cheekbones forced themselves out of the paper, then the thin aquiline nose, the full red lips and the impossibly black eyes. Then manually I burnt in the contrast of the white coat with the white shearling collar, until she looked just as she'd looked in the street. Except better.

"They're fantastic!" she pronounced. "No-one's ever managed to take a proper photograph of me before. I always end up looking like a little black blob or a devil. Can I keep them?"

"Sure. I'll print some more out for myself."

"Why would you want to keep pictures of me?"

"Because you're the most beautiful thing I've ever seen."

Then she came up to me, just as I'd come up to her in the street. But she didn't ask if she could take my portrait. No, she didn't ask at all. She just took.

She kissed me full on the lips.

And that was how we started.

I was saying: My Olumidé is a bit of a prick tease.

"Would you like to see my cunt then?" she asks in her best Mumbles Bay accent. I've managed to place the dialect now.

"Yes please," I mumble, answering in kind to her Welsh intonations.

When she opens it up for me the first time, all I can think of is the *Lepages* bottle. And we have to call the whole thing off.

"*Get them in the can!*" Sydney had exclaimed, or some such. I thought we must have been raided by the pigs and that he intended me to throw the sharpeners down the john. I had received clear and credible intelligence this week, as every week, now that I think about it, that the police had sixteen warrants to use up before the end of the month.

After I had flushed twenty quid's worth of Nepalese Temple balls down the toilet in a wild panic, Sydney explained that what he actually wanted was for me to start developing the negatives of that night's Satanic activities; apparently, "getting them in the can" was a phrase from the world of cinematography. But after all those substances, I couldn't face the spectral red light in my makeshift darkroom. It would have given me the *ebee jebees* and the tick that betokens worse. I will develop them tomorrow.

How can she be reading History of Art and Calligraphy with no eyes?

"Drop by my set after supper," Sydney had said, "and show me the rushes." It had taken me quite a while to twig that everyone in Cambridge referred to their rooms as their sets. The undergraduates, the graduates, the tutors and directors of studies, all the way up to the Fellows and the Dean and the Master of Peterhouse. They all called their rooms sets. I thought setts were what badgers lived in, not real people.

As the official photographer for Black Mass, I faced challenging lighting conditions as Sydney liked to perform his ceremonies in near-dark in the crowded souk that doubled as his bedsit in Gisborne Court seemingly transformed to the unquestioning eye by drapes and velvet swaggings. Sydney was sporting a floor length silk jellygown over his pyjama bottoms and bare torso, a matinee idol Prospero. Then he donned his negromancer's cloak over the jellygown.

And there, in the corner of his room, amongst all the other unusual *objets trouvés* and paraphernalia, was that infernal sedan chair with its two wooden poles, leaning up against the wall. So, it had not been a dream after all. At nights, dashing Syzygy did indeed traverse the city's alleys, borne aloft by four flunkies and the waft of marijuana. I don't really know why I was surprised to find the palanquin there; it would have been more surprising to have learned that he kept it in a lock-up garage underneath the arches in Kings Cross.

With all the swagging and the swirling and the dashing Sydney pontificating and gesticulating and genuflecting to the god Pan in his motheaten magician's cloak, trying to look serious, and with the rest of us protesting that our hysterical laughter was just the drugs speaking and not that Sydney was looking like a stupid cunt, the evening was full of promise. Sydney bore a passing resemblance to the subject of my Tripos dissertation: Blake's portrait of the Ghost of a Flea; with his demonic hooded eyes and his bowl dripping with what Sydney solemnly assured us was chicken's blood, but I thought tomato ketchup. Until I tasted it, and it tasted so foul, I was ready to believe him. But you can't make an omelette without breaking eggs. You want the god Pan, you have to do his bidding.

Lie down with dogs, wake up with fleas.

Can't Sydney and Calypso see that they are the only ones who even begin to take any of this Faust shit seriously? I am almost positive that the makeshift slab she was spatchcocked on was the bedder's ironing board draped in someone's duvet; I wanted to lift up the corner and check, but it would have been unspeakably rude in the circumstances. Like asking about Calypso's eyes.

The Catholic Burt is inept, but so that he has something to do with his hands during these ceremonies, Sydney entrusts him with an incense-filled thurible that Burt swings solemnly from left to right, broadcasting frankincense amongst the medley of other olfactory overload. He looks like the Prat and the Pendulum. Sydney gives Burt the censer in the same way that, if you were a musically talentless turd wanting to jam with your best mate who was a rock god, he'd give you a tambourine.

"But how did you persuade the four flunkies to carry you around in that contraption?" I find myself asking him.

"Well, it wasn't difficult really. They're members of the University rowing team. This year, under my management, Cambridge will definitely beat Oxford. Portering the sedan chair exercises every known muscle in the body, plus a few they haven't even discovered yet, and the rough poles harden up the skin on their hands, so it's good practice for the oars.

"Oh, they get a few blisters at first; but they persevere, and blisters grow on top of the blisters, and the callouses harden. They keep rubbing surgical spirit on their palms, and eventually their hands are weaponised like prehensile horns. After a few hours of that, they're ready for anything the Cam, the Thames or Isis can assault them with."

Then I remember. That was the other smell. The surgical, antiseptic smell, taking the edge off the sweet, thick aroma of the weed and the frankincense. Surgical spirit on their hands. Where they grasped the poles, the wood was heavy with the stink of rubbing alcohol; the staves acting as gigantic diffusers wafting disinfectant around Sydney's set, superimposing a hospital tang onto the narcotic note of the dope.

An assault by Isis. A Caliphate. A petition to change the name of the river. I am getting ahead of myself.

Who makes up the rules in these situations, and who bothers to follow them? I try to get things straight in my head, but they don't always come out right. I have been invited to a party in dashing Sydney's set. It's one of those spur of the moment things. When I arrive, after loosening up with appropriate substances, I am informed that we are going to attempt to conjure up the god Pan and my job is to attempt to photograph this enterprise. Well, it would have been impolite to have declined. I go along with it, as you would go along with it. For the crack; just for a laugh.

Not only do manners maketh the man, but they unmaketh him also. The instinct to join in. The instinct to defer, to go along with your mates in gregarious adventures, especially if you were a bit socially inadequate to start out with. One agrees to preposterous proposals, simply because it would be rude not to. Summoning the god Pan! Is that what we're doing tonight? But of course. Allow me. After you. No, no, please. Of course.

Dear Fuck! I didn't know they knew how to do it.

Every morning the rape court is filled with this. Girls going along with stuff, not realising what they were getting into, until they have passed the point of no return. It's a beam and a fulcrum, just like any other see-saw. You squeal in pleasure as you go up and up and up, until you don't even notice the point when things have turned around, and you're on the way down; but the momentum is too much for you to dismount.

Sydney Syzygy and his girlfriend, Calypso. Names to conjure with! Proper given names. We lived in a beige and vanilla age when we were given dull names like John and James, but we all dreamed of having names like The Man from Uncle. Every boy I know secretly wished he was called Napoleon Solo or Ilya Kuriyakin. And we all read superhero comics.

Except Ingram. Ingram thought that part of what had gone wrong with our society was that parents gave their children fucking stupid names drawn from inane films and TV programmes such as Napoleon Solo and Ilya Kuriyakin, so as they matured, they assumed more of the mantle of stupidity their names cast over them. A generation of kids living out their lives in the malign shadows of their own names.

"Where is the moral worth in calling a girl Amber or Saffron?" Ingram asks. "Why call your children Napoleon Solo or Ilya Kuriyakin? Look at Thackeray. His parents gave him the given name *Makepeace*. Isn't that a name that could come to define the man and make him offer more to the society in which we live? Isn't that a name to make your deeds aspire to?"

This shows to me that Ingram is just as good with names as he is with nicknames.

Catholic Burt Sully: Stan Lee reading, overweight geezer with a thurible. Burt Sully. But Surely. Oh, burt this too, too sullied flesh would melt, Thor, and resolve itself into a Jew.

When I asked Sydney who had given him his surname, he said the Nazis had given it to his grandad in Auschwitz. In the camps, they were stripped of everything, even their names, and given made-up names. What I found extraordinary is that of the few who made it out of the camps so many of them kept their given names after. In the same way that Spud brought his unflattering name with him to Cambridge, ignorant of the even less flattering name Ingram had dreamt up.

I am working with a 35mm Pentax with a manual focus. Sometimes, in these situations, I like to turn the focus ring all the way around to the position marked ∞, so as to capture the theoretical object located at the mythical point where the parallel rays of light meet. In the unimaginable event that Sydney was to succeed in producing the god Pan, would I have time to focus on him? Would he materialise at the point where the parallel rays converge? Would he be spectral, transparent, ethereal? How does one fix such an entity on cellulose when he might be cellular himself?

I had spent some time snapping Sydney, as he leafed magisterially through *The Book of Thoth*, looking for the right spell; I fire off a snap of Lyca, but generally I am parsimonious in my shots, because photography was more expensive in those days than it became later in the digital age of selfies and instant gratification.

After the imaginary heroes of pulp fiction, my real hero is David Bailey and my favourite film is Michelangelo Antonioni's Blow Up. I feel that I am a really special guy, standing out from the crowd, because I am a photographer. If someone had told me then that within thirty years' time no-one would dream of leaving the house without a camera, I'd have laughed in his face.

As I develop my prints, my mind is free to dwell on other things, and I find I really resent Burt for putting that fucking image in my head. I can't get rid of it. *Can she lick her own snatch?*

Blow Up was produced by Carlo Ponti. Ponti was married to Sophia Loren. Until I encountered Lyca, Sophia Loren was my idea of the perfect woman.

Thoth; the Egyptian god of Writing. What a diminished age we live in where we no longer have a god of Writing. I don't even know anyone who owns a proper fountain pen.

Reality Checkpoint is a lamppost in the Middle of Parker's Piece, so named because it marks the boundary between the University's "reality bubble" and the real world of the non-academics living beyond its Rubicon. When walking or cycling (or, for all I know, being carried in a litter) one is reminded to check the touchstone of one's reality before leaving the real world and crossing the frontier into the bubble.

It is a Cambridge landmark, as is the flagpole at Downing College.

I only have episodic recollection of how we got back from Reality Checkpoint. The only thing I remember is the black flag on the flagpole and that a blind girl showed us the way.

The first time I met dashing Sydney, after he had perceived my condition and then charged my glass, I asked him what he was reading at Cambridge. "The dark arts, dear boy," he whispered *sotto voce*, looking over his shoulder in pantomime paranoia. "The dark arts."

I later found out that the subject of the dissertation upon which he was working in his lucid moments when he was not seeking to summon Beelzebub, was *The Poetry of John Wilmot, Fifth Earl of Rochester*, although he confided to me that this was just a cover story. To my knowledge, he never went to a lecture in three years.

Everything about Sydney was *carpe diem*. Sydney taught us not to wait for anything. The only cuts that interested him were short cuts. If there was anything anyone might do, one should do it now. When I asked my nan for things, she used to say to me *Little word?* To which the answer in her vocabulary was Please. In Sydney's world, the little word was Now. Before I arrived at Cambridge, I had already learned that there was nothing wrong with not waiting for the evening and having a half pint at lunchtime.

When I met Sydney Syzygy, I learned that one need not wait until lunchtime. If one wanted alcohol or a cigarette or a joint, there was no time like the present. All time was meaningless to people who didn't go to bed and stayed up all night popping pills or sweeping through the streets on a howdah heaved by horn-handed porters. After Sydney, all of the disciplines and values by which I had hitherto conducted my life, ceased to have any meaning. With the benefit of hindsight, I believe this had a profound, ingrained and enduring deleterious effect upon me, because I need to have my life ordered and regimented, or things fall out of place. But at the time, it seemed like a grand idea.

When Calypso's arms were bound above her head, her tits—that had been minute to start with—disappeared altogether and her bony mons in her knickers stood up obscenely like a shark's fin. Sydney, the control freak, reduced her to a condition of slavery. The fanny shaved; the armpits unshaved; it was as if she was educating us that eroticism was completely transportable, reversible.

She could write the rules herself and we would all have to relearn them, starting with the rule that respectable, highly educated women weren't supposed to do this. Everything the media had educated me was supposed to excite was rendered unreliable by this girl.

Calypso is the paradigm of self-authorship.

Or so I thought until I encountered her previous boyfriend. I'm coming to that. I'm coming to Seth.

Eyeless in Gaza at the slave with pills.

Girls, they were just a commodity, like buying a cup of coffee at Joe Lyons Cornerhouse. You needed one on your arm. Even if you were gay, it would never have occurred to you in those days not to have a girlfriend. Before Ingram introduced the world to Human Rights, it was your basic human right to have a female partner for social occasions, if only as a cover story; enduring heterosexuality as an undercover agent for the Gay Movement. No wonder we were such a fucked-up generation.

But I had gone one better. I had a black girlfriend. And I had gone two better: she was a virgin, and I think she was so, because she was a lesbian. At least, that is what I accused her of every time she held back on me. How did I manage to find the only black, virgin lesbian in Cambridge?

I hadn't expected my exotic girlfriend to let me take those saucy snaps of her. I put it about amongst my peers that I would not deign to date anything Caucasian. No woman except a black one would do for me.

Oh dark, dark, dark. They all go into the dark.

"But come on, Nick, are you really asking us to believe that if you got a chance to get your leg over a white woman, you would turn her down?"

"Absolutely, Burt. Fucking a white woman is like making love to a skinned animal."

That went down well; but to tell you the truth, I hadn't fucked a woman of any hue.

But then along had come Olumidé, a nurse from the special clinic at Addenbrookes. If Ingram, the old name-changer, knew, he would sneer at me, but I was enthralled by the beauty of her name. I think I would have partnered her just for the pleasure of introducing her to my friends. *This is my girlfriend, O-lu-mi-dé.* The wide open vowels a premonition of wide-open limbs.

She kept me dangling on a string. Every night was going to be the night. But it never quite seemed to happen. She said she was a virgin, and I believed it. She had come to attach so much importance to her hymen that it became bigger than both of us. The only way I was going to make love to her was if someone else forced her first and took the decision-making out of it for me.

I think there are less girls like her nowadays. But at this time they were so common, there was a name for them: prick teasers. She would dress like a complete whore. It was her life's work to give men balls ache. But she was a virgin. She would reach inside your Levis like the best of them. She gobbled like a champ. You could put your hands up her jumper, your fingers in her fanny. But when it came to proper penetrative sex, she was *not quite ready*. She had made such a big thing of the submissive ultimate self-immolation of giving it to you that (too late) I came to appreciate that it was never going to happen. But, just as I was unlearning one girl, I was learning another.

"No, Nick, I'm not quite ready."

"You seem pretty ready to me." She was so wet and dilated, I was practically feeling for the head up there.

And then she would always deftly deflect the issue by tossing you off so expertly that the problem went away, or seemed to go away. She was very good at treating the symptoms, but not the underlying condition.

I guess that's why she was a nurse and not a doctor.

In hindsight, I am amazed at how I managed not to sleep with Olumidé for so long. We all operated out of and lived in bed sits with shared bathrooms. With the exception of Sydney's rooms that were furnished like a Moroccan souk, the only item of furniture in one's set was a bed and an arm chair. There was nowhere else to sit. Once you had persuaded the girl to come back to your room, you were halfway there.

I should have packed her in. But I had flaunted her at an earlier stage, when I was so proud of having bagged this dusky accessory. Everyone was jealous of what they wrongly assumed I had. How could I walk away from the legend I had spun? I was like Macbeth, so far steeped in blood that to go forward is as easy as to go back; but in my case, the blood was all menstrual; and going forward, she was always promising me completion.

"I'm so sorry, Nick. I've got my period again. But you can come in for a drink."

"What do you think I am? A vampire?"

It really wasn't that she didn't want to give it to me. I think I was just too much of a gentleman. With the benefit of hindsight, I probably needed a fluffer to break her in for me, and then everything would have been perfect. Although she had a lovely name, she came from Mumbles and spoke with a Welsh accent that grated.

"Do you really love me, Nick?" she would ask in that accent.

"I am glued to you like Lepages," was all I said, but it seemed to do.

But, forgive me, I am rambling again.

Albert Sully is bedding Bunty Brown, a fifth former from the Catholic school in town. It could almost be a poem. If it scanned properly. She doesn't look as though she is old enough to take into a pub, let alone have sex, and when Burt does take her into the pub she either has a lemonade or a Snowball. I'm not even sure that what he does with her in his bedroom is legal.

"Burt, why do you have to settle down with a girl who's so much younger than you?" I ask.

"Because, I want to make sure that, in later life, she's pushing my wheelchair and I'm not pushing hers," is his bizarre explanation.

"But Burt, later life doesn't have to be all about wheelchairs."

"Yes, it is," he says gloomily. "When I look into the future, all I see is wheelchairs, walking aids and mobility scooters."

The worst thing is that I hold myself responsible for Burt's statutory rape of Bunty.

"Nick," Burt cajoled in the run-up to St Valentine's Day, "there's this bird at the Catholic school in town, and I really fancy her. You've got a way with words. Can you write me a sort of love poem to give her? Just enough words to fit into a Valentine's Day card. Something that will get me into her knickers?"

"What's in it for me?"

"I've got a lid of Moroccan Blonde with your name on it here."

"Why not administer the Moroccan Blonde to the girl, and you'll get into her knickers that way."

"She doesn't smoke, and she only drinks Snowballs."

"What's a Snowball?"

"Advocaat and lemonade, but all she really likes are the cocktail cherries on top."

"OK. What's her name?"

"Bunty."

"Bunty?"

"Bunty Brown."

"Burt, I've never heard of anyone called Bunty. What's it short for?"

"It's not short for anything, Nick. That's her whole name. Bunty."

"It's not, like a pet name or a term of affection?"

"No. That is what she's called."

"OK. Come back same time tomorrow."

I shouldn't have accepted his retainer. I was racking my brains. What the fuck rhymes with Bunty? Well, I can think of one thing, but I can't use that. Anyway, I smoked his lid of dope, and I wrote the poem. He transcribed it onto his Valentine's card. It worked and he's been having his evil way with his under-aged squeeze ever since. I have aided and abetted a statutory rape.

We all share a common interest in Marvel superheroes. We exchange comics. We also share a common interest in recreational drugs, save in Sydney's case it probably goes beyond mere recreation. For him it is a profession or a necessary adjunct to his art. Aleister Crowley, mountaineer turned magician, was one of Cambridge's night climbers. He praised dope as a short cut to attaining mysticism, and short cuts were Sydney's stock-in-trade. In fact Crowley wrote an essay about it, *The Psychology of Hashish (1909)*. I wondered if Crowley handed it in as part of his course work.

I am an unreliable narrator. I shouldn't be the main protagonist. I should just be another voice in the Chorus. I jump about all over the place. I get confused. I was mildly epileptic before I suffered my concussion at the hands of Sydney's barrelling palanquin. I really shouldn't accept any of the substances Sydney offers me. No, I am not the best narrator. I'm a photographer, not a novelist. I am also a journalist. I can sell some doggerel verse to a mooncalf; I can write snappy copy to accompany my snappy snaps; but my mind doesn't flow along linear weylines. It ducks and dodges.

I take still photos, not movies. I will lay them all down in this great collage; but they are not a narrative. Each picture is an instant captured. How did Christopher Isherwood put it? That he was an aperture, that he was the shutter of a camera, and he walked around Berlin taking it all in, recording it, but not seeking to make any sense of it. I am just a medium on which stuff is being recorded. I am a walking Ouija board receiving signals from heaven knows where, but not seeking to interpret them. You are going to have to join the dots yourself.

No, I am not the best narrator; but nobody asked me if I wanted to tell the fucking story. I think all the other possible authors are now dead. But what worries me most of all is that I think it may have been me that killed them.

I smoke Burt's Moroccan Blonde, selfish, solitary in my set, illuminated by one candle on my desk. I don't know what got into my head, but I decided to stick my long plectrum thumbnail into the flame and see if it melted like one of Dali's soft watches. After ten seconds, the stink was gut-wrenching, and I fancied it glowed molten hot. *Flame on!* Then the searing heat arced right up my arm. I pressed the smouldering nail into my forearm, branding two neat crescents there; then turned my thumb up the other way and stamped two more: ∞.

2-Dimensional Printing

The stages of delivering a photographic image trace the evolution of life itself. In my makeshift darkroom illuminated only by the comforting glow of the red safety light, my three dishes are lined up in a row. I always have them arranged in the same order: the grey plastic tray to the left is for my developer liquid; the blue tray in the middle is water; the red tray on the right is fixer. I have to dilute the developer and fixer chemicals. But I also have to add wetting solution to the water as if water wasn't wet enough in itself. The wetting solution stops the prints from drying streaky when I peg them up on the clothes line.

Water, prehistoric *hyle*, the thing which is its own cause, Kant's *Ding an sich*, from which everything else is made, and which acts as midwife to my prints.

The red safety light; a primeval sun in an inchoate universe. As I agitate the coated paper in the developer, the grains rearrange themselves with the persistence of Brownian motion. Gradually, as I coax and tease at it with my rubber tongs, fleeting, amoeba-like life forms take shape; platelets harden and lift off, drifting away in the liquids; but take them out of the grey tray too soon and they will be still-born. Leave them in too long and they will be blackened, shrivelled.

When I see upright, sentient life assuming form and line beneath the red sun, I pluck it out of the grey tray and wash it in the contents of the blue, half expecting it to cry out as it comes to life and is christened. At this stage, if the print is ill-formed or irregular, we can still abort it before anyone knows. But if it is satisfactory, I dunk it in the fixer to arrest its growth. When I am satisfied with its stage of mutation, I stop it mutating further. It's more like a cancer than a hobby.

I enjoy best working in black and white, because it is only in the development of monotone prints that you have the luxury of being able to toil under the safety lamp and see what you are up to: the coated papers do not respond to the low wavelengths of the red light. I can also work in colour, but as colour films and papers register all bands of the spectrum, I have to perform my operations in total darkness. For this, I have a special black felt bag with elasticated holes for my hands.

Working like a keyhole surgeon, I extract the film from the camera in the big black bag, and using the sense of touch only, I twist the film onto the spool inside my developing tank before pouring in the chemicals. When I have developed the film, the papers are exposed under my Durst, but then it's back into the bag to slip the papers into my black plastic lightproof drum, working only by touch. Sometimes, as I do this, I wonder what it is like to be like Lyca. She could be my dark room assistant.

Under the red safety light, there are no parallel lines, no sharp edges.

Optophonetic Poetry

I am in Sydney's set, which Ingram has nicknamed Substance Abuse Central. Calypso is there, of course. And a joint is there, also of course. Even if no-one is smoking it, Sydney leaves a signature smouldering spliff in his Lalique ashtray, a sign of insouciant excess. Judging from the length of the ash that has formed at its end, it has been sitting there some time. I feel obliged to go to its rescue. I hate waste.

Sydney and his Lyca are burrowing around with their hands inside what seems to be a big black felt bag with a drawstring at its mouth. They are pulling characters out of the bag and squealing with delight. It reminds me of my black felt bag with the hand holes that I use when I am developing colour film.

"Is it a game?" I ask.

"Deadly serious," says Sydney.

"It's optophonetic poetry," explains Calypso.

"I'm none the wiser," I confess.

"According to the Dadaist, Hugo Ball, the poem is an act consisting of respiratory and auditive combinations, firmly tied to a unit of duration." Calypso explains further. "In order to express these elements typographically," she continues, "one has to use letters of varying sizes and thickness which take on the character of musical notation. Thus the optophonetic poem was born. The first step towards totally non-representational, abstract poetry."

"I collect newspapers and magazines from all around the world," Sydney informs me. "Because I don't approve of cutting up books. What did Thomas Lamb say? *The only way you can distinguish civilised man from the barbarian is in the way he treats his books.* Different languages, different typefaces. Just to make it more random than ever, I give them all to Lyca here, my Jewel of the Night, my Continuous One of the Heavens, and with a pair of pinking shears, she cuts them up, not even seeing what she is doing.

"Some are words, some letters, some mere calligraphic fragments. We put them all into this black sack, stir them up with this magic wand, and then we take turns picking them out and laying them on the page. The result is optophonetic poetry, and it has to be complete and utter rubbish."

"But I like order," I protest.

Quoting from Hugo Ball, Sydney says in his most stentorian tones:
Jolifanto bambla ô falli bambla
Grossiga m'pfa habla horem
Egiga goramen
Higo bloiko russula huju
"See what I mean?"
I didn't.
"Let me show you," says Calypso.
She gives the black hood a good shaking to shuffle its contents and then dips into it six times, on each occasion laying the product onto the adjacent blank sheet of A4 cartridge paper.
It says: Soiram Mezzanine Nebuchadnezzar Jeroboam o Ingles.
"Excellent!" exclaims Sydney. "Reward!"
She goes over to the Jelly Bean machine, cranks the handle and pops one in her mouth.
"And what do you do with these words?" I ask.
"I use them in my rituals," informs Sydney. "Black sack: negromancer's stash."
"So that mumbo jumbo that you pronounce…"
"Is optophonetic poetry." Extending his hood-holding hand in my direction: "You have a go for yourself," offers Sydney. "You should be a dab hand at this. All these fucking fonts! You pride yourself on being a printer, don't you?"
"Sydney," corrects Calypso, "he's a *photographic printer*. He isn't doing hot metal typesetting with antimony and tin." Then she reflects, "Although, thinking about it, maybe that wouldn't be such a bad idea."
Taking a last big drag on the doobie, I rest the bong back in the ashtray, and approach the bag seeing how long I can hold my breath for. I give it a good shake. Then I dip into its inky recesses six times as I'd watched Calypso do and lay the letters on the table like in a Scrabble game.
Sydney is appalled at the product.
"Oh!" he goes; and, "Oh! Oh! No!" He recoils physically from the characters on the cartridge paper as though they were coiled serpents.
"What's he written?" enquires Calypso, who can't see for herself.
"Well," says Sydney, "or not so well. In neat Times New Roman uppercase 12 point, he has written: WHEN ADAM DUG AND EVE SPAN."

"But the chances of that—" begins Calypso.

"—Of picking something that makes sense," completes Sydney, "are billions to fucking one. Forfeit! Forfeit!" he exclaims. "How dare you dip into that bag and make something coherent. It's arithmetically impossible!"

And with that, he has thrust the hood over my head, and is fastening its drawstring around my neck before he spins me round and round, blindfolded inside his black bag. My lungs are still full of the doobie and I exhale and rebreathe it from within the bag, the same way as you're supposed to do if you're hyperventilating. I don't know how long the episode lasted. Maybe 30 seconds that seem like 30 minutes.

To start off, it was unpleasant, claustrophobic and disorientating. Some of the glossier paper was sticking to my face; I felt I was suffering a million paper cuts from the matt papers. Then there was a phase when I thought I had been sewn up in a sack with a snake and a rooster, and a slathering dog, and chucked into the Cam.

But then, after I let myself get into the rhythm and adjust my breathing to the spinning, it wasn't so bad. I am a lift stuck in between floors. I don't want to be let out of the bag. If someone had come up to me and said *Nick Jobs, I am the geni of the hood; I am here to release you from the* bag, I would have picked a fight with him. At other times, I feel as though I am the sole inhabitant of a large bagpipe or someone has put a haggis in a spin drier.

The spinning seems to go faster and faster until I settle into a steady pace and realise that I am spinning myself and Sydney is no longer whipping me like a top. I am spinning, and the words in the bag are spinning round with me, and although it is pitch dark in the bag, I can make out the letters orbiting around me. The words are just beginning to make sense when I realise I am no longer spinning, and I am no longer standing.

I have passed out. But, of course, I didn't know that until I came round again. "Came round": a metaphor from spinning.

I don't know if this is a normal part of the forfeit, or if it is just me having one of my funny turns.

Clepsydra

From a dark bag to a dark room. What did Sydney say? *They all go into the dark.* I am back in my makeshift obscure workshop, dipping the photographic papers into their chemical baths, delivering into being the graven images from last night's festivities; grain regrouping beneath the developer liquid. There is something antiseptic about the smell of the chemicals. The red safety light illuminating the cramped workspace mimics the macabre quality of last night's events when Sydney was busy summoning the god Pan.

As I wait for the print to materialise, I reflect upon my misgivings concerning the ceremonies I seem to have stumbled into. I am concerned about the cocktails Sydney had us drinking last night. With all the Carnaby Street rubbish filling my lungs, and after Sydney had performed his sacrament with the chicken or the cock or whatever the fuck it was, I took him at face value when he said we had to drink the chicken's blood from the chalice mixed with cream cheese or cottage cheese or was it exceedingly live yoghurt? I forget.

But I am staring at the pleasing outline of Calypso's fanny, and as the image is coming to life under the fluid, I can just make out a string hanging out of it, or is it a hair on my lens or a scratch on the film? I am thinking to myself, Please God don't tell me that when I thought we were swilling chicken's blood to summon the god Pan, Sydney had us knocking back Lyca's menses and cottage cheese, please don't tell me that.

What if it wasn't cottage cheese?

And now I think back, I remember I had not liked the look of what was fomenting in Sydney's chalice, but a lot of things look strange when you are stoned and pissed and warding off the next convulsion. And now I think of it, I had even had the wit to ask Sydney what I had considered in my diminished state of alertness to be a pertinent and highly responsible question about the weird goings on and the chicken he had killed and whose blood we were supposed to be drinking.

But dashing Sydney had deflected my question with some rhetorical question of his own. "Nick," he had said, "Do you know the difference between a fetishist and a pervert?" to which I had said "No". Because I didn't. And he said to me: "The fetishist uses a feather. The pervert uses the entire chicken." And then we had all gotten the giggles, and I had forgotten that I was asking him about what was I drinking in my nightcap. *I got stoned and I missed it. I got stoned and I missed it.*

In the morning, just for the hell of it, I go to the Ward Library and look up the definition of tampon in the OED. It says it's a plug made from earth and bark that a bear sticks up his bum in the winter to stop the ants crawling up his arse when he's hibernating.

"Ingram," I say, "you're a bit of a cunt."

"Which bit do you mean?" The book-learned pedant asks me. "The labia, the clitoris, the Bartholin glands, the internal os, external os?" In fifteen years' time, it will become apparent to us that there is no such thing as Bartholin's glands, and women had been ashamed for nothing since that eponymous Danish doctor, Thomas Bartholin, first stamped his imprimatur on their anatomies in the seventeenth century by publishing his theory of the lymphatic system, accompanied by detailed illustrations of a part that only existed in his imagination.

For centuries, women have been unnecessarily consumed by the shame of possessing an anatomical feature that never even existed. Because a member of the opposite sex, who also didn't have one, told them they did. That old confidence trickster from Malmo realised that if you want to deceive the public into believing something exists, whether it be a body part, an ailment, a supposed common enemy, or a human right, the first thing you have to do is make up a name for it. Name it and shame it. The naming of the parts: control: *Logos.*

In the beginning, there was the word.

I am what I am. ‏הֶיְהָא רֶשָׁא הֶיְהָא‎.

The symmetry of the characters is fascinating: the vowels grouped beneath the consonants, like a parasitic life form drawing sustenance off the calligraphy.

ehyeh asher ehyeh. I am what I am.

In my big padlocked Bible that I have never read, but I was shown the pictures, this is what God says to Moses when Moses asks him for his name. When you give someone your name, you give him a measure of control over you, so it is wise to keep your name very secret. It's

Biblical identity theft, and God wasn't going to fall for that one. Oldest trick in the oldest Book. God has seven names in the Bible, but he didn't entrust any of them to Moses.

Ingram has learned all the names for the constituent parts of a fanny by rote, out of a book, but he has never seen one, and prefers boys.

Ingram is destined for high office.

I ask myself. What could be worse than having a non-existent part of a fandango named after you? The answer dawns on me: leaving all your money to Peterhouse and having it spent on a huge crapping complex bearing your name. Lord Birdwood. Master of Peterhouse (1931-1938.) Benefactor. The college took his money. But did they build a new theatre with it, a new library bearing his name, an eponymous science block? No, no, no. The foolish man left his endowment to Peterhouse, but didn't specify how it was to be spent, and they spent it on a shithouse bearing his name.

Worse still. It was not a posthumous gift. It was what Ingram would call an inter vivos gift. He left it during his lifetime, and in his lifetime he returned to his alma mater to see what they had spent his hard-earned funds upon. Oh, the shame of it, the horror, Iago, the horror! He returned, like a dog to its vomit, expecting a hero's welcome, as befits a benefactor. He had no idea how they had pissed his money up against the wall.

Ingram has this really annoying habit of having to tell you all the time what it is about you that annoys him. Why on earth does he think we should care? Usually, it's just the way you construct your sentences. When Burt Sully speaks, he intersperses the actual content of his sentences, by which I mean, the words, with tons of padding, mere words of supererogation that serve as filling for the time it takes whilst the cogs of his brain revolve and send the electronic signals to his mouth to form the next word in the sequence.

This isn't because he is stupid, but simply because his skull is organised in a different way. The electrical impulses from his cranial cortex have to travel through so many layers of fat before they arrive at his mouth, one has to allow longer. So, he is always saying *"Sort of"* or *"literally"* which words Ingram rightly points out, add nothing. Burt Sully would not dream of constructing a written sentence like that, but he does it when he speaks, because it is the connective tissue that gives him the time to work out the next half of his sentence. And I think that's not uncommon. Indeed Ingram begins a lot of his own sentences with *You know.*

Because Ingram intends to forge forward with a career in public speaking, first in the courts of law, next in the Houses of Parliament, these foibles are more important to him than they are to anybody else, and I think that he is honing his art by learning from Burt's faults. Every time Burt drops a redundant word into his sentence, Ingram makes a note not to do that himself.

Ingram regards Burt as a competitor for high political office, as they have both laid their cards on the table at a ridiculously early point. They have both set their sights on a unique job that no-one else in the country wants, so now they are like the two big maggots in Spud's jar, and one will have to consume the other. Sully, from his stature is the better evolved to consume Ingram. He could swallow him as an *amuse bouche*. Survival of the fattest. But Ingram never foregoes an opportunity to cast some *sotto voce* censure upon Burt. Indeed, he would never cast an aspersion, when he could get home with a full-blown disparagement.

Burt Sully has a certain lack of confidence the outward manifestation of which is that he tends not to initiate a conversation himself, but question the propositions by which others embark upon dialogue. So he will wait for someone else to throw his hat into the ring, and then say "But Surely-." Which, of course, is how he got his nick-name, just like in one of those *Just So* stories. Whenever Burt wishes to express a contrary opinion, he begins his sentence with *But Surely.* As a result of which, his real name has become elided into his soubriquet. Everyone calls Burt Sully "But Surely". The soubriquet was first conceived by Ingram, and it stuck.

It is regrettable that many of Sully's observations are insightful. If he had initiated them, they would probably go down in history. But because they are all responsive to less meaningful lines of enquiry initiated by others, his weighty observations tend to fall by the wayside whilst Ingram's ephemera sally forth and reach their targets.

It's stiflingly hot in Sydney's set. I think he keeps the windows closed so he can re-breathe all the dope everyone else is exhaling. It's back to his trick with the black felt bag. All his windows are dripping with condensation.

Ingram has to interrupt Burt when he is attempting to string his syntax together and say: "You know, I would really rather you didn't say that," or similar crap. And of course, But Surely is unaware of his affectation as he does it subconsciously, so he doesn't know what he's done wrong, and Ingram has to con-de-scend to explain it to him.

Unfortunately, this is not Sully's only affectation. I have noticed that apart from his habit of beginning many sentences with the words But surely, Burt also displays physical character traits. His hair is cut short and, indeed, shaved in at the sides, with a cowlick hanging over his forehead. This style of haircut was known as a pudding basin, because the hairdresser (invariably your dad) put a pudding basin on your head and shaved the area uncovered by the pudding basin.

Every now and then, Burt lowers his head, so his cowlick falls forward, and then he moves his jaw to the right and sticks the right hand side of his lower lip out proud of the upper lip, expelling a shot of air upwards in the direction of the cowlick, blowing it momentarily off his forehead. He reminds me of an elephant, sucking up water in his trunk, then hosing down his back with the contents of his own proboscis.

Sometimes, I have observed Burt practising the art of circular breathing, so that the zephyr from his lips is almost continuous, and the cowlick hovers perpetually in suspension, perpendicular in front of his brow, in the manner of a trained seal seeing how long it can balance the spinning ball on the end of its nose before the zookeeper rewards it by tossing a pilchard into its mouth.

Sydney could train seals with his system of rewards and forfeits. Every Good Boy Deserves Favour.

I swear Sully is completely unconscious of these mannerisms. If I had to guess, I would say that he probably started off flicking the cowlick back with his hand or a toss of his head; but, like all species, he became self-conscious of this, and he has evolved, so that he now uses this more efficient air spout technique. There are probably other members of the species like Sully, who did not evolve the spout technique and continued flicking until they became extinct. With sufficient interbreeding and a million years of evolution, Burt's progeny could develop upward pointing nostrils capable of storing rainwater in times of drought.

What is strange is that when I saw him on the TV in later years, after he had become the Chancellor of the Exchequer (which we will come to in due course), by which time Sully had lost all of his hair, he continued with this adolescent habit of blowing air upwards in the direction of a non-existent cowlick, which gave him the appearance of one who is constantly irritated and in a huff at something or other.

When he is involved in high-level negotiations with other heads of State, they are put on the defensive, wondering what crass mistake they have made that so vexes him, not realising it is just a nervous tick. This gives him a wholly undeserved advantage. I have read about soldiers who have lost their limbs; they have had arms or legs amputated, but they continue to experience sensations in them: the sensations are called phantoms. They feel itches or pain in parts of their anatomy that are no longer there. Like Bartholin's glands. In later life, Burt Sully was a bit like that, still seeking to tame a non-existent outcrop of hair years after it had all fallen out.

And the damnedest thing was that, unless you had known Burt, as I had, when he was a young man and still had his hair, you would have no idea what he was doing or why he was doing it, in the same way that archaeologists try to piece together the behaviour of extinct tribes from the *disjecta membra* they have left behind them, and come to absurd conclusions.

Of course, the backbiting Ingram, then Prime Minister to Sully's Chancellor, gave out that Sully was not actually bald, but had simply shaved off the rest of his pudding basin to trick the male voters into thinking he had gravitas, and the female voters into believing he was overflowing with testosterone. The way they bitched at each other, you wouldn't think they were both members of the same government. They had a gentleman's agreement that Ingram was supposed to make way for Sully at some point.

Looking back on it all with the benefit of hindsight, it is perfectly logical that Sully should have progressed to the position of Chancellor of the Exchequer. He always had a parsimonious streak, often expressed in platitudes, such as *Never a borrower nor a lender be!* Or *Look after the pennies and the pounds will look after themselves!*

Very politely, Sully always holds the pub door open, until everybody has entered, to ensure he is the last to reach the bar so that someone else has to get the first round in. Then he ensures that he leaves before it's his turn. In the three years we were together at Peterhouse, I don't think I ever saw him get a round in.

All of these foibles, mannerisms and vicious moles of character have not prevented Burt from achieving a girlfriend, and I use the word girl advisedly, because I am not entirely sure if she is of age. Bunty Brown is in the fifth form at St Mary's Catholic School, Cambridge. Looking at her, one would think that Burt had assembled her out of a flat pack marked *Burt Sully's Ideal Woman, One Size Fits All*, because she has everything Burt would want in a woman except a brain –or perhaps I do Burt a grave injustice here and the absence of a brain is one of Burt's *desideratum* in a female partner.

Her defining feature is her wobs. She has jugs like a Toby Jug, and she wears tight white slim-fit shirts with enough buttons undone so that you can see she has been sunbathing topless, whether at the swimming pool on Jesus Green, or in the tanning parlour in Trumpington, I couldn't say. She must have some kind of push-up bra that makes her tits spill out the top of the shirt in the same slightly sinister way that dry ice overflows the proscenium arch and then starts engulfing its audience.

With the white shirt, she always wears blue denim jeans tucked into white Courrèges cut-away boots. She has stuck-on mascara eyelashes, hair extensions and nail extensions. She clearly spends so much time on her appearance that she doesn't expect anyone to be interested in anything about her apart from her appearance. She doesn't understand most of the things we talk about. She lives with her mum and dad in a village just outside of Cambridge, and Burt's only allowed to see her at weekends because of her schoolwork.

I assume that when she leaves the house she has four of five more shirt buttons done up for her parents' sake, and all that it takes to turn her from an upstanding Catholic virgin to Burt's wet dream in white boots is the undoing of those fasteners on her blouse. Her shirt seems to be under such immense load-bearing strain that when you look at her at close quarters you need protective eyewear in case the buttons come pinging off.

When Burt and Bunty are together, she just wants to hold hands with him all the time, and Burt has this smug expression on his boat that makes me want to turn his face concave with my fist. The only way Burt could conceivably have landed such a catch is by pedalling his lies to her that he is destined for high office whilst passing off my poetry as his own work.

Anyway, where was I? Ah yes, I was telling you about Ingram's nasty little habit of picking on But Surely and telling him that he would really rather that he didn't say this and that.

Whereupon Calypso, rushing to the aid of the weak and defenceless, like the true super heroine she is, says: "But, Ingram, we all do that. Look at Sydney. Every other word is *fucking*. He uses the past participle of the word *fuck* as an adjective."

Sydney: "Not fucking true!"

Ingram: To be honest, I was—"

Calypso: "And Ingram, that's something that really pisses people off about you. You're always saying *To be honest*, and in my experience, only people who are intrinsically *dishonest* ever say that, which is not how you want to project yourself if you are going to be a hot shot barrister or a member of Parliament. It suggests that everything else you say, all the rest of your repertoire, is fundamentally *dishonest*, and the only time you deviate into honesty is when you specifically say so."

I love the way Calypso constructs her criticism, rather than just letting rip, as I would. She doesn't say that something about Ingram really pisses her off. No, she distances herself from the argument by reporting upon something that pisses other unidentified people off, thereby allowing herself a face-saving exit route, should the need arise. I am learning from her.

"But it's just an expression!" moans Ingram.

"They're all just expressions, Ingram," says Calypso. "So why are you rounding on Burt's?"

"Calypso, do you want my opinion?" asks Ingram.

"Not unless it's medical," she closes.

Ingram is rewinding Calypso's script to look for offensive expressions used by her that he can criticise, but he doesn't find any. She has thrown the first stone, because she is without sin. She has a way of harnessing the power of his name, addressing him as *Ingram* instead of *you*, that personalises it. Ingram wastes a lot of his time dreaming up nicknames to trivialise those with whom he deals. Calypso on the other hand weaponizes your own name.

Despite having learned all of the tricks in Cicero's book of rhetoric, Ingram decides it is safer simply to change the subject and talk about the weather.

"It's stiflingly hot in here," he says, and he dabs at his forehead with his handkerchief.

"Christ, Ingram!" she says. "You're like some menopausal Mediterranean matron seeking shelter from her hot flushes in the air conditioning of a smelly butchers shop!"

Ingram, soon to be hotshot barrister, subsequently to be Prime Minister of England, is left speechless, not so much because he is lost for words, as because he fears what use Calypso might make of them if he brings any more into play. The *angst* of reprisal. He feels like he's just been 12 rounds with Cassius Clay. Here he is learning a lesson that will stand him in good stead until he gets his own spin doctor. As if to illustrate that the subject is now closed, Lyca folds herself into a position that takes up so little space that no-one could possibly object to her. It is as though she has the ability to make herself disappear through an intricate system of creasing, folding, pleating and hemming her own limbs.

I am still conjuring with the image of the overheated matron amongst the slices of prime steak, when Ingram, in a weak parting shot, appealing to no-one at all, as he is the only person in the room who doesn't smoke dope, observes: "I thought that smoking that hashish was supposed to make you all docile; but in your case it seems to make you more aggressive."

"Actually, Ingram, that's what it was first used for," Calypso informs him. "We have records going back to the eleventh century that show that suicide assassins were fed on it to steel their nerves. That's the origin of the word hashish. It comes from *hashassin,* as in *assassin.*"

"*Christ on a bicycle*!" Ingram says in an aside as soon she is out of earshot. "What did I do to upset her?"

He is appealing to Burt. Strange how the politician in Ingram will immediately forge an alliance with the very bloke he had been taking the piss out of moments earlier. As in *my enemy's enemy is my friend.*

"She's not just a pretty face," confides Sully.

Looking back, I'm not sure Ingram was gay when he arrived at Cambridge. I think Calypso may have turned him.

We have by now left Sydney's set and we are just walking past Maurice Cowling's set in Fen Court, when Michael Portillo emerges. He has been participating in one of Cowling's whiskey-fuelled 10 pm tutorials.

"Have you learned anything?" enquires Ingram.

"Yes, I suppose I have," muses Portillo. "He told me to stop wasting my time reading history and to join the Conservative Research Department. Then he told me to Bugger Off. So here I am."

We continue on our way, leaving Portillo to ponder his future.

"I've read Cowling's work," says Ingram. "I'm a socialist, but I find myself agreeing with a lot of what he says." Then, quoting from Cowling's The Impact of Labour, he says: "*High politics [is] primarily a matter of rhetoric and manoeuvre.*" Then he adds, patting me on the shoulder as though we are fast friends: "And when I'm calling the shots, I think it would be useful to have someone like Nick Jobs behind me. He always has the *mot juste.*"

"You mean a sound bite?" I query.

"Sound bite," repeats Ingram. "You know what? I think I'll just write that one down." His skinny diary pencil is unholstered in the blink of an eye.

Ingram is reading the law, but did not abide by it or respect it. To him, the law was a set of rules such as one had in any other game of chance, and the law was a mind game for those who had outgrown the minor intellectual challenges of chess or bridge or the Times crossword. It was a hand of poker where the lawyers got to bet using the stakes provided by their clients.

"It's like a game of snakes and ladders," he once explained to me. "Sometimes you go up the ladders. Sometimes you go down the snakes. And sometimes the Judge confiscates the dice, and then you're really fucked and can't go anywhere."

"Do you aspire to be the Judge?" I enquired over a pint of light and bitter.

"No right-minded lawyer has ever aspired to be a Judge," he informs me. "The pay cut is mortally wounding. Tit-whipped second-rate barristers are pushed into office by their wives so that they can be called Lady-so-and-so and put on airs and graces in Waitrose. No, Nick, I aspire to be the Prime Minister of this fair country," he confided to me.

Then I understood that learning the rules, understanding all the discipline was just a means to an end for him. You have to master the rules before you can break them all with impunity. He needn't have wasted his youth at Cambridge. He should have been fast-tracked for private tuition by Niccolò Machiavelli.

"Do you really want to be Prime Minister?" enquires Burt Sully. Sully had earlier confided that he too wished to be Prime Minister, but they can't both be, at least, not at the same time.

Ingram, Burt and I are now standing underneath the crab apple tree in Gisborne Court.

"Passionately!" says Ingram, mocking a ham Italian accent from the movies and smiling as though he was starring in a Cornetto advertisement.

"But why should people vote for you instead of Grocer Heath?" asks Burt.

"Because," I offer, "more people worship the rising than the setting sun."

I see I have caught Ingram's imagination.

"But surely—" begins Burt.

"Where does that come from?" interrupts Ingram.

"It's what Pompey the Great, Rome's rising star, said to Sulla, its burnt-out tyrant. Pompey was on the way up, and he was saying that Sulla was a has-been."

I can see Ingram is conjuring with the phrase, committing it to memory.

"More people worship the rising than the setting sun," Ingram repeats. "I like it. Nick, when I'm running the shop, you are going to be my press secretary."

"And what am I going to be?" asks Burt.

Without batting an eye, Ingram responds: "My Chancellor of the Exchequer."

Normally, what Ingram has just said to Burt would be highly complementary. But in context, it's a nasty little put-down.

Ingram has the practiced air of insouciance radiated by a man who genuinely doesn't give a fuck, because he knows he's got it all made anyway. Meeting him the first time, I guess I was a bit overawed by his height. You don't do face-to-face with Ingram, more face to chest, which means that you have to look up to him, and he has to look down on you.

And to complement the looking down thing, he has evolved a round-shouldered sanctimonious stoop specifically for the purpose of condescending to listen to what you have to say, which he will find useful in the years to come when he pretends to listen to his constituents. When he assumes this listening pose, he also raises one eyebrow to show that he is being attentive. By the very gesture through which he seeks to elevate you, he makes you feel like a second class citizen. When I say that he looks down *on* you, as opposed to down at you, I was picking my words carefully as Calypso Sitzclarence might.

Weeks later, I saw him on the telly that someone had switched on in The Sex Club. He was appearing on the Young Debater of 1975 programme, the rising star of the new left. When they miked him up and asked him why we should listen to what he has to say and give him our vote instead of Edward Heath, he bent down with his rounded shoulders so that he was in the same frame as the interviewer, raised that eyebrow of his and just said, *"Because more people worship the rising than the setting sun."*

And did he give credit to me in his interview? In your dreams! But I guess the words were those of Pompey the Great, not mine, to start with.

Sydney's set in Gisborne Court is full of books and furniture. No-one else had really bothered to make a mark on their gaffs or personalise them beyond sticking an Athena poster on the walls, usually featuring either a female tennis player rubbing her arse, or Jane Fonda in Barbarella. Our rooms were transient hangouts, mere *embarcaderos* and caravanserai, because we knew that when each term finished we would have to remove everything so that the college could let the rooms out to Japanese tourists. Our homes were no more than stage sets. Indeed, perhaps that was why they called them sets. Shanty towns occupied no more than 12 weeks at a time.

But not so Sydney's set. Sydney looked like he had lived here all his life, and probably been in occupation for several previous lives also. Books everywhere, but not in a bookcase or scattered around: there are clumps of art books on matching gueridons, and some others with a clutch of old photos on the red japanned table; some wedged between a pair of bookends formed of curl-tailed monkeys; there is a bubbling silver samovar with eagle handles, a toaster for changing the smells in the room, a pianola at which he would pedal furiously in the only form of exercise he permitted himself; the Indiacraft sandalwood table that was dedicated to rolling joints on, as it would be sacrilege to risk harming the Louis XIV gueridons; the tapestry hanging on the wall depicting a Unicorn and a princess; the absinthe fountain filled with the Green Fairie with its three taps; the Cambridge amp and Technic turntable; the gigantic Bowers and Wilkins speakers.

He has silver candelabra on the baby grand just like Liberace, and he has proper things to put his joss sticks in so that the ash doesn't go all over the dhurrie. In the middle of the room, there is a leather pommel horse where there should be a settee; in the alcove, a burner charged with an amber glob of frankincense smoulders noiselessly. Sydney was going to die here. And he has one of those Jewish things on the door frame as you enter the set, but his is upside down.

Seeing me looking, Sydney says: "Omani frankincense, best in the world! Fruit of the Boswellia tree. So much better than Somali frankincense. You know the Bedouins used to use this as currency? When the three wise men brought the infant Jesus gifts of gold, frankincense and myrrh, you know, ounce for ounce, the frankincense was more valuable than the gold. I would say that this resin is my favourite resin after cannabis resin!"

It was as if the room had been designed to peel away your inhibitions by stages. Everyone of an athletic disposition who walked through the door gravitated towards the pommel horse and wanted to have a go but then backed down, because the commitment was just too great and the risk:reward ratio between impressing everyone with your athletic prowess:making a complete cunt of yourself, was too weighted in favour of making a complete cunt of yourself. Those not of the pommel horse persuasion, approached the pianola or the tapestry, the bubbling samovar or the Green Fairie.

The room held magnets for every taste, and the room was therefore a lodestone in itself. Every time I approached his front door with the inverted mezuzah I felt like an iron filing. Ingram had coined the name Substance Abuse Central for this magical space. Sydney was not just a mate you visited. He was a destination in his own right.

When the sixties started, without exception, I would say that we were a nation of racially prejudiced, misogynistic, queer-bashing bigots. What changed all that by the end of the sixties? It was India. India became cool: it was the ultimate gap year destination. Because you could get any sort of recreational drug you wanted there. Then the Beatles made it more cool. We all wanted to learn the sitar. Ravi Shankar was Top of the Pops, and yoga instructors were the forerunners to celebrity hairdressers and chefs.

What finally flushed all the detritus of racial prejudice and homophobia down the can, what we have to thank for the all-inclusive, tolerant society that we have since founded, is India and recreational drugs. India was to us are what the Italians were to Shakespeare and the Jacobeans. They were fascinating and they were feared.

On the one hand, Italy was the country of da Vinci and Michelangelo and the Renaissance. On the other hand it was the country of the Borgias and Machiavelli. Drugs and a generation of deep-thinking drug-takers at the finest Universities, shaped modern society, and then, pulling up the ladder after us, as if to prevent others gaining this sacred knowledge, we passed copious legislation to ensure that the ordinary bloke in the street didn't get his hands on any of it ever again. And in the van, shaping this new Age of Disenlightenment, 20 years on, these new Dark Ages, was Ingram Frazier.

I am wandering. I was trying to tell you that I thought I had no space for being any more impressed by Sydney's rooms and their contents - until I clapped eyes on the Recordati fireplace. What kind of person, on coming up to Cambridge, brings his own seventeenth century fireplace surround with him? I fed shillings and sixpences into the meter that provided indiscriminate gas to warm my rooms when I could afford it.

When I was a boy, we poured Aladdin pink paraffin into the heater, and in my head the feeling of pleasant warmth is still inseparable from the stink of kerosene fumes. It never occurred to me in those days that warmth could also be an ornament, a thing of beauty. It never occurred to me that by the time I came to commit these recollections to paper, there would be no such things as shillings and sixpences, and that even to mention them might be a criminal act. They would be gone, off to the fairies along with the silver sixpence and octagonal thrupenny bits that were already antiquities withdrawn from currency.

Sydney's windows are always perspiring with condensation, whatever the season. The bubbling of the water pipes, the steaming of the samovar. As the windows mist over, runes appear in the glass. I can make out dates, symbols, letters, but disjointed in meaning. I draw Sydney's attention to them. "What do they mean?" I ask.

"Must have been written by a previous occupant of this madhouse," he informs. "They appear when the windows mist up. I haven't the heart to rub them out. One day when I am in the right frame of mind, with the help of my Calligrapher-in-Chief here, Lyca, I will decipher them."

I am infinitely comforted that he too sees them. I could have been having one of my funny turns. What a cunt I would have looked if they weren't really there and were just in my imagination.

Then, harking back to Ingram, Sydney says, "It really is stifling in here!" He loosens his cravat.

I turn my head, viewing the hieroglyphics from different angles as they snap in and out of focus. Sydney's rooms have four huge picture windows over the prospect of Gisborne Court and the crab-apple tree planted firmly in its centre, and every inch of every window, from feet to forelock, is covered in these strange inscriptions. As though a madman was immured here for years with nothing but his index finger to keep him company. They are marshalled into some sort of order.

The words, if words they be, are broken up giving the appearance of sentences; sometimes there appear to be formulae; some of the letters are accented above, like French, some below like Hebrew vowels. There are series of dots and dashes like Morse code; there are flags, like semaphore. There must be meaning here, if one could but find it. Maybe it is written in a language only machines can understand. It is a series of instructions given to a computer to unscramble its meaning. *A sodden Bible written in the language of rooks.*

Perhaps a student previously occupying this set committed his year-end dissertation to the medium of windows. Maybe the topic of his dissertation was windows; but what could there possibly be of interest in Windows? There is one small space in the bottom right hand corner of the last window that has not been inscribed. It is as though the invisible author has left a space for me to finish his sentence when I finally come to understanding. Me and Sydney's window, like an old couple, finishing off one another's sentences.

Art in the Home.

"What does it all mean?" I ask again.

"It means *Don't write on the fucking windows*!" says Sydney.

Sydney feigns a kind of social *hauteur* so that he is always slightly abstracted from the action, detached, observing rather than immersing himself in it; encouraging others to participate whilst keeping a safe distance himself, so that he has the option of disowning it afterwards. Later on we would coin a word for this: *deniability*. He has clearly stuck that vaulting horse smack in the middle of his set as a challenge to others to assay it, but wouldn't dream of making a cunt of himself by having a go. It's Sydney's version of the Sword in the Stone. He is always bifurcating himself from the real action. When he is busy summoning up the Devil, he presides, but he doesn't participate. He makes others do his bidding.

But he doesn't quite pull it off. So instead of ending up like Fitzgerald's

Great Gatsby, he is more like Dali's Great Masturbator.

His detachment is voyeuristic, so that the true participants, those of us who have committed ourselves to the project, regard him with a certain equivocation. Sybaritically, Sydney and Calypso may have exhibitionistic tendencies, so the dynamic between them somehow works, like the bird that cleans the teeth of the crocodile. You can stare at Lyca as much as you like, because she can't see that you're doing it.

Obviously, Spud and Burt like the free bevvies and narcotic substances sempiternally available in Sydney's set, but Burt has a weather eye always on the lookout either for something better going on that he might be missing, or for someone coming to apprehend him for the illicit enjoyment he feels guilty about. His whole life is like a bloke watching cavorting lesbians in an Italian art house film. He doesn't know whether to look at the tits or pretend he's reading the subtitles.

Ingram Frazier takes the joint and I know it's going to be a Wildean moment of self-dramatization with him posing with the bong and wasting it when the rest of us would far prefer to smoke it

The joint's burning unevenly because it was badly packed, but commendable that it was packed at all given how stoned Spud was when he rolled the fucking thing. Ingram is flicking at it with his index finger nail with feigned nonchalance, attempting to pack it down into a cylinder of greater uniformity, as though we were sharing a biffer with Blake's Urizen; but all he is achieving is the expulsion of molten rocks of burning dope onto the arms of Sydney's armchair. Because I perceive that the joint isn't going to circulate until Ingram has finished having his Road to Damascus moment with it, I am transfixed by the irregular rotundity of the burn holes blistering up on the arms of the chair, like buboes erupting on the face of a victim of the Black Death.

My mind flips from burn holes to bullet holes.

If you filled your tank up with petrol that year Esso were giving away James Bond self-adhesive bullet holes to iron onto your car windscreen. Never before had so many lonely wankers outside their sad suburban semis, washed their cars and then *ironed* the pretend bullet holes onto the clean surface.

Obviously, feminism has come a long way, but in the sixties, the reason men were ironing fake bullet holes onto their car windscreens was because they thought women were gullible enough to believe they were secret agents if their motors were riddled with ersatz ordinance. They believed that they stood a greater prospect of enticing a girl into their Ford Anglia, if she thought she was going to get shot at! I guess we were witnessing the beginnings of feminism, the *fons et origo*: men doing the ironing, even if they were only ironing on bullet holes.

When Adam dug and Eve span.

My gaze reverts to Ingram, posing with the bong, but not sucking it, whilst all of its expensive ingredients are going up in smoke. I am thinking, *Is Frazier the same with fanny?* When he gets a promise, does he go for it like a man possessed, or does he assess it like a fine Havana cigar, doing everything in his power to make the poor woman feel as insecure as possible before he finds some means of holding her to account for his own inability to get a hard-on? He is going to make a great politician.

He is still tossing and flicking away at the reefer, like hemp grows on trees and it doesn't matter if it burns itself away consumed between his fingers and is never shared. Tossing and flicking. Tossing and flicking, we lay waste our powers.

He should be Prime Minister.

And when he finally stopped worrying the burning meteorites out of the doobie and lifted it to his lips, I swear everyone in the room leaned forward perceptibly.

I saw them and I knew them all. And yet
Dauntless the slug-horn to my lips I set,
And blew. "Childe Roland to the Dark Tower came."

Sydney seems unconcerned that Ingram is Bogarding his joint. He has lit a straight, so he has something else to damage his health with while he waits for the blunt to circulate, and he is typing away on his Olympia compact, abstracted from his surroundings. He has headphones on and is clearly clicking the typewriter keys in time with whatever he is listening to. His right foot keeps the rhythm. He is humming, but he has no idea that we can hear his hum.

Through Sydney's big speakers, Debussy's *L'Apres Midi d'un Faune* is playing. I've noticed this about Sydney. As part of his controlling personality, he likes to dictate what other people listen to. Sometimes it's Gustav Mahler. Sometimes it's Wagner. Today we've all got to appreciate L'Apres Midi d'un Faun. But inside his bins Sydney's probably enjoying Dr Hook's *I Got Stoned and I Missed It.*

The foggy air in the room is punctuated by the ping of the bell every time Sydney comes to the end of a line of type. Then he cranks back the carriage and is off again. I can hear from the ratchet that he is typing double-spaced.

Because he has a portable typewriter, he is slightly hunched over it, as if parodying Ingram's self-conscious stoop. If he had the bigger cash-register sort of typewriter, he would be more sit-up-and-beg, less guarded in his posture. *Homo Erectus.* More the upright bank clerk than the hunchbacked bellringer. I know he is working on his dissertation on the Poetry of John Wilmot, the Fifth Earl of Rochester, because, in between his humming along, he is snickering to himself as he types.

I also happen to know that the only reason that he chose that topic for his dissertation is because it gave him an excuse to spend his days copying down and commenting on a cannon of the utmost obscenity. It amuses him that his examiners are going to have to pore over so many C- words and so many F- words, and they are going to have to take him seriously, just as Sydney pretends what he is doing is serious when he tries to summon other-worldly beings. In truth, it's all a big joke for him.

The irony is that this English Earl in unexpurgated form is not even available in England because of the obscenity laws. Some of it Sydney buys in Paris and studiously translates himself. Right now he is working from a Yale University Press edition he sent away to America for. Ping! He reaches the end of another line. He is typing double-spaced so that his dissertation will look longer and weightier when he hands it in.

Now he is cussing. He has mistyped something and is trying to get the white correcting strip lined up so that he can erase it. This requires precision, so he plants his Marlboro in the groove of his Lalique ashtray freeing up both hands. The act of erasing the mistyped character involves threading the white Tip-Ex correcting tape in place of the red and black typewriter ribbon, and then backspacing and retyping the wrong letter repeatedly until the Tip-Ex whites out the black letter beneath it, thereby enabling one to type the correct letter on top. Maybe someday, Sydney's important opus will be put through the X Ray machine to reveal all its false starts.

But right now, it is a bit hit and miss, because concealing black type with white is seldom entirely successful. Sydney's technique is just to hammer down the key harder in an effort to attach as much white to the page as possible; but I can tell from his effing and blinding that it's not having the effect he desires. With his head full of Doctor Hook in his big headphones, he doesn't realise how loud he is. He thinks he is just cussing quietly to himself.

If he was not three quarters of the way down the page, I know he would just rip the paper out, carbon copy and all, and begin from the top again. But he has reached the point of no return. His repeated anvil blows with the same key are inscribing the outlines of his characters onto the typewriter platen, creating its own series of runes, just like the windows. It dawns on me that if I removed the battered platen and fed it into his pianola, it might play me the libretto of his dissertation.

There is a fascination in all the false starts, the beginnings concealed beneath the greatest works. What is particularly irritating to me is that Ingram is not inhaling the joint. He is just posing at being cool with it. Every now and then he holds it at arm's length and gives it a straight look as though the stick is a recalcitrant witness whom he is about to cross-examine. If it were my dope that he was wasting, I would say something. But as it is Sydney's generosity that he is abusing, I don't feel it is my place to tell tales. Ingram will make a great politician, skilled as he is in the art of dissipating other people's assets and contributing nothing himself.

I don't know why I am getting so irritated. Sydney with practiced nonchalance continues his typing. Lyca, with her permanently shut eyes, doesn't even realise the joint is bottlenecked. Eventually, the spliff passes to Sully, the overweight undergraduate. I swear Ingram just played with it all the while and never inhaled.

Sully steeples his fingers and then closes them as though he is going to attempt to use them as a vessel for carrying liquid. His stubby fingers start off in the position of *This is the Church and this is the steeple, Open the gates and here are all the little people*. But then he plants the cardboard filter of the joint in between his two small fingers, turning his hands into a makeshift bellows, and sucks the loco weed forcibly into the Aeolian windbag of his lungs from between a hole appearing between his two thumbs.

He has transformed the meat hooks of his metacarpi into a sheesha pipe. It occurs to me that Burt has two modes: in one mode his furious bellows are inhaling the Acapulco gold seeping through his steepled fingers; in the other mode, Burt is exhaling surreptitiously in his perennial attempts to keep his cows lick airborne. They are like the diastole/systole of the heart.

There must be a word for this act of making a human hookah out of your own dukes the better to inhale the old Dogberry and Verges; but, if there is, I don't know what it is. What the fuck do they teach you when you come to read English at Cambridge?

"But Surely, whatever are you doing?" asks Ingram, clearly perturbed that someone else has put the prop to better use than he did.

"It super-oxygenates the smoke so that more of the active ingredient goes into your lungs," explains Spud, polishing his large spectacles on the end of his tee shirt whilst waiting for the bong to reach him. "You see that bottle of Scotch over there? If I was to drink it neat, my oesophagus would have a heart attack and distribute it left, right and centre around my body, instead of getting it to the sweet spot where I want it to end up. But if I dilute it with water or coke, my oesophagus is caught off guard, and the alcohol hits its mark, getting me twice as pissed as if I had drunk it neat."

Spud, the engineering undergrad, understands stuff that the rest of us don't begin to understand, but he also doesn't mind explaining it to us morons, and he has a knack of being able to use metaphors and illustrations so as to make his explanations more accessible and comprehensible.

However, secretly, there is a kind of canker going around the room, because everyone is just thinking of Sully using both hands to force as much marijuana down himself as possible, thoroughly in keeping with Ingram's secret nickname. Anything that is not nailed to the table goes straight into Sully's gob. He loves his food, but he is completely indiscriminate.

If you have finished your dinner, he will politely ask if you are through, as though he is about to get up and wash the dishes, and when you say that you are, he turns your plate around so that it is facing him, and then he finishes it. Even if you have half-masticated it, and when no-one is looking, pulled it out of your mouth and tried to hide the product under your knife and fork. He is omnivorous. What I don't get about him is this little habit of always turning your plate around first so that it is facing him; and the reason I don't get it is because the plate is round.

And when he does this, Burt will tell you in a matter-of-fact sort of way: "My mother always used to say to me, never leave any food on the plate, as that lot that you have left would feed half the starving children in India."

"Well, why don't you send it to the starving children of India instead of scoffing it?" enquires Ingram.

"Actually, I'm working on that," interrupts Spud, taking the heat off Burt again. "The trouble is that the amount of energy required to get it to them is exactly the same as the amount of energy required to consume it. It's the same with water shortages or famines. The problem is always identical: the amount of energy that it takes to move the stuff from the place that's awash with it to the place that needs it, is the same amount of energy required to destroy it. That's the first law of entropy."

"What's the second law of entropy?" enquires Ingram.

"That the amount of energy required to understand the concept of entropy is the same amount of energy required to blow your head up," says Spud.

I am wondering to myself why Spud keeps taking the heat off Sully and stepping in to answer Sully's questions when Sully is in the hot chair and in difficulty. I think it must be because Spud identifies with

Burt as a larger form of himself. Spud is in a dull sublunary Platonic state of trying to stuff himself into a sausage skin container the size of Burt, but hasn't quite got there yet.

But he wishes to make a pre-emptive strike in anticipation of the time when he eats himself as big as Burt. I am thinking that I can see an opening for a professional that would fulfil this role; someone who would step in and deflect difficult questions fired at important people. I think on my feet. I could do that.

Whilst we are considering this puzzle, Spud elaborates further: "800 billion years ago," he says, grabbing our attention, "two giant neutron stars collided in a galaxy billions of light years away from where our galaxy would be if it existed then, but it hadn't yet been formed. The universe is unpopulated as yet, so it's like the sound of the tree falling in the forest with no-one there to hear it. It takes ten billion years for the sound waves communicating that collision to reach us by which time our universe has been created and, much more recently, mankind has evolved.

"Ten billion years just happens to be the time it takes us to develop the intellect to process that information so that we know that what we are hearing is the sound of two giant neutrons colliding ten billion years ago. If the sound waves had got here a year earlier, we wouldn't have understood what we were hearing. That's entropy."

"That's also a macrocosmic example of a double time scheme," observes Sydney.

In the meantime, until he has figured out the answer to this perennial problem of moving food from places where there is a surplus, to places where there is a shortage, Spud will continue to tip the food down his own neck. Those are life's little ironies for you: the more Spud eats, the fatter Burt becomes.

Through the lips, onto the hips. Spud is not as large as Burt, but he is certainly the next size down. I know I shouldn't say it, but, because of his appearance, Spud is doomed always to play second fiddle. If he makes a scientific breakthrough (as I'm sure he will), someone else is going to have to front it for him, do the presentation; step up to the plate and accept the Nobel Peace Prize.

The sad fact is that if Spud necked less food and drink and took more care of himself, people would pay more attention to what he says. We believe what good-looking people tell us more than we believe what bad-looking people tell us. This is why the most successful conmen are the best-looking. If he is going to be a success, Spud will either have to get himself into shape, or use his undoubted gifts, not for the benefit of mankind, but for its detriment. He is either going to have to become a slim scientist or an evil scientist.

Now Spud draws on the spliff. It's not so much that he actually likes the dope. It's just that if anything at all is being offered that you're supposed to take in the mouth, he wants some of it. If he gate-crashed Dignitas and came upon a couple in the act of fulfilling a suicide pact by quaffing cyanide, he would want to join in.

Ingram's secret nickname for Burt is *The Weapon of Mass Consumption.*

Someone has put the twenty-one and a half minute live version of Steppenwolf's Pusher on the deck, and it is at this point that I realise that the finest poem of the twentieth century is in fact a song. I can feel it all becoming too much for me, but I don't want to call it a day. I make it through the first seventeen minutes, then I think I must have blacked out. But I'm not sure for how long, and I'm not sure if anyone noticed. I think that it was the stripes in Ingram's corduroy jacket that brought it on.

"Very good," pronounces Sydney without removing the headphones. "Help yourself to a speedball," he says nodding towards the absinthe fountain. And why not? What could be finer than a shot of wormwood in the afternoon, active ingredient thujone, a neurotoxin and stimulant accounting for the instant upper-downer effect? I twist the tap and free the genie.

Soon the runes on the windows will all make perfect sense, I tell myself. Besides, I wanted to change the air in my mouth, and it was either the congenial, cleansing aniseed spritz of the Fairie fountain, or put a piece of toast into the toaster. To be completely candid with you, this preoccupation with cleaning my teeth never even occurred to me until Seth Godil came into my life. Sorry! I am getting ahead of myself again.

There is a blank square in the corner of the window just waiting for me to sign it.

Sydney, Burt, Spud and me. One thing we had in common was that we were all devotees of AC/DC and Marvel comics. Most of us wanted to be superheroes. One of us hankered to pen a superhero comic of his own. That was Burt Sully who thought it was wrong that all superheroes were American. He believed the quintessential superhero should be English.

"But surely, they could espouse English values…" he begins.

So there was SpiderMan, AntMan, BatMan, SuperMan, XMan, IronMan.

"But Surely, there should be…."

GentleMan.

"Gentleman," I muse. "I kinda like it. A superhero who is a proper English Lord. Maybe an Earl."

"Or a Diamond Geezer!" dismisses Sydney.

"Which superhero do you most identify with?" Calypso asks Sydney, humouring him. There is no way she can actually be interested.

Sydney, without even thinking: "Dr Charles Francis Xavier."

"But Surely, he's just a bald bloke in a wheelchair!" exclaims Burt. "He's not a proper super hero at all!"

"Ah," says Sydney. "But he surrounds himself with superheroes. He brings out the hero in others. That is how I see myself."

"And which superhero do you want to be?" Calypso asked Ingram, trying to bring him back into the fold of the conversation after having thoroughly alienated him moments earlier.

"Me?" Ingram looked genuinely surprised at the question. "I don't want to be any superhero. I told you. I want to be Prime Minister of England, a socialist Prime Minister, but not one driven by envy politics and jealousy of what the other bloke's got. I'll be a Neitzschean superman, a glorious affirmation of self. I will bring peace to the world and recognition of human rights. Those are the most superhuman deeds a mortal can do, and I plan to do them. The rest is bollocks and fantasy."

"Wow!" says Calypso. "Can you follow that Burt?"

Burt Sully: "I too will be socialist Prime Minister of England."

"Good heavens!" exclaims Sydney. "They're just like London buses. None come along for an age and then two come along at once."

"Don't take the piss out of them," says Calypso. "At least they've staked their claims. They're going for something that's ambitious, but it's just about achievable, whereas you're all tilting at windmills. Superheroes, my tush! You know what the first sign of madness is? Building castles in the sky. The second sign of madness is going to live in them. You're all at the secondary stage. Fuck knows what will become of you when it goes tertiary. It's a collective madness, shared psychosis, *folie á deux*."

Sydney has decided to get up from his typing and fetch something across the other side of his set, forgetting that he is still connected to his amp via the headphones cable. Momentarily, his head jerks sideways like he's dangling from the gallows, before the jack snaps out of the amp. He removes the bins and places them on his desk, pretending that nothing has happened.

"What's a tush?" Spud asks quietly, hoping that Sydney won't hear, but he does, because he has just had his headphones forcibly removed. Sydney, who has finished his typing and correcting had crossed the room to collect his copy of the JC and is now reading the small print in the Jewish Chronicle, looks up from it to stare Spud in the eye. "It's Yiddish for your backside," he says. "Tush, tooshka. Means arse."

"Or maybe vessel, container." Suddenly all eyes are on the one with shut eyes. Is Calypso second-guessing Sydney's knowledge of Yiddish? "As in Penta-Teuch," she says. "The five vessels of the law."

"Lyca! My Infinite Jewel of the Night!" intones Sydney, "Continuous One of the Heavens. Are you blasphemely suggesting that there is some correspondence between the Five Books of the Old Testament dictated by Jehovah, no less, to Moses—and your exquisite backside?"

No," she says, "*Blasphemously!*" Correcting him.

"But you do know," says Sydney, "that the original vessel, the original palanquin, was the Ark of the Covenant. This travelling about of mine in a howda is not some new-fangled craze. It's been going on since biblical times."

Once Sydney has put the big bins back on his ears and reconnected himself to the amp, so I think he can't hear what we are saying, I ask Spud: "What is it, do you think, that Sydney finds to read all day long in the Jewish Chronicle?"

"He doesn't read it," Spud explains. "It's the printer's ink. He uses it for cleaning the windows of his motor. He says that the ink in the JC is best, because the Jews are too greedy to put any fixative on the paper, so it comes off all over the place. It's the finest method ever devised for cleaning glass. Shame he doesn't use it to clean all that crap off his windows in here."

Spud is taking in the work of art that is Sydney's room. The paintings and tapestries on the walls, the Moroccan dhurries on the floor, the Murano glass mirrors and chandeliers.

"I've never seen anything like it!" pronounces Spud Mullins at length. "Every inch is decorated." Then, admiring Sydney's tapestry of the maiden and the unicorn, "I've got linoleum in my set; I don't even have carpet on the floor, but you've got it on the walls!"

"Not quite every inch. Look again, dear boy. There's the windows, and…" he averts his gaze upwards knowingly, "…the ceiling. To be fair, I couldn't really do much about the windows. I regard them as "listed". But, as for the ceiling. Well, that's another story, another story entirely. The ceiling is a work in progress. I left it blank for a good reason.

"You know those Brown Bars in Amsterdam, brown from exhaled smoke, encrusted with nicotine stains until they are no more than a metaphor for the smoker's own insides? I am trying to create a collaborative work of art here. Every memory of every cigarette, cigar, joint or chillum, smoked in this room is being transferred to the ceiling in spidery handwriting that scholars, less stoned than us, in hundreds of years' time, will be able to interpret.

"Cave paintings in Lascaux," Sydney continues. "Hieroglyphics in the Valley of the Kings, runes in Celtic cellars, cuneiform shapes on clay tablets; the Epic of Gilgamesh. Who knows what they will find up there? My ceiling is the DNA for every rowdy night that has passed here. All that it needs is an interpreter. The Sistine Chapel will be a mere bagatelle compared to this. A book written in the breath of heroes."

"Bollocks!" says Ingram. "It's all smoke and mirrors."

Sydney is correct. If you stare at his ceiling long enough, patterns emerge, faces appear, words write themselves. I find it calming to discern the shapes up there. As one would expect, at different times of day in the altered light, they are quite changed.

I lie on my back on the floor and take a photograph of Sydney's ceiling so that I can contemplate it later. Emotion recollected in tranquillity.

Ingram is retelling the story to Spud who wasn't paying attention.

"And you do not think it incongruous," Ingram whispers to Spud, safely out of Sydney's earshot, "that this self-styled Master of the Dark Arts is suddenly a qualified Talmudic scholar?"

"I thought he was kind of devout," says Spud. "I mean, he's always poring over the fine print in the Jewish Chronicle."

"That fucking *oven-dodger* isn't devout!" corrects Ingram, showing his true colours now Sydney has his headphones back over his ears. "He's reading the Obituaries! He's looking to see if someone has died and left him some geld, some money."

If Ingram seriously wants to become a socialist Prime Minister of England, he is going to have to do something about his ant-Semitic streak. Either that, or consign a lot of the electorate to the ovens.

My head is spinning as I contemplate the shapes in the brown ceiling.

Humber Super Snipe

Sydney drives a Humber Super Snipe. Somehow he has wangled his way into getting permission from the college to park it in St Peter's Terrace. This old man's car is an odd choice for a youth of comfortable means. Most of us aspired to a Mini or a Triumph Stag. Simon Templar in *The Saint* drove a Volvo, but even he couldn't make it sexy. The Snipe however was very large and Sydney is a gregarious type.

We are parked outside the White Swan at Fulbourn, wherein we have consumed a fine dinner. We are watching the rain piss down the windscreen, whilst Calypso rolls a joint on the Haynes Workshop Manual to steady Sydney's hands for the drive back to Cambridge. The car is fogging up nicely.

No-one would dream of taking the Super Snipe as far as Fulbourn, which must be all of 12 miles outside of Cambridge, without a workshop manual, explaining how to strip it down, because this motor is not famed for its reliability. In the boot there are jump leads for getting her started, and bottles of distilled water for topping up the battery; there are tyre levers for the tyres and wire brushes for scraping the spark plugs.

There is a jerry can of petrol to replenish the tank after someone has syphoned it out, and there are bottles of Duckhams, because this baby leaks oil as though she has come on heat. As a Renaissance *uomo universale*, Sydney would not venture out onto the roads were he not capable of stripping the engine down, extracting the viscera of the wiring loom and fixing everything in the pouring rain on a dark night. Ha-ha! Don't you believe it.

He buys a big car so that when it gives up on him, he can climb into the backseat and fall asleep, and he embraces the likes of Spud Mullins into his circle of devil-summoning acolytes, because Spud can take anything to bits and put it back together again, probably better than it was before.

Ingram, who still seems to be in a state of nervous shock following the ride down at breakneck speed, and who hasn't enjoyed the benefit of a joint to calm his nerves, is asking Sydney why he has to drive so fast.

"My theory," explains Sydney, "is that the less time I spend on the road, the less likely I am to have an accident."

We are having what passes in this company, after four joints and a quart of wormwood, as a serious discussion on the topic of why none of us have ever come across a girl who was remotely interested in reading superhero comics. Even when the makers offered up female heroines such as Supergirl and Wonder Woman, they weren't read by girls as role models, despite the fact that Wonder Woman is as high an IQ in hot pants as anyone could ask for.

They were read by men, as soft core pornography. "And when I say 'read'," says Sydney, "*I mean read as in the Aretino sense of a book so dirty you could only read it with one hand.*" We all agree that Wonder Woman is a male wet dream brought to life, and muse upon how AC comics can create such sensational heroines and such lamentable heroes, and conclude that is because they are all two-dimensional, unlike Stan Lee's creations. Stan is short for Stanley. So Stan Lee's correct name must be Stanley Lee. It has a ring to it.

And Marvel seems to have all the best costumes: Spiderman, the Fantastic Four, the X Men, Iron Man's suit, the Black Panther. But then once in a lifetime you come up against a costume like Wonder Woman's, as worn by the inimitable Lynda Carter on Saturday night TV, and the balance of super power shifts back to AC. Never mind that the plots were rubbish. Wonder Woman was in a class of her own. The red boots with the white socks foaming at the top, the hot pants made from the American flag; the impossibly pneumatic bustier; this is a woman with a golden lasso.

We all agree that she is the product of a very mixed-up psyche. And, indeed, she was created by an American psychologist, Walter Moulton Marston. A guy who knew what he was doing. She is a demi goddess. An Amazon, but one with both tits intact—the real Amazons used to have the right breast removed for better archery in a very early form of elective mastectomy.

Where she calls home, she is known as Princess Diana of Themyscira. In the US, she goes by the pseudonym, Diana Prince, a US agent at the Department for Metahuman affairs. But this is a US agent who likes to wipe her arse with the stars and stripes. She fights for gender equality. She endures heroism as an undercover agent for the Woman's Movement. Like Calypso, she has blue blood in her. And blue hot pants.

How prescient is that? That we were creaming our jeans for Princess Diana 9 years before we got our very own. The people's princess.

Lyca blames the introduction of the long bow for woman's slide into physical second place. Before that, she explains, the weapon of choice was the cross bow, and according to all the reliable records, women were pretty proficient at using it, and served on the front line. The long bow gained ascendancy because one could fire again in a fraction of the time it took to reload a cross bow, so it was more efficient if something was coming at you fast. But women couldn't draw the string of the long bow back far enough to use it lethally. Because their right breasts got in the way. That was the beginning of women staying at home with the kids and the man going out to work.

When Adam dug and Eve span...

Women weren't called upon again to aid the war effort for 1,000 years until we needed their assistance in the munitions factories. But my God, they had been nursing a list of demands during that 1,000 years, so that when we called upon their services, they had their wish list fully evolved and on tap. Thus came the Suffragettes.

Lyca is such a Golconda of knowledge. I could listen to her all night long. I would love that opportunity.

There is something rhythmic and comforting about the sound of the rain beating on the roof of the car. We are all getting very smashed, because we are both smoking and re-inhaling the narcotic within the sealed container of the Super Snipe's cabin. Of course, we could wind down a window, but that would be sacrilege. Not only would we get wet, but the likelihood was that the handle would come off in our hands.

The characters are forming. They are on every window. The same notations that appear on Sydney's windows at Gisborne Court. They seem to be in sets of four. What do the sequences mean? The windscreen wipers go swish-swish-swish. They erase the runes, like wiping the blackboard, but they come back again each time. I am searching for the key that unlocks all of this, that gives it meaning. There has to be a can opener.

It is as though it is my destiny. It follows me around everywhere; but I don't understand it. Just like Cassandra, the Trojan priestess who could foretell the future with unerring accuracy, but whose fate was that nobody ever believed her. So she never made any difference. All she could do was say *I told you so* afterwards.

I subscribed to Sydney's earlier story about a madman previously inhabiting his set with nothing to keep him company except his finger. But that doesn't begin to explain what similar markings are doing inside Sydney's Humber Super Snipe.

No-one else seems to notice. They are all too stoned to be attentive like me. I am in fine fettle.

Why do people name their daughters Cassandra?

As it's a weekday, Burt is without his child bride, but he still manages to take up two places in the Snipe's back bucket seat. Because his own requirements in a relationship with a female are so rudimentary, he makes the mistake of thinking that all women are like the shallow, vacuous, vain women he likes to date. Burt says that the reason women aren't interested in superhero comics is because they don't have enough imagination to identify with the characters.

An observation that was perhaps deliberately designed to get Calypso's goat. Calypso says it's because woman have too much imagination and occupy fantasy realms of their own making and don't need to sign up to Stan Lee's fulminations.

I am thinking, *What is she thinking when Sydney is fucking her? When Sydney is fulfilling his fantasies in his mumbo jumbo rituals, what is going through her head? Is she laughing at him and the rest of us? Are her closed eyes sealing her within her own fantasy realm?*

I am imagining her as Wonder Woman. But it doesn't fit. What does fit is if I imagine her as my vulnerable ballerina. Years later, emotion recollected in tranquillity, as they say, I can tell you this as your narrator, but I didn't make these connections at the time. I want to look after her. I want her to be at home whilst I go to the office.

Sir, I know she can read Latin and Greek, but can she spin?

We agree that women have a different kind of imagination.

Ingram says that they have the kind of imagination that will rifle through a man's private stuff in search of evidence of infidelity. His voice has the conviction of one who speaks from painful experience. Maybe that is what turned him off women.

Lyca says that Ingram is confusing imagination with curiosity, and the instinct to rifle through a guy's private things is just curiosity. She says that throughout literature women are punished for their curiosity. In Charlotte Bronte or de Sade or Pauline Reage, the woman in search of knowledge enters upon the man's secret lair or his private study, his den or his dungeon, the one room that she has been forbidden from entering. But the retribution for indulging this curiosity is always wholly disproportionate.

She is slain, or she has to spend the rest of her life in sexual servitude. But again and again in literature, the women do precisely that. Ingram says the endless repetition is because men endlessly repeat their shallow sexual preferences; and I say that history may repeat itself, but only ritual repeats itself precisely. And Ingram says that he likes the sound of that and will make a note of it and that I am destined to be his Press Secretary when he is Prime Minister.

But then Calypso points out that it all started with Eve, who was forbidden from eating from the tree that would give her knowledge of good and evil, but did so anyway. Seduced by the devil, she stuck two fingers up at God, and then we all fell from Grace. Adam and Eve, Eden's original *Start Rite kids* starting out on their long journey towards the spot where the parallel lines meet.

They were told by God that they could do anything, have anything; eat or drink anything; Paradise was theirs for the taking; they were beautiful and they were stark naked. There was only one thing that they must not do; one tiny thing no bigger than an apple, amongst the whole phantasmagorical magic of everything else in the universe, all of which was permitted.

So what did she do? You guessed it. Like when you see a sign that says Wet Paint. You just have to touch it to see if it's still wet.

When Adam dug…

Stoned Sydney is burbling on some horseshit about *the hegemony of curiosity*. He is rolling the words around on his tongue, so delighted with the auditory experience that it matters not to him that they communicate no sense to anybody else. What the words lack in meaning they make up in richness of sound and texture. They are the spoken equivalent of what is written on the inside of his set's and his car's windows. What the language lacks in meaning it makes up in plangency.

I am left wondering why so many men appear to have this essential accessory that I am lacking. Why don't I have a subterranean dungeon that woman can stumble upon to their eternal misfortune?

History repeating itself, becoming a tradition, until it repeats itself so often that it becomes an institution, and then it becomes reformed whilst history remoulds itself back into the same thing.

The Tree of Knowledge of Good and Evil. The serpent in the garden.

And that this place may thoroughly be thought
True Paradise I have the Serpent brought.

The Man of Letters

"Nick, have you brought your paper on Blake's *Ghost of a Flea*?" Dr Max Pfläfflin asks me.

He knows very well that I haven't brought the fucking paper, haven't written it yet and probably never will. He uses it as an instrument of control so that I am on the back foot from the beginning of the session.

Pfläfflin is Aryan, but too pudgy and pink-faced to be a fully subscribed member of the master race. So he plays at being an English country squire instead. Brown brogues. Harris tweeds. Knitted bowtie. All he is lacking is a William Evans side-by-side 12 bore broken in the crook of one arm, a brace of pheasants on the other, and a gundog slathering at his feet. He has to be a spy. No matter how he apes English manners, he can't quite rid himself of his clipped German accent. Sitting there in his wingback chair with his book open on his knees, he resembles a tub of taramosalata in a tweed suit.

Pfläfflin, my director of studies, is discussing the Faust legend with me and the rest of his acolytes.

"My problem," I say, "is that every time I get near to the ending, I realise the beginning is wrong, so I have to go back and start again."

Pfläfflin computes this proposition for a moment before dismissing it with the remark: "Hah! Sisyphus complex But with a biro instead of a boulder!" Pfläfflin is pleased to be belittling me in front of my mates and one other bloke who isn't my mate. In fact, I haven't set eyes on him before.

Yes, there is a new boy in our little clique. I am looking at him and thinking he reminds me of the *Ghost of a Flea*. I don't know his name, but he is wearing a sleeveless vest, and the contrast between the over-dressed squire-impersonating Pfläfflin and this guy who didn't even think to put on a whole shirt before coming to his first tutorial, is endearing. He looks like a body builder with a square jaw.

In fact, he looks like he has climbed out of the pages of a Marvel comic. He is impossibly musclebound. He is swarthy, of mixed race. He is so large he seems to fill the room, and the book we are considering resembles a postage stamp in his big hands. This is what the Mighty Thor would look like if his dad was Sidney Poitier instead of Odin.

He doesn't have a notebook, but he has a felt-tipped marker. If he considers something sufficiently important, he makes a note of it on his own skin. The notes are necessarily laconic, because there is not a lot of usable skin left on his body.

The most curious thing about this character (and I use the word 'character' advisedly) is that he has characters tattooed on every visible inch of his skin. Letters, symbols. I'd swear that the same author who made his mark in the condensation on Sydney's glazing gouged these glyphs into this guy's epidermis. I am finding it very hard to concentrate on whatever Pfläfflin is burbling on about, because my gaze keeps drifting back to the pictographs on this dude's integument, wondering what it all means. He could be a set text in his own right.

I'm not sure if he's written in an ancient language that no longer exists or if these are depictions of unrecognised zodiacs and extinct botanical species. He's a Sphinx to me.

It's like cheating at an exam: I keep stealing furtive glances at the big guy, trying to read what he has written on him. But not only do I not understand the words or the language they are written in, I don't even recognise the alphabet. It is a student's worse nightmare. You sit down at your desk and open your exam paper, and it is all gibberish, written in birdsong.

In those days, only sailors had tattoos, and they were all anchors or declarations of undying love for their mums. Apart from his face, every square centimetre of this guy's greenhide is tattooed; but none of it is pictures or avowals of love for his mother. It consists entirely of writing, but I can't understand a fucking word of it. I want to, because it must have been really important for him to have endured the discomfort of sitting still whilst, having this occult meaning transferred to his hide over so many hours and days.

I am trying to read it from left to right, side to side, up and down, portrait, landscape, tilting my head in different orientations. But it's a closed book to me, like the stuff on Sydney's windows. The difficulty is that the writing resembles recognisable characters, but isn't quite. Just like my girlfriend. It's a prick tease.

"The problem with the Faust legend," my director of studies, Dr Max Pfläfflin, says, "is structural."

I drift back into the session.

This is what Pfläfflin always does. He puts a proposition on the table, but we, as his students, then have to develop his own theory for him. We have to fill it in and put flesh on the bones of his skeleton, and then, when we have enthusiastically done all this hard work for him, he usually does one of two things: either he shoots it down in flames and says it's all a load of crap, forgetting that it was his hypothesis in the first place; or alternatively, he dismisses the topic and moves on; but then you find the theory that you have developed for him published shamelessly under his own name a few months later in an academic journal.

He has seminal ideas; he abuses his position of authority to seduce impressionable teenagers into incubating his false starts and bringing his fledgling suggestions to maturity, and he then steals the finished product. He is a real cuckoo. He's got all of us undergraduates sitting on his eggs. This is how I have justified to myself my inability to submit my paper to him. He is a plagiarist. He warehouses other people's dreams. These days, someone would say that we had been abused; but in those days we just regarded it as another incidence of everyday cannibalism.

"Yes, Nick." He is picking on me, as usual. I am going to have to develop his theory for him because I am *persona non grata* due to the fact that I haven't delivered my essay on the *Ghost of a Flea.*

Pfläfflin is the author of a short novel that is on the sixth form syllabus, because it is considered suitable for adolescents. Is it a commendable thing, I am thinking to myself, to have your deeply profound novel on the human condition relegated to something on the sixth form syllabus for a bunch of posturing wankers exploding with hormones to pontificate on? He hasn't written anything else.

It is possible that the novel he did succeed in publishing was only written as a result of the collegiate efforts I have described, which would explain why sixth formers like it: they probably wrote it. He could have had six different classes working on six different chapters, none of them comprehending the finished article, like workers in a car factory, toiling over different parts and panels with no vision of the finished whole. His success as an author is due to the absence of competition. Who else would want to write a short novel with a target audience of sixth formers? He is a one-book failure.

He is a sad bloke, but like all the best failed blokes, he is more likeable than those who made it in life. He is what Plato would describe as a failure at two removes. A bloke permanently in a Platonic state of trying to become a failure, but never quite making it in this imperfect sublunary world. If Pfläfflin could come to terms with his failure in the same way that I have come to terms with his failure, he would be a lot less objectionable.

Despite the fact that he wrote his stupid book ten years ago, he still has a stack of them on his desk as though he is about to start signing them for admiring adolescents. The stack isn't quite straight. Artfully, he has attempted to arrange the bricks casually so that when some unsuspecting undergraduate chances upon them in his set, she can say: *Oh, I didn't realise you were that Max Pfläfflin, the famous author!* as though there could be two people with that denomination.

Why did I automatically assume that his victim would be female? Did her curiosity bring her to his lair?

"It's just a male fantasy," I begin. "The protagonist gets 24 transitory years of pleasure in exchange for eternal damnation. Because this is essentially a male wankfest, whether we are analysing the works of Christopher Marlowe or Goethe or Mozart, it is the same old story. The Faust character acts out a number of very shallow male fantasies, which we enjoy with him; but he then gets carted off to hell for all eternity, which we don't experience with him, because, well, life's too short."

"Isn't that the whole point?" says Max. "That life is too short?"

There is no logical sequel to the Faust legend.

"Okay, let's go stream of consciousness for a while," says Pfläfflin, cracking his knuckles menacingly. These are everyday words for the rest of us, but because Pfläfflin is not speaking in his mother tongue, he arranges the words with possessive pride, as though he has picked them up in art house movies, and there follows a self-conscious Pinter-esque pause as though he's expecting applause.

Such turns of phrase, such locution, hold great value to him, but to my thinking, as a natural inhabitant of this realm, they are just so many fridge magnets. I wonder if he is going to read me Molly Bloom's soliloquy from Ulysses; but, no, he wants to talk about Christopher Marlowe on the pretext of the Faust association, but mainly because I haven't handed in my paper on the *Ghost of a Flea*.

"Kit Marlowe," he rolls the three syllables around in his mouth, "or should I say 'William Shakespeare'?" Pfläfflin pronounces his W's as V's, like a comic book Kraut.

"Mr Sully…" he says, picking on Burt.

"But surely…" stammers Burt, hoping someone else will pick up the subject. But there is no escape from Pfläfflin. Spud reads engineering, so there is no Spud Mullins in this English tutorial to come to Burt's rescue. This time the honour falls on Burt to develop Pfläfflin's thesis.

"Marlowe was born in 1564, the same year as Shakespeare," says Burt.

"That's what one would expect," says Pfläfflin. He looks from pupil to pupil, but we are all stumped, and none of us are in a position to develop his stream of consciousness. He's going to have to coax us a bit on this one. Having drawn a collective blank from his pupils, Pfläfflin has to continue alone: "Because they were one and the same fucking person! " he cries, going red in the face.

"Marlowe was a student at this very university, at Corpus Christi, but we know for a fact he was never here. It was just a front. He was a spy in Walsingham's army of spies and he spent all his time overseas spying. He was without a shadow of a doubt the most senior and accomplished undercover agent in Queen Elizabeth's network of spies of whom Walsingham was the handler.

"But in 1593, aged 29, his cover was blown. Walsingham therefore staged Marlowe's death in a preposterous cover story where Marlowe is involved in a dispute over the reckoning of a drinks bill at a Deptford tavern and ends up being stabbed through the eye with a dagger that kills him."

When Max Pfläfflin pronounces "the reckoning", he sounds like someone calling for the bill in a dodgy kebab house on the Reeperbahn:

die Rechnung bitte. I imagine that in his written work, he capitalises the first letters of all his nouns. For some reason this calls to my mind Ingram's reference to geld and *oven-dodger*s.

"At this point in time," Pfläfflin continues, "Marlowe has written the most amazing plays, Tamburlaine the Great Parts 1 and 2, Edward II, Dido Queen of Carthage, and of course, Doctor Faust. William Shakespeare, on the other hand, is a nobody, who by 1593 had written nothing but juvenilia."

He pronounces the Jew in juvenilia as though he is hankering to put it in the ovens himself. His face is turning deeper taramosalata as he warms to his subject.

"Nothing of stature: the Comedy of Errors, King John, Titus. They're all juvenilia and drunken collaborations with homosexuals." As Pfläfflin warms to his subject, his accent deteriorates. "Then Marlowe dies and suddenly Shakespeare starts producing a canon of the most profound and lyrical drama that has ever been written. *Hamlet, Othello, King Lear, Measure for Measure, The Tempest.* And the strangest thing about this guy, Shakespeare, is that he comes from nowhere. There is no record of his existence, until Marlowe supposedly ceases to exist. He is the original Hero from Zero. Shakespeare is Kit Marlowe in the witness protection programme."

Pfläfflin has developed his own theory for a change, or maybe the group that was leaving this room as we drifted in had contributed it and he was just regurgitating. I would like to shoot it down in flames, but our hour is up and Substance Abuse Central beckons. My body is telling me I need the Green Fairie and something to take the edge off it. However, as the others are filing out of his doorway, Max calls me back. There are just him and me, and the new boy, because the new boy doesn't know where he is supposed to go next. Obviously one thing he hasn't had tattooed onto his pellicle is the fucking timetable.

"Nick, one moment, please." Perfectly polite, but he clearly wants to aggravate me further because he waited until the others had left before putting the brogue in. Why does he call Burt Mr Sully and me plain Nick?

"What subject are you reading at Cambridge?"

I see. He wants to manoeuvre me into position with a couple of rhetorical questions I can't argue with, before making a complete cunt of me in front of the new boy.

"English literature," I answer. I didn't have anywhere else to go.

"English literature. Ah so." Again, the Ah so spoken like a Marvel comic book Fritz. "You declined my invitation to write a dissertation on Milton's Paradise Lost, and you have now been more than six weeks failing to hand in the paper you said you wished to write in its stead on Blake's The *Ghost of a Flea*. What I am struggling to understand here, Nick, is that Blake's *Ghost of a Flea* is not a work of English literature. It's a watercolour.

"And, Nick, *kein Blatt vor den Mund nehmen*, since you haven't even managed to perform for me the very small honour of writing one Blatt in six weeks, maybe you could be so kind as to introduce Seth here to your wide circle of friends. Seth Godil has been transferred from Warwick University. I'm sure you will make him very welcome here in Cambridge. Show him around. Show him the ropes, Nick."

"Can we talk about this first?" I ask.

"*There's nothing you can talk to me about that I don't already know,*" Pfläfflin replies.

I leave with my new charge in tow. Of all the fine upstanding students at this venerable institution to whom Pfläfflin could have entrusted Seth, why did he choose to condemn him to my circle of friends? Of all the alumni angels, why place him under my leathern wing?

How did I end up wet-nursing a muscleman who needs a cryptologist to unravel him?

The Birdwood

I go to speak as soon as I have closed the two front doors to Pfläfflin's rooms. It's a feature of Peterhouse that many of the entrances to the students' and Fellows' rooms have two sets of front doors sandwiched together for better noise and heat insulation. Seth puts his finger to his lips to keep me quiet as we take the lift down. It is not until we have completely exited not only Pfläfflin's rooms, but the entire building in which they are situated that Seth says confederately: "The meeting's never over 'til you've left the building."

Then he says: "Typical of Pfläfflin to have his rooms in the William Stone block instead of any of the more historic accommodation he could have chosen. When he asked you to show me the ropes, it was like the Spanish Inquisitor saying *Show him the Instruments.*"

We are now in the fine Deer Park leading down to the Fens. The gardeners have set the sprayer on the grass and the dappled light on the water droplets is revolving in the spokeshave, as though the garden designer was none other than Gerard Manley Hopkins. Some students are attempting to conduct a game of croquet, but they only have a casual acquaintance with the rules. It's more like a scene from Alice in Wonderland. The ball has gone into the camellia bushes. I place one lush-kept plush-capped shoe in front of the other. I have forgotten what I was going to say to Seth. I think that what has upset my equilibrium is Seth's scent. It had been raining in the night, but it was warm now. Blackbirds were pecking at the wet turf.

Bare ruin'd choirs where late the sweet birds sang

The sweet jasmine hanging on the walls between the Deer Park and the Old Park fused with the rank smells of the damp earth, the sharpness of the daffodils going past their prime; but there was also another note, a high citrus key with a tang of rosemary, warm and woody, amber with a shot of oak moss. After a moment, I realised it was coming from Seth.

"What's your aftershave?" I enquired.

"Huh?" he seemed genuinely surprised. "Oh, *Balafre...*"—he saw

I was confused by the unfamiliar foreign name, so he spelled it and then defined it further, "By Lancôme."

Until I met Seth, I had relied upon *That Man* by Revlon. It came in black plastic *hip flasks* with a gold silhouette of That Man stamped in the middle. The eponymous Man of That Man resembled the guy who surmounts all manner of obstacles to bring the lady the Cadbury's Milk Tray. If I didn't make out at once with the first girl, I would retire for a little, splash on some more That Man and try again.

If I still didn't score, I would just keep repeating the exercise until I had attained the correct formulation, until I had refined myself into abstraction, and was just utter distillation of after shave. Men didn't wear cologne or moisturiser in those days. That would have been considered effeminate. They wore after shave. Mainly because adolescence was not such a distant memory that we had yet forgotten our first shaves; so a showy après raisir was the male equivalent of a girl's first bra. Spud wore Aramis, Sydney wore Dunhill, Burt, Brut.

In his set, Burt has a Jeroboam of Brut mounted on wheels like a cannon, so that when he nods the barrel towards his hand a splash with a dash of spritz is dispensed into his palm, which Burt applies behind his ears. And the little girls seem to love it. *Springes to catch woodcocks.*

I wore *That Man.* I hadn't heard of this French upstart, *Balafre* by *Lancôme.*

We continue our perambulation along the back of the Fitzwilliam Museum and through the stone arch, trampling along gravel paths lined with gone-over daffodils.

We are walking through the Old Park when Seth speaks first:

"I thought that was a bit harsh of Pfläfflin," says he.

"No, no, I insist. Showing you around is no trouble at all. I thought the first thing you needed to know was where the Buttery is, which is why we're headed in that direction."

"I mean picking on you in that way about the *Ghost of a Flea* because it's a watercolour. I think that viewing a literary giant like Blake through the prism of his other artistic expressions is a perfectly valid exercise likely to throw new light on his literary output. It's biographical back story in the same way that we have to reassess Shakespeare when we learn that he left his wife his second best bed in his Will."

I am beginning to warm to Seth already.

"And what about *There's nothing you can talk to me about that I don't already know*?" asks Seth mimicking Max' German accent.

"What about it?" I query. "Where have I heard that line before?"

"There are two words missing from the end," explains Seth. "Mr and Bond."

"Of course!" I exclaim. "*There's nothing you can talk to me about that I don't already know, Mr Bond*. It's what Goldfinger says to Bond when he fires up the laser."

"Correct. And do you notice how the more animated he gets, the more Aryan he becomes? His mask of faux English squire slips and he even starts speaking in Deutsch."

"Hundred percent!" I agree.

"And I'm having an uphill struggle with Sisyphus Syndrome," Seth declares. "Oedipus Syndrome, I get, but where did Sisyphus Syndrome spring from?"

"The Underworld?" I venture.

I feel the need to shift the conversation back onto basics, or I am going to fall into the same error I fell into with Calypso, and never know Seth's basics.

"O—K. So, Seth, tell me, why did you leave Warwick?"

"Nothing left to climb. Cambridge is world-renowned for its night-climbing opportunities." As if to emphasise his words with feats of physical strength, he takes a run at a sheer brick wall, and succeeds in clinging to it for five or six vertical paces before he drops off. If each pace is a yard, he has run eighteen feet up a vertical wall before gravity takes over. Then he does it again; but this time he clings on for seven or eight steps.

Then he says: "Did our parents and our grandparents fight two world wars so that we could end up being taught English by some Jerry who thinks that William Shakespeare didn't exist?" He then emphasises this point by shimmying up a drainpipe, inspecting the guttering and then dropping off. It's like taking a stroll with the Amazing Spiderman.

"Seth, I think you had better tell me a few things about yourself so as to assist me in my duty of introducing you to my peers. Do you have any special skills or interests?"

"Night climbing," he says.

I gaze at him without comprehension. He nods in the direction of the Fitzwilliam Museum.

"You climb up that stuff," he says, "in the dark. And then once you're up there, you're in another realm. You find you can see things better in the dark. You can tune in to the thoughts of the stone masons who built it all 500 years ago. They've left their stuff everywhere up there. Down here, on ground zero, it's all been swept under the carpet. But up there, it was too much trouble for anyone to remove it. So it's all still there. The smouldering rocks of the past."

"But aren't you worried you might have an accident?" I ask.

"I have a special gift," Seth explained. "I can remember it all. Distances, spatial relationships of things to one another. So I know exactly where everything is vis a vis everything else, in the same way, say, that you could get dressed in the dark."

"Most of the time I look like I have gotten dressed in the dark!" I say.

"Just look at that!" Seth exclaims.

I don't see anything of note, so I have to follow his own sightline to make out what it is that is exciting him. He has been brought to a standstill by an orange and red-banded caterpillar on a glossy leaf.

"What about it?" I ask. "It's just a caterpillar."

"No, no. It's the colour scheme!" he explains. "Don't you see? It's a Catalan caterpillar!"

What is quickly becoming apparent to me is the fact that Seth, like me, makes connections in a way that is different from most other people.

Past the Fellows Garden. Through another arch, and opposite the William Morris Great Hall where we keep term by dining, set within its own arch, is the Buttery. The Buttery is run by Archie, a middle-aged townsman, who has worked within this arch all his life. As we enter his domain, he is standing on the customer's side of the counter.

He has the build of a Pez sweet-dispenser. In order to keep a respectable distance between us, he ducks under the hinged lid that lets him pass ghost-like through his counter and onto the service side, transitioning seamlessly between the apparent hinged lid of his Pez-like head and the actual hinge of his counter. His long shirt sleeves are rolled up with mathematical precision, and his forearms bulge out of them like Captain America when he is in civvies. He rests his arms on his counter and his large flat face opens up whilst he raises one eyebrow in the shopkeeper's expression that means *Can I help you?* He calls us *Sir* to make us feel important, to underline the fact that we are gown and he is town.

We are being groomed to rule the world, but he is in the service sector. We have all spent the formative years of our life calling other people *Sir*. It was a revelation to me to come to this place where everyone called me *Sir*. I still haven't got over it. Archibald is calling Seth *Sir*. He is taking his name and the details of his room and he is opening up an account for Seth at the Buttery.

Here, they stock everything an undergraduate might need. But no-one buys anything apart from biscuits, cigarettes, cigarette papers, cigarette tobacco, Clipper disposable lighters, Swan Vestas, alcohol, and occasionally some shaving foam, toothpaste or deodorant. A quick glance at the shelves reveals no *Balafre* by *Lancôme*.

It is amazing that a student can arrive here from nowhere with no income, no credit rating, no job, no history, no references and no permanent address, and he is immediately able to open up a credit account and buy hard liquor and cigarette papers without limit. Seth promptly takes advantage of his new status by purchasing a bottle of Hirondelle and a corkscrew. Although it is not yet noon, we uncork the bottle in Fen Court and take turns swigging from it as I lead him to the Birdwood.

Seth hasn't finished insulting the Germans. "I mean to say," he persists, "German is a vile language incapable of expressing anything well except the most mechanical grinding of repetitive acts such as a particularly pedestrian session of coitus in the missionary position. It doesn't recognise the tiny nuances that quicken literature. What decent thing was ever written in German?"

"Dr Faust?" I venture.

"Ah so! But we know that it is structurally flawed. Anyvay," he continues, mimicking Max Pfläfflin's accent and intonation, "vee now know it was vritten by Villiiam Shakespeare. Little Villie!"

"Wasn't Little Willie the name the Krauts gave to their gigantic cannon?" I query.

"You're absolutely right," confirms Seth. "The barrels used to burn so hot that they had forty seamen pissing on them at any time just to keep them cool enough so they didn't expand and crack."

"And all the piss was pissing down the length of the barrel and giving a shampoo to the poor sod who was attempting to load it at the other end," I added.

Then reverting to his normal voice: "Let me let you into a little secret, Nick: the German language was invented solely to give the speaker the opportunity of spitting at strangers under the guise of polite conversation."

The Birdwood is an architecturally abject building erected in 1932 with the benefit of a generous endowment from Lord Birdwood. However, when he visited the college to see how his benefaction had been spent, the Fellows who were taking him on the guided tour employed diversionary tactics so it would not come to his attention that his name graced the front of this ghastly slab of a brick shithouse obscuring the students' views to the Fens.

But worse surprises await inside. I pressed open the double swing doors as a cowboy enters a saloon. Automatically our voices drop to hushed whispers in the echoing space. Corridors lead off in every direction. There are literally hundreds of doors, one after the other. Seth, who, it seems, is naturally paranoid, presses against each ajar or closed door to see what is behind it before he converses lest we are overheard.

The Birdwood is a crapping complex, a cavernous bathhouse built in the days before the students' accommodation had been refurbished to yield *en suite* bathrooms or showers. As far as the eye can see, there are half open or shut doors, behind each one of which lies a white bath with brown stains from the iron content in the water, or a white crapper, also usually with brown stains. The place is warm and jungle-humid, but instead of the sound of parrots and howler monkeys, one hears only sloshing, singing, farting and the whirr of tumble driers pumping carbon monoxide into the enclosed space.

The Birdwood is my favourite place in Peterhouse; better than my set; better than the Ward Library or the Scholars Piece. I am comforted by the orderliness of its symmetrical construction. When I sit in the stall with the corridors stretching endlessly into the narrowing Canaletto perspectives, the serried ordered rows of crappers marching towards the point where the parallel lines meet, there is a place for everything and everything in its place, and *katharsis* comes naturally.

Like a prison or a madhouse, it is a building that is somehow intentionally incomplete in its interior. None of the doors or the partition walls reach quite to the floor or the ceiling. When the students are sloshing in their baths, if you catch the light right, the reflections of the moving bathwater dance in time to the plashing and humming as their shadows creep across the exposed walls above the bathrooms. This place is where Blackpool's glitterballs meet Plato's Parable of the Cave. I come here when my brain is on fire, and the orderly, symmetrical lines cool me down and bring me back to earth. The humidity, the steaminess, the whirr of the spin driers.

Many a time have I fallen unintentionally asleep in this bath-house. It comes naturally. To sleep, perchance to dream. For some reason, the place reminds me of my little ballerina. The broken beams of refracted light spin across the surfaces and my brain keeps time by spinning with them.

And there are words of infinite wisdom scrawled on the inside of every cubicle. We are in the days before meaningless spray paint and pointless vandalism. If someone wished to leave his mark, he had to gouge it painstakingly out of the wood, usually with the point of a compass, as though he were etching his very soul into the bog door.

Someone had considerately engraved the complete lyrics of the Pusher onto the door, and in truth, those words alone merited such a lifetime's undivided attention as could really only be given when one was seated on the crapper vacantly waiting for something to happen. It was rumoured that the graffiti had been laboriously scratched into the wood by the dropped-out decayed teeth of a crystal meth addict.

This may seem trivial or slight to you reading this now, but you can hardly imagine its impact when I first read it. It made me question everything and wonder why I was reading all this old Shakespearean shit at Cambridge when people were writing poetry like this in the here and now. This was something relevant at last.

As I didn't know if Seth's rooms had *en suite*, I thought it best not to ask intrusive questions, but to bring him to this place of learning and let him feel his way for himself. He is clearly as fascinated by it as I was when I first set foot. Row after row, of sanitary fittings as far as the eye can see, to the right, to the left and straight ahead, they stretch on to infinity.

Finally, after pushing lightly against several nearby doors to ensure no eavesdroppers lurk behind them, he pronounces: "It's amazing! It's an exercise in perspective where the unit of measurement is the crapper."

I have gained his confidence. I have shown him the ropes. We are fast friends, Seth and I.

Every stall wall is inscribed with erudite learning from scholars who have spent the best years of their lives in the Birdwood. I could quote them. You could blindfold me and lead me to any door, and I could tell you what graffiti lies beyond. I should be on University Challenge answering questions about the Birdwood. It doesn't matter if you are rich or poor, if you bribed your way into this place of privilege, or earned it with a scholarship or exhibition. In the Birdwood everyone is equal. We come here for a common purpose.

I share with Seth some of my favourite graffiti. He nods in agreement at the pithy and gnomic nuggets of wisdom carved into the doors and walls.

"You know," I confide in him, "sometimes I think that what drew me to reading English at Cambridge, is not the texts. I think I operate at a more molecular level. What I like is the letters themselves, their shapes, their function in stamping order upon the ephemera of the spoken word."

"Maybe you should have read calligraphy or maths" he says.

The mention of calligraphy stops me in my tracks for a moment. Does he know that I lust after Lyca? How could he? He doesn't even know her. It's just a coincidence. After all, the word would come naturally to him. He is a walking exponent of the calligrapher's art. I relax a little.

"You're probably right, but the problem is I'm crap at math, and I can't draw. That's why I take my refuge in photography."

The air is fragrant with the vinegar crisp stench of Izal. Izal medicated toilet paper, containing, according to the blurb that I would read when I had read everything there was to read on the walls, *a germicide to help kill bacteria and so aid better family hygiene.* Meaning, that when they pulped the trees in the paper mill, they added a few drops of iodine to better heal your arse from the smart of the splinters as you wiped it.

And they advertised it as the world's toughest toilet paper. As though their chosen market consisted of strongmen who wanted to retire to the jakes for the afternoon and test their strength by tearing toilet rolls in half.

What they really meant was: *You won't stick your finger through it.*

People who liked this also liked…

Jeyes toilet paper, shiny toilet paper, school toilet paper, Bronco, glossy on one side, matt on the other; just like photographic paper; but which side was which? Questions left unanswered when the manufacturers ceased production in 1989.

What did they all have in common? The odour of the germicide, a pungent cross between Nordic pine and iodine that suffused the halls of the Birdwood, and informed the wooden poles of Sydney's palanquin. You could inhale the smell of the paper and clear your head of a hangover. If your nose was blocked or if you had a cold, you could come to this place and inhale the camphor vapours. For extra efficacy, you could rub the glossy papers together to release the full strength of their olfactory onslaught.

Then it was as though you had sniffed a huge draught of your grandmother's smelling salts upon an attack of the vapours; or rubbed Vic into your chest. We washed our hair in Vosene and wiped our arses with Izal until they bled. When we got a chance of a fuck, we were so reassured by the comforting stench of the Vosene that we failed to notice the venereal discharge. It wasn't until after shiny toilet paper was banned in 1969 that we began to appreciate the pleasures of anal sex. Without soft toilet paper, there would have been no AIDS.

But now there is a new odour to factor into the olfactory compendium of the Birdwood: *Balafre* by *Lancôme.*

"Do you read comics?" I ask Seth.

"Sure, doesn't everyone?"

"Which is your favourite superhero?"

"Huh? No, I don't read Superman comics. I read Weird Tales and Fabulous Furry Freak Brothers."

I'm not sure he is going to fit in.

"Just so I can introduce you to my mates," I say, "you need to have some special powers. What do you want me to tell them?"

"I told you. I have a photographic memory."

"That's boring. Give me something racy."

"Tell them that I can foretell the future from reading tea leaves in a cup."

"Uh-huh! Can you really see the future?"

"Up to a point. I told you. I can map things out in my head, so I know that if I take so many steps in a certain direction, I am going to end up in a certain place. That's telling the future in the same way that a bird setting off on a 4,000 mile migration knows that it is travelling towards its future. The problem is that the future's all smudged with the fingerprints of the past. Tends to make the future a dangerous place."

"Yes, the future's scary. That's why there will always be a place in our lives for nostalgia."

"Yeh, yeh, I know. But even nostalgia ain't what it used to be."

The Following Morning

It is a morning of great promise as I stride through the Deer Park towards the Birdwood with my towel under my arm. It has been raining in the night but the sun is breaking through now. The light breeze is scattering the standing raindrops off the grass like some huge dog shaking himself dry. The bushes are flecked with dew and balls of cuckoo spittle. A blackbird is pecking busily for worms in the rain-sodden turf. I see it has the orange and red-banded Catalonian caterpillar in its golden beak. The air is crisp and cool, refreshing, unless you happen to be a caterpillar.

By contrast, the air inside the humming bath house is humid and viscous. As I pass from closed door to closed door, hearing the snuffling of the animals behind, I feel as though I am in a rainforest. The walls are dripping with photosynthetic spider veins reflected from the sloshing water in the baths. The light is architectural, tactile, honey-coloured, dappled with white ripples, as though a giant, diaphanous giraffe was rubbing itself up against the walls.

My resolution is to read new graffiti here every morning, and reflect upon it as though it were the day's sermon. Today I read the following gnomic inscription dug into a shithouse door:

Homosexuality

1952: Illegal
1969: Legalised
1986: Compulsory

I think Ingram is queer. He just hasn't come to terms with it yet.

I run the hot water and balance my washbag on the corner of the bath, placing its contents on the shelf beneath the steamed-up mirror: Gillette razor, Mitcham 48 hour anti-perspirant, Johnson's baby talc, 9-Flags heated shaving foam, and my newly purchased bottle-green bottle of *Balafre* by *Lancôme.*

I lie in the warm bath, bioluminescent, staring up at the patterns the plankton refract onto the walls and ceiling until I can't tell if it is phosphorescence in motion, or if the walls are standing still and it is my bath that is moving like a starlit bier slipping its cargo into an inky ocean for some Viking funeral. The tub drifts noiselessly into non-entity as I assemble the finishing touches to my superhero book in my mind. The dancing light: my little ballerina.

When I am done, I decide to save my precious *Balafre* for a special occasion. Besides, I might be bumping into Seth and didn't want him to think I was a copycat. I would make do with the smell of the 9-Flags thermal foam.

As I go to leave the bath house, I see that Seth is also there, following my example. He is cleaning his teeth. I decide it would be polite to ask him how he is fitting in and if there is anything else I can help him with. Not wanting to disturb him whilst he is brushing his teeth, I wait by the half-opened door of his cubicle. He is naked except for a white towel around his waist, which enables me to confirm that the tattoos cover only the circumference of his body: the outside of his arms, legs, neck and feet, but not the inside, and whoever the author was has resisted the temptation to write more expansively on the great slab of his chest.

As he raises his arm to brush his teeth, the characters on his biceps play out like film credits. Although the tooth-cleansing ritual seems to take some time, I am not bored. He brought along something for me to read.

I observe that he has a six pack like the Mighty Thor. He has powerful oxters and biceps swelled up so that the engorged blood vessels that are chewing all the haemoglobin pumped by his heart stand out like a circuit diagram stencilled onto his exoskeleton. There is no doubting the fact that he has created a commendable body for himself. Why did he choose to mess it up with all that graffiti?

The tooth-brushing ceremony seems to go on interminably. He has an electric toothbrush which he uses to polish his teeth with for a good five minutes, followed by a small soft brush, for buffing. He then deploys a series of inter-dental sticks of different thicknesses and colours, followed by vigorous flossing. Then, after a lot of spitting and rinsing, he gargles with Listerine.

The whole process goes on for at least fifteen minutes before he is satisfied. He then finishes off by putting a smear of Vaseline on his index finger and wiping it over his lips as if repairing them from the bruising session to which they have just been subjected. If Shakespeare had been a dentist instead of a playwright, this is what Lady Macbeth would have looked like.

I see that Seth is about to repeat the entire process from the beginning, so I decide to reveal myself.

"Hi there!" I say at length.

"Whoa!" says Seth. "How long have you been there?"

"No more than five minutes," I lie. "Everything OK?"

"Absolutely *Sir* Alfred Garnett!" says he. I haven't heard the expression before, but I assume it to be affirmatory. "I am very fastidious about cleaning my teeth," he says, "Because I use my mouth for a lot of very pleasant experiences: eating, kissing, drinking, smoking…"

"Going down on the lovely girls?" I offer uselessly. This is not even me; but I say it in the belief it may seek out part of him. But I have misjudged. It seems we are not a pair of jocks.

Ignoring my adolescent prurience, Seth continues, "I find I constantly want to change the air in my mouth. I do this at least five time a day, or my mouth tastes like the inside of a Turkish tram driver's jockstrap."

"So, I was right in assuming that you don't have an *en suite* on your staircase?"

"Oh yes, I do. But I like the ordered structure of this place. It's like going down to the gym. I mean, I could do my press-ups and sit-ups on the floor in my room. But if you make a positive effort to go down the gym and exercise in a collegiate environment, you push yourself harder."

Competitive tooth-cleaning. This is a new one on me. In the coming weeks, I would notice that Seth was always talking about the state of his mouth. If he's smoked a couple of cigarettes and hadn't cleaned his teeth, he would say that his mouth was like the inside of a parrot's cage, or that his tongue felt like those bits of dried cuttlefish they hang up for budgerigars.

I watch as he squeezes his piebald toothpaste out onto his brush. I see that he seems to be using patriotic toothpaste. It exits the tube in red, white and blue stripes as though he were extruding the Union Jack from a soft, cylindrical container. The stripes make my head go funny, just like the stripes in Ingram's pinstripe suit.

"What the fuck is that?" I ask.

Seth looks up from his brushing, genuinely puzzled by my ignorance.

"This?" he asks, prodding the tube. "Signal toothpaste."

"But how do they get those stripes in it?" I ask.

"Is this going to be another one of those stoned conversations?"
   he asks, foaming at the mouth.

"No, I'm not mashed this early in the morning.
   Genuinely, I've never seen anything like it."

"Help yourself." He extends the tube of friendship in my direction. Cautiously, I unscrew the white lid and depress the pipe. The red, white and blue stripes form. But how do they do that? I have a neat turd of toothpaste on my brush, but I carry on squeezing, because I have to get to the bottom of this phenomenon with the stripes. I have squeezed it out all the way up to the end of the toothbrush handle and continue onto the back of my hand. Then and only then do I stop; and I don't stop because I have gotten to the bottom of anything. I stop because it is giving me a migraine staring at the stripes and Seth is looking at me in a funny way, as if to say: *Hasn't this savage seen toothpaste before? Does he know what it's for? I expect he normally cleans his teeth with Brylcreem.*

"What are you going to do with that now?" Seth asks me.

I am feeling both queasy and squeezy, I think. I am worried that this stuff might be expensive and I have wasted a lot.

"I'll buy you another tube," I assure him. I smooth it out across my forearm, thinner and thinner, attenuating the stripes. *Like gold to airy thinness beat*, as Donne would say. Eventually, it's just one white goo, and as my arm doesn't seem to want to absorb it, I lick some off and wash away the rest. Then I look down at the prolapsed toothpaste tube with its sausage of multi-coloured shit pushed out and I start thinking about all the celebrities who have died on the can.

I feel the need to get out of the Birdwood before I have a nasty turn.

"I'm heading on over to Sydney Syzygy's set," I say. "Maybe I could introduce you to him and his girlfriend, Calypso Sitzclarence. He calls her Lyca and his Countenance Divine. I don't know all your preferences, but we call the place Substance Abuse Central." I feel like a cunt for pedalling Ingram's nicknames, but some of them are pretty good.

"Is that name, Sydney Syzygy, for real?" he asks.

"Yes. If Oscar Wilde had been Jewish, Sydney is what he would have been like."

"Sounds like he should be starring in a porn movie. I think I may have seen him around. Is he the guy that drives the big black hearse?"

"It's a Humber Super Snipe, but, yes, I see what you mean."

"He parks it in St Peter's Terrace, and he rubs Cornubia wax into it with his bare hands, lovingly, sexually, like he was curry-combing a thoroughbred horse, and then he cleans the windows with newsprint from the papers."

"Yes, the Jewish Chronicle to be precise. That's him."

"People say he's a bit of a control freak. Hands out free alcohol and drugs and gets others to participate in secret ceremonies just as a means of control. I've heard about him and I know his bendy girlfriend, and I've seen him around, but we haven't been introduced yet. Yes, I'd be interested to meet him. And his Countenance Divine. Calypso, you say?"

"Yes."

"Calypso Sitzclarence."

"Yes. You know her?"

"Means deceitful."

"And Lyca. What's that mean?"

"Italian. You can work it out for yourself."

A Visit to the Sex Club

I've shown Seth the Birdwood, so he knows where to go to perform his ablutions or contemplate the symmetry of parallel lines, and to imbibe gnomic graffiti wisdom from the haiku-spinning troubadours of all the bog doors that have preceded us. I have shown him the Buttery so that he knows whither he can resort if he has need of sustenance, wine or tobacco on tick. This mid-morning, en route to Substance Abuse Central, I must introduce him to the third necessity of Peterhouse undergraduate life, the Sex Club.

One generally visits the Sex Club in the mornings and in the evenings. Seth is looking confused and let down when he sees nothing but rows of pigeon holes, some guys noisily manning a table football machine, and a bar with a couple of beer pulls, but no student bartender, in light of the earliness of the hour.

I explain to him that the club was founded in the sixteenth century, and its title is simply short for the Sexcentenary Club. I think students have shared his disappointment for the last three centuries.

We discover his pigeon hole together. One checks one's pigeon hole each morning. The college will use it for publishing important announcements. Students will insert notes for one another, assignations, rendezvous, invitations to parties. The pigeon holes are also fed by the porters with external post, such as letters and post cards from the real world, or if one was very lucky, maybe a cheque or a postal order from your mum or your dad. It was a naïve system of communication, I appreciate, but I've never heard of anyone getting trolled by a pigeon hole.

There is one 24" screen black and white television with a huge rear tube. But it isn't switched on playing the endless loops of Sky News, as there were only three channels in those days, BBC1, the new BBC2 and ITV, and there is no broadcast until the evening. We were more gregarious in those days. I think it was the absence of refrigerators in our rooms. If you wanted a cold drink, you had to venture abroad to a bar. Sydney was the only undergrad with a fridge in his room.

One didn't go to a supermarket and buy booze and sit at home with it. One went out: either to the Sex Club, or a pub, or to someone else's set. As long as you brought a bottle or the makings of a joint with you,

you didn't need an invitation. But if you were planning something more formal, you could always put an announcement in someone's pigeon hole.

It's only Seth's second day. His pigeon hole is sadly empty. My pigeon hole on the other hand contains two items: one is an invitation to see a forthcoming production of The Who's rock opera, Tommy, being staged in the gardens at Gonville and Caius by undergraduates. I fold it up and slip it into the inside pocket of my corduroy jacket with the epaulettes. The other is an official envelope bearing the crossed keys seal of Peterhouse.

I scan the other pigeon holes. Hardly any have the flier stuffed in them. It has not been broadcast. I am one of the privileged few.

"Well," I say, "I've shown you the Buttery and the Birdwood. I guess it's not too early to take you to Substance Abuse Central. I need to pick up some papers from my room first. Meet back here in 30 minutes?"

"Aren't you going to open the envelope?" asks Seth. I rip open the envelope sealed with the keys. Inside lurks a card similarly embossed with the crossed keys.

"It's from the Proctor," I inform Seth. "He wants to see me."

"Sounds like bad news," says Seth.

"How so?" I enquired.

"Most people go through their three years sojourn at Cambridge without coming face to face with the Proctor," Seth informed me, suddenly knowing more about college life than I myself knew. "His job is to enforce discipline. The Proctors are university-wide. They're not specific to a college. They're overarching, like the FBI. There are only two of them for enforcement purposes, and there's a third whose duties are purely ceremonial.

"If the Proctor wants to see you, it's something serious. The police aren't allowed onto college property. That's why everyone smokes dope with impunity. The Proctors are supposed to enforce their own discipline, which they do through the Proctors and Marshalls office. If I were you, I would take this seriously, Nick."

The Fuck 4
Substance Abuse Central

I presented my *magnum opus* to Sydney like some trembling virgin, desperate for his approbation. In return for my glimpses into his world of advantage, I was his official biographer in words and film.

After all, Sydney had explained the situation to me quite early on, once he had discovered my journalistic ambitions: "Nick," he had said, "there are those of us who are destined to go down in history, and those of us whose job it is to record history in the making."

I was left in no doubt that I fell into the latter category, because I had not yet come to realise there was a third category: those whose destiny it was to rewrite the history of the future.

Now, here were the first chapters of my book, the tome I had been writing whilst neglecting my dissertation on Blake's *Ghost of a Flea*. I am Watson to his Holmes; Boswell to his Johnson.

We are in his rooms at Gisborne Court, where our collection of unconventional characters likes to congregate and discuss weighty matters, such as strip clubs and cigars, and whether Iron Man is mightier than the Mighty Thor.

As always, his grand sterling silver samovar with the eagle handles is bubbling away and combining with the vapours of unknown substances so that the condensation drips down his windows and forms pools on the wooden frames. I fancy that small reptiles breed in those warm pools.

The man who never changes his opinion is like standing water, and breeds reptiles of the mind...
Sydney has a huge Täschen edition of Dali's complete paintings spread open on his desk. Upside down, I see he is studying *The Hallucinogenic Toreador.*

Letters appear to me in the condensation, as if someone had written them on the window panes earlier and they only rematerialize in the smog: a secret vocabulary written in the language of water. The letters say: *I am trapped in the glass.*

My protégé, Seth, had followed me into the room, but I haven't had a chance to introduce him yet. He is wearing a white vest, grey tracksuit bottoms and trainers on his feet. The powerful biceps bulging out of the vest dwarf those of Sydney's palanquin-carrying oarsmen. Seeing the pommel horse, Seth went unhesitatingly up to it and began performing a gyroscopic gravity-defying gymnastic routine: sometimes his body is parallel to the horse and my eyes are straining to see the wires that must be holding him up as he sustains this impossible position for maybe thirty seconds; sometimes he is circulating like a giant turbine.

It occurs to me that he is a perfect complement to Lyca: whereas Lyca is a ground-based contortionist, Seth is more of an aerial performer. They should run off together and join the circus. The controlling Sydney could be the ringmaster. I imagine Sydney in a ringmaster's suit, cracking the whip in a top hat. It reminds me of the box that my John Bull Printing Press came in. There are more characters on the windows than there were in the printing press. There are even more characters on Seth.

Sydney has clearly taken a decision to ignore Seth's spinning antics and pretend he isn't there. The pommel horse is a decorative item of furniture to be admired: one is not supposed to embrace its intended use. Sydney is sat in his captain's chair: he rotates it so that he is busying himself with his *Hallucinogenic Toreador* spread on his orange fruitwood desk and pointedly offers his back to this athletic intruder.

What I now recognise as the opening strains of *Stella Blue from Wake of the Flood* are humming through Sydney's gargantuan speakers. The chords of the Wakeful Dead are punctuated by the whirring of Seth's body.

I want to read the cover notes on the Grateful Dead album, but Calypso is using it to roll a spliff. She is wearing an Indiacraft scarf tied around her boobs and pink hot pants. Bare feet. As always, her eyes are closed as though she is in ecstasy. She is rolling the joint with her eyes shut, in the same way that they train American navy seals to dismantle their guns and reassemble them in pitch darkness. It's intolerably hot, because, despite the heat, all the windows are sealed to keep the stench of the weed inside the room. What Ingram would call *stifling*. Sydney is like a salamander and doesn't seem to feel the heat. He is in constant training for the day when he is finally dragged off to his infernal charnel house after successfully summoning the Lord of the Flies.

"Sit down, dear boy; sit down." He swivelled his captain's chair and indicated the seat across from his desk on the other side of the coffee table overflowing with coffee table books. "What have we here?" Helping himself to my treasury-tagged pages with one hand, he twirled the index finger of the other in the air like a plate-spinner and thrust it into his moist mouth. For a minute I thought he was going to stick it up my exhaust. I was bordering on the disappointed when he used it to turn the pages. Sydney can do that to you. "Sherry, absinthe? I know what!" he exclaims. "White port."

Before you could say knife, Calypso had materialised at his side, bearing some chilled decanter. I thought this might be my opportunity to make a lunge for the album notes on Wake of the Flood, but I see she has left the makings on it, interrupting her important work to do Sydney's bidding. Sydney is the only undergraduate in Peterhouse who has a refrigerator in his set.

Lyca was pouring two crystal glasses from which I deduce that it's just Sydney and me partaking, *homo ad homo*, as though the other people in the room don't count. Beakers of the deep south with beaded bubbles winking at the brim. Despite what he may be offering me, I can tell from his mood that it is Pervitin that is coursing through Sydney's veins, that combination of self-assured confidence, distracted calmness and aggression.

This is the thing about Sydney. He may be a complete wanker, but he does wanker with such panache. "We'll be needing the Iranian pistachios," he cried out, as if it would be sacrilege to serve me white port without the Iranian pistachios, or greater sacrilege still to offer me pistachios from the wrong side of the Musandam Peninsula. He pings his finger against the glass and it hums back its reassuring echo so that we know it's the real leaded McCoy and not some shit you get free from the service station if you put enough gas in the car.

"I didn't know port came in any other colours," I quip.

"Achromatic is not a colour," observes Sydney. But his girlfriend tops this:

"What did Tristan Tzara say in his 1914 *Dadaist Manifesto Canabale*?" she asks.

Fucked if I know! I think to myself.

The more dashing Sydney has a response that makes him sound wiser whilst no more having the correct answer than me: "Lyca, Infinite

Jewel of the Night," he begins, playing for words and tapping his Dali *vademecum*, "you can see I am tuned into the surrealists; I cannot go back in time to the Dadaists. You will have to enlighten us all. What was it that Tzara wrote in his Manifesto?"

"*We demand the right to piss in different colours!*" she informs those assembled.

I am thinking to myself that only someone who is "doing" Calligraphy and History of Art at Girton would have such in-depth knowledge. I don't even know who Tristan Tzara is or was, but here is a woman who is able to quote from his manifesto and translate it for you at the same time. If only Max Pfläfflin was as knowledgeable and as helpful as Calypso, I could breeze through my tripos.

I am sucking an Iranian pistachio and thinking that, as far as boiled sweets go, this is not as good as a flying saucer or a humbug. Sydney dips his digits into the bowl and picks one out. He inspects it and cracks it open with his special plectrum thumb nail, before popping it into his gob. I see what I am doing wrong. We all cultivate a long plectrum thumbnail so that the girls think we are accomplished guitarists like Eric Clapton or Jeff Beck. It also comes in handy for slicing cigarette papers when assembling joints.

However, I now appreciate that its original evolutionary role was in de-husking Iranian pistachios. No problem there. In the future, Iran will be able to crack them open with nuclear fusion.

But I am looking into a bleak future after 9 Flags thermal shaving foam has been banned on environmental grounds. In the future, you can build a nuclear bomb, but you can't have warm shaving foam. What had Seth said about it? It's smudged with the fingerprints of the past.

"Pistachios and caviar," Sydney pronounces. "Only two good things ever to come out of fucking Iran. But there are a lot of bad things to come in the future. Won't be my problem though."

It is as though we have both been on the same astral plane at the same time, travelling two parallel paths. Sydney Syzygy and me: the *Start Rite kids*.

He has done everything he can to make me feel like the guest of honour before we get to the main event, which is my *catalogue raisonné* on the four of us. "*Tibidabo!*" he toasts me, clinking glasses. I am trying to work out what this toast means. The only Dabo I can think of is Mike D'Abo who is lead singer in Manfred Mann. He sang the hit single *5-4-3-2-1*. I can feel my dissertation on the 4 of us slipping away from me: 4-3-2-1-0.

"Is that what they say when they toast one another in Iran?" I enquire, because I know it is no embarrassment confessing one's limitations to Sydney, as he always likes to fill one in from his position of superior knowledge, especially if he has the adoring Calypso as his audience. There's no shame in allowing oneself to be controlled by a control freak.

"Oh, they'll be toasting a lot more than pistachios in that fucking country before long," is all he says.

Again, I have the feeling of treading parallel paths with him and not quite meeting up.

The foreplay over, it's time to read the book.

Sydney opens it up and smooths down the pages. As I was facing him on the opposite side of his desk and had placed the book on the tabletop my way up, he was reading it upside down. He read the opening sentence out loud:

"The Fuck 4."

That was the opening sentence, if one was minded to dignify it with the noun, Sentence. There followed one of Sydney's 10-second silences that feel like 60 seconds.

He looked up at me. "So, Nick, you restrained yourself until the second word of the book before descending into profanity?"

"I'm sorry, Sydney, but I felt it needed the definite article."

"Is it missing a question mark at the end, as in *What the fuck for?*"

"No."

"As in *What the fuck did you write this shit for?*"

"Constructive criticism is always appreciated."

"I see. So," he said, naughtily reading ahead several chapters, "the fuck 4 are the four of us, are they not?"

I am sheepish, because answering truthfully in the affirmative would suggest that Calypso is not one of the inner circle and upset her, him or both of them; but I cannot tell a lie: "Yes."

He was reading at the rate of a page every 5 seconds. I couldn't believe it. Especially because he was reading upside down. "And you've devoted two whole chapters to Ingram," he said with genuine astonishment. "And this whole section to Burt Sully?"

"Yes."

"I would just sketch them in lightly, dear boy. Just adumbrate them. They are not long for this world, and you will be their undoing. Candles that you will make to burn too brightly."

The Fuck 4 was intended to be me doffing my cap to The Fantastic Four. But Sydney was wholly dismissive.

"If you want to write like that, I mean, for the sake of it, why don't you write a book about the utter degeneration, the pernicious abasement of our language? The Fuck 4! A book that starts with a sentence with no verbs, nouns, pronouns, adjectives, adverbs, possessives, subject or object, and need I add, meaning?"

Lyca is clapping her hands with joy at Sydney's huge wit. For a brief moment, I don't know if the adjective for her is sycophantic or syphilitic. But she has a concealed fragility that I find unspeakably attractive. I want to protect her, but when I ask from whom, I can only think of myself.

"But Sydney," I protest, "That's precisely how you speak all the time!"

"I may speak like that," he says, "But I wouldn't fucking dream of writing like that!"

Sometimes Sydney is so far up his own arse, you'd need to be a turd to communicate with him, so it's best not to persevere, or he'll just make you look like an even bigger cunt. Calypso was annoying me with her sealed eyes and unquestioning approbation of everything Sydney, and I was sure that he was just grandstanding for her, so I thought I would not waste any more of my time with the written word, and I would switch to my photos, because one picture tells a thousand words, as they say, or, if you're as inarticulate as I seem to be, judging from Sydney's evaluation, probably more like a million. So I open up my portfolio and table the Infinity series of photos that had been worrying and puzzling me so much.

If I thought Sydney would be remotely interested in my findings when I laid the series of photographic prints out on his desk atop his *Hallucinogenic Toreador*, I should have had the sense to have broached the subject at a time after he had finished his supply of Nepalese Temple Balls and Pervitin.

"Did you really *have to* focus on her tampon?" asks Sydney.

"Well, we're not actually sure it is a tampon," I venture.

Sydney has grabbed the prints and he is striding towards his treasured Recordati fireplace, holding them up in front of the open fire that experienced drug users always seem to have to hand in case the Proctor comes knocking on the door and there is too much stash to flush down the john. I can see he is going to make some grandiose gesture to curry favour with his Lyca. I can see he is going to consign my prints to the flames. I am wondering if there is any other use for the verb consign apart from setting fire to things.

He holds the prints up at arm's length, as though they are infectious and he doesn't want them near him, inspecting them for 10 seconds. 10-second silence that feels like 30. Then he just says: "*C'est magnifique, mais c'est nais pas Daguerre!*" before he—what is the verb?—consigns them to the flames.

Ashes to ashes, dust to dust. If the Lord don't get you, the Devil must.

I am keeping a weather eye on the smoke alarm, living in constant dread that its piercing shriek will bring a ton of porters down on us, but it is quiescent, possibly disabled by a prescient Sydney.

Of course, Calypso is on hand to be Sydney's psychopompous through the underworld, to be Robin to his Batman. She has finished rolling a joint the size of a toilet roll and passes it to him so as to bring him down after the grave disappointment of my snaps. He directs a withering look of disapproval in the direction of the joint. "Told you never to use fucking Rizlas!" he says. "Where's Job?"

"We finished the Jobs."

"Well, how fucking far is it to the buttery?" He is giving Lyca a pasting for my ineptitude with the photographs.

Somehow, she has stretched the Indiacraft thing that was around her tits so it now just about covers her tits and arse as well. She scoops some loose change off the album cover I had been waiting to read, and she is out the door, but not before shooting a withering glance at me over her bony shoulder, as though she is telling me not to get any ideas: just because she is Sydney's slave, she is still infinitely superior to me in every way.

Still no shoes on. Maybe she needs the extra sensation she gathers from the soles of her feet to compensate for the closed eyes. I figure now is not an appropriate time to read the album cover. Sydney has kicked her out for a reason. He wants to have serious words with me now we are just *homo ad homo*, because he is pretending Seth doesn't exist.

This is the moment. This is it. The *Ipsissimus*.

I go to look him straight in the eye.

He's fast asleep. And the notion dawns on me that maybe Sydney isn't the big I am he pretends to be. Maybe Calypso is the puppet master. As soon as she departed, he went all floppy, as though someone had sucked his soul out and blown it into a bottle. Sydney Syzygy in his bottle green velvet smoking jacket and his monogrammed slippers. I take in the way his right arm flops down the side of the chair, fingers pointed straight at the impossibly green carpet, as though he had hoovered it with chlorophyll, the left hand protectively covering his groin.

He resembles an inanimate mannequin that has been dressed up by Lyca and arranged in his chair. And I begin to understand that somehow he feeds off Calypso like a succubus. When Calypso is by him, he is powerful and purposeful, striding, focussed like Blake's picture of The *Ghost of a Flea*. But without Calypso, he resembles one of those tailor's dummies that the artist, Chirico, loved to paint.

I am puzzled. Here is a couple who have devoted their Cambridge days to seeking unsuccessfully to conjure up the devil. When shown photographic evidence that they have not laboured all this time in vain, their first reaction is to destroy it. Maybe it is a sacrifice to summon up a bigger devil.

But Sydney does these things with such aplomb and gusto, how could I deny him his grandstanding, especially when we both know I have the negatives?

The extended fingers of his right hand insouciantly brushing the green carpet, as one brushes blades of grass on the Grantchester water meadows. As I see the hand moving, the rest of the body is reanimated; the eyes are open and he is continuing the conversation as though he had not been fast asleep for the last ten minutes. I hadn't heard when the bare-footed Calypso re-entered his set. It is as though she switches his lights back on. But hers are off. She has been to the buttery and back without opening her eyes.

"Got the Jobs?" he asks.

Calypso resumes her seated position with her slim legs tucked up beneath her and puts the Jobs on the album cover. I am cursing myself that I had ten minutes to read it, but the thought never crossed my mind. It was as though time stood still whilst she was out of the room. 10 minutes that feels like 30 minutes.

She is cutting and pasting the Jobs on *The Wake of the Flood*, dismantling the old toke and decanting the contents into the new one. I have heard of people being particular about the bhang they smoke or the tobacco they cut it with; but I have never before come across anyone so fastidious as to turn down a perfectly good sinsemilla just because it was rolled with the wrong papers. It's only as I study what she's doing that it occurs to me that the papers are my namesake.

"While I was gone," she begins, moistening the Jobs with her versatile tongue, "I was thinking just how stupid this Gentleman thing is. I see Nick as something much darker."

"Like Batman or Dr Strange?" asks Sydney.

"Not really," says Calypso. "Look, here's Nick Jobs. He's a photographer. As a photographer what does he do? He prints out images. That took me to thinking of a dark superhero. Let's call him "The Printer"."

"The Printer," I reflect. On one level it packs a certain punch; on another it's a bit daft.

"Marvellous!" cries Sydney. "Nick Jobs, the jobbing Printer!"

"That's not the spin we put on him," says Calypso. " I am thinking Printer's Devils, I am thinking William Blake; I am thinking twisted characters being brought to life in copper intaglio and lead collotype; mysterious symbols all written in back to front writing; acid etching onto sheets, galleys of print; the Proverbs of Hell. The Printer prints out creations, but because he has to organise all his leaden characters back to front, upside down, inside out, some of them don't work out quite right.

"Some of them are misshapen. Some of them he controls. Some of them control him. His brain is labyrinthine, but some of its chambers are twisted through his constant proximity to corrosive chemicals. He's all antimony and alloys. He is a deeply flawed character."

Talking of deeply flawed characters, re-enter Ingram Frazier, without even knocking on the door. He sits down on one of Sydney's Chesterfields and keeps his mouth shut for a while, taking the temperature of the room before making a fool of himself.

I am warming to this exchange with Lyca. It has overtones of the dark runes etched by human teeth onto the Birdwood doors. Or the scripts that adorn Seth's body.

Sydney isn't having this. "Don't listen to her!" he pronounces. "It's the calligrapher in her doing the talking. He's not a deeply flawed character, darling. He's not even a printer. What you are describing is a *Typesetter*! You can't have a superhero who's a typesetter."

"But I quite like the idea," I put in, casting back to my incomplete John Bull Printing Set made in the British Isles. "This guy toiling at night in the orange glow of some blazing blast furnace with sheets of molten lead dripping away, forming letters that organise themselves into coherence and spell out his next dangerous mission. Maybe the lead in his galleys of print is taken from the shell casings of bullets extracted from the bodies of the victims he is to avenge?"

"Oh, marvellous!" cries Sydney, "It's Shadrach, Meshach and Abednego in Nebuchadnezzar's fiery furnace. And your Printer won't even need a disguise like other superheroes, because he can lumber around in a blast furnace mask capable of withstanding unspeakable temperatures. And he'll have a huge pair of asbestos gloves. A hero for the factory workers at last!"

"He's quite a literary superhero, actually," says Calypso, trying to save her creation. "Because his missions will be auto-dictated by the letters that mysteriously take shape in his galleys of print. This is one comic that is going to be all about the written word."

"Well," says Sydney, "he's going to be a pretty obscene superhero, because the only written word this cunt knows is Fuck!"

No-one says anything for a few moments, whilst some of Calypso's tortured images sink through the basalt layers and into our brains. I am thinking to myself that this is a superhero that only a girl doing History of Art and Calligraphy at Girton could have conceived. Then Sydney continues as though no-one had said anything anyway. That's the thing about Sydney. He isn't receptive to ideas if they haven't originated from him.

"When Lyca was out of the room," says Sydney, "fetching the Jobs, you were wondering why I waste my days trying to conjure up the devil."

I feel a tingling down my spine. It's as if he can read my mind. I wonder if maybe it was Sydney who was awake and me that was asleep, and if I have been talking in my sleep. I know that sometimes my fantasy life becomes confused with my real life, like when I thought the faces in the lamppost at Reality Checkpoint were out to get me. All the alcohol and drugs probably don't help.

"It is a simple collaborative act," he continues, "Like putting on a play. It's learning how to interact with your fellow humanity. Everyone has a part. Everyone has meaning and purpose and is joined together by a single Mission Statement. It is what is lacking in the modern world. No-one seems to know who they are or what they are supposed to do anymore. Look at the pack of cards that is Happy Families. We have the Baker and the Butcher, the Barber and the Barber's wife, the Tailor, the Doctor, the Policeman, the Milkman. Everybody used to know who they were and what they were supposed to do.

"Where does the data analyst fit in? Where do the tele-marketeer, the brand ambassador, the photocopying clerk, the advertising executive, the unintelligible girl in the call centre on the other side of the world; where do they all fit in, or the bloke whose only purpose is to sell you shoddy goods you don't need?" He pauses for breath.

"The Printer can go fuck himself!" he continues. "Playing to the galleys. I still like Gentleman!"

After he has taken a few drags, Sydney wants to draw me a superhero costume for Gentleman. "This is going to be everything that a gentleman is not," he pronounces, as he begins sketching deftly with charcoal. My hero is crowned by a golden cap of curls, like Michelangelo's David. The washboard torso is a perfect six pack just like Seth's. As he continues to sketch, I realise that, indeed, in common with David, this superhero is bollock-naked. As if to emphasise the nudity, or more to the point, strip it even of innocence, he draws a kind of headdress for my dick, which passes through a metal ring with the concentric horns of a ram on either side of it.

The ram's head motif conceals the pubic hair or possibly lack of it: he may have shaved me. He paints large angel's wings sprouting from my shoulders, and then diminutive Hermes wings depending from the golden grieves encasing my ankles. The diminutive wings clearly would not credibly support flight, but they somehow balance the composition, like the tail fin on a jet. Then, deciding that something is missing, he gives me a metal amulet around my neck and arm bands in matching metal.

"There," he says, tearing the composition off the pad of cartridge paper and handing it to me, "I give you…Gentleman."

If I had Sydney's ego, I would reciprocate by chucking it in the fire, but I can't think of a put-down as good as *C'est magnifique, mais ce n'est pas Daguerre!* So, after I've rolled it into a scroll and planted it in the back pocket of my Levis, I have to content myself with words. "Don't you think it's a bit…" I am searching for the *mot juste*. I can only think of Kirk Douglas at the end of Spartacus, "…homosexual?"

"Well, I must be queer," says Calypso, "because I find him incredibly sexy."

That's because you can't see him, I think to myself, but I don't say it out loud. Why has she subordinated her magnificent, imaginative creation of the Printer, to Sydney's gay erotica of Gentleman?

"So do I," pronounces Sydney. "So I must be queer too. We're all as gay as geese!"

"And what are his powers?" I humour him, more out of my desire to prolong the conversation until the blunt reaches me, rather than genuine interest. Lyca, no doubt feeling it is due to her, as the one who rolled it, dismantled it, ran to the buttery in her knickers for Jobs, and re-rolled it, is Bogarding the joint.

"Apparently," says Sydney, looking out at me from those heavy-lidded eyes made all the heavier by the dope, "he has the power to make everyone fall in love with him."

"He can bring the dead back to life," says Calypso, finally passing me the zol, "but only by fucking them. That's why he has to have his cock hanging out. His seed is so potent, it can awaken the dead."

I am wondering, *How the hell can she know Sydney has sketched a naked superhero with his cock out?*

"Perfect!" cries Sydney. "But tragically, every time he fucks and spills his seed, a little bit of him dies too so that he immolates himself in bringing life to others. How did Shakespeare put it? *The expense of spirit in a waste of shame!*"

"But those others were dead in the first place," I complain. "Isn't he a bit of a Victor Frankenstein in the guise of an angel?"

"Oh, he's certainly very mixed up," says Sydney. "This is a complicated hero, but trying to make the delicate subject of necrophilia anything less than complicated is a bit like flogging a dead horse."

"Let's face it," says Calypso, "These dead that he brings back to life, they don't have to be, what? moribund. They can be recent, like roadkill."

"Look!" says Sydney, snatching back his crappy charcoal doodle from my arse pocket. "When they see you looking like this," brandishing his cartoon of bollock-naked, be-winged, shaved me, "when you make your grand entrance as a superhero, hundreds of beautiful young girls are going to get killed in the stampede just trying to get close to you. Those girls are going to be your focus group."

"Or…" chimes in Calypso, "should we say 'fuck us' group?"

"You are going to have to fuck back to life the very women who died impulsively, in the great wildebeest migration, just trying to get a few inches closer to you, women who would still be alive if you hadn't been so fantastically good-looking—"

"As in," interrupts Lyca, "*drop dead gorgeous*!"

"Or," continues Sydney, "some of them, because obviously there are going to be too many of them for you to resurrect every single one; so we will need to evolve selection criteria. We are witnessing evolution in the making. So many. I had not thought death had undone so many."

I have never really felt the need to create a selection hierarchy for the women I would fuck, because I have always felt that just to get a fuck would be a sufficient achievement in itself. "And how did he get these powers?" I ask. The stick is on its second circle.

"Most certainly from the devil" says Sydney. "This Gentleman is a good hero. He brings life. He looks beautiful. But in order to accomplish all the goodness Gentleman has in contemplation for mankind, he has to sell himself to the Prince of Darkness. Let's just say that Gentleman has a gentlemen's agreement with the Devil. Each time he sheds his seed, the devil tightens the noose a little more. This is the sad thing about the human condition; with diligence and devotion, it is possible to raise the devil and have an audience with him so that he might endow you with some of his earthly powers.

"God, on the other hand, has never been known to share an audience with any of his followers, save those that are institutionally insane, so no surprise then that people are falling back on the devil in desperation. We are driven to the devil, because the true God will not reveal Himself.

Is there any of that white port left, darling? I think we should raise a toast to Gentleman!" Sydney stuffs his scroll back in the back pocket of my jeans.

We raise our glasses and touch them with a clink. "*L'Chaim!*" cries Sydney, expelling some of his inner Yiddish. "And enough of all these superhero costumes. We can't be doing with any of that right now, because Lyca, my Continuous One of the Heavens, has her hands full designing the costumes for my palanquin porters."

"Oh yes?" I raise an eyebrow.

"Sydney's decided he wants them in livery," explains Calypso.

"Motivates them," puts in Sydney. "Give them a nice uniform and you create a value hierarchy. Why do you think all those *schnorers* from the Indian sub-continent wanted to come and work on the London Underground?"

"What is the theme of the costume?" I enquire.

"It's going to be themed around the King Street Run," Sydney informs me.

"Is that a test of which porter can run fastest down King Street carrying the litter?" I ask innocently.

"Ho no! Ho no!" Cries Sydney. "You'll see. Just you wait and see."

"Are you serious about all this devil stuff, Sydney?" I ask, passing the doobie.

"Nick, I am no different from you or anybody else. The old religion never really died out. It's all around you. Next time you go to Kings College Chapel or Ely Cathedral, take some binoculars and check out the roof bosses at the top of the ceiling, so high up the naked eye can't even see them. But they're all there! There are hundreds of little grinning green men hidden up there, supporting the entire structure. The stone masons who built these religious monoliths, working atop their giddy scaffolds, they still subscribed to the old religion; Christianity was trying to stamp it out everywhere, but none of the gilds, including the stone masons, were buying it.

"Up there, where no-one could see, they concealed their grinning gargoyles and green men, gods of the old religion; gods who are killed in the winter and come back to life in the spring. Every time you drink in a pub called The Green Man, that's the old pagan religion staring you in the face. Next time you sneeze and someone cries out

Bless You! That's the old religion. Here…" He is searching between his bookends for some relevant tome to underline his point with and swiftly extracts it. *"The Survival of the Pagan Gods* by Professor Jean Seznec, published 1953. I commend this to you, Nick."

He passes the book to me. He continues talking whilst I try to absorb what is written on the dust jacket. "It explains syncretism, the process by which one religion absorbs the attributes of another. It explains where the gods of Olympus hung out after the arrival of Christianity, what became of the pagan religions. They didn't disappear. They never disappeared. They simply went undercover. They took on more acceptable forms.

"Pagan man in the witness protection programme, as your director of studies would put it. I seek to control a resource that others sweep under the carpet, natural forces that inform everything on this planet and always have done. It's all around us, Nick, but up there, out of sight until you allow yourself to ascend. It's what drives the impulse for Cambridge night climbing. There's another world up there."

I am dwelling upon the coincidence that in the space of one morning two different people who don't know each other but are both now, unintroduced, sharing the same room, have told me that I will find all the answers I am searching for if I just climb high enough up old buildings. Maybe that's where they've hidden all the missing choir boys. Maybe they never left King's College Chapel. They were just translated into statuary, petrified Moai sentinels stuffed up in the rafters.

The conversation had taken a turn for the serious. I blamed it on the wrong dope. Sydney resumes his seat at his swivel chair, having handed me the precious book.

There is a gap in the conversation whilst those assembled in Sydney's set checked the levels in their glasses in anticipation of the toast. In that moment of quietude, it was as if all of us became conscious of the disturbance in our tranquillity at the same time. The first I noticed was that the curling plumes from the incense sticks were spinning off course; shattered.

At the same time, I became aware of a metronomic whirring. I stood and looked up at the ceiling, certain that someone must have turned on the overhead fan, an object that would have been entirely in place in Sydney's Kasbah. But there was no overhead fan. Just the brown nicotine stains on the ceiling. Feeling stupid, having risen for no apparent reason, I walked towards Sydney's bookends and pointedly reinserted Sezneck in its appointed place, instantly regretting this inane self-conscious gesture, because I hadn't read a page of it, and could hardly go back and collect it again now.

Sydney cannot pretend to ignore it anymore. He slams down his leaded crystal and swivels in his captain's chair at the same time that I turn to see what the commotion is.

Seth is rotating his lower body round and round the pommel horse as though his legs are the rotor blades of a helicopter. His feet are pointed as straight as a ballerina's.

"And, by the way," Sydney finally says, "who is that other cunt behind you?" He is referring to Seth, of course, who finally finishes his routine and crisply dismounts the pommel horse, having whirled like a Dervish for the last 15 minutes. He is so good, everyone has pretended to ignore him. The pommel horse is strictly for show. No-one has ever used it before.

Sydney's question was directed at me, because I was the one who brought the cunt into his set.

"Oh, I'm supposed to be introducing him to Cambridge." I say. "I'm his mentor. This is Seth Godil, everybody."

"Nice aftershave," comments Calypso. Seth has raised his body temperature with these exertions and his *Balafre* aftershave is evaporating from his skin and informing the many other odours lingering in Sydney's set.

Sydney, sensing that his aftershave may be under attack, resorts to his Dunhill, splashing it liberally around the back of his neck as though he were spicing a steak for the grill.

"And what special characteristics or attributes, pray, does Seth Godil have to set him apart from other individuals?" enquires Sydney.

"He brushes his teeth ten times a day with patriotic toothpaste," I ventured.

"Cleaning one's teeth isn't exactly a character-defining trait. What else does Seth Godil bring to the table?"

I look to Seth for inspiration, but his expression is as impenetrable as the glyphs on his mighty arms. He's not going to permit himself to be controlled by Syzygy.

"Seth Godil," I say, reflecting on my discussions in the cloister outside Max Pfläfflin's set, "has a very particular skill; he can predict your future from the faecal smear in your toilet bowl."

Sydney: "No shit?"

Calypso to Sydney: "You're not exactly very welcoming." To Seth: "What are you reading, Seth?"

Hearing her voice, I turn to look at the Countenance Divine, and I realise she is smoking the joint with her feet. She has twisted herself into a figure 8, but because she's recumbent, it resembles the infinity sign on my lens, and she is holding the thing between her hallux and second toe and raising her foot to her mouth to take a drag. But it's not *look at me* ostentatious. She's just doing it because she can. As casually as I can, I sidle slyly around so that I will be next in line for the joint when she finishes. I want to insert into my mouth what has been between her peedy loody and loody holly.

Seth: "Classics."

Sydney: "Then maybe you can help me translate this passage. What is the meaning of the phrase *Omne ignotum pro magnificio*?"

Seth: "Sorry, man. Can't help you."

Sydney: "Aha, is Greek your vice then, not Latin?"

Seth: "Little Latin and less Greek."

Calypso: "What were your set texts?"

Seth: "The Aeneid for Latin and the Odyssey for Greek."

Ingram: "You've got little Latin and less Greek, so how did you manage to translate them and get a place at Cambridge?"

Seth: "I have total recall. But only in English. I can't recall in other languages. So I memorised the Aeneid and the Odyssey in Penguin Classics translations, and just regurgitated the translations with a few colourable alterations so it didn't look like out and out plagiarism."

Sydney: "That's impossible. No-one could memorise the entire Odyssey."

Calypso: "Homer did."

Me: "And he said the Aeneid too."

Seth: "And the Epic of Gilgamesh."

The Epic of Gilgamesh is just penetrating my cranium and I am wondering what language it was written in the translation from which Seth has learned by rote when Calypso passes the doobie to me. With her foot. And I accept it straight into my mouth. I have kissed Calypso's feet. No-one notices, because Calypso sees nothing and everyone else is staring down Seth. I am high on that moment before I have even taken a drag.

Sydney to Seth: "Look, Master Godil, I may be a little stoned, but I haven't completely taken leave of my senses. When you were faced with the exam papers with the lengthy passages of Greek and Latin that you had to translate, how did you know what pages of the English translation they corresponded to so that you could regurgitate them?"

Seth: "From the occurrence of the proper names, usually of the gods and the heroes, or the cities. It was easy as they were all capitalised, staring out at you from the page. If I saw, say Dido and Ajax and Achilles and Zeus close to one another, then I could figure out where those proper nouns coalesced in the translation and just cut and paste it in. Names, names, names: Polyphemus, the Cyclops, Nausicaa, Circe, Hector, Agamemnon, the blind Tiresias—"

Calypso on cue: "Calypso."

Seth: "Indeed, the very beautiful and gifted Calypso."

I see the cloud pass visibly across Sydney's brow at the prospect that this athletic upstart could be coming on to his girlfriend. He fails to notice me passing the spliff back to her, bypassing a number of others in line, but I want to feel her toes again.

Sydney: "This is fucking ridiculous. No-one can remember everything." Reaching for his black felt hood that I had first encountered when he was doing the optophonetic poetry session with Lyca. "Do you mind if I conduct a little social experiment here, Seth?"

Seth: "What kind of experiment, Sydney?"

Sydney, circling behind Seth and putting the hood over his head "Let me just blindfold you, dear chap before I explain the rules. This is the first time you've been in this room, correct?"

Seth: "Correct."

Ingram: "Oh my God! Sydney, there are far too many valuable artefacts in the room for a game of blind man's bluff!"

"Buff!" corrects Sydney. "Bluff is a malapropism. Buff is old English for push, as in *God damn the pusher man!*"

"Couldn't we just have a game of Murder in the Dark?" protests Ingram.

"Later, Ingram, later!" Sydney assures. Continuing: "Let me just spin you around, Master Godil, three or four times. Just to lose your bearings, as it were. Now," adjusting the hood to ensure no light can penetrate, "this is a room with a great many, how shall I put this? *Objets trouvée…*"

Seth: "I told you, I don't do foreign; only English."

Sydney: "What I am trying to say is that there is a lot of stuff in this room. If you really have total recall, let's see how many of the items in the room you can remember."

Seth: "Oh, like a parlour game, you mean?"

Sydney: "The same."

Seth: "After I've just spent the last fifteen minutes doing my routine on the pommel horse and not looking at anything?"

Sydney: "If that's how you chose to spend your time in my set, squandering the many opportunities to better yourself."

Seth, from within the bag: "You do realise that when one spins on the pommel horse, like a ballerina, one focusses on one point only, or one would become dizzy and fall off, so I only paid the most glancing attention possible to your, what did you call them? *Objets trouvée…*"

Sydney, going to remove the hood: "So you don't intend to rise to the challenge and prove your credentials?"

Seth, holding down the hood: "Joint please."

Blind Calypso extends her foot holding the joint en point in the direction of the blindfolded Seth. In the kingdom of the blind, the one-eyed man is king; so I collect the joint from between Calypso's toes and put it in Seth's hand, stealing a deep drag of purloined paradise en route. The benighted Calypso and the blindfolded Seth with his head in the sack are never going to know a thing about the theft. I've committed the perfect crime!

Having relieved her of her burden, so that she is once again footloose and fancy-free, Calypso assumes a complex yoga position. Seth raises the hem of the hood just enough so his mouth is free and takes a long drag. Then he extends his arm offering the spliff for the next in line. As I seem to have appointed myself the torch bearer for this little gathering, I relieve him and take a toke whilst trying to remember which direction it was supposed to be travelling in before I got involved with it.

Seth holds the smoke inside the black hood for so long I wonder if he has stopped breathing. I am also wondering to myself whether all the cut-out letters are still in the black bag. I am concerned that they could superimpose themselves atop the other characters etched into Seth's skin. It would be like one of those Rudyard Kipling Just So stories.

A further exercise in overwriting, just the same as Sydney's typewriter platen. *And this is how Seth Godil got to have letters all over his forehead. He kept his head in the bag of letters for too long whilst inhaling bad gear…*

Then his muffled voice within the black hood says: "Pommel horse."

"Well, of course, you remember the fucking pommel horse!" exclaims Sydney. "What sort of a fucking feat of memory is that?"

Seth holds his powerful arm out again, the same way the Mighty Thor does when he is waiting for his hammer to return to his hand. I interpret the gesture as meaning he wants another drag before embarking upon the parlour game. I pass the bong back to him. It may not be Thor's hammer, but it will get him hammered, as sure as Rose Kennedy has a black dress.

He ups the hem of the hood and takes another long draw on the doobie and then starts walking purposefully but sightlessly, as his head is still in the sack. I remember how he had explained to me earlier the way he could remember distances and spatial relationships between objects when he was climbing buildings in the dark.

"Where are you going now?" asks Sydney.

Seth from within the bag: "I am avoiding the George II Dolphin Pier Table. Now I am taking four steps that bring me to the wing backed swivel chair and partner's desk in fruit wood." He tosses the smouldering joint expertly, from memory, not being able to see where he is flicking it. "Lalique glass ashtray," he says, "weighing down the papyrus scroll with the Prayer for the Dead beneath it." I marvel at the trajectory of the reefer as it traces its elliptical arc, before it plops perfectly into the unseen Lalique ashtray. Then a second later the cylinder of grey ash on its end shuffles off its mortal coil neatly into the receptacle.

"Coming into the door," Seth continues, "inverted brass *mezuzah*, limited boxed edition of The Arabian Nights, Silver Samovar with Imperial eagle motif and insignia of Tsar Nicholas XII, Furry Freak Brothers Compendium Edition, Job Rolling Papers XXL, matched pair Louis XIV *gueridon* tables, carton of Marlboro Lights with the top ripped off for roach material, Dr Strange edition #35, a scene depicting the Crucifixion from the Byzantine school—oil on wood—Congo original in watercolour; a mosaic gecko paperweight from Gaudi's Park Guell, upright pianola; Steinway baby grand piano; Jelly Bean Machine, absinthe fountain; programme from La Palau de Musica Catalan Summer Festival August 1969, Sedan Chair and two wooden pall-bearer poles, Nepalese Temple Ball, approximate weight 4 ounces in original aluminium foil, a Ladekh Prayer Drum almost certainly from the Thirska Monastery, Iron Man edition#14, a Corby Trouser press, 4 cedarwood clothes hangers, 1 wire coat hanger; incense burner, inscribed Aramaic curse-bowl from fifth century Mesopotamia, Montegrappa skeleton pen, incomplete set of terracotta warriors from Xian scale 1:24, save the archer is missing; spare pianola music roll *Angelus* 65 Note; Olivetti portable typewriter with black and red ribbon, pair of signed Japanese Meiji Period Bronze Elephant Head Bookends, containing the following books from left to right: Blake's *The Marriage of Heaven and Hell*, Trianon Press edition 1952, numbered 24, The Magical Record of the Beast 666 by Aleister Crowley 1914-1920, The Devil and All His Works by Dennis Wheatley; Compendium Maleficarum by Guazzo, Facsimile Reprint published by Frederick Muller Limited 1970, Nicholas Remy's Demonolatry in 3 Volumes bound in human skin; Poe's Tales of Mystery and Imagination illustrated by Harry Clarke; and The Survival of the Pagan Gods by Professor Jean Sezneck."

Sydney's jaw has dropped. He allows himself to be off-guard, because he knows Calypso can't see him, Seth is blindfolded, and Ingram and I don't really count.

"May I continue?" Seth is eager to resume his inventory. Without waiting for an answer from the speechless Sydney: "A pair of wooden Telemark skis; Fantastic Four Meet the Silver Surfer; propelling pencil; Alpenstock full length; amulet carved from rare red coral from Cap de Creus depicting the head of the god Pan; Tapestry featuring a Unicorn and a Princess, 15th century French; Anglepoise lamp; roach clip depicting grinning green man; oxblood Chesterfield sofa; Moroccan silver bookmark with red tassel; Chinese calligraphy set with lacquers, ink and brushes; print of Millais' Angelus; brick purloined from the Great Wall of China, Badaling section, if I'm not mistaken; coffee table made from a Tibetan ox cart; Wake of the Flood, Grateful Dead; Pentateuch;

The Mighty Thor edition #42; Aspergillum and vat of Holy Water from the Sanctuary of Loreto; two massive candlesticks; hallmarked silver cruet; a box for the host in crystal and gold of exquisite workmanship from the Cathedral of Metz; fireplace surround after Recordati."

Sydney: "What do you mean, after Recordati? I was personally assured by John Partridge of Partridge Fine Arts that this is a genuine Recordati."

Seth: "They don't call him Bodge of Bond Street for nothing. It's a copy of one belonging to the Sotheby's director, Mr Mavromatis."

Sydney: "OK, OK." Removing the sack and looking him in the eye. "Well, you are Mr Memory Man. You really are. All we have to do now is figure out what use we can make of this amazing gift. Amongst this gathering of putative superheroes, how can we package your unique abilities?"

Seth: "Cheating at exams?"

"You know what he reminds me of?" Sydney addresses his question to the room generally. Since I'm accepting his hospitality, I feel obliged to play his straight man.

"No," I say. "What?"

"That joke about the Indian Memory Man," he says.

I am in the mood now for a joke. "How does it go?" I ask.

"I can't remember," says Sydney.

Calypso snickers.

The samovar gurgles like my lava lamp. The glazed sections of Sydney's room are dripping with condensation. The writing appears again in the window panes: *Set me free. I am in the glass.*

"Sydney," I venture. "you seem to have some party pieces of your own. How were you able to read my story so quickly when it was the wrong way up?"

"Oh that!" says Sydney dismissively. "When I was little, my father used to sit at the breakfast table opposite me reading his daily newspaper every morning. He was Austrian. English was not his mother tongue. You know, we yids got thrown out of every place. It was painful watching him try to read the fucking thing every morning, wanting to fit in. So I would read it at the same time, but upside down, because I was on the other side of the table.

"Anyway, the upshot is that I can read just as fast, whether it's up the right way or upside down. I can also read from left to right, like in English, or from right to left, like in Hebrew. I can also read and write back to front, as in our discussion earlier concerning the Printer and printing presses. I can also read in columns, which we use for certain demonic scripts, and it goes without saying that I have an inverted *mezuzah* on my door lintel, and I can also write with both hands when I don't chose to type.

"But that doesn't make me bisexual. You could put that cunt in a spin drier," nodding in the direction of my protégé, Seth, "and I could still read what's written on him; but I couldn't tell you what the fuck it means, because it's unintelligible shit. Oh, and I'm dating a calligrapher."

Seth to Sydney: "One thing confuses me, Sydney. Why does a man obviously as fastidious as you give house room to a wire coat hanger?"

Sydney looks across at his partner pleated into her impossible yoga position: "Who said anything about wire coat hangers? Haven't you heard of "the coil"? It's the latest form of female contraception"

"You're joking?"

"Lyca practices oral contraception," continues Sydney. "When I ask her for a fuck, she says No."

Sydney looks around for reaction, but no-one seems to get it, except Lyca, who has obviously heard it before and is looking bored, if it is actually possible for someone to maintain so complex a yoga posture and still radiate ennui at what she hears; so Sydney seeks to draw her out of her yoga position and into the conversation, and indeed, into the wire coat hanger.

"Oh Countenance Divine," says he, "Continuous Jewel of the Night, Lyca, show the newcomer your party piece with the wire coat hanger."

Obediently, Calypso exits the yoga position and strides in precise balletic steps in the direction of the wire coat hanger draped from the back of the Corby trouser press. My mouth drops open in disbelief, as I watch her climb through the coat hanger. First she places it on the dhurrie and stands both bare feet in it, and then she shimmies it up, above her knees; as it approaches her hips she rotates her upper body, and from there it seems to rise as if by its own capillary action; somehow she gets her shoulders through it, then shrugs it off and over her head. Every movement was graceful, exquisite.

She is like my little ballerina. Whilst it was in contact with her, the wire coat hanger took on its own life. Now she has finished, it is just a dead thing, lying on the woven rug, resuming its earlier state of inanimacy. She bends down and goes to pick up the lifeless object and drape it back on the Corby; but then she seems to think better of it. Leaving it on the rug, she walks away from the hanger; three paces; four paces; five paces. The whole process has been carried out without her opening her eyes. Ingram claps his hands in applause.

"Pretty neat!" he says. "Pretty good, pretty neat!"

"Hush!" purrs Sydney. "You'll spoil her concentration."

It appears, to our mounting amazement, that the party piece isn't over yet. Eyes still closed, she executes two back flips and then lowers herself from a handstand into a headstand and from a headstand, burrows straight back into the coat hanger and reverses the routine head-first. Whereas before the hanger had climbed up the monkey puzzle of her body as if by capillary action, this time she dives into it and it seems to move up her body by peristaltic motion. Her routine finished, she detaches the coat hanger from the bare foot that is level with my eyes, rights herself and deposits it back on the Corby. No-one is clapping. We are all just gob-smacked.

"Reward," pronounces Sydney.

She goes over to the Jelly Bean machine and helps herself to one. It dawns on me that these aren't Jelly Beans. They're multi-coloured tabs of all shapes, colours and sizes. It's a lottery. One has no idea what pill will be dispensed when one cranks the handle. Least of all Calypso, as her eyes are closed. She pops it into her mouth.

Sydney passes her a fluted crystal of Ruinart, and she swallows. I hadn't heard him uncorking it. We had all been so transfixed by Lyca's routine with the coat hanger that, for all I know, Sydney could have opened the Ruinart with a sharp downward slice of a Cossack sabre and I wouldn't have noticed.

"What's she got?" I ask him.

"Time will tell," says Sydney. "Maybe acid; maybe peyote. Did you know there are 40 different types of LSD in that machine?"

"Wow! Talk about hiding in plain sight!"

"I've never seen anything like it!" mutters Ingram, eventually recovering from the spectacle.

"That's nothing!" Sydney assured him. "Wait until you see her packanatomicalisation."

"Pach-what?" asks Ingram. "Are we in Elephant Man territory?"

"Packanatomicalisation," explains Sydney, "is one of the accomplishments that contortionists, such as Calypso, keep in their repertoire. Packanatomicalisation is a derivative of enterology whereby the gifted performer folds her body over and over until she is able to squeeze herself into an impossibly small box, preferably a glass box, so that the audience can see there's nothing up her sleeve. I've also seen the trick performed with a Balthazar of Bollie. Related skills are splits, oversplits, front and backbending and minor dislocations. The Countenance Divine can do them all."

"But she can't do Human Flag," observes Seth.

"Indeed," replies Sydney. "Human Flag requires profound upper body strength. Calypso's forte is flexibility, not brute strength."

"Well," says Ingram, "maybe I wasn't so wide of the mark when I said Elephant Man. She should be in a circus."

"And you should be in a fucking institution!" responds Sydney.

Seth has finished wiping himself down after his exertions and has rolled his towel up.

"What did the Proctor want?" Seth enquires of me.

"Oh, it was to do with the missing choir boys from Kings," I explain.

"They're interviewing everybody!" interrupts Sydney. "They called me in, because someone had told them that I practice the Dark Arts, so they thought that I might be doing something to pubescent boys in my ceremonies. I ask you, don't they know the fucking difference between demonolatry and paedophilia?"

"But what's the connection with Nick?" enquired Seth.

"It was the photographic angle," I explained. "I take a lot of photographs around Cambridge. They're interested in anything that might amount to 'evidence'."

"You know," began Ingram. "They're all poor kids that go missing. Imagine the unholy row if they'd actually been anyone important. They receive a special scholarship from King's College to come and learn how to sing as choristers. The kids come from problem backgrounds where the parents are glad to get shut of them—assuming, that is, there actually are two parents. Instead of having to sell them into the sex trade, they imagine that they are doing something akin to putting them into holy orders.

"They've been disappearing at the rate of about one a month, and everyone's clueless as to what's become of them. Apart from being in the choir, there's no feature to connect their disappearances. No-one's come forward. No bodies have been found. No ransoms have been demanded. Nobody even took the remotest interest until the local rag revealed that 20 had disappeared. And they're a commodity! There's an endless supply of the little bleeders! The choir never gets any smaller, because the College just goes out and recruits 20 more. They seem to have vanished off the face of the earth. I think we have the free press to thank for the fact that their story is at last coming to the forefront."

"Bollocks!" Exclaimed Sydney, changing the subject. "It's all just Chinese whispers. And where are you headed with that towel under your arm?" The devil-worshipper in him has had enough of listening to gossip about missing choir boys. He doesn't appreciate that Seth has already used his towel and was now on his way back from the Birdwood. Sydney rises so late that it doesn't cross his mind that someone else might already have performed all of his morning ablutions.

"I'm going down the gym," Seth says.

"Making a temple of your body?" asks Calypso.

"More of a library than a temple," says Sydney referring to the calligraphic glyphs.

"I try," says Seth.

"You know," muses Calypso. "Never mind the lost boys! There's a whole generation of lost men out there. They can't get jobs or women, so they are seeking to achieve their ambitions upon themselves. They think that if they get sufficiently ripped, that's an end in itself. That's why I call them my Lost Boys. Somewhere along the path of their development between boys and men, they lost their way. They have no fucking idea where they are going or where they belong, or how they fit in. They don't want to join the army or go to war or box or wrestle in the ring. They just want to create the body of a warrior as an end in itself.

"They take the by-product of a martial existence, and want to use it to be pretty boys. No-one could ever love them as much as they love themselves, so life is a permanent disappointment for them. It's all about fucking form and no fucking function. The trouble with you guys," she concludes with an embracive gesture that seems to include everyone in the room, "Is that what you really want is to be chicks."

"What sort of chicks?" asks Seth.

"Chicks with dicks," replies Calypso curtly.

"And what about you?" asks Seth. "How did you get to be so toned?"

"Fucking," she says.

It is one of those conversations that just ties my brain up in knots. First you elevate a woman to a position of semi-deity in your head, the Countenance Divine, the Continuous Jewel of the Night, whatever. But then you superimpose upon that image the visceral reality of Lyca, her proximity: her choreographed, unseeing flexibility. If I could only extend my finger a centimetre further, I could touch her, refine her and burn off all her imperfections: I could be her cupping glass. I could twist her into new shapes in my furnace.

Shadrach, Meshach and a Bendy Girl.

Somewhere I hear Ingram belittling Seth: "It's just a bad case of arrested development," he says. "He's already covered himself in tattoos and now he can never change. Why would anybody want to make themselves so finite at such an early age?"

I stride purposefully towards the great stained glass windows of King's College chapel, the Printer, a lifeless doll in the crook of my arm, like a bundle of rags. I set the rags on the floor, but they jump up, animated. It's Lyca!

On all fours, forked and bearded, I crawl through a mass of iridescent colours, following in the footsteps of Blake's Nebuchadnezzar. It's stiflingly hot in here.

When I walk amongst the fish ponds of my garden, methinks I see a thing armed with a rake that seems to strike at me.

Everyone is staring at me. The jagged glass is snapped. *I bleed, sir. Strangling is a very quiet death.*

That is what Ferdinand says in *The Duchess of Malfi,* before he descends into lycanthropy.

Sydney is barking orders to Calypso. "Get that stoned maniac patched up before he bleeds all over the Egyptian Ankh rug!"

The cut in my hand seems deep, but clean. I have no recollection whatsoever of how it got there. I feel no pain.

I am unwell. Reader, dear Reader, I have delivered a proxy to Björn

Agen to stand in as narrator during my indisposition. Yes, I know, you haven't been introduced to him yet; but he can introduce himself. He's the only one I can trust.

Björn Takes Up the Narrative: Flag 1

Oh man! Oh man!

The morning awakes and shakes the bedsores from its eyes
And loans its long wings on the black ponchos of the wind.

Shit! I must have fallen asleep with all the lights on.

I don't know where those words come from. It's as if I've been composing some doggerel verse in my sleep. And what a deep sleep. As I crawl out of bed, I realise it's only six in the morning. I am wondering how I can need so badly to micturate whilst at the same time feeling totally dehydrated and consumed by a parching thirst. I can't decide whether to go to the tap and drink a gallon of water or go to the can and make room for it first.

Then I see her in the half-light, still strapped to the bed, and I think Oh fuck! and last night starts snapping into focus. She's still attached to the bedhead by my set of physiotherapy deadlift yoga squat rubber bands, which were the only things I had available when she kept asking me to tie her up. *Hurt me! Hurt me!* She kept saying. But I went to public school: I could never strike a woman.

Anyway, not anywhere her regular boyfriend would notice. I'm not into S&M and hadn't been prepared for any of this, so I had to make do with the tools at hand, in the good, old English tradition, even though I'm not English, and she seemed to be Welsh. So we'd contented ourselves with some candles. I'd restrained her to the bed with my physiotherapy rubber bands, dripped molten wax all over her belly and tits and then stuck the candle up her arse before fucking her.

I think the candle was still in there. It was a joke candle my brother had given me for Christmas. It had wicks on both ends. In the middle of the candle it said 0; then radiating out from the candle in both directions from the 0, it had 1, 2, 3 printed on it through to 12 o'clock. In the box the candle came in, it said: *Patent Alarm Clock Candle. Select the desired time, light one end and insert the other end up your arse.* I'd never thought I'd actually use it, but she'd been like someone who had been bottling up all her libido all her life until it all gushed out at once last night.

I piss furiously in the gyp sink and then stick my head under the tap, guzzling. Then I hear her voice.

"Björn," she says.

It's Olumidé.

"If you don't let me out of this contraption, I think I'm going to wet myself."

I finish slurping the water and approach the bed, fumbling with all the intertwinements. It's hopeless. It's like trying to undo the knots in a tiny gold link necklace. As soon as you think you've undone one tangle, you find you've just made two more. Then I hear a light hissing.

"I'm afraid I've just had a little tinkle," she says.

I am wondering what the bedder is going to think when she finds the waterlogged mattress; but that shouldn't be my first priority. My first priority should be detaching the naked girl covered in wax from said waterlogged mattress. But for some reason, I find I'm getting hard again, and suddenly dealing with that is my first priority.

I fuck the life out of her, and somewhere between pissing and biting and screaming, we both come together. Fuck me! She's still got the candle up her arse, but at least it's not alight.

"Again?" she asks.

I pull my jeans and top on and decide to step out and get some air. She's still cuffed to the bed. I unlock my cycle, cursing myself for not having thought to padlock her to the bed instead of wasting my physio bands. But then someone would have pinched my bicycle.

I am cycling down Trumpington Street when I am nearly knocked off my bike by someone's exceedingly large feet colliding with my face. As I myself am over six feet in height, this is an uncommon and unwelcome experience. The owner of the feet is hanging on to a lamppost, but his body is at 90 degrees to it, forming an L shaped bracket protruding into the highway. His feet, pointed like a ballerina's, graze my chin as I cycle past. The only parts of him that are connected to the lamppost are his hands. His strength is so prodigious that he seems to defy the laws of gravity.

"What's going on, man?" I ask.

The tall stranger who has curious markings all over his body, falls off the lamppost as though he were a leech that has sucked all the electricity out of it before crumpling onto the pavement beside my supine cycle. But he doesn't release his grip on the lamppost. It never leaves his embrace. I am reminded of Odysseus having his crew strap him to the mast of his ship so that he could hear the song of the Sirens.

"How long was that?" he asks, breathless.

"How long was what, man?" I ask.

"I am seeking to establish a new world record in the discipline of Human Flag," the athlete informs me. "One uses one's upper body strength to impersonate a flag; with the arms fully extended and one's body parallel to the ground, one must see how long one can hold that most demanding of all gymnastic positions. The pommel horse is nothing compared to this. The Flag exercises to breaking point every known muscle in the body."

"Have you tried crucifixion?"

"Do I know you?"

"Nobody knows me yet. We haven't been introduced."

"Seth Godil. I'd shake your hand, but then I'd have to release the lamppost."

"Is it resisting arrest? We can do this in the street, or we can take the lamppost down to the station. Björn Agen at your service."

"Seriously, how long?"

"I would say about 30 seconds."

"For a new world record, I need at least forty-two," he says. "Let's try it again." And no sooner has he said that than he has leapt back up the lamppost, and is gripping it with his huge hands and uncurling his body into the flag position, parallel to the pavement. From the blue bulging veins in his neck, all down his oxters and arms, his torso and legs, he is total concentration attached to a streetlight. I have no stopwatch, so I am counting *one little second, two little seconds, three little seconds* until the limpet's energy seeps out of him and he slithers down to the pavement again.

"Well?" he asks.

"Thirty-five seconds," I guess.

Looking up at me from the pavement: "Shit!"

"Seth, you can't expect to smash the world record every time."

"Björn, I am not leaving this fucking lamppost until I am over forty seconds."

"Well then, I'd better roll me a bong as I can see I may be here some time."

"Don't you think it's a bit early for that? You wanna have a go at the Flag?"

"Me? Buddy, I'm still in physio since I bust my sciatic nerve doing bum burpee jumps."

Then I remember: the bird's still strapped to my wee-soaked bed. It'll be hours before the gyp arrives.

"Do you believe in Buddhism?" I ask, crumbling away at my stash.

"Maybe, Björn. I don't know. Why do you ask?"

"It's the lamppost thing," I say. "If you come back, you should come back as a dog."

"Very funny!"

"And get yourself a proper lamppost next time. Visit Reality Checkpoint."

Further down the same street, I fall into step with Ingram Frazier. Early riser. Everyone knows Ingram, the guy who wants to be Prime Minister. When he grows up. He has a copy of *Megarry's Manual of Real Property* under his arm. It's like wearing a badge that says I am reading the law. Maybe I could have a tee-shirt printed with Do you want to score? written above a big question mark. Ingram could probably get sent down just for shooting the breeze with the likes of me.

Even though I was present myself, he feels the need to recount to me the events of yesterday culminating in Nick Jobs trying to dig the hidden letters out of Sydney's window pane and practically slicing his hand off. Ingram seems to have a very low opinion of Sydney who he refers to as Shylock Syzygy and *oven-dodger*, and an even lower opinion of his girlfriend, Calypso. Personally speaking, I like her. Geddit? Lyca!

But Ingram is bubbling over with vitriol and invective. I don't know if it's aimed at her personally or womankind in general. I draw on the doobie and let his shit wash over me.

"And that party-piece with the coat hanger!" Ingram exclaims. "What was it that Samuel Johnson said about woman preachers?"

I take a toke and hold it down. "I believe he likened them to a dog walking on its hind legs," I offer.

"Yes, not that it is done well, but that it is done at all."

"I don't quite follow how your metaphor works, man," I point out.

Not condescending to answer my question, he continues his rambling misogyny. "Sydney Syzygy is welcome to his double-jointed two-timing cuntortionist pachyderm!" he declares, loving the sound of his own voice, delighted at his play on words, positively revelling in his court room rhetoric.

"Ingram," I say, "do I look like a jury to you?"

"She's nothing but flesh and freckles!" he continues, "She's all skin and bones. There's precious little of her as it is and what there is, is all pointing in the wrong directions! Toned by fucking! My fanny! Making love to her would be like trying to have sex with a deckchair!"

"Don't knock it if you've never tried it. Lyca's the height of cool. She is the ablative absolute."

"Must be the dope talking!" He sneers.

"Don't anthropomorphise the dope!" I respond.

I conclude that Ingram is both an anti-Semite and a misogynist.

Returning to my set, Olumidé is still fastened to my bedstead, awash in candlewax and bodily fluids and offering to receive more; but I'm wasted and all out of jis. The expense of spirit in a waste of shame. I cut the Gordian knot with a Stan Lee knife I find in the drawer, and set her free. Woman's Lib! She rubs her wrists, restoring the circulation, and as soon as she can feel her hands again, she uses them to slap me really hard on the cheek before gobbing in my face, picking up her things and leaving.

Once she's left, I heave the mattress over 180 degrees and crash out for 30 minutes before the gyp starts hammering on my door.

A Brief History of the Peloponnesian War

One step below Herodotus, the Father of Lies, stands Thucydides. Thucydides embellishes history with nice touches, such as Pericles' Funeral Speech, an encomium of democracy and the dead. Some would say it is closer to embroidery than embellishment. Thucydides explains that he wasn't actually there to hear the speech himself, but he's sure this is what Pericles would have said in the circumstances. He then makes it up word for word, *verbatim*.

I wasn't present at the following meeting between Detective Inspector Dix of the Cambridge Police and the Proctor; because I'd passed out in Substance Abuse Central. But I'm sure this is what they would have said if I had been:

"The College Statutes going back to the fifteenth century require that there should be 16 choristers who are to be chosen from the ranks of the "poor and needy boys of sound condition and honest conversation… knowing completely how to read and sing.""

"They have to be under the age of 12 at admission, and are generally admitted about 8 years old, and they get turved out once their voices break."

"Then what happens to them?"

"I dread to think. These days the boys are educated at King's College School, but there is still a lot of bias in favour of poor and needy lads, and a variety of bursaries are available. So it's a way of getting into Cambridge University even if your family's destitute and your lad's not the sharpest knife in the drawer."

"And how many have gone missing altogether?"

"56 at last count."

"But if there are only supposed to be 16 of them?"

"That's the thing. The Provost keeps topping them up. He calls it an imprest system."

"What? Like in petty cash?"

"Yes. He always keeps a balance of 16 of the little buggers in hand or the choir wouldn't sound right."

"So, if 8 of them disappeared in mysterious circumstances?"

"He'd just go out and get 8 more, and so on *ad infinitum*. He doesn't seem to have concerned himself with where they were disappearing to, why they were disappearing, or what became of them once they'd disappeared."

"Because they were just a commodity that was going to get chucked onto the dung heap anyway as soon as their voices broke and be replaced by others. They're the ultimate transients."

"And their parents?"

"Were pleased to get shot of them. As I say, they're hand-picked from disadvantaged homes."

"And their friends?"

"Their only friends are in the choir and disappear with them."

"It's the perfect crime."

"Did you interview the Provost?"

"I did."

"And what did he say?"

"Well, these weren't his exact words, but the gist of it was that God moves in mysterious circles."

Kir Royale; Nick Jobs Resumes His Role as Narrator

"How much is the damage?" I ask.

I am back in Sydney's set, looking at the obscene hardboard that has been tacked to the window frame until the glaziers find a slot in their busy schedule. I can tell he has been reading Othello. He has a Moroccan sterling silver bookmark with a red silk tassel, and it is always in the book he is currently reading. He wouldn't dream of dog-earing the page or, worse still, damaging the spine of the book by leaving it open upside down, as I would.

"Oh, don't worry about it," says Sydney. "The college have said they will pay."

Despite the veneer of feigned easy-going insouciance, I can tell Sydney is really irritated. It's not the cost. The ugly hardboard offends his aesthetic sensibilities. It's my fault. I must have lost control.

"How's your hand?" he asks.

"They had to stitch it."

"Should've asked me," Sydney says. "I'm told my needlework is very good."

"Really?" I don't know what he's talking about.

"Perhaps," he ventures, "In your condition, you shouldn't indulge as liberally as the rest of us. I read about epilepsy in the Ward library, and I would say you are doing absolutely everything you should avoid doing if you don't want to have seizures. Flashing lights, drugs, alcohol, not to mention living under the constant stress of this paper about the Ghost of a fucking Flea that you're obviously never going to hand in."

"If every cloud has a silver lining, I guess the upside is that now I've got a perfect excuse. I can't write with my hand all bandaged up like this. Look, I'm really sorry about the window, Sydney."

"No, no. Don't even mention it. You interest me, Nick, because it seems that what happens to you spontaneously, is what I am working so hard to achieve through artificial stimulants. You flit in and out of the Astral Plane at will, whereas I have to strive to achieve it through a combination of dedicated professionalism and abandonment to mind-altering substances."

"More window pane than Astral Plane," I joke.

"Seriously, Nick, are you able to control it?"

"In the short term, yes, I can usually cheat it; but eventually, it always gets the better of me. It's like I can tell I'm about to heave up and it's inevitable, but I have just enough self-control to get myself to a private place and a bucket."

"No, I didn't mean *Can you control it not happening?* I meant: *Can you make it happen?*"

"The answer is No, but I guess we've been having a pretty good try, haven't we? I'm normally able to control it. I usually get signals in advance, little muscle contractions, nervous tick, dryness in the mouth, smacking the lips. There are lots of signs that the neurons are lining themselves up in the wrong order, and I can generally concentrate on other forms of order, and I master it. It is important to me that I am in control. So I have to expose myself to the stimuli that threaten it. Like Milton saying he couldn't praise a fugitive and cloistered virtue."

Sydney is dismissive: "Milton was simply plagiarising Socrates," he snaps. "It seems to me," says Sydney, "that your brain is just like the engine in my Super Snipe. You know that the cylinders fire in a specific sequence? When you have a fit, groups of neurons start firing in an abnormal and excessive order. It's all to do with sets of numbers, things arranged in sets"

"Maybe, but it's fully synchronised. It's the synchronisation that is the problem, but if I immerse myself in something else, something ordered, if only the contemplation of a row of objects in a line, that usually does it."

"I must take you to Wells-next-the-Sea one day," he pronounces. "They have these rows of piebald bathing huts all in lines. You can contemplate them and marshal your thoughts."

"I would very much like that," I determine. "By the way, where's Calypso?"

"She's doing one of her lectures at the Sedgwick Site this morning."

"Oh, I didn't know she lectured. I thought she was another undergrad."

"She's not just a pretty face, you know."

"Well, if I can't offer you something for the damage," I persist, "I suppose I had better get back to my darkroom."

"Well, it's almost eleven o'clock; you can't leave without a sharpener, old chap."

Having taken the trouble to thoroughly research his subject in the Ward Library, so that he knew all the worst things to do to me, he now put the theory into action, producing a large spliff from the rose-veined marble top of his finest *gueridon* and firing it up with his Dunhill lighter.

"Isn't it rather early in the day?" I queried.

"Indeed, Nick. That's why we call it wake n bake. Be a good chap and bring that Crème de Cassis over here, whilst I find some cold Cava. Prosecco's too sweet. I think the time is right for a Kir with beaded bubbles winking at the brim. Sorry about the Cava, but the Buttery's out of Bolli."

"Sydney, where do you get all this gear from?"

"Nick, well, obviously, from my man, from my dealer, Björn Agen."

"God damn the pusher man!" I start the quote off but we both end it together.

"Yes, God damn him, but he has his uses. If you want gear, you want to deal with the engine driver, not the oily rag. The more middlemen, the more risk of bad gear and the higher the price."

"So you deal with the engine driver?"

"Yes, *el Hombre.*"

"I'd like to meet him."

"You will, Nick, you will."

I hold the joint whilst he fiddles with the wire around the cork on the Cava. I take a deep and satisfying drag on the doobie, filling my lungs. Just then the cork explodes and I feel the neurons in my brain performing precisely the sort of abnormal and excessive activities that Sydney had just described. I am also conscious of the fact that I have lost an armful of blood recently. In my mind I try to concentrate on the order of the Birdwood until I take back control. I imagine my little ballerina dancing in the straight corridors of the Birdwood in the dappled lights.

"Did you know that Shakespeare's Othello is epileptic?" Sydney abruptly asks me, as he relieves me of the bong whilst depositing the kir royale in my good hand.

"Certainly not. It has never crossed my mind."

"Read the text, Nick, read the text. You'd be surprised what you can learn by reading the text."

"But why would he be an epileptic?"

"Why not? It's more common than people think. One in every one hundred. You should have been a Hell's Angel, Nick. You are the one percent!"

"What do you mean?"

"Don't you know? It was a comment made by a member of the AMA—American Motorcyclists Association—he said that 99% of motorcyclists were law-abiding citizens. That meant that 1% were outlaws. The Hell's Angels adopted that, and proudly referred to themselves as the 1%. It's an example of taking hold of something that's supposed to be an insult and proudly adopting it. Like Euripides turning the Erinyes into the Eumenides. Turns it on its head, so the guy who insulted you ends up feeling inadequate himself. We should get Calypso to make you a patch, commemorating that you are one of the 1%."

My word, that Kir Royale hits the spot! It's barely 11.30 and I'm already *ausgeflipt*.

I feel emboldened to ask Sydney a very direct question, especially as Lyca isn't here. No beating around the bush.

"Sydney, let me come straight out with it. I'm sick and tired of imbibing hearsay and Ingram-esque rumours. Can you please tell me, what happened to Calypso's eyes?"

Sydney looks up and then looks down, flicking through his beloved John Wilmott.

"Here we are," he says. "Page 136. *The Mock Song*. Read it!" He holds the opened Rochester up to me. "Please. I'd like to hear it again. Please read it out loud. If you've cut your hand and can't write, you must read!"

I take the book. I don't get it, but I recite it. It's one of those Phyllis and Amyntas pastorals that they loved to write in the seventeenth century.

I cannot change as others do,
Though you unjustly scorn,
Since that poor swain that sighs for you
For you alone was born.

No, Phyllis, no, your heart to move
A surer way I'll try,

And to revenge my slighted love,
Will still love on, will still love on, and die.

"*Will still love on, will still love on, and die!*" echoes Sydney. "Again, Nick!" he pleads, practically swooning with delight. He takes the spliff from my hand, fills his lungs, hands it back to me, and flops into his chair. "Just that lilting last line again, Nick."

I draw on the bong again and reread in the halting rhythm the verse requires:

And to revenge my slighted love,
Will still love on, will still love on, and die.

I mean to ask what the hell this has to do with Lyca's eyes, but Sydney is clapping his hands with delight at my rendition. "Second verse, Nick! Second verse!" he cries out.

My eyes lower to the page and I continue:

When killed with grief Amyntas lies,
And you to mind shall call
The sighs that now unpitied rise,
The tears that vainly fall,
That welcome hour that ends his smart
Will then begin your pain,
For such a faithful, tender heart
Can never break, can never break, in vain.

I don't get it. I hand him the book back. And the joint.

"*Can never break, can never break, in vain!*" Emotes Sydney, and he wipes his eyes on the sleeve of his crushed velvet jacket, transported with the lilting rhythm and the inanity of the doggerel he has had me reciting. "It's killing me!"

"But what's Rochester got to do with Lyca's eyes, Sydney?" I ask.

"No, no! You don't get it, dear boy! That wasn't Rochester. Those pathetic verses were written by Rochester's enemy, Sir Carr Scroope and addressed to Scroope's mistress, Cary Frazier. The point is that Rochester satirised Scroope's delicate lyric in his Mock Song, and that

approaches the answer to your query about Lyca's eyes. Here, here…"
He is rifling through the pages. "Read this please."

I see that he has opened the book to Rochester's satire of Scroope's lyric. I read as requested, but not before I have fortified myself with further spliff. I clear my voice for Rochester's response.

"*I swive*," I begin. "*What's swive?*"

"Fuck. Swive means fuck, Nick. Fuck, shag. Read on, please. Read Rochester's version."

I swive as well as others do;
I'm young, not yet deformed;
My tender heart, sincere and true,
Deserves not to be scorned.
Why, Phyllis, then, why will you swive
With forty lovers more?"
"Can I," said she, "with nature strive?
Alas I am, alas I am, a whore.

"Were all my body larded o'er
With darts of love so thick
That you might find in every pore
A well-stuck standing prick,
Whilst yet my eyes alone were free,
My heart would never doubt,
In amorous rage and ecstasy,
To wish those eyes, to wish those eyes, fucked out."

I close the book and hand it back to him. "Very funny!" I say. "Who was Cary Frazier?"

"Probably Ingram's great great great grandmother but he doesn't know it," splutters Sydney. "She was a Maid of Honour to Queen Catherine and the Countenance Divine of Charles II's court. She was the daughter of Sir Alexander Frazier, who was the King's principal physician. *Principal physician*, I emphasise. How many different strains of syphilis do we think Charles II was suffering from? You know what Rochester wrote of Cary? I can recite it from memory:

"Her father…that's Sir Alexander Frazier…" Starting again:
Her father gave her dildoes six;
Her mother made 'em up a score;
But she loves nought but living pricks,
And swears by God she'll frig no more.

"Nick, where has all this exuberance disappeared to in the present day and age? Why don't we have characters like this or writers celebrating them like Rochester? When I read the papers…" He is stabbing his index finger at the JC, "And they say that their columnists are vitriolic; they don't even approach this. The cunts don't know what fucking vitriol is!"

"Sydney, are you telling me Lyca's eyes were fucked out?"

"Don't be so ridiculous, Nick! Is that the dope talking? I just wanted to share *the Mock Song* with you. Fuck the Ghost of a Fucking Flea! Give me 500 words on The Mock Song!"

Just then, the Countenance Divine comes through the door. Using her big toe, one by one she shrugs the heels of her shoes off and steps out of them, so that she is barefoot on the dhurrie, and helps herself to the joint out of my hand as I had previously helped myself to it from between her toes. She plants her bag, overflowing with papers and manuscript notes down on one of the two gueridons, and takes a good, healthy suck as though her life depended on it. She then wipes sundry strands of tobacco filings off the tip of her tongue with the back of her hand.

"Who packed this fucking thing?" she asks, looking at it in disgust.

"What was the talk at Sedgwick Site all about today?" asks Sydney, answering a question with another question.

"I was doing Millais' *Angelus*," she answers.

"Ah, Millais' *Angelus*!" muses Sydney. "Dali had a great deal to say on that topic. And were your students receptive?"

"Honey, when I first started delivering this course of lectures, I realised that most of the students were just as much off their fucking faces as you are. My lectures are designed to cater for what people in that emotional condition can handle, and, yes, I think they all handled it very well, especially the over-painting, which, as you say, we shall approach via Dali." Then, acknowledging my presence for the first time: "Nurse Hilda patch you up OK, Nick?"

"I've got to keep it dry," I say, immediately wondering why the fuck I volunteered that useless piece of information.

Angels and over-painting. I have no idea what they are talking about. I don't know if it's the epilepsy, the dope, or my innate stupidity that sets me apart from the other people in the room.

My heart would never doubt,
In amorous rage and ecstasy
I'm fucked if I know, I'm fucked if I know,
what this is all about.

Just then Sydney puts Dylan's *Ballad of a Thin Man* onto his gramophone. I identify with its sentiments. I could have been Mr Jones.

I feel I'm in the way. I will retire to my makeshift darkroom and see what turns up. The tongs will replace my bandaged limb. I tell Sydney that I am going off to my set to read Othello.

1st Interview by the Proctor

"Have you seen this lad before?" The Proctor slid a glossy photo across the desk in my direction. It was one of those crap portraits that the school photographer takes. After he's done the form shot (the plenary session with the entire school printed on an endless bog roll), he tries to sell the parents individual portraits of their kids. The subject of this cameo was in his school V-necked pullover and sat up so rigidly for the camera that you'd think the photographer had stuck his tripod up his arse. It looked like every other school photograph I'd ever seen, except the Proctor's thumb print was smudged on the high gloss. I buffed it with my bandage. Has its uses.

"No," I said.

"Are you sure about that?" persevered the Proctor. "It's just that this lad was one of two lads. This one's gone missing; but the other one made a positive identification of you. He says you came up to them when they were crossing Parker's Piece, and that you were the worse for wear."

"Oh," I say, staring at the photograph again. "I may have some dim recollection, yeh."

"The other one says you offered him a cigarette."

"Did I?"

"We're talking of 11-year-old boys, Mr Jobs. Why would you be offering cigarettes to 11-year-old boys?"

"I felt sorry for him."

"But earlier you said you'd never seen him."

"Well, it wasn't an important thing to remember; but when you'd mentioned the two of them being on Parker's Piece, it came back. Why is it important?"

"Because you're the last adult who saw the two of them together, and now the one in the photo's gone missing. That makes 60 King's College Chapel choir boys who have disappeared in the last few years."

"Ah, the Lost Boys!"

"What are you referring to, Mr Jobs? What Lost Boys are these?"

"It's just a literary allusion, sir. Nothing to get excited about."

"Mr Jobs, I am told that you keep blacking out, that you have spells when you can't account for your actions."

"Sir, are you accusing me of doing something with 60 missing choir boys?"

"I am simply pointing out, Mr Jobs, that if you had done, you may not even remember it."

"Do I need a lawyer, sir?

Little Girl Lost

"I don't even know what it is you think you see in this Wilhelm Blake," says Dr Max Pfläfflin in our private tutorial, "that you vant to vaste your time vriting about him."

Since Seth pointed the trait out, I have noticed that when there are just the two of us in the tutorial, Pfläfflin seems to drop his guard so that his German accent is much more pronounced.

"He was a visionary poet," I say.

"He was a paedophile poetaster with tendencies to bestiality," says Pfläfflin.

"What on earth are you talking about?"

"Read *The Little Girl Lost*!"

He is quite red in the face.

"I have read *The Little Girl Lost*."

His index finger is running along the spines of the books on his shelf. I see that he has Blake's *Songs of Innocence and Experience* on his top shelf, as though he is making a sincere attempt to keep it out of the reach of children. Standing on tiptoe, he pulls it out and goes to the page he has in mind.

"Vread it out loud!" he exclaims. "From where my finger is."

I seem to be developing a complex: first Sydney wanted me to read Rochester's *The Mock Song* out loud to him. Now Pfläfflin wants me to recite *The Little Girl Lost*.

Taking the page from beneath his fricative finger, I vread it to him:

Leopards, tygers play,
Round her as she lay;
While the Lion old,
Bow'd his mane of gold,
And her bosom lick,
And upon her neck,
From his eyes of flame,
Ruby tears there came;

While the lioness
Loos'd her slender dress,
And naked they conveyed
To caves the sleeping maid.

"It's deviant!" Pfläfflin cries. "All this, and the Little Girl is only seven summers old!"

"No, I don't read it like that," I say. "It's quite normal. You have to read it together with *The Little Girl Found.*"

"I vill tell you the one and only normal thing about this poem," blurts Pfläfflin. "That the Little Girl is stripped off by the lioness and not the lion! That is his only concession to decency!"

As I walk away from his set, I am coiled in confusion as to why someone who seems to have nothing but contempt for English writers and can't even pronounce the English language without gobbing on you should have been put in a position of authority from which he might corrupt others with his vile views. The only explanation that I can come to that makes any sort of sense is that he was put here as some sort of an *agent provocateur* to make the rest of us more steadfast in our opinions.

3-Dimensional Printing in 1972

My makeshift darkroom is assembled by blu-tacking a *Do not Disturb* sign up outside my door for the benefit of the gyp and covering the windows with black bin liners, whilst I arrange my developer dishes around the sink in the corner, cloaked in further bin bags. My hand is still bandaged up, so I'm careful to keep it dry. I prod the photographic papers with my rubber tongs protruding from the end of my dressing and ponder what it would be like to have bionic rubber tongs instead of opposable thumbs.

Johnny Storm, the Human Torch in *The Fantastic Four* cries *Flame on!*, before he turns himself into a fireball. Rubber on! wouldn't have the same ring. The Human Contraceptive. But he'd still be a Johnny.

Beneath the red glow of the safety light, I was coaxing to life another print from the ∞ series.

I noticed a lozenge-shaped blemish on the paper, like a small scab. As I continued to agitate the chemicals, the scab became crustier, taking on definition, and then it lifted off the paper altogether, suspended in the chemicals. It was growing; now it was the size of a tab of acid; now the size of a thrupenny bit; now it was the size of a seed pod. It was forming a serpentine tail and the tail was moving. I stopped agitating the chemicals, because the tail was thrashing around doing the agitation for me: whatever it was, it was developing itself.

Prehensile arms sprouted from the other end of the seed-pod, and what resembled the back of a furry head, but I could not be sure, as it was face down in the liquid. With its little arms, and its hammering tail, it was swimming the crawl towards the edge of the developer tray. Now two legs were sprouting from either side of the tail. It was becoming an accomplished swimmer. Each stroke was more self-assured than the last. It had reached the edge of the dish, and the hands at the ends of those sinewy arms were clutching the rim.

I watched in amazement as this imperfection within the picture took on sentient life and crawled out of the dish. It was upright now, with one leg outside the tray, planted on the draining board and the other still inside. Then, balancing with its tail, it climbed right out of the developing dish and onto the Formica laminate top next my draining board, leaving shallow pools of liquid behind it. If it wasn't so scary, it would be like Loony Tunes. Dear God, the thing was staring at me, and as it grew in size, it grew in confidence. I wanted to run, but it transfixed me in its gaze.

It continued to increase in stature until it was of equal height with me. From somewhere, it produced one of those red Catalan caps that Salvador Dali liked to be photographed in and popped it onto its head. Then it put its hand on my shoulder and looked me up and down, as though I were the one that was abnormal and deserved contemplation and consolation, as though it was me who had just climbed out of the developer. The thought passed through my head that I should have popped him into the tray of fixer to stop him growing any more. Or called the police. A case of arrested development.

He shouldered aside the black bin liners and emerged into the perpetual twilight of my bedsit, which was a relief, because it was getting crowded with the two of us around the sink. He picked up the framed photograph of topless Olumidé on the mantelpiece over my fireplace with the electric coal-effect fire.

"Who's this?" he enquired.

He had shown scarce interest in who I was. Perhaps, he was more fascinated by graven images.

"My girlfriend, Olumidé. I took it around the swimming pool at Jesus Green."

This information seemed to annoy him, because his brow furrowed and his hand went up to screw his red cap more firmly to his head.

For some reason I added, "She's a nurse in the special clinic at Addenbrookes Hospital. Very exclusive, trend-setting for a white guy to have a black girlfriend."

He raised his eyebrow and looked at me like the fucking idiot that I was. "In twenty years' time, you won't be able to move for them," was all he said.

Then he was onto my lava lamp. I thought that maybe he was enjoying it, as it reminded him of the fiery furnaces of his homeland. But he just said "Tawdry geegaw, like the crap they sell to the *religiosi* at Lourdes or Santiago de Compostella. I suppose you've got a three dimensional representation of the Last Supper where the halo lights up if you insert enough batteries into the apostle's arse"

Oh no, now he was studying my 8-track quadrophonic stereo. None of my peers had quadrophonic. In fact, it had been a difficult time for me, because after I had blown all my money on quadrophonic, it became apparent to me that no group apart from Pink Floyd had released anything in quadrophonic stereo to play upon it.

"You are a cipher defined by your attributes," he said.

"Well, what about you and that stupid red hat?" I enquired.

"It covers up the horns," was all he said. Censorious hat of a cardinal, or Urizen, or the Bols fellah.

"Who are you?" I muttered in bewilderment, not expecting him to condescend to answer a mere cipher. But to my amazement, the thing replied:

"I am the god Set."

"Where did you come from?"

"I think you know the answer to that one. You made me yourself. You grew me in that dish like a tumour, and now I will continue to grow in you. I will express myself through you."

"You mean, like I am your 'host'?"

"I don't like that word. It has Catholic overtones."

"Look, Mr Set. I didn't summon you. It was Sydney who was always trying to summon you."

"Ah, poor Sydney."

"If I want to—what is the appropriate word in these circumstances? 'banish' you, how do I get the geni back in the lamp?"

"Very simple. I came from the place where the parallel lines meet. If you arrive at the place where the parallel lines meet, you will find a person sitting there; you simply hand that person, who, I should add, will be completely defenceless, the Book that we shall author together in due course, and I am out of your life again. The person seated where the parallel lines meet will become your successor."

"But the whole point about parallel lines is that they don't meet!"

"Parallel lines; crossed keys! Work it out for yourself, son!"

"And what do you do whilst you are here?"

"I do your bidding, of course. Anything you have ever imagined, your wildest conceit, I can make it happen."

"You mean, like I get the customary stipend of twenty-four years of transitory pleasure, and then you come for me and drag me to roast in the charnel houses of hell in perpetuity?"

"Not at all. That is the rubbish of the Faust legend. I don't have to take you anywhere. With the powers that I will give to you, we can safely rely upon you to create your own hell."

"But I'm not a bad person. I just want everything to go on getting better."

"That is fastest autobahn to hell. What do you want? Ask me for anything?"

"I don't know. I can't think."

"Here." He handed me a cassette. It was Emerson Lake and Palmer in quadrophonic stereo. "Wow!" I said. "I didn't know that had been released yet."

"It hasn't."

He handed me another cassette: "Santana," he said, "featuring Soul Sacrifice in quadrophonic."

"But this is exactly the cheap crap that Faust gets," I pointed out. "What did you say about the souvenir shops at Lourdes and the geegaws?"

"You are correct," he said. "In the future all this will be meaningless. In the future that you are about to write, music will be streamed seamlessly across the ether with no interfaces. This is what we are here to do. We are here to write the history of the future in a large Book that it will be your life's work to complete."

"And how does one put an end to the future?"

"Very simple. Where I come from, we have an entirely flat management structure. You simply have to confront your successor at the point where the parallel lines meet; you deliver the Book, and you thereby put an end to your artefact. It may be that you like your artefact, or think it is no worse than your predecessor's grand design, so you postpone the confrontation. But sooner or later, the inevitable occurs."

"And what became of my predecessor?"

"Nick, this is a work in progress. There can only be one of you at a time. Not for any theosophical reasons, but simply because we haven't yet worked out how to have more than one of you at a time logged on to work remotely from Hell. But we are hoping that this is something that you will achieve during the period of your stewardship.

"We have engineered a situation where husbands and wife are both working; our corporate goals now look forward to a future where they are both working all the time, wherever they are. And for why? Because the aphorism that the devil finds work for idle hands could not be more wrong. The more work humankind does, the more of it is bad work. We have fed this into our business model, and we generally find that the greater opportunity and power we commit to any project, the more harm it creates. There is a direct correspondence between the quantum of beneficial intent and the volume of collateral corruption produced in its realisation.

"I believe your fat friend would call it entropy. It will not make a blind bit of difference to you, because you are young and idealistic, so now that you know that you can have limitless powers and not have to roast in the charnel house for perpetuity, you are going to rise to the challenge, and, despite my undeniable and persuasive eloquence, there is absolutely nothing I could do to talk you out of this gigantic vanity project.

"Our IT systems are improving, but we've got a long way to go yet. Trouble is we're still playing catch-up because no scientific advancements were made between the time of the ancient Greeks and the seventeenth century. Know why?"

"Enlighten me."

"Because religion had them all under its jackboot. If you've successfully been brainwashed into believing that all wisdom is contained in the Bible, why enquire further?

"The delivery of the Book is nothing new. But we have to write it first, don't we? This isn't predestination. You have free will. But our USP is that there is only one place where you can launch your successor, and that is at the point where the parallel lines meet. This isn't a riddle. It's a clue. He wants the job, but he can't tell you. He's busy trying to write it himself, but there is no collaboration between all the protagonists attempting to write the same Book. Each of you has the opportunity to accept endless powers and make the world a different place. Each of you will accept those powers and proceed to fuck everything up. Same old. Same old."

"And this person you refer to as my successor…"

"He will set out to achieve world peace and harmony like they all do, but everybody fucks it up, just like you will."

"So much for my predecessor. When I present my successor with this Book you mentioned, what happens to him? Does he go to hell for all eternity?"

"Nick, I really have no idea what happens to him after you give him the Book, because it all depends on what you've written in the fucking Book! Look, I'm willing to free up your time for you by doing all your course work, writing your dissertation for you; I can assist you by writing everything else for you. But the Book, the Book, is the one fucking thing that you have to write for yourself. It's no different from when you used to glue Brooke Bond tea cards in your sticker book. I don't know how it ends. All I can tell you is that if there was such a thing as an afterlife, we wouldn't be having this conversation, because someone better than me would have stopped me doing this by now.

"Imagine an engine. Yes. Imagine that Spud Mullins, your ingenious engineering *compardre*, has built an engine as big as the universe consisting of an infinite number of concentric cyclones each spinning in the opposite direction to its predecessor and successor. There are an infinite number of trap doors through which you can enter the engine, because each cyclone has its own opening, but, once inside, you have to spin within the cyclone you have entered, just like a ball bearing in an infinite pin ball machine. An infinite number of other protagonists are also spinning within the other cyclones, but you aren't aware of anything beyond the cyclone you have chanced to enter.

"Just as spiders spin webs, or silkworms spin silk, or authors spin tales, so the protagonists within these revolving rings are all busy writing up their Book. When a Book is completed, that ring stops spinning, and it falls out of the engine. Its absence from the grand design results in minute adjustments to the infinite number of remaining cyclones that continue spinning.

"You can subtract 1 from Infinity, but the product still remains infinite for the simple reason that there is no number that is 1 less than Infinity. To put it another way, once you have achieved the Infinite, there is no number that you can deduct from Infinity that will make it finite or any less whole. But nonetheless, there is an end to Infinity."

"At the point where the parallel lines meet?"

"Exactly, and that is where all the plates stop spinning, and they crash to earth."

"But parallel lines don't meet."

"Nick, you're only saying that because you've been inculcated. If you can accept that there is such a place as Infinity, you must accept that there is also a place where Infinity culminates. That terminus is the point where the parallel lines meet. And, by the way, Nick, you realise who it was who inculcated you?"

"No."

"The same cunt who made you believe that you were tied to this earth by the force of gravity. But it's merely laws of physics. We can do whatever we want. It's all just programming and mapping. Whether a law is a moral law that governs your relationship with other beings, or a law of physics that governs your relationship with time and space, it can be rewritten, and that is what the Book is all about."

I felt the need to do something assertive; after all, we were in my room, but the newcomer had completely usurped my space. I strode purposefully across my minute bedsit, lord of all I surveyed, until I was face to face with the only piece of furniture apart from my Habitat coffee table and the bed: an armchair with cigarette burns in the upholstery. I seated myself and contemplated the god Set. He didn't seem to like being stared at. He retreated a couple of paces away from the sink and perched himself on the edge of my bed. There was something invasive about this unclean creature annexing my bed.

"You're talking in riddles," I said. "Parallel lines don't meet."

"Ah, but they will do. Just you wait and see."

"And what is in this Book?"

"Nothing as yet. You have to write it up with your own deeds, Nick; there are those who are destined to make history; there are those who are destined to write it; and there are those who are destined to rewrite it."

"What is the book called?"

"It doesn't have a name as such. Its title is a symbol." And then he rose from the bed and crossed the room so that he was standing above me, seated as I was in my armchair. Bending over, he exposed an area of my damaged forearm beneath the bandages and pressed the horny yellow nail of his long index finger against my skin and burned into it the mark ∞.

He picked up a stack of my Marvel pulp fictions from my prized Habitat coffee table. "Which is your favourite hero?" he asked. "With whom do you most identify?" He was skimming the titles and tossing them aside. "Spiderman, the Incredible Hulk, the Mighty Thor, Iron Man, Daredevil, Silent Knight, Dr Strange?"

We were picking up where the conversation with the guys and Calypso had petered out. "Design your own superhero," he said. "Whatever powers you can imagine, I will give them to you. Do you want to lift heavy objects, seduce beautiful women, fly like a bird, travel through time? Whatever you seek, I can give it to you."

"But I will use my powers for good."

"We are inventing the future. The past shows us that we can always rely on a superfluity of good to ensure the supremacy of evil."

He handed me a scroll with a kind of corporate tree on it. As I squinted down at the tree, I saw it was a hierarchy of superpowers, so that one useful power was associated with another. It said "X Ray Vision." Then it said, "Those who liked X Ray Vision also liked The Ability to Enrapture Women."

"What's this?" I asked.

"It's an organogram. Every known super power is listed here. "

"Who designed this flowchart?" I asked.

"Why, Mr Tree, of course. He has branches everywhere."

I decided to focus my thinking by lighting a cigarette. "Marlboro?" I offer him. Then I called to mind the choir boys on Parker's Piece, and thought that I shouldn't go around offering cigarettes to strangers. He takes one. He smokes like a woman.

"In the future you are about to write," he says, "we won't be able to do this."

"What, not even Marlboro Light?" I ask.

"Smoke indoors," says he as he manages to exhale a series of perfect smoke rings without having inhaled in the first place. With his head tilted back 90 degrees to the upright of his neck, he blows a mushroom cloud like he's exhaling Hiroshima.

The English student in me speaks: "Maybe I would like the power to write amazing dramatic works like William Shakespeare."

"Shakespeare didn't write any of those fucking plays," he says. "Christopher Marlowe wrote them under a *nom de plume*. You don't have to make a decision now. Think on it overnight. I'll be back tomorrow."

He was halfway through doffing his cap and making a mock bow, a regular little Artful Dodger, when I interrupted his exit.

"Just a minute." At the moment I said this, I didn't know what else

I was going to say, but I needed to make some sort of concession to being master of my own destiny in my own set. He raised his eyebrows expectantly from the mock bow.

"Where are the missing choir boys?"

From the expression on his face, he was clearly despairing of teaching me anything.

"Choir boys are not a topic that chimes well with my disposition," he said.

"You don't even know what I'm talking about," I pressed on.

"You are referring to the 60 missing choristers from the King's College Chapel choir."

I was impressed. "Yes."

"They're in the fucking chapel where they're supposed to be, Nick. It's the chapel that's gone walkies, not the boys. As I explained just now, everything's relative. It's all remapping and perception. You'll see."

"But the chapel's still there! I walked past it this morning."

"You think you saw it this morning. Why do you think they call the fronts of buildings façades? Because you've walked past it a million times, you took it for granted that it was still there, but you didn't actually take it in or regard it. The only events that actually receive any degree of attention are unexpected events, which is why you're paying attention to me. Now, I really must be off."

He was then overcome by a coughing fit. It sounded like Hell clearing its throat. When he caught his breath again, he said, "Fucking Marlboro Lights!" As a devil-may-care parting word or two, quoting Kit Marlowe, he said to me with a wink in his eye and a downward nod at his codpiece: "*All those who love not tobacco and boys are fools!*" Then he took another huge drag and sucked his being into the cigarette and disappeared into it.

And then he wasn't there anymore. Nothing except the smouldering butt of the Marlboro Light in my ashtray. And I didn't really know if he ever had been there, or if he was the product of too much dope and absinthe and *kir royale*, and all the stress of the smashed window and the bandaged hand, and the paper on the *Ghost of a Flea* that I hadn't handed in or started. I didn't know if he was a façade, as he would put it, that had surfaced from my memories. But there was no doubt that I was holding a scroll of super powers in my hand and Emmerson Lake and Palmer were playing on the quadrophonic 8 track.

Indian Memory Man

The wisdom on the Birdwood bog door this morning says:

You can divide the world into two sorts of people. Those who divide the world into two sorts of people…

I shuffle down the corridor to where memory man, Seth, is performing his lengthy ablutions to his mouth. He rinses and spits so violently, you would think he was trying to fill the sink with his teeth.

"Morning," I say.

He expectorates, looks up at me and says, "Good morning, Nick."

"Seth," I begin, "do you know the one about the Indian Memory Man?" I ask.

"Of course."

"How does it go?"

"Well, like most jokes, it begins There's this guy…"

"And how does it continue to the punch line?"

A young scouser is touring the US of A in his gap year. He has disembarked the 'plane; he has had a long rail journey; he has hopped off a bus and walked God knows how many miles into the remotest corner of the Nevada desert. Eventually, he is about a million miles from anywhere else when he sees a bar materialising out of the layers of heat as though it was a mirage. He goes through the swing doors and there's no-one inside except the bartender and a red Indian sitting on a stool in the corner.

The Indian looks about a thousand years old. He is wearing tribal headgear; he has long white plaits; a profoundly wrinkled face like the skin of a tortoise. He is smoking a clay pipe and minding his own business.

The scouser orders a beer and asks the bartender what the story is about the ancient Indian in the corner. 'Oh, him?' says the bartender. 'He's the Indian Memory Man. He remembers every fact known to mankind. Go and try him out for yourself.'

So the scouser goes up to the desiccated Indian, thinking he won't know fuck all about English football, and he asks, 'Who won the 1965

FA cup final?'

Without missing a blink, the Memory Man takes the pipe from between his parched lips and says, 'Liverpool.'

Well, the scouser is amazed, so he pushes the envelope a bit further: 'Who did they beat?' he asks.

'Leeds', comes the answer.

'And what was the score?'

'2-1.'

'And who scored the winning goal?'

'Ian St John,' comes the reply.

Well, the young scouser is gobsmacked by this. He leaves the bar. He completes his gap year tour. He starts work, and he becomes a big important man, but he can never get that image of the Indian Memory Man out of his head. He carries it with him all his life.

Eventually, sixty years later, the young scouser is approaching his eightieth birthday and he feels his time on earth is almost up, but he is troubled by some unfinished business. He just knows that he has to make the pilgrimage again to exorcise the image of the Indian Memory Man from his mind. He won't get any rest until then.

So, he jets off to Phoenix Arizona; he takes the long, long train ride; he hops on and off the bus, and then he trudges for mile after weary mile into the Nevada desert with nothing to keep him company except the circling vultures and the picked-over bones of decaying bison, and then it begins to materialise on the horizon: the very same bar. He reaches it and pushes through the swing doors, and to his amazement, the same Indian Memory Man in his tribal gear with the white plaits and headdress is still sitting in exactly the same spot, drawing on his clay pipe.

The scouser decides that it would be polite to greet the Indian in his native tongue, so he goes up to him and says, 'How!'

'Diving header in the six-yard box,' says the Memory Man.

It takes me a minute, but then I get it.

"That's a really clever joke, Seth," I say. "You know, when you were doing the memory test in the felt sack in Sydney's set, I got most of the objects in the room, but I didn't get it when you said *original Congo in watercolour*. What's that? Tintin or something?"

"No. It's the light blue and dark blue painting on the wall above the pianola. It's by Congo."

"Who's Congo?"

"I'm not sure if it's a who or a what. Congo was a chimpanzee. Died in 1964. Used to churn out paintings. They took on quite a novelty value."

"Sydney's giving wall space to a painting by a chimpanzee?"

"Nothing to be ashamed of. Salvador Dali kind of put him on the map when he compared Congo to Jackson Pollock. He said something about Congo the chimpanzee's hand being quasi human, as opposed to the hand of Jackson Pollock, which is totally animal."

2nd **Interview with the Proctor**

"He's got an alibi, sir."

It's round two with the Proctor; but this time I have barrister-in-making, Ingram Frazier, alongside to help me.

"Oh bloody marvellous!" exclaimed the Proctor profanely. "He's got a devil-worshipper and his mistress for an alibi. They're probably all involved in it. They're probably all part of a ring. How do I know you're not all in on this together?"

"I have come along today," asserts Ingram undaunted, "to act as Mackenzie friend and legal counsel to Mr Jobs here, not to be the recipient of *sotto voce* allegations of impropriety myself, if you don't mind!"

In Ingram, I recognise the voice of authority, and I remember that is what the missing choir boy had mistaken in me which caused him to stub his cigarette out. Ingram has self-belief, where I have self-doubt. But I could fool a naive young chorister.

"Now," continues Ingram, "the alibi for the night may not be completely watertight, because it seems that Mr Syzygy and Miss Sitzclarence probably encountered him about 5 minutes later, as long as it took Mr Jobs to cross the other half of Parker's Piece and enter Trumpington Street."

Where I was knocked down by a sedan chair with four footmen, I am thinking to myself. Ingram doesn't mention that part of the story. So early in his political career, he has already begun being selective with his truths.

"But on top of that," Ingram continues in full flow, "two further choir boys have gone missing since and, as we have seen, Mr Jobs does have completely watertight alibis for the two subsequent disappearances. And," continues Ingram, positive menace now rising in his voice, "so do I."

Sidgwick Site

It was my protégé, Seth, who took me to my first lecture at Cambridge. I had been there two terms and never attended a single lecture. There seemed no point. I didn't want to approach the texts via the erudition of the thousands of scholars who had read them before me. I wanted to form my own opinions. This wasn't arrogance. It was humility. I just wanted to listen to the words on the page.

"But you've gotta hear this," urges Seth.

Have I taught my pupil everything I know? Am I now condemned to learn from him? As I follow Seth towards the Sidgwick Site for my first Cambridge lecture, I am reflecting on what we have taught one another. I have shown him the Deer Park and the Buttery, the Birdwood and my small circle of friends. He has shown me night climbing and introduced me to *Balafre* by *Lancôme*. We are probably about even; but I am about to become indebted to him.

There she stands at the lectern, eyes closed, in complete mastery of the room, talking so quietly you scarcely dare draw breath lest you miss a syllable. Heads are craning forward to catch the honey that drips from her lips. It had never occurred to me that Lyca was a lecturer. In her Indiacraft cheesecloth shirt, an Alice band around her red hair, she holds the auditorium in her hand. Sydney is fucking a lecturer. The envy puts me into sensory overload. I feel the blood rushing to the right-hand side of my brain, the side that controls the irrational, the part of my brain that processes threat.

"We often use the term 'fabrication' in a pejorative sense. We use it as a euphemism for lying, because we're saying the story is 'made up'."

She pauses. Ten seconds that seem like…

"But everything is made up; everything is fabrication. These fabrications are fabricated by our brains. If you detect a ghostly presence at the foot of your bed in the night, it is fabricated by your senses, in just the same way that your perception of that building…" she gestures sightlessly to something beyond the window, "…on the other side of the Quadrant, is fabricated; in the same way that chair is fabricated."

I feel as though she is talking just to me.

"Amputees report continued feelings, sensations, pains in their missing limbs, because the pain is fabricated. The sense of loss…If I slice off my fingers…"

She pauses with her hand held up as the audience comes to terms with the violent imagery of self-mutilation. But what is it? Balletic. The one hand held above her head. There must be a name for that gesture. Everything has been catalogued and named. I can feel a fit coming on. I need to get back, but I can't explain to Seth. All of my concentration is directed to staving off the inevitable. Her words wash over me. Her missing fingers. Her closed eyes. The sense of loss.

"I have simply removed some of the apparatus by which our brains interpret the objects they are continually fabricating. But the fabrication is still there. All that is missing are some of the receptors that transmit the fabrications to my brain for processing.

"I choose to go around with my eyes glued shut, because I wish to hone my other receptors. The eyes are so predominant they overwhelm the other senses and dull them. If you put your dogs' eyes out, it will make little difference to him, because he has not allowed sight to assume the ascendancy.

"We perceive things that are man-made and things that are fabricated by God or the Devil or Nature. Sir Thomas Browne in his *Religio Medici says All Nature is artificial, because it is the art of God*. It's all fabrication."

Lyca's eyes! Lyca's eyes! I'm trying to concentrate on what she's saying, but I've got Sydney's fucking poem on the brain:

To wish those eyes, to wish those eyes…

Seth nudges me and says: "Isn't she fantastic? She's her own *magnum opus.*"

I am asking myself, *How did I miss it? How could I have missed it?*

The name for the gesture she has assumed with her hand held up is Fourth Position in ballet.

Meeting the Man

The next time I'm in Sydney's rooms, Sydney is sat in his captain's chair reading from his big book of Spells, and Seth and Calypso are gathered around his card table with a third guy I haven't seen before. I feel a faint sense of loss at the realisation that Seth so quickly feels that he is entitled to walk into Substance Abuse Central unaccompanied by me, in the same way that a parent experiences disquiet at his child's growing independence.

Seth is shuffling a deck of cards in his huge hands, and then slaps them face down in a block on the table. There is a long bong as wide as a wrist, smouldering in the Lalique ashtray and another being handed around by the stranger. Also on the table are a range of substances wrapped in screwed up tin foil and some piebald pills and tabs.

The stranger is tall, slim and upright and his tanned face is valenced by long, blonde, leonine locks that reach down to his shoulders, and a gold beard. He looks kind of Scandinavian. He's wearing a white military double-breasted jacket from Lawrence Corner. I can't see his trousers, because they're under the green baize of the card table. With the white jacket buttoned up so tightly surmounted by his gold hair and beard, he reminds me of a bottle of milk with a gold top, the Jersey ones with gobs of thick cream; the ones I used to save up to buy a blind dog with.

"What are they playing?" I ask Sydney.

"*Ombre*," he informs me.

"What's *Ombre*?"

"You asked to meet the man, didn't you?" says Sydney. "Well, this is the man, so when the man comes around, we play *Ombre* as in *Hombre*. Get it?"

"You mean this is *the man as in the man*?"

"This is the man," says Sydney. "As in Velvet Underground's *I'm Waiting for my Man.*"

"Ciao!" says the man by way of greeting to me; but I haven't come across this form of greeting before.

"Chow?" I query.

"Shall I cut?" asks the man.

"You're the dealer," says Calypso. "You deal. I like to cut."

Seth raises his eyebrow.

Calypso cuts. "Spades," she says.

"Oh!" quotes Sydney, "*Let Spades be trumps, she said, and trumps they were!*"

"Can I play?" I ask.

"Dear boy," says Sydney, "you cannot play for the same reason that I cannot play."

"And what reason is that?" I enquire.

"*Ombre* is a card game for three players only," explains Sydney. "There is a variation for four people, but it's complicated enough with three people."

"So," I say, sidling over to the dealer, "you are the God damn the pusher man?"

"I don't like being called that," says the stranger. "I don't do this for financial gain. I regard myself as a not-for-profit charitable foundation, whose object is to educate people in the beneficial uses of marijuana. I do it so as to enrich other people's lives. I am a co-operative. I don't go down the docks with guns and knives. The ware in my pockets, during my vacation time, I have personally selected and imported at considerable risk to myself from the Lebanon, Morocco, Yemen, the Indian subcontinent and the Milkweg."

"And where did you import all that aluminium foil from?" asks Seth.
"Tesco's."

Why is it that all dealers want to insinuate themselves in your lives as your mates? I think—"

"So what are you called, man?" I ask.

"My name, man," he says, trumping Seth at *Ombre*, "is Björn Agen." And he places his trick in the neat stack of tricks by his right hand. The action of winning the trick seems to call for some sort of a celebration, so he draws on the bong until the smoke is practically lifting his epaulettes off his shoulders. Then he turns over a court card and says Mine, stacking up another trick. I think I have the hang of this game. It's just knock-out whist with cannabis.

"Is that name for real?" I query.

"Do you want to see his birth certificate?" asks Sydney.

"I don't think that would help, buddy," says the dude who claims his name is Björn. "Unless you can understand Scandinavian."

"So," I say, "Björn, what are you reading at Cambridge? Norse myths?" He does bear an uncanny resemblance to the Mighty Thor.

"I'm reading modern languages."

That was a real conversation-stopper. Trying to break the ice, I try again: "So, Björn, what's trending in the world of psychotropic drugs?"

"Sonoran Toad."

I can't tell if he's taking the piss out of me, so I try a topic closer to home: "What's new in the world of cannabis resin?"

He looks up from his hand of cards at me like I'm a cretin, then reels off: "Lebanese Gold, Nepalese Temple Balls (the jewel in the crown because there's no organised market, so it has to be self-imported by me); butane hash oil, Durban Poison, Bubblegum, Hindu Kush, Northern Lights, Shiva. Or maybe you prefer tincture of cannabis (drops of shit under the tongue).or we can even do it in suppository form– very quickly absorbed into the bloodstream, but don't ask me to share it with you."

"The way you reeled that off," I say, "you could be reading History of Marijuana."

"If it was on the syllabus, man, I probably would be", he says. "It has a chequered history going back to Herodotus. Herodotus in his *Histories* (440 BC) makes the first historical reference to cannabis. He says the Scythians took steam baths of cannabis, throwing hemp seeds upon red hot stones in an enclosed cave of felt sackings."

"Similar to when we put your head in the felt sack, Nick." I hear Sydney making an aside from his book of Spells. "During the optophonetic poetry reading."

Ignoring Sydney, I address the man: "440 BC," I say. "Well that's really something, because before I met you, I had been labouring under the misapprehension that the earliest reference to marijuana had been in the eleventh century when hashassins used it to steel their nerves." I made this contribution so that the beautiful Lyca would know how much I pay attention to her when she's speaking, but she doesn't register any reaction.

"Well there you go," says Sydney. "It seems that everything between 440BC and the eleventh century is the Dark Ages, no doubt because everyone was stoned and recorded nothing for posterity. How does that song go?"

Calypso answers him sing-song:

I got stoned and I missed it, I got stoned and I missed it. I was stoned and it rolled right by.

"Thank you, Lyca."

"Sydney," I venture, recalling my conversation with the god Set. "don't you think that an explanation for the Dark Ages might be that the jackboot of religion kept everyone in ignorance for centuries?"

"Some people are determined to remain ignorant," Sydney points out.

"You are determined to educate me, Sydney," I say. "You've taught me the optophonetic poetry and now you're teaching me *Ombre*."

"Fuck it!" says Seth, as Björn stacks up yet another trick. "Let's play Happy Families." Addressing Calypso: "Do you mind?"

"Not at all, Seth. You deal and I'll cut."

"Don't you think I've been cut up enough?" the tattooed man asks her. The air is charged, as though you could feel volts zagging between Seth and Lyca. Some sort of shared knowledge that no-one else in the room shares.

An Unexpected Meeting at the Sex Club

It's 11.30 pm. I don't really feel like getting shit-faced with Sydney not only in the middle of the day, but also at the end of it. Nor do I feel like going abroad at night and being bounced into the ditch by his sedan chair or run over by his Humber Super Snipe. So I head towards the Sex Club to take in some asinine television.

There are some sad lonely wankers playing table footie. That they are sad, lonely wankers is confirmed by the fact that they complement one another on their superb wrist action; but I am the only wanker who is so sad and so lonely that I don't even have a compatriot to play table footie with. Olumidé told me that she is working nights again.

I get a pint of Newcastle Brown from the friendly barman, who I think is reading engineering because I've seen him shooting the breeze with Spud. He volunteers to serve behind the bar because it gives him an opportunity to give you short change so I check mine. I balance my pint on my pigeon hole. What was it that I had seen on the Birdwood cubicle doors this morning? Ah yes.

Newcastle Brown
Makes you shit
Brown sauce

Contemplating my pint with enhanced anxiety, I go across to turn on the telly. I have to stand up on tip toe as it is mounted on a lofty bracket in the corner of the room. I press the On button with my good hand. The On button used to be green and the Off button red, but both buttons have been greyed out by the onslaught of countless thumbs. After the excesses of the middle of the day, I feel a constriction across my chest, stretching up to reach the controls.

I wait for its valves to warm up and the black and white picture to fill the tube, and I watch mindlessly, just because it's company, and so I can pretend I am not a sadder lonelier wanker than the rest of them. I'd like to see what's on the other channels, but that would involve stretching up again to reach the buttons, so I'll have to watch what I'm given. It's Ben Cartwright and Hoss in a late night repeat of the Ponderosa.

Just as I am purporting to watch, sipping my arse-widening pint and wondering to myself why Hoss Cartwright has such a stupid hat, in comes my new Mackenzie friend, Ingram Frazier, looking smug and pleased with himself. I register mild surprise as he belongs to Trinity Hall and should be in his own common room at this time of night, but maybe he is out cottaging. Who was it who coined the phrase about a man who could look like he was swaggering even when he was sitting down? That's Ingram's posture.

He purchases a pint of Abbot Ale, checking the shrapnel of change in his palm carefully, and comes over to me. I can't understand why anyone would buy bottled Abbot Ale when there is so much better Green King on tap, but perhaps his father being a man of the cloth drew him to the Abbot Ale.

"What are you watching?" says he.

I'm embarrassed to own up to watching such crap, but Ingram has observed the first rule of all barristers in cross-examining their witnesses, which is never to ask a question to which you don't already know the answer.

"Bonanza," I admit, although I haven't been looking at the telly because the strobe lights make me come over all queer. I'd just turned it on, as the old folks say, *for company*; but I can't tell him that. That would be tantamount to confessing that I am a sadder, lonelier wanker than all the rest of them, than the lonely wankers on the table footee machine, the short-changing bartender and Ingram Frazier himself. So magnanimously, in my shame, I say to him:

"Ingram, please treat my home as your home. Please feel free to change the programme as takes your fancy."

Because this is simpler than admitting that I am just staring mindlessly at a space somewhere behind the telly. I am as bad as the people on the telly. They are actors; they have to do this for a living, but I am the unpaid Billie Muggins acting out that I am watching them.

"There's an interview of Jeremy Carbon I wouldn't mind watching," he says. "But it's on the other channel."

Jeremy Carbon, well-named politician, because he is just a photocopy of every Trotskyite cunt who has gone before him.

"Feel free," I say.

Being taller than me, Ingram manages effortlessly to change the channel on the elevated Grundig cantilevered on its wall-bracket. There is no evidence of any tightness across the chest or imminent heart attack. But his shirt does come out of his pants, causing him to stuff it back in, yard by yard, so that it is all scrunched up in his pinstriped trousers. Christ! His shirt must be as long as a winding-sheet! I think it's a status thing.

People wear exceedingly long shirts to pretend that they are country squires who spend their time ambling around their manicured estates shooting at stratospheric partridges, which would cause their shirts to fall out of their trousers if they had shirts as short as mine. So they need long wheelbase blouses. Let's face it, I'm just a short guy with a short shirt. I try to concentrate on his shirt and not the stripes on his trousers, because I feel that the stripes in the trousers bring on my condition. But then the double jeopardy hits me: it's a striped shirt.

Carbon is spouting away about owning the means of production and nationalising the air we breathe and squeezing the rich until their pips squeak and all the usual stock-in-trade shit.

"I forgot you were interested in politics," I say. Because he had recently assisted me as my lawyer, I had overlooked his longer term plans.

"Interested? I intend to be Prime Minister one day, Nick. Can't come too quickly for this country."

"I am sure the populace will be rightly grateful," I say. "I thought your subject was the law."

"Yes, Nick, but law is just a discipline. A way of marshalling the arguments in your head so that you can think more clearly. If you want to lead others, first of all you need to know where you're going yourself. That's what's wrong with politicians these days. They want to lead, but they have no fucking idea what direction they're travelling in. Just spinning around in circles.

"Reading the law is not a destination in itself. The law was never intended to be more than an intermediate step." And he puts this kind of emphasis on the law and gives me a knowing look as though to say that we are complicit, in this thing together, both of us knowing the law is only there to be broken, as if we each know what I really did to all those choristers from King's.

"Ah!" I say. And then for reasons I do not even know, I add, "A mere *embarcadero*." Being another word for a staging post or stopping off quay, or something. Maybe it's Spanish. I don't remember how I came across it. Probably written on a bog door in the Birdwood like so much of my erudition these days.

"*Embarcadero*!" ponders Ingram. "Good word, man. I like it! Copy! Copy!"

And we clink our glasses. "Cheers!" in unison.

"But this guy, Carbon," I say. "He is not very mainstream or electable."

"From the viewpoint of a student," says Ingram. "He has sound ideas. We just need to extend the franchise to students. There are guys at the top of the pole earning a million a year. They don't need it; they can't spend it, and anyway, it's unearned, underserved and often inherited. If we just squeeze them a bit more, the waterfall cascades down so that all the less well-off people can benefit.

"There are always going to be more poor people than wealthy people, so all we have to do is attract the votes of the poorest members of society and we are in power. That's democracy. How do you do that? By being a demagogic Robin Hood and taking the money off the rich to give to the poor."

"But Ingram," I say, "don't you see? It's a sliding scale that slides the wrong way. These wealthy guys that you talk about, they account for, what, 0.001% of the population? You could strip them of everything they have and leave them destitute in their cufflinks and underpants; you could forfeit their estates and stick their heads on poles, but how is that going to benefit the remaining 99.9999%? There can never be enough to go around. If you just give the branches at the top of the tree a haircut, it won't help the roots. The roots just spread out further with less water to nourish them."

I see from his expression that he is genuinely considering this proposition, and I further deduce from his continued silence that his previous discussions on this weighty social topic have been either internally within himself or with like-minded stooges who have never challenged him. Carbon copies, just like I said. He is having a Road to Damascus moment.

"By God, Nick!" he says. "You're right. A sliding scale that slides the wrong way! I love it! Nick, when I am Prime Minister of this Sceptred Isle, I am going to pay you a visit and I am going to say to you, *Jobs, Nick Jobs.*"

I can't believe he is so lightheaded on half a pint of Abbot Ale.

"I am going to say, *Nick Jobs, I want you to be my spin doctor.*"

"What's that?"

"Like a press secretary. Everyone who's anyone in the village of Westminster has one. Look, Nick, what are we going to do if the sliding scale is sliding the wrong way?"

"We have to find a middle way."

"A middle way." He lifts his cloudy tankard of Abbot Ale up to eye level and stares at it as though it holds the answers. I am unclear if he intends to drink it, administer an eye bath to himself, or baptise me. *All these things will become clearer. All manner of things will become clear.*

Through a glass darkly, is what I am thinking. I could never have imagined Ingram Frazier could be so pissed on so little but still talking so much shit.

"Nick, to be honest, you know, I've forgotten what the two things are that we have to find *the middle way* through. But I have to tell you, I find I am drawn to your way of expressing it. You know what I mean? The middle way. It makes the listener think he understands all sorts of stuff that in fact he doesn't and that it would expose his ignorance were he to ask.

"It makes a, how shall I put this? It makes a *consiglieri* out of your audience, because they think that by sharing in what are frankly meaningless platitudes, they are part of your inner circle and have the whip hand on those who are not. So, after they have listened to you, they will sally forth and they will just drop into conversation ideas such as *middle ways* and *sliding scales that slide the wrong way*; and because these expressions sound plangent and meaningful, they will be adopted and repeated by others until half the electorate is mouthing your mantras even though they have no actual meaning.

"Nick, you are a fucking genius. Do you have more of these?"

Do I have more of these? What did Kit Marlowe write in his great play, King Lear? I have *beyond all manner of so much.*

It was really just shit off a shit house door, so all I could say to Ingram was: "Does Rose Kennedy have a black dress?" which he also thought was brilliant.

He has his long, slim Letts diary in the breast pocket of his pinstripe jacket, and he takes it out. In the spine lurks one of those thin, diary pencils, secreted, stiletto-like, such as an emissary of the Venetian Doge would go abroad with if he had an appointment to do you harm. He plucks it out from his inside pocket and jots down notes of these pithy words.

In between scrawling, he licks and sucks the tip of his pencil so as to ensure a darker impression on the page, whilst also giving himself mild lead poisoning. When he sucks it, his eyeballs revolve upwards, like a bent copper considering how best to embroider his story before he and his dodgy mate record the same false account in their notebooks. What he is committing to paper, is simply the banalities I have amassed from my study of boghouse doors in the Birdwood. But to Ingram, who is from Trinity Hall, not Peterhouse, and who has no knowledge of the Birdwood, the rubbish I impart seems to contain valuable information.

I can't bear to look at him. The uniformity of his pinstripes is giving me a headache.

"And what are you doing here in Peterhouse?" I ask him in a polite voice, so that he does not read into it a criticism that he is not within his own barrio of Trinity Hall.

"TV was broken at Tit Hall," he says. "Shush, here comes Carbon again!"

For six minutes that seem like sixty minutes, we have to listen to Carbon blurbing on about how the future is technology and how we need more evil scientists, and how all Chinese are plagiarists, copying everything we do in flagrant disregard of the laws of patent and copyright; about China doing repetitive tasks more cheaply than the west so we will soon all be unemployed hausfrau arsewiping the robots of the East. And I pass out briefly at about the point where he is talking about arsewiping your own bot.

When I wake up, after maybe sixty seconds, or six seconds that just seem like sixty, I notice that Ingram has his moistened pencil at the ready to record any notable phrases emanating from Carbon's lips; but none issue forth, and at the end of the interview, he holsters his pencil up the arse of his diary. Then he looks at me as though he had forgotten I was there.

"What are you thinking?" says he.

I realise that I must have fitted off somewhere looking at his orderly pinstripes.

"I was thinking," I improvise, "that I am listening to Carbon talking about the complexities of the modern world, and I don't even have the faintest idea how rudimentary household objects such as that pencil of yours are made. I mean to say, Ingram, for crying out loud, why the fuck didn't they teach us all that stuff before they sent us up to Cambridge?"

Ingram stares down its wooden shaft inserted in his diary's spine suspiciously as though the lead it harbours might be of the percussive variety and about to fire at him. He then gives me a most profound look: "You're absolutely right, Nick. You know something? Neither do I."

He has licked the lead of his pencil too many times until he has poisoned his disposition with it. He has become Saturnine. In the world of medieval humours, he is a repository of black bile. He pops his diminutive notebook back into his pocket.

"But, Nick, what did you make of Carbon's vision of a future of robots taking all the jobs away from the humans?"

"If you want to make it in the future," I improvise, "you have to be the man who owns the machines. If you aren't one of the men who owns the machines then you will be one of the men who is replaced by them."

Ingram raises his Abbot Ale and cools the side of his cheek as though turning this concept over in his head was making his brain boil.

"Nick," he says, "forgive me, but I'm really going to have to write that down as well." And he finds a surface to balance his pint on, whilst slipping his diary out of his jacket pocket and licking his pencil again.

"Ingram," I say, flickering on the edge of consciousness, "when you are Prime Minister, I will be honoured to be your spin drier."

"Doctor," he corrects.

I regret having thought ill of him for becoming lightheaded on a half of Abbot Ale. We are all in this together.

"Tell you what, Ingram," I begin, "can I buy you a chaser to wash that Abbot Ale down with? How about a nice shot of Tequila."

"Good idea, Nick," he says. "I'll have a Barney."

"Eh?"

"Barney Rubble," says Ingram. "A double."

He must have written that down in his fucking diary when a character I haven't even introduced yet mentioned it. Some of us have come to Cambridge to study English at the highest level, and what are we learning? Cockney rhyming slang from a fucking moron.

Double-Timing

"No sign of the *Ghost of a Flea* then?" Pfläfflin asks rhetorically.

"Just don't seem to be enough hours in the day," I blag.

"Maybe what you need in your life," ventures Pfläfflin, " is a double time scheme; like in *Othello*." I am conscious that there was a distinct pause before he pronounced the word *life*, as though he was weighing whether to qualify the noun by one of the usual adjectives; such as *contemptible or sad or pointless.*

I am wondering why people keep telling me about Othello. It's not even related to anything I'm reading.

"You must have come across it," continues Pfläfflin. "A.C Bradley wrote an essay about it at least 500 years ago. Shakespeare uses long time and short time. There's a long time scheme, because the audience has to believe that Desdemona has committed adultery with Cassio at least a thousand times.

"But Shakespeare also needs to compress the action so that Othello's reaction is the more extreme, so he has two time schemes running in the same play, each pointing in opposite directions. The play is entirely impossible, just like a play about The Moor of Venice, which doesn't even feature a single canal. And I was just saying, if you think you are strapped for time, why not take a leaf out of the Bard's book, and run a double time scheme?"

"Hold on," I am trying to come to grips with this. "You are referring to A.C Bradley's essay. But you say he wrote it at least 500 years ago, which puts the essay on Othello back before Othello. I'm sorry; I don't get it. Surely Bradley was nineteenth or twentieth century?"

"Double time scheme, Nick! Double time scheme!" If Pfläfflin's grin were any broader, it would slice his face in two.

I think about this for 30 seconds. 30 seconds that seems like 30 minutes.

I'll never understand the German sense of humour.

"Seriously, Jobs," Pfläfflin says, "If you're so interested in art, forget about Villiam Shakespeare. Forget even about Villiam Blake. You write me an essay about Villiam Morris. The Victorian *uomo universale* who decorated the Great Hall in Peterhouse where you keep term by having your dinners. If you fancy yourself as a printer, you could learn a lot from him. Yes, submit me an expository essay of five thousand words entitled *Art in the Home*. Hand it in within the fortnight, and we'll overlook the missing *Ghost of a Flea* dissertation. Expository, mind you! Not imaginative! Must be expository! *Art in the Home!*"

Calypso Accepts an Invitation

I can't believe that I have managed to persuade the Countenance Divine to come back to my humble set, but I draw confidence from the knowledge that she sees nothing. I won't even need to tidy up. Sydney was not in his rooms when I rapped on his door. The sun was shining, and he was busy rubbing his special wax made of gold, frankincense and myrrh onto the glistening shanks of his Humber Super Snipe; so when I knocked, Lyca had come to his door with the inverted *mezuzah* on its lintel. I had her all to myself.

I didn't want to waste the moment, so I started blurting out stuff that I should really have kept the lid on. I told her about my new, imaginary friend. I had intrigued her. As she herself had observed so recently, female curiosity got us all chucked out of Paradise. I had told her about the appearance of the god Set, how he had climbed out of my dish of developer fluid and started expounding his management philosophy at me. Unsurprisingly, she said that my story required not only willing suspension of disbelief, but moreover, willing suspension of intelligence.

But then I played my master card. "That," I said, "had been my own initial reaction, but I was convinced otherwise by the fact that he left me with an 8-track Emmerson Lake and Palmer cassette in quadrophonic stereo."

This persuaded her to suggest we repair to my set so that she could verify this claim, because the one thing that Sydney did not possess in his set was the equipment on which to play an 8-track quadrophonic stereo cassette. Thus, the trap was baited and I had lured her into my lair.

My rooms in St Peter's Terrace are separated from Sydney's set in Gisborne Court by the Deer Park. As she is unsighted, like the hero, GentleMan that I am when I am not the more sinister Printer, I offer to take her by the arm, which she accepts. I walk as slowly as possible, because it is a lovely day, and I have the loveliest woman in Cambridge on my arm.

I want the moment to extend into infinity and for as many jealous undergraduates as possible to drink it in. If, by a one in a million chance, Olumidé (who is working nights and should be resting at this time of day) were to see us, it would appear a simple act of courtesy, like helping a blind man cross the road. As we are walking through the Deer Park, I confide in Lyca: "My Director of Studies has told me that if I don't hand in five thousand words on *Art in the Home* within a fortnight, I'm going to be rusticated or something."

"I wouldn't worry," she says. "Pfläfflin's all mouth and trousers. You know, Cambridge Dons; they're like a swimming pool. All the noise comes from the shallow end."

"This insight coming from a fellow academic is very reassuring," I confess.

"Well, that's Pfläfflin parked," she pronounces. "Is the Proctor still on your back about the choir boys?"

"Lyca," I say, "you are my poison and my antidote in the same cocktail. At the very moment, you put my mind to rest about one problem, you remind me of my other one."

"Without contraries, there is no progression," she shrugs, quoting from the subject of my dissertation that I haven't written.

"Tell me something," I ventured. "Is Sydney's name for real?"

"Sydney Syzygy?"

"Yes. Sydney Syzygy. Is that his real name or is it a made up one?"

"Not only is it real. It's double real. He's Sydney Syzygy the Second."

"What happened to Sydney Syzygy the First?"

"That was his younger brother. He died of childhood leukaemia within six months. It put quite a weight on Sydney's shoulders, adding to his existing stock of Jewish guilt. His mother used to take him down to the Hoop Lane cemetery almost every day after school, and it must have been as though he was staring down at his own headstone."

"I thought Jews don't name their children after an existing member of the family."

"Correct. It's considered very bad luck. But this wasn't an existing member of the family. He was deceased. Best thing that ever happened to Sydney was getting into Cambridge and away from that family. But we all love him, don't we? Love him for his common touch, his ability to reach out to everybody; his theatricality."

"Right. He's a showman searching for a show."

"More shaman than showman, I think."

This conversation has taken us to my front door. In my set, we shared a joint of my Moroccan blond earned from writing doggerel verse for Burt.

I was flattered when she said, "Nice gear, Nick. Where does it come from?"

"It was a commission," I informed her mysteriously.

We listened to the superb drum solo that leads into *Tank*. Then we listened to all of *Tank*, sat side by side on my single item of furniture, the bed (I didn't tell her that I also boasted an armchair) and listened as that amazing riff visited every corner of my minute auditorium. I lean forward as though I am trying to climb into my speakers, but I'm really ascertaining if I can see all the way up her skirt.

When it was over, she said: "That's not quadrophonic, Nick. It's just stereo coming out of four speakers."

"But if it's coming out of four speakers, it must be quadrophonic!" I protested.

"Don't let yourself be taken in, Nick. It's all a question of cause and effect and you mustn't confuse the cause with the effect. A guy can see hosts of angels that give him instructions as to how he should conduct his life. He could be a true visionary; he could be Christ risen again; or he could just be fitting."

Taking advantage of her shut eyes, I looked her up and down to see if she was taking the piss; but from the expression on her face, she seemed to be making this observation at a general level. It wasn't aimed at me. Looking her up and down was not without its own gratification.

"And I guess you can hear things better with your eyes closed?" I said.

"I also find I can see things better," she added; and she pulled the hem of her skirt down, as though she could sense I was trying to stare up it. She didn't pull it down so far as to curtail my enjoyment, and in any case, it rode straight back up. It was just an empty gesture, a nod in the direction of decorum, letting me know that she knew. Inexplicably, that made it all the sexier.

I let this sink in for a moment, not sure where we should take it. I decided the safest thing to do was continue where we had left off earlier, before she started talking about people who thought they saw things.

"So, the Emmerson Lake and Palmer, thing, you mean, it's a geegaw?" I said.

"If you like, yes, a geegaw."

"But I was looking at him as I am looking at you now. He was wearing one of those traditional Catalan hats that Salvador Dali wears."

"The Barretina."

"Like a toque? Is that what it's called?"

"It's not just Dali who wears a Barretina," pointed out Calypso. "It's also the traditional headdress of the *caganer.*"

"What's a *caganer*?"

"I suggest you find out for yourself before you publish your story more widely. It can be a voyage of discovery for you. A warm-up for your piece on the *Ghost of a Flea* or *Art in the Home*."

And with that, she showed herself out of my set. Had she displayed any inclination for a fuck, I would have betrayed both Sydney and Olumidé without a moment's hesitation, Sydney, because he had sexualised his girlfriend to such a degree that he deserved it, and Olumidé because she was such an undelivering prick-tease that she also deserved it. But unfortunately fortune did not favour me that day, and I would have to acquire many more earthly powers before she did.

I acquired those earthly powers from the god Set. Calypso was very sexy and desirable; but she was both blind and deaf. It was definitely quadrophonic.

There was still the unanswered question. What's a *caganer*?

In the Kingdom of the Blind

"What does it all mean?"

Seth is stripped to the waist in the Birdwood. He has rubbed a hole in the condensation on the mirror so that he can see to shave himself.

I nod at the direction of the strange markings that are all over his torso, and the sides of his arms and legs. The characters seem to need to be read in columns, not across. They are grouped in sets. "The writing," I say.

"That's what I'm trying to find out," answers Seth.

Seeing my confused look, he adds: "I wasn't the author."

Two questions come to mind. Who did it, and why did he let that person do this to his body? But I content myself with one question at a time.

"Who is?"

"Calypso Sitzclarence."

"Fuck me!" Calypso, doing History of Art and Calligraphy at Girton. How could I have been so blind? I'm as benighted as Lyca.

"We were together most of my gap year. She's older than me. She was post-grad. We were in India. I was out of it for a long time. Whilst I was out of it, she cut a bit more each day. I figured if that's what she wanted to read in the morning when she woke up, that was ok with me. We were an item. But we're not an item anymore."

"And you followed her here to Cambridge?"

"To find out."

"You know she can't see?"

"Yes, I know all about it."

Leica

"Jap Crap!" Set pronounces his verdict on my prized Nikon SLR. "Cheap Jap crap like this is what devastated the European rangefinder camera market, the best on the planet. If you want a proper street camera, do you know what you should get?"

"Hasselblad?" I venture.

"Hasselblad!" Set bites the end off his cigar and spits it onto the floor. "No better than a fucking cuckoo clock! When did a Hasselblad ever fetch millions of pounds at an auction?"

"You telling men that any camera has fetched millions of pounds?"

"Yes, consistently, Leica. A 1923 Leica fetched €2.6 million in auction not so long ago."

"What's a euro?"

"Leica has always been regarded as the best street camera. Henri Cartier-Bresson, Alex Webb, Mark Cohen, Joel Meyerowitz—the list is infinite."

The View from The Top
Anthropodermic Bibliopegy

"Look at this." Seth has got me up onto the roof, but fortunately, not the roof of the Senate House; only the roof of Gisborne Court, to which we are supposed to retire in any event if the building is on fire. He seems to be doing his best to set it alight. It's not vertiginous like one of his usual climbs. He just needs sufficient height to conduct the experiment. I have friends in high places.

Methodically, he is tying big knots in a black plastic bin liner, similar to the ones I use to assemble my makeshift darkroom. I guess it's a logical progression. First my photographic prints are consigned to the flames by Sydney; then Seth torches my entire darkroom. *C'est magnifique!* Sometimes, Seth seems to reflect on what he is doing and concludes the knot is inadequate, so he ties a double knot, just as a careful mother would teach her child to tie a double bow in his laces so his shoes don't fall off.

In secondary school days, we used to do something similar with sodden towels: tie huge ligatures in them, heavy with the capillary weight, and then beat the crap out of fellow bathers around the edge of the swimming pool. One only went swimming to get a sound beating. I remember how I used to come home from the public baths black and blue with bruises, and smitten with athlete's foot and verrucas, after having been frotted in the changing room by the teachers; and we thought absolutely nothing of it.

It was all in a day's work and part of life's rich tapestry. And we all longed for next Thursday so that we could have the crap beaten out of us again during another swimming sessions invigilated by a Socratising paedophile. Never did me any harm. In fact they gave me a Bronze survival medal. But now, we are living in enlightened times, so Seth is tying knots in his huge plastic condom.

We are hanging over the edge of the tiled roof. It's the first day I'm out of my bandages, so I'm feeling invulnerable like the super hero I am. The sheer drop looks worse than it is. Seth is barefoot for better grip. I am wearing plimsolls with toes curled around the gutter to stop me sliding right off the edge. Seth's arm is hanging over the side. He asks me for my Clipper, which I provide, and he sets fire to the knotted bag.

Agog, we wonder as its flaming shards drip to the ground; the fire licks up to the next big knot in the bin liner, then the knot catches fires and plummets flaming earthwards, as though he was knitting and purling and casting off stitches with needles of fire. The molten gobs of burning bin liner impact at ground zero with satisfying thwacks. They are like the fallen angels in *Paradise Lost.*

In the dark, it's quite a spectacle. I hope no-one is walking underneath.

"Why did you say that earlier?" he asks.

"What?"

There is something possibly menacing in his voice, and here I am sat out on a rooftop in the company of a massively strong, tattooed mountaineer with a death wish, hurling flaming firebrands from the firmament. I look to his face, trying to discern from the expression whether I have anything to be worried about. But the momentary illuminations from the burning binbag are too brief to yield a proper reading.

"About me telling fortunes from the stains in a toilet bowl."

"Did I say that?"

"Yes."

"Didn't you tell me that?"

"No."

"What did you tell me?"

"That I can tell your fortune from reading tea leaves."

"Sorry. I sometimes get things muddled up in my head. I think we were headed for the Birdwood shithouse, and you must have been talking about telling fortunes, and I've managed to run the two together. I do it so often, I even have a name for it. I call it *enjambement.* Are you going to chuck me off the roof?"

He seems to think about it as a serious proposition. I begin to wish I hadn't put the idea in his head. Under his breath, he is counting out the seconds it takes for the next fireball to drip off the bulk of the bag and hit the ground. Then he seems to get fed up, and lets go of the whole garbage sack before it burns his hand. It lies on the pavement below, smouldering, stinking and belching black smoke for a while.

"No, " he announces considerately. "Not high enough up to do any real harm."

I don't know if he's joking.

Trying to change the subject, I ask: "Did she sign it?"

He turns to face me. "Did who sign what?"

"Calypso. Did she sign her *magnum opus*?"

"I told you, I don't do Latin."

"The gap year *War and Peace* she inscribed on your body."

"I don't know if it's a signature, but I can show you where she left off."

"OK. Show me."

His left leg is fully extended with the heel in the gutter. He lifts his foot up to show me his big toe. I can't make it out. I take back the Clipper lighter and illuminate the scene as though we are two guys in a Flemish painting consisting almost entirely of chiaroscuro and sfumatzo. We are The Night Watchmen but without the big hats, or barretinas as Lyca would say.

On his big toe, it's an 8. I don't get it.

Then I realise that he can't twist his foot around any further without falling off the roof, so I am reading it in landscape. In A4 portrait mode, it says ∞. It's an ambigram.

"What does it mean?" I ask him.

"I thought it was like two dots, you know, dot dot: TBC. To be continued, if she found any more skin to continue it on. Or if I kept growing. But then we ended; so it's just two full stops. The end of everything. "

"If you did Latin, we'd say it's the *Ultima Thules*."

"No doubt we would." He says. Then after a pause: "You know, Nick, I think that's when I realised that life is finite, and that I'd turned the corner and it was downhill all the way ahead of me. Up until then, I had my youth and some of my innocence, and the rest of my life stretched before me into infinity, you know, like the *Start Rite kids* in the shoes advert. She used to call me her Lost Boy; after the kids in *Peter Pan* who never grow up.

"Up until then, every year that went by, I could look back and I'd grown bigger and taller and more powerful. You remember how your parents used to stand you up against the wall and chalk in your height, so that you could see how much bigger you were than last month? And you wondered where it would all end. Would you go through the ceiling if you ate enough of your greens? And there was everything to look forward to.

"So when she filled up all my skin, I guess I just thought, well, I'm in a relationship; I'll grow some more. Next year I'll be bigger than ever and there will be more skin for her to write on. I'd never been out with a girl for a whole year.

"But there wasn't. It's when it dawns on you that the limitless is transitioning into the limited, and there's nothing to look forward to anymore. The things she'd written on me increased in stature, as I expanded into the finite mass of my skin; I grew, but I never grew any more skin. It was the same finite issue of skin becoming more stretched and attenuated with each passing year.

"My skin had been a canvas on which she painted; and she turned the screws and stretched the canvas tighter and tighter. But there comes a time, when the bolts start turning counter-clockwise, and all the old tightness is on the way out, and from then on, it's a process of loosening and yellowing until it's all hanging off your bones like cerements; a winding sheet. I never made any more skin. The writing grew with me. It didn't make any more space. I really was a Lost Boy. She made me into one. Somewhere in my past, I'd lost my future."

The stinking black mass on the pathway beneath us squelches, belches and burns out. Suddenly it is very dark up on the roof. Seth doesn't seem to notice. He just continues with his fireside narrative even though the fire has gone out.

"Two full stops, Nick. Two full stops. For added finality. I suppose she could have done one full stop and underlined it."

"No. It's supposed to be what it is."

"And what is it?"

I roll up my shirt sleeve, newly rid of its dressing, to expose my forearm beneath the bandage. I flick the Clipper alight, showing him the corresponding mark Set had clawed onto my skin.

"Snap!" I say.

**

In the morning, it's a real mess. It looks like some pterodactyl that has been feasting on volcanic ash has taken a dump on Gisborne Court from a great height. But the splatter pattern where it landed is in the shape of Calypso's signature, ∞. This is the sort of symmetry that I find very calming. This morning I don't even need to go as far as the Birdwood to achieve *catharsis*.

I rub my forearm under my shirtsleeve. My fingers trace the same shape in cicatrices on my skin.

You've got to have some skin in the game, I think to myself.

Seth and me. We're like two books bound in anthropodermic bibliopegy.

The Mathematical Bridge

The morning after the burning of the bin bags, instead of hanging over the gutters of Gisborne Court, Seth and I are hanging over the edge of Etheridge's Mathematical Bridge, chucking stale bread at the ducks ploughing the Cam below. The complexity of the bridge reminds me of the unsolved puzzle that is Calypso. Or maybe too many things remind me of Calypso.

"Calypso is OK," I grudgingly concede to Seth. "But I think that affectation of keeping her eyes shut all the fucking time is a bit pretentious."

"She has no choice," Seth leaps to her defence. His arms are resting on the tangent and radial trussing of this renowned bridge, but I can see that he is restless. I am wondering if he is thinking of throwing himself off the bridge. Sometimes Seth is self-confident; sometimes he seems suicidal. Did Lyca do this to him?

"Why not? Don't tell me she's blind."

"No. Her eyelids are just sealed shut."

"Like the bloke who couldn't tell shit from putty?"

"Yeh, yeh, I know. His windows fell out! Calypso thought she was putting anti-histamine drops into her eyes."

"And what the fuck was she putting in?"

"Super glue. They used to package it in very similar containers."

"Jesus Christ! Is she blinded?"

"No, the blink reaction stopped the glue reaching the eyeball, but her eyelids are glued shut. Her mum took her to visit specialists at Moorfields. One guy was going to cut a few millimetres of her upper eyelids away. She would have been able to see; but she'd never be able to blink, so she would have to keep her eyes moistened by dripping drops in them every few seconds.

"And knowing her, she'd reach for the wrong phial when she was stoned and glue them together again. Another doctor said the glue would wear off eventually, but he couldn't say exactly when. That option was called—here we go again—'Wait and see'—And that's what she's doing. She's become reconciled to the situation like someone who sews his mouth up voluntarily for a hunger strike."

"Or a diet."

"She says she is experiencing everything a different way."

"She is cleansing her doors of perception."

"Whatever. I thought you knew. You must have read about it," yawns Seth. "It was all over Exchange & Mart."

And then, unable to restrain his exuberant energy any longer, his huge fists seize the arc of the wooden bridge, and he raises himself into a handstand. Now I am genuinely concerned that he is going to complete the manoeuvre with a diving handstand; but he merely scissors his legs a couple of times, and then dismounts. Just letting off steam.

The trouble is that when I'm with Seth and he does these things, it's me that feels embarrassed.

Next Meeting with Set

I am proceeding down Trumpington Street, with Sydney's cartoon of GentleMan rolled up in my back jeans pocket, heading for a meeting at Downing's flagpole, when I notice he is walking alongside me again. The *Start Rite kids*.

"Why so glum, Dilly boy?" he asks. "You've got an ecaf as long as a suet pudding."

"My director of studies has told me I have to write an expository essay entitled *Art in the Home*, and I have absolutely nothing to say upon the subject."

"Don't you worry, bud. I'll screeve the essay for you. You need all your spare clock to plan your Grand Entrance. You don't need no dogshit distractions about *Art in the Home*. Your manager here will screeve it for you. I don't know why you waste your time on this English lit. I call it English shit. None of it will have any relevance in the future."

"In the future, we'll all be speaking English lite. Mankind began communicating their basic needs with grunts and monosyllables. Then language evolved with ever more creative flourishes: made-up words, confections imported from other languages, reaching its apotheosis in England with Marlowe. In other countries, such as France, they actually had to pass laws to restrain the exuberance of their own language and stop it evolving. But in the future, it's all going back to the monosyllables and grunts it grew from, and everything you're learning now will be consigned to the rubbish heap."

"How come?"

"Because in the future we're all going to be communicating with robots, and robots have very rudimentary vocabularies. Also, their programs are written by geeks who speak in monosyllables and grunts themselves. If you want to make yourself understood to a machine, you have to descend to its level and speak to it in the vocabulary it has been given; so we will all become accustomed to speaking like automatons ourselves. It's already happening. I suggest you forget all about *Art in the Home*, and leave it to me. I'll write it. You concentrate on writing the script for your Grand Entrance."

"And where do we set the stage for this Grand Entrance?" I ask the god Set, after having shown him the cartoon charcoaled by Sydney for my superhero, and explained his power of fucking the dead back to life.

"What do you have in mind?" he asks. "Oops!" he says, putting his hand across his mouth. "I have committed the cardinal sin of answering a question with another question. But to hell with it, if I can't sin, who can?"

I am thinking of the most sophisticated place I can imagine. It hits me. "Dubai!"

"No, no," says Set, as though I have made a terrible *faux pas*. "You need something simpler, so as not to steal the thunder from your entrance. Besides, I have other plans for Dubai: the myth of the Tower of Babel coming to life. But not yet. Somewhere else. Simpler, purer, starker. I'll zhoosh it up for you. Somewhere that makes a bold statement. And plenty of open space to land PJ's, choppers, spaceships; lots of *lebensraum* for all the paparazzi and ajax film crews, gaffers, grips, continuity men. This is going to be mega!"

This is taking shape in my imagination.

"And the angel wings," Set adds. "They're impractical."

I sense it's the association with heavenly hosts that he doesn't approve of; not the wings themselves.

"What are you going to do with them when you go to bed, when you want to lie on your back, when you want to charve? And you'll be doing a lot of charver if this hero of yours is in the business of fucking the dead back to life. No. The wings don't work. If you have aspirations for angel wings, why don't we have you arrive on a winged horse, Pegasus?"

"Or a winged unicorn…"

"Indeed. Why do things by halves?"

It occurs to me that he is adapting his language to the gay undertones of GentleMan, as though his brain continues to evolve and assimilate after his body stopped growing.

I believe this may be insulting but I can't quite figure it out. I can detect we are drawing up the blueprint for the gayest superhero that ever trailed a mincing gait upon the earth, or flew in the sky, or sat atop a winged unicorn. This is Liberace on horseback.

"And the name of this superhero, GentleMan."

"No, no, no. GentleMan is hopeless. And it sounds too Yiddish. Swap names with me. You will be the God Set, and I will in future be

Old Nick."

"You would be prepared to give me your name?" I am touched.

The God Set. It has a ring to it. The swapping of names. "In the future," Set explains, "everyone will be doing it. It's called Identity Theft."

Why would anyone want to steal my identity? He seems to talk a lot of shit.

"I will tell you what we will do with this GentleMan," he informs me. "In return for all these earthly powers beyond your wildest dreams. In recompense, you and I will have a gentleman's agreement. That's the deal. Just think about it."

A gentleman's agreement.

Game. Set. Match. I am having a road to Downing moment.

Following Meeting with Set

I am walking along Trumpington Street the following morning, and there he is again, the god Set. He is holding a walking cane topped with a silver death's head and poking out the cat's eyes in the road.

"I would like to make a Grand Entrance," I inform him.

I have followed his advice and thought about things overnight, and I have decided that I want to be my own work of art. I will take all the powers the devil gives me and use them for good. In other words, I have listened to all the warnings he gave me, but I propose to learn nothing from the mistakes of others and proceed to make my own. He said this isn't predestination, but I just can't help myself. We are the stars' tennis balls.

"I want to summon all the evil dictators and oppressors in the world and give them the ultimatum to reform. If they do not, I will destroy them. I need the Grand Entrance so that they take me seriously, so they know I am a force to be reckoned with."

"You will have the imagination and powers of expression of Christopher Marlowe and Stan Lee combined," says he. "No-one will ever make a grander entrance."

"I will need some sort of harbinger; someone to announce me and prepare the world for me, so that I don't have to do it myself and seem conceited."

"I shall be honoured to be your chronicle. I will be your manager. I will prepare the ground for your Grand Entrance."

"And I want a huge army."

"Armed with what?"

"Not necessarily armed with anything at all. An army of fans, like I'm the Rolling Stones or Emmerson Lake and Palmer; groupies, but groupies who follow me from planet to planet."

"Ah, you're arriving from another planet with an army of devoted admirers. I believe this is resembling a cult and they would be described as "followers". Intergalactic groupies, no problem at all."

"Where are you going to get all these people from?"

"How about we go raid the King's College Chapel choir again?"

"No, no, no. I don't want real people. Yesterday you were talking about automata."

"Smoke and mirrors. CGI. No-one even expects real people any more. Just so long as everybody *thinks* you've got a real army. It's the appearance that matters. But the first thing any super hero needs," says Set, "is a name. Have you thought further upon the name swap?"

"What's wrong with my own name?"

"Nick Jobs?" He pulls a face. "Do you know what Jobs is? A job is a thrust of the penis. Your friend, Sydney, is writing a treatise on the divine Rochester's A Ramble in St James' Park, and I quote: *Had she picked out to rub her arse on/Some stiff prick'd clown or well-hung parson/Each job of whose spermatic juice/Had filled her cunt with wholesome juice...*

"This is a tragic poem when the aged libertine walks in St James' Park and finds his former mistress consorting with an unworthy beau. But also, Job has biblical overtones. The Book of Job, a story of senseless persecution and martyrdom for no reason at all. People will think it's the second coming. Despite your grand entrance, no-one would take you seriously. Nick; it would be like something you assemble yourself in a flat pack. You can't have a superhero from IKEA."

"But I want folks to know it's me."

"Well, there's no harm in them knowing that you used to be you before you transcended yourself. I assume you're going to want to be different in appearance, at least six inches taller; we can do away with the love handles; you'll be needing a six pack, golden locks blowing in the wind. What we are penning together here is a supreme work of self-authorship. In the future, it will be all the trend.

"People won't be content to be the gender they were born into. It will be all comings and goings, of omi polonis and hobbledehoys. The looming age is an age of uncertainty; people won't even be sure what sex they are. Their bodies will simply be canvases for their self-expression. In the future, the high street will consist entirely of tattoo parlours, because everything else will be delivered. You should look like Michelangelo's David. People will know that you used to be Nick Jobs before you defeated the god Set and took on his powers."

"I defeated the god Set and took on his powers," I repeated, already warming to the script.

"...and his name."

"But I like my name. That's the name everybody knows me by."

"Changing your name is nothing at all. Names are nothing. *Tell me gentle hobbledehoy,*" he quotes. *"Art thou girl or art thou boy?* In the future that we are writing, people will change their sex as simply as they change their underwear. They will shed their skin like snakes."

Strange. I have been through my entire life without using the words anthropodermic bibliopegy, and now my head is ringing with them two days running.

Once more, I find myself unrolling the cartridge paper with Sydney's charcoal drawing of GentleMan on it.

"Well, this is you to a T," says the god Set, focussing on it this time around. "And obviously, if you were simply going to say that this monument to homoerotica is Nick Jobs, you may find that embarrassing. But if what the press (who you will obviously control) say is that the amazing Nick Jobs has defeated the god Set and taken on his powers, and come back looking like this after years of training on another planet, well, as your manager, I don't think this would be embarrassing to the former Mr Jobs, before he acquired his powers."

"Years of training on another planet?"

"But of course! Intergalactic boot camp."

"Yes," I said, "it does make sense. He defeats the god Set, and takes on his powers, and his looks."

"His *good looks*!"

"Of course, his *good looks*."

"And his name."

"His good name."

"No, Nick. His bad name."

"And in his bad name, I do good things."

"Nick, you're going to do marvellous things, but the collateral damage will be mega!"

"How come?"

"Vada, vada! Read Malthus. I think he went to this very university. He says that population growth is exponential, whereas the means of sustaining it, the capability to make food, is linear, so we need wars, disease, pandemics, pestilence and huge natural catastrophes, to keep the population under control, or we'll eat ourselves into extinction. Malthus was writing at the end of the 18th century, but the big bang in population came in the 20th.

"At the same time, life expectancy is a third longer than it was in the 18th century; doctors have cured or contained most illnesses; generally speaking, we don't have any more plagues, and if we go to war, it's frowned upon to kill anybody, so we just blow up a few airfields and buildings. As a result of these lifestyle adjustments, population is totally out of control; there's not enough food to feed it, and now here you come along with a plan to charve the dead back to life. You're an unsustainable superhero. End of!"

The Blind Girl

The blinds are drawn in the main lecture theatre on Sidgwick Site. Seth and I are seated at the rear looking down into the cockpit. I recognise the backs of a few heads in front of us. There's Ingram bunking out from his study of the law, and But Surely is sitting up at the front with the teachers pets. The only light source is the beam from the projector, plunging Calypso into a series of dramatic chiaroscuros and sfumatzos. She is wearing a red shawl. She is so still she looks as though she is a fresco painted onto the wall by Fra Angelico but with the lighting done by Vermeer.

Lyca stands by the lectern, waiting for all of us to shut up. The slide which she has chosen and which is the theme of her talk for today is projected onto the huge screen right next to her, so large that the dimensions of the girl in the painting are precisely the same as hers, and I am immediately struck by the uncanny resemblance. She must have done this on purpose.

It was raining outside; the kind of summer rain that can soak you through. As a result, there is a warm dampness in the room, also mirroring the subject of the painting.

"John Francis Millais," she begins confidently in her cut glass accent, once we have stilled, "painted 'The Blind Girl' between 1854 and 1856, and I wish to use this canvas as an introduction to the more far-reaching talk I will be giving on the composition he painted 3 years later. But for today, we are reflecting on 'The Blind Girl'.

"Look at the slightly unnatural rotundity of her face, and the way it is tilted upwards. The Blind Girl's head mirrors the movements of the heliotropic sun-tracking wildflowers she brushes with the back of her right hand. She is another sunflower.

"The rainbows, of which there are two, signify that it has been raining before the artist takes his snapshot. It's a clever little trick. Although a painting must necessarily be frozen in time, he manages to show us what was going on before the shutter clicked. The grass must be wet. Her other senses, sharpened by the lack of sight, must be taking in the scent of the flowers she is brushing against.

"A tortoiseshell butterfly has alighted on her shawl. The girl is sitting so still that the butterfly mistakes her for a sunflower.

"And doesn't she resemble the sun? Her hair is red. Her face is suffused with a golden glow. Is the warm orange incandescence the reflection of the sun on her face, or is she herself the light source of the painting?"

She has a point. As an *amateur photographer*, I understand it well. The Pre-Raphaelite canvasses are so intensely illuminated that it can be difficult to tell by what, or as Calypso would have it, by whom. Ironically, the source of light in this composition may well be the subject of the painting who cannot see it. There is something uncanny about sitting in this blackened room, smelling the damp jackets of the students in the dark, and listening to a benighted red-headed lecturer deliver this dissection of a work of art that she cannot see. I am wondering when she last saw it.

"One of the most interesting things about Millais," she continues, "Is his overpainting of his canvasses by which you can see his thought processes evolving—and we are going to reflect upon that when we come to '*The Angelus*' later in my little series of talks. In this canvas we see a double rainbow, a very rare phenomenon. In fact so rare that I would suggest Millais has never even seen one himself, which is why he got it wrong. In a double rainbow, the hierarchy of colours in the inner bow is reversed, so that whereas the outer bow is R-O-Y-G-B-I-V, the inner bow should be V-I-B-G-Y-O-R.

"When Millais first hung the canvas, someone who had seen a double rainbow told him he'd gotten it wrong. What are the odds against that? Someone who had actually seen a double rainbow being present when he first hung his canvas that happened to feature a double rainbow? So Millais overpainted the inner bow to give the painting a naturalistic integrity. Which makes one wonder, why was this symbol of the double rainbow considered so important to him, that he insisted on depicting it even though he didn't know what it looked like. Why take that risk? What does it stand for, bearing in mind that the subject of his painting cannot see it?"

Calypso is not afraid of the gaps between words, the silences that fools like to fill with the sound of their own voices. She speaks without notes, quietly but confidently in the darkened room. It is as though she is extinguishing herself into the painting, the three dimensional taking on two dimensions, akin to the talk about fabrication she had given the previous week. I feel one of my headaches coming on, but I don't want to miss out on anything. It's probably the flickering light of the projector. I am thinking that everyone in this auditorium is thinking to himself or herself what Millais is trying to say to us with these two rainbows. Millais has no more seen a double rainbow than the little blind girl in his painting.

If anyone thought she was going to answer her own question, they have another think coming, because, for the time being at least, she leaves it hanging there; but we already have the promise of a lot of things becoming clearer when she tells us about *The Angelus*. Maybe both rainbows are overpainted and something else lies beneath.

She continues: "The Blind Girl combines supreme sensitivity with utter crassness." The words are strident and harsh. They make my head throb harder. "The sensitivity lies in the narrative skill that we have observed; the way the artist conveys the girl's disability through a number of subtle hints: the lightly closed eyes drawing in the warmth of the sun; the face illuminated by the golden glow; the stillness communicated by the tortoiseshell butterfly, a stillness that betrays self-confidence and self-sufficiency despite her disability; the heightened sensory perception of the hand releasing the fragrance from the wildflowers: all the details that silently hint that the subject of the painting is blind.

"But then, as if to trash all this subtlety and nuance, he hangs a label around the girl's neck with *Pity the Blind* written on it in capital letters. He entitles the painting "The Blind Girl", those words being etched onto the frame of the canvas, and he endows her with the schmaltzy stage prop of a concertina, from which we may deduce that she intends to earn a living for herself by busking with her squeeze-box when she reaches the town of Winchelsea discernible in the background.

"There is a kind of schiamachy between the subtlety and the crassness in this canvas."

No-one disagrees with her, because no-one knows what schiamachy is.

"There is something intensely voyeuristic about the theme of this painting," she pronounces. "The beautiful blind girl. You can look at her for as long as you like, as closely as you like, because she can't see what you're doing."

Her words are hitting home. I feel as though I've been "found out" by her, my guilty little secret. What I do with her every time I see her, undressing her with my eyes. The blood is drip-dripping into the right hand side of my brain. I can hear it in my ears. I have to tilt my head to the left to try to drain some of it back into the other hemisphere of my skull before I fit. Satisfyingly, I can hear it percolating back and refilling the chambers on the left, as one tops up the battery of one's car. It must be the flickering light from the projector. There is nothing I can do about it. I am about to black out, at least, when suddenly the bell rings, marking the end of her lecture.

"Wow!" says Seth. "You know, most lecturers play a slideshow of 20 or 30 slides and say a few words about each canvas, such as when they were painted and what museum they are hanging in. She spoke for a full 60 minutes with no notes on just one painting that she couldn't see."

"And she was just getting started when the bell went," I added.

"More than that," adds Seth, "remember this was all just context. This was merely the *mis en scene* for something else.

"*The Angelus.*"

"And the overpainting. The secrets that lie beneath."

"She must have done all this from memory. It's incredible." I forget that I am addressing the man who memorised *the Iliad, the Odyssey and the Epic of Gilgamesh.*

"Do you think," Seth queries, "that's why she forgot about the other girl in the picture?"

"Don't know. Shall we ask her?"

A group of students had converged around Lyca at the front of the hall. We were looking down on them from the back of the raked auditorium. They were in animated conversation with her. I didn't know if it was easier firing questions to a lecturer who was a close friend, or to a total stranger. I was worried about getting the tone right.

It didn't matter if you agreed with Calypso or violently disagreed with her. She was hugely stimulating either way. She hadn't bothered to call for the lights to be turned back on after the bell had interrupted her. She may not even know they were still off. The students were gathering in the shadows of the dusty light from the projector beam that no-one had killed, making eerie halos around their heads. From the back of the cockpit, where Seth and I were now standing, they resembled a congregation of UFO watchers come together on Nevada

State Route 375 for a night of infinite promise.

As they had their moments in the limelight and dispersed, so we crept forward, a step at a time, wanting to have her all to ourselves. Silently, we passed Ingram ascending the steps by which we descend. Worrying that he might miss something, he hangs around like the Grand Old Duke of York's Men, halfway up and halfway down. Eventually we had ambled all the way to the front, but Burt Sully was still there, laboriously organising his question that would be less a search for the truth than a proclamation of his own smartness. Seth wasn't hanging around for it:

"But surely—"

Seth cut in: "I wanted to ask you," Seth began. Very smart opening, just enough verbiage to steal the floor from But Surely but without wasting any important words in case Sully continued and didn't shut up. But he did.

"Why you didn't mention the *other* girl in the painting."

"Ah," says Calypso, as she moves her face like the heliotropic flower towards her interrogator, "you mean the blind girl."

Seth's double take is like the double rainbow.

"I was coming to that," she says, "when the bell rang. Problem with having my eyes glued shut is that I can't see the fucking clock on the back wall. It felt like 10 minutes."

Ten minutes that feel like sixty minutes.

But Surely has finally composed his question:

"But surely—"

This time it's my turn to interrupt.

"So what you were working up to," I butt in, feeling justified as I am continuing her point rather than attempting to make some self-serving point of my own, "is a hypothesis that the subject of the painting is the other girl, the one who is looking at the double rainbow, but missing the million, tiny, beautiful things that the unsighted girl perceives."

"What I was working up to," says Calypso, cutting me off this time, "was a far more important painting, *The Angelus*." Clearly, she's not going to let me steal the punch line from her lecture.

"But surely—"

Seth cuts him off again. "This riddle of the double rainbow," he begins. "I don't know what it means in other cultures, but in Christianity, from the Bible to D H Lawrence via Milton and Browning, it's a symbol of redemption, of God's covenant with man that he won't unleash another inundation."

"An important covenant," observes Calypso, "when you consider that the biblical inundation was triggered by a relatively insignificant incident, if you think of the number of major transgressions that are occurring now every millisecond, it's a very important covenant."

"Doesn't mean to say He won't dream up another way to punish us," notes Seth.

I see the silhouette of Ingram's head, halfway up the auditorium in the projector's beam. It's been turned on for too long and the heat from the bulb is melting the transparency of The Blind Girl. For a few seconds the image is projected onto Ingram's face; then it begins to bubble up obscenely like a huge boil before it bursts. Then there is no more Blind Girl; just the white searchlight from the projector. Then someone kills it. But the image of Ingram's head blowing up plays on in my own head. I can't seem to change the reel. Maybe this is the overpainting. If you strip it all down, what do you get? A would-be politician with an exploding head.

Attendees for the next lecture have started arriving in the auditorium. Someone has turned the lights on. Calypso presses her eyes tighter shut and brings her whole arm up to cover them, again assuming that fourth position. It appears that the light hurts her. In the background, I hear the bass rumble of the summer thunder outside.

"…so the two rainbows…?" Seth urges.

Lowering her arms, now a hand on each hip: "They cancel one another out," she says.

This would be an ideal time for Burt to say, "But Surely…" but he has either forgotten what his question was or is in a hurry to get to his next lecture. He has disappeared.

As we go back up the steps to leave by the door at the back of the cockpit, I notice there is no clock on the wall.

Outside, the streets are awash. We tip out into a circular courtyard, refulgent in the bright sunlight that acts as a blinding mirror. I am feeling proud of myself for my self-control in not passing out and making another scene. We could take cover, but the torrential rain shows no sign of easing up, so Seth and I resign ourselves to getting drenched.

After I've dried out in my room, I head for the Ward library. I want to look up "schiamachy" in the big fourteen volume OED. How humiliating for Cambridge to have to look everything up in the Oxford English Dictionary! I realise I am hanging on to every word she speaks. Am I falling in love with my best mate's girl?

As I duck into the doorway of the staircase leading up to the Ward Library, I realise there's a rainbow. Only one of them though. I'm not impressed.

Maybe if I ask her nicely, she will explain to me what Blake's "*Ghost of a Flea*" means.

Self-Harming Harry

Next time I drop by Sydney's set with my recent charge, Seth, in tow, there is a new face sitting atop a new body sat on the *chaise longue* and reading a *Fantastic Four* comic. He has black hair in tight curls. His features are negroid, but his skin colour is too light. He is smoking a *Guards* cigarette, and every time he turns the page in his comic, he rewards himself with a swig from whatever is in his hip flask.

"Gentlemen," says Sydney, "allow me to introduce Self-Harming Harry." Harry looks from face to face, suspiciously and then drops his nose back into his comic.

"How do you do, Harry?" Ingram ask politely.

Harry looks up at Ingram from his comic. "I'm cream crackered!" he exclaims. "I've just worked a Barney."

Seeing the lack of comprehension on Ingram's face, Sydney translates: "Cream-crackered means he's knackered. Why is he knackered? Because he's worked a Barney. Barney Rubble equals Double. Double Shift." He works at the hotel. He's had to do a double shift so that he can spend quality time here being personally instructed at the feet of the Master. And his Mistress," Sydney adds, nodding in the direction of Lyca. "Although not born within the sound of Bow Bells, Harry here likes to speak in Cockney rhyming slang. I'm afraid he's not very needle."

"Needle?" Ingram asks.

"Needle and thread," translates Sydney. "He's not very well read."

"No," corrects Harry, "needle and thread is bread."

"Wilfulness in the pupil!" exclaims Sydney. "Needle and thread means fucking Dead, if I say so. As long as it scans and rhymes, you don't have to follow what some other ignorant cunt said it means!"

"Hi, Harry," I say, trying to defuse a threatening situation. You can never tell if Sydney is being ironic or if he is in the grip of psychotic substances and beyond his senses. "What are you reading?"

"Fantastic Four," he informs.

"No. I mean what are you reading at Cambridge?"

Harry looks genuinely confused, and his forehead exhibits unnaturally deep furrows of consternation, wrinkles deep enough for a flea to break a leg in.

"As yet, Harry isn't reading anything at Cambridge," intervenes

Sydney. "He is town, not gown. There's some rhyming slang for you! He hails from the other side of the bubble beyond Reality Checkpoint, *where there be dragons*," Sydney adds in an ersatz yokel accent. "I am looking after him. I am the socialite, Bruce Wayne, and Harry is my youthful ward."

I can't believe this. Less than 48 hours since Pfläfflin entrusted Seth Godil to me, Sydney has had to go and get himself a protégé of his own, even if it meant picking up some drunken dotard off the pavement of Trumpington Street.

"Let's just say that Harry is my Eliza Doolittle," Sydney continues. "I propose to take personal charge of his education. Obviously, he hasn't sat, let alone passed, any entrance exams, so the university won't admit him. However, they have agreed that he can sit the tripos exams, provided I pay an enhanced entrance fee. We shall see if it is possible for someone who begins his education at the age of—How old are you, Harry?"

"Twenty-six."

"Twenty-six; didn't you tell us that Frank Whittle didn't start here until he was twenty-seven, Spud? This is an experiment to see if Harry can pick up enough learning to get a Cambridge degree from a complete standing start, under my expert tutelage, of course."

"And what have you taught him so far?" I ask.

"Well, he has to start at the bottom, like everyone else," answers Sydney. For the first few weeks he's going to be carrying the sedan chair. Harry, make a note of that!" exclaims Sydney, thrusting a pencil into his hand. "Look at the way he holds a pencil!" cries Sydney in delight. "Like it's a knife and fork!"

"What do you think of the livery?" asks Calypso.

Harry is wearing a maroon crushed velvet jacket with green and gold braided lapels, frogging and cuffs, and dark blue and green blackwatch tartan trousers. Tucked into them is an avocado coloured tailored shirt, and hanging down from the collar of that shirt is a dark blue silk tie featuring a motif of a lighter blue frothing tankard with a crown atop. On his feet he wears white plimsolls.

"I'm impressed," I say truthfully. "What does the tie mean?"

"The tie denotes hierarchy amongst my porters," explains Sydney. "This is the tie awarded to those who have done the King Street Run, a pub crawl consisting of the thirteen pubs in King Street (used to be eight, but that's rampant inflation for you). Harry has downed a yard of ale at each of the thirteen pubs in less than two hours. The absence of any P lettering on his tie indicates that he didn't stop along the way for a pee or a puke.

"Had he done so, a P embroidered above the tankard in yellow would indicate the stopping for a pee, and a P embroidered in green below the tankard would signify a puke. Many participants have to carry the shame of multiple P's below and above the tankard. To Harry's eternal credit, his reputation and his piss is intact, immediately catapulting him to the position of Head Porter, which is why there is a small gold crown above the frothing tankard."

"Congratulations," I say, showing that it is possible to be impressed and totally mystified at the same time.

"Cheers," says Harry.

"How are you going to follow that?" I ask Harry.

"Sydney has enrolled me for the Jacob's Cream Cracker cramming competition."

"Being?" I question.

"Swallowing sixty Jacob's Cream Crackers in 60 minutes without liquid," explains Sydney. "The first few go down easily enough, but I understand the going gets a bit drier after twenty or so, and each time you have to fool your swallow mechanism if you want to keep them down. They say it's like being constantly fucked up the arse with no pomard. Metaphor for life really!"

"Except it's with your mouth," points out Spud.

Over the ensuing days, I learn that Harry is an unusual mix. His mother was a highly respectable Jewess from Stamford Hill. She allowed herself to get bedded by a schwarzer while she was still in her teens, and Half-Cast Harry was the result. His mother named him Harry after the popular black musician, Harry Belafonte who had a number one hit with *Island in the Sun*. But that didn't stop her family telling her never to darken their door again. Of course, the father ran off to continue sewing his oats elsewhere. Leaving Harry with Sydney for a role model.

Despite his inauspicious beginnings, the mother attempted to do everything right, for Harry, including having him schnickled: after all, he was Jewish, as it passes down the distaff side. The schnickling was the only harm anybody else had done to Harry and all the rest he did to himself. As a negro Jew, he is a permanent outsider. He doesn't fit in anywhere. They used to say that when they circumcised Harry they threw away the best bit of him. He feels shunned and an outsider and the only living thing he really identifies with is Snowflake, the albino gorilla in Barcelona zoo, whom he has seen photos of in *National Geographic*.

As a schoolboy and adolescent, he was known as Half-Cast Harry. When he arrived in Cambridge to work in the kitchens at the freshly rebuilt Garden House Hotel after the students had burnt it down, he wanted to turn a new page. No-one from his past life had followed him to Cambridge, so he was free to cast off the shackles of Half-Cast Harry. The sobriquet, Half-Cast Harry, fell into desuetude, and the folks at Cambridge started calling him Self-Harming Harry, strangely enough being the nickname he devised for himself, presumably on the principle that anything is better than Half-Cast Harry.

I would say that Harry has low self-esteem. I have seen him cutting himself with a Stanley knife. He is quite open about it. He does it without embarrassment, and why not? People pierce themselves, have themselves tattooed, put rings through their nipples, noses and ears. If Harry wants to slice collops out of his forearm, good luck to him, I say.

"But he cuts himself!" whispers Ingram, disapprovingly, to Sydney.

"Harry has dealt himself a hard hand," interrupts Lyca. "He was already hammered out upon humanity's anvil before he decided to take a mezzaluna to himself."

Once again, I find my brain conjuring with one of Calypso's images. I remember what Seth told me she had done to him. Harry cuts himself. She cuts others.

"But why are you wasting your time with that self-harming simpleton?" perseveres Ingram.

"Simple people can be complicated too, you know," says Sydney. "It may surprise you to learn that undergrads at Oxford and Cambridge don't hold the cartel on complexity. I find that Harry can be quite insightful. Having him around is like having your own Reality Checkpoint to keep you company, make sure you don't get too far up your own arse, eh what, Ingram? I feel like the Roman emperor who had his slave remind him every day that he was only human."

"Did you know," puts in Lyca, continuing her mezzaluna metaphor, "that 99.99% of the statistics you read in the media for Female Genital Mutilation consist of grown women who gladly and consensually pay to have it done to themselves?"

"Absolutely correct!" exclaims Sydney. "The old Nigerian crone or wrinkled Haitian fishwife with a boat hook and a two day old baby girl, are just urban myths. It's all middle-aged BDSM fans doing it to one another voluntarily. After they've tattooed every inch of skin, they start slicing it off, as though they could start over again."

I cast a sidelong glance at Seth, but he's not meeting my gaze.

Most of the harm Harry does to himself is through alcohol. He gets mullahed and walks into things, falls down things, crashes into things. But today is different. He hasn't collided with anything, but he is leaking blood from the inside. You can see the thin red track etching its way under his skin, searching for the line of least resistance. It's like one of those old films where you are supposed to believe the actors are moving from one exotic destination to another, although it's all taking place in Elstree studio.

There's some stock footage of an aeroplane propeller spinning around, and then they cut to a yellowing parchment map of the world, and a moving red line indicates that the 'plane is flying to some far-flung clime such as Timbuctoo. Harry's bloodline resembles the red line in the travel animation in one of those Road To…movies with Bing Crosby and Bob Hope and Dorothy Lamour: *The Road to Mandalay, The Road to Morocco, The Road to Rio, the Road to Zanzibar.*

The Road to fucking Perdition.

And then it starts spurting out of his eye, a very fine mist of sanguine lachrymosity. And as the haemoglobin seeps out of his face, his erstwhile dusky hue starts taking on a pallor, which Harry quite likes, because, apart from his curly hair, he is beginning to resemble a white Caucasian instead of being neither one thing nor the other. Because he approves of the result, he puts off seeing the doctor for far too long, until he is so anaemic he is passing out for want of blood and needs a transfusion.

Whilst yet my eyes alone were free,
My heart would never doubt,

In amorous rage and ecstasy,
To wish those eyes, to wish those eyes, fucked out.

When the transfusion is on hand, Harry eschews it, claiming he is a Jehovah's Witness. He has cast his eyes on that vial of bright red blood and this is not what he wants. He wants white blood. If you can get white Toblerones and Milky Bars, why doesn't blood come in different colours? What he needs is a transfusion from an albino.

Self-harming Harry is sat opposite Hilda. Hilda is the nurse at Peterhouse. She is a woman of a certain age, but nothing else is certain about her. If not for the bleeding eye, you would swear he was giving Hilda the come on. Despite his manifest faults, some women find his striking, unnaturalised features attractive in the same way that someone might want to have sex with a lyre bird.

"And this happened entirely without trauma?" she questions.

It takes Harry a moment to adjust to trauma being used in this way. What she means is *Didn't anyone sock you in the face?*

"No, miss. I was in Gisborne Court, drinking my Grey Goose and Cranberry Classic from my hip flask and the person opposite me told me I was bleeding from the eye."

"How many Grey Geese had you sunk?" she asks, probing him to get to the truth.

It takes Harry a moment to adjust to sunk being used in this way, and the pluralisation of Goose like this. What she means is *How many vodkas had you consumed?*

"I would say two or three," he lies. She is supposed to think glasses. He means *hip flasks*. How appropriate for Harry to be telling white lies.

The nurse knows that alcoholics are always mendacious, mixing large measures of hooch with much smaller measures of truth, so she compensates. She knows there is no such thing as alcohol lite only alcohol litotes; so she reads *eight or ten large ones* for Harry's two or three. She should have been a translator at the United Nations. "Had you been on a protracted bout?" She perseveres.

It takes Harry another while to adjust to bout not being used in connection with a boxing match. What she means is *Had you been on a bender?*

"Well, miss, that is my normal level of consumption of the demon alcohol."

"It's relatively uncommon," she edges towards her diagnosis, "But excessive consumption of alcohol can cause the platelets in the blood to become realigned, and thinned, like with paint thinner," she offers. "I think this is what has happened to you. It's changed your complexion. You are tending towards…" she searches for a word that won't offend him, "…the achromatic. You must dramatically reduce your consumption."

Not only had Harry not heard achromatic used in that way before. He hadn't heard it used at all, but when he got back he looked it up in a dictionary and found out it meant devoid of colour. From that day, he upped his consumption of alcohol, trying to drink himself white, white like his mother, white like Snowflake, the albino gorilla in Barcelona zoo. Drink himself as far away as possible from his useless cunt of an absentee dad, who had contributed nothing to his upbringing save the wrong pigmentation. Pursuing this quest, he had drunk himself into the arms of Sydney Syzygy.

For additional achromaticity, Self-Harming Harry also likes to cut himself. Some people do this for the scarring, but Harry does it because he is physically trying to empty the blood out of himself so that he will be paler of hue. The constant blood-letting bleaching his skin.

"Harry," says Sydney, asking Harry a question simply because someone else is thereby forced to answer it, which is a means of control, "Who is your favourite musician?"

"Michael Jackson," replies Harry, without missing a blink.

"And do you play a musical instrument yourself?" probes Sydney.

"Sure," says Harry. "I jam with a number of other guys in a band."

"And does this band have a name?" enquires Sydney.

"Sure. We call ourselves The Damson Jam."

"What sort of a name is that?" asks Sydney.

"It's a nom de plum," replies Harry.

This exchange, featuring a bilingual pun, led me to the conclusion that Harry had hidden depths. This was on a level with his master's *C'est magnifique, mais c'est ne pas Daguerre.*

And so it was that Seth and I were looking at this uncharacteristically pale negro Jew sat on the chaise longue in Sydney's rooms. He has discarded the Fantastic Four comic and is seemingly sketching something in his rough book whilst toking on the passing joint. But he wasn't using the whole rough book, just a tiny area in the top right hand corner of each page. He had one of those 4 colour biros, where you clicked through red, blue, green, violet.

This made the biro very fat, which caused Sydney to remark that he held the pen like a knife and fork. I dare say that the manufacturer would have liked to have packed an entire rainbow into the shaft, but then you'd need two hands to write with it. Harry was concentrating very hard on whatever he was doing so that the deep wrinkles in his forehead got even deeper. He reminded me of what it was supposed to be like in the old days when children made their own amusement. *The Rainy Day Book for Boys.*

Spud is making his own amusement, flicking through the pages of a *Fantastic Four Omnibus Edition*. Spud is very gifted at engineering works, electronics, mechanical stuff; but I don't think he's a great reader. He is okay with the Marvel comic as most of it is pictorial; but I saw he was reading it with his finger and his lips were moving, forming the words. In one of those moments when the conversation goes all quiet, I hear him mumble: Flame on! Just like I do, if I know no-one can hear.

Harry is still doodling in his rough book. I think to myself that Sydney has got his work cut out if he is going to make this one pass his exams. But maybe Sydney is just leading him on so that he gets a stand-by porter when the first eight are rowing away and he needs to bring on the reserves.

Suddenly, Sydney seems quite restless and picks on his protégé.

"So," says Sydney, grabbing Harry's rough book, "Let me have a look at your course work, and I'll mark it out of 10! Harry, do you understand me?" Then shifting his attention from Harry and addressing the whole room: "Mark it out of ten! It's like the joke about the scrubber who walks into a bar and a guy says I'll give her one, and the scrubber overhears him and says, *How dare you assume I am an object of sexual gratification. I wouldn't dream of having sex with you if you were the last man on earth. To which the guy replies: I'd rather bite my own cock off than have sex with you, darling. When I said I'd give you one, I meant one out of ten."*

Sydney is holding the book upside down, as is his custom. "It's totally fucking blank!" he says. "Is this my guerdon for hours of extra-curricular education and initiation into the black arts?" He chucks the empty book back into Harry's lap, snatching the doobie from Harry's grip as he does so.

Just then Seth hops up onto that pommel horse again and starts his circular swishing, so that all the different smoke patterns from the candles, from the joints, from the incense stick, all fragment in Brownian movement and are scattered in the motes of light and spiralling dust particles. If he isn't practising to be a human flag, he is honing his skills on the vaulting horse. It is a fine spectacle of a man at the peak of his physical abilities, but it also makes a fucking draft in the room that offends Sydney's sensibilities.

"Lyca," he exclaims, "let's go outside and harvest the crab apples from the tree in Gisborne Court." I fancy making crab apple bitter dope marmalade before the crows eat all the berries."

He doesn't wait for a response, but grabs Calypso in the same way that he had grabbed Harry's rough book; in the same way that he had reclaimed the joint from Harry's hand; and he drags her through the door. As she passes the lintel inlaid with Sydney's inverted mezuzah, she turns around and addresses the whirling Dervish that is Seth: "Bitter crab apple jelly." She repeats, "Something to change the taste in your mouth. No more parrot's cage, huh?"

The revolving Seth respond under his breath: "Sure beats Damson Jam!"

Sydney isn't sure he likes where this conversation is going, and he pulls her out of his set. The outer and inner door suck shut and we are again sealed within Sydney's strange parallel universe of *objets trouvee* and whirling Dervishes.

Then, just as suddenly as it had shut, the door reopens and in marches Sydney. He had forgotten he was still smoking the stick. He hands the joint to the nearest person, which, unfortunately for the rest of us, happens to be the arch-Bogarder, Ingram, and he completes his exit, this time not immediately returning.

"I made this for you, actually," says Harry, passing me the rough book.

I am perplexed, but not wishing to be ungrateful or discourage this fledgling student in his studies, I take it. I inspect it, but its significance is lost on me. I see beyond what Sydney saw, because it's not totally blank; there is a tiny motif sketched in the top right hand corner of each page. It's just repetition. The same doodle in the same position on each page, replicated *ad infinitum*, and the rest of the page blank. I gave him a look of profound non-comprehension. Why has he wasted so much paper?

"Like this," he says. Harry takes the book and holds it as if it was a giant deck of cards. He grabs the right hand corner between the thumb and forefinger of his left hand and then rifles through the corners with his right thumb. Then it dawns on me. He's made a flicker book. An evil, stocky, green and black lizard of profound apparent strength seems to stride forward across the pages, concentrating on a bowl of over-spilling blood in his grip. It puts one leg before the other, sloshing the blood bowl from side to side in the process. I am amazed.

"It's Blake's The *Ghost of a Flea*!" I cry.

"I thought you might like it," says Harry. "Maybe inspire you to finish your thesis! Sydney told me about your writer's block."

"Can I keep it?" I ask.

"It's yours."

The Maryjane has reached me. I take a drag on it whilst I flick through the pages as though I'm a proper card sharp. It moves like a motion picture.

"Where did you learn this?" I ask.

"I can just do stuff like this," he says.

"What else can you do?" I ask.

"This," Harry says. He puts his hands in front of his eyes, opening and shutting the fingers as though they were the bars of a cell, or maybe the Doors of Perception even. He is changing the speed at which he is opening and shutting them.

Once again, I don't get it, but Spud has looked up from his perusal of Stan Lee's finest, presumably having despaired of getting his thumb to burst into flames. "You have to look at what he's looking at," explains Spud.

I follow the line of Harry's gaze. He is looking at the revolving Seth, spinning on the vaulting horse, but through the prism of his opening and shutting digits.

"He's making a zoetrope with his fingers," explains Spud. "You know, like when the wheels on your bicycle seem to be going backwards."

"I can read it," whispers Harry, so that Seth cannot hear him. "I can read the shit that's written on him."

The Swimming Pool on Jesus Green

It's a beautiful Sunday in the middle of June. When I walked through the Old Deer Park to the Birdwood this morning, there were traces of fog slithering around on the grass in the process of being burnt off by the sun. A day of infinite promise, and as it was a Sunday, Olumidé wasn't working until her night shift started in the evening.

Today's gnomic wisdom on the bog door was apparently written by one of the engineering undergraduates, such as Spud. It said:

Yesterday I couldn't even spell engineer. Now I are one.

In the Birdwood, I bumped into Seth doing his Lady Macbeth tooth-washing regime. "Why don't we go swimming today?" he suggested, foaming his patriotic toothpaste at the mouth.

"Good idea," I agreed. "Let's ask the others." By which we both understood whoever was hanging out in Substance Abuse Central.

Our ablutions done, we sauntered over to Gisborne Court, radiating around the central feature of the old crab-apple tree whose fruits Sydney was threatening to turn into mind-altering marmalade at the appropriate time. We walked into Substance Abuse Central without knocking, figuring that if anything private was going on Sydney would have locked the door. We were greeted by a fog of Omani frankincense, but through the pother I discern the form of my prickteasing girlfriend, Olumidé, and wonder what she is doing in here before I am. Absurdly protective, I realise that I am concerned that she has fallen in with a bad crowd. My friends.

The smoke is curling up from a china burner chaffed by a tea light, and Sydney was busying himself fiddling with the molten rock in the brazier, turning it around deftly with his plectrum thumbnail to expose new facets to the heat, as though he was a Venetian glassblower. A golden syrupy strand of frankincense joined his thumbnail to the dish in an amber umbilical composed of pure aroma. Compared to this, even Seth's *Balafre* gave up the fight for recognition.

We all burned joss sticks all the time because there was always some illicit smell to conceal. Sometimes the penetrative smell of damp; rarely cooking; occasionally bodily eruptions, but usually dope. I don't know why we bothered as the smell of joss sticks was like putting up a sign outside your door saying you were smoking marijuana. But it was one of the college's many customs, such as the custom that only scholars were allowed to walk on the scholar's piece; but it was nice to make up new customs, so, in idle moments, we dreamt up new customs or traditions, such as the custom that from next Wednesday all porters should wear bowler hats.

The burning of incense was certainly a custom that had probably started when the Beatles discovered India. I think a lot of people really believed that. I am sure Self-Harming Harry did. There was Christopher Columbus and there was Vasco de Gama and Magellan, Scott of the Antarctic, and all the rest, discovering the Americas, the New World, the South Pole. But the Beatles discovered India for the twentieth century.

"Fuck it!" A glob of molten frankincense had attached itself to Sydney's thumb. He couldn't dislodge it, so he had to endure the pain, waiting for it to cool down. However, frankincense holds its heat, thereby prolonging Sydney's discomfort. Eventually, he stuck his thumb in his mouth to calm it down. "I'm worse than fucking Harry!" he snarled. Then, staring accusingly at his damaged digit, he broke into verse: "He stuck in his thumb, and made it go numb, and said *What a stupid cunt am I!*"

Lyca was sitting on the floor in one of her impossible yoga positions. She must have been quadruple jointed. Burt Sully was there. Sydney had a Morphy Richards electric toaster and, competing against the Omani frankincense was the appetising smell of warm toast. It was apparent that everyone, apart from Seth and I, had been out on the razzle last night and missed breakfast in hall, so Sydney, who knew the recipe for toast, was hosting a late breakfast.

"Mmmm," says Seth, "Is that toast I smell? I'd love a piece of hot, buttered toast, if only to change the air in my palette. My mouth tastes like Bombay Duck!"

"Well, you had certainly better have some toast then, dear boy." Says Sydney, now having left off his worrying the frankincense with the blunt end of a burnt-out matchstick, and vigorously buttering slices of toast as they pop up from the toaster.

Seth bites into the mouth-watering morsel. "Mmmm, mmm, thanks, Sydney. Anyone for swimming today?" Seth is still holding his rolled-up towel from the Birdwood under his arm, so it looks as though he is on his way at this very moment.

"I'm afraid not," announces Sydney. "Duty calls."

"If it's a Sunday," informs Lyca, "and if the sun is shining, Sydney has to clean his fucking car. This is a ceremony that wastes the whole day known as Tantric car wash, because first of all he has to get it all wet, then he has to lather it up with a mild solution of Fairy Liquid, not strong, mind you, so as not to harm the paintwork. He has to use a sponge from the Greek island of Kos, no synthetic crap. Then the suds have to be washed off thoroughly or they corrode the paint. Then the car has to be all chamoised down, but quickly, or it will dry streaky.

"The chamois has to be sourced from the French medieval town of Rocamador, or it will smear. Then he has to rub this fucking wax from the Cornubia tree into it with his bare hands, practically creaming himself off as he fondles the flanks of his car with his second favourite form of resin, after cannabis resin that is. Then he has to buff it off with the red cloth. Not the black cloth, mind you, because that's the microfiber only to be used for the interior trim.

"Then he has to polish all the windows with the Jewish Chronicle. And by the time he's done all that, the day's wasted and it's time for him to get stoned."

"I would really rather you didn't insult my wax!" says Sydney. "It's the most expensive form of resin I've ever come across. It's more expensive than this Omani frankincense or Spanish saffron. And it won't take all day on this occasion, because my new friend, Harry, has agreed to take the day off and help me, so it will only take half a day."

"But surely…" says Burt Sully, champion-to-be of worker's rights: "Harry has to work today?"

"Yes," says Sydney. "Being in the hospitality industry, Harry has to work weekends. Harry has 15 days holiday a year plus Bank Holidays, and he has kindly elected to take a day's unpaid leave today to help me wax the Snipe. Cleaning the windows with newsprint is good current affairs teaching for Harry's syllabus. "

"I'm up for a swim," announces Calypso.

"So am I," jumps in Olumidé, not wanting to be left out, but I am not entirely clear to whom she is grandstanding. I didn't think she even knew how to swim.

"Count me in!" cries Burt.

"I may join you later," announces Sydney, simply as a face-saving way to terminate the topic. He hands me a piece of burnt toast. I see the face of Christ is etched into it like the Turin shroud. No-one else seems to have noticed. When I pop it into my mouth, I feel like I am self-administering the Host.

"By the way," adds Sydney, addressing his words to his Countenance Divine, "you forgot to tell them what I do to the white wall tyres."

**

We are lying on the brown border of shrivelled-up turf edging the pool. From burnt toast to burnt grass. After the border of burnt grass, there is a margin of paving stones, and beyond the paving stones, what is known as a rumble strip. The paving stones are reserved for true sun worshippers, flags hard enough to make your piles bleed, and relentlessly hot. Olumidé's olive skin is looking fabulous in a khaki-coloured bikini.

Strangely, Calypso, who is so quick to take her clothes off indoors, now that we are outdoors, where nudity would be more natural, is wearing a halter neck one-piece swimsuit in powder blue. But it's very high cut up the thighs. I realise that my girlfriend's desire to accompany us to the pool is more about her displaying her unviolated charms in a minute bikini than doing the butterfly or the crawl. But for whose benefit, I ask myself?

Seth is sporting a pair of Vince black and white striped swimming trunks with a belt ending in a plate gold-buckle, featuring a V motif for Vince. An *ubi sunt* brand. He looks like a swimwear advert with his own copy written on him. The parallel black and white stripes are making me go dizzy.

"Take your top off!" I keep stage-whispering to Olumidé. If she would just tell me to fuck off, I would stop. But she is ignoring me. Calypso is lying on her back on the grass. Seth is next to her. Then Seth gets up, adjusts his belted black and white briefs to make sure they don't fall off on impact, and noiselessly slips into the pool like a water vole.

"He's a nepton," declares Calypso, although she remains motionless on her back with her eyes closed. She must have heard Seth disturbing the waters.

"What's a nepton?" asks Olumidé. The same question was on my lips, but I was too vain to articulate it.

"An animal that swims against the current." Calypso educates both of us. Judging by the colour scheme of his trunks, I am thinking the animal is a zebra.

Seth ploughs two full lengths under water holding his breath, then swims a few lengths of crawl, before heaving himself out of the side of the pool with his upper body strength using only one arm, ignoring the convenient steps considerately placed immediately to his side. He throws himself back on his towel, face up, next to Calypso. He is rubbing at his eyes, which I see are red and inflamed.

"Jesus Christ!" he exclaims. "That pool must be 90% chlorine and 10% water!"

"Take your top off," I urge Olumidé. "Look, lots of other girls have their tops off." And it was true. One or two scrubbers did.

Seth was correct. They had just started the pool as the weather had improved suddenly and unexpectedly, and they had shocked it. They should have put a sign up. It was like chemical warfare. Surely, chlorine was a weapon of mass destruction? But no-one bothered in those days. If you went swimming, you expected to come back with verrucas, athlete's foot, crotch rot from the mouldy towel, and to be propositioned in the changing room by your form master. But you didn't expect your eyes to be cremated.

"Flame on!"

"I can't see a fucking thing!" says Seth, rubbing at his eyes, making it worse. "Jesus, and to top it all, the inside of my mouth tastes like the inside of a Turkish tram driver's jockstrap. I'm going to get an ice cream. Anyone else want an ice cream?"

Burt Sully is on the point of raising his hand affirmatively for a Mivi, but just then, before Seth can get up, Calypso pulls down the front of her bathing suit and rolls over on top of Seth on her tummy. She presses both her palms flat on his chest, like she's pinning him down, and glues her mouth to his for a fifteen-second kiss that feels like thirty seconds. Then she rolls off again, and resumes her position lying on her back beside him on the grass, except now her breasts are exposed.

"Wow!" says Seth. "What was that for?"

"I just wanted to find out what the inside of a Turkish tram driver's jockstrap tasted like," says Calypso, licking her lips like the cat that got the cream.

Seth doesn't seem to have a snappy comeback, so he gets to his feet, and still rubbing his smarting eyes, but now also nursing a noticeable hard-on in his Vince's, stumbles off in the direction of the café to find some ice creams.

Unprompted by me, Olumidé takes her top off. "And what *did* it taste like?" she asks Lyca.

"What?" Calypso has pulled her top back up and doesn't have any idea what she's talking about.

"Turkish tram driver's jockstrap," says Olumidé.

Calypso tunes into her for a moment. "Oh," she says, "no different to an Albanian's."

Seth returns with two fistfuls of melting choc ices. He looks like a Dalinian *gelato* vendor. His full frontal hard-on has been downgraded into an *ubi sunt* kind of an erection. I can't get out of my head the notion that the only way that he could have gotten it to subside so quickly was by secreting into his Vince's the erection-numbing choc-ice that he is now offering me.

"Put your top on!" I command Olumidé. But she is in disobedient mode. She reaches out to Seth to take one of his deliquescent confections in her hand, giving him an eyeful. As it melts all over her hand and dribbles down onto her bare tits, obscenely she licks her sticky fist from every angle as though she were auditioning to be the next Cadbury's flake girl. "This is just what the doctor ordered!" pronounces my nurse from Addenbrookes.

Having got everyone's attention, with her left hand she lifts up her right breast and laps the leaking lactose from where it has dripped like candle wax around her nipple. The head of my cock pops out of my Speedos. To cause a distraction from the act of stuffing it back in, I stretch my other hand up to grab one of Seth's choc ices, despite my grave misgivings that it has been secreted in his Vince trunks. He notices the mark on my forearm, and he grabs my arm staring intently at the ∞.

"How long have you had that?" he says.

I am struggling to answer his question, because I had forgotten I had it myself. I thought I had already showed it to him when we were on the roof of Gisborne Court burning bin liners; but maybe that never happened. I know I had thought I had imagined Set pressing it onto my arm, but I thought that was all in my mixed up head and not for real. I am trying to remind myself when the strange lemniscate mark first appeared.

Spud's spectacles are sitting on his forehead, denoting fierce concentration. The object of his concentration is the markings on Seth. "You know," says Spud, "if you don't mind me making personal remarks, but I do know that you are keen to solve the riddle of your writings…have you noticed they are grouped in sets of four?"

"Yes," says Seth, "we've done that, been there, got the t-shirt. We supposed they were semaphore and tried cracking the code that way. Didn't get us anywhere. Remains a riddle."

"Have you heard of Georg Cantor?"

"The German philosopher?"

"No, you're thinking of Immanuel Kant. George Ferdinand Ludwig Philipp Cantor was a German mathematician who died early on in this century."

"And what does he have to say for himself when he's at home?" asked Seth, his interest beginning to be roused. Fortunately, this turn in the conversation is making my cock slither back down into my trunks and behave itself.

"He invented Set Theory. It's a branch of mathematical logic that studies sets. I mention it for two reasons. Firstly, your markings seem to be gathered in groups of four, which Cantor would regard as sets."

"Yes…"

"But secondly, the culmination of his work on the Set Theory was that he posited a hierarchy of infinite sets according to their cardinal numbers. He appears to have been mildly epileptic or at least bipolar. He said that the Set Theory was dictated to him by God Himself. He was ridiculed at the time, but now everyone accepts Set Theory and it's on the maths syllabus if you read maths at a sufficiently high level.

"Set Theory was applied philosophically and demonstrates how one infinity can be greater than another infinity. Cantor was obsessed with the conviction that he could measure infinity. He came up with the notion that there needn't be a *One Size Fits All Infinity*. There are an infinite number of infinities. But the reason I am being so impolite as to bore you with all this is because the only marking on you that isn't grouped in a set of four is the signature marking on your toe, which, not being grouped, is irregular and therefore stands out from the rest.

"I am wondering to myself if it is just a coincidence that the one symbol that isn't contained within a set is itself the symbol for Infinity; you know, in the same way that an artist might leave hidden clues in his painting to help you understand deeper meanings. Indeed at various periods in history, artists had to conceal their true meaning or they would have been burned at the stake."

"Wow!" exclaims Burt. "That's the longest I've ever heard Spud talking. So we must be onto something."

I am pleased to report that, after this exegesis on Set theory, there is no trace left of the massy construction that was my erection. *Look on my works, ye mighty, and despair…Round the decay of that colossal wreck…*

Seth glances at the Weapon of Mass Consumption in his cut-off denim shorts. It's not a pretty sight, so he returns his attention to Spud.

"Where do we go from here?" asks Seth.

"Set Theory is ludicrously complicated," explains Spud. "I couldn't even begin to describe it to you. Your head would pop. What I would suggest is that if Nick here could take some photos of you and print them out for me, I could work on them back in my set and see where that takes us. Any objections?"

"None at all," says Seth.

To get the shot, I am going to have to stand up; but I'm still not quite in a respectable state to do so. Maybe if I stare at Burt instead of Olumidé, it will go down. In a flash of inspiration, I decide to roll over onto my tummy, getting closer to Seth, so that the casual bystander would assume I was just scoping out my shot.

Just then, before I can unholster my camera from its leather carry case, Sydney arrives late with Self-Harming Harry.

Harry, who is accustomed to slicing up his own skin, instantly takes in the situation, noticing that a guy with ∞ written on his big toe (Seth) is visually interrogating the forearm of a guy similarly marked (me), and he defuses the situation by saying, "Well, Snap!" I have a sense of *déjà vu*, but I'm not sure if the first déjà on the roof with the bin bags ever happened. If the thing with the real person on the roof never happened, the strange correlative would seem to be that the thing with the imaginary person when he burned the lemniscate into my arm, did happen.

Sensing that Harry's arrival means that Sydney has also arrived, Calypso enters the conversation.

"Have you finished rubbing massage oil into the hearse?" she asks.

"I have indeed," he replies. "We finished early. This guy," nodding towards Self-Harming Harry, "is a bloody miracle! He's so strong he practically lifted the engine block out with his bare hands, and he's done the timing, the compression ratios, the spark plugs. All I meant to do was valet it. She's running like new again!"

"How did you know how to do that?" asks Spud, keen to ascertain if Harry might be of any use to him in his own engineering endeavours.

"There was a Haines Workshop manual behind the seat," explains Harry. "I don't understand all the words. But I understand the pictures. The manual is mainly…"

Lyca supplies the word he is searching for: "Pictorial."

"Yes, I guess so."

"Maybe you can understand that lot," says Burt nodding his head in the general direction of all the runes etched onto Seth's body.

"We need to give her a good run to blast the carburettors out," pronounces Sydney. "We'll fine tune the details later." Then, noticing my girlfriend, topless: "Nice wobs! Are you doing anything later on?"

"How do you mean?" she asks in her best Mumbles accent.

"A few of us will be seeking to raise the god Pan after dinner," he says matter-of-factly, as though he were saying we were off for a kebab. "Your boyfriend, old Nick there, I very much trust, will be on hand to document the proceedings on celluloid, if not participate himself. I would be delighted if you were able to assist Calypso in the ceremonials."

"I don't need any assistance," pronounces Calypso. I swear her lips never parted.

"I'm working nights tonight," says Olumidé. I breathe a sigh of relief.

"We all are, my dear," remarks Sydney. "Needs must when the devil drives. Why don't you throw a little sickie and drop by my set at the witching hour?" Then, finally acknowledging what he has been pretending does not exist for so long, he takes in the script covering Seth's body. He is genuinely surprised. He has been trying so hard for so long to ignore Seth that now that he actually condescends to consider him, it is circuit-popping.

I guess the rest of us had seen a wrist here, a glimpse of lower torso there; but here was Sydney, for the first time, coming to terms with the full text of Seth's body, naked save for his Vince Swimming Trunks, and ignorant of the hand who had made those markings.

To Sydney's eternal credit, now that he has finally seen it, he does not shy away. He does not look in the other direction, as one does when tramps and junkies approach you, or the bloke trying to sell you a copy of The *Big Issue*. He does not ignore him, afraid that if he pays Seth too much attention someone might think him a cottager. No. He rolls over until his eyeballs are centimetres away from the markings, and then he prods his digits at them as though he were some Doubting Thomas, and he traces the outlines of the runes with his index finger.

His lips are moving, like he is reading to himself. But in a tongue he does not himself understand. The dead man's Bible written in the language of rooks. It reminds me of the prayers I've seen when I've been invited into Jewish synagogues, when everybody is davening and bowing their heads and mouthing unheard meaning under their breath because they all know the words, so it doesn't matter that the listeners can't hear or understand the shibboleths. They are tuning in to a shared ideology. Turn up; tune in; drop out, as we used to say,

Sydney's finger is tracing the characters on Seth. "I haven't seen this since my Bar mitzvah," he says. "It's the old Hebrew script as we learnt it, but it's like it was when I had to read it from the Torah. The vowels should be here underneath the consonants, but they're not there. I guess there was no room for them."

"Meaning what?" asks Olumidé.

"Meaning what indeed?" says Sydney. "That is the question. He's like a fucking Sphinx! What you have here, is a treatise of some sort, but it's written entirely in consonants. The vowels that should go underneath the consonants are missing. This is normal in biblical Hebrew. But in biblical Hebrew, there are only a few hundred words, so you can usually figure out the vowels, just like Seth told us he could figure out the set texts from the names of the gods and heroes. This essay is far more extensive than the Bible. It's modern, but without the vowels, it could take years to decipher." To Seth: "Would you mind awfully rolling over?"

Obligingly, Seth rolls onto his tummy, leaving Sydney to try his textual analysis upon Seth's back. But the back is without inscription, so he rolls over again.

"Do you need a piss?" asks Sydney.

Seth considers his Vince's for any leakage. He is confused by the directness of the question. At length, he answers simply: "No. Why do you ask?"

"Because," says Sydney, "this may take some time."

There is a section of script on Seth's forehead, consisting of two short words, almost hidden beneath the hair line, as though it contained hidden knowledge that the author only wanted to be revealed as Seth grew older and his dark hair receded. There are two more words below his omphalos; but apart from these, the author has resisted the temptation to cover the huge slab of his chest or his back in the hieroglyphics, which is what would have been easiest. All of the writing is written on his outer extremities: the outside of his arms and legs, his fingers, his neck, and the signature on his big toe. As though he is supposed to be viewed from a particular perspective.

Sydney beavers away at his task until there is no more warmth in the sun, and Seth, eager for answers, lies motionless, co-operating. Sydney inspects; he frowns; he prods; he licks the end of his pencil (an unpleasant trait he seems to have picked up from Ingram) and makes notes, arranging and rearranging the characters on the back of his copy of this week's JC. It crosses my mind that Sydney has no idea what he is doing and this is simply an attempt to grandstand and impose control upon Seth.

Eventually, Sydney is beaten. "The good news," he says, "is that I can inform you that whatever is written on the front of your left leg is in old Hebrew, but I mean, very old, like The Dead Sea Scrolls. And I can inform you that it is very important. The bad news is, it's encrypted. As if it wasn't difficult enough to decipher anyway, it seems to be encoded, and I think the answers to the code may be found in the Pentateuch. "

"What's the Pentateuch?" asks Seth.

"Penta mean five," begins Sydney.

"As in the Pentagram," adds Calypso, swiftly turning the Holy Bible on its head by association with the sign of the devil.

"Penta is five, and teuch is vessels," continues Sydney. "The five vessels, or five books of the law dictated by God to Moses. It's the Torah. The first five books of the Old Testament. I had to practice them for my Bar mitzvah and read to the congregation from the Torah. But, at my Bar mitzvah, the rabbi he said to me, 'Sydney Syzygy', he said-". Sydney is speaking in a cartoon Jewish accent. 'Sydney, up until this day, you have come to *schul* with your mother and your father. Now you are a man. You make your own decisions.' And I haven't been to *schul* since; and I haven't read any Hebrew since."

"So why do you think the code is in the Pentateuch?" asks Olumidé, eager for any excuse to prolong the conversation so she can carry on staring at Seth's musculature before he puts his shirt back on. Seth is sitting up on his elbows now.

"Well, I understand enough to follow the letters that keep repeating: ג G is Gimmel for Genesis; ה E is He for Exodus, ל L is Lamed for Leviticus, נ N is Nun for Numbers, and ד D is Dalet for Deuteronomy. The reason it seems to stand out is because ה is the only time the author uses any vowels here. But Hebrew is written from right to left, as is the rest of the Hebrew text. But whenever this G,E,L,N,D sequence occurs, it's written from left to right, and it's preceded each time by αντι, which is Greek, written round the right way."

"Meaning what?" enquires Seth.

"Anti," explains Sydney.

"Anti-Bible?"

"Yes, Seth," nods Sydney. "And as if to emphasise the point, it's always written the wrong way round. I think it's demonic, like inverting the crucifix. It's the five books of the Law as dictated by God to Moses on Mount Sinai, but written backwards."

Seth has stood up and is climbing into his track suit bottoms, maybe because it is getting cold, or maybe because he is ashamed of the uncleanliness of what is written upon his person, the same way that Adam and Eve were okay going around naked until they acquired Knowledge.

"That's about as far as I can take it, man. If you want to go further, we're going to need some sort of Talmudic scholar."

"Where am I going to find one of those?"

"You're in Cambridge, Seth. There's got to be every sort of scholar imaginable here. I can't be the only yid in Cambridge. There must be someone studying to become a rabbi."

"And how am I supposed to find him out of the thousands of pupils here?"

Sydney wants to help Seth, because he perceives that Seth's text may further his own calling of summoning the devil. It's as though the reversed religious writing adorning Seth's skin corresponds to Sydney's inverted mezuzah. "I'll get to the bottom of this," he says, tapping Seth with his rolled up copy of the JC for emphasis. "Either I'll telephone the Jewish Chronicle and ask them where the nearest rabbi is, or I'll get Pfläfflin to raise enquiries amongst other fellows and directors of studies. There must be lots of people reading the Bible and archaeology and stuff like that, and someone's bound to know a classical Hebrew scholar. "

"But surely," says Burt Sully, "you don't have to have a Cambridge University degree to become a man of the cloth?"

"Shame upon you, Burt!" says Calypso. "You think that a rabbi should be less qualified than a vet or an engineer?"

"And before you know it," continues Sydney, "Job Done! That's your left leg. You realise that the other parts of your body are written in different languages?"

"It's not all as difficult as that," remarks Harry.

Out of the mouths of babes, as they say. Harry is looking at Seth's hairline, and he is doing that thing again where he makes shutters out of his fingers and opens and closes them. What did Spud call it? A zoetrope. Everyone has gone silent and is looking expectantly at Harry. Harry had never stripped down to his swimmers because the last thing he wants to do is expose his skin to the sun's rays and tan it.

"Those two sections," says Harry, moving the long fingers of his two hands before his eyes and gazing through the moving gaps in them. He is indicating short pieces of script, one written on Seth's forehead up by the hairline, and the other on his belly, beneath his naval. "They're in English."

Sydney moves closer to inspect them. "This one on his head?" he asks. Harry nods. "And this one on his tummy?" A second nod.

"Well, if it's English, the top one says DNE WOLLAHS and the lower one says DNE PEED. What the fuck is that supposed to mean?"

"You're not looking at it the right way," explains Harry. "I've seen it before, today—here."

"Here?" queries Sydney. "In the swimming pool."

Everyone is looking up and down for clues when the clues are written on Seth.

"It's under your nose," explains Harry. "Look what's written on the paving stones." And he points it out.

SHALLOW END

DEEP END

"Fuck me!" exclaims Sydney. "He's right. We were just looking at it upside down!"

"Do you understand any more of it?" asks Calypso.

Harry does this thing with making shutters out of his fingers and looking at Seth through them as he opens and closes them like Venetian blinds.

"Sure," pronounces Harry self-evidently. "He's an Instruction Manual."

"Am I some sort of joke?" asks Seth.

"I don't know about joke, my friend," says Sydney. "But you're certainly a riddle."

As we thread our way back to our rooms, I am thinking to myself: *How to keep an Irishman amused for hours; see other wall.*

It's not a riddle. What was the word I used earlier? Ambigram: SWIMS.

Ingram is just shaking his head in that way he has as if he is really despairing of us. "Deep End," he says, "Shallow End! What do you think he has written down there?" nodding in the direction of Seth's tracksuit bottoms. "Bell End?"

"Instruction Manual for what?" I ask Harry as we are walking back across Parker's Piece, past Reality Checkpoint.

"An Instruction Manual for the Eternal Night," Harry whispers to me.

"Can you really read him?"

"I need an apparatus," he says.

"What sort of apparatus?" I ask.

"Something to read him with as he is spinning around," says Harry. "You know, like Spud said; like in the movies when the wheels on your bike look like they're going around backwards."

"A zoetrope."

"We need to build a zoetrope big enough to put him in, and then he has to spin around one way whilst the pinwheel spins the other."

Stairway to Heaven

Sydney and I find ourselves outside Millers Music Store in Sussex Street.

"Nick," he says, "do you know that this music shop has been here in Cambridge for longer than some of the redbrick colleges? Shall we check it out? Shall we just go and have a little practice ahead of Ingram's musical *soiree*? A warm-up."

"God! It's tonight! I'd forgotten."

Inside, Sydney threads somnambulistically and unwaveringly towards a Fender Stratocaster as though it had summoned him into the shop. The middle aged assistant glides towards him as though he's on rollers.

"Mr Worthing," he introduces himself. "May I help you?"

"Mind if I try it, Mr Worthing?" Sydney nods his head in the direction of the Fender.

"Go ahead, sir," he says. "Let me just make a few adjustments."

We watch as the assistant hooks Sydney up to the amp and then inserts the headphone jack in the socket and mounts the bins over Sydney's ears. Sydney catches my eye and looks down. I follow his gaze and observe the toe of his stacked leather Cuban-heeled Chelsea boot mischievously removing the jack from the amp. Whatever Sydney plays at Millers is supposed to stay in Sydney's head, but it's going to wake the dead. I look from left to right and take in the infant prodigy frizz-headed crypto-Mozart wunderkind auditioning the harpsichord in the corner, his eyes closed in bliss as the music he is making washes over him. He's in for a nasty surprise.

Sydney's plectrum nail strikes the metal strings and Jimmy Page's composition immediately shakes the store. The assistant is practically knocked off his feet. The ersatz prodigy on the harpsichord looks as if someone has shat in his earphones.

"For God's sake, man!" exclaims the assistant, grasping the neck of the guitar so as to silence its strings. "Have you no respect?"

"Well, as a matter of fact," begins Sydney. "The answer to that one is probably *No*; but, pray tell me, what is it that we are supposed to be respecting today?"

"It's 12 noon," explains Mr Worthing, gesticulating at the wall clock. "Cambridge is supposed to be observing 60 seconds silence for the 60 missing choristers."

"To lose one chorister, Mr Worthing," begins Sydney, "may be regarded as a misfortune. To lose 60, smacks of a paedophile ring to me."

"Why is it," the assistant appeals to me, apparently having despaired of Sydney, "that every time someone comes in here and asks to try out a Stratocaster, they launch into *Stairway to Heaven*?"

"Because it is," says Sydney, "to the guitar *what the quick brown fox jumps over the lazy dog* is to the typewriter keyboard."

"What's that?" asks the assistant, suddenly displaced from being in charge of his shop to being out of his depth.

"It's a mnemonic," says Sydney. "I love mnemonics. Don't you?"

"What's a mnemonic?" queries the assistant.

"I could tell you," says Sydney, "But it wouldn't necessarily be helpful. You might find it ambiguous."

"Why?" asks the assistant.

"Because," teases Sydney, "as Jimmy Page says, *sometimes words have two meanings.*"

After a pause, the assistant asks: "Are you going to take it?"

"Mr Worthing, I was thinking of it," says Sydney, "but I have decided that I am going to play classical tonight, thank you." He hands the axe back to the assistant and then says to me: "Ingram's expecting me to kick up rowdy so that he can moan and complain and ask me if I've been smoking that wacky-baccy again, as he puts it. So I think I'll just disappoint him."

"Why change the habits of a lifetime?" is all I can say.

Fit Happens

As they say, *Fit Happens!* But I am learning to control it. Like the superhero, GentleMan, inside me, I find I am able to harness the gamma oscillations in my head and put them to good use. If it's going to be a full-blown seizure, I think about nice, ordered things like the Birdwood, and I have mixed success in warding it off. Of that, I am not fully in control. But there is an intermediate state of reverie that I find I can bring on, and in that reverie I meet up with old imaginary friends like the god Set, friends who are more reliable than the wankers that real life has to offer. The trouble is that I find I am drawn back towards this state of reverie more and more often, so that it is becoming a kind of alternative reality for me.

But when it's so much better than the dull diurnal round, why not, eh? Bring it on!

In my dreams, I find I can take control. I wake up frequently in the night, but when I go back to sleep I can rewind my last dream and resume from where I left off. I can conjure up a dream sequence that lasts over hours or even days, but when I wake up and consult the luminous watch on my wrist, it is only minutes later than when I woke up the last time. I can make one night last for an eternity. I am living in a double time scheme.

I saw Eternity the other night…

My dreams have a pause button. Alas, my nightmares do not.

When Burt comes into an important meeting, such as with his tutor or director of studies, he removes his luminous Timex watch from his wrist and sets it down on the table, as if to say that he is committing to this meeting and will give it his full attention. I would be worried that I would trance off and forget my watch. They advertise the Timex watch on ITV. Someone fastens it to a propeller on an outboard motor.

I ask you, why would anybody want to do that? The motor is lowered into the sea; the engine is gunned up and off the boat goes as fast as it can. After a quick spin around the bay, they kill the motor and crank the outboard back up, and through the moisture droplets clinging to its glass, you can see the sweep second hand still keeping good time. Then the voiceover bloke growls: *And his Timex watch is still going.*

If I am expecting to have sex, I take my luminous watch off my wrist and tie it around my cock for half an hour or so beforehand. I read instructions on the Birdwood door that the radioactivity in the luminous paint will deaden the sperm count in my ejaculate so that I am firing blanks for the next few hours. This is a very useful form of birth control, especially for Catholics.

Time and the bell have buried the day
The black cloud carries the sun away.

"Where do you get all this homespun crap from?" the god Set asks me.

"It's written on the bog doors in the Birdwood," I inform him. "The sum of all human knowledge is there."

"And the bog door told you to wrap a Timex around your lunchbox before sex?"

"Right on."

"In the future, which we are about to write, all knowledge will be shared digitally. Shall I tell you what? Let's start writing the future now. Let's make the very first entry in this huge harvest of human knowledge that will be shared by the online community. The very first helpful hint that we will record in the endless register of things will be your useful tip about wrapping a wristwatch around your willy as a form of birth control."

"What's this register of things called in the future?"

"Let's call it Wankipedia."

"Wankipedia?"

"I am joking. It is called The Great Book of Thoth. It's the book that you must build up and pass on to the person waiting at the point where the parallel lines meet."

"And what happens if I don't make it to that point?"

"I am afraid that you will be locked inside this book forever. Never able to climb out."

Of course, Olumidé found it. I hadn't expected her to stuff her hand down my pants so soon. I thought I would have time to excuse myself and put the watch back on my wrist.

"Nick," she goes, "why are you wearing your watch, you know, down there?"

"I got dressed in the dark," I lied.

If I had been Sydney, I would have said "*Tempus fugit!*" And if Olumidé had been me, she would have gotten it and laughed. But I am not Sydney and she is not me, so the words would have been wasted. She removed the watch deftly, working by touch alone; never letting go of my cock, like that trick where the magician pulls two solid metal rings apart. Then she told me to put it back on my wrist.

"Has your watch got a second hand?" she asked.

"Yes."

"Time this," she said.

"Forty seconds," I said, as she wiped her hand with the Kleenex.

Digital sex. Without full penetration. Alas, Olumidé and I were destined never to know if this form of Birdwood birth control worked or not.

In Max Pfläfflin's little session this afternoon, we're discussing a 15th century poem of only some 616 lines written by a Scotsman, Robert Henryson, *The Testament of Cresseid*. The content is appalling, and one wonders what sadistic pleasure Pfläfflin derives from making us read this shit. It's a kind of misogynistic sequel to Shakespeare's Troilus and Cressida, where the once beautiful Cressida is portrayed as a syphilitic whore who goes blind and becomes leprous and ekes out her days physically disintegrating in a leper colony. She has to go out begging with a little bell and a clapper so that gentlefolk hear the ringing and the clapping and don't venture anywhere near the lepers.

Troilus and Cressida were like Antony and Cleopatra, lovers of epic proportions, the kind of love that can span continents and bridge the years, love that has no bounds. But Henryson is only interested in reducing his female lead to abject misery.

Troilus, her former fabled lover, just then, is riding by on his horse leading the garrisons of Troy. She is so disfigured with syphilitic sores and leprosy that Troilus doesn't know it's his former lover, although there is some faint glimmer of recognition that he can't quite place in his memory. Cressida would have recognised him, because he's still as handsome as ever. But the syphilis has left her blind. So he rides on by. Two ships passing in the night.

But then something about her prompts him to an act of charitable kindness. He takes off his belt full of gold and gives it to the lepers, and then he rides on by. The blind Cressida enquires of the identity of their benefactor, and when another leper tells her it was Troilus, she is overcome with emotion and dies.

I find this little poem deeply disturbing. I keep waking up in the night, its horrifying images leaking out of my head, and feel nothing but resentment for Pfläfflin who put them there. As I say, I can control my dreams, but not my nightmares. The blind girl in the Testament ringing her bell keeps coming back to me and forms an association with my lost mother and my own little bell that I could do without. I could very happily have gone through life without reading this sanctimonious proselytizing little poem by some Calvinist Scots cunt. Nothing would have been missing.

I have to wonder whether the Proctor has had Max Pfläfflin in for questioning about the missing choir boys.

When I turn over in the night, by the radioactive glow of my watch, I can pick out my little Tinkerbell, the hoop-skirted silver ballerina that will summon my mother. But when I reach out for the bell, like the little fairy she is, there is nothing there. But the tintinnabulation keeps ringing in my head.

Art in the Home

"Are you serious?" asks Pfläfflin looking up from the essay my manager, Set, wrote whilst I was off on my reverie.

"What's wrong with it?" I enquire. To tell you the truth, I hadn't even bothered to read what he had written before I handed it in. I just accepted it when he had told me that the future was all about plagiarism and let him get on with it. I had my hands full planning my Grand Entrance.

Pfläfflin gave me *The Testament of Cresseid.* I'll retaliate by filling his head with *Art in the Home.*

"I asked you to write an essay entitled *Art in the Home.* This was to be an expository essay about William Morris." He continued to pronounce his W's as V's—Villiam Morris. His voice cracks on the second syllable of expository. "Expository. That means a factual essay, not an imaginative work of fiction. At Peterhouse, you are reading English Literature. You are not writing it! Your five thousand words that you handed in entitled *Art in the Home* is an imaginative work about your brother, Arthur, in the mental home!"

I can see he's really annoyed, and thinks I am taking the piss. For a moment, I fear he is going to consign it to the flames, Sydney style. But, after staring at it for a while as though it is something he has used to wipe a mess off his shoe with, he just thrusts the papers back at me, and rasps through his clenched teeth, "*Ghost of a Flea.*" So the reprise is over and we're back on the same old same old.

I decide to indulge myself in one of my little reveries. I lower my lids and let it wash over me whilst Pfläfflin burbles on.

On the Birdwood door this morning when I performed my ablutions, the following words were carved:

If the doors of perception were cleansed, everything would appear to man as it is, Infinite.

I had committed these fine words to memory, my thought for the day fresh off the shit house door, and proceeded towards my meeting with my director of studies.

I am secretly fitting in his Barcelona chair and thinking to myself that I should do Radio 4's *Thought for the Day.* Instead of their usual diet of vicars and the occasional rabbi for diversity's sake, aged anchorman, John Humphreys, could interview me.

Today's Thought for the Day is coming to us from the Birdwood and is curated by the God Set. Mighty one, what words of wisdom do you have for us this morning?

"If the doors of perception were cleansed everything would appear to man as it is, Infinite," I pronounce sagely.

Everyone else is looking around at me as though I am the man who ordered rare meat in the macrobiotic restaurant. I realise that I must have been talking out loud in my little reverie. I search from eye to eye for clues. After a pause of 30 seconds that seems like 30 minutes, Dr Max Pfläfflin gives me an enquiring look as though he is waiting for the rest of the quote and says: "And?"

"What do you mean And?" I question.

"Nick, you are supposed to be studying the works of William Blake. You have just delivered a very well-known quote from Blake's Parables of Hell in *The Marriage of Heaven and Hell*. As our renowned Blake scholar in this group, I assumed you were going to impart some useful information to the rest of us."

Sydney saves me: "The full quote," he says, "is *if the doors of perception were cleansed, everything would appear to man as it is, Infinite. For man has closed himself up, till he sees all things thro' narrow chinks of his cavern.* It's one of Calypso's favourite quotes. She uses it in her seminars.

"The reason everyone knows the quote (except, it seems, Nick, who is our Emeritus Blake Scholar) is because the rock group, The Doors, named themselves after it. However, whether or not Jim Morrison even read Blake is dubious, because it has also come down to us via Aldous Huxley's short story *The Doors of Perception* which describes his experience on a mescaline trip."

It's only when we arrive at the penultimate word in Sydney's little address on the doors of perception that I realise Sydney's interest: he approaches Blake via mescaline.

Clearly, Pfläfflin doesn't want to discuss anything as modern as Huxley, so he cuts off further discussion by wearily consulting his watch and announcing: "Time's up."

I roll up the rigmarole of my essay and exeunt with Sydney. *Art in the Home*! Fucking Set!

Once safely outside, I ask Sydney where mescaline fits into the great hierarchy of Class A drugs.

"It's peyote, a psychedelic drug, similar to LSD or psilocybin. It induces altered thinking processes, including altered sense of time. The user may experience checkerboard effects, pinstripes, recurrent patterns, multicolour pixels, angular spikes and fractals."

"What's a fractal?"

"Nick, I have just given you a list of experiences associated with mescaline all of which are highly deleterious to your epileptic inclinations. Why explore fractals?"

"What's a fractal?" I persist.

"A fractal is a recurrent pattern: a simple pattern that under the effects of the drug can become very complex; like shaking up a kaleidoscope. Aldous Huxley described it as a vision of stained glass illuminated from behind the eyelids."

"Far out, far fucking out! Where can I get some mescaline?"

"Why do you think the buttons on my loon pants are this colour, dear boy? I have cyanide stitched into my lapel seams for particularly desperate occasions, but my middle button is peyote for wilder occasions. Here."

He plucks one of the buttons off his trousers and raises it to his nose as though he had just picked a flower. Then he gives it to me. "You might as well start chewing now," he says, "It will last for hours. It's bitter. Suck a sugar cube or something as soon as you can."

"What's the worst that can happen?" I ask him as I pop the pill.

"My trousers could fall down," is all he says.

Thorough De-Coke

"The Super Snipe needs to stretch her legs," announces Sydney, referring to his beloved motor. "Harry says her carburettors are coked-up with pottering around Cambridge traffic all the time. She needs a good blasting out on the motorway."

"Where shall we go?" asks Harry.

"To the seaside," pronounces Calypso.

"But surely…" begins Burt, "there's no sea anywhere near Cambridge."

"That is the whole point," informs Sydney, rifling through his library. "We need to get away from Cambridge."

Finding his *AA Book of the Road*, he locates Cambridge in the index, opens up to the corresponding page, and butterflies the book with the palms of his hands. "Thumb tack?" he enquires.

Lyca passes him a drawing pin from his desk drawer.

"Thread?"

Sightless, she passes him some darning cotton from the same drawer. It is wound around a card with *Hotel Ista, Amritsar* written on it. He ties the thread to the thumbtack and plunges the thumb tack through the very heart of Cambridge with the commitment of a vampire hunter thrusting a stake into the undead. He then attempts unsuccessfully and inaccurately to perform an orbit of Cambridge with the uniform length of the cotton thread.

"What's he doing?" asks Harry. "Playing Find the Donkey?"

"He's trying to find the blue bit on his map that's nearest to Cambridge," informs Spud. "But he's not doing it very well. Here, use my compass."

Spud Mullins is the only person we know who would carry a hazardously sharp pair of compasses in his shirt pocket where it could shear his nipple off at the least provocation. But they have in the past come in useful as roach clips. Harry might harm himself on purpose, but only Spud would recklessly expose himself in this way to the risk of an involuntary piercing of his mammary papilla.

Sydney takes the compass and inserts a red pencil from his wooden pencil case in the hole; he then repeats the encircling manoeuvre, but not before he has stabbed himself in the thumb and cursed mildly. The compass describes a radius in smeared blood around Cambridge. The point where the blue area on the map signifying the sea is nearest to the centre of the circle is Wells-next-the-Sea. Sydney looks dubious, but then, as if for emphasis, a large, sticky glob of blood from his stabbed finger drops prophetically smack centre upon that very destination.

"It's Wells-next-the-Sea," he informs us, mystified at his own prescience. And then, sucking his thumb: "Blood marks the spot." He looks at the scale in the bottom left page, measuring it against his stigmatised thumb, and announces that it's about 70 miles away.

"Nowhere in England is more than 80 miles from the sea," Spud informs us helpfully. He is a veritable Golconda of useless information.

I seem to remember that Sydney had once mentioned Wells-next-the-Sea to me, but I can't remember in what context. Apart from that, none of us have ever heard of the place. We know the beaches of Brighton, Devon and Cornwall. Some of us have even heard of Portmeiron because of the long-running Prisoner TV series starring Patrick McGoohan. But no-one seems familiar with Wells-next-the-Sea.

"So, it will be a proper adventure then," observes Sydney. "Since none of you have ever heard of the fucking place. So we'll be needing lots of supplies."

By which, I assume he means dope and alcohol.

After the others have drifted off, Seth slides down off his customary perch on the vaulting horse and sidles up to Sydney with the demeanour of someone who doesn't actually like Sydney, but is resolved to entering into a symbiotic relationship with him. Sydney has convinced Seth that Seth needs Sydney's assistance in decrypting the riddle he wears upon his person.

"Did you have any luck finding a Talmudic scholar?" Seth enquires, his voice lowered.

"Well, yes and no," says Sydney. "I found the ideal bloke, except he was Ashkenazi, which would not be my personal preference. Anyway, leaving aside my own preferences, I contacted him, but he says he only comes out for schnicklings. Are you circumcised, Seth?"

"No," says Calypso.

For once, Sydney is lost for words. The great control freak is no longer in control. Regaining composure, he tries to turn it into a joke: "Would you like to be? I mean, we can get the Ashkenazi out on a pretext."

"Don't you think I've been cut up enough?" he asks.

Sydney doesn't follow why Seth seems to be aiming the rhetorical question at Calypso.

Back in my own set, I make myself a mug of Maxwell House and sit down to a first reading of my essay *Art in the Home*. It's a fucking gas! I should enter it for the Booker Prize.

The Music Evening at Trinity Hall

Ingram has organised what he calls a Symposium at Trinity Hall. He takes himself very seriously. The format of the evening is that we will already have dined in Hall, so there will be no need for Ingram to worry his pretty head about catering arrangements. There will be red and white wine and all attendees have to do what Ingram calls "a piece" or "a turn". Ideally, that means a musical rendition on their chosen instrument, but when Ingram learns to his genuine and bottomless disbelief that not all of us have mastered an instrument, with the clemency of Caesar, he relaxes the rules so that other forms of artistic contribution will be tolerated. He describes this bending of the rules as a derogation.

I don't own a musical instrument, so I am clutching my Nikon for support. If I am required to perform, I will assert my own authority by requiring everyone to assemble for a group photograph.

To soak up the wine and the better to demonstrate his sophistication, Ingram has assembled some Libby's tinned pineapple chunks surmounted by cubes of cheddar cheese affixed with toothpicks. He has also emptied a tub of taramosalata into one dish and into another shaken out the broken contents of a past-its-sell-by-date Ritz Crackers packet because he couldn't get his hands on any pitta bread. Bear in mind that we are still in 1972, in culinary terms, the Dark Ages, when people believed spaghetti grew on spaghetti trees. In those days, if you wanted to buy olive oil, you had to go to the chemist and convince him that your ear infection was sufficiently serious. Then he would give you a prescription for it. Yes, England's largest distributor of olive oil was the NHS.

Unfortunately, the only way I could face such an evening was with the assistance of Sydney's bitter button. I am wondering how long it will be before its effects kick in and my eyes turn into stained glass windows.

Ingram's room is a complete contrast from Sydney's. Whereas Sydney's is an Aladdin's cave of *objets trouveé*, Ingram's room by contrast is sparse. There is his single bed, one arm chair, one stool, a chair by his desk for writing on, a few lawbooks, an upright piano and a beanbag. His guitar case stands upright in a corner. His single monastic bed has no headboard and a candlewick bedspread. Where Sydney has a tapestry of a maiden and a unicorn on his wall, the only ornament to Ingram's wall is a big sign saying *No smoking*, and if one had wanted to smoke, there are no ashtrays, although there is a sink and washstand beside the bed, which one wouldn't want to use, as it is bound to be the place where Ingram pisses when he can't be bothered to walk down the corridor at night.

There aren't enough chairs for everybody. I am lying on the floor atop Ingram's bean bag, presenting myself as one presents oneself to one's gynaecologist for a proctorial examination. Ingram obviously thinks every cool home should have a bean bag. I am just thinking *How the fuck am I ever going to get out of this again?*

Also, I feel a splitting headache coming on, and maybe even a little fit. I think it is all the parallel lines in Ingram's room, as if he is trying to impose order on everything. The mescaline appears to be accentuating their regularity. The few objects in the room seem to be arranging themselves in grids and checkerboards. Ingram has these wooden Venetian blinds from Habitat that he is obviously very proud of, so he has them lowered during daylight hours, although he keeps striding over to them and tugging the string to open them a crack, *rere regardant*, and then snap them shut again.

I find that if I stare at the blinds for more than a few seconds, I feel queer. Also, Ingram wears this pinstripe suit most of the time, although this evening, in a concession to Boho chic he is only wearing the jacket with blue denim jeans below. But it still gives me a headache.

When he tugs on the cord as though summoning his butler, the blinds revolve open, but as Ingram's room is in a basement, all one sees, when he parts the shutters, are the rows of iron railings outside, painted black with gold dagger motifs mounted on top. It's like living in a jail. I find myself focussing unwillingly on the horizontal parallel blinds and the vertical parallel iron railings beyond, and my brain thinks it has to make sense of this, like the puzzles in *The Rainy Day Book for Boys*, where you have to stare at the bird until it ends up in the cage, or at the two lines that look to be of different lengths, but are in fact the same.

This makes the cogs in my cerebral cortex revolve like his blinds, and if I then abandon my perusal of Ingram's inanimate objects and look to Ingram for light relief, I find I am staring at the parallel pinstripes of his suit jacket, which is the final twist of the blade in my skull; the daggers that started life mounted atop the iron railings, penetrate into Ingram's room through his wooden blinds, become incarnate in his infernal jacket, and drive themselves one by one into my cranium. I want to get out of his set, but I have only just arrived, so I close my eyes and try to imagine the sloshing and dancing shadows of the Birdwood in a hopeless attempt to fend off the inevitable. I should have listened to Sydney's sage advice and not taken his shilling.

What you have got to understand, because I appreciate some of you will be reading these journals many years in the future, is that in those days, people liked the Beatles or the Rolling Stones in the same way as they liked AC/DC or Marvel Comics, and some teenybopper girls aped the symptoms of Beatlemania. But these groups weren't held in awe by men. Every one of us believed we could go out tomorrow and form a band at least as good as the Beatles or the Rolling Stones, and in our spare time we were all busy writing the material.

The only thing holding us back was that our dads had told us that we must get our degrees first so that we had something to fall back upon just in case our preferred career choice of being a rock god didn't go entirely according to plan. No-one wanted to do what he was actually doing. We were all marking time until we emerged from our chrysalises. We all wanted to be rock stars or idols of the silver screen, but our parents had persuaded us to postpone those earthly pleasures whilst we completed our education.

So we underwent a kind of twilight existence acquiring skills to fall back upon in the unlikely event that we weren't the next Grateful Dead or the Doors. Our careers were in postponement. If we plunged off the pyramid stage at Glastonbury and broke our necks, it was important to have a profession to have recourse to, so that when one was wheelchair bound, one could earn a crust as a lawyer or a dentist. Or in the case of Charles Francis Xavier, Professor X, the genius behind X-Men, one could be wheelchair bound and a superhero.

Yes, university was an insurance policy in case our lives didn't go to plan. But, with the exception of Ingram, who wanted to graduate in law, practice law for a few years and then go into politics, no-one had a plan.

Things seem to have fallen apart later, for the next generation. Partly, it was the lack of fathers and the lack of role models; partly it was a generation of fathers who wanted to suck up to us and be our mates instead of our dads. And it was student's loans and tuition fees and mountains of debt. If we were paying for it ourselves, we had nothing to look up to our parents or our tutors for; no reason to heed their advice, owe them any debt of gratitude, or learn from their experience.

And it ceased to be a wonderful, dreamful game, a three year sojourn upon the banks of the Cam, absorbing wisdom and making contacts. Once we were paying for it, it became a callous business transaction like anything else. Oh, I can see so well, where it all went wrong. It was Blake's Songs of Innocence and Experience in microcosm.

Some of the lads have dressed up as befits what is being billed by its host, Ingram, as an evening of great sophistication. Sydney, of course, has a white tailcoat on top of his distrained and ripped jeans. Burt Sully, on the other hand, is wearing his Cool Hand Luke T-shirt which has a stencilled picture of the cop astride his hog looking through his Aviator sunglasses at Luke and the caption from the Paul Newman film: *What we have here is a total lack of respect for the law.*

I remember reading somewhere that wives in America's rustbelt didn't even know there was such an animal as a hog. The only hogs they knew were their husband's Harleys. Someone with Burt's beer gut should wear the T-shirt outside his pants, but he has it tucked in, just like Fat Freddy in the Furry Freak Brothers, trying to slim himself down by tightening his belt. A body of two halves divided by a one inch strip of leather ending in a huge buckle. In the same way that females evolved fleshy *mons veneres* so that the male and female pubic girdles didn't grind themselves into arthritis during prolonged shagging, Burt has evolved a barrier beer gut so as not to castrate himself with his belt buckle when he bends down to tie his shoelace.

Burt's bum is fairly compact and his legs are quite slim, in contrast to his moobs and his pot belly like a Vietnamese truffle-pig. Viewed from behind, Burt looks pretty trim. Burt scoops up a glob of taramosalata with a Ritz cracker, but the desiccated wafer is too friable and over-laden, with the result that half of the phosphorescent pink gloop slides off the cracker and onto Ingram's carpet. Burt sees that no-one else has noticed, so he slyly scuffs it out with his brothel creepers as though it were a dead cigarette, whilst creating a diversion by blowing up his cows lick. In a few days' time, Ingram is going to be puzzled at where the nasty pong of rotting cod's roe in his set is coming from.

Olumidé seems to be in some sort of competition with Lyca to see who can get the boy's pulses racing faster. I have been noticing this building up for a while. On every occasion they meet, their hems are higher. I can't imagine why Lyca would participate, as she can't see what the other one is wearing, and she's far too smart anyway. As for Olumidé, I'm unsure why she bothers, as she's just a prick tease and a virgin. But it is distracting, especially from my near-horizontal vantage point in the bean bag. So I close my eyes to hear the music better, thereby becoming kind of complicit in Lyca's world of darkness. But when I close my eyes, I just imagine the two of them with their skirts off.

Talking of the music, although we were given to understand that this was an evening of classical music, *Sticky Fingers* is sat on Ingram's turntable. I say *sat*, rather than *spinning*, because Ingram obviously wanted us to hear every track from the beginning, so he doesn't insert the needle into the groove until everyone has arrived and is listening attentively. There is no question of any pleasant ambient music playing in the background to oil the cogs of conversation. When Ingram plays music, he expects us all to shut up and listen to it. Right now, he wants to be edgy by playing the Stones.

If he actually knew how to do edgy, Country Joe and the Fish, or the Mothers of Invention, or Captain Beefheart would be on that turntable. Ingram thinks that coolness is measured by the fact that the Stones refused to rotate on the carousel that used to close Sunday Night at the London Palladium. No performer had ever paid Bruce Forsyth such disrespect before. They took the producer's money, but they wouldn't make themselves look like pillocks rotating behind the big letters whilst the credits rolled. If Bruce Forsyth had asked me, I'd have been up there in a trice, spinning like my ballerina.

Seth arrives. I know that Seth plays the drums, but I am not surprised to find that he hasn't brought his drum kit with him. We shall see what he has planned. For the immediate future, he ejects *Axis Bold as Love* from his Sony Walkman and proffers the cassette to Ingram who shuns it.

"Only vinyl and needle here," pronounces Ingram, resting the stylus on the spinning disc and coaxing the music and lyrics of *Dead Flowers* out of it. Everyone starts tapping his foot. I notice that Seth momentarily drops his gaze to take in the needlework tapestry that is his skin.

Just then Björn Agen lets himself in. Judging from the scowl on Ingram's face, he doesn't appear to have been invited, in any event, not by Ingram. When Ingram challenges him as to where his instrument is, he produces a tiny set of brass scales from his inside pocket. By flicking at them with his thumbnail, he manages to convince Ingram that they are miniature Tibetan prayer cymbals, although I recognise them as the tools of his trade: a set of dope scales. As everyone else is eager to accept Björn Agen's contribution, Ingram submits to majority opinion like the wily politician he is in training to be, even though the majority are in the wrong, as is usually the case.

Sydney is first to perform, not electively, but because he is picked on by Ingram and too polite to refuse. Ingram obviously intends to use the highly gifted Sydney as the warm-up act for himself. Sydney, being the *uomo universale* that he is, is an accomplished musician, so he takes his place on the piano stool in front of Ingram's upright. Sydney plays Beethoven's Piano Sonata # 14 which the rude multitude call Moonlight. There is no pretentious prelude or introduction.

Sydney just seems to size up the piano that he has not played before. The piece needs no introduction. So he cracks his knuckles a few times and goes straight into it. It is magical. One can close one's eyes and be transported to another world. There is no *"look at me, see how clever I am"*. Sydney is a true artist. He loses himself in his art. He is the humble servant of his chosen instrument. The notes seem to come naturally from the ivory keys in the same way that rubbing an aromatic herb between one's fingers will release its fragrance. I am so pleased he decided against *Stairway to Heaven*.

When he finishes, I feel fulfilled, but also let down. I don't know if this is because I would have wanted it to go on for longer, or if it is the upper-downer effect of the rollercoaster button from Sydney's trousers. I realise that I have been sitting on the floor in Ingram's bean bag all this time with my eyes closed. There was absolutely no justification for having them open. No-one seems to know quite what to do.

The rendition of Moonlight was a thing of such exquisite beauty nobody wants to do anything to spoil the moment, not speak nor cough, not applaud; even to cross one's legs seems like an aberration. I am trying to understand why that should be. It is because any such movement would be presumptive, egotistical, a challenge to the completeness of that moment. Who knows but the dying chord may still be audible somewhere in the universe to some beast blessed with sufficiently acute hearing?

Perhaps all the music from every age is still playing somewhere, but we lack the perception to hear it. If we could retune our senses, maybe Mozart is still to be heard playing in real time. Perhaps Calypso can hear it. Perhaps dogs, with their heightened aural awareness can hear it, and that is why their tails are wagging: they are still listening to the dying embers of live performances from Tchaikovsky and Beethoven.

If only the doors of perception were cleansed…

At length, Ingram concludes that a decent interval has elapsed and asserts himself, more playing the part of moderator than compere. "Thank you so much, Sydney. That was so, so professional. I hope we can look forward to some more of that later. Calypso. What have you got for us?"

Ingram is trying to exert control over Sydney. He will have to try harder than that if he wants to control a control freak. The thing about Sydney is that he does it without even trying.

Calypso can't play any musical instrument, so she recites a poem from memory.

"This poem is called 'In the Stump of an Old Tree'," she announces, "by Hugh Sykes Davies." She stands up to recite the poem. As I am sitting on the floor, buried in the bean bag, this affords me a good view up her hemline. It reminds me of when I used to upturn my silver bell and look up the hoops of the ballerina's skirt, only to find that her legs were tied on to the inside of the bell with rivets. Olumidé sees what I am doing and scowls at me, so I close my eyes again, the better to use my ears.

I have never heard of the poem or the poet, but, as I am sitting on the floor with my eyes closed, I surrender myself to the sensation. I am utterly smitten by it. I cannot believe that I have immersed myself in English literature for so many years and never come across this masterpiece which she recites so beautifully.

She continues to the end, but my mind is locked on the image of the sodden bible written in the language of rooks and the leaves turning to lace, recited in Calypso's cut glass accent.

I am beginning to understand what Sydney and Calypso contribute to one another as a couple. Calypso's reading was the ornament to Sydney's piece. Sydney had immolated himself upon the altar of the piano, so that he was the Ouija board through which the spirits of the notes trapped inside the keys lived. Calypso did the same with her words. In each case they reduced themselves to no more than the organs through which expression flowed. They became invisible, refined out of existence. I was completely dislocated from the speaker and perceived only her words.

I am also beginning to understand Calypso (obviously not all of her, but she is no longer a closed book to me) as a world of intelligence and eroticism fused into one, and the intelligence is inseparable from the eroticism.

Ingram had clearly planned that he would do his piece next, after Calypso had wearied the company with some crass reading from Mill on the Floss, or something. But she had done nothing of the sort. She has elated the gathering, taken the evening to the next level, so that it was now difficult for Ingram to follow. So he attempted to turn the clock back by asking Sydney to do another turn, after all he had indicated that as a distinct possibility earlier.

Sydney is far too clever. He can see where this is going.

"Would you mind awfully, if I did a poem also?" he says as though butter wouldn't melt in his mouth. He then proceeds to recite from his American edition of John Wilmot, 5th Earl of Rochester, which, of course, he knows by heart, as it is the subject of his dissertation:

> *Much wine had passed, with grave discourse*
> *Of who fucks who and who does worse*
> *(Such as you usually do hear*
> *From those that diet at the Bear)*
> *When I, who still care to see*
> *Drunkenness relieved by lechery,*
> *Went out into St James' Park*
> *To cool my head and fire my heart.*
> *But though St James has th'honour on't,*
> *'Tis consecrate to prick and cunt.*
> *There, by a most incestuous birth,*
> *Strange woods spring from the teeming earth;*

For they relate how heretofore,
When ancient Pict began to whore,
Deluded of his assignation
(Jilting, it seems, was then in fashion),
Poor pensive lover, in this place
Would frig upon his mother's face;
Whence rows of mandrakes tall did rise
Whose lewd tops fucked the very skies…

Poker-faced, Sydney continued with this long verse narrative from Rochester's early maturity whilst the rest of us doubled up with laughter, with the exception of Ingram who saw the gravity of his soireé undermined and grew resentful. Everything that Calypso's poem had been, Sydney's was not. The poem was entitled *A Ramble in St James's Park*.

It tells the tale of the poet, John Wilmot, 5th Earl of Rochester, who rambles drunkenly into St James' Park in search of one of the many prostitutes who used to ply their trade beneath the bushes of the royal park, only to stumble upon a former love of his, Corinna, in the company of *Three knights of the elbow and the slur*, knights of the elbow being swindling gamblers, and the slur a method of cheating at dice by sliding the die out of the box so that it does not tumble. Corinna flirts with these unworthy characters to hurt her former lover, Rochester, who cannot comprehend how she has stooped from his worthy love to fraternise with such base individuals, how her fall from grace can have been so profound.

Gods! That a thing admired by me
Should fall to so much infamy.
Had she picked out, to rub her arse on
Some stiff-pricked clown or well-hung parson,
Each job of whose spermatic sluice
Had filled her cunt with wholesome juice,
I the proceedings should have praised
In hope sh'had quenched a fire I raised…

Sydney's recital by heart of the entire *A Ramble in St James's Park c. September 1680* lasts a full 20 minutes, longer if one counts the pauses in Sydney's deadpan delivery that he has to insert if his words are to be heard over the uproarious laughter. When it comes to an end, our eyes are watering; our sides are positively painful with the hilarity, the profanity, but most of all the dead-pan delivery and its incongruity with the type of evening we all know Ingram had planned. Sydney has asserted control in the teeth of Ingram's attempts to control him.

It occurs to me that if Sydney could commit this long verse narrative to memory, there is nothing so unusual about Seth memorising the Epic of Gilgamesh, but Sydney had doubted him.

In order to get things back on an even keel, Ingram feels obliged to allow a short comfort break for those so inclined to leave his set for a smoke. On that note, only our host is left solitary in his room. We all withdraw to the staircase and proceed to get stoned with the generous assistance of late-comer, Björn Agen. I had not realised how dependent I had become on the stuff, even though I already had the peyote from Sydney's pants button performing its good works. Here we were. It was after ten at night and I hadn't had a single joint. My body was calling out for it to such an extent that miraculously I somehow managed to climb out of the fucking bean bag and achieve sentience.

We return in one clump, trying to look serious. The bong has done its work, because I collapse back into the bean bag, already having forgotten how difficult it was to escape from. Sydney makes a bee line for the piano stool. Everybody else proceeds in single file to take their places on Ingram's monastic bed, except Calypso who can't see the conga line in front of her, so she doesn't join it. She stands up, unsure where a seat is. Sydney, who now has the munchies, scoops up a handful of dry Ritz crackers, pops most of them in his mouth, and then crosses the room, facing Lyca.

"The Body and the Blood," he says, administering the cracker onto her outstretched tongue.

"That's enough of that profanity!" says Ingram. "Seth, what have you got for us?"

Seth had arrived with a violin case and I remember thinking how Lilliputian it looked in his huge hands. But he makes no move towards the violin case. After a short dramatic pause, Seth finds two desert spoons in Ingram's drawer, inserts one between the knuckles of the first and second digits of his right hand and the other between his thumb and first finger of the same hand, convex to convex; in other words, not spooning the spoons.

Within seconds he has set up a foot-tapping rhythm by clapping them against his thigh. He then makes the percussion more complex by using other parts of his tattooed body as the skin to this human drum, fanning it with the back of his left hand like a gunfighter in a western, setting up complex cross-rhythms. In a momentary break in the percussion, I become aware of the fact that *Sticky Fingers* has been playing in the background throughout. When we left the room for our comfort break, Ingram had put the record back to the beginning.

I would say that most of us are impressed at what Seth can do with household cutlery, but Ingram is dismissive. "I don't remember inviting Bud Flanagan and the Crazy Gang!" he sneers.

Seth stops his rendition and puts the pudding spoons back in the drawer. Ingram removes them from the drawer and places them in the sink. I think Ingram was a tad unfair, because Seth is a fine drummer. Obviously, he couldn't bring his whole drum kit to Ingram's set, but he has demonstrated his sense of rhythm in microcosm. However, this is clearly lost on Ingram.

So Seth has concluded his warm-up act with the cutlery and is just getting his violin out of his case.

"This is a waltz by Strauss," he begins. I open my eyes a crack. Calypso is still standing above me. I feel my cock hardening in my jeans, but not at Calypso: at the mere hint of *The Blue Danube*.

"Not now." Ingram bluntly dismisses Seth's second attempt at making his contribution. Ingram is exasperated at the Mongol horde he has invited to his sophisticated soirée, but we're the only mates he has. What he should do is thank us politely for coming, insult us a little more, and send us all packing. But he still harbours an overweening desire to educate us and to show how his own skills surpass ours. One wonders for whose benefit is this display? If he were a lyre bird, or a toad or an opossum, we would understand it as part of some complex mating ritual. But as a human being, in this company, why does he feel the need to compete?

Björn Agen is laughing and rolling a spliff at the same time.

"What's so funny?" asks Ingram.

"It's the music," explains Björn Agen. "Don't you get it, buddy?

You're in your basement room with some needles and a spoon?"

"I'm very sorry, old man," says Ingram, "but, no, I don't get it."

Then the chorus from *Dead Flowers rings out: Take me down, little Suzie, take me down! I know you think you're the queen of the underground.*

I get the spoons and the basement, I don't know if the needle is a reference to the stylus playing *the Stones* or Seth's needlework; but I can see the possibilities, and I find Björn's observation amusing: not belly-laugh material, but the sort of things that delivers a lingering smile and a warm feeling in your gut. Ingram however clearly wants to attempt to keep control over his own evening. He stares pointedly at Burt to help him out, but Burt misinterprets this as a signal for him to take the floor.

"I'm next then," says Burt, rising to his feet with his squeeze box. Ingram gives him a withering look that makes Burt's accordion positively detumesce in his pudgy hands. Burt sits down again.

Ingram is clearly going to play his guitar, because he is unlocking it from its case of body armour. If the IRA were to chuck a pipe bomb into Ingram's room, the safest place to be would be inside his guitar case. But Lyca's the only one of us bendy enough to fit in.

It was obviously not how Ingram had planned his evening, but, as his evening wasn't going to plan, it was best for Ingram to cut his losses before it deteriorated further into farce with Sully's piano accordion. Six hinges on Ingram's guitar case snap open. In fact, at first, I thought that was his piece, the percussion of those six twangs. Then out comes the acoustic guitar. But if you had any belief that he was going to play it, you would have to suppress those beliefs for a while yet, because first of all, he must show us what a huge personal sacrifice it is to share one's life with such a temperamental instrument.

Ingram has to have a special comfy chair in which to sit before he can strum his gat. This entailed kicking Seth out of the chair he was in, so Seth has to fall into the bean bag beside me, his limp violin dangling from his huge hand. Calypso, who had been standing, deposits herself lightly onto the bean bag between Seth and me, but the bean bag makes a farting noise, so Ingram has to scowl and wait for the class to come to attention before he addresses his instrument again.

He tucks his acoustic guitar into his thigh and leans forward over it as though trying to protect it from our philistine company. We are all ready, but before the recital can commence, Ingram has to have a footstool to elevate his foot to just the right height for the guitar to rest upon his knee. There's three of us squashed into a beanbag and the rest of us perched on a single bed, but Ingram's axe has to have a footstool all to itself. And it is not enough for Ingram to have an acoustic guitar. It has to be a Spanish acoustic guitar.

And then he has to introduce us to his lump of wood so that we are fully versed in its progeny and provenance. It seems he knows the manufacturer in Segovia; the very forest near Albacete, deep in deepest Don Quixote country where the tree was chopped down; he tells us what sort of wood the instrument is hewn from, and what part of the tree. He is not going to play the fucking thing until we are all on first name terms with it.

Play it, did I say? Sir, you can fret me, but you cannot play upon me. No, no, no. Before he can play it, and once he is very comfortably composed around it in his comfy chair and footstool, he must tune it, because, Heaven knows, in the last 30 minutes, when he was arranging his Libby's pineapple chunks on their toothpicks, his instrument may have un-tuned itself. The same thought is going around in everyone's head: *Why didn't he tune the fucking thing whilst we were outside smoking Björn's bong?* In a failed attempt at control, because Sydney is still seated beside the piano, he asks

"Sydney, could you just give us an E?"

Sydney turns around to face him and suggests: "I could give you a little C."

This is not how Ingram had wanted it to spool out. Despairing of getting Sydney to follow his line, he clears his throat.

"This is a piece by Albéniz. Albéniz was a native of Girona in northern Spain." And then he proceeds to tell us the life history of Albéniz.

"He wrote very little for the guitar."

So this is obviously going to be a privilege. His language suggests that, had he written more for the guitar, Ingram is such a doyen, that he would be playing everything else for us too. But we get the message that there isn't a lot more where this one came from, so we are supposed to lean in attentively. We then have to wait a little longer whilst he affixes a kind of clothes peg to the frets of his guitar before he is willing to play it. His recital is circumscribed only by the lack of oeuvre of Albéniz, who didn't write enough for the fucking guitar.

And finally, he strums. And, I have to say, it is very fine, although I do believe it is simply the intro to The Doors' *Spanish Caravan* and not Albéniz at all. From the sanctimonious smirk on his face, Ingram obviously knows he has impressed. He has probably been practising this one piece all his life and can play nothing else.

It is all over too soon. Presumably because Albéniz didn't write enough for the guitar.

When his last chords have died down, Ingram holds his five fingers across the strings to still his instrument, and exert control over its desire to continue yielding musical harmony, whilst he shuts his eyes and lets his lower lip quiver in a moment of existential epiphany. This is clearly intended to be a moment like in Greek tragedy, when everything ends in quiescence after all the most serious murders and disembowellings have been committed offstage. But this is not to be.

The final notes of one of the few pieces that Albéniz wrote for the guitar are still floating in the lacqueria when Burt Sully jumps up with his piano accordion and squeezes out the theme tune from *Z Cars*.

Burt doesn't understand bathos and anti-climax. I don't know if it is the fact that his chosen piece has absolutely no intellectual or artistic pretensions (it's not even a film theme; it's a TV series, and it's not on the BBC; it's on commercial television!) or the sight of Sully's tits in his Cool Hand Luke T-shirt, getting caught up in the concertina mechanism; but everyone is reduced to helpless fits of the giggles again, but now with the added propellant of the dope. Except, of course, Ingram, who doesn't get it and is furious, and except, of course me. Harry puts Dylan's *Ballad of a Thin Man* onto the record player.

I am not reduced to helpless fits of laughter, because when I see Burt with his squeeze box, it reminds me of Millais' *The Blind Girl*, and that reminds me of Calypso, who is now pressed between Seth and me in the bean bag, and I find I am getting the hots for her again instead of allowing the clean waves of laughter to wash over me.

"Is that the time?" asks Sydney rhetorically. He crosses the space to Calypso and yanks her up out of the bean bag, as though he had been reading my salacious thoughts. "You must excuse us, but we have a ceremony to perform. Nick, we'll see you and your camera at the appointed hour." He leaves the room with Lyca and Self-Harmer.

I was on the point of using this as my cue to exit also, but just then bloody Olumidé, who had been seated on Ingram's monastic bed, plonks herself down in the vacant space on the bean bag between Seth and me, making it awkward for me to take my leave. Seth, however, has no such inhibitions, so he springs up out of the bag and informs the room: "Gotta dash! Buildings to climb, places to go, things to see!" And he's gone.

The door safely closed, the conversation naturally turns unfavourably towards the recently departed.

"*Ceremony to perform*," repeats Ingram. "He's just a pound shop Aleister Crowley."

"Or a pound shop Ezra Pound," quips Burt, disconsolately fiddling with his crumpled-up squeeze box on the bed.

"Maybe you're being a bit harsh on him," I say. "It's not all about him. He regards it as a collaborative act in which a number of us are involved, like any other major initiative requiring a team. We could be on the brink of a breakthrough."

"It's all mumbo jumbo," declares Ingram.

"But how can you dismiss it out of hand?" asks Olumidé, apparently calling upon a knowledge of Sydney's secret ceremonies that I was unaware she possessed. "After all you're a Christian. Your dad was a preacher man. I know for a fact you go to church on Sundays."

"What my girlfriend is saying," I feel the need to explain. "Is how can you believe passionately in God, but not believe in the devil? I am probably not the best person to be doing the explaining because I've never even read the Bible, but I have looked at the pictures. My knowledge of the Bible comes largely from close-reading Milton's *Paradise Lost* as a set text for A-level. But, my understanding derived from that impeccable source is that there are good angels and there a bad angels, and the bad ones were led by Satan, and they live in a place called Hell, and he tempted Eve in the shape of a serpent and it's him we have to thank for the fact that we are all inhabiting this dull, postlapsarian, sublunary world with nothing to relieve the ennui of our humdrum existence apart from indiscriminate sexual encounters, recreational dope and attempts to summon up the Prince of Darkness. How can you buy into God and deny the existence of the Devil?"

I am impressed by my own burst of eloquence. It must be the button from Sydney's loons doing its work. My eyes are stained glass windows. My tongue is tipped with gold. But Ingram isn't as impressed as I am.

"I'm not discussing theology with some idolatrous cunt who's never even read the Bible!" says Ingram.

Olumidé's mouth falls open. I thought she was going to round on Ingram for using the c-word, which (thanks to the 5th Earl of Rochester) seems to have had a good airing in the space of one evening; but instead she extends her shapely arm holding out her empty plastic cup and asks: "Is there any more of that sauvignon Blanc in the bottle?"

I am in no hurry to leave. Sydney's trouser button is doing its work very nicely, thank you. I am controlling the known universe from the helm of Ingram's bean bag whilst pontificating authoritatively upon a book I've never read.

"Weren't you supposed to be working nights tonight?" I ask my girlfriend.

"Oh, I threw a sickie!" she says.

The Gathering

I have seen Trafalgar Square at times of protests. I have seen it on New Year's revels and holidays. But I have never seen it as comprehensively overflowing with humanity as it is today. Onlookers sardined so close you couldn't get a Job cigarette paper between them, spilling out down Northumberland Avenue, leaking into the Strand and the Mall, dribbling up Cockspur Street. So many. I had not thought death had undone so many. Were they the CGI and was what I was about to do the reality? I can't tell the fucking difference anymore.

Their views of these once-in-a-lifetime Setan landings would have been wholly obscured by the sheer density of the spacecraft the god Set had thrown up into the skies had I not had the prescience (as befits my photographic and humble origins) to illuminate the scene with dozens of new suns ascending into the atmosphere like Chinese lanterns, their each gaseous ball of flame anchored to the earth by massy chains and hempen hawsers.

The impression one took away was of the contrast between the fluxional lightness of the buoyant suns, so spiritual and ethereal that they needed guy ropes to stop them floating away into nothingness, and the impenetrable leaden mass of the huge starships tethered to their larger still mothercraft by umbilical hoses pumping fresh fuel into their veins; spacecraft teeming with Setan infantrymen and defying the laws of physics by hanging motionless in the atmosphere, borne aloft only by the palpable sound waves emitted from their vast engines thrumming at idle, each craft a perfect circular tryst of invasion from a distant sun.

Whilst the ships are moving into formation, you will be wanting to know what I was doing on this historic eve. Dear Reader, stoned beyond comprehension, supported by the solid mass of Reality Checkpoint, I am completing 14 circumnavigations of the earth, as Set had suggested. I am flying faster than a speeding bullet, faster than a particle lapping the large Hadron collider, faster than the speed of light, and I am scattering the spent particles behind me, as the sonic boom shuts the skies in my wake.

The viscous air is fragmented into the colours of the prism. On my first circumnavigation, I leave a shimmering red wake, the next is an orange vapour trail; the next is yellow furrow ploughed into the night.

I am spinning a web around the planet in the colours of the rainbow. When I reach violet, I turn around the other way and reverse the palette, just as Millais did in his Blind Girl. Because, if there is a twin rainbow, the bands must always ascend counter-chromatically.

I hear Set's voice, my evil angel on my shoulder: "Not if it's a black rainbow."

I wipe the delirious spittle from the corner of my mouth. The grass is sodden with bodily leakages.

The planet is festooned in fourteen concentric rings. Cross-gartered. It's a work of art, and I've signed it.

Save for the search lights casting about from the spaceships, the new suns were the only light source after the gathering of spacecraft had inked out the normal sun. The *basso profundo* of their huge engines at idle made the ground shake, so that everything seemed uncertain when you couldn't even rely on the earth beneath your feet to support you. The bass was so tangible, it was difficult to catch your breath: it was like walking into an Aztec wall composed of bricks of sound.

And still they hovered there for sixty seconds that seemed like sixty minutes, impossibly suspended. The crowd gazed up. There is a kind of inherent subjugation implicit in any upward look, from the smaller man looking up to the taller man; from the tall man looking up to the idol; here from the whole crowd gazing upwards at the heavens, apprehending the coming of a new Messiah; questioning the intentions of the visitors from another world, but nonetheless rooted to the spot. They shielded their eyes and caught their breath as the deadweight of the huge engines throbbed upon their chests.

The Special Air Service of the British army had also gathered, armed to the teeth, eyes scanning the heavens, focussing on that point where the parallel lines meet. They had light arms, heavy arms, water cannons. Did they think they were going to stop an alien invasion with water cannons and flush the jetsam and flotsam of space into their puny sewers?

Then, in a balletic manoeuvre, sufficient of the ships broke formation so as to reveal glimpses of the dark vault. As the spaceship cluster fragmented, increasingly larger chunks of the heavens revealed themselves in the gaps between. A trapdoor in the sky then opened and from that trapdoor the stages of Set's stairway, hewn of coagulated slabs of welkin, materialised. Treading downwards, one by one, each tread on each step broader and deeper than the last.

An army of giants passed through the celestial doorway, descending step by step. At the same time, landing gear in the bottoms of the circular spacecraft opened and link after link of ponderous chains clattered out towards the ground. Hitting the pavement, they pooled in great whorls of iron. The inhabitants of the ships slithered down the chains.

Once sufficient of the Setan infantrymen had assembled on the ground, they divided into separate units of ten men apiece and each unit set about its appointed task of hauling down on its appointed chain like bell ringers, dragging the connected spacecraft link by clanking link to its docking position on the ground.

The armed forces held their fire, uncertain of the reaction if their body language was hostile. They were taking stock. The situation could change at any second.

Once landed, it became apparent that the composition of the craft differed. Some were hooped in metal; some in wood. And each metal and wood differed: in metal: copper, brass, pewter, platinum, gold; and in wood: teak, rosewood, mahogany, ebony, oak and takamaka. Each was a huge rotunda capped with tautly stretched skin. The Setan teams set about upending the landed craft like tortoises, so that their stretched skins were facing up.

With great effort, the Setan infantry dragged down about half of the ships. Then the trap doors in the base of those craft remaining airborne opened. Instead of chains, sentient beings emerged, Setans. Head first, feet first, tumbling, promiscuous, cartwheeling, they dropped out of the craft like paratroopers exiting the mother ship. Falling bodies. Golconda. Down and down. That is, until their impact with the skins of the landed craft. The sound of a million gigantic drums. This was an exercise in percussion on a scale previously unknown. The upturned landed craft were giant kettledrums.

The Setan drummers fell onto them with resounding bangs and then trampolined from one craft's skin to the next, somehow managing to avoid mid-air collisions. Sentient life reduced to being the hammers in gigantic bells. The drumming of the jumping dancers; whirling dervishes, their skirts spinning; the humming of the idling engines of the hovering ships, frozen in their holding pattern: the music of the spheres. The music heard so deeply it is not heard at all.

And at last, through the sinkhole in the sky, emerged your narrator, Nick Jobs AKA the God Set with his Was-Sceptre probing the integrity of each huge rung of the celestial stairway before descending to the next. The sounding taps of his Was-Sceptre were the oboe for the orchestra of tumbling Setans ricocheting from skin to skin.

And I descend the stairway with the fourteen concentric rings behind me bleeding their colours into one another and falling as coloured rain. As the droplets enter the atmosphere, they solidify into Jelly Beans, eagerly scooped up by the waiting crowd. Despite the police warning them not to eat the beans, greedily, they ignore that sage advice and do so anyway, and through their mouths I enter their collective unconsciousness. They are the screens for Set's great projection. Houdini has never done anything on this scale, nor David Copperfield. I am in a league of my own.

"Nick, are you OK?" It's Olumidé. Fuck me but I have a crick in the neck from that beanbag and a searing migraine.

"Must have dropped off," I say, rubbing my eyes. Everyone has left except Olumidé, Björn and me and, of course, Ingram.

"Well, Nick," says Ingram, picking on me, "are you going to do your piece before you leave?"

It takes me a few moments to adjust. Then I say, "No, thank you. I've just done it. But I did it in my own head. It was quite spectacular," I add. "I've never seen anything like it."

I have never expelled the jumbled characters from my head with such peristaltic force before. I must be getting good at this.

Olumidé and I are pressed shoulder to shoulder. We resemble the contorted figures of Michelangelo's Prisoners as we struggle to extricate ourselves from the beanbag. Ingram busies himself with taking the uneaten tinned pineapple chunks and squares of cheddar cheese and wrapping them in aluminium foil for his next soirée. I suppose we could have offered to help him with the washing up.

But we don't.

"My go now."

The three of us turn around. Somehow we had forgotten that Björn was in the room. He has taken his minute brass dope scales out of his jacket pocket. Holding them at arm's length in his right hand, he pings one scale with the thumbnail of his other. One confident note that sums up Jainism, Buddhism and Hinduism expands to fill the room with Om and brings the evening to an end. As I depart Ingram's set, I am thinking of the ballerina inside my little silver bell.

Cambridge Night Climbing

I am walking back along Trumpington Street, having nobly escorted Olumidé to the nurse's quarters at Addenbrookes after the excitement of Ingram's music evening. It is a night of the full moon. I have my Nikon with the 200mm non-prismatic zoom lens, slung casually on its strap across my shoulder, when I hear a whistling high above me in front of the Fitzwilliam Museum. It's two in the morning. I can't believe any bird would be singing its song at this time of night.

The complete circle of a full moon, perched on the rooftops of the Fitzwilliam Museum, resembles one of those old silver nitrate photographs. If not for the lunar caustic phosphorescence, and the fact that he intended by his whistling to attract my attention, I would never have noticed him, folded as he was, in his black Ninja outfit, like a pleat in the fluting of the Corinthian columns. Then when he realised that he had my attention, he stopped whistling.

Seth was at least 100 feet up, above the stone lions, squashed in between two ornamental pillars on the facade of the Fitzwilliam, a living, breathing gargoyle. His back was pressed against one pillar; his feet against the other. And that was all that was keeping him up, less gravity and more capillary motion; a human spring, squeezed beneath the entablature.

As the light from the moon was half decent, I focussed the 200mm lens and stopped it down to Bulb action to keep the aperture open for long enough for some guttering wavelengths of light to maybe find their meandering path onto the surface of the film. Holding the unwieldy lens as steady as I could, not even breathing for 10 seconds that felt like 10 minutes, I slowly squeezed the button until Seth's likeness was flattened onto the light-sensitive emulsion drawn taught in its black box.

I continue my perambulation towards Gisborne Court.

Into The Dark

Oh dark, dark, dark! They all go into the dark.

Sydney's rooms were customarily dark when he performed his ceremonies; but tonight he plumbed new depths of obscurity. I could scarcely see my own hand. My Nikon hung redundant on its strap around my neck. Just how did he expect me to get a shot off in an almost total absence of light?

It's turning out to be a long night. Good job I swallowed Sydney's button.

Maybe the darkness was intended to preserve the modesty of his Jewel of the Night, Continuous One of the Heavens, stretched out stark naked on Sydney's velvet draped altar, wearing nothing but his black felt hood over her head to conceal her blushes, whilst we tried desperately to adjust our eyes to the absence of light in time to steal glimpses of her. Everything looked darker than usual. Even Lyca looked much darker than usual. I find the stark contrast between her in-your-face nudity and the fact that she is modestly wearing a burqa, most becoming.

A metallic crash followed by a *What the fuck?* from the lips of the Ipsissimus, signalled that a stoned Burt must have careered into the samovar in these inky conditions. Judging from the smell, Sydney has entrusted the thurible-swinging Burt with his finest Omani frankincense, and, in the dark, I would guess Burt has over-swung his thurible impacting the chafing dish, resulting in percussive consequences. Sydney was holding his Almanack de Goethe Grand Compendium of Spells spread open between the hugely flared sleeves of his Thai silk kaftan.

Also present to observe the unobservable were substance-dispenser-in-chief, Björn (the Man) Agen and a benighted Spud Mullins. Spud, through his engorged spectacles, is staring so intently at the darkened vision of female sexuality before him that I can almost hear his pupils dilating in their attempts to leech more light from the atmosphere, so as to register a higher reading on his index of utmost lubricity.

Sydney relieved himself of his great Book of Thoth (How could he possibly read it in the dark?), placing it upon one of his gueridons, and asked me: "Nick, did you get that?"

"Get what? I ask innocently. "I can't see a fucking thing!"

"Just then. The god Pan. I heard him in the chimney *up the Recordati fireplace*. He said he would show himself in the shape of a bird."

I'm trying in the dark to keep a straight face, but all I can think is that "Up the Recordati fireplace" sounds like a Frankie Howerd skit.

"Sydney, if I can't see anything, you can safely assume my camera can't either."

"What?" he barks, genuinely irritated. "Can't you get some faster film or something?"

"No-one makes film fast enough for these conditions, Sydney. You'd need to turn the light on."

"Over my dead body!" He cries, but in a grudging concession, he lights another joss stick. In the momentary sulphur flare of his Swan Vesta, I see his girlfriend's thighs look darker than usual; must have been all that sunbathing on Jesus Green.

"Did you take all the pain-killers?" he asks her.

Really! I have heard some chat-up lines in my time, but what sort of a chat-up line is that?

I can just about discern her head inside the black felt bag, nodding affirmatively.

Sydney is vigorously shaking an analgesic aerosol in a can. He depresses the nozzle and sprays the contents straight onto her fanny. There is a sharp intake of air from inside the black bag. Whatever he is spraying on her must be very cold. Just like the seed of the Devil, I think.

"If your fucking camera doesn't work," says Sydney, "You'll have to make yourself useful some other way." He has placed the aerosol on the other gueridon of the pair and now I can just about make out that he has a large needle in one hand and a bobbin of silk yarn in the other. If the needle was any larger it would be a fucking syringe. "Stick your label out!" He says.

I stick my tongue out just like I used to for my nan. Sydney offers up the end of the yarn to my tongue as though he were administering the Host, moistens the tip, and deftly threads it through the eye of his needle in almost total darkness. If I was wearing a hat, I would take it off at such dexterity. Maybe he really can do magic.

"Pass me that goblet, Spud."

Spud dutifully bears the silver vessel with a smear of scabrous liquid sloshing in its base and hands it to Sydney. I can see that he is trying just as hard as I am to see what is going on, especially in the vicinity of the naked, supine form before us.

Going behind his patient, Sydney cradles her head hidden inside the felt Abaya in one hand, and lifts the goblet to her mouth with the other. We hear the sound of her swallowing the contents, then Sydney passes the vessel back to Spud, who doesn't know what to do with it, so he just hangs onto it. Satisfied that she has drained the philtre, Sydney returns her head to the cushion on which it rests, moves down to her other end and begins plumping her labia between forefinger and thumb like a junkie searching for a vein. Perceiving no signs of sentience down there, dear Christ! He starts sewing her cunt up. After the third stitch, there is an almighty commotion in the fireplace as though someone has fallen down the chimney, but this just encourages Sydney to redouble his efforts.

"This is hurting me more than it's hurting you!" he declares, as he draws the thread through its new aperture and reverses his grip to go back in the opposite direction. I can just about make out the considerable physical exertion that is required of Sydney to make his punctures of her flesh, such that he pierces his own in the process: the blunt end of the needle has ruptured his thumb which is dripping blood, just as it did earlier that day when he stuck a pin in his *AA Book of the Road* and we decided to go to Wells-Next-the-Sea, an imminent outing. Four more neat stitches, and then he sticks his bloody thumb in his mouth to suck on it like a fruit bat.

Removing his opposable digit from his gob, he forms a loop and threads the yarn back on itself, making a knot and then says: "Finger, Nick. Put your finger there."

I place my finger on the most exquisite, plump, yielding, but strangely cold elastic of her labia, feeling Sydney draw the knot atop my digit, and then, reluctantly, I slip my finger away, as he tightens the ligature. She is sewn up.

"There!" cries Sydney, clearly very pleased with his work. "You're quite a little Queen's Scout, Nick, aren't you? Take her away, and let's see if the Devil can pick those locks!"

Calypso emerges from the shadows. She must have been in the room all the time, that way she has of making herself so small and quiet and invisible that you don't know she's there. She sits the poor girl on the altar upright, and then helps her swing her legs over the edge and unsteadily to the floor. She must be drugged out of her skull. Lyca puts the girl's arm around her shoulder and guides her towards the *en-suite* bedroom.

On the other side of the door, Lyca has turned on the light, because a fine pencil of luminescence slithers out from under the doorway, illuminating the tormented carcass of a huge black raven, tergiversating in the unlit fireplace, one wing broken and snapped back unnaturally. It is wearing something around its neck that is choking it. The bird seems to be driving the blunt instrument of its beak into its own ceratoid artery in its attempts to dislodge the ornament; succeeding in nothing save its own violent immolation; but I can't make out what's written on the choker. Then the door closes shut, and everything is inky black again. I feel like a patient drifting in and out of consciousness.

I hear the scrofulous scuff of Sydney's shoes between the shag pile and the parquet as he crosses to the fireplace and then the snap of his breaking the chain around the raven's throat, before passing the necklace to me, but only after he has balled it up in blood-smeared waxed paper from some delicatessen or butchers.

"Here, Nick," he says, "Waxed cotton. The demon Barbour! Put this in your scrapbook!"

Quitting his rooms, holding his parcel between my palms, somehow made complicit by his little party bag, I pause in the corridor beneath the inverted mezuzah, and unwrap the waxed paper. Inside there is a gold medal on a short gold link chain, the sort you used to see around the necks of the bottles on my dad's bar, informing that their contents were whiskey, port, brandy or whatever. The medal has the words '*Sequimini me*' engraved on it. *Follow me*. I stuff the chain and medal into my loons pocket and wipe the waxed paper down my trouser leg. It smells of mortality. As I set off towards my set, wrapped in thought, there is only one thought on my mind.

Who the fuck was it in the felt sack?

A Wedding Announcement

Burt Sully has only gone and got Bunty up the duff. So now she is Bun in the Oven Bunty. One can just picture the scene when she tells Burt that she's missed her period.

"But surely," Burt Sully would have begun, "You're on the pill?"

"Burt, I'm a Catholic."

Burt hadn't been so indelicate as to ask beforehand. Strange things taboo hierarchies are. They had got naked; they had rutted like animals and climaxed, grunting and sweating; but he never thought to ask her if she was on anything, because "I didn't like to ask her personal questions."

Anyway, we're in the seventies, not the naughty nineties, so there's nothing else to be done about it: the wedding announcement goes in The Times and also in Melody Maker, Exchange & Mart and the NME.

Burt takes little interest in the wedding which is going to be a private ceremony in Gretna Green to which none of us are invited. After all, he's just doing the decent thing. He does however take considerable interest in planning his stag night. After suitable research, Sydney decides that we're all off to Barcelona for a long weekend the highlight of which is going to be getting trashed and watching a bullfight.

"Isn't it wonderful?" Sydney asks me. "Burt being the first to tie the knot! And when I say we're off to Barcelona, I mean that we *fly* to Barcelona, but our pilgrimage is actually to Port Lligat, near Barcelona, home of the incomparable Salvador Dali. Port Lligat—means the Tied Port, as in a ligature. What better place to tie a knot?"

"I've had enough of ligatures and knots, thank you very much, Sydney."

"How so?"

"What you- I hasten to add—with my assistance, did to that poor girl the other night is known as FGM!"

"And who is FGM when he is at home?"

"Female Genital Mutilation."

"Don't be ridiculous, Nick. It was nothing more than a minor episiotomy. A procedure performed at least a million times a second!"

"Come off it, Sydney! A million times a second?"

"Did I say a million times a second, Nick? So sorry. Must be what Pfläfflin would call a double torn seam!"

A Day at the Seaside

The two Zenith Stromberg carburettors on Sydney's Series V Humber Super Snipe were presumably receiving a thorough de-coking, because Sydney's shoe has been mashing the throttle to the floor from the moment we hit the open road. *The open road! The dusty highway!* Sydney did bear a resemblance to Toad of Toad Hall. The new improved Harry Westlake-tuned cylinder head was delivering its upgraded 137.5 brake horse power.

The journey of around 70 miles was accomplished in just under an hour. In those days the cars were much slower but we made up for it by getting there faster. The open road! The thrill of just climbing into your car and driving around aimlessly for the pure joy of it before the tossers in their town halls turned all the roads into dangerous chicanes and obstacle courses. It's as if they've forgotten what the fucking roads are for. The minority who are actually licensed and insured to use the Queen's highways are milked road tax that funds an insidious plan of making them unusable as roads before handing them over to those who are not.

At the helm sat Sydney, his musician's hands encased in string-backed suede-fronted fingerless driving gloves. In the front passenger seat was Seth, because, to Sydney's ire, he was so big he wouldn't fit in the back, so he had the pleasure of the flexible Lyca perched on his lap. She is the smallest passenger and has this ability to fold herself up until she is almost not there. In the rear were Spud, Ingram and me.

Harry has to work today, which sorted out the problem of trying to squash him in as well. Olumidé is also working. I tried to steal a snog off her before I departed with the others on my journey, in the same way that a medieval knight would sew his oats before departing on a Crusade; but she wouldn't let me put my hand down there.

"I've got the curse!" she said.

"But you had your period last week," I pointed out.

"Oh, we're keeping a diary now, are we?" was how she closed the topic.

I think she must have been seeing too much of Ingram. He's the only person we know who keeps a diary.

So, banished from my girlfriend's snatch, I find myself in the back of Sydney's Snipe, nursing unfulfilled desires whilst the lucky Seth balances Lyca on his manhood that we now know to be uncircumcised.

As the huge mass of the chassis rolls from side to side like a steamship, I make myself useful in the rear by lining up some joints to enjoy when we reach our destination, using the Haynes Workshop Manual as my table. Sydney is most particular about not drinking and driving, so I had brought additional dope. The car interior is soon filled with the usual illegal fog.

"Oh God!" invokes the censorious Ingram under his breath. "Do you have to smoke that pot all of the time?" Ingram is the only person I know of our generation who calls it *pot*. That's what they call it in *the Daily Express*, a newspaper consisting almost entirely of adverts for incontinence pants and stair lifts, so judge for yourself who reads it.

"Have you ever considered the advantages of public transport?" Burt enquires of Sydney.

"I'm a man who needs a machine, Burt."

"Is that why you have aligned yourself with Spud?" asks Burt.

"You have to be the man that owns the machines. If you aren't one of the men who owns the machines then you will be one of the men who is replaced by them," offers Ingram.

Not for the first time, I have a strange feeling of *déjà vu*.

"Ingram, you are right as rain!" cries Sydney. "If you don't have a machine, in the future, you'll find your job has been snatched away, and you've been replaced by a fucking algorithm; and, yes, that is one of the many virtues that I observe in Spud Mullins, which is why I like to spend time with him, as I like to spend time with all of you, my friends."

Sydney is really chipper. I don't know where he gets all his energy from. I had had the benefit of a power nap in Ingram's bean bag, but Sydney has been stoned since 11-o-clock yesterday morning; he drank copious wine at dinner in Hall, because we had been warned not to expect any food at Ingram's little Symposium; he then drank and got smashed at said Symposium; he was then up all night summoning a dead crow into his chimney piece whilst dexterously sewing up some poor cunt, and was now driving like Stirling Moss.

We park in the car park by the pine forest and exit the Snipe. I can see that the lucky Seth has a hard-on in his Levis after having endured the lovely Lyca wriggling her ass around on his lap for almost an hour. He pretends to take an interest in the Haynes workshop manual so as to cover the swelling. Ironically, it falls open to the page entitled *Hard Wiring.*

The joint-rolling factory in the backseat stretches its legs whilst Sydney bounces around inside the car, pressing down all the door locks before exiting through the driver's door and locking that and the boot and the petrol cap from the outside, each with a different key. We then head off through the woodland in search of the beach and a shop selling stickers for the car rear window that say we've been here, there and everywhere, and as a result can't see out of the back. But we don't find either.

The beach is as silted up as the carburettors of the vehicle that brought us here.

After what seems like an eternity of placing one foot in front of the other whilst being spat upon by an east wind carrying the debris of ice particles in its wake, we stumble across a row of brightly coloured clapboard beach huts. They are raised, so that one has to climb up a flight of weathered wooden steps to the front door, presumably because the high tide used to come all the way up to the steps. But there is no high tide today. In fact there is no sea at Wells-next-the-Sea. It's just mile after mile of tidal silt, punctuated by the odd crabhole ornamented by semi-symmetrical splatter patterns of minute silica balls displaced by burrowing claws. The Nazca holes of Norfolk. A pound shop Patagonia.

After we have been solemnly trudging in the direction where the sea should be for about 40 minutes, Sydney throws his great head back with his Chinese queue almost touching his arse, and he laughs a warm, baritone laugh from the bottom of his stomach. Then the rest of us join in, although there is nothing specific to laugh at, just the general theme of it all. A biting Hyperborean wind is making our eyes water, and burning comets of dope are flying off the end of the joint in every direction. "It's utterly surreal!" he pronounces. "That whoever it is whose job it is to think up names for towns went to the trouble of emphasising the very close associations between this place and its missing attribute!"

"It's like a crime novel," says Spud, "Where someone has stolen— the sea! Let's say they start out on smaller things, petty crime, such as the hygroscopic absorption of little puddles with blotting paper; before they know where they are, they have graduated to hoovering up garden fishponds, and, sooner or later, it had to come, grand larceny: they steal an entire ocean!"

"Another case of 'now you sea it, now you don't'," offers Ingram, trying to get in on the act. Weak smiles but no belly laughter. Too clever by half. That one's not going in his diary any time soon.

Spud continues his metaphor: "If we keep walking, at some point we must come to some yellow and black police incident ribbon, or a huge chalk outline of the crime scene, where the sea used to be."

"Maybe the sandy beach is that yellow ribbon," says Lyca, "So we are already compromising the integrity of the crime scene."

Calypso has elevated the conversation from the camaraderie of stoned jocks and feeble puns to the realm of lyrical and mysterious images, and I reflect on that for a moment.

Giving up on playing for any laughs, Ingram states: "Seriously, if it's called Wells-next-the-Sea, and we saw the big blue border on the map in the *AA Book of the Road*, it has to be here somewhere."

Sydney: "Yes, now let me think, where did I leave it?" He taps down his pockets. "I have my keys, my lighter…"

"Maybe," says Seth, "it's like it is in Calypso's talk. Maybe, it's all fabricated, like she says. Maybe we're standing in the ocean up to our waists right now, but our circuitry isn't wired correctly, so we are interpreting this as silt."

I am not sure that I like the way that things are developing with Seth acting up sycophantically to Calypso after she has been sitting on his knee for so long in the car breathing in his *Balafre*. Sydney obviously thinks that the situation needs taking down a peg, because he calls for calm: "What you say," says Sydney, "resonates deeply, not least because you are quoting the authority of my dear partner. I think this certainly merits a pause for another boo whilst we contemplate these mysteries."

The advantage of Sydney's fingerless driving gloves is that he can roll a doobie without removing them. The pipe of peace is passed around, and I would guess that if someone was observing this congregation, we look rather out of place, five undergraduates, dressed in the gaudy colours of as many beach huts, planted in the middle of nowhere, gathered in the omphalos of this flat, brown, continuous landscape, watching the sun set over a non-existent sea.

"Wells-next-the-Sea," pronounces Ingram, "is a fraud, just like the Isle of Wight."

"Why is the Isle of Wight a fraud?" provides Spud.

"Because," explains Ingram, "it has Cowes you can't milk, Needles you can't thread, Freshwater you can't drink, Newport you can't bottle and Ryde where you have to walk."

I am still wondering how Sydney managed to thread that needle in the pitch dark last night. As we pass the joint around, minute soapy bubbles blow up from the bore holes of the crab and the whelk, and the waterlogged silt takes on an altogether more viscous density. For a moment, there is a film of water around our shoes, and then within seconds our feet are submerged in quicksand.

Seth grabs hold of Calypso, scooping her up just as she is about to be sucked out by the tide that comes in with the roar of a lion. From nowhere. The world has been turned upside down from a flat disc to a terrifying maelstrom in a matter of milliseconds. We turn our backs on the huge sea, the violent determinative sea that we had arrogantly ridiculed in our stoned jokes. The only incident tape will be around our sodden carcasses if we don't run away from it fast enough. And we sprint for all we are worth back to the pine forest, Seth carrying Calypso on his huge shoulders like a circus strongman.

After we have made it back to the safety of the pine forest, after Ingram has finished making his nervous braggardly jokes about our near escape, I just feel resentment at Seth. He has had the pleasure of Calypso sitting on his knee all the drive down, and then he rescues her in a fireman's lift on the way back, carrying his trophy away from the danger, one part superhero, three parts caveman. She doesn't know what he looks like. She doesn't even know what colour he is or that he is covered in incomprehensible characters. To her, he's just an aroma with strong arms.

Balafre.

Balls ache. Why has Olumidé not let me near her fanny the last few days?

I'm not coming back here in a hurry.

The Spinning Room

It's unbelievable that Sydney has permitted his refined sense of the aesthetic to be compromised by allowing his beloved set in Gisborne Court to be used for Harry's scientific experiment. It also bears witness to what Harry had learned at the feet of his master. No more does he have to make up one of a number of Sydney's sycophantic litter-bearers. Since his knowledge of things mechanical became apparent, he has been treated as an equal, and Sydney is as receptive to any idea coming out of Harry's head as he is to Spud's.

Today, Harry is calling the shots. As if to underline the point, he is sat in one of those folding director's chairs, and he has a megaphone that the Peterhouse coach uses to shout encouragement to the oarsmen as he cycles along the towing path.

Moreover, because Harry is now being promoted by the campus as a role model for what can be achieved in the absence of any formal educational system, the University have created a Chair for Harry and a fat cheque that goes with it. The subject of Harry's doctoral thesis at Cambridge is the decryption of the markings upon Seth's body, and if he actually manages to deliver on this near-impossible quest for knowledge, he gets a substantial compensatory package that is known as an *honorarium*, followed by recurrent emoluments, and thenceforth he will be entitled to call himself Doctor Self-Harming Harry.

So as to cause minimal disruption to the academic year, the experiment is being carried out on Twelfth Night and those present in Sydney's room have all come up early from the Christmas holidays.

The four static treadmills from the Cambridge University Athletics Club are in place in Sydney's set and have been bolted to the floor, so they don't slip or slide during the experiment. Spud and Burt Sully are overseeing the joining together of the giant slatted rotunda in the centre of which the pommel horse is rooted. I am seated inside the rotunda beside the pommel horse.

My camera sitting on top of its motor drive and the motor drive sitting atop my tripod are on the outside, looking into the drum. The camera's aperture will be triggered by the depression of a black rubber bulb in my hand whereupon the Nikon will expose the film stock at 60 frames per second. At the appointed time a single puff of air will begin its journey from the rubber bulb in my fist to the camera's motor-drive, and the rest will be history in the making. *Get them in the can!* I have wound my own monochrome film stock onto the spool, so as to ensure I can capture several hundred shots and not the standard 24 or 36 on shop-bought items.

There are other cameras outside the zoetrope, but I am not in charge of them. It seems that almost everyone who has come along to watch, has come with a camera. This is what Set would call a glimpse into a future where no-one would dream of leaving the house without a camera. A series of gears and cogs and wheels connect the treadmills to the big cogged wheel exactly in the middle of the rotunda's drum, and Spud is busy screwing the steel spokes from the centre of the wheel to the circumference of the rotunda, making sure each one is the same length.

At exact intervals of every 18", the wall of the rotunda is slitted like an archer's crenulation, and it is through these slits that the characters on the spinning body of Seth as he goes through his revolving routine on the pommel horse, are to be frozen by my camera, and subsequently viewed and interpreted. It is just a giant version of the thing Harry had done when he made shutters, opening and closing his fingers. Or like living in a spin drier.

Or a particle accelerator.

Amazingly, Harry has obtained a grant from Peterhouse to pay for all this paraphernalia.

Sydney's rugs and carpets and many items of furniture are pushed back against the walls, because the huge drum takes up most of the space. Calypso has folded herself up smaller than ever, so that, as usual, no-one could accuse her of occupying more space than she was entitled to. Because this is an official event, that qualifies towards Harry's continuous assessment as an undergraduate—indeed, if it works, he could graduate cum laude this afternoon—four bowler-hatted porters are in attendance. I don't know how it happened, but one minute we were dreaming up a tradition that all porters should wear bowler hats, and now they were.

Dr Max Pfläfflin is there also as an observer, as is Sydney's Director of Studies, and Spud's Tutor from the Engineering Faculty. The four litter bearers, each one a member of the Peterhouse first VIII, are standing by on the four treadmills, and the College general practitioner and nurse,

Hilda, are also standing by to deal with any medical emergencies. The pall-bearers have metal discs glued to their chests, necks and legs. The discs are connected by lengths of rubber tubing to monitors measuring their blood pressure and heart rates. What with all the pall-bearers tubes and my camera's hose pipe from the rubber bulb in my hand, it's like cutting into an *Andouilette* sausage and watching all its intestines spew out across the room.

The Dean of Peterhouse is in attendance in his dog-collar in recognition of the vaguely religious overtones to this unique decrypting event.

Ingram is slouching against the wall, so that he can criticise the event afterwards, but it has not stopped him from bringing his Kodak camera along.

There had been a small interrogation from the porters wanting to know what the stringent odour was. In his attempt to make his rooms smell slightly less like an opium den, Sydney has had the wooden poles of his palanquin pickling in surgical spirits all night long. It dawned upon me that these must be the largest diffusers in existence. There were always so many other interesting diversions in Sydney's rooms that I had paid scant regard to the humble palanquin-bearing poles; but as the stink they were emanating seemed to cry out for attention, I did pay them more than a casual glance.

In doing so, I saw that one end of each stick, largely rubbed away by the grip and perspiration of the bearers, was coloured blue, although the remnants of the dye were the mere traces one might encounter in an ancient flaking fresco. They were Scudamore punt poles. Who, apart from Sydney Syzygy, would dream of stealing punt poles?

"It's Spud," Sydney confides. "Spud Mullins there. For his acne. Please don't let on you can smell it or I daresay he'll die of embarrassment."

Max Pfläfflin is explaining to Björn Agen that the zoetrope device was originally known as a Daedatelum, after the legendary Greek craftsman Daedalus, the architect of the Minotaur's maze, who unintentionally stumbled 2000 years later into what Pfläfflin would regard as James Joyce's juvenilia, although it was later renamed zoetrope after the Greek word roots zoo for animal life and trope for "things that turn".

Calypso disagrees with Pfläfflin and says that the trope signifies a word, and words are what the crowd has assembled today to seek to read. The girl with the sealed eyes, explains to Pfläfflin and Agen that the human retina retains images for about a tenth of a second, so that if a new image appears in place of a previous image within that tenth of a second span, it appears continuous and uninterrupted, which is how all motion photography works. The object of the experiment is to get Seth spinning and then view the markings on his skin through crenulations in the spinning drum, so that they appear frozen again. The Dean shrugs his shoulders and says: "It's just the great whirligig of Time."

A tenth of a second that feels like ten seconds.

But both Seth and the giant drum have to be spinning at precisely the right number of revolutions per second if this is going to stand any prospect of working. Also, the experiment requires a lot of light, but not stark shadows, so it is happening mid-morning.

All of Sydney's narcotic substances have been tidied away, I have no idea where, and the only odour in the room, apart from Seth's *Balafre*, is the sandalwood joss sticks and surgical spirit. It smells as though an aspiring taxidermist has stuffed a whore house in a field hospital.

Seth is wearing a bathrobe, so at the moment, we can't see all of the markings on his body. The ∞ symbol on his big toe is visible as his feet are bare. Because everyone in the room is in a state of heightened apprehension, there is a susurrus of nervous speculation about its meaning.

"It's a symbol of Christ," the Dean mutters, "like the fish, ichthus."

"Like a *prawn again* Christian?" quips Harry from his director's chair. The Dean emits a sanctimonious chuckle.

"It's a bicycle," pronounces someone else.

"Christ on a bicycle!" mutters Sydney in a kind of stage whisper. Sydney doesn't like anybody else being the centre of attention, which is why he has offered his room as the venue for the experiment, so that at least he will get a mention in the dispatches if anything actually happens. I can't tell if Sydney was rebuking Harry or following up on the bloke who had said *Christ on a bicycle*. But I sense that Sydney is a little jealous of his *protégé*. Either this is going to be Harry's day, or Seth's. Or maybe both of them; but I can't see how it can end up being Sydney's day.

I know Harry's *prawn again Christian* was just a humble pun, but when you bear in mind that a month ago Harry was barely articulate, I feel he's come a long way in a short time, so maybe rote learning at the feet of the master isn't so bad. Maybe if I started out at the bottom, humping the litter around for a few weeks followed by private tuition from Sydney and the Divine Calypso, I would be able to finish my dissertation on the *Ghost of a Flea*.

Also, I can't help noticing that Harry isn't in uniform. He's not wearing his livery or his King Street necktie. I think Sydney regards this as an evil manifestation of the 3 i's: ingratitude, insubordination and insolence. I regard it as the 4th i: independence.

Still expressing their collective nervousness by speculating upon the true meaning of the ∞ sign:

"It's an 8 that's fallen over," says a member of the 1st VIII.

"It's a pair of spectacles," says Pfläfflin, removing his own spectacles and polishing them on his tie, so as to be sure not to miss any detail of whatever is about to unfold.

"Well, it certainly has an affinity with spectacles and lenses," states Ingram definitively. "It's the sign for infinity that you find on camera lenses."

This marks the end of the idle speculation, because it seems that the time has arrived for the experiment to begin. So from now on it will be rotation instead of speculation.

"OK," pronounces Spud, having satisfied himself with his last minute preparations. "We're ready."

A couple of helpers, lift up a corner of the giant pinwheel and Seth slides underneath it, naked, having brushed off the bathrobe. He and I are now inside the cockpit. Everyone else and my camera, connected to me by the length of rubber tubing culminating in the bulb in my hand, is on the outside. Harry is sitting in the director's chair, observing the embodiment of his vision, and snapping his fingers open and shut before his eyes. "Go for it!" he says.

You can hear a collective audible intake of breath, as each one of the spectators of this momentous occasion, rearranges his posture infinitesimally. The porters uncross their arms that were akimbo upon their chests, stiffen slightly and place their big open hands on the fronts of their thighs, inclining towards the centre of activity in the manner of Wimbledon linesmen. Pfläfflin's head bows towards the drum as though he has come to listen to it; Sydney looks all around the room, as though making some sort of last minute adjustments. Ingram raises his eyebrow, as if to say *What are the children up to now?*

And they're off. The pall bearers work the treadmills, slowly at first as they gain traction, then faster. Like marching soldiers, they are all in perfect unison, setting each leg down upon the rubberised road at exactly the same second, and without realising it, everyone in the room unconsciously keeps time with them, so that I am surprised to find that I have adjusted my breathing to the diastole systole of the runners' hearts.

Seth has mounted the pommel horse and he is rotating counter-clockwise; the drum spins clockwise. They have to achieve synchronicity.

"Stop! Stop," exclaims Sydney. His great tapestry is lifting off the wall. All of his paintings are getting blown out of kilter. His numerous objects recently memorised and catalogued by this very Seth are flying all over the place. There is a 30 minute break whilst the paintings and the tapestry are gaffer-taped to the walls, although the porters complain that only blu-tack is allowed. The other paraphernalia are weighted down or stowed away in the bathroom, and then the experiment can resume.

Spud inspects his stopwatch. Harry regards the spectacle through the flicker book of his fingers. Dauntless, the slug-horn to his lips he raises: "Runners, faster!" he orders. "Seth, a little slower."

I hear the great drum creak up a notch. The medical practitioner is viewing the heart rates of the runners on his consoles. Nurse Hilda looks over his shoulder at the monitors. The room is beginning to hum, but it is impossible to tell if it is Harry or the zoetrope that is making the humming, or if it is in fact the combination of their two wavelengths interacting and setting up some kind of a bow wave.

"Hold it steady there, Seth!" says Harry. "Runners, give it a little more wellie please."

The running pall-bearers with the sensors screwed into them and all the electrical leads hanging out of their bodies are plugged into the machines monitoring their performance. My camera on its tripod is plugged into the rubber bulb in my hand, awaiting my signal. The pall-bearers are wearing different coloured shorts. The one with the black shorts seems to set the pace for the others, so that when Harry tells them to *Mush* like a pack of huskies, the one with the black shorts appears to hang in mid-air for a split second and then bring his right foot down with a pronounced slam, readjusting the pace that the other three fall in with.

And everybody in the room unconsciously adjusts their breathing so as to keep time with them. Every fourth pace is the heavy one. I am trying to think what sort of a dance has three light paces and then one heavier one.

My head is beginning to spin like the drum. I have tried to focus on one fixed spot whilst the rest of the room is rotating, which is what I understand ballerinas are supposed to do, so they don't get dizzy. But that just made it worse. I tried focussing on Seth, but that was even worse. I then tried focussing on the little slits in the zoetrope and trying to see the people and objects in the room on the other side, but that was worse than ever, and I just know I'm going to convulse any moment.

This low bow wave hum is getting more oppressive by the second. My breathing has adjusted itself to the rhythm of the runners, and I find it is stifling me. But when I try to break the rhythm, I can't catch my breath. It's suffocating. My fist is clenched around the rubber bulb waiting to depress the fucking thing and have done with this loathsome experiment.

To take my mind off things, I try counting. *One little second. Two little seconds. Three little seconds.* Three little seconds that seem like thirty seconds. I wonder how long this has been going on for. But then I realise I have become out of time with the footmen and it feels wrong and uncomfortable, so I adjust my breathing back to their rhythm again. Seth shows no signs of flagging I wonder if the runners should break their step, like soldiers crossing a bridge. *Tap-tap-tap-Wham!* All four right feet stamp down at the same time following the lead of the oarsman in the black shorts.

The light is flickering. The resonance is unbearable. I can't tell if it is affecting anybody else, or if it's just me.

"Stand byyyyy…"

Harry's voice through his loudhailer. The "y" at the end of "by" trails off, hanging there, letting us know we have almost arrived at the moment. He is opening and closing those digits of his and tilting his head sideways as he looks through them.

The vibration is lifting, bringing to mind those performers who run their wet fingers around the rims of wine glasses, making sounds as though they could have meaningful conversations with whales. I realise that the noise the oscillating Seth makes each time he completes a circuit is now timed exactly to the footfall of the pall-bearers. I am foaming at the mouth. Four bodies revolving around a single primary. Maybe the markings on Seth's body are not writings at all. Maybe they are wavelengths.

Everything is throbbing. The soundwave is resonating at a higher frequency. I am just thinking to myself that this must be the vocal chord of an angel when Harry barks "*Now!*"

Unthinkingly, I squeeze the bulb. A thousand other flashlights are popping on the outside of the rotating drum. The last thing I hear before I pass out is a gigantic crack as all of Sydney's windows disintegrate, followed by a series of thwacks as shards of glass rain down on the spectators.

In my dream, as Seth is whirling round and round in the huge cyclone, the wind is getting under the edges of his letters, and lifting them up a centimetre at a time, until, one by one, they become unglued and fly off his revolving figure, until he is clean of their obscene texts.

And there the lion's ruddy eyes,
Shall flow with tears of gold:
And pitying the tender cries,
And walking round the fold:
Saying: wrath by his meekness
And by his health, sickness,
Is driven away
From our immortal day.

And now beside thee, bleating lamb,
I can lie down and sleep;
Or think on him who bore thy name,
Graze after thee and weep.
For wash'd in life's river,
My bright mane for ever,
Shall shine like the gold,
As I guard o'er the fold.

When I come around, my mouth is very dry. I look up and the letters SHALLOW END come into focus. The naked Seth is cradling my head in his arms. He is regarding my eyes intently with his own, as though he is searching for signs of life. There is a gigantic jagged pane of glass, resembling one of Jove's thunderbolts, embedded in the floor, inches away from my head. I take the rolled up extract from Sydney's Jewish Chronicle out of my mouth and spit drily.

"Sorry, man," says Seth. "I thought that's what you're supposed to do to stop you biting your tongue out. That's what Iago does to Othello in Olivier's film version."

I look at the paper in disgust.

It's the obituaries page.

An Indian Head Massage

"His forehead's as hot as hell, but there's no perspiration."

Inside my addled noodle, I am aware that Seth is speaking those words. Cautiously, I squint half an eye open. I can hear the blood ticking in Seth's engorged muscles, like a huge machine cooling down. With my head cradled in his powerful arms, we must resemble Michelangelo's *Pieta*.

"In-inside my head," I stammer. "It's all still spinning, and the spinning is overheating my brain."

"Let's get you sat down properly, old chap." Seth scrapes me up off the floor and plants me in Sydney's revolving chair. I am aware of an absence of people. All the supernumeraries—the porters, the palanquin-bearing rowers on their treadmills the Dean, the doctor, the Directors of Studies—have evaporated, how long ago, I could not say. Sydney's set is back to normal. Our revels now have ended. Of course, Ingram is still lurking. Ingram would never leave until last knockings.

"Lyca!"

It's Sydney calling to her. "Why don't you give old Nick one of your shampoos?"

Where did Sydney get the idea that he could cool down my head by having his girlfriend wash it?

"Shampoo?" I query.

"Shampoo and Set!" exclaims Sydney. "Set. Don't you remember? That's the word you kept muttering when you were down and out! Game, Set and Match!"

"*Champissage.*"

Champissage. I don't know what the word means, but the beautiful Calypso is standing right behind me in the chair and whispering it in my ear, her breath cooling down the heat in my brain. Then I feel her cool, urgent fingers enclosing my spinning head and stilling it.

"*Champissage,*" she repeats. "Sydney calls it shampoo. It's the Indian word for an Indian head massage.

"It's about as much fun as you can have," pipes up Sydney, "with your clothes on."

"Take a deep breath." She instructs me. "Again. Hold it in. Longer. Now let it out, slowly. Again."

As she instructs me in breathing, she talks me through what she is doing whilst she does it, so I don't get anxious.

"I'm going to start with light pressure and circular movements around the trapezius muscle at the base of your neck, circling outwards towards your shoulders." And so she does, and she reaches around and unbuttons the top two buttons of my shirt and then resumes her work at the back of my neck.

"Now, I'm pressing with my thumbs on either side of your backbone just beneath the base of your collar. My little Printer, you're very stiff; must be because you're such a GentleMan. Stiff upper lip…"

My eyes are closed. I'm drifting back towards when my mum used to read me bedtime stories and stroke my forehead and rough up my hair. I can feel all the plates on sticks that I had kept spinning in my head, slow down, revolving slower and slower as one by one they clutter to the floor. Somewhere at the back of my skull, her probing thumbs along the upper ridges of my spine, find each spinning plate and becalm it. In my imagination, I am collecting the tin foil tops from the milk bottles to make spinning decorations.

Now she is massaging the tops of my shoulders either side of my neck with her forearms, and I can feel her pointed breasts against the back of my neck as she reaches around. Her arms are cool and sensuous. Just like Sydney said, it's about as much fun as you can have keeping your clothes on.

"Nick, I'm pressing little rotations with my thumbs up your neck to the base of your skull. And here, I've arrived at the place where your skull was formed. From the moment your fontanelle closed, you had to keep your head open to new experiences."

"And this is one!" I didn't even notice those words leaving her lips. I think they must have formed themselves in my skull.

Now one of her hands is around the front of my head. "I'm supporting your forehead with my left hand," she says, "So it doesn't fall forwards and hurt your neck. With my right hand, I'm running up and down the back of your neck. Just like a little mouse."

And she whispers in my left ear a nursery tale rhyme, but in the most sensuous of tones: "*Hickory-dickory dock; the mouse ran up the…*"

I couldn't be sure if she said *Clock or Cock*.

"…Until I reach your hairline. You're still very tense, Nick. So I'm just going to have to do this again. *Hickory-dickory dock…*" and her skilful mouse is running up and down the ridges in my spine as though they are bubbles from which she is expelling all the air, making me smooth.

"Keeping my right hand touching your hairline, I'll let your head tilt forward, just a few degrees, as if you're nodding off to sleep. I'm holding the meridians of your head, pressing them with my thumbs, and channelling the Chi with my fingers."

She's brought me down from insanity to Nirvana in a few masterful movements, and now my only anxiety is that this is all going to be over in a few moments,

"I'm lifting your head back to vertical, ever so gently, allowing your brain to spin naturally on its own axis."

Then she stroked my forehead and ruffled my hair up, and ever so gently, I felt her fingers slipping away from me and the connection to her ebbing away. With it came the sensation that she had drained everything bad out of me and I was being reborn beneath her hand.

"Now just sit there for 30 seconds"

Thirty seconds that feel like one second. It's all over too quickly.

"How do you feel?" she asks.

I feel like my head was a useless lump of clay until she span it and shaped it into something worthwhile.

I am thinking *When Adam dug, and Eve span…*

"I had no idea that the crown of my head was such an erogenous area," I said.

"Oh yes, dear boy," piped up Sydney. "Of course it is. Lyca! Over here! Me next!"

And whilst he leans back and has his head expertly manipulated by Calypso's cool fingers, Sydney expounds upon his theory of heads.

"Yes," he begins, "the head is a very erotic area. Why do you think yids wear yarmulkes? Not to do so would be as rude as going to schull with your kishkas hanging out the front of your pants! And I'll tell you another thing, something that Seth will be able to verify, because he's memorised Homer like the back of his hand: when Odysseus goes down to the Underworld and meets all the ghosts, we call them ghosts, but the Greek word Homer uses for them translates as *Dead Heads*. And he also refers to them as being composed of pure *Psuke*.

"Now, *Psuke* is a word for which we have no direct translation, so we have to translate it from the context in which the ancient Greeks used it. If it's a cold day and your breath vaporises when it leaves your mouth, the word they use for that vapour is *Psuke*. When a hero has worn himself out in battle, they say that he has expended a lot of *Psuke*. If he then takes a bath, the liquid restores his balance of *Psuke*, so he's as right as ninepence again.

"*Psuke* is stored in various parts of the human body. In ancient Greek philosophy, it's stored in the knees and elbows, in the balls, but the main reservoir of it is in the head. The *Psuke* reservoirs correspond exactly with the areas that are gilded in ancient statuary, not just Greek, but Roman and Egyptian also. They believed that when you cum, the *Psuke* drains out from the central reservoir in the head and races down the spinal marrow (which is why we experience a shuddering all down our spines when we cum); from there it progresses to a kind of holding chamber in your bollocks, until it's overflowing, and then the *Psuke* goes rocketing out of your cock, after which, you are temporarily exhausted at having wasted so much of the fucking stuff.

"Shakespeare must have had it in mind when he wrote about *the expense of spirit in a waste of shame,* because *spirit* is Shakespearean for *jism*, in the same way that *Psuke* is ancient Greek for cum. So that, Nick, is why Jews cover their heads in synagogue. It's a sign of respect, just the same as keeping your cock in your keks. Lyca, that's absolutely divine!"

I think that Sydney is grandstanding. He needs to regain some of his ground after the trip to the seaside, what with Lyca wriggling on Seth's lap and being scooped up and carried off by him. Sydney needs to do something to assert his superiority. It's as though he is saying that Seth might be big and strong, but let's not forget who it is in this little group who has the towering intellect. Also, Sydney deliberately led Seth into this: first of all, he pretended to put himself on the same level as Seth by referring to Seth's wide reading of the classics, but we all know that Seth could only read them in translation, whereas Sydney is translating not only the text, but the sub-texts within the text for which no known translation exists.

And in doing so, he also manages to dangle a carrot out in front of Seth. At the swimming pool, he had said that he would help him translate the script on his skin. After this exegesis on the topic of Heads, who could doubt that there could be anyone in Cambridge better suited to that task than Sydney?

"Pretty good! Pretty good! Pretty neat! Pretty neat!" Sydney is making approbatory noises in praise of Lyca's deft strokes. "It's the thumbs up for Lyca's Indian Head Massage! It was in India that I first acquired my interest in palanquins. Did you know that in my spare time (of which there is precious little) I'm working on a book entitled *The History of Howdahs?* My bendy friend here, Calypso, Infinite One of the Heavens, Countenance Divine, knows all about it, don't you?"

"How much can there be to know about a howdah?" It's Ingram asking.

"You'd be surprised!" says Calypso.

"Go on then, surprise me." Says Ingram.

"Did you know, there's a whole museum of howdahs in Udaipur?" she asks.

"Well no."

"The Maharajah fell off his horse and was paralysed from the waist down." It's Lyca talking. "So he had to be carried about in a litter, and then visiting potentates kept making him gifts of more and more elaborate litters, because they didn't know what the fuck else to buy him. I mean, what gift do you buy for the cripple whose got everything except his legs? They're all there in the museum in the City Palace. After his accident, he couldn't father any children, and a dynasty that claimed its bloodline from the sun was going to die out, so he adopted."

"In her mis-spent youth," continues Sydney referring to Lyca, "in her years BS, that is *Before Sydney*, she spent a lot of time in India with a mystery man, and it was her who told me about the Museum of Palanquins, and how even a fucking museum of Palanquins could seem interesting after a nice Opium Lasse. Just think of it! Getting smashed out of your head and spending the afternoon in the Museum of Sedan Chairs!

"That adopted son of the Maharajah, he married a fucking *shiksa*! What a thing to do! He married a *goy* who made him shave his whiskers off! The dynasty claimed direct descent from the Sun itself. Their royal symbol, emblazoned on everything, was the sun with a fine pair of whiskers, and now, after thousands of years and a fall off a horse,

314

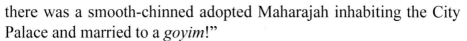

there was a smooth-chinned adopted Maharajah inhabiting the City Palace and married to a *goyim*!"

"Is he making this up?" I ask generally.

"Not at all," says Seth. "He's right on the money. I can vouch for everything he says."

"I have to go," announces Ingram. "Can I give you a shoulder to lean on on your way to your set, Nick?"

"That would be great, Ingram. Thanks a lot."

As we are walking back through the Deer Park, my right arm straining to reach up to Ingram's shoulder for support, Ingram says: "You know, Nick, that must have been a load of bollocks about a museum of palanquins in Udaipur and the dynasty coming to an end because the maharajah couldn't reproduce."

"Actually, it hit a bit of a raw nerve that I'd forgotten I even had until they told the story. I can't reproduce either."

I don't know what got into me that made me confide to Ingram Frazier, of all people, the story about my childhood visit to the doctor and my father telling me there would never be any more names in the big Bible and squeezing my wrist so forcibly that the impression of his thumbs was still there a week later. It's not that I can't reproduce, but that I mustn't, or there might be another person like me. So I will continue religiously to fasten my luminous watch around my dick before embarking upon sexual liaisons.

We had reached my room in St Peter's Terrace. Realising that I had let him into a confidence, Ingram felt compelled to reciprocate with a confidence of his own.

"Well, you know, Nick, to be honest, I think that the great Frazier bloodline may well come to an end with yours truly here. You know, I've never—*been with*—a woman, and I fear I never will. So maybe you and I are the end of the line, the terminus. We're St Pancras fucking station."

Because I have my arm around his neck, and because I think that Ingram has just got about as close as he's ever got to confessing that he bats for the other side, I decide that it could be misinterpreted if I invite him into my set, so I thank him for the loan of his shoulder and bid him goodnight.

Aegrotat

After the others have departed, Dr Max Pfläfflin asks me to stay behind with him for another one of our little *tête-á-têtes*.

"Have you considered an *aegrotat*?" He seems to be addressing the question to his brogues. He doesn't meet me in the eye.

I have not considered an *aegrotat* because I have no fucking idea what an *aegrotat* is. I don't want to be humiliated by admitting that I don't know what an *aegrotat* is, but I consider I will be snookered further down the line if I attempt to brazen it out by embarking upon a conversation concerning an unknown subject. So it's a choice between being humiliated now or being snookered later.

"What's an *aegrotat*? " I ask him, giving in.

"An *aegrotat*," he begins, "is a kind of degree that this University dispenses to a student who is too sick to sit his exams. And we call that," the sanctimonious cunt smirks, "an *aegrotat*."

"I'm not sick!" I cry, affronted.

"But Nick, you keep blacking out."

"No, I don't. I just get tired sometimes."

"Nick, maybe you should get your blood pressure checked, or take some iron pills."

He's going to send me to the gas chambers, pretending I'm off for a shower. I am comforted by the thought that very soon Self-Harming Harry, the wretch that Sydney had dragged out of Hobson's gutters, will be Pfläfflin's better. Pfläfflin doesn't have a doctorate. He's just another jock with an overgrown ego. But Dr Self-Harming Harry has a ring to it. If I am having my blood checked, I could provide a transfusion to Harry.

"I intend to pass my exams fair and square," I declare. Complete bollocks, of course. I intend to get the god Set to sit them for me and obtain a first and a Senior Scholarship.

"Nick, please, just to humour me, if you won't see the doctor, see the nurse. She'll take a specimen." He deeply inflects the *humour me* with his Aryan accent. Nothing humorous about it at all.

I can see in his eye that, with the aid of his demented nurse, he intends to skin me and turn me into a lampshade. Me first, Seth next. Seth's lampshade could revolve and we could read his characters from their shadows on the wall, as in Plato's the Parable of the Cave. Or Pfläfflin might render me into one of Sydney's integumental tomes, his books bound in human kip.

"I intend to sit my tripos like a gentleman," I say to call an end to the debate.

"When Adam delved and Eve span, who was then the Gentleman?" Pfläfflin enquires inscrutably.

He sets me thinking of my little ballerina, spinning in her bottle.

"Or you could take another year and sit your exams after four years," he continues.

"I'll tell you what I'll do," I retort. "I'll spend four years at Cambridge, but I'll sit my exams in the third. And you know what we call that?" I ask him rhetorically.

"Keele? University?" he ventures.

"We call that a Barney! Barney Rubble, Double Time Scheme!" I reply, smirking to myself as I leave his rooms.

A Bullfight; The Hallucinogenic Toreador

The Iberia jet touches down at Barcelona's El Prat de Llobregat airport. In those days, the passengers still clapped the pilot on a decent landing, so we give him a hand as though it was Vaudeville, and he turns around and gives us a little bow from the cockpit. They live for applause.

In the airport, there is a Tabac shop, so we stock up on duty-free Marlboros whilst Harry thumbs through the post cards in the rack outside, ultimately buying a card depicting Snowflake, the famous albino gorilla in Barcelona zoo.

Set had suggested we stay at the Hotel Arts in the Olympic Village, but, as it turns out that hasn't been built yet, we check into the Hotel Majestic in Passeig de Gracia, which is a nice wide boulevard with many a fine lamp post that reminds us of the ornate ironwork planted in the middle of Parkers Piece. We therefore conclude that if, at any stage, anyone gets homesick or lost, they should embrace one of these lamp posts and imagine they are at Reality Checkpoint. From his guide book, Professor Harry manages to tell us that they date from 1906 and were designed by Pere Falqués. To Harry, the Guide to Barcelona is just another workshop manual.

We have a pretty hectic schedule designed around the fact that we wouldn't allow Sydney to bring any gear onto the flight in case we all end up in Spanish clink, scuppering Burt's stag-do. So, after lunch, we have to cram in some sightseeing before early evening which Sydney considers an appropriate time to go down the docks and score, because the idea is that at sundown we go to a bullfight, and Sydney refuses to attend such a spectacle unless he is stoned. We then have a late dinner planned.

For lunch, we take the funicular up to Tibidabo and absorb the fine mirador of the City and Mediterranean sea from that vantage. We have a reservation at El Vent Restaurant. Although the day belongs to Burt, Sydney takes charge, glancing at the menu and addressing the company:

"Would you mind if I ordered for everyone?"

After general nods of approbation (none of us understand the menu, and there are no photographs of the fare), Sydney calls the waiter over and begins practising his finest Castilian Spanish on him, to which the waiter responds:

Habla Catalan?

"You're in Catalonia," Ingram explains. "He doesn't understand you."

Nonetheless, despite the language difficulties, we are soon feasting on finger food: *tallerines* in *ajo* and parsley, fried *calamares*, succulent baby *polpo* in garlic and chilli, and the main course is sea bass baked in salt. Burt, Ingram, Self-Harming Harry, Seth, Sydney and I enjoy the spectacle of the white-jacketed waiter chipping away at the plaster to release the inner bass, as if it was four and twenty blackbirds baked in a pie. More applause and expressions of regret from Sydney that he is having to enjoy this spectacle when he isn't smashed, but we try to compensate by necking more Sangria.

Our Self-Harmer proves to be the exception. As Harry is, let us say, closer to the grass roots, despite being beholden to Sydney in many ways, not least the cost of his air fare and lodgings, he doesn't embrace girlie-stuff such as the helpful suggestion that Sydney should order food for all of us. Harry regards that as unmanly. As a hunter-gatherer, he will order his own food, and, in an ideal world, he would go out and kill it also.

Harry sees some people at a table over the way eating something theatrical and asks what it is.

"Erico de Mar," declares the white-jacketed waiter.

"Eric of the sea," explains Ingram, as though no-one could figure that out for himself.

"*Mismo*," states Harry, and the waiter heads off with Harry's order.

"*Mismo*?" asks Burt.

"Means the same," Harry informs him. Clearly, Harry has taken the trip more seriously than the rest of us, and gone to the trouble of conning a few words from the back of his phrasebook.

Rik of the Sea turns out to be sea urchin served in its own circular anemone shell. When they plate him up, I understand what has attracted Harry to that dish. It's completely white, etiolated; what Ancient Pistol would have called *exsanguinated*. Which is Harry's destination. I look at the confection and recognise that white, fragile shell from my unfinished Fish of the Deep sticker book: Paracentrotus Urchin. It really is an exquisite work of art; except it's not art; it's natural.

What did Sir Thomas Browne say in Religio Medici?—"*All Nature is artificial, because it is the Art of God*". If Hermès or Louis Vuitton had invented it, we would all be falling over ourselves with admiration, because to all intents and purposes we were looking at a blanched cylindrical object with multiple, regular striations as though someone had fashioned an annular Ostrich hide. I could see why it appealed to Harry. Under the ocean, it started out life as brown; but above sea level, it became white. It lost its colour in the sunlight. I could also recognise why it appealed to me.

The cavity of the urchin was hollowed out and then refilled with a digitally-enhanced version of what they had eviscerated. I don't mean to sound like an old queen, but when I say *digitally enhanced*, I mean it in the old way. The chef had done it with his fingers. This was the precious heart of the *garaguella* that someone had ripped off the side of a rock.

During its life, it had grown longer and longer and deadlier spikes. But some cowardly picador with a padded glove had pulled it off the rock and upended it like a defenceless tortoise. The chef (and this is the digital enhancement) had excavated the succulent guts, repacked them within the blanched shell, cracked an organic egg on top, poured *Carlos Tres* brandy atop that, and then set fire to the whole fucking conflagration at the tableside with a miniature flamethrower.

I am fascinated as I watch the egg veneer grow gradually opaque, bubble up, then grow transparent, then glossy, then caramelised. It was as if someone had taken a blow torch to your eye. My mind drifts back to the day when they left the projector running after Lyca had finished her lecture. Lyca! I'm missing her already, but it's boys only on this trip.

The waiter, in his smelly white bumfreezer, is hanging around, waiting for a tip for not setting fire to the curtains. "Come on, guys," I say, "and after I have rattled them up a bit, we manage to produce a decent few pesetas tip in shrapnel.

Sydney, the control freak, had taken the liberty of ordering for everyone else, and he had ordered the sea bass baked in salt. His disloyal protégé had been beguiled by the blanched carapace on the neighbouring table and sought to express his individuality over his master by ordering the *garaguella*. So we were faced with the intense competition of Sydney with his waiters chip-chipping away at the salt-waistcoat of the *loup de mer* on the one hand versus the pyrotechnics of his protégé's party piece on the other.

Not wanting to risk losing control and being outdone, Sydney had produced a Marlboro from behind his right ear, stuck it in his mouth and then applied the Marlboro to the blow torch that was working on the *garaguella*, trying to upstage his own apprentice. In doing so, he singed the tip of his Shaolin goatee which momentarily glowed like a dud firework before deliquescing into a foul-smelling taper.

It was as though he had lit the fuse on his own head, and in mine I was counting off the seconds, waiting for it to explode, raining brain material down upon the white tablecloths. The company applauded the spectacle of Sydney's glowing tip, and Sydney, clearly in pain, had to grin as though it was all intentional, before lowering it into his glass of *Vichy Catalan*.

"That will be a hard act for the bullfight to follow," commented Ingram.

Pudding is *crema Catalana* for most of us, save I note that Harry has to go off menu again, ordering the smoked bacon ice cream pierced with anchovy reinforcing rods. He asks for two spoons in sign language, and I have to tell you it actually tastes a lot better than it sounds. But I am conscious of the fact that Harry's menu choices are dictated by their colours not their tastes.

The ice cream was the only thing on the pudding menu that was white. Let me hasten to add that Harry is not a White Supremacist. He is whatever the opposite is. He feels wholly inadequate because he is not white, but he is in a permanent state of striving to attain whiteness. In that state, inappropriate menu decisions would include ordering red meat.

The blowtorches come out again to glaze the *crema Catalanas*, and I am thinking that, whilst this was entertaining first time around, it is now repetitive and dull; but I accept the waiters' tomfoolery in good spirit, smiling thinly. As does Sydney, stroking his caramelised stubble. No split ends there.

After a digestive *Carlos Tres* and *café solo*, it's outside for another look at the view, then we're all clanking down the funicular to ground zero. We take in Park Guell, pause for tapas, Sagrada Familia, pause for more tapas, *la Pedrera*, and over tapas we agree to separate, because Burt wants to go back to the Majestic for a siesta, Seth needs some exercise after all that food, so he's off for a swim, and Sydney wants to go straight down to the docks to score. So Harry and I decide to pay a visit to the zoo in the late afternoon, and then we'll all meet up at a bar beside the Plaza de Toros and get *ausgeflipt* before taking in the bullfight, followed by a very late Spanish style dinner.

Harry and I are enjoying a sun-dappled promenade through the swishing bamboo-lined paths of the zoological gardens. Harry is wearing a Barcelona FC beaky cap to keep the sun off his face as he remains dedicated to his pursuit of the achromatic by alcohol abuse, daily blood-lettings, the consumption of monochromatic food, and lemonade facials, so he certainly doesn't want to undo all this good work by exposing his still swarthy face to the Spanish sun. We have chuckled at a few chimps and admired a mandrill displaying his arse in the colours of the Union Jack; and we have watched a near-toothless hippo with a hosepipe playing into its huge mouth whilst the keeper attempts to floss the stumps of its remaining teeth with a yard brush, and we are shooting the breeze as guys do when Harry is suddenly rooted to the spot and can't proceed any further.

What has captivated him is Snowflake, the albino gorilla, whose cage is more like a large stage set that he has all to himself, because there's nothing else like him in nature, and if he was to share his cage with a regular gorilla, the regular gorilla would probably kill him. And this Snowflake is putting on a bit of a performance for his admirers, theatrical, almost balletic; but I can see he's sad, because he's never going to find a mate, and he is destined to be shunned by the normal gorilla community. But Harry is riveted and can't tear his eyes away from this vision of achromacity attained. An anaemic ape! What will they think of next?

I watch Snowflake for a while, being polite and patient, as I was at the restaurant when the waiters wielded their blow torches second time around; but after 10 minutes or so I suggest we go on, as we have to get across to the other side of town and meet up with the guys so as to allow good time to get mashed before the bullfight. If I have to make a choice between getting *ausgeflipt* with the lads or shooting the breeze with an ashen ape, I would like to get mullahed first and keep my date with evolution later. After all, if it's evolution, it can wait.

Harry says "You go on without me." Self-Harming Harry has a kind of saddened look in his drooping eyelids, as though he has met up with a kindred spirit and wants to spend more time contemplating the albino gorilla. He is not looking at me as I talk to him. He has come to the conclusion, maybe with justification, that he can get a better quality of discourse with a primate.

"Look, Harry," I say, "I can wait another five minutes, if you like."

"Nick, I'm in for the marathon, not the sprint. I know you guys are all in a hurry to get to your lofty destinations as fast as possible, and good luck to you; but for me, this gorilla isn't something I can do in five minutes. This is like staring evolution in the face."

Five minutes that feel like five million years.

So, no more Genesis, and Adam and Eve for Harry. His feet are now firmly in the Charles Darwin camp. Farewell, the spinning Eve and the digging Adam.

I remind him of where we will be later if he wants to join up, and I go stalking off towards the exit where there is a taxi rank and I can jump into a green and yellow Barcelona cab towards the Plaza de Toros.

"*Hace uno recibo?*" he asks me.

I have no idea what he's on about, but, not wanting to be impolite, I say Si. As a result of my positive attitude, I have to hang around whilst he finds his biro amongst the crucifixes, beads, Holy relics, photographs of grandchildren and assorted debris on his dashboard and then composes a receipt on a piece of paper as big as the old, white £5.00 notes. He writes the date, the time, the amount of the fare in pesetas, the pick-up point and the drop-off point with religious precision for its accuracy, all the time whilst the guys behind him are beeping their horns.

He seems indifferent to this, but I find I am breaking into a mild sweat with anxiety on his behalf. I am beginning to wonder if he is going to add illustrations to whatever he is composing on the dashboard, in the fashion of a medieval monk. Is he going to hand me an illuminated manuscript? Am I being driven around the sights of Barcelona by the ghost of William Blake?

Then he rips it out of his book with a flourish and gives it to me.

One day this humble taxi driver will tell his amigos that he had none other than the god Set in the back of his cab once.

And what did you say to him? His amigos will say.
I ask him if Adam had a navel.

I am feeling pretty good, but thinking to myself that *a fast green and yellow* doesn't have the same ring as *a fast black*, but then again, there are all sorts of connotations to the latter phrase, so maybe I am better off with a fast green and yellow. The circuitry in my head is all firing good and no fits or passing out today. I've been clean since we boarded the 'plane at Heathrow. However, Sydney has been successful in his mission, and, in the Bar Gaudi, by the bullring, I am staring down at the tennis ball-sized lump of dope in his hand and wondering how we are going to manage to consume it all before we have to go home tomorrow evening, and how we will manage to talk Sydney out of trying to bring it back into the country if we don't.

We smoke the first joint in a side street around the back of the bullring as, although we believe it is not illegal to use gear in Spain, we are unsure of the legality of an individual being in possession of a carbuncle the size that Sydney has in his trouser pocket. We then join a queue for the tickets and having acquired the means of entry, Sydney shows the prescience to get in another queue for some cushions.

"Having become comfortably numb," he says, "We don't want our arses to go numb, sitting on those stone seats for a couple of hours." This is the sort of initiative they teach us at Cambridge.

So Sydney distributes the zabutons, and we file into the arena with our pillows under our arms. To an objective onlooker, we probably resemble a bunch of naughty schoolboys ascending the steps to their dormitory. We take our places. After a while, there is a fine fanfare of trumpets. Out comes the bull, pawing the ground and snorting, black as Sydney's palanquin the night he knocked me into the gutter. Up comes the picador, a fat bastard with a sideways hat riding a cart horse in a stab jacket; and for a while he and the matadors stick unpleasant things in the bull until he is good and angry, before there is another fanfare and out comes the Toreador.

My head is spinning with the dope, but also, the regularity of the arena is getting me down, because I find myself contemplating the architectural unity of the bullring. As far as I can see it's a Roman amphitheatre. We sit in sets in serried ranks of pigeonholes just like the Sexcentenary Club, round and round, up and up to the open-topped O, and then it dawns on me. The Plaza de Toros is the Birdwood in

360 degrees. It's a bigger version of the spinning cylinder Harry had installed in Sydney's set. In my head, it's a spinning crenelated pinwheel. It's Poe's *Descent into the Maelstrom*. Then I am swept away by the symmetry of the place and before I know it, I am in another world.

The Toreador with his suit of lights and his red hat like the censorious old cunt on the Bols bottle is whirling his cape and goading the bull, who is stamping his front hooves in the sand and working up a real head of steam. Then I notice that it is not just the bull that has cloven hooves. The Toreador does too.

I rise in applause as the god Set dispatches the huge black bastard and tosses its sawn-off ears in the direction of the crowd. Then the arena is spinning around like a gigantic zoetrope as the flunkies tie the bull to a horse-drawn yoke and drag him out of the cockpit. It's Harry's pyrotechnic lunch with the *garaguella*. The whole Plaza is a gigantic spinning anemone shell, rising and whirling in the welkin. I watch as it rotates in the direction of Tibidabo in a helical arc. Then it bursts into flames.

Shielding my eyes from the sun, I glance at the newcomer in fancy dress who has asked if the seat next to me is free.

"Nice suit of lights," I say.

The god Set sits in the spare seat beside me. "Make the most of it," he says. "In the future, you won't be able to do this."

"What, smoke dope?" I ask.

"Visit a bullfight," he says.

I believe there were two or three more bouts with bulls before the main event, but I have no idea what was happening, because I was off on a culinary event with Seth.

"Look," I tell him. I have figured it out. "If we put you in a pie, like the sea bass at lunch time, and bake you in the oven, then I can chip the salt coating off you and the letters will come off and be stuck to the pie crust. Your skin will be clean."

So we get a bucket of flour and water and a lot of salt and we make it all sticky with an egg and bind it into a dough, before Seth takes all his clothes off and we roll him in the batter until he is coated all over, and then we pop him in the oven with just his head sticking out like a toad in the hole.

In the background I hear a shout of *Olé*! Hats off!

He comes out of the oven with the salt coating all hard and compacted like some bloated meringue, and I start chipping away at the shell of this tortoise very carefully along the fault lines. I get the carapace off neatly in two halves, and Seth is clean and rid of the words underneath, and all the letters are preserved on the salt and flour coating, and I am tracing them with my stubby finger; and I begin to understand them. I am beginning to write The Great Book of Thoth.

After the bullfights, Sydney announces that he intends to get mashed early in the morning and go to the Dali museum in Figueres in search of the painting known as *The Hallucinogenic Toreador* which happens to feature just such a bullring as we have been sat in for the last couple of hours. We are deeply unsure that the work is actually to be found in that museum; but he has made his mind up. He says so.

"I've made my mind up! Don't bother me with facts!"

To complete the evening, prefatory to a little siesta back at the Majestic before a late, Spanish dinner, we decide to take an open top bus tour of the City, enjoying a nice spliff from the upper deck.

Basically, there are only so many things to do in Barcelona, so we are redoing them, but from a different perspective, now from the top of a bus. And this is a worthwhile exercise, because we come to appreciate that there could be two cities; the same as Cambridge: an upper and lower city; the city seen by the walkers, cyclists and drivers; and the city seen from higher up.

The elevated city is all about night climbing. It is populated by statuary invisible from the ground, grinning gargoyles, characters of unclear import that must have had significance for the stone masons who laboriously carved them whilst perched unsteadily on giddy scaffolds. It's impressive. And after a few joints, it's very scary. I feel as though I'm taking a bus ride around Gotham City and the bus driver is Set. We hop off before the end of the tour as the bus is going down our street past our hotel, and we are all wasted and looking forward to some shuteye.

Alighting from the bus, Sydney announces: "I'll book a table at Casa Botin. It's Spain's oldest restaurant. Hemingway used to dine there."

Sweeping into reception, Sydney goes up to the concierge: "Can you book us a table for late dinner at Casa Botin?"

"Sir, it will have to be a very late dinner," the concierge replies sycophantically.

"No problem," says Sydney.

"Casa Botin is in Madrid, sir."

"Oh!"

The concierge recommends the restaurant 7 Portes. The restaurant of the 7 doors. We are told that it is very historic and one of the oldest in Barcelona. We book it for 7 persons at 11.00 pm.

Sydney does a head count: "Seth, Nick, Ingram, Burt, Spud, me. Where's Harry?"

"Fuck me!" I say. "He must still be down the zoo."

"Well, assuming the zoo shuts by 11.00, there will be seven of us at the restaurant of the 7 doors," observes Sydney.

"We can each enter by a different door, like in a spaghetti Western," suggests Burt.

"Cracking idea!" cries Sydney. "Let's meet up here at 10.00 so we can go on a bar crawl first. Seth, since we don't have any pigeonholes here, will you stick a note under Harry's door?"

It dawns on me that this is slightly territorial. As Sydney's protégé is absent, he is giving orders to mine.

I don't know where he gets the energy. I'm pooped already. Back in my room, I get out the Lepages, and stick the taxi receipt in my book, the ticket to the bullfight and the admission tickets to the zoo, Park Guell, the Sagrada Familia, la Pedrera and the funicular. My book is coming along.

As soon as my head hits the pillow, I'm off with the fairies, and I would never have got up for late dinner except two big lesbians with a skeleton key unpick the lock on my door to perform something called turn-down service. If I thought turn-down service had overtones of a happy ending, I was disappointed. They turfed me out of the bed, placed a biscuit on the fluffed up pillows, found a crappy tray and put the TV remote on it, flushed the john a couple of times, and marched out, leaving me naked and nursing my stiffie on the floor.

After our little rest, we're all met up at the appointed rendezvous which is a bar in *Las Ramblas* at the opposite end to the Christopher Colon statue, and we're ambling along past the stalls selling flowers and parrots when Sydney realises his protégé is missing.

"But just a minute," he says, "where's Harry?" He immediately points the finger of blame at my protégé. "Seth, did you push that note under his door?"

"I certainly did, but I don't think he came back from the zoo."

"He seems to have become emotionally involved with that albino gorilla that's in all the postcards," I explain.

"What?" cries Sydney. "Harry's in a relationship with a Vanilla Gorilla?"

"Yes," I say, "that seems to be the case."

"But is it a male gorilla or a female gorilla?" He enquires.

"Sydney," I say, "it's a fucking gorilla. It doesn't make it any the more acceptable if it's a female gorilla."

Despite lots of stoned false jocularity, dinner is tense. Sydney had asked me to organise the defining shot of the stag weekend, which was going to involve the 7 revellers entering the restaurant through the 7 different doors. How he thought I was going to do this with only 6 of us, and 5 of us if we counted on 1 of us having to take the shot, and the fact that the shot would have to be captured in 360 degrees, I have no idea.

But he had this bee in his bonnet about getting the shot in the can, and now its inevitable absence, like Harry's, hovered unspoken like a pall over the evening, probably not aided and abetted by the false highs and lows of all the gear and alcohol beginning to take their cumulative toll.

In an effort to escape from what has suddenly become the lacklustre present, Sydney starts seeking to organise the future. And why not? If the present is shit, live life in the future. What Max Pfläfflin would call a double time scheme. Barney Rubble! Live fast, die young. But even the future is falling through his fingers, because Ingram announces that he really wants to see the Palau de Musica Catalan, especially as tomorrow is Sunday and there's going to be a recital there, probably, I think, of Albéniz, that cunt who wrote very little for the guitar.

Spud and Sully want to join Ingram, they say, for the architecture and the rampant stone Pegasus's sprouting from the ceiling; but if truth be told, I think they are just a little over-Sydney'd. Not to be outdone, Sydney confirms that, following our delightful bullfight, he is going to the Dali Museum in Figueres to view *The Hallucinogenic Toreador*, but only after he has got well and truly smashed. He had trailed this earlier to test our reactions, but now, it seems, he is going through with it, even though it is highly unlikely that *The Hallucinogenic Toreador* is to be found there.

I agree to accompany him, whether out of sympathy or the desire to help him consume his weight of dope before he gets on the plane, who knows? There is still no sign of Harry. Seth just wants to go for another swim. "Anyone for a bracing dip?" he asks. *Bracing!* It's two-thirty in the fucking morning.

"As an Englishman, I wouldn't consider swimming in the Med," begins Burt, "unless my Spitfire had been shot down."

"It's disgusting!" exclaims Ingram. "In the Med, you don't so much swim as go through the motions."

I am conscious of the fact that what is supposed to be Sully's stag is fragmenting and it's more like seven psychopaths visit Barcelona and all go off doing their own thing; but I don't know what else I can do. 7 guys. 7 different doors. They have their entrances and their exits, but what Shakespeare didn't tell us was that they were all through the same door. The body is a temple; but everyone leaves through its anus.

It's 3.00 am. As Harry's door at the Majestic is next to mine, I knock on it lightly before retiring, and to my surprise, after looking through the spyhole, he opens it.

"Hi, Nick."

"You OK, Harry?"

"Yes, Nick, I'm great. Just couldn't face Sydney and that lot at dinner. I knew they'd be taking the piss out of me, so it seemed simpler to go off and have a bocadillo on my own."

"We thought you were sleeping in the zoo."

"They chucked me out at nine."

"You were there 'til nine? Harry, you were in the zoo for five hours."

"Yeh, five hours alone with my thoughts and Snowflake. And you know what, Nick?"

"What?"

"It seemed like one hour. I'm going back there tomorrow. I've got a date. Here, Nick," he says. "You can have the guidebook. I've read it."

I take his book and go back to my room.

In the morning, Ingram has already made his artistic intentions clear: he is sloping off to the *Palau Catalan Musica*, and taking most of the gathering with him; Seth is swimming, and Harry is going back to the zoo to fawn on his new soul-mate, Snowflake, so I find that I am, partly by default, and partly drawn by the lodestone of the ganja ball that has to be consumed before we return to the airport, joining Sydney on the early morning Catalan Talgo to Figueres and the *Teatre-Museu Salvador Dali* in search of *The Hallucinogenic Toreador* that we know isn't there, but we are going all the same.

After all, it wouldn't be much of a fucking hallucination if it really was there, would it? Sydney, arch-master of manipulation, had got Seth to carry his bag to the station before he takes his early morning dip. As Sydney had to check out the Majestic before going to the station, he must schlep his bag with him to Figueres. He had made some desultory efforts to carry it after a breakfast of chocolate-dipped churros, then despaired in exhaustion; then challenged the mighty Seth to see if he could lift it. Seth had felt obliged to demonstrate his physical supremacy.

The result was that Seth ended up carrying Sydney's bag to the railway station. What wasn't clear to me was why Sydney needed such a large bag for a stag weekend, but then I rationalised it by noting that Sydney likes to take a huge wardrobe with him wherever he may go, because he always needs to be just right for the occasion.

Seth nearly gives himself a hernia hoisting the heavy bag into the overhead rack in the train compartment, then bids us farewell and agrees to meet us at the airport. So we are off to Figueres in pursuit of The *Hallucinogenic Toreador*.

After Seth has departed, Sydney says to me: "Monkeys, Herodotus," and winks in the direction of the departing strongman.

"I don't get it," I admit.

"Herodotus, in his *Histories*, tells how the Abyssinians trained monkeys to get the banana harvest in. The humans go for the low hanging fruit. They pick a couple of nice easy bananas off the bottom of the tree, look at them with disdain and then throw them on the ground in feigned disgust. The monkeys are very imitative. Before you can say *knife* the monkeys have stripped all the difficult, high branches of bananas and thrown them on the ground too. Then the humans pick them up. Job done.

"Monkeys have harvested the bananas. I just pulled that trick on Seth. Muscles like that, he should be in a circus, not a university. Nick, word to the wise. Always go for the low-hanging fruit."

After this lesson in porterage from the past-master of palanquins, I settle down to read Harry's guidebook, It says that Guifré el Pelòs, meaning Wilfred the Hairy, a warrior baron living in the middle of the ninth century, is credited with the invention of the Catalan flag consisting of four crimson stripes on a gold background.

Originally, the Catalan flag was plain gold, and so was Guifré's shield and the shields of his troops. Fighting in the Siege of Barcelona, he was badly wounded. King Louis the Pious, under whom Guifré was serving, saw his brave warrior, Guifré, bleeding out and wondered what device he could give him for his shield by way of recognition for his heroic deeds. The King dipped his fingers in Guifré's wound and dragged the four gory digits down the gold shield. Thus was born in blood the Catalan flag, the gold background with four parallel strips running down it.

The train sets off. I am wondering if the wheels are spinning backwards like in the movies. With a name like *the Catalan Talgo*, I had been expecting something luxurious, at the very least a Japanese bullet train, but instead the Talgo is all grotty plastic seats and wooden floorboards littered with pistachio kernels and cigarette butts. Sydney takes a look around, checking out whether anyone would be likely to take exception if he fires up a spliff.

The carriage is pretty empty. The only other occupant is an old walrus in a blue reefer jacket whose face is a road-map of broken blood vessels, sucking on a huge Meerschaum pipe. We conclude that he is living in peace with his pipe and indifferent to what we might put in ours, so it makes sense to smoke as many joints as possible before anyone else enters the carriage.

Sydney and I are enjoying the first joint when Sydney says, "Nick, before we get too stoned, would you be so kind as to give me a hand with my case that Seth stowed in the overhead rack? There's something I need to get out."

The two of us heft the suitcase down amidst instructions from Sydney for me to be careful and *Easy does it*, as though there is something very fragile inside. Sydney has us set it down on the wooden floor like it's eggshells. He unzips it carefully, and, fuck me, there's nothing inside it except Calypso. Out she pops like a Jack-in-the-Box.

"Dear boy," he says, "you didn't think I was going to endure a stag weekend of male company and a trip to the Dali Museum in Figueres in search of *The Hallucinogenic Toreador* without my little Muse. Arise, Jewel of the Night, my Continuous One of the Heavens. Nick, you can throw the guidebook away; we have brought with us our own expert on surrealist art."

And she emerges from the case as though it were the most normal thing in the world. She's wearing suede hot pants and white Courréges cutaway boots. She looks like Wonder Woman with red hair. Or the genie of the lamp. She is the neatest thing I have ever seen. I want to put her back in the bag and run off with it. But I am worried. "Don't you think you could come to some harm, packing yourself into a bag like that? You could come a cropper one day," I point out.

"I think we've just invented a new way of fare-dodging," she says.

"Suppose an inspector comes aboard?" I ask.

"Easy," says Sydney. "We'll blame it on Seth. I had no idea there was a woman in the bag he carried on, and she had no idea where she was being taken to."

"After Port Bou, this train goes on all the way to Geneva," she says.

"My Pocket Venus knows everything," pronounces Sydney. "I'll bet you she could recite the fucking timetable."

"Pocket Venus needs a pee," she says and skips down the corridor. The green light above the door goes red for a while and I feel myself drifting back to the comfort of my dark room, and the moment when the god Set first materialised in my developer dish.

When Pocket Venus returns she informs us, "There are no less than 28 Venus de Milos in *The Hallucinogenic Toreador*. I've counted them."

"Why?" asks Sydney.

"I can't tell you why there are 28 of them," she says, "but I do know where they came from. In New York, Dali was presented with a box of English Venus pencils, and they used to come in cartons with the image of the Venus de Milo on them, and his cracked brain discovered the image of the toreador latent in the image of the Venus. You know how Dali was very famous for seeing double images."

Fuck me, I think. It's another Barney!

Sydney, me and our pocket Venus fare dodger alight at Figueres and follow the signs to the Dali Theatre Museum. After a short queue, we are inside.

I can see I am going to like this place. The Dali Museum has no hard edges. From the square outside with all the round Michelin men and eggs, to the bulbous Cadillac full of snails, to the pumped-up lips in the Mae West room, everything is soft, feminine.

Of course, *The Hallucinogenic Toreador* isn't here. None of the good stuff is. It's all been sold off to rich Yanks, or, in the case of *The Hallucinogenic Toreador*, a museum in St Petersburg. But they have a life size copy of it. The three of us study it.

"I don't get it," pronounces Sydney after a while. "I can't see the toreador."

I can't see it either.

Sydney continues more graphically: "It's just a seething mass of saffron and red like someone has eaten *paella* and drunk *Sangria* and then chucked it all up. Calypso, can you see it?"

"In my mind's eye, I see it," she says. Then Sydney's muse draws us into the narrative of the picture. She is like a blind guide leading me through the underworld and making sense of it. And as she explains it, all the hidden images on the huge canvas start to snap into focus as she draws me into the painting.

"The red and yellow colouring you refer to is a reference to the Catalan flag. Concentrate on the two largest Venuses, draped in green and saffron," she instructs us, but she doesn't know that Sydney has already wandered off and is looking at other exhibits.

If Sydney can't access something immediately, his attention span is too short and he moves on. I think that's what made Sydney a high achiever and good at exams. He doesn't waste his time trying to figure out questions that he doesn't know the answer to immediately; he just tosses them aside and keeps moving on until he arrives at something he knows he can do, then he executes it superbly. Others come up against a puzzle they can't solve and just freeze. *How to keep an Irishman amused for hours: see other wall.*

"Look at the right breast of the left Venus; the one in green. That forms the nose of the toreador, but his head is on its side at an angle. Once you've adjusted to the fact that his head is on its side (as it would be, because he is dying, recumbent), everything else should reveal itself. Now you can make out his lips under the nose, and Venus' belly button is his chin.

"Once you've grasped that, you'll be able to make out that the green draping is in fact his necktie, and once you've seen the tie, then you'll see the collar of his shirt, and on the left, down a bit, the shirt sort of bleeds out into the dead bull. You see the horns and the snout? The bull is dying, dripping blood, snot and saliva into the sand, stuck everywhere with bandalleras, scraping the arena with his nose."

One by one, each of the features she describes reveal themselves to me, like hidden meanings.

"Can you see the toreador's eyes? There is just one tear. Both the toreador and the bull are dead or dying. The dead toreador is a classic theme in Spanish painting, but this one evokes all of Dali's friends and family who have gone before, especially his elder brother who died before he was born, and his great friend Garcia Lorca who was executed by firing squad at the beginning of the Civil War, for the crime of being gay. Lorca wrote a very famous poem about a dying toreador, *Lament for the Death of a Bullfighter*. This picture works on so many different levels, not least, because every image is a double or triple image, so Dali is packing more into the canvas than other artists can achieve. It's like everyone else is working in 2D but he is working in 3D."

I am thinking to myself: it's a Barney. But I don't want to appear crass by saying it out loud.

"In the top left-hand corner, Dali's wife, Gala, looks on frowning, because she disapproves of bullfights, and diagonally opposed to the vision of Gala, in the bottom right-hand corner, is another familiar theme from Dali's paintings, Dali as a young boy, looking on at the crazy world he is causing to unfold. Dali, the toddler, juxtaposed to his wife, old enough to be his grandmother.

"In the middle bottom, there is a patch of blue water where the blood dripping from the bull transforms into the sea and a figure on a li-lo. This is *Cala Fridosa* beach on Cap de Creus, the rocky suburb of Dali's home town of Cadaqués, which forms the backdrop to most of Dali's greatest paintings, and whose weird rock formations dominate *Sleep* and *The Great Masturbator*. The Cadaqués mayor had just sold off this unique beauty spot to Club Med, and this is Dali's protest at the corruption.

"The picture is framed by the arena of the bullring and is dominated by swarms of flies. Dali loved flies, but only the glistening flies of the region. He used to smother himself in anchovy extract, so that they would crawl all over his skin whilst he was painting; the flies of shit, putrefaction and death, and as Sydney will know," nodding her head in the direction of her friend who was no longer there, "Beelzebub."

The warm sun is on my back. I am reclining on my side like the dying Toreador, on a li-lo floating on the gin-clear waters of *Cala Fridosa* at Cap de Creus. It's a big li-lo. Calypso, naked, is lying next to me.

Now we are the *Start Rite Kids*. We are walking hand in hand down an endless avenue, a wide, cypress-lined boulevard. From the pet shops and the flower stalls, I realise it's *Las Ramblas*. I have a large satchel on my back. No, it's a great big book that I am carrying as a back-pack. I am stooped with the weight of it. A heavy black motor car is careering towards us, weaving from side to side. At first I think it's Dali's Cadillac, but then it begins to look more like Sydney's Humber Super Snipe.

It's driven by a giant black snail with Sydney's fleshy features, putrefying at the wheel and erasing the tourists in the pavement cafés, upending the tables. It's headed straight for us. I can get out of the way, but Calypso can't see it. I have to protect her. It mustn't end like this.

I see millions of Catalans gathered in a square, unfurling mile after mile of gold and blood red flag, shouting, marching. *See, see Christ's blood streaming in the firmament. One drop, one drop...* I watch the jackboot of Madrid descending. Plastic bullets. Tear gas. Civil War. Thousands of little yellow bows.

So strong is my resistance to the inevitable ending of the story, I pull myself out of my fit and I am awake again standing in front of the painting, shaking.

"Nick, you're hurting me."

I realise that I am gripping her hand tightly, too tightly. I loosen my grip, but I don't want to let go of her altogether. The two of us are staring at the painting, holding hands, a boy and a girl, about to begin their journey into the painting. The *Start Rite Kids*.

"You were calling out my name," says Calypso.

The Hallucinogenic Toreador marks a turning point for me. I can induce my own reveries, and I can also walk away from them. Like Dali's double images, I can carry on two lives at the same time.

I can live in a double time scheme. It's a Barney Rubble!

Sydney has returned to the fold. "Having come all this way," he announces, "we may as well finish the job off by visiting Dali's hometown of Cadaqués. It's only a short hop down the road and over the mountain. Nick can immortalise us in some holiday snaps."

Tick tock, tick tock

Everything is measured now.
The beat of my heart,
The watch on my wrist,
The clock on the wall,
The display on my phone,
The read-out on my microwave,
The dashboard on my car,
The output when I fire up my PC,

The photos on my camera all filed away by time and date and place,
Every new gadget you buy; the first thing it wants to know is the time, but then the gadgets started telling the time for themselves.

The captain on the aircraft always tells you the time at your destination "Should you wish to adjust your watches". But your watches have already adjusted themselves before he said it. In that time in the future that your watch that is supposed to know all about time, has not even dreamed of yet.

A world in the future that the instruments of measuring destiny, have never imagined as being part of the future.

Every step I take.
It never used to be like this. It's creepy.

But at my back I always hear
Time's winged chariot drawing near...

I am reduced to nothing more than a unit of measurement, a cog in a double-time scheme.

It's getting worse;
My brain's upended.
I'm off to the Nurse,
As Max recommended.

Fucking doggerel!

A Visit to the Nurse

The nurse, Hilda, isn't full-time, but she is full-on. She has the use of two interconnecting rooms in the part of Peterhouse known as Noah's Ark. There are eye-shaped windows, but too high up to look out of. I am in the waiting room, and there's nothing to read except pamphlets on venereal diseases. I've enjoyed *Gonorrhoea; What it Means to You*, and I've thumbed through *Syphilis Through the Ages*, and I'm actually just about to dip into *Non-Specific Urethritis* when the previous bloke comes out and she invites me in. The previous bloke is walking like he's shit his pants, and my guess is that the nurse has pumped an enormous injection of some arse-tightening serum into his backside so that he has to walk numb-bumbed. Obviously didn't have Sydney's foresight to collect some cushions before he went in.

I didn't know parents still gave their children names like Hilda.

Nurse Hilda is easy on the eye. She is as wholesome as Mrs. Beaton, what with her starched uniform and her watch hanging from her breast. She has to be some kind of undercover deviant. Why else would she have installed herself here amongst all these male youths exploding with hormones? I want to discover her hidden depths.

Reading my name from the card in her hand, like the name was part of the problem, she says "Mr Jobs." And although she doesn't pronounce it as a question, when she says it, she raises her eyes and looks around, as if to say *Is anyone going to own up to being the owner of such a fucking stupid name?* even though she can see that there is only her and me present. I am thinking, *Should I tell her I have swapped names with the god Set?* Then, fixing me with her eyes, she says: "I'll see you now."

Nurse Hilda has got my trews and kecks down and is holding my balls in the palm of her hand as though I have ambled in to the assay office and she is going to weigh them before stamping a hallmark on them. I had always taken it for granted that one sought out a partner around one's own age so that you shared the same favourite pop groups, books and movies; but looking at this nurse, who is of a certain age, who is pretty fit, and who moreover has my kishkas in her hand, I am thinking to myself that I am up for an affair with an older woman. What did Pfläfflin say? Show him the ropes. Yes, she could show me her ropes. I am concentrating on getting my prick as rigid as possible so that she can't ignore it, and we'll see how she deals with it.

"Cough," she says.

I cough.

"Well, Mr Jobs," she says, as though we were in a *Carry On* film, staring down at my ludicrously engorged todger. "As far as I can see," and I swear she is addressing this to my cock, "There's nothing I can see that's wrong with you. Why did your director of studies suggest you should have an *aegrotat*?"

"It's not really physical," I say. "I suffer from epilepsy, and he seems to think I need longer."

"What did Pascal say when he finished his lengthy book?" she asks rhetorically, but I am conscious of the fact that she is still holding my balls and addressing her remarks to my cock. "If I had longer, it would have been shorter."

For a person who spends a lot of his time voluntarily abstracting himself from reality, even I am having difficulty in believing this conversation is happening. Why can't nurse be my director of studies instead of Pfläfflin, and I could have all my tutorials with my balls cupped in her hand?

"Is that what you call a double time scheme?" I ask her.

"All I know," she says, "is that the older you get, the faster the years spin by, but the gaps waiting for your holidays to come around seem to get longer and longer."

Double time schemes! It's a Barney! I don't want this conversation ever to end. I want to spend the rest of my days, standing here in this high-windowed room with this beautiful woman balancing my *putz* in her palm and misquoting Pascal to me.

"How old are you?" I ask.

"Old enough to know better, but still young enough to enjoy it," she replies without missing a stroke.

"You need to avoid straight lines, parallel lines, Venetian blinds, radiators, and…"—emphatically to my cock—"…hard edges. They exacerbate your condition. Embrace the soft," she advises. Then, with an alarming and detumescing crack, she has released my balls and is snapping off her latex gloves and tossing them into her bin with the contempt they deserve.

"There you go," she says, nodding at my flaccid tube. "I see you've made a start already."

I can't allow it to be over so soon. "Pfläfflin said you would want to take a specimen," I offer.

"I've taken it," she says. "It's on my glove."

My God, I hadn't even realised I had come off!

After I have pulled my Y-fronts and trousers back up, in an effort to regain some of the lost composure that is deposited on her discarded glove, I say to her: "I am told my condition is hereditary."

"Who told you that?"

"My dad."

"Is your dad epileptic?"

"Not to my knowledge."

"Well, there you go. "

"So it's not hereditary?"

"Absolutely not. Just bad luck."

I'm still unsure of how to bring our little meeting to a finish after having become intimate so quickly. Stupidly, I ask her if it's okay to take one of her brochures on *Living with Chlamydia*.

"Sure," she says. "Why not? After all, everybody's suffering from the same thing. Life is just a sexually transmitted disease, and I'm afraid it's terminal."

When I get downstairs, I chuck her brochure in the bin, overcome by foreboding at my own mortality, and regretful at the smear of my dynasty discarded in her dustbin. Just like my father said. End of the line.

A Gentleman's Agreement

"Couldn't you just make it happen for him once? It would be the summation of his life."

The god Set is looking at me like the madman I am. He is reading the Fabulous Furry Freak Brothers Compendium edition, and specifically the strip when Fat Freddie's Cat shits in his stereo headphones, and he is holding his demonic little pot belly and positively wetting himself with laughter. We are met together planning the future of the universe as we know it, and he is reading Fat Freddie's Cat, and is visibly pissed when I interrupt him. I can always tell when he's lying, because his ears go red.

"It's just that Sydney's spent his entire adolescent life trying to summon up the devil. Each day is a new assault on the unknown that ends in disappointment for him. Someone else would have stopped doing it years ago, but not Sydney. Each time, Sydney thinks he's just got one tiny thing wrong; that he just needs to make one minor adjustment, turn one more page in his Book of Spells, change the order of the words, and it will be right next time.

"He's not capable of stepping back and realising that he has a flawed business model. Don't you understand? He's invested too much in this for it to fail. He can't turn around and try something else. He has to make this work. If you are, as it were, mine to command, why don't you just let him conjure up one little demon; just so that his CV doesn't look so pathetic when Il Commendatore invites him for work experience in Hell?"

"Nick, I am the god Set. I am not the Careers Advisory Service; and summoning up the Devil isn't like an episode of *It'll be Alright on the Night*. I am not the genie of the fucking lamp. Look at me. Do I look like a pantomime dame to you?"

"You can't do it. You are expecting me to put my trust in you and undergo gruelling training and as close as it gets to gender reassignment, but you can't even summon up the devil."

"Holy Jism of the Redeemer! Of course I can summon up the fucking devil. But why would anyone want to do that? What good ever came of summoning up the devil?"

"Sydney has spent his waking life and probably his sleeping life, trying to summon up the devil. Is it really too much to ask that you make his dreams come true for just one night and fix him an audience with the devil?!"

"You serious about this?"

"As if my life depended upon it."

"Be it on your conscience. Let's just say that we have a gentleman's agreement. It's done. We don't speak of this again. Don't come asking me to undo this."

Girl Talk

"I think Nick may be two-timing on me," Olumidé confides to Bunty.

Now that Bun-in-the-Oven Bunty is a married woman, this ups the stakes for everybody else. Other girls start acting as though they are incomplete, because Bunty is wed in holy matrimony whilst they are still wasting their youths on Lotharios in search of transient thrills and the lure of ephemeral ejaculate. After Burt's untimely coupling, all the men are now stalking around looking over their shoulders, apprehensive that the women in their lives want to get knocked up so they can get spliced. Spliced, of course, being a term from the world of film-making, because such things only ever happen in films.

After the stag weekend in Barcelona, Burt and Bunty had taken the train to Gretna Green and got married there. There's only one reason that couples get married in Gretna Green.

"Why do you think so?"

"Well," says Olumidé, "he's just hardly ever there, and when he is there, it's as though he isn't all there. I come to his set at night and knock on the door. He doesn't answer it, but he swears he was inside and must have been dreaming."

"It's just the gear," Bunty assures her. "Makes them sleep more deeply. Cambridge! The whole city's like a fucking opium den!"

"And the other day I found these spots of cum in his pants, like he'd been fucking someone and had to pull his Y Fronts up real quick while he was still, you know, dripping."

"Are you sure he wasn't fucking you, Olumidé?"

"I just reached for his junk in his pants and it was already sticky down there."

"Just a bit of premature leakage, darling. I'd put him on rations."

"So you don't think he's two-timing?"

"Nick? He lacks guile."

Tibidabo

"Come with me."

"Where are we going?"

"We are already there in a twinkle, before you can even ask."

"Then where are we?"

"We are at the funicular at the bottom of Tibidabo in Barcelona. I could have whisked you straight to the top of Tibidabo, but I thought it would be passing fair to ride the funicular together."

Is it not passing fair to be a king
And ride in triumph through Persepolis?

The funicular is a cross between a fairground big dipper and a ski drag lift and, for one who is able to teleport himself at will, the God Set seems childishly excited at the prospect of his ride. He chooses the seat at the bottom of the carriage, facing downwards, whereas I would have chosen the top, facing upwards, but it seems he is accustomed to staring into the abyss. Seated, we cling to the hand bars watching the parallel rails of the point of our departure shrink away from us.

All the time, amidst the mechanical clatter and clunking of the device, he never stops chattering. What with him and the clattering of the funicular, it's like being shaken up inside a box of Mah-jong tiles. People are looking at us. I should be embarrassed, but I know I am soon to change beyond recognition, so I am in a devil-may-care frame of mind.

"Some days," Set pronounces, "you can see the whole of Barcelona. The vantage point is the old funfair on the Collserola massif behind the city, known as Tibidabo."

He is right. I can see the viaduct de Parc Guell, the Torre de Collserola, Ciutat Vella, the old cable car, the Palau de la Musica Catalana, the statute of Christopher Colon at the head of the Ramblas, the nodding and dipping derricks in the Port Vel and the big ships on the alley-alley-o. It is a clear day. I feel as though before I have been seeing things through a glass darkly.

"All this I will give to you. That is what this place means. Shall we ride the big wheel like Harry Lime?"

"Wasn't that in Vienna?"

"Then Goodnight, Vienna!" Set exclaims, removing his red cap for applause, and into the carts we hop.

My head was spinning before we climbed aboard. We are like two children side by side in a revolving pram. The phrase 'to hell in a handcart' is ringing in my ears.

"This is puerile!" I exclaim. "Why are you so fascinated by this fucking place?"

"But it is my address!" he says. "Here." He hands me a printed card. "I turn it over and over, but there is nothing inscribed on it except Set@tibidabo.es.

"That isn't an address," I complain.

"Oh, but it will be," says he. "And when you type it, it will change colour from black to blue and underline itself without you having to do anything at all. I promised you, all these things shall become clear."

Then he says: "See that down there? It's Barcelona zoo. Would you believe it? they've got a gorilla in there called Snowflake. Let's go and take a look at him!"

"How do we get back down again?" I ask.

"It's a leap of faith," says he. "As you requested, I have been making the preparations to make the Devil appear to Sydney Syzygy. I'm afraid there is always collateral damage."

I wake up. Someone is banging on my door. I hear Olumidé's voice calling out.

"Nick, I know you're in there."

Just for a change, I get up and answer the door. She's been acting quite strange recently. If she wasn't a virgin, I might think she was two-timing on me. A double time scheme.

The Senate House Leap

For some weeks now, in between his other engagements, Seth has been carrying an eight foot wooden plank around, like Christ on his way to Golgotha. He takes it out to Midsummer Common or Parkers Piece. He lays it on the ground, and sometimes he runs alongside of it and does a long jump. Then he measures his leap against the known length of the plank.

"8 foot," he says. "That's the distance of the Senate House Leap. An 8 foot jump sounds easy when you're down here, but when you're jumping between two buildings eighty foot up in the dark, it's not so clever."

"Why not?"

"Because there's no room to take a run up. You have to make the jump from a standing start."

"Then why do it?"

"Because it is the summation of any night-climber's career. The final Leap of Faith. I think I'm ready for it tomorrow night. Can you bring the camera and record this for posterity? It's a full moon tomorrow."

I imagine the 8 foot gap between the buildings, the figure suspended between them, not in contact with either, at the point where he has disconnected himself from one ledge and not yet arrived at the other, the silver disc of the moon behind him the only light source. I am not going to need a tripod, because this is going to be a lightning quick shot. Correct exposure is going to pose a problem. I'll need a 200mm telephoto lens, but that is going to absorb what little light there is. The flash won't carry that far.

"If this is going to work," I tell him, "you're going to have to illuminate yourself."

"Paraffin?" he asks seriously.

"Like the Human Torch?"

Flame on!

"I think not. What about that luminous watch paint that made the American factory girls glow in the dark?"

"Didn't it also give them all sorts of new cancers that hadn't been discovered before? They used to lick the paintbrushes they applied it with to get them in a nice, fine point for writing the numerals on the watch faces. Didn't one girl's jaw disintegrate when the dentist touched it to see why her teeth were glowing in the dark?"

"I see you are particular about the way in which you dice with death," I say. I would like to have followed up with the quote from the Duchess of Malfi when her persecutors are asking her if she doesn't fear the manner of her death, and she goes on about whether she might prefer being strangled with pearls or smothered in cassia; but I can't get it quite right in my head, so I keep silent.

Seth unfolds an A3 sheet of cartridge paper. Every inch of it is covered in his scrawls just like his body. It resembles the grid of a city, and I realise that's what it is, but as if the picture had been taken through an oculus in the firmament.

"It's a road map of the rooftops of Cambridge," he explains, "drawn in my own fair hand and painstakingly compiled over several months' worth of night climbing."

As far as I can make out, every altitudinous switchback is there, lovingly rendered to scale. I can see that he has graduated from the precise Canaletto perspectives of the Birdwood to something far more dangerous. He has mapped out and measured each perpendicular path and moreover the gaps between them, the vertiginous jumps that excite the night climbers.

Marvel comics have nothing to equal this and I find that I am thrown back on AC comics for my comparison. "It looks like a circuit diagram of Gotham City drawn up by Batman," is all I can say.

Cambridge Stegophilia

"Stegophilia," pronounces Sydney solemnly, rapping his knuckles upon the now out-of-print leading authority on the subject that he has acquired, *Night Climbing in Cambridge*, published under the pseudonym, Whipplesnaith in 1937. "Should we be more worried that it is going on right now above our very heads, or that it is common enough for a word to exist to describe it?"

The question that he has posed is more plangent than any of the rhetorical questions that our directors of studies have put to us over the last three years in their attempts to stimulate our raddled brains into creative activity. Looking around the room, I can see that Seth would do anything to get his hands on the rare gem that Sydney is rapping his knuckles on. It's been out of print since 1952.

First of all Sydney had to trump my protégé with his protégé. Now he has to trump Seth's night climbing proclivities by acquiring the definitive tome on the subject. If only the competitiveness had ended there, how different things might have turned out. But Set had indicated that there would be a price to pay.

"Stegophilia," Sydney continues for our benefit. "The practice of climbing tall buildings, in the instant case, the spires and steeples of Cambridge edifices, at night. It has to be done at night for many reasons: firstly, it's illegal, but it's hard to get caught if the authorities can't see you or reach you; secondly, it's a different world up there at night; thirdly, the challenge is all the greater.

"On any given night, unbeknown to us, the rooftops of Cambridge are alive. Shimmying up drainpipes, hugging onto gables, negotiating metal grates. It is more prevalent than we suspect. Under cover of the dark, there is a whole ant-like parallel world up there, with climber after climber scurrying around well-trodden ways and passages.

"Stegophilia: it sounds like a perversion, and perhaps," glancing across at his competitor, Seth, "it is."

"It seems there are two great prizes in the realm of the Cambridge night climber," Sydney pontificates, idly flicking through the pages. "The O'Hara Pinnacle at Trinity Hall, otherwise known as the Tottering Tower, and the Senate House Leap. Those who assay these climbs and jumps, must have their feats recorded on film. They also leave their mark on their conquests like true mountaineers. The author here," he taps on the cover of his book for greater authority, "tells of the stegophile who draped a Union Jack on the rooftop." Now reading from the text: "Upon descending, the porter told him to shoot it down. 'Sir,' he replies. 'I cannot shoot upon the Union Jack.'"

I can see that Sydney is offering us these glimpses in between the covers of his prized book to wind up Seth, who would clearly love to borrow it, or better still, own it. Then he could access all the anecdotes, folklore, useful tips and street cred that belong more naturally to him, and which Sydney has no use of, because he would never have the balls to go night climbing. He is locking horns with Seth, because Seth has been hitting on Calypso. Sydney is very happy for his mates to see his girlfriend naked when it suits him; but if anyone should attempt to follow through the process he has himself begun, he is highly territorial. That is what control is all about.

I can see that Spud also would dearly love to get his hands on this book. It may contain inside knowledge as to how they got that Austin 7 onto the roof of the Senate House.

The Austin 7

With the assistance of Seth, I have gained access to the turret room at Gonville, being the launching point for the Senate House Leap. I am looking across the 8 foot void to the Senate House roof. It's true that jumping 8 foot in a long jump is no big deal, but this jump is done illuminated only by the moon, and there is no room to take a run up. My stomach churns with dread, and I feel myself slipping into one of my reveries.

I am squatting on the roof of the turret room with the god Set beside me. The two of us are staring down into the 80 foot drop. We look like two stone gargoyles. I am scoping out the scene for when I have to film Seth doing the leap. Contemplating the Senate House roof, I ask Set if he knows how they got an Austin 7 up there in June 1958, because this is a riddle that is driving Spud mad, and someone needs to explain it to him so that he can get on with the rest of his life.

"Oh that," says Set, "Everyone knows about it in the future. Fifty years later to the day in June 2008, the ringleader called a press conference, came clean about the stunt, and staged a re-enactment.

"In June 1958, according to what he told the reporter of the Daily Telegraph, the week of the May Bumps boat race, Peter Davey, an engineering undergraduate at Gonville and Caius performed the most ingenious stunt ever witnessed in Cambridge. His rooms at college looked out over the Senate House roof, eighty feet above Trumpington Street pavement. Davey felt the roof "cried out" for some further adornment.

"Davey recruited 11 confederates to assist him in his enterprise, or 13 if you count the two girls in short skirts. They chose the week of the May Bumps, as what they were about to do would be partly visible from the river, but in those days before mass tourism, they figured the only people using the river would be drunken oarsmen celebrating their victories in the Bumps.

"Davey decided that the architectural purity of the Senate House roof, which for some reason has always been a magnet to undergraduates, would benefit from the further ornamentation of having a motor car on top of it.

"The pranksters towed a broken-down Austin 7 through the streets of

Cambridge and parked it beneath their destination. In order to explain its presence, they hung advertisements on it for a May Ball, so that it appeared to be a marketing stunt.

"Under cover of night, one group of Davey's assistants hoisted the car aloft using a makeshift A-shaped crane made out of scaffolding poles and steel cable, all of which materials they had "borrowed" from building sites. Another group bridged the famous gap between the Senate House roof and this turret window at Caius, famously known as The Senate House Leap, with a scaffolding board, and shoved the vehicle across the deadly gap with ropes, hooks and pulleys. Three drunken rowers who spotted the activity were persuaded it was a tethered balloon. Any possible onlookers from the Trumpington Street side were distracted by the two girl students who had agreed to hoist up their hemlines.

"The following day, the onlookers gazed in awe at the sight of the Austin 7 parked on the roof of the Senate House. It took the authorities a week to figure out how to remove it. They had to use scaffolding to get up there before cutting the car into manageable pieces with blowtorches. The then Dean of Caius, the Right Reverend Hugh Montefiore, had an inkling who was responsible and sent a case of champagne to his staircase by way of congratulations.

"Davey, himself a prodigious night climber, went on to establish electronic automaton and robotic companies in England, Heidelberg and California, and was awarded a CBE. He said his only regret was that the car wasn't left there forever."

**

Electronic automaton and robotic companies. Where do these words come from? What do they mean? It is as if I have already started writing the book of the future I am inventing that the God Set warned me I must author.

"Are you alright?" Seth has to ask the question twice before I slip out of my reverie. Our arms are resting on the window ledge of the turret room. These little attacks are becoming more common. I realise I am using drug abuse as a front to conceal my predicament. That way everyone just treats it as a joke: *Old Nick was wasted again!*

"How long was I gone for?" I ask.

"Well, I couldn't say exactly when you left us," says Seth. "It was like one of those phone calls when it dawns on you that you have been cut off because the person on the other end has not contributed anything useful to the conversation for some time. Anyway, where did you go to?"

"I was just thinking about that stunt when they got the Austin 7 onto the Senate House roof."

"Oh, that. You've been spending too much time with Spud. That's all he ever thinks about."

"I know how they did it."

"Well, don't tell Spud. He would be devastated."

My gaze falls onto Seth's massive forearm. I could swear that some of the characters are missing: *Electronic automaton and robotic companies*. Sounds like a fine business for a control freak like Sydney.

Zoetrope

I have exposed the first contact strip and glued it to the inside of a cardboard drum, as recommended by the god Set. Holding it by its spindle, I rotate the images of Seth's tortured body, more out of idle curiosity than anything else really. One by one, the letters detach themselves from him and form at the back of my retina. It says *The Book of Thoth*. And if you rotate the same contact prints in the opposite direction, it says, By *Nick Jobs*.

I suspect that it is going to take me a great deal of time to come to terms with this.

A Transcendental Punt Trip to the Orchard Tea Rooms

One thing I will definitely say for Sydney. He doesn't do things by halves. Having announced a punt trip along the Upper River to Grantchester, he has lined the inside of the punt with rugs and carpets. Several bottles of champagne are tied to the sides to chill in the Granta, and for those in need of a hot drink, he has brought the silver samovar aboard. A Thermos flask just wouldn't have cut it. His porters *schlepped* all the stuff to the Scudamore's dock in his sedan chair. There are black candles on every horizontal surface and disposable lighters a-plenty, because the candles are obviously going to blow out every few minutes. At the prow is a vintage wind-up gramophone with a horn speaker and a collection of Glen Miller 78s.

Although our destination is the Orchard Tea Rooms, this has not stopped Sydney from also shipping a large wicker hamper of other culinary delights. There are rolled up towels in case anyone fancies a dip; there are tea-cloths to wipe the river slime from the necks of the bottles when we crack them open.

Having gone to so much trouble to lay this on, there is no question whatsoever of Sydney doing any manual labour such as punting, so he has arranged himself, in a fez hat with his queue streaming out the back, his best Indiacraft shirt and rolled up linen trouser bottoms, on a pile of ornately decorated scatter cushions at the prow in front of the platform for the punter. He looks like a cross between Colonel Gadhafi and Tommy Cooper. He is smoking an Imperial Russian in an ivory holder, and has so many large rings on every finger that if he were to take a dip their weight would certainly drag him straight to the bottom.

Seated between his open knees is Calypso. I can't tell if she's in her underwear or a bikini. She is so still. She calms me down whilst she raises my pulse. A tortoiseshell butterfly rests on her lifeless hand. No motion hath she now, no force. She neither hears nor sees.

Rolled around in earth's diurnal course…

Sydney drops the Imperial Russian over the side, where it fizzles momentarily in the Cam before he fires up the first of many spliffs.

Ingram is welcomed aboard, as is Self-Harming Harry, Burt Sully and your narrator. Burt volunteers to take the first watch with the punt pole, because that way he figures, due to the configuration of the punt's occupants, he can stand behind the seated Sydney and Calypso and stare at Calypso's tits and tummy without her or Sydney knowing. He should take up photography like me. Then he would have a perfect excuse all the time. However, to Burt's chagrin, Sydney countermands Burt's offer, saying that his protégé, Harry, has to be schooled in the noble art of punting, and besides, since he has been promoted and relieved of his duties portering the palanquin, his hands have started going soft. So Harry grasps the punt pole and steps up to the plate.

Seth was invited, but has gone back for his swimming trunks as the heat is already shimmering on the meniscus of the Upper River. Now that we are enlightened as to his being a nepton, we appreciate he would not want to miss an opportunity to swim against the current. He says he will cycle down and join us en route, no doubt wishing to make his own grand entrance.

When he broke the news about going back for his trunks, Calypso teased him: "Why bother? They're all guys except me, and I can't see."

Seth appeared to see the logic in what she was saying, but then decided to go for his trunks anyway. I think it wasn't her he was worried about, but Ingram.

"I'll go all the same," he announced.

"What's your mouth taste like today?" she asked.

Sydney looked from one to the other, sensing something was going on that he didn't altogether approve of. Seth went off at a run. Self-Harming Harry shoved the boat away from the dock with the punt pole.

I am excused punting, because my hand is still mending from my encounter with Sydney's window. But I am not excused the bong. My word, that's strong gear!

When Calypso asks Sydney why he needed to bring so many provisions aboard when our destination is a tea house, Sydney replies by quoting King Lear in Stentorian tones:

O, reason not the need! Our basest beggars
Are in the poorest things superfluous.
...Thou art a lady;
If only to go warm were gorgeous

Why, nature needs not what thou gorgeous wear'st
Which scarcely keeps thee warm.

After the first bend, Calypso announces that she wants to take a stand at the punt. The tortoiseshell butterfly takes weightless flight. Self-Harming Harry passes the baton on to her whilst Sydney passes the joint on to me. Sightless, Calypso glides us through the slippery water between the shades of weeping willow trees. She is using the punt pole as a blind man uses his cane.

After taking the helm for maybe twenty minutes, Calypso expertly docks the vessel at the appointed spot where Seth is to join us, planting the pole firmly against the side of the boat to keep it in place. There is no sign of Seth yet. She slips out of her bikini and slides into the water, silently, like a vole. She is not seen again.

The god Set is swimming strongly up the river, just as he swam in my developer tray. With his considerable upper body strength, he pulls himself up onto the back of the punt and grasps the pole in his hands. He is naked and dripping wet. Sydney has not turned around. He must be thinking his Lyca has climbed aboard after her swim and is resuming her position on the punt counter. Set plants the pole and off we go. The others, too drunk or too stoned to notice the substitution gaze ahead with glassy eyes. Maybe they are just being polite and making a point of not staring at the naked swimmer when she emerges.

The god Set plants the punt pole with such determination and sheer force as though he were sticking a pig, and he holds the boat with the pole in the mud whilst the muscles and veins in his sinewy oxters stand out in relief, causing the boat to revolve on its own axis of evil. I have never seen this before: a handbrake turn in a punt. Someone else, one of the stoned voyagers calls it a three punt turn. It must be Self-Harming Harry; but the turn is brutal. Everything is going round and round. My head is spinning.

Set is so powerful. The muscles on his musculature ripple with each shove of the pole, and then the punt seems to glide on for an eternity before it needs another shove. His prehensile tail is trailing in the water behind him, acting as a rudder. Then with an almighty push of the pole I become aware of the fact that there is no longer any sound of the bubbling water slapping against the flanks of the boat. Frictionless, we are riding above the water.

Perched on the huff, he pushes the punt again, and we are maybe six feet high. Why has no-one else noticed? Now we are above the willow trees, all the clanking champagne bottles tied to the side of the coracle bobbing like the corks on a bushman's hat. I pass the spliff to Burt and marvel at the magic carpet ride to the strains of Glen Miller's String of Pearls on Sydney's wind-up gramophone.

Because he has rotated the vessel, we are no longer headed downriver. Now, we are soaring above the Backs, the water meadows and the Cotswold stone turrets of Kings, St John's and Trinity. We are looking down on the prized terrain of the night climbers of Cambridge. I can see the King's College choristers streaming towards the East.

"Everyone got drenched to the skin!"

Ingram is retelling the story of the transcendental stoned punt passage to Grantchester in the Cricketers Arms.

"Luckily for Nick, when Calypso parked the boat and went for her swim, he had decided to disembark and have a pleasant forty winks on the river bank, or his camera would have been ruined. Seth arrived at the ordained meeting point and in his efforts to get his bicycle on board overturned the bloody punt.

"All of Sydney's contraband went to the bottom of the river; our finger sandwiches were sodden, all the rugs and soft furnishings were waterlogged and the cushions went bobbing down the river like ducks in formation. It was Calypso, who was already in the water, who managed to right it again, but all the towels were soaking wet, so we had to dry ourselves on the sharp grass in the sun between taking turns to dive down searching for missing parts of the gramophone and samovar."

"And what of Nick?" asks Spud, who had attended his lectures that day and not participated in the doomed voyage.

"Nick? Nick Jobs? He was lying all the while in what the Gawain Poet calls his *erbe grene*, his herb garden of the green genie, on the banks of the Cam," answers Sydney.

"But surely, it is a Grene Knichte, not an Erber Grene?" pipes up shallow Burt Sully.

"No," explains Seth, whose gift of total recall compartmentalises every epic poem in the chambers of his brain. "He's not quoting from Gawain and The Green Knight, but from the other, lesser known and far more mystical work by the same author, *Pearl*."

"Never heard of it."

"It was lost for many years."

"What's it all about, Seth?"

Seth looks around the room. He could recite the entire poem if he wanted to, but the mnemonic feat of mechanical recall is far easier than the intellectual activity required to explain it.

"Well…" He is trying to articulate to the non-cognoscenti what a great work is all about in one word. No-one has asked him what the plot is or who the protagonists are. He has been asked what it is about.

"It is about…" He looks from face to face as the word materialises in his psyche: "Loss."

We look at one another, from face to face, as this simple proposition sinks in.

Lying on the banks of an unfordable river, gazing to the other side.

It dawns on us that every meaningful book that has ever been written from the time of The Bible to my work-in-progress, *The Book of Thoth*, is upon the same subject: loss. The only thing that ever changes is how much of yourself you lose when you set it down.

The Senate House Leap

To get the shot, I am lying on my back on the pavement in the 8-foot gap between Gonville and Caius College and the Senate House. The Nikon shutter speed is dialled in to 1/200 of a second and I am using my rubber remote bulb to depress the shutter because squeezing the button on the camera would give rise to shake. Seth will be launching himself from the Caius side. I hear the whistle of *Old Man River* 80 feet up in the night sky and brace myself for the shot.

If I don't catch it, and Seth survives, he will kill me. If he doesn't make it, he will kill himself. Then it happens. The *jeteé*, like the Enzo Plazotta statue approaching the Tate Gallery in Millbank. Balletic, beautiful, framed by the silver disc of the full moon, dispensing light like the chiliagon spokes of a wheel. It is over in the blink of an eye, but somehow it is also lingering, as if he has been frozen between the two buildings, as hopefully the camera will reveal.

The Nikon's shutter is fired by the remote bulb of air in my fist. One two hundredth of a second that feels like five seconds. The reassuring click of the aperture and the more reassuring thud as Seth lands safely on the Senate House roof.

"What do you think?" I ask Sydney, tabling the prints of Seth's Senate House leap against the backdrop of the full moon. I am half-expecting him to consign them to the flames. Calypso is gathering around, smoothing down the prints with her hands as though she might read them by adsorption. The way she is doing it is the same way as the waiters in a posh restaurant smooth down a new tablecloth before they seat you.

At length, Sydney delivers his verdict, but resentfully, because it is not him: neither he nor his protégé are the star of this show. It's my camerawork and my protégé. "They are fucking amazing!" he says. For a moment, I am thinking that this is one for the books. For a change, Sydney is jealous of me, instead of me being jealous of him. But then I realise that it is Seth that Sydney is jealous of: his brute masculinity. Sydney fills a room with presence, because he has studied it and rehearsed it and is busy turning himself into a work of art. Seth just does it naturally because he is huge. As soon as he enters a room, the room is full.

And I have to say the snaps are pretty stunning. Illuminated by a full moon, it looks as though someone has hurled a nitrate discus at Seth's head, which is the light source, and none of Seth's four limbs are in contact with anything else as he jumps between the two buildings. It is a stunning moment suspended in time.

After more compliments—all to the performer, I should add, and none to the photographer who recorded it—eventually everybody leaves the set except for Sydney and Calypso and me. Then Sydney takes me to one side and says, "I have to do it, but better."

"Do what?"

"The Senate House leap."

"Sydney," I protest, "you're not cut out for that sort of thing. It takes years of training. It's very dangerous."

"I've been reading Whipplesnaith," he says. "It's all psychological preparation. Do you know that photograph of the scaffolders eating their lunch balanced on an RSJ at the top of the Empire State Building?"

I am familiar with the photograph he is referring to.

"If the steel beam were on the ground, everyone would walk up and down it with ease. It's just the fabrication of our minds that makes us frightened because it's high up; but the width of the beam is constant. Doesn't matter if it's on the ground or a hundred yards up. And because it's at night time, we won't even be able to see what we're doing, so we won't worry about it. Anyway, I have prescribed myself some Dutch courage. I want you to take the shot; but it has to be a better shot than Seth's."

"How are we supposed to make it better?"

"I'll do it in my white tailcoat," says he. "Then you will have the cruciform limbs plus the two matching arcs of the tails. I'll hold my right hand up thus…"—he shows me the fourth position at ballet—"and if shot from the right angle so that the moon is above my right hand, it will look as though I'm a butler in outer space, holding a silver tray aloft."

"But, Sydney, why would you want to be a butler in outer space?" I ask.

"Because it's not been done before."

"Sydney, where did you get this crazy idea?"

"The devil put it in my head."

"Sydney, why don't you start out with something simpler? The O'Hara pinnacle is difficult enough, but you can climb that carefully, and if you change your mind halfway up, you can shimmy down again. You don't have to commit yourself to making that jump into the dark."

"I most certainly do, and you must film it."

"But, Sydney, after tonight, there won't be another full moon for a month."

"Then we must put our skates on, mustn't we?"

Flag

This morning, on the door of today's cubicle in the Birdwood, I saw some psychotic had inscribed a fairly lengthy quotation from *The Waste Land*:

A woman drew her long black hair out tight
And fiddled whisper music on those strings
And bats with baby faces in the violet light
Whistled, and beat their wings
And crawled head downward down a blackened wall
And upside down in air were towers
Tolling reminiscent bells, that kept the hours
And voices singing out of empty cisterns and exhausted wells.

I read it two or three times. It kind of set the scene for how the latter part of the day was to unfold.

But I promised earlier to explain what we were doing in a psychotic state at Reality Checkpoint. I am so sorry. I jump around all over the place. I am worse than Seth.

As was our wont, we had arranged to meet at the flagpole at Wolfson College. Amidst the mouldering, medieval megaliths of Cambridge, Wolfson was a beacon of modernity. As it was not an example of Cambridge trophy architecture, it had to try harder to lure people towards itself. Thus it had an excellent dancehall promoting new bands, events, concerts. It also hosted gastronomic dining events. It was coeducational, and not only did the sexes mingle in harmony as in Eden before the Fall, but undergraduates mixed freely with postgraduates and mature students.

Many an evening started off at the flagpole outside Wolfson College, just as one might say, *Meet me under the clock at Waterloo Station*. Sydney was prepared to leave the gentleman's club that masqueraded as his rooms to go there, because he regarded the journey as a kind of *hajj* in the direction of Judaism. After its benefactor, Lord Wolfson, it was in Sydney's warped mind Cambridge's equivalent to the Judea. For Burt Sully, a bike ride or perambulation to Wolfson was probably the only exercise he got.

For Calypso, it was on the way to Girton, if she ever went to Girton anymore. For those seeking escapism from the historic centre, Wolfson held the promise of an unruly border town, an *embarcadero*. One would meet up there to "go on" somewhere else. We knew no-one who was a student there. It was just a jumping off point.

Tonight was the night designated by Sydney as being the night of the Great Cambridge Mandrake Hunt, and we had arranged to meet up at the flagpole before embarking upon whatever was involved in such an enterprise. The word was that Sydney had sealed instructions in envelopes from Smythsons of Bond Street.

I was sauntering along with Björn Agen. It was dusk. He had the collar of his reefer jacket turned up. The winter's day had been bright and clear with our shapes casting Giacommetti silhouettes, but as soon as the sun had gone down, there was no warmth, and a chill breeze had started blowing in from the Fens, the sort of damp coldness that penetrates one to the very marrow.

Björn and I had already broken the journey with stopovers in two public houses. In the second hostelry, it being so cold, there was no-one else in the beer garden, we had considered it safe to light up some of Björn's Moroccan blond; and then, after another pint, I felt it would have been rude not to reciprocate with the remains of my Nepalese Temple Balls.

There was a tall ewe hedge in the beer garden. If it is possible for something to throw a shadow in the dark, that sepulchral ewe hedge achieved that paradox. It seemed to multiply the darkness until it was palpable. Then, from a high tree beyond the ewe hedge, we heard the hoot of an owl that sent shivers down our spines. There was that old full moon that cast little light as it was seemingly being sliced in two by a scythe-shaped cloud. Then, to add to this sense of foreboding, vampire bats began streaming incessantly out of that infernal ewe. The black hedge seemed to be breeding the unclean things. They were swarming as though we had stumbled upon their forcing-house.

"Where do bats live?" asked Björn.

"I believe, in a set," I replied, guessing, but I liked the word Set.

"What is the collective noun for a swarm of bats?" asked Björn, deferring to my supposedly greater knowledge of English, either because I was English and he was not, or because I was supposed to be studying

English. This reminded me that I still hadn't written a word of my essay on the *Ghost of a Flea*, and as I dwelt upon that sad failure, I swear I saw the image that haunted Blake come creeping out of the hedge, contemplating the contents of its bowl.

"A colony," I said, my mind stretching back to my learned studies of Batman comics. But the only colony I could visualise was a leper colony from that fucking Henryson poem. "It's also known as a cloud."

"The cloud of unknowing," remarked Björn.

The vile things were dive-bombing us, brushing against my face and lips. I spat forcibly and spat again.

"There's only one thing to do," pronounced Björn.

I thought he was going to say that we should go inside. But no, his solution was to fire up another joint. He said the smoke would keep them at bay. And they did withdraw momentarily. They rose and passed across the face of the moon like a plague of locusts. But they were simply regrouping for their next assault.

They had stopped brushing against my head. But only because they were now inside it.

Just as the bats elevated themselves, the ground game made its appearance. The keening of foxes; the arcing gait of an hare with burning coals for eyes; then something large and damp-smelling with black fur against the blacker cloth of the night, rubbing its filthy coat against the poisonous hedge; the webbed feet of Canada Geese pat-pat-patting on the wet grass, setting free a host of smaller beings infesting the lawn. The earth seemed alive and swarming with a million seething maggots busily going about their business. This was collective madness because Björn saw it too. "Let's go!" he said.

And go we did.

In this state of heightened apprehension, we were jogging along the Barton Road about to turn right at the Tango and Salsa Society corner towards the Wolfson college flagpole, when we noticed that the crepuscular bats had followed us and continued to dart around. It was quite creepy, but we could just discern the reassuring shape of the flagpole ahead. We knew the Sydney was approaching it from Selwyn Gardens, the opposite side.

Aware that we would soon be in company, and not just any company, but the company of Sydney Syzygy, Björn and I were attempting to make braggadocio demon-exorcising conversation, discussing whether to go for a dodgy kebab to soak up the beers and dope, or see what was on at the Arts Cinema. I believe it's called small talk.

Sydney is always punctual, and as we drew closer to the flagpole, we saw his four porters bearing his black sedan chair at a trot. Self-Harming Harry was one of their number, but not bearing the litter. He was carrying a flambeau as evidence of his promotion. To Sydney's barked instructions from within the dark velvet-lined cabin, the porters lowered their burden, and he emerged with Calypso on his arm, as though they were headed for an evening at the opera. Both of them were dressed to the nines.

Harry's self-induced pale face in the guttering *sfumato* of the flambeau cast some dim light on the proceedings. Spud was already seated at the bottom of the flagpole, resembling one of Bacon's studies of the figures at the base of the crucifix. Harry's words were slurred, so I assume that he had been smoking with Sydney. Sydney's style, when he was stoned, was to work harder at his enunciation trying to over-compensate for it and act normal; what my nan used to call *putting on your telephone voice*; so I could tell that he was stoned too.

"Why do you think the flag is flying at half-mast?" asked Sydney. "Has someone important passed away?"

To tell you the truth, I hadn't noticed. The flagpole was just the appointed meeting place. I hadn't really paid it any more attention. I hadn't analysed its quiddity as a flagpole, or what Socrates would have called its *areté*, as perhaps I should have done.

"Has someone died?" Calypso asked.

The accursed colony of bats darted by again as if to answer her question. Yes, they had died and risen from the dead. What other infernal gathering shares this collective noun? There is only a colony of bats, and a colony of lepers.

"Christ, I'm *ausgeflipt*!" remarked Björn.

"Aus-what?" asked Harry.

"*Ausgeflipt*. German word," offered Sydney. "Means the state of being smashed out of your head. Off your face. Put that in your commonplace book. Fuck me, I am a great mentor for you! The only aus he knows is *Aus widersehen pet!*"

"At least it's not Yiddish," said Spud, rising from his position at the base of the flagpole.

Now that Sydney had drawn our attention to the flagpole, our stoned and vacant brains tried to focus on the flag at half-mast.

"Something's wrong with it," said Sydney.

There was something not quite right, but I couldn't put my finger on it at first. I blamed my lack of alertness on the distraction of the cloud of bats that rushed past again, colonising my perception.

"There's a brisk wind," said Björn, "but the flag's not moving at all. It's facing the wind when it should be blowing in the direction of the wind."

"Maybe they used too much starch when they ironed it," joked Calypso, who couldn't see it, but was entering into the spirit.

The flag was solid black.

I was just thinking back to my collection of Flags of the World from bubble-gum, and thinking to myself *I've never seen a flag like this before. Who has an all-black flag?*

Then the most uncanny thing happened. The flag slithered down from the flagpole and started walking towards us on two legs. Harry was the first to scream and start running. Sydney followed suit with Calypso, although Calypso was just being dragged along and didn't know why she was running. I followed them at a brisk pace. Björn fled in a different direction. Spud screamed and followed us. What a fine collection of superheroes we were!

I think Calypso, who couldn't see the frightening apparition, must have directed Sydney's steps towards Reality Checkpoint, as she would have assumed that we were having a bad trip and imagined that a flag that had taken on sentient life was coming to claim our souls. So Calypso figured that the eponymous Reality Checkpoint was a sensible place to bring us all back to earth.

"Jesus Christ!" exclaimed Harry. "The thing was pointing towards me! He was coming for me."

"No!" cried Sydney. "He was definitely coming for me. It was like the Appointment in Samara. You know that old Mesopotamian folktale, where the king's gardener sees Death making a threatening gesture at him in the garden, and he runs terrified to the king and begs the king to lend him his swiftest horse to flee far away from Death, to Samara. And the king lends him his fastest horse and the gardener gallops to

Samara.

"Later in the evening, the king is walking in his garden, when he too comes face to face with Death. 'Why did you make a threatening gesture to my gardener?' the King asks him. 'That was not a threatening gesture,' says Death. 'It was a gesture of surprise to see him here, because I have an appointment with him in Samara tonight.'"

As we are contemplating this, we discern the sentient flag approaching. To make sure that it's not my imagination playing tricks on me, I ask Spud if he sees it too. His exclaimed, "Oh, Jesus Christ, no!" confirms that he sees it too. Just as we are about to run away again, it starts talking.

"It's only me! It's me, Seth Godil!" We are under starter's orders to scarper again, but Calypso holds us steady.

"I was practising my human flag," he explains.

Spud is the first one to make the connection. "How long can you hold it for?" he asks.

"That was forty-one seconds," answers Seth.

"It has to be a new world record," says Spud.

And that, dear Reader, is how the four of us (and Calypso) came to be slumped around the base of the lamppost on Parkers Piece that is known as Reality Checkpoint, in a state of heightened collective paranoia on the Night of the Great Cambridge Mandrake Hunt.

Fearful Symmetry

My days are taking on a structure at last, a symmetry. I need things to be orderly in my life if I am to withstand the ghostly, forked visitor that comes to the end of my bed and disturbs my rem sleep, and stop it from taking over my waking life. I need to stamp my days with a routine.

So in the mornings, I get up and go to the Birdwood where I contemplate the parallel lines of the cubicles and imbibe the words of wisdom written on their walls. Next, a full English breakfast in Hall, served by flunkies who call me Sir until they know me better and then, when they know me better, they call me *Mr Jobs*. I have learned that you can score off the assistant chef. He's not a real chef. He just dishes out the food; but they let him wear a toque. His acned forehead is all red and sore from it, but he won't take it off, because it signifies his status. And I think to myself that he hides his stash up there. If the toque was red, he would remind me of the censorious cunt on the Bols bottle. Or the god Set.

Then I go to Calypso's next lecture to have my intellect tickled at the same time as my fancy. Then I go to Hall for lunch and chat with whoever is hanging out there. Then I go around to Sydney's set and get trashed. Then in the evenings, it's dinner in the Hall, after which I repair to the Sex Club for some bevvies and maybe a round of table football, if I can find a partner. After, I collect my camera from my room. Then I go back to Sydney's to help him raise the devil. This also gives a fearful symmetry to my day. Raising the devil by night and seeking to push him away in the morning.

Rolled around in earth's diurnal course.

Same old. Same old.

At the weekends, I get to see Olumidé, because her schedule is now more complicated than mine. She says she's so stressed out it's giving her dysmenorrhea. Every time she sees me, she has her period.

In the lacunae in my hectic schedule, I might develop some photos of the goings-on. Apart from Calypso's, I've been here two years now and not been to a single lecture.

This morning, the words of wisdom on the bog door say:

How to keep an Irishman amused for hours –See opposite wall
And on the opposite wall it says:

How to keep an Irishman amused for hours—See opposite wall

I'm not Irish, but to tell you the truth, it amused me for a good 5 minutes. I liked the symmetry of it. Symmetry is what I need to fight the demons.

After breakfast, Calypso's talk is entitled:

The Overpainting of the Angelus

Proverbs of Hell

The next morning in the Birdwood, as I lift the seat up to pee, someone has written on the underneath of the seat:

Thank God! A man at last!
Above the bog roll, someone else has written:
Sociology degrees; please take one.

Then I go to dry my hands on the Towelmaster, which is a machine manufactured, as I see from the brass plate on its front, by a company called Advance, that never dispenses a sufficient length of towel for you to dry anything properly. In a felt tip pen, someone has written *AND BE RECOGNISED* beneath the brass plate. The Birdwood is just like Seth's body. It is written on everywhere. The more you delve into it, the more you are rewarded by its gnomic wisdom.

A Game of Murder in the Dark After Magritte's *The Threatened Assassin*

Richard Brokenshaw is a Fellow of Selwyn. His field is Rococo and Neo-Classicism. Somehow or other Sydney, with his ability to chat to anyone, has widened his circle further so that Brokenshaw enters his orbit. Brokenshaw has a large Gothic pile and formal gardens in Grantchester, but he's not using it this weekend, because he is paying a visit to Sans Souci in Potsdam, preparatory to contributing a preface to a large tome about its architecture to be published by Taschen.

He will be staying in both the East and the West of Berlin and he has a special pass from the Master of Peterhouse to cross the Berlin Wall. Brokenshaw is a judge on the RIBA panel for aspiring new British architect of the year, but clearly Brokenshaw lacks judgment, because, whilst he is away in Potsdam, he has given the keys to his house to Sydney, telling him to make free use of it for the weekend.

Grantchester may only be 5 miles away from the centre of Cambridge, but the weekend has a real holiday feel to it. We aren't to sleep in Brokenshaw's beds, so we have sleeping bags. Olumidé and I are sharing a sleeping bag and she has whispered to me that tonight she intends to give me her virginity. I don't know if I am feeling excited or exploited by her for giving the occasion such a big build up. This life-defining event has been hyped up for so long that I am not even sure I can rise to the occasion. But to set me off in the right direction I have anointed myself liberally with *Balafre*.

Sydney is driving Lyca to Grantchester in his Humber Super Snipe, because Sydney needs a car with a huge boot to carry all his belongings, because whatever house he goes to, he has to make it his house, like a cat spraying out its territory. They are giving a lift to Self-Harming Harry, because Harry is Sydney's *protégé*, so that makes sense. Ingram has managed to borrow his father's car for the weekend in an effort to impress us, even though it means that he is going to have to drive it back 150 miles on Sunday night, and hitch hike back to Cambridge, because his dad needs it for Monday morning.

Unfortunately, he has drawn the short straw as there was nobody left to impress apart from Olumidé and me, Burt Sully and his *enceinte* wife, Bunty. Olumidé and I are squashed into the backseat with Bunty, because it makes more sense to put Burt in the front with Ingram. Ingram is giving us a display of his driving skills.

His father's car is a Ford Prefect with the gear shift in the steering column. People know it as a Dagenham Dustbin. He is over-revving it to impress us. It has no overtaking power, especially with But Surely and the three of us shoehorned in, so he just keeps cussing and saying "Not safe to overtake" every time he noses her out into the suicide lane and then has to retire ignominiously. But we're there before we know it.

We arrive at dusk and are gathered in the living room, having filled the fridge up with wine, beer and pizzas. Seth has disappeared somewhere, no doubt searching for new structures to climb. He has taken his citrus tang of *Balafre* with him, so that I now have no competition for my after-shave.

The house is huge and rambling. I have never come across a house with two staircases before. It is set hundreds of yards back from the road, but the back garden is even bigger, featuring infinite clusters of formal Italianate gardens nested one within another and culminating in a huge sunken garden like a sink hole. We can enjoy complete seclusion whilst Olumidé attempts to lose her virginity.

Both Olumidé and Calypso are wearing very short skirts. Olumidé has a mini-kilt that wraps around her snaky hips and the only thing that seems to be holding it together is a big safety pin at the front. Calypso has a gold halter top and a minute frothy concoction like a denim tutu, scarcely any bigger than a belt. Her bare legs seem to go on forever, incredibly pale.

She is sitting cross-legged on the floor, but she has managed to fold her ankles in on themselves in a feat of human Origami that provides a scintilla of modesty. I can't believe it. In a day when *debutantes* graduated from Lucy Clayton finishing school having learned nothing except how to get out of an E-Type Jaguar without showing their knickers, here was the 39th in line for the throne, Calypso Sitzclarence, looking like a delicious edible pretzel in a microskirt.

Sydney, with his innate sense of propriety, is attempting to involve the gathering in an intelligent conversation before it degenerates into the usual stoned giggling and munchies. He is holding court on Stanley Kubrick and how *2001* changed his life when it was released in 1968, how one just knew one was staring the making of history in the face from that fantastic beginning when the primates throw that bone into the sky to the strains of *Also Sprach Zarathustra*.

Someone has found an LP with the soundtrack to the movie, and, after a difference of opinion as to whether we are supposed to put it on the turntable or use it to roll joints on, we are listening to the plangent opening chords of *Also Sprach Zarathustra* whilst Sydney pontificates about evolution and existentialism, artificial intelligence and whether *2001* is a better work than *A Clockwork Orange*, even though there is more sex and violence in the Orange.

It would appear that Burty and Bunty haven't seen the film. Not wanting to be left out of the conversation, Burt tries to change the subject by proposing a game of Truth or Dare. After breaking up some matchsticks which we draw by way of lots, Ingram draws the short straw of being the interrogator and Sydney draws the still shorter straw of being the object of the first round. But Surely is visibly disappointed at the all-male result, undoubtedly having hoped for an opportunity to listen to the girls' Truths or watch the girls' Dares.

Ingram to Sydney: "Truth or dare?"

"Truth."

"OK. I'm going to ask you twenty questions."

"That was your first question."

"What was?"

"You asked if I wanted truth or dare; your second question was *What was?*"

"No, that doesn't count. That was all just to establish which choice you pick."

"You may have thirteen questions. One for Christ and each disciple."

"OK. Let's start with a simple question to check you are telling the truth. What is your name?"

"Sydney Syzygy."

"What is your calling?"

"I am a magician."

"Why practice magic?"

"It's the only means available to mere mortals to rise above the gravity that chains us all to the human condition."

"How proficient a magician would you say you are?

"I would say I am at the level of Magus."

"Is that the highest level?"

"No, the highest level is Ipsissimus. That is beyond all the others and also beyond all comprehension of those of the lower orders."

"What sort of magic do you practice?"

"Sexual Magic. I have tried Ceremonial Magic, but its ascent to the Astral Plane is too slow and the materials too expensive. It is possible to arrive at the same destination using Sex and Drugs, which is quicker and much cheaper. It was created by Theodor Russ in Germany and developed by Aleister Crowley not so long ago at this very university. He teaches that *Matter is an illusion created by Will through Mind, and consequently susceptible of alteration at the behest of the Creator.*"

"What is its goal?"

"True Knowledge of Self."

"What drives people to have recourse to magic?"

"We live in an age of uncertainty where the number of maniacs who could bring one's own life and all of humanity to an abrupt end are so legion that one takes to magic to quell the mortal fears in wildness and excess."

"What are its tenets?"

"First, that there exists a parallel universe known as the Astral Plane. This is a timeless realm. The Astral Plane is a medium more fluid than the real world and consequently more susceptible to alteration by the Magician. It is the existence of the Astral Plane that enables soothsayers to predict and clairvoyants to communicate. Secondly, that there is a correlation between the seen and the hidden, the microcosm of man and the macrocosm of the universe. This is known as The Doctrine of Signatures. Thirdly, that the powers of the true magician are limitless."

"Do you have a Guardian Angel in the Astral Plane, a Tutelary Spirit?"

"But of course. Every magician must have one."

"What's he called?"

"*Angelus.*"

"Is he a red Indian?"

"No. She is a dead child."

"And what does she do?"

"She is dictating *the Book of Thoth* to me."

Ingram Frazier, barrister-in-training, with his dry questioning, has managed to reduce what should be a party game more fun than naked Twister into a fustian session on the psychiatrist's couch.

Attempting to lighten up the ennui, having seen neither 2001 nor A Clockwork Orange and therefore not wanting to return to them, and not understanding the truths that Sydney sententiously recounts, But Surely next suggests we play Consequences, but no-one can find any pens or paper. Then somebody suggests a game of Charades, but that seems to require too much intelligence. Then Sydney says we could play Murder in the Dark.

I glance over at Calypso in her tutu, the doll-like legs hanging out of the bottom as though she were a Pelham puppet. I am thinking that she would have an unfair advantage at Murder in the Dark, as she has chosen to spend her Cambridge years with her eyes glued firmly shut.

Without me noticing, she has risen from her cross-legged position on the floor. She is jigging about, dancing to herself, like girls do, on their own, around their handbags. She has one arm higher than the other in a balletic movement; she pirouettes, unaware that I am watching her. I feel both very protective towards her whilst at the same time obsessed with the idea of fucking her.

Then I realise the *2001* film soundtrack has moved on from *Also Sprach Zarathustra*. It is *The Blue Danube*. I'd forgotten it was part of the score. I feel myself taking a very funny turn. But the blood isn't emptying from one side of my head to the other this time. It's emptying from my brain and going straight to my dick.

"I've never played," says Olumidé. "Can we do an open hand or something?"

"As there are a number of different versions of the game, let us first establish the rules to which we will play," announces Sydney. "Here is a deck of cards." He is already busy shuffling them like a slimy croupier. "I am removing the jokers, and dealing out the rest of the deck face down" which he proceeds to do to those seated around the table. "Whatever you do, upon your life, do not show your cards to anybody else. The person who draws the Ace of Spades is the Murderer. The person who draws the Jack of Hearts is the Detective. If the Detective is murdered, the person who has drawn the King of Hearts will be the Detective. Next—"

"Wait," says Ingram, "we need to legislate for the possibility that more than one detective might get murdered."

"That should not be possible," explains Sydney. "Because after the first murder, the victim must cry out *Murder in the Dark!* at which point the person nearest to the light switch must turn all the lights on. As I was saying, the person who draws the King of Hearts will be the Policeman."

"What does the Policeman do?"

"Why do we need a Policeman and a Detective?"

"I don't rightly know. Let's forget about the Policeman then, shall we? Where was I? As I was saying, we turn out all the lights so that the house is pitch black…"

"Whoa there!" says Ingram. "Why do we need to deal out the entire pack? Surely all we need to deal is the Ace of Spades and a couple of Court Cards."

"But then it would be too obvious who is who," suggests Spud.

"Well, what happens if the same person is dealt the Murderer and the Detective?"

This has even Sydney stumped for a moment, but then he says, "That person must declare himself, and we will redeal. Where was I?"

"You had turned out all the lights," says the permanently benighted Calypso.

"Ah yes, we turn out all the lights. The players then disperse themselves around the premises and conceal themselves how they will. The Murderer counts to 100 to give them time to do so, and then he stalks them. When he finds a victim, he touches that person on the shoulder and whispers *You're dead.*

"The victim must then count to 50 to enable the Murderer to put some space between himself and the victim, and then the victim must cry out *Murder in the Dark!* at which sound the person or persons nearest the lights must turn on the lights and everyone must remain in the positions in which they are in when the lights come on, save for the Victim, who may lie down upon the floor or a bed or other suitable receptacle…"

"…Such as a coffin," giggles Bunty.

"The Detective then assesses the situation; the attitude of the Victim, the whereabouts of the sundry persons in juxtaposition to the Victim, and he can ask questions of everybody, save of course the Victim, who is dead, such as *Where were you when you heard the cry of Murder?* And other questions of a more forensic disposition that you can dream up for yourselves. All answers must be truthful, save the Murderer can lie. Eventually, the detective has to accuse someone of Murder. If he is right, he has won the game. If he is wrong, he loses."

"And what spoils belong to the victor?" asks Ingram.

"Fuck knows!" says Sydney. "Let's just play the game and see what happens, shall we?"

"What happens if someone doesn't want to play?" asks Harry, the someone in question clearly being him.

"We all need to play," informs Sydney. "If the numbers are too low, it will be obvious who the Murderer is."

"OK," says Harry reluctantly. "Do you want me to give the deck a little extra shuffle, or shall I cut?"

"First of all," says Sydney, "let's have another joint, shall we?"

Ingram complains that Calypso has an unfair advantage in the dark. Calypso offers not to participate, pleased to be rid of the stupid game, but everyone insists, so she relents.

"Sometimes," she says, "people can have their eyes wide open, but miss things." And she is looking at me with her closed eyes. "Take Millais' *Angelus*, a painting of two peasants in the potato harvest at Barbizon in France. They are in a field, heads bowed over a basket of potatoes. They look like they are praying. But Salvador Dali saw something different from everybody else. He said that the painting wasn't a spiritual painting of a husband and wife peasant, heads bowed in silent prayer. He said it was a funeral.

He got so agitated that, having regard to what was by then his huge reputation, he absolutely insisted the Louvre X-Ray it to see if it had been overpainted. They relented. He was right. The potato basket between the husband and wife peasants with their bowed heads had been overpainted. Beneath it was a child's coffin. How could Dali have seen that?"

A child's coffin overpainted. I am horrified by the sense of loss.

The cards are dealt. In this first round, I have nothing in my hand, which I suppose makes me a natural Victim. Calypso is making eyes at me. I can't tell if she is giving me the come on, or if she is scrutinising me because she thinks I am the Murderer.

Harry announces that he is the Detective. Burt announces that he has the King of Hearts, so if we had a Policeman, he would be Policeman. But we haven't. So he is another cipher, as far as we know.

The lights go off and there is a mass exodus. The exodus starts swiftly, because everyone knows where the door to the room is, but once they get out of the door, things slow down, because everyone is fumbling in the dark, unfamiliar with the layout of the house. Apart from the Detective, who stays in the room, Calypso and I are the last to leave. I follow Calypso out.

I have decided to head upstairs and hide in a bathroom. That way, if the waiting is protracted, I can always do a slash, or negotiate terms of entry with others who didn't have the foresight to think of that for themselves. I am feeling for something that I think is the rounded wooden spindle to the staircase banister, but it is too smooth. I realise it must be Calypso's leg in the short skirt. She has had the same idea as me to head upstairs.

After five seconds that feel like five minutes, I realise that I am still stroking her leg and she is putting up no resistance, so I decide to let my hand wander higher. I am in her knickers and she is already sopping wet. I swear it is the most exquisite fanny in Christendom. I don't know whether to fuck it or drink from it.

"Parlour games are so fucking boring!" she purrs in my ear, and then she traces the shape of my mouth with her finger and plants her mouth to mine as though she intended to suck out my soul. Her other hand is reaching inside my trousers and she has my todger out. "So," she whispers, "just like old times, eh?"

I am drawing her gusset to one side and about to enter her on the staircase when some cunt cries out *Murder in the dark!* and we both realise the lights are about to go on. In fact, it seems all the potential victims and the Murderer must also have headed upstairs, because when the lights go on, they only go on in the upper rooms. I have just managed to rearrange my jeans when Harry the Detective emerges from the kitchen shining a torch at us, as the downstairs is still in darkness.

He walks past us, unconcerned, because, of course, he first needs to find his dead body, and he will then take it from there. The victim is evidently upstairs somewhere. We follow him to the next storey.

It's Olumidé. Of course, it's Olumidé. Always is. One of life's natural victims. She is sprawled out across the bed in the Master Bedroom, her short skirt riding indecently high. She is face down, positioned like one of those crime scene caricatures in the movies. She should be defined by chalk lines and incident tape. She is probably taking the opportunity to catch up on her sleep. She has been doing night shifts at the hospital.

The person nearest to her, and therefore the natural suspect for Murderer is Sydney Syzygy, who is sitting on the avocado crapper in the bathroom *en suite* to the bedroom's crime scene, his feet buried in a fluffy rug meant to stop drops of wee marking the bathroom carpet. His fists, resting on his thighs, are clenched together, possibly concealing a murder weapon of some sort. Our Detective assesses the crime scene, probably coming to the conclusion that Sydney is just too obvious and a decent Murderer would have put more space between his Victim and himself.

Our intrepid Detective begins with Sydney.

"So, sir," says our Sleuth. "What are you doing sitting on the can with the lid down and your trousers up?"

"I was attempting to hone my skills at rolling a joint in total darkness," ventures Sydney. "One never knows when one may be called upon to roll a spliff in the dark."

"And where is this spliff?" asks the Detective.

Sydney opens his right fist which encloses a Clipper lighter and a cigarette sawn down the middle by Syzygy's thumbnail; he opens his left fist to reveal the misshapen beginnings of a joint. It is not a pretty sight; but it also dawns on the Detective that a clever Murderer could have thrown this alibi together in the seconds between carrying out the murder and the cry of *Murder in the Dark!* Its very misshapenness was because the Murderer had little time to act.

The Detective finds a pair of bathroom tweezers in the light-up mirrored cupboard on the wall.

"Would you move your feet, please?" Sydney opens his thighs wider and plants his feet a few inches further apart. Our detective pokes around in the tufts of the fluffy white wee rag beneath Sydney's monogrammed slippers. Combing the strands aside, he reveals a series of microscopic burn holes in the acrylic rug. In the crater of each hole, lies a near-invisible smouldering meteorite of dope that Sydney would have been heating with his Clipper lighter and which has fallen out of the ill-made joint. Sydney then presumably stamped out his elven bush fires in the wee rag before we had a serious conflagration on our hands.

Sydney's story seems to stack up. Having ascertained that Sydney is not the Murderer, the Detective proceeds to pump him for information, in the confidence that the answers he gets from this witness will be honest, as opposed to the mendacious crock of shit he would get from the Murderer.

To Calypso: "Describe the route you took to get to where you are."

"I got to the top of the stairs, feeling my way up the bannisters; then I got the munchies, so I was coming back down again, headed for the kitchen for another slice of the dope cake, when I bumped into someone coming up the stairs, and then someone else got murdered and the light came on."

"And who was it you bumped into?" quizzes our intrepid sleuth.

"I couldn't see," Calypso answers.

Her account probably had the ring of truth, because it probably was true, except she had omitted the part that rang most resonantly with me.

To Sydney Syzygy: "And you, Sydney, describe how you came to be sitting on the can."

"I felt my way up the bannisters like everyone else. Calypso and Nick were behind me. Olumidé and Ingram were ahead of me. I don't know where Burty and Bunty were. I didn't see what happened to Seth. When I got to the top of the stairs there were a lot of unfamiliar rooms, so I fired up my Clipper lighter to see my way and walked through the bedroom where Ingram was murdering Olumidé, went into the *en suite*, sat down on the john and started rolling this joint."

"You say you actually saw the Murderer carrying out the murder?"

"Well, on the assumption that Olumidé is the victim, she was murdered before my very eyes by Ingram."

The Detective informs Ingram that he is arresting him for murder and that anything he says may be taken down in evidence and so forth.

"Well, that wasn't much sport," Ingram complains. "This is supposed to be murder in the dark. It's not exactly going to stretch your powers of detection if you've got a stool pigeon with a searchlight illuminating all the nefarious goings on, is it?"

The Detective and Sydney having been duly disgraced in this first attempt at murder in the dark, no-one except me has much appetite to try another hand at the game, but I am keen to get them engaged before they all stuff their faces on the hash cake and get *ausgeflipt*. I am keen to complete my unfinished business with Calypso.

I keep brushing the fingers of my right hand, the one that came into contact with her sex, nonchalantly under my nose, like I am just stroking my upper lip, breathing in her musk, her heady scent that makes me oblivious to the deep disloyalty I am planning against my best male friend and my best female friend at the same time. Two birds with one stone. Calypso must know what I am doing and I swear she keeps giving me knowing looks, even through shut eyes, like she's saying there's more where that came from, and more is what I want more of. More is even better than enough.

The perfume of Calypso's arousal hovers like a miasma in front of my keen nostrils, combining with the *Balafre* and the lingering sweetness of the dope, whilst the fading chords of *The Blue Danube* have my cock uncurling and straining at its jockeys as though a hooded cobra is squaring up to Rikki-Tikki-Tavvi for the battle to end all battles. Just So.

"Well," I venture, "we had better redefine the rules a little, if we are going to assay another round of murder in the dark. This is a variation that I learned in the States."

I have never been to the States, but the god Set is doing the talking.

"In this version, we don't have a Detective. He is replaced by the District Attorney. We don't bother to draw cards for DA. Sydney is DA as punishment for messing up the last round. The DA has to sit outside the house at the bottom of the sunken garden to give the Murderer more time and make it more challenging for the crime to be solved. The DA stays at the bottom of the garden until he either hears the victim cry out *Murder in the dark!* or he sees the lights going on. Then he comes in and carries out his investigation. If he wishes to play with his Clipper lighter or roll joints in the garden, that will not compromise the integrity of the crime scene."

Reader, dear Reader, as you will have gathered, the variation is simply intended to keep Sydney as far away as possible, to enable me to extract every last droplet of enjoyment from his enchanting paramour, Calypso.

I continue with further rules intended to prolong my anticipated moment of ecstasy.

"When someone gets murdered," I continue, trying to hold their interest, "They have to count to 1,000 before calling out *Murder in the Dark!*"

This raises a few eyebrows, except I can see Calypso is getting it already. She is looking straight at me and she is raising the three fingers of her left hand to her mouth as if in the inchoate preparation of a blown kiss. "Because," and here I come to my *piece de resistance*, "the Murderer is allowed to commit more than one murder. He can in theory commit as many murders as can be committed in the space of 1,000 seconds, being his window of opportunity before the hue and cry goes up."

"But surely," complains Burt Sully, "in that time he could murder everyone except the Detective, I beg your pardon, the DA, and the only reason he doesn't murder him, is because you've stuck him outside at the end of the garden."

"Well then, that would be the perfect crime, wouldn't it?" I improvise, "But in practice he would not do so, because if he murders everyone except the DA, it will be very obvious that he is the Murderer. But because the odds of finding the Murderer increase in favour of the DA with each murder, as the pool of suspects is diminished, the Murderer is allowed to move his victims."

"Move his victims?"

"Yes, he can put the bodies in different places or situations, just to make it more difficult for the DA."

What I am trying to do, and I have already removed the Ace of Spades from the deck to ensure that I am the Murderer and thereby in control of the pace of the game, is ensure that I can remove anybody else who happens to be in the room and steal at least 1,000 seconds of bliss between Calypso's thighs before the hue and cry goes up. 1,000 seconds. That is 16.6666666 minutes. I probably don't need quite as long as that, even allowing for tissuing her down afterwards. Is she on the pill? It would be ill-mannered to ask her so personal a question, and waste precious time. I'll just fuck her. Where is all this invention coming from? I ask myself. It's not me. It is the god Set asserting himself in me. He is on the ascendant. I hear my evil angel whispering in my ear.

*Put out the light, and then put out the light…*Turn up; tune in; turn on the double time scheme.

They are all sat around the kitchen table as if we are going to have a séance. I deal out the cards confident in the knowledge the Ace of Spades is removed. I realise my hands are shaking. If anyone notices, they will assume it is the dope. My mouth is also very dry. That probably is the dope.

I go through the motion of dealing out the whole deck, totally pointless, as we already have our DA, and the Ace of Spades has been deftly palmed by your narrator. Then my good angel whispers in my other ear.

Take no part in and have no fellowship with the fruitless deeds and enterprises of darkness.

With the DA appointed without election and the only card in the deck that has any meaning removed, I complete the dealing, ask everyone to remember their card if they have the murderous Ace, and I then escort the DA to a stone bench in the sunken garden at the end of the reassuringly infinite series of formal Italianate gardens.

Furthermore, there are lots of ornamental boxes and arches of honeysuckle and rose, so he can't even run in a straight line. He has to climb out of the sunken garden, which is worse than getting out of a bath with an arthritic hip, even if he wasn't trashed (which he is) and then dodge around the shrubs and rockeries, weave past things in terracotta pots, prickly cacti and, for all I know, man-eating plants.

The route he would have to take would be like the route of a steel bearing in a pinball machine, so his journey will take him far longer. I explain to him that he needs to be as far back from the house as possible, so that he can command a view of the whole house and see in which room the light first goes on. That may aid him in his deliberations.

Then re-entering the kitchen, I note everyone's position, especially Calypso's. She is still doing this thing with the three fingers of her left hand and giving me meaningful looks with her eyes shut. I consider actually locking the back door so that the DA can't get in at all, but reject the idea as being a step too far even for me and Set.

Olumidé is quaffing the cabernet sauvignon because she doesn't use dope. Burt is grabbing a last mouthful of cake before flicking the light switch off. This is usually as much exercise as he takes. He is holding

Bunty by the hand, but I tell them they must split up or it isn't fair.

As the room enters blackout mode I am taking a mental stock-taking of everyone's position and where they appear to be headed. Calypso will have gone straight up the stairs. No ifs, no buts. I am bounding up them two at a time, a dog on scent. I continue taking the human inventory: Sydney, we know about: he is at the end of the garden staring from the outside upon the dark canvas of the house inside which the love of his life is about to get fucked by me.

She wants it as badly as I do. She will have gone straight to the bedroom. No more rumpy-pumpy on the stairs like in round 1. No, this is going to be the real thing this time. What is it that they say about marriage? Exchanging the hurly burly of the *chaise longue* for the deep, deep peace of the double bed. But Brokenshaw's house has 8 bedrooms.

Burty and Bunty will be too lazy to mount the stairs. Despite my injunction not to hold hands, they will have secreted themselves somewhere on the ground floor, probably not too far from the hash cake. If Sully had assayed the stairs, I would be able to hear him puffing and breathless, which I do not; the diastole systole of his heart pumping the blood into unfamiliar parts of his body, the unfamiliar parts in question being any part that is neither his arse nor his mouth. Bunty wouldn't have strayed far from him. So that's Burty and Bunty ticked off.

As for Olumidé, she has already been murdered once. What worse could happen to her? She is a creature of habit. She will go for safety and familiarity. Last time she was found in the middle of the bed, and I would guess she would go back to exactly the same place. She feels safe there. If she is murdered, she has a nice squishy mattress to fall into. She will go back to precisely the same spot, like a dog returning to its vomit.

Ingram, he thinks he is a clever cunt, so he will have to hide himself in more complex obscurity than anybody else would ever bother with, and then get bored at the length of time it takes us to find him. As if we give a fuck where he is. He is the sort of bloke who would open a window and go to the trouble of standing on tiptoe on an uncomfortable window ledge, entering fully into the spirit. No need to worry about him. He will have concealed himself into total abstraction. He won't get in the way.

Seth? Well, he disappeared before we started. He is probably shimmying up the drainpipes and night climbing Brokenshaw's Gothic heap as we speak.

All I have to do is find Calypso before I find anyone else, and swive her to my heart's content, doing the deed of darkness one thousand times, without the incessant worry of wondering how many of those precious one thousand seconds have expired, because they won't even have started. I will take my pleasure with Calypso and go on my murderous spree afterwards. The D.A will be rolling joints at the end of the garden inhaling the night scented stocks.

At the top of the stairs, I have to make a decision to turn right or left. Then it dawns on me. She was giving me a coded signal. The three fingers of her left hand passing over her mouth suggestively. I have to turn left and go to the third room. I should have been the fucking DA. I am smarter than all of them. This isn't like me. It is the god Set asserting himself.

They should never have put that fucking music on the turntable. I can't be held to blame if other people play provocative jingles. I feel my way past the frames of three doors. I enter the third door and inch my way, waiting to encounter the soft obstacle of the bed, my terminus. I can sense another animal presence in the room. I swear I can smell her sex. Although it is as dark as fuck, my pupils dilate involuntarily, trying to extract any shards of luminosity remaining from these finite bands of the spectrum.

And then I encounter it: the bed. As I mount it with one knee and both palms flat, I feel her shifting her weight to accommodate me. She has extended her arm, like a signpost, so that I can get my bearing. My fingers trace their way to the top of her arm. Her armpits are unshaven, which I find inexplicably sexy. Straying on, it is no distance at all to her breasts. The halter top just pulls down and she is wearing no bra. We are French kissing as I feel her nipples stiffening. She has unzipped me and has both of her hands around my cock, flattering me as though its girth requires two hands. As I let out an involuntary gasp of pleasure, I hear someone giggling in the dark. There is someone else in the room. I will have to get rid of that person.

The giggle had come from under the bed. Someone must have entered the bedroom in the dark before Calypso and hidden herself under the bed before Calypso climbed on top of it. "Keep my place,"

I whisper to Calypso. "I'll be right back." I then swing across the side of the bed and pull out the giggler by the ankles.

When I have him or her all the way out, I say, "Consider yourself dead and start counting. Get to your feet." The victim rises, mumbling "5,6,7,8,9…" I pick the victim up and hoist him over my shoulder in a fireman's lift and shamble along the corridor. I'm certain it's a man, and it's a man that weighs a fucking ton. I'm sure I must have murdered Burt, he's so heavy. It's like carrying two sacks of wet cement. I have no idea where I am finding such reserves of strength.

I enter the fourth room to the right and throw Burt into the empty space where I was expecting the bed to be in a similar position to the bedroom I'd just left. But it isn't. He lands on the wooden floor with a thud and also with a crack, but I can't tell if the crack is a minor bone such as a tibia or a fibula, or maybe a stick of furniture he has broken. But he can't be badly injured because he's still counting: He's up to 149 already. I have to move fast. Time's winged chariot is hurrying near.

I am back in the adjoining bedroom. My heart is pounding in my chest, partly with the exertion of humping the dead body down the corridor and partly with lustful anticipation. I snuggle up against Calypso on the bed. "Did you keep my place?" I ask her *sotto voce*. By way of answer, having found my knob, she draws me towards her, where she has thoughtfully removed her knickers. Her pussy is a vortex. I feel myself being inexorably sucked into it cock first.

But then she stiffens up. "What was that?" she says.

"I didn't hear anything," I lie, not wanting to hear anything that will come between me and the satisfaction of my carnal urges towards Calypso. But then it happens again, and this time even I can't ignore it. Someone is suppressing a sneeze. Our activity has been shaking dust out of the mattress and some hay fever sufferer is underneath it. Jesus Christ, there must have been two people under the bed, not one. They were probably giggling, because they were probably doing under the bed the same as we were trying to do on it, probably more successfully.

Zipping myself up, I pull out the second victim. "You're dead," I inform him or her. "Onto your feet and start counting." I hoist the next victim up into the fireman's lift, as I go stumbling along the by-now familiar corridor. Thankfully, this victim is slightly lighter than the predecessor. It must be a girl. Or maybe I am just getting better at this.

She only feels like one sack of wet cement. It must be Bunty.

In the adjacent room, I hear But Surely counting away. Jumping Jehosophat, he's up to the 500's already! My pleasure is slipping through my fingers by the second. I sling the other victim onto the floor. Another almighty thud and a splintering of something or other. To tell you the truth, I am so in the thrall of lust, I couldn't give a toss if I've broken her neck. I care about nothing, nothing except Calypso in the room next door. The second victim is up to 200. I must be slowing down with the physical effort of dragging dead bodies around the house, or the younger generation must be counting more quickly. I must put a hop in my step.

Not wanting to waste a precious second, I already have my erect todger out as I fly along the pitch black corridor. It is guiding my way to the Divine Calypso like a water diviner's stick, but straighter and harder. She lies exactly where I left her. In one deft move, I pull the gusset of her knickers aside and thrust my cock into her roughly, as though my life depended upon it, and in my head, I am counting the seconds from where Sully left off in the other room, doing the mental arithmetic for how long my visit to Paradise will last, when suddenly a cry splits the night.

"Rape!"

I can't believe this. After all the signs of encouragement she has given me. I'm fucked if I'm going to stop now. But, more loudly, "Rape!" and she has expelled me from her fanny so forcibly the recoil sends me off the bed and onto the floor, which is good, because I can feel her arms propeller-ing, her talons searching for flesh to bloody, her shoes flailing about for calves to connect with. Than it dawns on me, she shouldn't be wearing any knickers.

Then I realise that I know that voice. It's not Calypso. I've just deflowered my own girlfriend, Olumidé. I have to get away. I toy with the idea of carrying myself to the room next door and throwing myself onto the floor atop the heap of other dead bodies I am accumulating; but the deception would be all too obvious as they would know that the third person had entered the room after the cry of Rape.

Why am I worrying about losing the game, when I have just committed the criminal act of rape? My mind isn't thinking straight. It is the god Set messing me up again.

There is only one thing for it, as I'm on the floor anyway. I slide silently under the bed from where I had just dragged the two other bodies. No sooner have I bestowed myself there than the lights come on in the adjacent room of dead bodies, followed by Olumidé turning on the lights in the bedroom. She hasn't figured out that her rapist is under the bed.

After a delay of about thirty seconds, there is a banging downstairs as our stoned DA, Sydney Syzygy, enters and closes the garden door, having seen off the numerous box hedges, statuary, fountain, ornamental koi carp pond and assorted watering cans and wheelbarrows as deftly as he negotiated the glasses, cutlery and candelabra on the tabletop the first time I set eyes on him.

One by one all the lights are coming on until the house resembles a prison break. I hear him stomping up the stairs. As he bounds into the room, I realise the wooden floor is sprung, so my supine body is bouncing up and down under the bed in time with his footsteps.

Sydney enters the room, his caricature joint glued to his lower lip. "Well, well, well," he says, although policemen are supposed to say "Hello, hello, hello". To Olumidé: "What's happened here?"

"I've just been fucking well raped!" she screams in an outburst of uncharacteristic vulgarity.

I poke my head out from under the bed. "Is it okay to come out now?" I ask.

"Stay where you are," he snarls with unexpected authority.

"And what about me?" What's this? Another disembodied voice from under the bed. This is Calypso. Why the fuck did she get off the bed and end up underneath it? Olumidé must have entered the room and got onto the bed, and Calypso, with her benighted vision, knowing that I was about to come into the room and fuck her, had sought to avoid that happening in such close proximity to my sainted girlfriend, by swiftly removing herself from the *locus in quo*.

Burty and Bunty come wandering into the bedroom from the lumber room next door where I'd chucked them. Burt is bleeding profusely from the nose. Bunty has some sort of minor head wound. The DA objects: "Go back where you both came from; you are disturbing the integrity of the crime scene. You're supposed to stay where you were at the time of the murder, not saunter around like you own the fucking place."

They waddle back to the next door room, hand in hand. Tweedledum and Tweedledee.

Now it's time for Ingram to object. He has been concealing himself behind the curtain in a window alcove, the window being in the hall midway between the bedroom where the rape has occurred and the lumber room where the bodies were stashed.

Olumidé: "I'm not joking. I'm telling you I've just been raped!"

Ingram to Sydney: "The rape is all very interesting, but you're supposed to be investigating a murder."

Sydney: "Who's been murdered?"

Ingram: "You tell me. You're the fucking detective."

But Surely (from the other room): "I have."

Bunty (from the other room): "Me too."

Sydney slides me out from under the bed by my ears as though I am on ball bearings: "Did you see anything, Nick?"

Mendacious me: "No use asking me. I'm dead too."

Sydney: "Who's that under the bed with you?"

Calypso (emerging): "Me."

Sydney: "I don't suppose you saw anything."

Calypso: "No, but I heard things."

Sydney: "Oh yes?"

Calypso: "Yes, I heard her cry out *Rape*."

Sydney: "Did you hear anything before that?"

Calypso: "Yes, I heard someone come into the room, get onto the bed, and then rush out of the room after the cry."

Interesting. She is giving me an alibi.

Sydney (to Olumidé): "Forgive me for asking such a personal question, but did penetration take place?"

Ingram: "Of course it did. It wouldn't be a rape without penetration, would it? It would just be a bit of slap and tickle."

Sydney: "I am not asking Olumidé for a legal definition of rape. I am asking the victim what she experienced."

Olumidé: "Yes."

Sydney: "So, our suspect is a male, which means that we can rule out Calypso and Bunty."

Ingram: "And we can rule out Nick and Burt, because they're dead.

And we can rule out Bunty for the additional reason that not only is she the wrong sex, but she is also deceased."

Sydney: "I'm not entirely sure that follows. You are allowing the fictional world of the parlour game to encroach upon the painful reality of what has just happened to this poor girl."

Ingram: "And you, sir, are allowing the world of the Belgian surrealist, René Magritte to impinge upon the world of the French fictional detective, Maigret."

Ingram has a point. Sydney is approaching this very much like a TV sleuth. He is even speaking in a mildly French accent. I am wondering if he is going to say next that he is going to turn out the lights and the rapist will reveal himself.

Sydney: "OK. We can rule out the two girls, and we can rule out the victim herself. I think we can rule out Nick for two reasons. Firstly, Calypso said she heard someone come into and then leave the room, that person presumably being the rapist, and Nick was still in the room. Also, Nick is Olumidé's partner, so he has no motive for raping her, as he would have the amenity of consensual sex with her whenever he wants."

Little does he know. Olumidé isn't going to correct him.

Sydney: "So that leaves Ingram and Harry."

Ingram bats for the other side, but can see how he is being fitted up for a heterosexual rape, and doesn't appreciate the way the odds are narrowing in his favour: "For Christ's sake, Sydney! Does she even want to press charges?"

Sydney: "I'm not her interlocutor. I suggest you ask her yourself."

Ingram: "Well?"

Olumidé: "Yes."

Ingram: "Look, Ollie, I'm not trying to trivialise your trauma, but, not to put too fine a point on it, we're all friends, we're all pissed and stoned, and we're playing a game. That carries with it the legal concept of *volens*, as in the tag *volenti non fit injuria*. If you agree to play a game, you're also signing up to the possibility of a certain measure of collateral damage. It's like agreeing to play Naked Twister and then complaining that someone has groped your tits."

Sydney: "Well, thank you, Mr Frazier. We are indebted to you for that learned exegesis on the law of *volens*. But if a girl agrees to play a game where she may be murdered, that does not mean that she is also consenting to a little collateral rape and non-consensual violation. I have noted that you show no remorse. Now, if I may continue with my peripatetic investigation, Burt, you were in the room next door with Bunty. How long had you been there?"

But Surely: "Am I allowed to answer?"

Sydney: "Yes, dear boy. We are investigating the rape, not the murder, so you may forget about the fact that you are playing the part of the victim and come forward as a witness."

But Surely: "I got murdered by the Murderer in the bedroom next door where the rape occurred, and I was then picked up bodily by the Murderer and carried down the hall into the room next door, and tossed unceremoniously onto the floor. Precisely 640 seconds later, she (pointing at Bunty) was thrown on top of me. I know that because I was counting from 1 to 1,000 pursuant to the new rules, as I had to cry out the Murder on attaining 1,000 seconds. Then, a further 250 seconds later, I heard the cry of Rape."

Bunty: "Yes, he was counting out loud. I can vouch for that."

Sydney: "In that case, we can indeed exclude Burty and Bunty as they cross-alibi one another. It is likely that we can also exclude the Murderer."

Ingram: "Why can we exclude the Murderer?"

Dear Reader, I was about to ask the same.

Sydney: "Because he would hardly have commenced upon a rape knowing that he had scant 110 seconds left in which to enjoy it before the lights would go on. By the way, who is the Murderer?"

Now, I am in a quandary, lying on my back, half in, half out of the bed, staring up Sydney's nostrils. I am already excluded according to Sydney's sophistry by virtue of being Olumidé's paramour. I could be excluded still further by owning up to being the Murderer. But as I have already falsely claimed to be one of the Murderer's victims, I would sacrifice credibility, if I was now to resile from my own story and confess to being the Murderer in the game as well as his victim, although that would clear me of the crime of rape in real life.

Sydney: No takers then?

He is looking from face to face. Perhaps his gaze rests over-long on Ingram, because Ingram starts laughing unnecessarily in what may be a sign of nervous guilt, and then realising that he is drawing attention to himself, stops.

Sydney: "The Murderer won't reveal himself. That suggests that, contrary to my initial theory, the Murderer is one and the same person as the rapist. The Murderer, knowing the new rules, knew that he had a full 110 seconds left to perpetrate the rape."

Ingram: "Oh! So now it's a *full* 110 seconds! A minute ago, it was a *scant* 110 seconds."

Sydney: "110 seconds is almost two full minutes, which is longer than most men perform for in the best of circumstances."

Me: "But if the Murderer is the rapist, and if he had planned this meticulously down to a T, why did he murder 2 people first? Why didn't he just proceed straight away to the rape? Why set the clock ticking against himself by murdering twice, so that he then had to start his nefarious business of rape constrained by the 1,000 second rule. If he hadn't murdered anyone, he could have raped to his heart's content."

Sydney: "3."

Me: "3 what?"

Sydney: "Three victims. He killed 3 times before he raped."

Jesus Christ! In my stoned state, I'd forgotten that I'd just murdered myself. I also have a numbing balls ache of an unresolved ejaculation that is preventing me from concentrating fully on anything except completing the rape.

Fortunately, Ingram, who has never managed to keep his mouth shut for more than a few seconds, wades in and takes the heat off me. The good thing about Ingram is the blink mechanism. Ingram has tight skin. Every time he closes his eyes, his mouth opens.

Ingram: "Maybe that is what excites him. Maybe he doesn't plan it meticulously to a T. Maybe it is the act of murdering that he has a hard-on for. Maybe it is a spontaneous act—which should certainly be a mitigating factor."

Sydney: "Ingram, we haven't got a suspect yet, and you're already doing a plea in mitigation!" Then, addressing me: "By the way, what number did *you* count up to?"

Oh, superbly dealt! It's always the little throwaway lines that carry the crippling weight. My addled brain and aching balls are computing wildly. Is it better to be an early victim or a late victim and how do I make this consistent with Burt's anally retentive countdown?

Ingram must have closed his eyes, because his big mouth opens again, saving me: "Look, Sydney, you've already told us that we're blurring the distinction between the game and the reality, so why are we all deferring to you and letting you ask the questions like you're a real Detective when you're just a pretend Detective? Suppose I want to ask the questions?"

Sydney: "You are deferring to me because I am the only one who is above suspicion, because I was not in the house."

Burt, trying to be clever: "We've only got your word for that."

Ingram: "You've only got Olumidé's word that she was raped in the first place. Maybe she was just bored with this fucking stupid game and wanted to shake things up to relieve the ennui!"

Ingram gets a slap in the face from Olumidé and then she follows up by spitting on him. Ingram's cheek is smarting, but he rubs the gob off it and continues: "And aren't we all missing something here?"

Everyone: "Like what?"

Ingram: "Like where the fuck are Seth and Self-Harming Harry, the only guys here who could carry But Surely down the corridor without breaking a sweat?"

Calypso: "You mean to say that Seth isn't here in the room with the rest of us?"

Sydney: "I'm afraid not."

Ingram has a good point. They are nowhere to be found and have been absent at all material times, except possibly the most material of all. I see a shadow of doubt and confusion move across Calypso's lovely face at the news that Seth is not present. After we have collectively turned the house upside down looking for them without success, we are torn as to whether we are convinced one of them is the rapist, or whether we are concerned at what worse fate may have befallen them. So we patrol the curtilage of the house, after which Sydney, albeit a Detective of shreds and patches, proves he is still the best Detective we have, because he spots both of them sitting on top of the chimney like Santa Claus.

Or Mr Bols.

Whilst Bunty tries to talk him down, concerned he might be a jumper, which Harry isn't, although, if he were the rapist, he might be, Sydney continues with his anastomosis. The drawing in of all the threads.

Bunty is shouting up to them, asking them what they are doing up there. It seems that Seth went into night-climbing mode, and Self-Harming Harry, who didn't want to play the stupid game to start with, went wandering off after him, and arrived at the same destination, but by ascending the wisteria, rather than scaling the sheer face of the masonry, and they had been sitting on the warmth of the chimney, shooting the breeze throughout.

Sydney: "We can rule them both out, because it's impossible for either of them to have committed the rape and got up there in the time available. In that case, the rapist is Ingram."

Ingram, panicking, sensing that the game is becoming a reality: "I'm not a fucking rapist! I'm not even straight. I'm queer!" Unless I'm mistaken, we all harboured our doubts, but this is the first time Ingram has made it plain. Ingram Frazier has just outed himself to avoid a charge of rape.

Sydney: "Let's face it, you've been obstructing my investigation from the outset."

The next thing that happens takes everyone by surprise. Calypso grabs Olumidé by the hand and leads her out of the room for what Calypso describes as "a straight talk *homo ad homo*". They are gone a couple of minutes that seems like 10 minutes during which it would appear Calypso upbraids Olumidé for letting down the values of feminism and behaving like the weaker vessel. Olumidé is told in no uncertain terms that she has "to take one for the team".

Calypso: "For fuck's sake, Olumidé, if you don't stop grandstanding and drop this thing, he's finished."

Olumidé: "What do you mean?"

Calypso: "He's reading the law. He may go on to be a great barrister or a judge. He fucking well wants to be the Prime Minister of England. If you go ahead with this rape thing, his career is dead in the water. He's finished. He'll go straight down the pan without even touching the sides, just because you're pissed and he's pissed and everybody else is stoned."

Olumidé: "Ingram wants to be the Prime Minister?"

Calypso: "Yes. He's gone public on it. He's said so."

Olumidé: "What are the chances of that?"

Calypso: "Well, pretty damned good, I should think, because who the fuck else wants to do the fucking job? Of all the poisoned chalices you could pick up, who in his right mind would want to pick up that one?"

Olumidé: "A socialist Prime Minister of England."

Calypso: "A socialist PM, a human rights lawyer."

Olumidé: "And I hold his future in my hands?"

Calypso: "You hold the future of the future Prime Minister of England in your hands."

Olumidé: "Fuck me! I've been raped by the future socialist Prime Minister of England!"

Reluctantly, Olumidé agrees in principle subject to one condition, namely that I have to have the last word on the subject. The logic behind this is that what Olumidé has lost is a treasure that she was saving for me, so the fate of the rapist is in my disposition.

Olumidé then takes me into the private room where she had her straight talk with Calypso and she tells me she is minded to let it drop rather than ruin the remainder of the house party, provided I am okay with the decision.

Me: "Why wouldn't I be okay?"

Olumidé: "Because he's forcibly taken what I was planning to give freely to you tonight."

Me, tapping my head: "Virginity is what's up here." And me, stroking her fanny: "Not what's down there. If you didn't agree to it, it never happened."

"What's that smell?" She grabs the fingers that have been in Calypso. She is turned on.

"*Balafre*," I lie, "by *Lancôme*."

"I like it," she says, pointedly licking my fingers as if in promise of things to come.

In this topsy-turvy world where a tap on the tush passes for foreplay, one thing leads to another, and I end up finishing off the job I inadvertently started before the cry of rape went up, separated from the DA and the Judge and hanging jury in the room next door by only a partition wall and a closed door.

It's not how I wanted it to play out, and it hasn't satisfied my unforeseen appetency for Calypso, but on a purely anatomical level, it relieves the godawful pressure on my kishkas. We come together like a couple for whom a lot more practice has made perfect. Olumidé is looking absolutely radiant. With the benefit of hindsight, she now seems delighted that someone else has broken her in so that she could at last give herself to me.

"By the way," I ask, "how long did that take?"

"110 seconds."

A Room with a Ruse

This morning when I perform my ablutions in the Birdwood, written on the back of the door, it says:

To be is to do—Socrates

To do is to be—Jean-Paul Sartre

Do-be-do-be-do—Frank Sinatra

Finding an opportunity and a pretext to get Calypso back to my room a second time to complete the unfinished business wasn't at all easy. It had to be on a Sunday when Sydney would be waxing the Super Snipe. But Olumidé usually had Sundays off in return for working nights during the week. However, as luck would have it, this week she only worked three night shifts and had to work Sunday morning as a result. I prayed to the god Set for good weather, because Sydney couldn't apply the Cornubia lotion in the rain, and Set heard my prayers. It was a morning of warmth and great promise.

Finding an excuse to entice her out of Gisborne Court and over to my rooms was more difficult. I couldn't say that I had something there I wanted to show her, because she wouldn't be able to look at it. So when I knocked on Sydney's mazoosa'd door before walking in, I had to deceive her by informing her that I had recorded a broadcast about Millais' *Angelus*.

"Why don't you bring it around?" she asked.

"It's recorded in quadrophonic 8 track," I lied.

This wasn't like me at all. Set made me do these evil things.

Back at my room, she said, "Well, where is it?" I made a show of fumbling around a bit, and then came up behind her and grabbed her tits, whilst whispering in her ear, "I must have pressed the wrong button."

"What do you think you're doing?" she demanded, breaking away.

"Just trying to follow up on what we began at Grantchester," I said, instantly regretting that I seemed to be sounding like a such an oleaginous Lothario, but the craving for her was pulling my strings.

"Nick, I'm sorry if I encouraged you. I genuinely like you, and maybe in a different time and a different place, who knows? But Grantchester was a case of mistaken identity."

"Who did you think I was?"

"I'm sorry. It was the aftershave. When did you start wearing *Balafre* by Lancôme?"

She is the blind one, but the scales are falling off my eyes.

How could I have been such a vain, egotistical, stupid cunt?

After she's left my set, my friend pops up to console me in my loss.

"Didn't I tell you?" says the god Set. "That the future would be full of identity theft?"

"You did indeed."

"Don't worry. You'll get her in the end. But look at it this way, what a fantastic fucking advert for *Balafre* by Lancôme! There's the things that happen to that poor woman after a *Badedas* bath, and there's the Lady that Loves Milk Tray. But this is on a different level altogether!"

"Yeh," I think, composing the copy in my head: "You get ballsache with *Balafre* by Lancôme."

"Remember the Grand Entrance that we worked on?" Set reminds me. "After you arrive on the planet earth with your retinue of Space Groupies. Remember that the earthlings don't know if you come in peace or war, and one trigger finger on one hand of one member of the Special Forces gets twitchy and fires off a round that enters the head of a beautiful girl just as she is rushing to get a better look at you. That girl could be Calypso."

"And I fuck her back to life."

"Exactly. You fuck her back to life. Maybe not literally; maybe it will be metaphorically; but I promise you, after an exile in the wilderness, you get to fuck Lyca back to life."

Tommy

It's the premiere of Sydney's Syzygy's adaptation of the Who's rock opera, Tommy. It should have occurred to me earlier that, if he didn't succeed in his Plan A which was to summon up the devil, with a name like Sydney Syzygy, there had to be a Plan B career waiting for him as a theatrical impresario. He had wangled permission to erect a small stage in the centre of Gisborne Court. By arranging the seating so that the audience sat with their backs to the Birdwood, he managed to avoid them looking at that eyesore whilst also ensuring that the absolute minimum number of rubberneckers could get a free look from the windows of the rooms in the Court.

The first night was a low-key affair, the audience consisting largely of the friends of the performers. In a masterly stroke of casting, Sydney has cast Calypso as the blind, dumb, deaf and moreover eponymous protagonist, whom Sydney contrives to be born in an elegiac opening sequence when the prodigiously strong Seth carries a *papier mâché* egg on his shoulder, which he sets down centre stage and from which impossibly small object she hatches, and of course, she is stark naked. I am asking myself, how could I possibly have missed the obvious fact that the male Tommy was going to be played by a girl and, not just that, but, in case any of the audience was in any doubt, a naked girl.

Looking back on things, I know it seems hard to credit, but in those days after the abolition of the Lord Chamberlain's censorship powers under The Theatres Act 1968, no self-respecting director would have dreamed of putting a play on the stage or a film on the screen unless the leading lady stripped off at the least provocation. Even if it was a comedy, someone had to lose his trousers.

I am thinking to myself how lucky Seth is. I am wondering how they are going to repair the egg for tomorrow night's performance. My mind is working overtime, imagining the origami-like shapes some lucky person must have folded Calypso into before they enclosed her in the eggshell.

Let us begin at the beginning. It's dusk. A new moon illuminates our little diorama. The opening chords of the Who's Overture see Seth costumed as what appears to be a giant Nubian with a fantastical headpiece carrying the elliptical object shoulder high. The egg is no more than a metre from base to apex, and, due to the cunning lighting, it seems to have a kind of semi-pellucid transparency, so that you can discern some hint of pumping life throbbing within it.

He sets it down centre stage and, over the course of a full minute, the foetal form within the egg, tears strips after strip away, undressing itself from its own cocoon, until an elbow thrusts out, then a whole arm; the head is born; the shoulders. And I am just bewildered and thinking to myself: how did she possibly shrink herself into that tiny space. But then the wonder at the feat of contortionism is supplanted by wonder at her boyish beauty.

Calypso emerges into sentient life from the ovoid structure, and, just like a frail little bird, she is sightless, and she is naked. It is beautiful and tasteful, but if the audience thought that Calypso was going to put her clothes on after the initial scene of Tommy's birth, they are in for a mistake, as she stays in role until the last dying chords have drifted above the Birdwood and into the lacquaeria.

I give her a standing ovation. I clap until I feel the pins and needles in my palms. Believing in fairies is twice as much fun as trying to summon the devil. I do believe in fairies.

The word gets around that the 39th in line for the throne who also lectures on Calligraphy and History of Art at the Sedgwick Site is performing naked in Gisborne Court and the following 5 days of tickets for the very limited run are fully sold out by 10.00 the next morning, and being resold at astronomical prices on the black market. But on the second night, it is closed down by the Performing Rights Society.

It appears that Sydney hadn't considered that the law of copyright applied within the inner sanctum of the college, or he thought that his enormous and artistic original contribution in adapting the piece and in particular casting a naked woman in the lead male role, was sufficient to amount to a work of joint authorship. But Robert Tear and his Performing Rights Society didn't see it that way, and the show is pulled.

Sydney is facing a situation where he has taken in and already dissipated a lot of money in advance ticket sales. A lot of hard-up students have wasted their hard-earned cash in hope of seeing something that would give them a hard-on. If Sydney shuts his doors in the face of so many paying customers, there is concern that Sydney may not be able to see the sun for writs, so *The Show Must Go On!* Calypso agrees to perform the remaining performances unaccompanied by the music, and none of the paying audience have any complaints.

As we know, I am the official photographer for all things Syzygy; but it seems that another paparazzi slipped in to one of the shows and to our horror we see that nude photos of the 39th in line for the throne are on the front page of the Cambridge Gleaner. Sydney, ever the control freak, swiftly takes charge and a deputation is deployed to reconnoitre every newsagent and buy up every copy.

The four rowers from the 1st VIII race from shop to shop bearing their sedan chair, weighted down, not this time with the sepulchral Sydney, but with reams of newspapers destined for conflagration. *C'est magnifique!* But it is a hopeless task. There are too many. The more they seize, the more demand the newspapers think there is, so they just print more and more copies. The photos get syndicated. They reach the nationals. Calypso is disowned and disinherited, told never to darken her parents' door again.

Girton rusticate her. I didn't think the rustication would make a great deal of difference, as she cohabited with Sydney anyway at Peterhouse. However, I called it wrong. Girton put the squeeze on the Dean of Peterhouse, and Lyca achieved the questionable feat of being blackballed and banned from Peterhouse, a college she had never belonged to in the first place.

Encouraged by the Master of Girton, the Dean sent the Head Porter around to Sydney's set in Gisborne Court and had Calypso led to his rooms.

"Sit there," said the Dean to Lyca. Reginald, the Head Porter, accompanied the sightless girl to the heavy oak chair on the opposite side of the Dean's desk and sat her down.

"You can wait outside, Reginald," the Dean said to the Head Porter, who retired, as requested. On his desk was a green button and a red button. The Dean pressed the red one, which lit up a red light outside his door meaning *No Entry*.

Once he heard the click of the door, the Dean opened up all the newspapers to the appointed pages that he had flagged up earlier with Post-It notes: the Daily Mail, *the Daily Express*, the Times, the Telegraph and the Sun, and spread them across his desk. He looked from Lyca, sitting facing him in the wooden chair to the lurid pictures of her on his desk.

"What do you have to say about these, young lady?" he asked.

"I can't see what you're referring to," she replied.

"I thought as much!" sneered the old misogynist as he noiselessly tossed himself into a tissue.

The Dean thought he had a real way with words when he told her in a short speech that he had no doubt been rehearsing with his scriptwriters all day long:

This is Peterhouse, not Penthouse!

Then he dropped the tissue into his wastebasket, closed the newspapers, and pressed a green button on his desk which made the green light outside his door light up, the signal for the Head Porter to come in.

"Go with her to collect her things and then escort her off the premises, Reginald."

Sydney, who had spent his years at Cambridge on a quest to become possessed, was now well and truly like a man possessed. He worked relentlessly but ultimately impotently attempting to summon the devil, aiming for that limitless power that would put him back in control and able to fashion different consequences. But it eluded him. No matter how many crucifixes he spat upon, no matter how many hosts he defiled, Lucifer refused to make his presence known.

"I just can't believe it!" he declared at last. "That she could spend every waking hour openly abusing herself with every narcotic substance known to mankind, and she gets sent down for undressing!"

Sydney's plan was to install her in a love nest in Grantchester to which he would only be allowed access by invitation, like Gala in her castle in Pubol, he explained. But Calypso wasn't the mistress type. Overnight, she simply disappeared. I don't know who was the most upset, Sydney or me. Months later, we heard rumours that she had run away to join the circus, that she was performing in Montreal.

The Senate House Leap V2

From morn
To noon, he fell, from morn to dewy eve
A summer's day; and with the setting sun
Dropped from the zenith like a falling star.

This morning, on the Birdwood, high above the urinal, it says:
If you can reach this far, you should be in the fire brigade.
  And on the wall it said:
T S Eliot is an anagram for Toilets.
  It's been a lunar month since I recorded Seth's feat on film. Once again, I am on my back staring through the viewfinder at the 8-foot crack in the buildings. This time I have mounted the Nikon on a tripod to eliminate all wobble, and I have the rubber bulb in my right hand, ready to detonate the shutter when the action starts.
  Somehow, Sydney's warped and competitive mind has come to the conclusion that if he outperforms Seth in feats of night climbing, his Lyca will miraculously reappear with the full moon.
  "Nick," says a disembodied voice from a maniac in a tailcoat a long way up. "Are you ready?"
  "Sydney, I'm ready, but it's not too late to change your mind and come down the same way you came up."
  "Fortune favours the brave," says the disembodied voice. "Here's to Dutch courage, and here goes!"
  Before I can say anything else to talk him out of it, or before his own sound judgment might prevail and talk himself out of it, it has all happened in a moment, but also in slow motion, and I am squeezing the bulb.
  And I manage to squeeze it four times before he hits the ground with a sickening crack as I hear his bones fracturing. That noise that resembles no other noise, will never leave me.
  With hideous ruin and combustion down.
  I am hoping it is one of those floppy falls that drunks do where they drop out of trees without breaking anything, because they are so relaxed and bendy, but the crack suggests otherwise. At least he isn't dead, because he is able to move his facial muscles in grimace at the

pain he must be in.

"Are you alright?" I ask. As the words leave my lips, I realise how inane they are. How could anybody possibly do what he has just done and be alright? But I didn't know what else to say in the circumstances.

His first thought is for me. "Get out of here!" he whispers. "Or you'll get into trouble too. I'm fucked. I can't move anything except my mouth."

"I can't just leave you here. What can I do to make it better?"

"Just make sure the shots come out well, and scarper. I'll only slow you down. I'm seriously buggered here. They'll judge that whatever I have done to myself is punishment enough, but if they know someone else was involved, he'll be in big trouble."

"I'll make an anonymous call to the hospital from the Sex Club payphone."

"Fine! Now get the fuck out of here!"

I run off to the Sex Club and ring Olumidé. I tell her to get an ambulance at once to the foot of the Senate House.

When I develop the photos, the disc of the moon doesn't look like a butler's tray. It is flattened, resembling the base of an upturned glass, and Sydney is illuminated inside it. And in the sequence of shots as he falls, the light elongates, until he is completely enclosed within the glass, his right hand aloft, the tails of his jacket thrashing the night like a dragon's tail. And there is another dark shape above him, falling with him, or maybe it is pushing him, an old man in a red hat.

I tell Sydney the photos didn't come out. That it was all over too quick.

Now that Calypso's gone anyway, he doesn't really seem to care. In whatever the competition was between him and Seth, neither of them won.

A Fistful of Keys

After his accident, there were a few months when Sydney Syzygy thought that he might get better, if he did the exercises and ate the right stuff, but after about six months of trying very hard and no noticeable difference, he reconciled himself to the fact that no amount of present medical knowledge was going to fix him, and the only way he was going to rise from his wheelchair was by magic. So he devoted himself more and more to that search for forbidden knowledge, but always along the broken, twisted, left hand path. His beloved Lyca had disappeared. His mates had all gotten their degrees and gone off to well-paid jobs in the City or into politics. I was retaking. There was just him and me as hangers-on. The caravan has moved on and we are still here.

There is a network known as The Peterhouse Register, which keeps one informed as to what one's former colleagues are getting up to. Few of those in my circle get a mention, because we spent all our time getting wasted and thereby frittered away our opportunities. Spud is in the Register. The bonkers boffin. He is quite famous in the world of robotics and electronics. You can't turn on *Tomorrow's World* or *Blue Peter* without seeing the things he is working on.

But Surely went straight into politics as a special advisor to the Labour party constituent for Bootle North. He is biding his time, gaining experience, because what constituents would want to be represented by an overweight professional career politician fresh out of university who has never seen active service or worked as a captain of industry? The idea is risible. He must serve his apprenticeship, before he makes his move.

Ingram didn't attend Peterhouse. He was at Trinity Hall, but through following glimpses of Burt, one manages to keep track of Ingram. He is destined for politics, but first he has to carve a name for himself as a Human Rights lawyer. Human Rights are new things that had presumably always been out there somewhere, but no-one had bothered to think up a trendy name for them before.

Giving a name to something is the first stage in the process of controlling it. It only took someone to come up with the smart-ass name Human Rights before sods like Ingram could start coining money out of it. It was always out there, but he packaged it into an industry. There are very few Human Rights cases, but those that there are, are all very high profile, and every time one hits the news, Ingram's fingerprints are always all over it.

As the god Set became more ascendant in me, Seth waned, until he disappeared altogether. Then it dawned on me that Seth had never really existed. Seth was just a figment of my imagination. The real one was the god Set.

Or was it the other way around?

Professor Self-Harming Harry, Sydney's fine weather friend. What had happened to him? He was like the Fool who becomes King for the Day before they execute him. It didn't dawn on him that his sinecure office might not last forever. For one year he had a Chair. Then they pulled it away from beneath him, and he was back on his arse again. Not much of a protégé.

He was stripped of his gown and for a year or two, he worked as a Cambridge taxi driver. An extreme case of the Knowledge: having a Cambridge don as your chauffeur. I suppose it was a step up from portering the fucking sedan chair. He wasn't there to be counted when Sydney needed someone to push his wheelchair. But the lodestone of Cambridge was such that Harry couldn't quite bring himself to leave it, so he just circled it in his taxi, like some lovelorn satellite forever orbiting a planet. However, it seemed that his mind was still working as the wheels on his taxi span around, and it wasn't long before he returned to the world of academe.

Of course, I have opportunities. I am just hanging around because I have to complete my training as a superhero. I am like some mooncalf in a Jane Austen novel, telling the heroine's father that I have prospects. *Sir, I have four acres in entail in Dorset and an income of forty guineas.* It's just that I never get around to pursuing these prospects. Olumidé took the job in London and left me. After her prized virginity had finally been rudely wrested from her, she made up for all the lost time by behaving like an utter whore. I was relieved when she left. It was a weight off my shoulders.

I've started writing stuff for the local paper. I'm not on the payroll yet. I'm what they call free-lance. Also I take photographs of what I'm writing about, so they publish my shots as well as my copy. Rather supererogatory really. If one picture is worth a thousand words, why have both? I might write that yesterday was the coldest day of the year in Cambridge and the ducks had to walk on the frozen lake. Then, just in case nobody believed what they read in the papers, underneath the copy, you can look at my photo—of ducks waddling on the frozen lake. Do they think I'm smart enough to tell lies in print, but not smart enough to fake the accompanying photograph?

Ingram Frazier, Human Rights counsel at the Inner Temple, man on a mission to rekindle his relationship with me. What could he possibly want with me? We never really got on when we had Cambridge in common. Now we don't even have that, but he sought me out.

"It's just…" he begins to poke around the delicate subject diplomatically, "To be honest, I remember you explaining to me that you'd never actually had intercourse…"

"Ingram," I interrupt, "where is this heading?"

"Nick, please. Please, Nick. No offence. If I may confide in you as you once confided in me, I've never had intercourse either. But with me, it is a physiological thing. For you, it is psychological. I remember that you told me that your father told you that you must never reproduce. He spoke those words threateningly and they were accompanied by trauma in the form of damage to your wrist."

"Ingram," I repeat, "where is this heading?"

"Nick, it is my belief that we can sue. In addition to bringing finality to this cloud you have lived under for years, we can also make some money. Believe me, there's enough there for everybody."

"Sorry to disappoint you, Ingram. My dad never had any money."

"Of course he didn't, Nick. That's why we're going to sue the National Health Service."

"How so?"

"What your doctor told you about your condition was confidential. It was your human right that it shouldn't go any further. You have a human right to privacy. The doctor told your dad. Your dad used that confidential information to traumatise you with threats of the terrible things that would happen if you ever attempted to live a normal life. And what has happened?

"You have been a substance-abusing, damaged individual hovering around the margins of society ever since. You flit in and out of a fantasy world unable to distinguish between the real and the imaginary, and the only place you feel safe is in that fucking bathhouse built by Birdwood. You have never enjoyed consortium or coitus. You have conducted yourself in the belief that you harbour some sort of condition that can be passed on in your genes."

"And don't I?"

"Epilepsy is not hereditary, Nick."

"So, Ingram, I get it that we bring this case against the NHS and you become part of the syllabus, and further develop this inchoate Human Rights field that you are the country's leading exponent on. Apart from the humiliation of being outed as the jock who's never shagged, what's in it for me?"

"To be honest, Nick, in addition to substantial compensatory damages, I would, I would obviously, well, be personally in your debt."

"Because you are the country's leading exponent of a non-existent area of the law, and you want someone to take it to Strasbourg? Tell me, Ingram, do you have any other clients, apart from me?"

"You're alluding to the missing choir boys? You know, to this day, they're still going missing."

"Makes you wonder why any parent would allow his son to apply to be a member of King's College Chapel choir. Why not just sell them straight into the sex trade and cut out the middlemen?"

"Yes, I read your investigative journalistic treatise on the topic. I still don't get it, how you fulfil so many impossible deadlines now and couldn't hand in your essay throughout three years at Cambridge. Good headline by the way. I wrote it in my diary."

"*Going for a Song!* Yes, I was very pleased with that. But, Ingram, it's all ephemera. What are you doing still remembering headlines months after they should've been wrapping up your fish and chips?"

"Nick, leaving that, doubtless, interesting question aside, and just getting back to your original question: to be perfectly honest, you know, I think you have always known, you know, that this lawyering thing is not the be all and the end all for Ingram Frazier. After Cambridge, the next thing I wanted was a seat in Parliament. I have that. I expect ministerial office to follow swiftly as I've got a lot to offer.

"If I take up your case and become the youngest ever barrister to be entertained by the European Court in Strasbourg, trailblazing an area of the law that doesn't even exist yet, Human Rights, I think we will be off to a flying start, don't you? Nick, I have never made any secret of the fact that I am going to be Prime Minister. When I am Prime Minister, I would like you to be my Director of Communications. Like a, you know, Press Handler."

"And, if I go through with this, Ingram, how do we make this deal stick?"

"To be honest, Nick, you just have to believe me. We would have what they call a gentleman's agreement."

"Okay, Ingram. Deal."

One day Sydney asked me to drive him to Wells-next-the-Sea in the Super Snipe, just like old times, except I'll be doing the driving. He doesn't realise that I don't have a licence or insurance, but what worse could happen to him? We put the wheelchair in the back and find a nice, convenient disabled parking space in the car park. I have to carry him out of the car, the same as Seth carried Calypso last time we came to this place. Where did everybody go?

I help him into the wheelchair and ask "Shall I push?" and he gives me the customary answer: "God damn the pusher man!" and off we go along the endless beach that he seems to love so much. I notice the rictus of pain as he transfers his broken arse from the passenger seat to the wheelchair. His sharp eyes detect my concern at his discomfort and he is addressing my inchoate thoughts.

"It doesn't matter. It really doesn't matter, old chap. It just means that I must focus more than ever on what I wasn't doing well enough before. I'm virtually there, at the level of Ipsissimus, after which I'll be in control of everything. I feel like one of those early doctors who injected themselves with deadly venom because it was the only way they could find out if their antidotes worked."

I am fiddling with the fistful of keys, locking the doors, locking the petrol cap, locking the boot.

"You might as well keep they keys," he says after a while. "I can't see that I'll ever be able to drive it again. I have put my name down for one of those three-wheeled blue cripple cars. There's a nine month wait whilst the NHS extrude it from some fucking fibreglass moulding machine."

The crossed keys, just like St Peter, the founder saint of Peterhouse. I am the proud possessor of a Humber Super Snipe Mark V. "I'll look after it for you, until you're better," I say.

"Whatever," he dismisses. "You'll need to put yourself on the insurance. And I want you to promise me you'll look after it, and do the thing with the Cornubia wax every week. The cleaning kit is in the boot save for the chamois. That has to hang up in the air to dry or it will go slimy and, as with all slimy things, once it's gone slimy, you can never get it out. The white wall tyres…"

"Sydney, why are you telling me all this shit about your car? You never gave me a fraction of this shit when you told me about your own circumstances and asked me to push the chair."

"Transference, I guess," he says as though he is coming to this realisation for himself for the first time also. "Transferred Munchausen syndrome by vehicle."

Then, after a while, he starts talking about the accident. He hasn't spoken to me about it before.

"I was a stupid cunt," he says. "I was jealous of that new boy, Seth. Or not such a new boy as I came to discover. I hadn't realised. I mean, of course, I knew that someone like Lyca must come with some baggage, but it was the coming to terms with the specificity of it that was unnerving. I lost my judgment. I let Lyca get too close to him under my very nose.

"Then I found myself in a competitive situation with him, trying to do all the physical stuff to impress her, the Cambridge night climbing, the Senate House leap—none of which she could even see, I should add; so whatever was I thinking of enlisting you to chronicle the events in a series of photographs for a woman who couldn't see them? Now I'm a fucking paraplegic, and she fucked off anyway!"

"All seems pointless now," I offer. I am in his debt, because of the car. I guess I will have to take him to the seaside whenever he pleases.

"I really can't accept the car," I say.

"Take it. It's no fucking use to me. It would just be a liability. You can get some pleasure out of it, and maybe push me around from time to time. Be company."

It's no fucking use to me either. I don't have a driving licence. I don't think I'm allowed to drive, because of my condition, so there was no way I was going to get insurance; but I can't tell him that. I am thinking to myself that I had also compromised myself. I had put myself in a competitive situation with Seth, because I could tell Calypso had the hots for him, and I had figured that if I assumed the mantle of his after shave, I could fool her I was him. I am an imposter. I am a plagiarist. But at least I rose above all this, and I am becoming the god Set. I am on the ascendant.

What did the young Caesar say to the elderly Pompey?

More people worship the rising than the setting sun.

I am the rising sun.

Plagiarism

This morning on the Birdwood door, it says:

I like sadism, necrophilia and bestiality. Am I flogging a dead horse?

"I'll write the fucking essay for you, and you can get on with your training."

The god Set is negotiating with me. Neither of us can face the idea of me having to do a 5th year at Cambridge trying to write my dissertation.

"But that would be plagiarism," I remark.

"Just because there's a name for it, doesn't mean you shouldn't do it. Do you think that any genuine plagiarist would even have such a word in his vocabulary? Plagiarism, onanism, masochism. Just because it ends in "ism", it doesn't have to be filthy. Do you know what "ism" is short for?"

After a pause for thought: "Jism?"

"No, no, no. There you go again. Ism is short for schism. A break with the past. Like the Road out of Eden. Plagiarism is the new originality. In the future everybody's going to be plagiarising everybody else. It's going to be an art form in itself."

"But creativity, originality will be lost."

"That doesn't necessarily have to follow. It's just a redistribution. Somebody's still got to be writing all those fucking dissertations. Everything about them will be absolutely kosher except the author's name at the end. It's inevitable. In the future, mini-cab drivers are going to have to write dissertations about Blake's *Ghost of a Flea* in a foreign language if they want to get a licence to carry passengers. Who do you think's going to help them? Someone like you. Someone who went to Oxford and Cambridge."

"OK. You write it. I'll do my training."

And So, It Came to Pass

We pick up our story some years ahead, because I felt I owed it to my director of studies and all the people who had enabled this poor schmuck to get a scholarship to read English literature at Cambridge, that I should finish off my Tripos, re-sit my exams and pass them with no *aegrotat* before embarking upon my superhero duties.

It was a lonely year, as all my friends had moved on by now, except for my new best friend, the god Set, and except for Self-Harming Harry and Sydney.

Unfortunately, I got a 2.2. The god Set had promised me he could fix me a 1st without me batting an eyelid. When I finally handed in my paper on Blake, it was not well received. Set had persuaded me to abandon the *Ghost of a Flea* project and to write a dissertation instead upon Blake's visionary *The Book of Los,* because it was more to do, as he put it, with the human condition. The sense of loss. But no-one got it. Even worse received was my thesis upon Kit Marlowe in the witness protection programme.

My new best friend had informed me it didn't matter a fig. More people would identify with the poor boy from Peterhouse who only scraped a 2.2 but transcended his humble beginnings to defeat the god Set and become the most powerful being in the Universe.

My training took some months. Despite my new found powers, marshalling them and getting used to my new body and face required considerable rehabilitation and practice. I have never beheld anything so beguilingly beautiful as my new self. I get a hard-on just looking at it in the mirror. It is difficult to leave the mirror and get on with the business of saving the world.

I spend five hours a day in the gym. I have to become a work of art, or I will not receive my powers from the god Set. I have a washboard stomach, even though I don't know what a washboard is. I think it was something housewives used in the fifties before household appliances became available. I know that the opposite of a washboard stomach would be a beer gut, the main exponent of which was Burt Sully.

I pushed Sydney's wheelchair across Midsummer Common, not confiding my own situation to him. It would have seemed unjust in the circumstances that I had graduated from Cambridge a superhero, whilst he was crippled *cum laude* and didn't even have his bendy Lyca to push him around; so I kept it to myself. We have a customary address now and a response. Our own little catechism.

I say to him: *Shall I push?* And he answers: *God damn, God damn the pusher man.* And then off we go, pushing and chatting. What is worse, he is losing his hair. The once dashing Sydney Syzygy is now more bald and less dash. He is turning into Professor Charles Francis Xavier, just like he had predicted. He didn't seem unduly concerned that he had permanently disabled himself. In fact he was quite chipper. All he could say was *Well, I did it, Nick!*

When he said that, bearing in mind the pitiable condition to which he had reduced himself, he reminded me of those two bankers in the Wall Street Crash who threw themselves off the Empire State Building. After they have plummeted 33 floors and are 3 floors shy of the pavement, one says to the other *How's it going?* And the other one says *So far so good.*

"How are you coping with your disability?" I feel emboldened to ask him.

""You start out being too embarrassed to mention it, thinking it's temporary and will go away soon, but you end up regarding it as normal. Like some bloke getting used to having a fucking great goitre on his head."

I couldn't tell if Sydney was smiling or not, because I was pushing his chair and he was paralysed, so he couldn't twist his neck, and besides, only half of his face worked now, so his expressions were unclear. I think he was still in denial. But he sounded like a man who had achieved all his ambitions before the age of twenty. And paid the price. I wondered if I could use my new-found powers at the appropriate time to restore him, make him whole again.

I discussed this with Set during my training. He said that of course it was possible, and indeed, I could bring the dead back to life if I wanted, but he recommended extreme caution: "If you give an inch," he said, "they'll take a mile. Once it gets around that you healed one leper, you'll never get any fucking peace. Colonies of lepers will be knocking on your door 24/7."

"But if my ambitions are to mend this broken planet," I said, "why not begin with the individuals who inhabit it?"

"Because they are too fucking many. The sum of the parts is more than the whole. It's a sliding scale that slides the wrong way, Nick. This isn't a project that you can micro-manage."

People keep disappearing. People keep dying. When did the minor irritation of a burning sensation on peeing, cured by a shot of penicillin, mutate into full-blown AIDS? Things are supposed to get better.

With the benefit of hindsight, things seemed to change for the worse about the time I began mending the world with my second class degree from Cambridge. How did I ever think I was qualified? I should have gone straight into politics like Ingram, or signed up for the Department of Metahuman Affairs.

But then I remembered that my successor was still alive and waiting for me to release him as soon as I could find the point where the parallel lines met, and I thought to myself, things weren't so bad. Things were getting better. I would make things better.

I am careful not to fall into the sophistry of what the god Set has explained to me is known as *post hoc ergo propter hoc* reasoning, that is to say that Because B comes after A, A is the cause of B; or I would start thinking that I am the cause of all the great evils in the world. This is the fallacy of *a priori logic*. The tendency to look back to a nostalgic golden age that in truth never existed. There have always been evils. No-one has ever been the author of any of them. It's just the human condition. Original sin that used to get washed away in the confirmatory font under the jackboot of the Church, but in the modern age of enlightenment, lingers on, like a bad smell in the elevator.

Every day another maniac in a suicide vest blows himself and other innocent people up, or drives a lorry load of explosives into the marketplace. It's as though some puppeteer is controlling their movements, a puppeteer who has marshalled an army of masochists.

Where would one find an army of masochists?

This is the sort of philosophical shit I discuss with Sydney as I push his wheelchair across Parker's Piece and past Reality Checkpoint. How had a lamp post come to symbolise our mis-spent youth? Now that the others had left us, there were only two points on our compass. Maybe that is what happens when you lose your moral compass. It is replaced with an axis of evil. I feel as if I'm a bumpkin being dragged down the hill by a wheel of cheese.

Forgetting the promises I have just made to myself, I say: "I have been given boundless powers," I explain to him. "I was endowed with these powers by the devil; but I intend to use these powers for the good of mankind. I intend to outwit the devil. I will take all his boundless powers and use them for good."

"But don't you have some sort of compact with the devil?" asks Sydney, entering into the spirit of the game. "Isn't part if the deal that you must use the powers for evil? Usually, you have to sign an agreement with the devil in blood."

"No, we have nothing like that," I explain. "The devil and I, we have a gentleman's agreement."

Peace

"How do you see yourself?"

"I've never really thought."

"But the first act of self-authorship," the god Set informs me, "is to see yourself. Until you see yourself, you cannot see yourself as others do."

"I'd like to be a peacemaker. I'd like to put an end to war."

"But wars are necessary. The planet doesn't produce enough food to meet the demands of an ageing population bent on ageless procreation. Wars, famine, pestilence, natural disasters—these are the checks and balances that Nature has introduced. That is precisely why, those parts of the planet that produce most offspring suffer the most natural disasters. It is Nature's symmetry. Without them there would be so many of you that in the peacetime you wish to introduce, you would have to resort to cannibalism for the species to survive."

"Perhaps I could deliver the peace, but with casualties. The bad men would have to go."

Set spits out a sputum ball and rolls it around between his claws until it grows into the size of a globe suspended in the air, and I see the nations of the earth are all stamped upon it. As it revolves, he is gesticulating towards the different areas of conflict.

Disappointed, he concludes: "The map of the world hasn't really changed in the last 50 years. No world wars; no-one invades anybody else's territory any more, because it's politically incorrect; it's all nickel and dime stuff; skirmish here, dirty bomb there; crowdfunded warfare; a hollow strutting up and down the stage of Armageddon by another tin pot dictator firing blanks at his neighbour. There are no problems out there that you would want to put your name to solving. The enemy has become abstracted."

He is spinning the world on the long horny nail of his index claw. "Wouldn't it be good if the world asked you for an Update and Restart every few weeks? Or every morning when the sun came up, everything had changed. You just wake up one morning and find that Cambridge isn't there anymore. It's been uploaded to the Cloud."

"A regional *war* would do," I plead. "It's not the body count. It's the issues that the conflict represents. If the media stoke up enough public feeling first and then I go in and sort it all out. What is important is what the *war* represents."

"There are plenty of local skirmishes. Which one are you planning to resolve?"

"What about Peace in the Middle East?"

"Peace in the Middle East! Holy Mother of Mephistopheles! Blessed jism of the Redeemer! Why is it that every fucking politician wants to try his hand at that one? Peace in the Middle East! Nick, it's like a turd that won't flush! Whatever you do, steer well clear of Peace in the Middle East. Whatever you do, you'll upset more people than you please. Don't go there!"

I prod a territory on his globe. "What about there?" I ask.

"Well, if you attempt to bring peace there, you'll kick off a *war* over there."

"Here then?"

"Go there and the Chinese will have to invade around here. If the Chinese invade there, the Russians will have to invade there, and it doesn't matter whether you go here or there, because either way all the displaced refugees are going to cause a crisis everywhere else."

"So wherever I try to bring peace—"

"Incubates a worse war."

"So if I really want to bring peace—"

"You're going to have to start a war of your own."

The Top of the Greasy Pole

The curious thing about pushing Sydney is that he is always in the lead. For the first few years after I eventually graduated, I used to return to Cambridge to visit Sydney. He stayed on with his disability money in a pokey bedsit on Parker's Piece, not seemingly knowing where he was headed. I'd push him along and shoot the breeze until we ran out of things to say to one another, and my visits became less frequent. With the benefit of hindsight, I think the only reason I sought out his company in the first place was to hang out with the beautiful Calypso.

After Ingram's success with my legal case against the National Health Service, I had some money in my pocket, and we had that bit of news to talk about. Then there wasn't really anything else to justify paying him a visit until Ingram Frazier was suddenly elected Prime Minister.

That was the occasion for my last visit to Sydney Syzygy.

"I can't believe he just swept to power like that," I say.

"…with that meaningless slogan," says Sydney continuing my sentence for me; we are getting to be like an old married couple: "*Take back control*. Control of what, I ask you?"

"I suppose he was aided and abetted by the incompetence of the Tories."

"Well, that toe-sucking tosspot in the Home Office, didn't help, incapable of turning down a shag with a free prostitute paid for by the red top rags. No control there!"

"The scandal!"

"That's not a fucking scandal!" exclaims Sydney. "At least it was a prostitute of the other sex! I don't smell even a sniff of a real scandal unless at least a couple of rent boys are involved. Take back control! What was the first thing he did after he came to office? Get himself fucked up the arse by the American President Rash."

"Literally?"

"Metaphorically, but the only reason it wasn't literally is because Rash is straight."

"Being urinated on in a hotel bedroom by two Russian prostitutes is what counts as straight these days?"

"He gargled with it, but he did not swallow."

"Rash hopes to have his features carved onto Mount Rushmore."

"Rash on Rushmore. What could be more offensive to the environment? The guy looks like a Croque Monsieur with a rug on!"

"Sydney, are you going to, you know, are you going to stay here forever?"

"Good point. Push me over there please. That way. I know a shortcut."

"No, I mean, stay here in Cambridge."

"What finer place could there be?"

"I mean, are you going to get a job or something? After the State's spent so much money honing your skills, educating you at its premier academic institutions, don't you think that you should, you know, sally forth and lead others?"

"Like fucking Ingram, you mean? And Burt Sully, his iron Chancellor? Iron Chancellor! You know what an Iron is in cockney rhyming slang? Iron Hoof. Poof. Queer! And what was the second thing Ingram Frazier did after being fucked up the arse by President Rash? Legalise sodomy! Nick, all those years I spent trying to summon the devil, I never dreamt of anything as deviant as Ingram. And they're in control. You want me to be a leader of the country like Ingram and Sully?"

"Well, those jobs are already taken. But a man of your skills can't spend the rest of his life on disability benefits, loitering around in Cambridge after the caravan has moved on. Don't you ever think you're a bit like, how can I put this? Like a dog returning to its own vomit?"

"Nick. I can't be like a dog returning to its vomit when I never went away. I am the *status quo.*"

"But the *status quo* doesn't have to be static. Why not have a dynamic *status quo*?"

"A dynamic *status quo*! That is a very interesting concept that I will reflect upon in my wheelchair."

"And why didn't you go to your graduation ceremony and collect your degree after working so hard for it? Surely you owed that to your parents, to let them see you grabbing the praelector's *sticky fingers* and snatching your scroll."

"Now, that *would have been* returning to my vomit! In case you hadn't noticed, the graduation ceremony takes place inside the Senate House!"

"But surely, you could have arranged to collect it somewhere else, somewhere with fewer legacy issues for you, Sydney?"

"Two Surely's in two sentences! You know who you're beginning to remind me of?"

"But you could've done! Could've used the wheelchair as an excuse if you needed one."

"Unfortunately, Nick, there was the small matter of an unpaid buttery bill."

"What?"

"They wouldn't let me collect my degree until I'd squared up my account with the buttery. Obviously, I passed my exams, so I'm a BA. But they won't let me graduate, and they won't let my BA ever mature into an MA until I've cleared the buttery bill. I'm like one of dear Lyca's Lost Boys who never grow up. I've got a BA that can never become an MA."

"How much is the bill?"

"Sixteen thousand pounds."

"Fuck me sideways, Sydney! Sixteen thousand pounds! I've never even seen what sixteen thousand pounds looks like. Sixteen thousand pounds would buy you a semi-detached four-bedroom house in Ealing."

"And what the fuck would I want to do with a four-bedroom semi-detached house in Ealing, Nick?"

"How did you manage to run up a bill of sixteen thousand pounds in three years?"

"I didn't. I paid my way in the first two years. I ran up a bill of sixteen thousand pounds with the buttery in my third year. You kindly assisted me, dear boy. I suppose I just wanted to see what I could get away with before they called a halt to it. And because I'd been such a big spender in the previous two years and paid them, they thought I was a good credit risk, so they never turned off the tap.

"You know, there was a scientific experiment not so long ago where they put these white mice in a contraption where they soon learnt that if they pressed a certain red button it gave them a tiny electric shock that their brains equated with pleasure. And of course, they just kept pressing the button until they were all dead. I'm like that. No restraint! If there's a slate, and if they let me put it on the slate, then I'll just keep on taking it. If I'd failed my exams and had to re-sit the following year, I'd have got the bill up to fifty grand!"

"But didn't you ever stand back and think to yourself, *how am I going to pay for all this?"*

"Of course, I'll fucking pay for it! But I'm not interested in nickel and diming it. I'm not interested in a conventional job. As we speak, I am working on something. In my head. A game changer. Maybe it will even change me. You remember how everyone always used to ask you *What are you working on?*"

"Yes, and Ingram was the only one who took the question seriously and used to tell you about his unfinished magnum opus or whatever."

"Well, I'm working on something. Nick. I'm interested in one big bang, not reporting for work 9 to 5 to some arsehole boss. I am working on one idea that will change everyone's lives starting with my own and will make me a fortune in the process. You remember Kim Roo? Graduated from Caius. Did fuck all for ten years during which time no-one ever heard of him; then, like shit off a shovel, he has a No 1 hit with *Walking on Sunshine*. Then he falls off the face of the earth again. That's me. I'm only interested in making history, and I don't propose to let myself get distracted from my calling by wasting my energies performing some mundane job for the benefit of some cunt in the buttery. Milton didn't write Paradise Lost until he was in his fifties.

"Do you think he would have created that masterpiece if some sanctimonious scrote had said to him: *John, don't you think you should stop writing that masterpiece and get a newspaper round so that you can square up your buttery bill?* Why do you think I spent so much fucking time trying to summon the devil? I'm ineluctably drawn to short cuts, even if it means selling my soul. Like running up the buttery bill. I'll do it first, and worry about how to sort it out after. I want it all and I want it now.

"I want my place in history, but I mean the real timeline of history, not the self-chronicled soi disant bullshit of Ingram and Sully. For God's sake, who writes that shit for them? What an age we live in where being a Prime Minister or even a President of the United States is no more significant than participating in a tawdry reality TV show. Just like Andy Warhol said, they're all famous for 15 minutes. Just like Professor Self-Harming Harry was. A curiosity. It's like a new rule of physics: *Nothing Changes Anything.*"

We come to a halt. Suddenly, I can't see the purpose in pushing his fucking wheelchair aimlessly around Cambridge any more. I feel like

I've become Lyca's stand-in. Her stunt double.

"What do you want to be when you grow up, Nick?"

"I don't want to grow up, Sydney. I'm one of Calypso's Lost Boys."

"Stop pushing this fucking contraption and come around the front where I can see if you're laughing at me or not!"

I do as he asks. I bend over with my hands grasping the arms of his chair and we look one another in the eye.

"Don't tell me you did three years at Cambridge and a retake to make a career of pushing a fucking wheelchair. If you'd gotten better grades, you could have been a dog walker."

"I've decided I'm going into journalism. I seem to have a knack of coming up with pithy headlines and I take good photos. I've been dabbling in it; but I think I can make a living doing it full time."

"Why the fuck did you waste four years at Cambridge doing a three-year course if your exit strategy was to become a fucking journalist?" He stared me in the eye with a fixed concentration. "Nick," he said, "our revels here are ended."

I am the all-powerful God Set; but I have the feeling I have just been dismissed by a bloke in a wheelchair.

BOOK THREE
SPIN DOCTORS

Scoop

It's a bit like life at the Daily Bugle must have been for Peter Parker. The Foreign Editor loves me. I'm what she calls a Twofor, meaning Two For the Price of One, because not only do I write fantastic copy (as one would expect from a graduate boasting a degree in English from Cambridge University), but I also illustrate my copy with my own stunning photographs. I am beginning to wonder why I was ever so ashamed of the low 2.2 degree Set saddled me with. I have a degree from Cambridge; that's all they care about.

Little does the Foreign Editor know, but if the truth is to be told, I am actually a Threefor, because the reason I am always in the right place at the right time to pen the best copy quickened by the finest images is because I am making the news up myself as I go along. Strikes, demonstrations, plagues, wars, pestilence. These are my stock-in-trade. Each day when I open up the great leather-bound Book of Thoth in my bleached oak empanelled study, new ideas leak off its pages. Tortures, abductions, terrorism. These are just some of the jaunty numbers in my retinue.

"Excuse me, Nick. Do you know the nuking of Pyongyang?"

"No, but if you hum the first few bars, I'm sure I can pick it up."

Every day I'm off somewhere different. I spend more time writing up my expenses than I do writing my copy. It's the only way my editor knows of squashing a journalist and a photographer into one economy class seat on the aeroplane. "Send Nick!" Goes up the cry. I just blow my nose and don my stab vest, and I'm ready for action.

Underneath the headline, it says:

Story by Nick Jobs.
Photos by Nick Jobs.

It's all Fake News. At night, as the god Set, I plan it all out and make it happen. By day, as Nick Jobs, I record it for posterity. One day I'll be able to show my hand, but for the time being, I am operating "under the radar". At the moment, I am controlling the combination of Ingram Frazier and Burt Sully in their ineluctable ascent from the primeval reptilian swamp of the Bar and the barroom into the cesspit of public life and politics.

Although I prefer wars and pestilence, I also cover English politics, and especially anything to do with Ingram and Burt. Anything that someone else does wrong that I can spin to show them in a better light by comparison, I do. So if a member of the government fucks something up, I don't rest, as lesser mortals would, in just recounting the story with glee; no, I go further: I seek out something vaguely comparable that Ingram or Burt has done that has gone well, so that I am constantly offering the electorate an alternative. If John Major picks up a baby for a photo opportunity and nearly pokes his finger through its fontanelle, I dig up some footage of Ingram holding a baby correctly, supporting its head in the crook of his arm.

If Ingram commits some inexcusable gaff or if Burt puts his big foot in it, I spin the stories and the photos so they come out smelling of roses. When Burt walks away from the manky Glaswegian harridan with whom he has been commiserating on camera for the last five minutes, telling his aide that she's a stupid old cunt, not realising that he's still miked up, I spin him out of trouble because these guys are headed for the top jobs, and I am writing and filming them into those niches.

I am the Kingmaker. Once I've installed them, then, as the god Set, I will act through them. They will perform my will.

In between, in addition to making my name as a journalist, I am building up a huge portfolio of photographic out-takes, and I've had one-man exhibitions in London, Paris, Barcelona and New York. I am a household name, like David Bailey or Lord Snowden. Nick Jobs. Jobbing Photographer. No Job too small. Weddings, Bar Mitzvahs, Funereal Deathmasks.

What had Sydney told me a job was?

I understand this is quite unusual: for a photographer to be the one who is constantly ambushed by the paparazzi. The hunter becoming the hunted. But this is because I make news, so the wannabees sidle up to me, trying to inch their way into the frame one shoulder at a time, just the same way a new-born enters the world. I get interviewed. I have been on the One Show, Thought for the Day, Graham Norton and Desert Island Discs.

I have been on the cover of Forbes Magazine and on the inside of Vogue magazine. I turned down an occasion to pose naked in Cosmopolitan

Magazine, but was very flattered to receive the offer. I get invited to the dinner parties of the rich and famous. If a Russian oligarch's son is getting bar-mitzvah'd, or if a Hollywood film star is getting married, they beat a path to my door to record the event for posterity. Of course, they could purchase an equivalent elsewhere, but then the ungrateful little shits would accuse their benefactors of humiliating them in front of their peer group.

I have published a book of my photographs so large that the reviewers said it was not so much a coffee table book as a coffee table in its own right. The books are walking off the shelves; the printers can't print them fast enough. Because the book is so big, no-one can carry it out the store. They are all delivered by DHL. We don't bother with requesting alternate means of delivery if the purchaser isn't home, because none of the fucking things would fit through anyone's letterbox anyway. DHL dump them by your wheelie bins whether you ask them to or not. The books are monolithic tombstones bigger than the bins they try to hide them behind.

Pulp Fiction!

It's a work-in progress. The Great Book of Thoth.

Today, I am reading about myself in the papers. The Sunday Times art critic, Waldemar Janusszczak, has done a two page review of my *War* exhibition at the Photographers Gallery. Of course, he completely misses the fucking point. *War* features images too violent to print in the newspapers, so he has to resort to words. We know that one picture tells a thousand words, but he can't use pictures, so he is going to have to be fucking bombastic. In one room there is a gigantic collage of every abomination known to mankind plus a few they haven't thought of yet, and my intention was to trivialise it. A *reductio ad absurdam*.

But of course, Janusszczak doesn't get it. If one displays brutal images of war, the critics always fall into the error of believing that this is because we want to demonstrate war's pointlessness. It doesn't occur to the critic that this photographer took so many snaps of the abyss because it appealed to his perverse tastes.

Janusszczak, with approval, has reproduced the passage I had written on the blank wall as you enter the exhibition. I had used a special font. I don't know its name. It's the one Calypso had used to ornament Seth:

There was an Athenian soldier who had fought bravely in the Battle of Marathon in the warm September of 490 BCE when the Greeks repulsed the first Persian invasion. He knew that hundreds of his friends had been slaughtered by Darius' men, and were lying unburied, scattered across the plain of Marathon. He wanted to go and look at all his butchered comrades, but he knew the sight would upset him.

Try as he could to persuade his eyes not to look, eventually, he could resist the urge no longer. He ran out onto the battlefield and beheld the acres of mangled limbs, hacked off heads, broken bodies, continuing to throw up the contents of his stomach, even after it was empty. And he screamed out: "There, eyes, have you seen enough? Have you had your fill? Are you content now?" And he thrust his fingers into those eyes and blinded himself.

Herodotus

I'm not actually sure if it was Herodotus or Thucydidides, but if one makes one's living by purveying Fake News, who gives a fuck? It was kind of appropriate to quote from the Father of Lies.

These words in the strange typeface were written on the wall above the door. I made the characters big deliberately, so that they filled most of the wall, leaving little room for the door. Then I made the door little, Alice in Wonderland little. So one had to bend over double to pass through the door, like a supplicant, approaching with humility; and once you had negotiated the door, just as you were straightening up, you were immediately confronted by a vast depiction of what could well have doubled as the plain of Marathon after that memorable battle. The photograph had been blown up to 30'x25', and everybody in the photograph had also been blown up. They were children. It was done in sepia. But all the blood was bright red. *Children, they blow up so quickly!*

Unless you are one of Calypso's Lost Boys.

The image was considered so horrifying that the members of the public attending the exhibition, having just passed through the little door and straightened up, were stopped dead in their tracks. This meant that the people behind them in the queue, who had paid good money to view the abomination, were stuck half in and half out of the little doorway, and couldn't get through.

Gradually, they became impatient, animated and started pushing the people on the other side of the door out of the way. Some of the people

427

who had viewed the first image wanted to turn around and leave, but they couldn't because of all the people trying to push their way in. It was, as Webster says in The Duchess of Malfi, like a bird cage in a summer garden. All the birds outside the cage want to get in, and all the birds inside the cage want to get out.

"Ten People Crushed to Death in *War* Exhibition," it says. I am making the headlines again. We haven't had a good shooting *war* in ages. More people perished trying to gain admission to an exhibition about *war* than have actually perished in waging any *war* on the soil of this continent in the last 50 years. Malthus would have approved.

The quote about the eyes from Herodotus made me think about Calypso. Women were easily available as I was a minor celebrity now. They were a commodity, like going out and grabbing a cup of coffee at Starbucks. I do a lot of shagging around with different women, and it feels close to right but not quite right, like the way you feel when you start descending the down escalator and then realise it isn't moving.

I'll take it because it's there, but in my little reveries, there was only one woman who haunted me. I secretly hoped that one day she would come to one of my exhibitions and I would see her again. But she never came. No-one I knew knew of her whereabouts. It was a though she had disappeared off the face of the earth.

Since I began my secret life as the god Set, I haven't felt the need to sublimate my inner superhero by staring at my finger and muttering Flame On! But I do find myself regressing to the *Peter Pan* story. Do you believe in fairies? I ask myself. I picture Sydney's Lyca, my little Tinkerbell. *Don't let Tinkerbell die*, I hear the voices in my head saying. *Clap if you believe in fairies*. And I try to imagine Lyca back into my life.

I *do* believe in fairies!

War

Set is lying on his back. We are on a patch of dried up yellow grass that he has found after having led me off the Strand, down a puke-ridden staircase into John Adam Street, and then down another puke-ridden staircase to the Embankment. We are not alone, as there seem to be lots of tramps sprawled all over the place. I am staring at a wall illuminated by the full moon where a graffiti artist is making his mark. I think it might be Banksie, because he is not just festooning the walls with pointless shit from a spray can.

He has a design and he is executing it well. It's kind of stencilled, but I can see the outline of the twin Trade Towers in New York, and in some of the windows there are lights and some are dark. And two planes are making their way towards the towers and he has done it in Roy Liechtenstein-style grainy magazine pointillism with a balloon saying "KERPLOW!" coming out of the first 'plane, reminding me of the good old Marvel Comics. Set is balancing on his hoof the big spitball of the globe that he had extruded earlier.

After a while, he seems to grow bored. He gets up and dribbles the ball for a while and then gives it an almighty kick against the wall. It explodes on impact. It takes out the Banksie. The lights in the towers go out and they are falling over.

I am looking at the patterns forming in the dark crimson smear running down the wall. I see that the map of the world has been transferred from the burst globe onto the brick wall, obeying some unknown law of physics that says that the DNA of the planet is preserved and transferred in a collision. But, as I stare at it, I see that the map of the world has been subtly redrawn.

"Shut down and Update," says Set.

"If there are no regions that we can usefully bring peace to," I say hesitantly getting to grips with the concept, "and if we have to start our own *war* in order to resolve it with peace, on whom should we declare war?"

"Clearly, you need an abstract war. A war against a universal enemy that is not circumscribed in one place so that you don't make yourself unpopular invading any sovereign territories. A war that we can conduct in other people's lands, harming other people, people that we only ever see on the telly; a war that is like an augmented reality game; a war against no specific enemy; a proxy war conducted by generals in arm chairs with remote controllers, by drones and droning politicians in television studios, with nobody coming home in body bags. A fake war.

"A war on terror."

A War on Terror

"Nick, you are a fucking genius! You are the ablative absolute!"

I knew Ingram would love it. The old queen is clapping his hands together, applauding the idea.

I do believe in fairies.

"A war on terror!"

"And, of course, Ingram, that's not *real* terror. Real terror is when you wake up one morning and realise your high school class are running the country."

"Is that one of yours?"

"No, Kurt Vonnegut's, but it seemed apt in the circumstances. And, Ingram," I add, "if one leader of the civilised world were to wage a war on terror, you'd think he was delusional, tilting at windmills. But if you get enough of your allies to sign up to it, then everyone's going to start thinking it's for real."

"So we forge new strategic alliances and trading partnerships—"

"Uniting to fight a common, non-existent enemy."

"And that's how we keep the peace."

"That's how we keep the peace."

A College Reunion

Who would have believed it? After 13 years of Tory misrule, I have installed a young Socialist government in Downing Street. I have made their wishes come true. Didn't Ingram say he wanted to be Prime Minister of England? And didn't But Surely say the same thing? Well, I have made Ingram PM with Sully his Iron Chancellor, but, wait for it, they have a gentleman's agreement that at a certain time, Ingram will move over so that Sully gets his turn at the helm.

It is a college reunion of the Sexcentenary Club. Normally, I eschew these events. No-one who has made anything of himself in life ever turns up. It's just a bunch of sad professionals hoping to network until the organiser wants you to get your cheque book out to endow the college with, who knows what? Another crapping complex like the Birdwood.

But this time I attend, because Ingram and Sully are going to be there, so it's kind of required of me, toeing the party line. Indeed, their party are sponsoring the event, and we have them to thank for the freely flowing socialist champagne I am pouring down my throat. Maybe I will even get a scoop for my newspaper. Ingram is going for an historic third term, and Burt is champing at the bit, desperate to taste the tang of real power popping on his lips like cardamoms pods before he grows any longer in the tooth.

I see there is a scattering of stage and screen actors, musicians who have topped the charts and the odd celebrity chef and hairdresser. Ingram loves to surround himself with these people in the same way he liked to mingle with edgy dudes like Sydney and me at Cambridge. But at Cambridge he had to hang out with the in crowd. Now he's in himself, they're forming a line to hang out with him. It's a toss-up as to whether he'd rather be in *Vanity Fair* or in power. I don't think anyone in the room is even wearing a tie.

To show how cool he is, Ingram has instructed the DJ to play Dr Hook's 1975 hit, *I Got Stoned and I Missed it*. Takes me back to my mis-spent youth. Sometimes when I cast my mind back to my years at Cambridge, it's just a blurred bubble of substance abuse, and that song sums up how I feel about it all, that I must have been stoned and missed it. It's fortunate that I won a scholarship and did it for myself, because if my dad had paid for it, and if, after three years and a retake I'd told him that I couldn't remember a fucking thing about Cambridge, he'd have taken his belt to me. But Ingram has his DJ put Dr Hook on the deck, because he thinks it makes him cool and edgy. Who the fuck is Dr Hook, anyway? A villain from *Peter Pan*. Don't they ever grow up?

Now it took me seven months of urging just to get that local virgin
With the sweet face up to my place to fool around a bit
Next day she woke up rosy and she snuggled up so cosy
When she asked me how I liked it Lord it hurt me to admit
I was stoned and I missed it
I was stoned and I missed it
I was stoned and it rolled right by...

As if on cue, I realise Björn Agen is standing by my shoulder. Typical of Ingram, fulfilling his destiny as the architect of edginess, to ensure he has a multi-lingual drug dealer in attendance, even if he doesn't use it himself.

"Bonjour, Björn!"

"Ciao, Nick. Que tal?"

"Is that what they call a whistle-stop tour? We've just covered three languages in six words!"

"I've been following your exhibitions," he says. "Good works, especially if you're stoned before you walk in."

"And what are you working on?" I ask the pusher man. I don't do gear any more if I can help it. Sometimes you have to pop a few pills just to be polite. But I don't feed the crazy god Set out of choice.

"I'm struggling with my first novel."

"Why does it have to be a struggle?" I feel the question was invited. I had to ask it.

"I decided to write it in French."

"Pourquoi?"

"So that I could get paid again for translating it back into English. As it's French, I decided it had to observe the three French Unities, like in Racine."

"Aha! Unity of Action, Unity of Time and Unity of Place."

"Yes, the whole thing unfolds in one afternoon."

"And why is it so difficult?"

"I decided to make the narrator a mobile phone."

"So, I suppose it's written in the third person?"

"No, it's written in the first person singular."

"Why?"

"It's an iPhone."

"OK. So we've got a novel narrated by a telephone written in French where all the action takes place in one afternoon. What you going to call it?"

"*L'apres midi d'un phone.*"

"I just love it! That's the best thing I've heard in French since Sydney consigned my pages to the flames in Gisborne Court."

"Ah, Sydney Syzygy!" He sighed wistfully. "Well, there's a mobile phone success story for you!"

"Really?"

"You'll have to excuse me."

Over my shoulder, his sensitive antennae have noticed a very attractive young lady, making a discrete gesture that means she wants to score a line of coke off him, so he goes towards her and then the two of them head off towards the john. I am left standing on my jack in the middle of the room like Norman no-mates, but I am rescued by none other than the Prime Minister himself. Ingram Frazier makes his way towards me and somehow manages to pump my hand at the same time as he is patting my back as though he were trying to burp me.

After the formalities, I am asking Ingram about this gentleman's agreement he has with his Iron Chancellor. He looks over his shoulder like a pantomime villain ensuring Sully is out of earshot and no mikes are turned on, letting me know he is about to share a confidence with me, not for everyone's ears. Like a true lawyer, *sotto voce*, he says to me:

"A gentleman's agreement is an agreement that each side expects *the other side* to be bound by." And he gives me an almost imperceptible wink of complicity.

This gets me thinking about my own gentleman's agreement.

During the campaign, the Saatchi & Saatchi advertising agency put up a poster showing Ingram with devil red eyes in an attempt to frighten people. It just made them vote for him. As many have observed since Milton's Satan, the devil has all the best lines. I am just thinking how much better Ingram looked in the poster, like when Superman turns on his X-ray vision and the red lasers blaze from his burnt out eye sockets, when someone I used to know sidles up and takes Ingram by the hand.

"I believe you know my fiancée?" he says.

Fuck me! It's Olumidé! He didn't even have the originality to get his own girlfriend. He has obviously chosen her for her colour so that he can demonstrate to the country his fine liberal proclivities for the wonderful inclusive society I have helped him build.

For some reason, the only thing I can think of to say just then is, "Well, the apple doesn't fall far from the tree." But I'm not sure what that means.

There is a short embarrassing silence when I can see Ingram looking over my shoulder, always checking that he's not missing out on something better, someone more interesting to talk to. During this uncomfortable interlude, a waiter comes around offering a tray of Lamberhurst Malbec. Then I say to him: "Well, Ingram, you finally made it to the top of the greasy pole."

"My word!" says Ingram. "A quote from Gladstone, I believe? "

Actually, it's what Benjamin Disraeli said when the old Yid story spinner was finally elected Prime Minister, but I don't correct him. Ingram was ever the Philistine. His greatest natural gift was his ability to make up nicknames for people.

"And Fat Boy as your Number 2," I add.

"We don't call him that anymore," corrects Ingram. "Besides, he never was obese, not really. Just more stout than the rest of us." I see that he has already begun rewriting the past without the aid of his press handlers. Political correctness. Fat Boy not fat! But staring across the crowded room at him, I have to admit that he does look as though he's lost about four stone in a very short space of time. Type 2 diabetes, I guess.

"And what about you, Nick? Your press coverage of foreign affairs is always laid out on my breakfast table before I read anything else in the morning; and my fiancé and I visited the War exhibition. I am also mindful of the fact that when everyone else has nothing good to say about me and Burt in the media, you always manage to turn the story on its head, so that we end up looking alright. What are you working on these days, Nick?"

They don't call me Nick any more. I am the god Set; but I don't tell him that. "I am directing," I say. And so I am. The whole world is my stage and I am moving the players into position, including Ingram and Fat Boy, building a better world, cheating the devil.

"So, you've moved from stills to the movies," he concludes incorrectly. "And what's the film all about?" For some reason, Olumidé's face is set in a rictus. She looks like she wants to put my head on a spike.

"It's about an epileptic photographer who inadvertently summons up the devil and prints him out in a session of 3D printing, and about the effect it has on his life and the lives of everyone else."

Then something over my left shoulder distracts the Prime Minister and he is off with an "You'll have to excuse me." I am left standing beside my old girlfriend. You can still see that she used to be attractive, but she has assumed the matronliness of office. I am trying to remember if I packed her in or she me. She is beginning to grow those dark pockets of Mediterranean granny under her eyes. In ten years' time, she'll look like a tobacco pouch. I got out while the going was good.

For some reason, all I can think of is Lyca's quip about the menopausal Mediterranean fishwives cooling themselves down in the butchers shop. My Olumidé has gone from sushi to rotting fish.

"Well," she says, looking me up and down, "how is the Lost Boy who never got fucked? How is the great superhero, GentleMan, who made a name for himself by dragging my name through the mud?"

"I may have made a fool of myself," I say, "but how did I drag your name through the mud?"

"I'm the woman that you were dating for three years and a retake year! You kiss-and-tell shit. I've never been so humiliated in all my life! Everyone knows that I am the O in NJ v NHS. I'm on the fucking syllabus!"

She is just so off-piste that I am lost for words. Because I am trying so hard to follow her broken logic and see it her way, I can't even begin to compute it my way, so as to tell her she is talking bollocks. So I am simply tongue-tied.

"I want those photos back!" she hisses. "And the negatives."

She is concerned that now that she is within spitting distance of becoming rich and famous, I will publish the private photos she had encouraged me to take of her with her clothes off so many years ago. The idea had never even crossed my mind. I am grossly insulted that she should entertain such uncharitable thoughts. But now she has set the hare running, perhaps I will find out how much I can get for them.

Thinking back to that game of Murder in the Dark at Brokenshaw's house in Grantchester, I ask her: "What draws a woman to marry her own rapist?"

The colour visibly drains from her face. Self-Harming Harry would have been proud of her.

Because she hasn't got a snappy comeback or a neat put-me-down, she too pretends she sees something over her shoulder. "You'll have to excuse me too."

I'm not going to let her get away as easily as that.

"You know," I say to her, just as she is readying to walk away from me. "I've always thought that Sydney would have done a lot better if he'd sewn your mouth up instead of your cunt!"

She was in the process of leaving when these words stop her in her tracks. She has taken a couple of steps away from me in the broad direction of her fiancé, but then she spins on her heel like my little ballerina of old and she hawks a sputum that lands on my cheek. Betraying her Creole roots, I have just been gobbed on by the Prime Minister's fiancé. She sashays off in the direction of her husband-to-be whilst I dab at her DNA with my pocket handkerchief. I should never have let her get within spitting distance. I wonder if she knows Ingram is a cottager.

So that is what passes for a snappy comeback in her mind.

Ingram really has no idea that I am pulling the strings now.

I had taken a stroll around the old place. Most of it remained as it had been for the last seven centuries. After all, if it ain't broke, as they say, why fix it? But they had demolished the Birdwood. I suppose they will shortly be passing the bowl around for contributions to build something to replace that ghastly carbuncle that sat at the end of Gisborne Court blocking out the view of the Fens for so many years; but I will miss it fondly.

It used to keep me in order. Now it's gone, all I have is the god Set and the restless *psychomakkia* in my soul.

Just as I was leaving, I bumped into Self-Harming Harry, or Dr Self-Harming Harry, as we must call him now. I didn't recognise him at first because his complexion is as white as ivory. It looks surreal juxtaposed to his black curls.

"Hey, Harry!" I cry out, catching his attention. "I didn't think you were the type to attend college reunions."

"You're right, Nick. I guess I just wanted to show off the new me. My Goth look."

"I'm impressed," I tell him truthfully. "How did you manage to achieve it?" I think the how is a politer form of enquiry than the why.

"Illegal stem cell transplants from Snowflake."

"Who's Snowflake."

"The albino gorilla in Barcelona zoo. Remember?"

"Why is it illegal?"

"He couldn't give an informed consent to the operation. Because he was a beast. And he's dead now. So this is as white as it gets."

"You are a supreme work of self-authorship," I tell him.

"And what are you working on?" he asks politely. "I visited your exhibition at the Photographers Gallery. Those images of warfare were really powerful."

"Thanks. I'm working on a book."

"Has it got a title?"

"The Book of Thoth."

"Heavy, man!"

I change the subject before he asks me what it's about: "And what are you up to now that your honorary professorship has run out?"

"Me? Oh, eventually I got a college grant for another project."

"Wow! So you get to eat cake for another year."

"No, this one is a long-term study of an endangered species."

"You mean, the sort of project where you hang tiny cameras around animals' necks and observe how they behave in real life? Get the animals, who aren't even members of any union, to make your film for you without getting paid?"

"Close, except in my case, the long-term study was cheaper to fund, because the objects of the study bought all the cameras for themselves."

"An endangered species that buys itself cameras. Who are they?"

"Males. Just like Lyca predicted. We're all wounded animals. Our sperm count has been devalued to the extent that it's not even currency deposits of which will be accepted by any self-respecting sperm bank."

"Too much quantitative easing and too many early withdrawals?"

"Spot on! In the study, we take the feed and the geo-tagging from their' phones and analyse it all. Try to find out where we went wrong. It'll keep me busy for the rest of my life. In fact I'm doing it right now."

"Hear anything of the others? "

"Generation that disappeared, man. Lost Boys. So far we've got nothing to show for ourselves."

"You mean, apart from a Prime Minister and a Chancellor of the Exchequer?" I point out.

"I didn't mean it like that. I mean, no-one I know's married or having children, at least, not legitimate ones. Must be all that emancipation caused by the pill. Given the choice, why would any woman want to undergo the pains of childbirth?"

"Procreation? Motherhood? Ingram's engaged to be married."

"Well, la-dee-fucking-dah! Of all our straight friends, the only guy we know who's tying the knot is a fucking fairy!"

"Seth?" I enquire demurely, as if I didn't know.

"Seth? He disappeared off the face of the earth. I thought you would know as he was like your protégé."

"Nada. And you were Sydney's protégé. What news of the Great Gatsby?"

"Haven't you heard? Sydney is as rich as Croesus. He's got a chromium-plated Rolls Royce with a liveried chauffeur. He joined up with Spud Mullins, the engineer. Remember him?"

"Sure! The guy who was as fascinated by the art of lifting heavy objects up onto the rooftops of Cambridge as Sydney was in falling off them."

"The same. First of all they did The Cellulite Hotel and Spa at—wait for it—Wells-Next-the-Sea."

"What's that?"

"The original concept was a fat farm with a difference. They liposuction-ed you in the spa and then used the fat they'd extracted from you to cook your meals in the restaurant. It was a Sydney joke, but it turned out to be highly popular especially when some nutritionist wrote a paper about it: turned out there's less fat in our own fat than in butter, vegetable oil, olive oil, coconut oil, or for all I know, Duckham's oil. It's like one of those perfect crimes where you eat the murder weapon. Didn't you hear? That's how old Sully shed four stone in four weeks."

"At The Cellulite Hotel?"

"Actually, at it's more extreme successor—Spa Cellulite Lite. They had him on a high-protein low-calorie diet of umbilical poached in cellulite broth."

"Yuk!"

"That was just the beginning. Sydney used the income stream from the fat farms to fund other more capital-intensive ventures. Bear in mind that the Cellulite Hotel and Spa is a low investment high return business structure, so you can use the cashflow from that to fund something else. The clients at the Cellulite Hotel were basically providing their own means of production. They have the fat extracted out of one end and pay to have it shoved up their other ends. It's an amazing business model that keeps on giving. Sydney took the money from the Cellulite Hotel and sunk it into his transponder business."

"What's that?"

"It began as a decent enough attempt on Sydney's part to develop something for the benefit of mankind: transponders that would stimulate dead nerves and muscles into motion to overcome his paralysis and help others in the same situation. But it didn't work on him, because his muscles and nerves were already too dead. You realise that, in deadness, there are degrees, just like in anything else? So, it seems, on a scale of 1 to 10 dead, Sydney was an 11.

"But then he got into the spin-offs. They formed a company called SM Art Phones Inc. Get it? They developed an app for smartphones aimed at the BDSM market. Sydney dreamt it up, but he had to enlist Spud to do all the technical stuff. Basically, it's Sydney still trying to recreate his lost flexible friend, Calypso.

"In S&M relationships, it appears that there is a dominant partner and a submissive one. The submissive one has to attend before one of the panel of approved doctors who have consented to work with the app. After running through a script of specially constructed questions that Snowflake was never asked, to make sure they understand the procedure and are over eighteen and agreeable, the doctor installs a series of transponders into key nerve endings of the submissive one that enable the dominant partner to control essential muscle movements of the submissive one with his or her telephone.

"You start off in beginner mode, which basically enables you to make the other one open his or her mouth and legs wherever he or she may be, just by tapping on the photograph of that person in the contacts list on your 'phone. You then progress through public humiliation and uploading and sharing images until you become more and more advanced until eventually you achieve the status of Magus where, basically, the other person doesn't even have any control of his or her own bowels.

"The submissive partner is entirely dependent on the dominant one for performing even the most basic bodily functions. You can even override the gag function, so that you don't choke when foreign objects are thrust down your throat.

"And the domination thing is all the more acute, because, whilst the submissive partner is writhing around naked on the floor in a pool of his or her own bodily fluids, the dominant one is abstracted, remote, fiddling around with his 'phone; so that, like, maybe he sends a few texts, catches up on his e mail, does a bit of shopping online, and in between, initiates violent spasms in his consenting partner with a jab of his index finger. The detachment through the medium of the phone screen, the utter feigned disinterestedness, makes it all the better for both of them, apparently. Plus, every second of it is being recorded on the phone to be enjoyed later or uploaded and swapped.

"Sydney's original idea, after he realised he couldn't use it to cure his own paralysis, was to be in control of another person's movements, so he could bend and manipulate a girl around the way he could in the good old days with Calypso. But it went viral on the BDSM market, which is when they changed the company's name to SM Art, and it seems it's primarily used by lesbians and gays."

"Is the procedure reversible?"

"Oh, that's the money-spinning aspect of it. You have to take out a subscription to renew it each year or the transponders self-dissolve harmlessly in the body. The subscribers sign a direct debit, and Sydney and Spud are building up a gigantic order book after which they will sell the company for billions. It's bigger than Facebook."

"I've never heard of it. What's the app called?"

"Appy Bendings. Get it?"

"Yuk. It's sick! Yet another ingenious invention designed for good that ends up doing bad."

"Well, I was a bit like that when I first heard about it, but then I thought how different is that from me changing my appearance, or transgender or Botox and breast implants? It's more common than you would imagine, which is why Sydney's making so much dough, and it's all consensual. You ask the submissive ones what they want most of all for their birthdays or Christmas, and all they want is more fucking transponders fitted so they can demonstrate their devotion more completely.

"Did you read about that case recently where some gay managed to fold himself up inside a small hand-luggage size wheelie-bag and zip himself up inside, and then died when he couldn't get out again?"

"Yeh, I did read about that. In fact, I think I may even have covered the story."

"Well, you remember, the big mystery was, how did he manage to get himself inside the bag? I can tell you that it was done with the Appy Bending App, but SM Art used social media to spread a rumour that the victim was an MI6 spy to take the heat off them before someone like Ingram started passing legislation to outlaw it."

"You mean, the guy didn't want to get in the bag?"

"No. His partner controlled his movements on his phone."

"But, what happens at the end of a relationship?"

"Oh, Sydney's got that all figured out. He has a master switch and he can turn anyone on and off for another fee. But the creepy Big Brother thing is some people say that Sydney's master switch can control all of the users, and we're talking about more than forty million subscribers already. Some people say that Sydney is in a position to mobilise an entire army, and the army is getting bigger every day.

"An army that he could sell to the highest bidder. An army of mercenaries where the only bloke who actually gets paid is Sydney. And we are talking here about an army that could do a lot of damage, regardless of the hurt to themselves, because, let's face it, it's an army consisting entirely of masochists."

"I can just about see how a mind like Sydney's could have dreamt up such a thing," I say. "But how in the name of fuck did Spud manage to put it into execution?"

"Spud created an algorithm based on a very high level mathematical concept known as Set Theory."

My mind drifts back.

"Dear God! When you look back on the old days, those silly games, summoning up the god Pan, Reality Checkpoint, bending Calypso inside that papier mâché egg in Tommy, folding her up into that wheelie bag on the Catalan Talgo—all the seeds were there, just germinating."

"We were so innocent," he says.

"Yes," I say. "Looking back, it's quite a logical progression really. Sydney always was a control freak."

"Correct," observes Harry. "And now he's a CTRL+ALT+DEL freak!"

"Nostalgia ain't what it used to be!" I remark.

"Yes," said Harry before adding, "The apple doesn't fall far from the tree."

I didn't know what the expression meant before when I used it, and I was none the wiser when Harry used it.

"And you say Sydney's got a chromium-plated Rolls?"

"Absolutely! He's had a series of supercars all of which he had specially adapted for his disability; but then one night he drives his Aston Martin to his local pub. In his local, he proceeds to get totally smashed, and then he gets back into his motor even though his house is only 400 metres away. He puts his foot down and drunkenly drives it straight through the wall of his neighbour's house. He is sitting on the floor of the neighbour's house when the police arrive and you know what they say to him?"

"No."

"They say, *You were only 400 metres from your house. Why did you get into the car and drive? And he says Because I was too fucking drunk to walk!* Well, as you can imagine, the pigs don't like a disrespectful answer like that, so they throw the book at him. He is amazingly lucky to escape a custodial sentence, but he gets a huge fine and is banned from driving for 24 months.

"Sydney doesn't take that lying down. He hires that lawyer they call Mr Loophole and, at astronomical expense, gets it reduced to 23 months. On the 23rd month he climbs into his eagerly-awaited specially adapted McLaren and is just exiting his house nice and carefully when a drunken driver in a HiLux drives straight into him, writing off the McLaren and pushing his liver through his ear and, as if he wasn't badly damaged enough already from his night climbing fall, he spends the next 3 months in intensive care and the rest of his life in physio and, of course, back in his wheelchair. And the irony is—"

"That if he hadn't successfully appealed, he'd have been off the road and it would never have happened."

"Correct. Anyway, now he's got this chromium-plated Rolls Royce, but he prefers to use the services of his chauffeur rather than attempt to drive it himself."

"Bit ostentatious."

"He says it's just 'cos the suicide doors are easier with the wheelchair and all. Same reason he bought the McLaren: dihedral doors. "

"And how is Sydney looking, physically I mean?"

"In appearance? You know the stories of how people grow to resemble their dogs over the years? Well, it's a bit like that. Out the back, he's still got his ponytail, but now it's mangy and looks more like the tail of a syphilitic fox; but upfront, he's lost all his hair and his face is bloated, so each day he seems to be growing more like the Aleister Crowley he emulated so much in his days at Cambridge."

"But what about his famous Shaolin goatee beard?"

"Well that's another weird thing. You remember how the cleaners at the Cairo museum broke off Tutankhamun's blue and gold beard from his death mask and stuck it back on with Lepages, hoping no-one would notice?"

"Yes, I remember. It happened in 2015."

"That's what it looks like."

"Like his beard has been snapped off and stuck back on with Lepages?"

"Yes."

So, Sydney wanted to be like Professor Xavier in X Men, but he has grown up more like Dr Doom in the Fantastic Four. Another one of those experiments for the good of mankind that go terribly wrong.

An army of masochists. Where had I heard that one before?

"And what of the others?" I ask. "Are you still in touch with any of them? Calypso?" I ventured hopefully.

"Lyca? Disappeared off the face of the earth. She's like that Agatha Christie story, you know?"

"*The Lady Vanishes.*"

"Just so."

"We were her Lost Boys," I remember. "Now she's Little Girl Lost."

For a moment, we both just stand there, rolling back the years, not embarrassed by the silence. Then I continue: " And you've really heard nothing of Seth Godil?"

"Seth? No. Like I said, he was your mate. Seemed to evaporate when you came down from Cambridge. Did they ever crack the code that was printed on his skin?"

"It's a work-in-progress," I hint.

"I remember!" says Harry. "The day we all went swimming at the pool on Jesus Green. I arrived late with Sydney after helping him wax his car, and Spud was in the middle of a lecture about some German mathematician, and he thought he could translate the characters using the theory of the mathematician. What was it called now?"

"Oh God! Oh my God! You just said it yourself! Set Theory!"

"Of course! As I was just saying. You were supposed to take photographs and give the prints to Spud so that he could do the translation using the Set theory and we would be enlightened as to what it all meant."

Harry is looking at me, and he can see the loss in my eyes.

"You didn't follow it up?"

"Oh fuck!" is all I can say. "Oh fuck, fuck, fuck!"

The music seems to get louder, as if reminding me of where I went wrong:

Now I ain't makin' no excuses for the many things I uses
Just to sweeten my relationships and brighten up my day
But when my earthly race is over and I'm ready for the clover
And they ask me how my life has been I guess I'll have to say:
I got stoned and I missed it
I got stoned and I missed it
I was stoned and it rolled right by ...

They had taken the algorithm that should have decrypted Seth and recycled it into Appy Bendings. And it's all my fault.

Just as I am attempting to make my excuses and leave for the second or third time, Ingram makes a bee line for me. His fiancé has faded into the scrum. He is unaware of the slight unpleasantness that we exchanged recently, but the memory of which is germinating in my handkerchief.

"You know," he says, "you know, I've noticed how Ingram begins a lot of sentences with those two words. But I'm not sure they are mere empty padding whilst he warms to his subject. By introducing his propositions with prepositions in this way, he seeks to put his listener in a position of knowledge because *they know*, even though they do not know yet, and he is about to bring them into his state of knowing. It's an insidious kind of political flattery, a harbinger announcing that you are about to become a member of the *cognoscenti*. Its effect is to prick up your ears.

"You know, Nick, I've noticed how, as a reporter, you're always there before the news arrives. As though you were making the news. Like Jimmy Olsen in those *penny dreadfuls* you used to read."

Still do, I am thinking. I can tell he is working himself up to something, so I decide I might as well accept another glass of champagne from the silver tray borne aloft by the liveried flunky.

"Yeh," I mutter, "scoop!" The champagne is in one of those big dishes that you need a steady hand for or it will slop all over the place. Just thinking about this responsibility makes me nervous. I decide it is best to look away from the glass, so I meet Ingram in the eye, like I am interested in listening to his crap.

"Seriously, Nick, you're always one step ahead of the posse. The old days when ministers reached out for the newspapers in the morning over their toast and tawny marmalade, fingers trembling with trepidation, not knowing if their acts and omissions were going to be praised or denigrated by the media—are over."

I have taken a sip from the champagne dish, and an alien body floating in it has brushed against my lips. Instinctively, my gaze drops, and I notice there is an effervescent lozenge fizzing on the surface of the liquid. It has Ingram's initials, "IF". I had never made that connection before between his initials and the conditionality of everything. On the lozenge, it says "IF" and beneath the "IF" it says "x3", presumably alluding to Ingram Frazier serving an historic third term. The cretin who dreamt it up probably wanted to write more, but there wasn't enough space on the Alka Seltzer.

Seeing me looking at it, he says, "What do you reckon?"

To tell the truth, I think it's awful and reminds me of those Love Heart sweets we used to give the girls at primary school. But I know it would be impolite to mention any of this to Ingram, so, remembering his Catholic upbringing, instead I say: "It's a bit Holy Communion, like administering the Host."

He gives me a straight look, not sure whether taking the Host was really taking the piss, or if I have offered him a glimpse into something bigger than both of us.

"You know, Nick, it's just those sorts of insights I'm after. The old Punch and Judy days with the media are dead and buried. End of the pier stuff! It's all so bloody amateur. In the modern age, we've got to tell the media what to write. And for that, I need a Director of Communications, a DOC."

"A Spin Doctor."

"There you go. First the Host, then the Spin Doctor. Nick, you know, you can't help yourself: you just do it naturally. Spin Doctor is a very good description of what I'm after; but let's keep that to ourselves, shall we? Someone who is both a journalist himself and mixes with other journalists. Someone who has the ear of the media, but will also be its mouthpiece."

He can see he hasn't gotten my attention yet.

"You know, the job carries a six figure salary, plus there's a grace-and-favour terraced 5-bedroom mews house within earshot of the Division Bell. So, if you already own a house, you know, you rent it out and live in the free one that comes with the job. All paid for by the taxpayer. Plus, you get your own dedicated policeman at the end of your street, not intrusive or spooking you by standing right outside your front door if you feel the need to light up a bong or do a line of coke, but near enough for comfort, and you can speed-dial him on your phone."

"I need a garage for the car."

"I see I have your attention at last."

"OK," I say. "Let's go and make the news."

"I thought you'd see it my way, Nick."

"No, Ingram, thinking I'd see it your way is just a thought I put into your head that you think is your own."

"I see you've already got started, Nick. Good. Very good indeed. So the thoughts I think are my thoughts are really your thoughts that you think I ought to be thinking."

"No, they're not even mine. Someone else who is pulling the strings put the thought into my head that I should put into your head that thought and the thought that you had thought it yourself. It's all post-truth post-hypnotic suggestion."

Fucking Set! I see him standing behind Ingram, giving me the old slow hand clap.

Ingram takes a chromium credit card holder out of his jacket pocket. It has a sliding contraption like a casino card shoe that enables him to extrude his business card towards me. I inspect it.

THE RT HON INGRAM FRAZIER, QC, PM, MP, PC

I take it.

It may come in handy someday.

I have decided to go undercover. I will take control of the English Prime Minister and run things through him. I will become Ingram's parasite. He will think that the things that are happening are the consequences of the decisions he is taking. But I will be taking them for him. I will be calling the shots from now on.

On the way out, I pass by the god Set.

What was all that clapping about? I ask him.

Answering my question with another question, he just says *Don't you believe in fairies?*

Cadaqués in China

"I'd like you to cover this, Nick. Give it some of your inimitable spin."

She had her office window open the width of a wrist, using the great outdoors as her ashtray.

I grasped the transparent folder of documents the foreign editor was proffering me. I saw it was labelled "Cadaqués in China".

"What's it all about?" I asked her.

"Well," she began, drawing breath, "where to begin? Everybody's known for a long, long time that the Chinese are world class plagiarists. They rip off our intellectual property, perpetrate industrial espionage, copy our designs, reverse-engineer our electronic devices, manufacture pandemics in their laboratories, tear gas our colonies. Anything we've invented or created in the west, the Chinks have found a way to misappropriate it, poach it, pinch it, pass it off as their own, when it isn't, and now we're buying cheap counterfeit imitations of our own stuff back from them, putting our own native industries out of business in the process.

"That's all old hat. Western death wish. Everyone knows that, so we ain't going to hold the front page for that. But now, it seems, they've counterfeited an entire Mediterranean fishing village."

Now she can see she has my interest.

"The village of Cadaqués. It's at the foot of the Pyrenees in Spanish Catalonia."

"Yes, I know it."

"The artist, Salvador Dali, put it on the global map when he declared it the most beautiful place on earth. It's also the most north eastern point in Spain, so it gets the light before anywhere else on the Iberian Peninsula gets a look in, which made it very popular with artists.

"Anyway, it seems that a team of architects from a conglomerate known as China Merchants Zhangzon visited Cadaqués in June 2010 and fell in love with the place, so now they're building an entire replica village halfway around the globe in Xiamen Bay looking out towards Taiwan.

"The architects identified Xiamen Bay as an area geographically very similar to the Costa Brava and Cadaqués, and they started work in October. They're building 15,000 homes on a 100 acre site, which is going to feature all the best things about Cadaqués, but none of the bad things, such as the inconvenient 6,500 mile trip to get there, jellyfish or the infernal Tramuntana wind blowing all day and all night.

"It seems that logistically their biggest problem was working out how to squeeze a regulation-size Chinese fire engine into the narrow streets if there was a conflagration, because they may be very *laissez-faire* in China, but one thing they are inflexible about is the uniform dimensions of their fire engines. Most of the houses are already pre-sold.

"I'd like you to get your cute little arse over to Xiamen Bay and cover the story, speak to the people who purchased the holiday homes; find out what it feels like to live in a fake, live a counterfeit life, inhabit a forgery."

"What for?"

"The USP, Nick, is that this isn't a one-off. It appears the Chinese have already built a replica Paris complete with Eiffel Tower, boulevards and homes for 100,000 people. They've built a counterfeit of Thomas Hardy's Dorchester in Changdu which they call "British Town". They've also built the Himalayan utopia of Shangri-la, which has been declared a compulsory tourist paradise by the Chinese government, and some guy's working on a replica of Michael Jackson's Neverland ranch near Shanghai.

"I think there could be a lot of interest in the piece, and it lends itself to your photographic flair. We can set out the pictures of the rip offs side by side with the originals, like a kind of Parallel Lives. In fact we might even call it that. I've fixed you up an appointment with Mu Zheng, one of the architects. Here's your tickets."

I turned over the voucher. "6,500 miles in economy class?" I queried.

"When I said there could be a lot of interest, Nick, I didn't mean as much interest as all that. I thought it could be like a piece for the magazine, you know. But once you get back, I've got you premium economy for the Barcelona leg."

Good, I think to myself. I've already got footage of Cadaqués from Sully's stag do. I'll flog the Barcelona ticket.

Cattle Ranch

Ingram has not seen a 600,000-acre cattle ranch before. In fact, at this stage of his career, he hasn't even been invited to Tuscany for a bunga-bunga party with Berlusconi. Ingram is proudly sporting the Jaxon and James Sedona Stetson Cowboy Hat in Buffalo with the brown band that President Ivor Rash had given him on his arrival. He isn't wearing it just to be polite. He is wearing it because at last he feels he belongs.

He took morning prayers with Rash in the President's private chapel this morning, and he was still able to remember the many passages from the Bible his cleric father had drummed into him. They had got on like a house on fire, the President of the United States and Ingram, the Prime Minister of Great Britain. They had taken Communion together, and when Ingram had placed the wafer on his tongue, he had imagined it had "IFx3" engraved on it.

He is leaning on a fence, shoulder to shoulder with President Rash. Both men have Levi jeans and curling toed cowboy boots. Ingram is shooting the breeze with the most powerful man on the planet. They share common values. He has found a like-minded spirit who doesn't make him feel inadequate if he doesn't want to pretend to smoke dope and drink himself paralytic every evening; a man who goes to church on Sundays, and promotes clean family values; someone who wouldn't recognise a quotation from Shakespeare or Milton if it was branded onto a hamburger bun, or make you feel like an outsider, because you didn't; someone who wants to eat rare steak and burgers every day of his existence with no vegetables. Local steak: no Wagyu or Argentinian crap.

This is life as it should be. Ivor Rash is a glorious affirmation of self. He is what Nietzsche would have written about himself if Nietzsche had ever written an autobiography.

President Rash dips his two middle fingers into the grey gunk on the inside of a flunky cowhand's cocked Stetson. Ingram doesn't know if he is more surprised to see the President of the United States proprietorially smearing the product with his ungloved hand into the ass of a gold palomino on heat, or by the fact that the cowpoke puts his hat back on his head deferentially afterwards.

Ingram has scarcely stepped out of the way before a gigantic stallion mounts the palomino, stamping up a blizzard of swirling dust motes with his hind hooves. Rescuing him by the shoulder, Rash says: "Let's walk and talk, Frazier. Let us discuss the nature of pure evil."

Both men look down at their dusty boots as they pace forward, lost in weighty peripatetic deliberations.

"The Contranistas are holding ten of our boys hostage in the north," says Rash. "I want to bring them home to their folks. It's like a mission. No ifs. No buts. I have to bring them back, and I don't mean in body bags!"

"Most commendable, Mr President."

"I want to bring my boys back home, because each hour that passes, it's like walking with a stone in my boot, reminding me every day I haven't brought my boys back home to their folks. Plus, it was kinda like an election pledge. But when you want something, like you are running for the highest office in the civilised world, you make a lotta promises, and after you have sleepless nights wondering how you're going to make them all come true.

"The great American electorate, they're like children. You can make them the most impossible promises, and the more impossible they are, the more fervently they want to believe in you. But when I made those promises, I meant them, or some of them at least. It's just that I really believed that if I was elected to the highest office in the country, I would hold it in my hand to deliver on all those promises.

"But now I'm at the top of the greasy pole, I realise it ain't as simple as that. The Contranistas are armed to the teeth (not with the latest arms, mind you, but the dirtiest and most unpleasant), and I come to realise that I can't bring my boys back home without putting more and more boots on the ground, which would result in the Contranistas just taking more and more hostages, 'cos it's not a terrain where you can fight a clean stand-up shootin' war. These guys have never even heard of the Marquis of Queensland."

"So, Mr President, would you like me to put some battalions of my maddest Scotsman's boots on the ground? They have a very low life expectancy anyway."

"No, son. It hasn't come to that yet, but thankyou deeply for that pledge of earnest. I fear I am going to have to negotiate with this filth; but the problem is, it was like another central plank of my election campaign that we don't negotiate with terrorists."

"You know, if you don't negotiate with terrorists, how can you deal with people like that? You saw how I brought the IRA back into the fold. I mean, terrorists don't have armies; they don't have bases you can blow up; they're embedded behind human shields and they marshal their ranks at the click of a mouse. The only way you can ever make any progress with people hiding in the shadows like that is if you speak with them; if you seduce them with trappings of credibility, with the notion that they have the ear of President Rash.

"Make them think you'll meet their demands halfway. The souk is what they're used to. If it hasn't got a price label on it, it's open for debate. You saw what I achieved in Northern Ireland? Just what are these Contranistas demanding?"

"They asked for a trillion dollars."

"And what are they going to do with a trillion dollars?"

"Well, it seems these guys are fighting their own battle with the TerraMoto Group in the south, and if we gave them a trillion dollars for the return of our boys, then, I suppose that, after allowing for shrinkage in terms of inevitable payments to corrupt officials and *consiglieri*, there might still maybe be a quarter of a trillion dollars left to buy arms to enable them to fight the TerraMoto boys in the South.

"And it wouldn't be as though it was wasted money, because they would use the money we give them to buy arms from us, so we wouldn't just be tearing up a trillion dollars. We get a lot of it back again in arms sales and software maintenance licences for the GPS systems that make them hit their targets. And if they used those arms to wipe out the TerraMoto Group, they would be doing the whole world a favour, because quite frankly that group is ten times worse than the Contranistas, and I wouldn't even want to send any of my boys out there on the ground to deal with that scourge, because they would confiscate their iPods. These guys are remorseless."

"But the TerraMoto aren't our enemies, Ivor."

"No, Ingram, but they are very evil guys, so we should rid the world of them. No one could argue with the logic of that. Live by the sword, die by the sword. Know what I mean?

"It seems the way these guys are organised—not the TerraMoto; I'm back on the Contranistas now—there's no national army as such.

It's more like a franchise. If you have wealth and want to be a general, you just buy your own army, and it's like a shareholding: the army enables you not only legitimately to rape and pillage the enemy, but also your own people. You extort money in fines with your army, but you also defeat the Contranistas."

"Like private vehicle clamping?" He pronounced it "ve-hi-cule".

"A Denver boot, yes."

"Wouldn't it be simpler, Mr President, just to swap the arms for the hostages? Give the Contranistas the weapons they need to fight the TerraMoto. In return, they release your boys, and do your dirty work for you in vanquishing an even worse bunch of guys. And in the future, you have their allegiance, because they'll need to come back to you to buy spare parts for the weapons. Terrorists have their needs, just like other people. They're only human you know. Terrorists get out of bed every morning. They have their good days and their bad days."

"Arms for hostages! You know, I kinda like that. But isn't that tantamount to negotiating with terrorists?"

"No negotiations involved. This is you tabling your own wish list to them; although your guys coming home unharmed happens to be linked to that. You initiate an arms trade agreement; they expunge the TerraMoto from the annals of history. What's not to like? The more weaponry you give them, the more TerraMoto guys you wipe off the face of the earth. If they ask you for a trillion, you insist they have— what's the next thing after a trillion?"

"I don't know that it even exists, so I'm just gonna call it an Ingram! You are so very deep. But if people think I have been supplying arms to the Contranistas, I am going to be in deep do-do!"

"Well, that's public opinion for you, Ivor, and political correctness. In the east, they're burning our pilots alive in iron cages and filming it with their phones, but in the west there's moral outrage if a French policeman asks a Muslim woman to remove her burqa on the beach."

"Sure, but as I'm facing re-election next month, public opinion happens to be quite important to me, Ingram."

"Well, use me, Mr President. I'm not facing re-election because I've just been re-elected for an historic third term in office, and Great Britain's not at war with the Contranistas. What do you need to move arms around the world?"

"Fake End User's Certificates."

"Is there any other kind of End User's Certificate?"

"Ingram, you really think out of the box. I have to take my hat off to you! Who would have thought it? Providing a trillion dollars' worth of arms to our enemies. I'm sorry, an Ingram's worth of arms to our enemies!"

"Yes, but they are not going to unleash those weapons on us. They are going to unleash them on their greater enemies, the TerraMoto group. They are going to use it to go to war with TerraMoto and wipe that evil bunch of cretins off the face of the planet."

"The TerraMoto being the worse enemy of the two, even though they pose no immediate threat to us, but they are a despicable people led by a bloody dictator."

"Yes, the world would be a better place without him."

"And in return my boys will come home, enabling me to fulfil my election pledge."

"Except there will be no linkage. This will not be a post hoc ergo propter hoc situation. The British will sell arms to the Contranistas, and, as it happens, shortly thereafter, your boys will come home to their folks."

"Ingram, you are a true friend! I owe you a million!"

"Let's just call it a straight Ingram, Ivor."

Xiamen Bay

The replica's identical to the original. I don't know why I let the foreign editor persuade me to waste my time coming all this way. I could just have palmed off my old Cadaqués photos as being footage of the Chinese rip-off and no-one would have been any the wiser. That's how it is with counterfeits. Sell her some fake news about a fake village by passing off the original as the fake. Buy some fake receipts or print your own, and reclaim all the expenses of a trip to China I never made in the first place.

I am letting my imagination run free. If I get some receipts for Chinese call girls and expensive meals, will my foreign editor become distracted, poring over the detail of these minutiae whilst not noticing that I never even made the trip to China? I'm not dishonest, but when you enter the realms of counterfeit, where does it all end?

I take a couple of snaps of the architect, Mu Zheng, just so my editor knows I really came here.

"He says," says my translator, "that if you're so interested in this sort of thing, you should check out Shiga Mountain."

"And what will I find at Shiga Mountain?" I ask.

"Apparently, a very wealthy businessman who adores choral music has built a replica of King's College Chapel."

"King's College Chapel, Cambridge?"

"Yes."

"Why?"

I wait whilst he puts the question to the architect.

"He says the guy is very secretive, but the answer is the only way he could replicate the acoustics was to copy the entire building."

"How far is it from here?"

"He says it's a 20-hour train journey."

"I'm on my way."

Quanzhou Province

My editor had been very pleased with my proposition. Why travel six and a half thousand miles to cover Cadaqués in China when I could also cover Cambridge in China at the same time? It was a Twofor, two for the price of one. Nick Jobs stock-in-trade.

After 21 hours aboard a cattle truck, I disembark, and a bone-rattling rickshaw ride later, I check into the Nan'ao Qiyunge Guesthouse for a shave, shower and general freshen up before my trip to Shiga Mountain. I emerge from my room spritzed with *Balafre* and begin my enquiries.

No-one at the Nan'ao Qiyunge Guesthouse knows anything about a replica Cambridge university building or King's College; but the foreign editor has agreed to push the boat out and engage me a dedicated local driver who knows every inch of Quanzhou Province, and we are going to explore the area in the morning.

Next day, at first light, appropriately, my English-speaking Chinese driver, Chung, shows up in a replica Range Rover known as a Hongqi LS5. I ask him if he knows anything about a secretive billionaire and King's College chapel, but he just stares at me like I've been eating loco weed. However, to humour me, he holds open the car door and bows politely, recognising in me the air of authority. I chuck my photographic bag onto the back seat and get in the front with Chung.

By the time we've knocked on almost every door in Quanzhou Province eliciting the same blank stares Chung had given me back at the Nan'ao Qiyunge Guesthouse, Chung wants to turn his rip-off Range Rover around and drive back to the Guesthouse for a late dinner of Raman noodles, when in the twilight, I spot a glimmering reflection.

"Is that water down there?" I ask him.

"A reservoir. This area's dotted with reservoirs."

I'm impressed with his grasp of the English language. How many foreigners would quicken their syntax with a word like "dotted"? And this guy is just a chauffeur in the back of beyond.

"If someone's really built an ersatz King's College here," I explain to Chung, "for authenticity, he might want to build it next to some water and water meadows. You know, King's College runs down to the Backs."

"You go Back now, sir?"

"No, the Backs. It's what they call the lower river. Let's check out the water down there; then we can go back."

Of course, the reservoirs that dotted the area were a lot farther away than they had seemed. It's getting dark before it reveals itself to us; but, as we inch closer, there is no mistaking the imposing bulk of those great buttressed shoulders in biscuit-coloured brickwork. Mu Zheng hadn't been hallucinating. In a clearing in the dense forest, in the middle of nowhere, in the shadow of a mountain, a Chinese madman had pirated the Plantagenet architectural masterpiece begun by King Henry VI and finished 20 years later after the interruption of the Wars of the Roses, and rebuilt it here, after an interruption of a further 500 years. It's a Barney.

Chung is scared. He won't leave the car. So I grab my camera bag and start the walk. The journey takes longer than I was expecting, because I'd got my perspective wrong. I'd assumed the replica would be scaled down; but it was full size. The walk took me half an hour.

By the time I get there, it's pitch dark, but a faint light is shining through the delicate tracery of the stained glass windows. I am right there, beside the monolithic structure clad in white Yorkshire limestone. About 100 metres to the right is a low-built concrete compound and to the right of that what looks like a toilet block.

The chapel and the compound are surrounded by dense forestry, save for the water meadow leading down to the reservoir. You could be 100 yards away and have no idea it was there. Why would anyone build such a vanity project in a place where no-one else could ever see it?

With a boring inevitability, there are guards armed with Type 56 Assault Rifles (the Chinese Kalashnikov counterfeit), patrolling the grounds. This leads me to conclude that the secretive gentleman is very secretive indeed. The question is, *Is he trying to keep me out, or someone else in?*

I open the door a crack, and gaze up into the honey-hued fan vault of the ceiling atop the filigree stone frames encasing jewel-like windows, reflecting the flames from a hundred flickering candles, and from within I hear the sound of choir music. It is simultaneously exquisite whilst being obscene in its incongruity. I recognise the strains of Gregorio Allegri's *Miserere Mei Deus*, drifting from the dummy chapel in the depth of the forest by the reservoir in the middle of the night. I poke my lens through the gap in the door and start clicking away.

"What're you doing?"

So enchanted am I by what I hear and see that I nearly jump out of my skin when I realise someone is standing right beside me. He must have come from the compound. It's a young English boy, no more than 8 or 9 years of age, Leeds accent, National Health specs, dressed in a white surplice over a red full-length vestment.

"How many of you are there?" I ask him.

An Exoculation in Judea

"I brought this one to add to your collection."

With his crustacean claw, he pushes a 10 x 8 glossy photograph across the desk in my direction. I slide it around so that it's up the right way. Touching it, I realise it's not been printed on photographic paper. In fact I don't know what the recording medium is. If I had to make a guess, I'd say that Set had carefully peeled the silver nitrate off the back of a very ancient mirror. I take a look. There are three guys on a mount nailed to crosses. Beneath them, there's a crowd of onlookers wearing expressions covering the whole spectrum from agony to ecstasy; there are a few Roman soldiers and a woman.

"It's a crucifixion," I observe.

"Not just any old crucifixion," corrects Set. "The crucifixion."

"Impossible!" I exclaim. "Cameras weren't invented. "And this is in full colour. How could it have been taken?"

Set points his claw at one of the centurions with his back to us in the middle foreground. His red cloak thrown over his shoulder is like one of those splashes of expensive pigment that a Venetian Doge would order by the litre when commissioning his portrait.

"He took it."

"How? What with?"

"He observed it. He was disgusted with the spectacle that he was participating in. He blinded himself. I performed a neat exoculation upon him on that very spot, and I kept the eye whilst it was still fresh from his skull. The image was frozen on his retina. I used the lens of his eye to print the image, like your pin-hole camera in a shoe box; and now I give it to you to paste into your scrapbook."

I study the image more carefully. Set is standing next to the soldier, watching the proceedings.

"So, it really happened?"

"Of course it happened. In Judea in 32 AD. As you can see, I was there. Without good angels, there wouldn't be any bad ones."

"And that's the face of Christ."

I can't take my eyes off it. I want to avert my gaze, but His keeps drawing me in. The wound at his side, the sign affixed to the top of the cross, saying, "Jesus of Nazareth, King of the Jews". He bears the marks of a flogging. Flanked by two convicted criminals, their legs broken to hasten their deaths, their faces etched in suffering, His visage radiating translucent peace and calmness. He is looking straight at me, as though he is saying *You did this to me*. I know that this is an image that will calm me down when the demons short circuit the wiring in my head.

Pulling my focus away from the action in the centre, I look at the background.

"What's happening with the weather?" I ask. The sky is tinged with fire.

"You can see for yourself. In Hebrew, the words for blood and red share a common origin; *dm* means red and *dom* means blood."

"I remember the different eyewitnesses refer to ominous portents in the skies. One even said there was an earthquake during the six hours He was on the cross. Others talk about the sky going dark and storms of meteors."

Seth raps his claw on the glossy image. "Well, as you can see, it was none of those things. That's how it was."

"It's a double rainbow."

"No look closer at the colours."

I do look closer, but I don't know what it is.

"What is it?"

"It's a double *black* rainbow."

The bands of the spectrum are reversed.

"How rare is that?" I ask.

"Must be pretty fucking rare," replies Set. "I haven't seen another one in the last two thousand years."

"And you were there."

"I was there. But you don't have to believe me. Believe the proof of someone else's eyes."

"And the negative?"

"-Was the soldier's eye. It can't be printed again. This is the only one."

"I will treasure it."

Twofor

I show my editor the prints.

Her left hand is absent-mindedly corralling some Danish pastry crumbs on her desktop, memories of elevenses. Her right hand is resting on the window ledge, clutching her vaping pen. I notice that her left shoe has become partially decoupled from her foot. Her toes are still in the vamp, hanging on by a thread, but her heel has come adrift.

In a circular motion below her desk mirroring the crumb corralling that is happening on the desk, she is trying to coax her wayward heel back into the shoe. But then the vamp gives way and the whole shoe clutters to the floor. This reveals a seam across the toes of her stocking which for reasons I can't explain is giving me a fledgling stiffie, although I don't fancy her in the least.

"There's 300 of them," I tell her, "living in a cement compound alongside a replica of King's College Chapel. They can't leave because they've got no money or passports and they're in the middle of nowhere, locked up during the day and only let out to sing evensong. The Chinese billionaire who built the carbon-copy Kings is a collector. He came to King's College on vacation in the 70s and took in a performance of the choir, and he's been collecting the kids ever since.

"He kidnaps them at between 8 to 13 years old. After that, they're no use to him. As they grow up, he has them surgically castrated, so they keep their voices, but apart from that, he doesn't lay a finger on them. All that he wants is to listen to the celestial music they make. And, get this, just like the Abominable Doctor Phibes, he plays the organ.

"King's College, Cambridge ran special scholarships to attract these boys from disadvantaged homes, so their disappearances didn't trigger the same hue and cry you'd expect if middle class or wealthy kids were picked off. These kids didn't count. Plus, they came from working class homes in the north of England, so the parents had already washed their hands of them.

"Just think of it, if the kids had gone into the sex industry, their parents would be looking for them relentlessly; but because they were working class kids who had chosen to dress up in girlie clothes and sing in a choir, they'd been told never to darken their parent's thresholds again. The Chinese oligarch has been harvesting 10 a year for the last

15 years."

My editor is gobsmacked. Her vaping pen is quivering in her hand. Nothing happens for maybe 20 seconds that feels like 20 minutes. Then she exhales ripe apple, buttered popcorn, cinnamon and burnt vanilla. It's difficult to reconcile how something that smells so wholesome can be impairing the ability of her lungs to rid themselves of mucus and severely compromising her ability to manufacture interleukin-6.

"The authorities," I continue, "have spent the last 15 years infiltrating every paedophile ring in the world, whereas it turns out no paedophiles were involved. Just a well-heeled Chinese music junkie who took a vacation in Cambridge that stuck in his mind for the rest of his life."

"Nick, this is amazing. I sent you to Xiamen Bay to cover a copy of Dali's village, and you uncover something weirder than Dali himself could have dreamed up. And, in the process, you solve a major crime that has spanned the twentieth and twenty first centuries, baffling the authorities for more than 15 years. This was going to be a cute little confection for the Travel section in the glossy magazine, but you've delivered a—"

"Scoop?"

"Scoop."

"What are we going to do with it?"

"Publish it, of course."

"As in *Publish and be damned*?"

"Yes. Why ever not?"

"I think I'd just like to run this one by Ingram Frazier first."

"Why is that, Nick?"

"Let's just say some things are too big to do on your own. Finding them is half the story, and we can take the credit for that; but if we're going to bring them back home, we're going to have to bring in the government."

Yes, I'd solved the crime that had bridged a century, but it was a crime I'd been accused of. I wasn't going to take that lying down.

A Welcome Contortion

I was a cameraman. I preferred that title to *photographer*. There are just so many photographers, but only one or two Helmut Newtons or David Baileys. When there is a good war going on, the editor sends me all over the place. First, I make the news as the god Set. Then I get sent off to photograph the news that I myself have made. One could think of it as demeaning, taking orders in this way. But I just think of myself as Peter Parker, confident in the knowledge that I know I am really Spiderman.

But now, I have this additional lamination: I am also the PM's Director of Communications. So, having made the news myself, I tell everybody else how to write it up. And if they don't do what I tell them, they don't get any more news. They don't get invited into No 10 to sit on the couch with Ingram and Sully and me, and watch pure, unadulterated strategy seeping from our craniums. And now, Ingram's Spin Doctor is writing tomorrow's news. Ingram and the Foreign Secretary are liaising with their Chinese counterparts, practising the lost art of diplomacy, and my newspaper has chartered a plane to fly them back. Fucking Business Class.

My photographic work is highly regarded amongst the *cognoscenti*. I started off with a boutique exhibition in Shoreditch. But then came my War Exhibition at the Photographers Gallery, followed by the Loss exhibition at the Tate Modern, the only venue large enough to house one of the exhibits known as Start Rite. And the money comes flowing in, unexpectedly. I didn't know you could earn a good living out of this.

People are actually buying posters of my work. I learnt that my images are selling more than anything else, and I wonder at what a sad world I have contributed to creating, where students' walls are no longer enlivened by posters of Jane Fonda in Barbarella or the tennis player with no knickers rubbing her bum as she approaches the net. Instead they have my photographs of war and post-war apocalyptic meltdown and dystopian hopelessness.

All my images share a common theme. Someone is beginning a journey along an endless landscape. The Sunday Times art critic said: *"The sheer enormity of the task ahead shrinks the viewer into insignificance."* I usually feel that way when I get out of bed in the morning. I don't know what my message is, but it's a message that a whole generation is buying into.

I told the Sunday Times art critic to write that.

And the royalties are rolling in. I have rented out my grace and favour five bedroom terraced house within earshot of the Division Bell, courtesy of the PM, Ingram Frazier, and I am able to buy an expensive high ceilinged mews house on the South Bank, looking across the Thames towards Charing Cross and the Embankment. I have taken my dedicated uniformed policeman with me from the grace and favour house and he now stands guard at the end of my cobbled mews.

I buy before the trend for riverbank living takes off after which the property speculators can't find enough riverside to develop. I buy before Docklands and Canary Wharf. I watch from my floor to ceiling windows as they build the footbridge across the Thames like a Blade of Light. It could be an image from one of my photographs. I watch as British Airways float the components for their gigantic Ferris Wheel down the Thames and spend three months assembling them before my very eyes, right in front of my window. It looks like a gigantic zoetrope or *Camera Obscura*.

I think how fitting it is that someone should decide to plant a gigantic revolving lens outside the house of this famous photographer. It is called The London Eye, but I call it The London Lens.

I am planning my next exhibition which is going to take place in a Women's Prison.

There are no wars to photograph today, so I have been sent to the London Wonderground Tent on the South Bank of the Thames to cover the first appearance in England of *Le Cirque du Soleil*. The London Mayor has banned circuses with animals, so instead we have to put up with the degrading spectacle of human beings reducing themselves to the status of beasts. Progress. Or that's what my editor had told me.

I start off in a bad mood, because I feel that covering the local news is beneath me. Nick Jobs, the journalist who cracked the 15 year riddle of the missing choristers, covering a circus! However, contrary to the obscurantist beliefs of my editor, this turns out to be the finest circus I have ever seen. It is an aerial ballet on bungee elastic, seemingly lit by a Renaissance grand master and performed to the accompaniment of very fine live music.

I am just thinking to myself that this has to be the best show in town since *The Coming of the god Set* when I see that the strong man has rolled a Nebuchadnezzar into a follow spot, and there is nothing else on the stage apart from this huge bottle of wine, revolving, turn after turn, until it comes to a full stop on its side, centre stage. And the music stops, as it does just before the trapeze artists perform their most terrifying plunges into the void; the signal for the audience to be hushed and gaze up in awe whilst the acrobats de-grease their palms with talc for the next leap of faith.

Yes, the music stops, and then there is a low drum roll, building up the anticipation that something out of the usual is about to happen. But what can possibly happen to a big bottle occupying the follow spot centre stage?

And the bottle that was reclining on its side begins to wobble, of its own accord. Like a jumping bean. Until it has wobbled itself upright. There isn't a sound in the auditorium. Then a small door in the bottle is opened from the inside, and out comes a foot shod in a satin ballet shoe. The audience gasp in amazement as, limb by limb, an entire women emerges from the bottle, clad in a flesh coloured leotard. Like the Venus of Botticelli, but with shorter red hair. A contortionist. And I gasp in amazement.

Little Girl Found.

Taking Stock

Reader, dear Reader, I fully understand that there are a number of targets that I have set myself, and which you are entirely justified in expecting me to deliver on, because I would be a cocksucker if I didn't. So that there are no arguments over the tally later, so that no aspiring Kit Marlowes have their eyes put out over the reckoning; no ifs; no IFx3's; no buts; let's just take stock and make a little list, shall we?

First and foremost, you are expecting me to take you to the place where the parallel lines meet.

Secondly, you want to know what all that shit written on Seth means.

Thirdly, and this is a new one that's only cropped up recently, you want me to describe the Face of Christ.

May I point out in my own defence that I never promised to tell you what had become of the missing choir boys. But I gave you that one *gratis* as a loss-leader, as a sweetener for the bitter pill yet to come.

Taking the last one first, let me tell you what His face *didn't* look like.

It bore no resemblance to the ghostly image on the Turin shroud, or indeed to any of the depictions I can think of in paintings from the Byzantine, the pre-Raphaelites, the Renaissance or Francis Bacon. And before you ask me, no, he wasn't black. He had no beard, and he was much younger than I'd expected. He had shoulder-length auburn hair.

I believe this hair colour has previously been claimed by a number of commentators, wishing to prove that the King of the Jews was in fact a Welshman or a Scot. Plenty of Yids have red hair. Also, he looked underfed with a protruding ribcage, but I guess most of us would look like that if we were forced to adopt that posture for six hours. It was that gaze, that still, firm, penetrating, understanding, forgiving but playful gaze, more compelling than the Mona Lisa, the gaze that drew you in and made you keep returning to it every time you thought you had moved on.

Reader, the only way that I can describe Him is to say that He looked like what She would have looked like if Lyca could have opened her eyes.

Next, the characters written all over Seth. As we now know, if you take a snapshot of them, as we did, they read *The Book of Thoth* and ∞. I don't know what all the individual runes mean or say, except that they are instructions for a pathway that takes you to ∞, Infiniti, the place where the parallel lines meet. And when Calypso put that mark there, I no longer think it was her signing off or like a full stop. I think it was more like the frontispiece or title page, being the subject of the book. Seth was the object of the book and ∞ was the subject.

Lastly, this place where the parallel lines meet; well, obviously, it's one and the same place as ∞; and Reader, dear Reader, I promise you, we are going there.

∞: it's just like two wheels. And if you're on two wheels, all I know is that you have to keep pedalling. Because if you ever stop, you'll fall straight over.

For Old Time's Sake: A Doobie with a Special Roach on the Blade of Light

I hadn't had a spliff in years. My days of turning up, tuning in and dropping out were long gone. But I didn't want to seem impolite.

Harry was alternating between trying to roll his joint and turning the business card I had given him over and over between his thumb and forefinger as if he was practising to become a card sharp. I hasten to say that it wasn't my business card; it was Ingram's. Harry frowned down at the rubric on it in the same way that we used to concentrate on all the shit that was written on Seth Godil, before he disappeared. I remembered how the wrinkles in Harry's forehead were so deep that we used to think an ant could twist his ankle in them.

When we met up at the Sex Club reunion, in addition to covering a lot of important topics such as weight loss and Appy Bendings, we must have mouthed some stock footage about how we shouldn't leave it so long next time. No-one takes that shit seriously. But a month later Self-Harming Harry had texted me and fixed a meet.

So, here we were at noon shooting the breeze on the new bridge connecting Tate Modern to the South Bank, the pedestrian bridge that was now known as The Blade of Light, but which used to be known as The Wobbling Bridge, due to the way it responded unfavourably to the pedestrians' footfalls. Weather-wise, it's what the French meteorologists would call *un temps couvert*. One of those overcast days that Magritte used to paint with the sky full of torsos and burning tubas. But every now and then a veritable blade of light breaks through to irradiate our eponymous bridge.

Down below on the Thames, the vessels slip by under Blackfriars Bridge and railway station. Water taxis, Thames Clippers, workboats, and in between seagulls circle. Snatches of a nursery school rhyme keep tickling my memory:

From the Cotswolds, and the Chilterns
From your fountains and your springs,
Flow down, O London river
To the seagull's silver wings.
Isis, or Ock or Thame

Forget your olden name
And the lilies and the willows,
And the weirs from which you came.

"Why did you chose to meet here?" I asked. "In the intermezzo of this bridge. Are we going to be trading hostages?"

"I thought that you might fancy a wee tincture of Nepalese Temple Ball for old time's sake," he said. "And standing here, as we are, as you put it but more elegantly than me, bang in the middle of the bridge, we can see all the way to the south and all the way to the north, so that, when the time comes to smoke this joint, we can be as sure as shit that there are no pigs or undercover scum anywhere near, and if any should materialise, we just drop the gear over the side of the bridge."

"Harry, don't you think that's a bit paranoid?"

"Nick, even paranoids have enemies."

I couldn't tell for sure if he had his heart in rolling the joint, or if he just felt obliged to get hammered with me for old time's sake. But, as there was no doubt that he had all the makings with him, I figured that he must have been intending to get lashed anyway, and getting lashed solitarily is the first sign of addiction, so I should keep him company and help keep his habit under control in the same way that no-one should have to make the pilgrimage to Dignitas alone.

But, if you have a friend who cares enough about you to travel with you, why go in the first place? Maybe it's all about the journey and not the destination. Anyway, this was Self-Harming Harry that we were talking about, so, it went without saying that he wanted to go the whole nine yards.

The card read:

The Rt Hon Ingram Frazier, QC, PM, MP, PC

"When did he get to be a QC?" asked Harry. "Last I heard, he was an old hack running a human rights factory on CFA's because no-one valued his services enough to pay for them. The only noteworthy case he ever did was yours."

"He's in the cabinet, Harry," I explained. "If you're in the cabinet, and if you're a junior barrister, you automatically get upgraded to Queen's Counsel."

"You mean, like with Hertz and Avis?"

"Yes, just like that, as Tommy Cooper would say."

"And PC. What's that? Politically correct?"

"Harry, you could be forgiven for thinking so. No; it means he's a member of the Privy Council."

"And who are they when they're at home?"

"In theory, they advise the Monarch; but, quite frankly, if the Queen wants advice, I think she would go to a firm like Ince."

"And is that an automatic upgrade too?"

"Fuck knows. There's a Privy Council to which rights of appeal lie from the judgments of the courts of some of our more obscure colonies."

"You mean like leper colonies?"

"No, Harry, I mean one of the Dominions of Great Britain."

We contemplated the circling gulls for a moment whilst Harry assimilated this information.

"So you get to appeal to a second rate barrister like Ingram Frazier –"

"Because, so the theory goes, even a legal hack like Frazier is better than some monkey in a wig Judge in the British Commonwealth."

"But that's awful. And does it really happen?

"Do they have kangaroo courts in Australia? Harry, in practice, it happens very rarely. The insult of having to refer your appeal to someone like Ingram is considered so contumelious that most Defendants would rather do a few years shovel."

"Well, you know what I'm going to do with his card, my friend?"

"I've got a fair idea. I think you're going to put it in your pipe and smoke it."

"Spot on! Spot on!"

Harry had concluded his rolling of the joint, and all that was lacking was the roach, for which purpose Ingram's illustrious business card was well-suited. Harry curled it up and shoved it up the spliff's exhaust.

"I think this is what the Frogs call le toque Final," he said. "I couldn't think of anything else to do with it as it was too small to wipe my arse with!"

And with that reflection, he looked to his left and right, the length of the bridge, and, having checked that it was safe in both directions, lit the joint, and we shared the pipe of peace again. Fortunately, we had done most of our philosophising before we got mullahed.

After flicking the toke containing Ingram's abused business card over the side of the bridge, Harry reached robotically into his jacket pocket. Grasping a bottle-green weathered glass phial in his fist, he dabbed the button, releasing a fine mist of cologne from the vaporiser. Due to my proximity and the direction of the wind, a few fine pearls settled on me. As if the simple act of seeing Harry again after all these years wasn't enough, the scent sent me off on a Proustian descent into my olfactory past. I feel Time's tentacles tightening her tourniquet.

"*Balafre*?" I query.

"By Lancôme," answers Harry.

"I haven't smelt that in 20 years," I say. "I didn't know they still made it."

"Not sure they do," observes Harry, inspecting the bottle at arm's length. "I've been stock-piling it for Brexit. This is from my private reserve. My wife would leave me if she knew I was still smoking cigarettes, and if she knew I was still smoking this gear, she'd kill me before leaving me."

Then, he produced a travel-size bottle of Listerine, the measure they manufacture specially so people can pay more for less and take it on the 'plane in their hand baggage. Harry swigs, rinses, gargles for about 20 seconds that seems like 20 minutes, and then spits it over the side of the bridge into Old Father Thames, Isis or Ock. One silver thread of saliva, attached to his lower lip, growing longer and heavier, refulgent like a spider's web in the solitary string of light cracking out through the covered slates of the sky. He didn't want to let it go.

In fact, neither of us wanted to let it go, and the inert gob itself didn't want to let him go: it was as if the two of us were watching our past hammered out into some barnacled umbilical tethering us to our beginnings. We both beheld it attenuating, like gold to aerie thinness beat, as John Donne would have said; or like a job of jism, as I would have said; and neither of us wanted to bring that moment to an end by the act of snipping the last tenacious thread clinging to his lower lip.

As the two of us contemplated the caterpillar-fine skein of sputum penduluming in the wind, it occurred to me that this elasticated drool contained the stencil for Harry's whole life in its unique DNA. In the future, that I must write, there wouldn't be any money or credit cards, just a gigantic electronic register of everyone's unique DNA. At the supermarket checkout, you'd just gob on the attendant and your bank account would automatically be debited. Things were already swinging in that direction. The Spit and the Pendulum.

I realised that I must have been locked in some time capsule, where the past never moves on. Until last month's reunion, I hadn't seen Harry for 10 years, but here I was taking it for granted that nothing had changed in the intervening years. He was so easy to talk to. It was just like conversing with myself. Or Set. It was like the Indian Memory Man joke, where the guy returns to the same saloon 40 years later and the same Red Indian is sitting in the same corner and finishes the sentence the guy started 40 years earlier. Suspended animation.

From the covered skies, one thin lance of piercing light breaks out, illuminating Harry's drool, as endless and hierarchical as the medieval Great Chain of Being. Beneath us, I see the god Set. He is floating on a li-lo in the Thames, wearing nothing except his red barretina and a Christ-like loin cloth. Shit! It's been ages since I've seen him. It's the fucking gear! He catches the other end of Harry's hoick, and he starts shimmying up it, dragging himself metre by metre, as though performing the Indian Rope Trick. His li-lo drifts away towards Blackfriars.

Why had it never occurred to me that Harry might have a wife; that Harry's life might have moved on. Not only does Harry have a wife, but he has a wife who doesn't approve of us. Self-Harming Harry had taken to wed, but nothing had really changed. Like all the best superheroes, he was just concealing his true identity from her. With *Balafre* and Listerine.

Set is halfway up Harry's rope. Fuck knows what's going to happen when he reaches the bridge. I feel the need to get out of here.

Finally, in order to continue the conversation, Harry releases the spittle skipping rope, and I watch as Set uncomprehendingly spirals down its length and disappears into the murky depths from which he rose.

"What's her name?" I asked.

"Hilda."

I didn't think women were called Hilda anymore.

"The only woman named Hilda I've ever met was the nurse at Peterhouse."

"That's her."

"You're married to—"

"Hilda."

I couldn't believe it. In the telescopy of time, I am remembering his wife holding my nuts in her hand and telling me to cough. And Harry was married to her.

"And we have a little girl."

I snapped out of it as Harry resumed the thread.

"And what's she called?"

"We called her Lyca. After Calypso."

"How cool is that!" I mused.

"Except that we don't use words like cool."

"How'd you mean?"

"Well, she says Cool all of the time. Not Hilda, I mean—Lyca. It's almost the only word in her vocabulary. I think it was the first thing she said after she said *Mummy* or *Daddy*. She said Cool. Because she overuses it, I say to her: *You don't even know the meaning of the word 'Cool'*. She uses it as a filler the same way people us *Sort of or You Know or To Be Honest.*

"And I say to her *That's my word. That word belongs to my generation. Why don't your generation make up some words of your own?* And she looks at me like I'm a crazy man. I didn't realise how ridiculous I'd become, trying to arrogate vocabulary to myself, to my generation. I mean, we just used it. It wasn't as though we'd personally made it up or anything. God knows who made it up. But there I was getting proprietorial about a word. And then I met up with you again, and it was like what they call a salutary experience, a trip down Memory Lane."

"What does Hamlet say? *Words, words, words.*"

"Yeh, what the fuck."

"I can see how that would annoy someone. Having your kids appropriating your words, and using your own language to look down on you. And here you are, a secret smoker. Hilda must be, what, ten years older than you?"

"Fifteen. Cradle-snatcher, Sully, definitely wouldn't approve."

"You've married a woman fifteen years older than you, and she thinks you've moved on, but you've never really grown up."

"What did Lyca used to say? We're *Peter Pan*'s *Lost Boys*. Here we are in the future, still mouthing the platitudes of the past."

"Yeh, weird how time makes ventriloquists of us all."

"Gottle o'geer?"

"Yeh, let's get one in!"

The Passover

Ingram tossed his copy of today's Daily Mail onto the coffee table and gave me, his Spin Doctor, a straight look like I was responsible for the terrorist atrocities.

"Another nail bomb on the underground!" He cried. "Twenty-nine dead; more injured. What are we going to do about it?"

"There's one every week," I observed. "Statistically, the chances of you getting roasted alive on the underground are higher than your chances of winning the lottery. Catching a train is no different to going to the casino. It's just another game of chance."

"What I object to is that it's become so frequent everyone just takes it for granted. Being blown up has become a normal incident of the daily commute."

"Yes, we've become inured. We've been indoctrinated. We've been as radicalised into accepting it as the cunts who do it."

"But, Nick, what are we going to do about it? Every time I'm on *Any Questions* that's the first question I get asked, and I fob them off with all the usual shit about my COBRA committee meeting to discuss it next week, being vigilant, putting more bobbies on the beat, CCTV cameras on every lamppost.

"Nick, you're a famous photographer. When you got into that game as a teenager, did it ever dawn on you that by the time you were middle aged, everyone would be recording everything all of the time? There's a camera on every dashboard, on every policeman, every lamp post; every cyclist's helmet. You can't even take a shit anymore without someone filming it!"

"Yes, I daresay there's one on Reality Checkpoint now. We need to beat them at their own game."

"How do you mean?"

"We've got to radicalise the good guys. Yes, I am evolving a policy as we think about it. And in radicalising the good guys, we get all this obese human detritus off the streets; we provide purpose and meaning to meaningless lives; we give aimless youth something to aim for. We are going to raise a gigantic peace time army."

"To what end?"

I have to consider my words carefully, and the impact they will have on their audience. My immediate audience is my boss, Ingram Frazier. My ultimate audience is the British electorate.

"Give me a moment to marshal my thoughts," I request.

"Well, while you're doing that, talking of photographs, you might care to take a look at this." He removes a 10" x 8" brown paper envelope from his man bag and pushes it towards me. The envelope's not glued down. I pull out the contents. It's a large glossy photograph date stamped at noon yesterday, featuring two guys standing in the middle of the Blade of Light footbridge sharing a large bong. You could see quite clearly who the two guys were.

"How did they take this?" I ask.

"Ultra-high definition police drone," says Frazier. "It's okay. I used my influence with the Home Secretary to get it pulled. That's one for the books, eh? Me acting as your Spin Doctor."

"Thanks, Ingram."

"Have you marshalled your thoughts?"

"You know, Ingram, when you spoke about a war on terrorism…" I can't actually remember if he spoke, or if I put the words in his mouth.

"Yes, Nick. On the joint podium with President Rash."

Mealy-mouthed lickspittle euphemisms. How do I tell him this truth that combines his political convictions with his suppressed sexuality?

"Prime Minister…" I realise I am just playing for time. I am never so formal even when I am addressing the Prince of Darkness. "When we spoke of a War on Terror, that was a kind of euphemism. It was part of conditioning the public for what we really meant."

"What did I really mean, Nick?"

"Ingram, how can I put this?" Then it comes to me. "It's the hatred that dare not speak its name."

"What do you mean?"

"When we spoke of a War on Terror, we were being politically correct. What we really meant was a War on Islam."

Ingram is looking blankly at me. I realise that my words will not sit easily on him. Against his better convictions, he married my Islamic ex-girlfriend and was voted into power by the black vote, although I think I can sustain him in power with the pink vote if we have to put him to his election.

"War on Islam, Ingram. It's the only thing."

"What, back to the crusades?"

"Exactly. Everyone's been pussyfooting around the subject for years, because they would rather carry on being blown up than pronounce those three words, War on Islam. You are going to announce it and start recruiting. Every hoodie and skinhead will suddenly become useful. They will be our own Knights Templars. I'm not talking about the Knights Templars after they became a corrupt institution. I'm talking about the purpose for which they were first founded, to provide protection to pilgrims wanting to visit the Holy Land without being raped, murdered and robbed by Arabs *en route*.

"They were highly trained, at the peak of physical fitness; they were deeply religious, abstained worldly possessions, wealth and alcohol; totally virtuous, but also completely murderous. They were like a cross between the Automobile Association and having your own private ninja. We give these aimless lost souls something to believe in. We sell them the prospect of turning them into comic book heroes, but they must buy into the whole life style, which includes abstinence, charitable acts, western religious convictions, and being indoctrinated to murder non-believers."

"So who are these guys going to murder?"

"Well, everybody else, of course. If you're not one of the chosen, you're on the outside. We'll give all the good guys a shibboleth, like that thing Sydney used to have on his doorpost."

"A mezuzah?"

"Yes, a mezuzah, except his was upside down, of course. When War on Islam is declared, there will be a night of the Passover. If you haven't got the signpost on your door, you're finished. The problem with the present age is that the Jihadists have the monopoly on ideals and beliefs. The west are all just sitting on their arses, watching Internet porn and football. They don't have any convictions, except criminal ones; no beliefs.

"So they are just cannon fodder for the Jihadists; sitting ducks. We are going to abolish apathy. Why are all these people reclining at home on their fat arses, clogging up their arteries with junk food and clogging up all the roads by dialling for everything to be delivered to their houses whilst they squat in front of 120 inch TV's until their diabetic limbs drop off one by one onto the shag pile carpet? Because they know if they go out to watch a football match or a pop concert, or visit a Christmas market, they're going to be blown to smithereens. We're going to take back the streets."

"So you are putting obesity down to terrorism?"

"It's a one-stop shop, Ingram. That's the beauty of it. Blame the same old bogeyman for everything. A one-size-fits-all eidolon."

"What you're describing sounds like ethnic cleansing."

"No, that's got a bad name for itself. Stick with War on Islam. Cometh the moment; cometh the man. The time is right. We've had enough of getting blown up or stabbed every time we walk out the front door. We get kicked around from pillar to post: first of all we take a pasting from some madman in an exploding waistcoat, then we have to take it up the arse from some sanctimonious cunt telling us that it's a small price to pay for our freedom.

"Then the politicians try to put us into lockdown for our own safety. But we're not free. We've all become prisoners in our own homes, spied on by police with ultra-high definition drones, because it's too dangerous for policemen to actually walk the streets; and, yes, obesity, diabetes and all the fucking rest are caused by terrorism. You declare War on Islam and you can bank £35 billion a year into the NHS. Go for it, Ingram!"

"Nick, I really think this may be a step too far."

"Then let's do it one step at a time. First of all, we roll out the Order of the New Knights Templar. It's government backed. It's compulsory national service, but we'll spin it so it's like an apprenticeship. We pick up all these Lost Boys and we train them in a blend of martial arts and religious fanaticism. They get a recognised qualification for turning themselves into characters from PlayStation; and then we set them loose in the community to supplement the dwindling numbers of our police force. They aren't vigilantes, but they are vigilant.

"What did it say on the Birdwood Door? *Be Alert. England needs more Lerts.* We are going to create an army of state informers, paid for by the state, doing something useful, and people who will continue to vote you back into power, because otherwise they'd be in the gutter where we found them. Having an army of Consiglieri never did the Venetian Doges any harm! I say, less Influencers and more Informers. They will speak out.

"You know what's wrong with the English? They're too fucking polite. They would rather be cremated on the tube than ask the bloke with the big beard sitting next to them why he feels the need to carry a tub bomb in a Lidl bag on the underground. But for the New Knights Templars, this will be part of their job. So instead of trying to keep this rabble off the streets, we will put them back on the streets and use them as our eyes and ears, and if they get a whiff of jihad, they will stamp it out, and when they come to be adjudged for their murderous tendencies in the courts, they will be rewarded."

"Nick, we may have the germ of an idea here, but we have to do a lot more work on it."

"Ingram, it's all incremental. I tell you what. Why don't we repatriate the missing King's College Choir Boys into the New Knights Templars?"

"How so, Nick?"

"What the fuck else are we going to do with them? We've somehow got to get 300 radicalised, castrated choirboys back into the community. This would give them something to belong to, a sense of civic community. Let's roll out the Order of the New Knights Templars first, and see how that goes down with everybody before we roll out the crusades."

"Nick, don't you think that could, sort of, you know, push me over the edge? There's quite a groundswell of opinion that I should resign and let Sully have a go."

"And do you want to do that?"

"Not in a million years, Nick. He's got no charisma. He couldn't run a whelk stall, let alone a country. The old style left love him. He's an anti-Semitic closet Trot."

"But Burt's lost all that fat, honing himself for high office. I thought you had an agreement that you were supposed to resign at a certain point, and he was supposed to have his turn."

"Nick, that was just a gentleman's agreement."

"Ingram, I'll see what I can do."

"You know, Nick. Things have to be different."

"Ingram, dear Ingram, You are coming up for an historic fourth term. We must be doing something right. If it ain't broke, don't fix it."

"But people want change, just for the sake of it. You know, plus ca change…"

"Yes, yes, of course. Ingram. If you want things to stay the same, things are going to have to be different."

I'll be revenged on the whole pack of you.

The Happiest Days of My Life

People were always telling me that one's days at Cambridge were the happiest days. But nothing prepared me for the sempiternal joy of having Calypso in my life, and the fact that it seemed as though I had waited all my life for her to arrive in it, just made it all the better. I can't get enough of her. Like Marc Antony's passion for Cleopatra, the appetite increased with what it fed upon.

On that first night, the night of the soft opening, I scouted all around the tent and established that there was only one way in and out of the big top, so I just waited there, like a stage door Johnny, waited; fifty minutes after the show had closed, fifty minutes that seemed like fifty years; until she appeared. Her eyes were no longer glued shut. That same doll-like fragility.

She was dragging a wheelie-bag behind her; that genuine red hair and the alabaster skin; the slight frame. She was unchanged and as gorgeous as ever. The only thing that was different about her was that she had her eyes open. They were the most beautiful eyes: greenish-yellow, as though her face glowed with its own patina.

She saw me and made a slight detour in my direction.

"Nick Jobs! I can't believe my eyes! You came to see the circus?"

"Calypso Sitzclarence! I can't believe my ears, because how can you believe your eyes when they were never open when we used to know each other? How can you recognise me?"

"Because you're all over the papers, you bell end! Did you see the performance?"

"Yes; it was sheer magic; you were fantastic. When that giant brings the bottle onstage and you think he's going to drink it all, or juggle with it, or throw it at a clown. But he sets it down. Then when it wobbles and eventually sets itself upright, it reminded me of those Mexican jumping beans we used to have as kids. You know, the ones you roll in the palm of your hand and the weight of the bean gives them a strange lurching motion. And then when your body parts start emerging from the chrysalis, I thought of Dali's painting of the Geopoliticus Child watching the Birth of the New Man emerging from the Egg…"

" Don't remind me of Fucking Tommy!" She was serious, bitter.

"Oh, my God, I'm so sorry!"

"Doing what that control freak, Sydney Syzygy, wanted me to do every day until my quite promising life ended in my twenties and I had to run away for shame and join the circus."

"And do you know what he's doing now?"

"No fucking idea!"

"Well," I said, "the apple doesn't fall far from the tree." And then I proceeded to tell her what I'd learned from Harry about Appy Bendings, and the latest reincarnation of the control freak.

After which she said: "…And it's supposed to be some sort of a tribute to me? It's the sickest thing I've ever heard of."

"Me too. I couldn't believe it at first. But then it all snapped into focus."

The word "focus" seemed to remind her of who I was, and she said that she'd followed my work, and how delighted she was that I'd decided to become the Printer and not GentleMan; how moved she'd been by the War exhibition and how the Loss Installation at the Tate Modern had brought her to tears. In fact her words were that once she got the use of her eyes back, the first things she took herself to see were my exhibitions.

"Some of your images from the Loss Exhibition haunt me," she confided. "That gigantic blow-up the size of Guernica with the two children in that endless grey landscape of towering burnt-out batteries. What was it called?"

"The Start Rite Kids."

"That's it. And the one with the endless beach and the two parallel lines?"

"Ah, that one doesn't have a word for a title. But it's where the Start Rite kids are travelling to. It's the frontispiece for a book."

"And what's the book called?"

"Well, that's the thing, the book doesn't have a title either. It's title is just a symbol." And with my fingernail, I drew the ∞ on the back of her hand. When I touched her, it felt like an electric shock that had been bottled up inside me for ten years.

Then I remembered that is how she had signed off on Seth.

"That should be the title of your next exhibition," she declared. "Logical title for someone who lives by the lens."

"Well," I mused, "we'd better start a mutual admiration society, because I'm coming back here tomorrow, and every night until my money runs out!"

"Oh!" and she added, "Still wearing *Balafre*!"

I hadn't even thought about it, but I guess I was. It had just become a part of my daily routine. Shit, shower, shave, *Balafre*. I had completely forgotten all the legacy issues. When I came down from Cambridge I'd given it up; but then when I'd had my dribbling reunion with Self-Harming Harry on the Blade of Light, out of nostalgia for a golden age that probably never existed, I'd resumed it. *Balafre* came with baggage. She had hers symbolised by the wheelie-bag in her hand. I had mine.

"And where are you living?" I asked.

"Well, I was disinherited after the Tommy business, told never to darken my family's doorstep again. When I'm at the *Cirque de Soleil* base in Montreal, I've got a very nice Airstream; feel like I'm a film star on location; but we're on tour now, so I'm looking for somewhere to crash tonight. They've given me a list of places."

"You can crash at mine," I ventured.

I couldn't believe it when she said, "OK."

Ananda.

"Where do you live?" she asked.

"By the lens," I said. "Like you said. Come on, I'll show you." I thought it was one of the wittiest things I'd said. If I was Ingram, I'd be licking my pencil lead and making a note of it.

Alas, those who live by the lens die by the lens.

That's the wonderful thing about Sydney Syzygy. Two people who haven't seen one another in ten years, can meet up, and they'll immediately start talking about him. And from that common denominator, extends a thread of all the other things you discover you have in common that you would never have discussed without the catalyst of Syzygy. And I think back to the time when he first made his entrance in my life on the tabletop at dinner time in Peterhouse, and I thought, yes, that's what he is, a catalyst. He brings about reactions in others.

And I didn't try it on with Calypso. I was too much in awe of her and fearful of doing anything that might upset the *status quo* and make her leave. I wanted to hold on to this new life forever. Now that I had gone digital, I took about a million photographs of her—with her clothes on, I should add, because, despite what she said about the Printer, I am sublimating the god Set in me and living the life of GentleMan.

And we discussed politics, and the things I photographed; the choir boys that had disappeared, and the man who had brought them back and rehabilitated them into society. We talked about art and music, books and the performing arts; we talked about the God Old Days, and when they had ceased to be so good; about China, about Cadaqués and Cambridge, and we talked about Calypso's work, the circus; how she could make her body do those impossible things. And we criticised Sydney. What more could I want?

We didn't patronise one another. She was genuinely interested in my work, and I in hers. I couldn't have been more fascinated if she'd been a *prima ballerina* or an Olympic gymnast. She seemed to combine all those roles. She worked on new performances and different routines and she tried them out on me; but I was a hopeless critic, because I unquestioningly adored every step she took. She trained for 4 hours a day.

I had a spare room with fabulous views across the Thames to the Houses of Parliament, the Coliseum and the London Eye, which I had intended should one day become my gym. However, I had too much in common with the wit who said that whenever he felt the urge to exercise, he would lie down until the feeling passed away. I'd gotten as far as buying an exercise bike, which, quite frankly, plonked down there in the middle of the large room with the huge windows over the river, looked ridiculous, and I would have felt ridiculous to mount it.

It was as intimidating as Sydney's vaulting horse had been to everyone except long lost Seth. So I insisted that the room became Lyca's workout room. For four hours every day to the accompaniment of a soundtrack that hadn't changed much since the sixties, she twisted herself into impossible balletic shapes in there whilst I got the next meal ready.

She went out to work. A matinee and an evening performance six days a week. I loved her for the fact that she was willing to work so hard and not be a kept woman, although she deserved to be. If any part of her had ever wanted that, she had used it all up with Sydney. I had *aperitifs* waiting for her when she walked through the door, and dinner cooking in the oven. She wanted to contribute to the housekeeping and pay for her board, but I wouldn't hear of it. I would have paid her any amount of money just for the pleasure of another moment of her company. If she had any complimentary tickets going, I would always take them. If she didn't have, I would buy one. I was living in dread of what would happen when the circus left town.

Against time, I tried to work harder and harder to consolidate her into my life so that when the caravan moved on she would remain. I live in terror of being without her, but I know if I told her, she would leave. I have a recurring nightmare that seems to betray my ineptitude. In the nightmare she tells me it's time for her to move on, and I beg her not to go. *After all*, I say in my dream, *It's not as though performing in a circus is a real job!* And then she spins on her heel and walks out of my life, dragging her wheelie bag behind her. I keep replaying the scene. It fills me with utter dread and foreboding. Night after night, I wake up in a cold sweat.

I am building the huge photographic montage known as *The Ballet*. It's so large I had to break it down into eight sections that screw together, or it wouldn't go through the door. Tens of thousands of images of Calypso as a ballerina pasted to both sides of a series of parallel vertical wooden strips in the gigantic frame, so that as one walks around it (and it's so large it takes some time to walk around) she moves through the linear zoetrope of her positions, a storyboard ballerina come to life.

She starts out in a foetal ball on the floor; she rises to full height, she lifts her right hand above her head, she spins, she stretches, and then she collapses back onto the floor at the end of the sequence. Every undulation, every microscopic nuance of her body, is exquisite. I have fixed her in the frame. From a thousand motionless images, I have brought her to life. The imprisoned ballerina is free at last.

Then I realise that I am trying to keep her captive. I'm just as bad as Sydney. Maybe she has that effect on people. Yes, of course, why did it take me so fucking long to come to the conclusion that it's her fault?

After her exhausting work, she liked an Aperol Spritz as soon as she walked in through the door. I glowed in smug delight at the act of gentle proprietorship as she let herself in and slung down the set of keys I'd given her onto the radiator cover. She wasn't some sort of a tenant: she belonged here. The Aperol went so well with her colouring. But Aperol Spritz just with Aperol, ice and Prosecco. No tonic.

She would allow herself two or three gulps as soon as she came to the place I am now delighted she refers to as home, and then take the glass to the wet room to remove her makeup, take a shower and carry on drinking it. Then she would come back wrapped in a towel and finish the drink off around the table with me. I adored every second of it. We shared all the intimacy of a married couple even if we didn't have the sex. And that was more than I could have asked for. So I didn't upset the apple cart by reaching out for the sex as well. The ticking in my head had disappeared.

Ingram was proving a disappointing host for my activities, and I could see that I was going to have to move on if I was going to set the world to rights. But for the time being, I was complete. What is the Latin word for complete? Perfect. Yes, everything was perfect. Olumidé had been a useful rehearsal for the Platonic life. What is the phrase for it? A dry run.

Lyca confided to me about the stabbing pains she suffers horizontally across her shoulders and up and down the top of her spine. Making a bad Ingram-style pun, I said she'd had *too many years in the bottle,* as opposed to *on the bottle*. I was referring to all the time she had to spend twisted up inside that Jeroboam in the arena before she emerged from it like a butterfly from a chrysalis.

"Let me help you, please," I said. "As you helped me when my head was spinning all the time. Teach me how to do that *champissage* thing, so that I can make you feel the way you made me feel."

"Don't be so silly. That's for me to do and you to enjoy."

"What did you say to me?" I asked, reaching back ten years into my recall, and fishing out the right words from the great soup of muddled memories in a way that would have made the master mnemonist, Seth Godil, proud of me. "From the moment your fontanelle closes, you have to keep your head open to new experiences."

She looked at me. She registered her own words from the past. She evaluated the fact that I had remembered both the experience and also her voiceover from so many years ago. So she knew I was serious.

"OK," was all she said. And then over the course of the next fortnight, she taught me, dividing our heads into their meridians and learning one sector at a time. She couldn't teach me on her own head, so she had to do mine, and then I had to copy it onto her head.

As they say, the best method of learning is still by rote, and I wouldn't have had it any other way. There was a Shaman-like knowledge and intensity to the discipline of spending an evening focussing on a one inch square patch on the nape of her neck, trying to apply the correct motion and pressure that would draw out all the toxins of her day into my probing fingers. Sydney's words held true: this was still the greatest enjoyment you could have with your clothes on.

Before I get to work on the next section of her head, she has to show me how to do that section on my own. As she drained all the bad thoughts from my cranium in this way each night, I asked her, "What are you doing to me?"

She said: "I am the Spin Doctor's Spin Doctor."

Then I dug my fingers into her scalp.

When Adam dug and Eve span.

I continue to be the perfect GentleMan.

One evening, after I'd mastered the *champissage*, I tried her out on a Hugo, being an Aperol-related elderflower alternative cut with Catalan Cava from Perelada, which I found drier than prosecco, and which I hoped might even remind her of Spain and holding my hand in front of *the Hallucinogenic Toreador*. Just to keep her on her toes, so we don't fall into a rut, I add a splash of Gabriel Boudier lychee liquor to give it that certain *je ne sais quoi*.

Her legs are folded up underneath herself in that way she has, and from the approval on her face, I feel the time is right to ask her some questions that have been troubling me for some considerable time. She is sitting in one of my Barcelona chairs. Her glass is hanging from her hand carelessly as though it were a bracelet. You would think the contents are about to spill over the edge at any given moment. But she has such grace, it never happens.

Even the way that she holds her glass is an master class in poise and balance. Maybe in the good old days when young ladies went to Lucy Clayton and learned how to walk around with books on their heads and how to get in and out of E-Type Jaguars without showing their knickers, maybe they were also taught how to hold their glasses in this sexy, careless, come-hither kind of way.

So she is sitting there, balancing the precarious Hugo in her right hand; and I am behind her, now an experienced head doctor, unlocking each neuron of her brain, detoxifying each hair cell faultlessly with the techniques I have rote-learned from her. I consider the time is ripe to pop the question.

"Do you have a problem talking about Seth?" I ask.

"Seth? Why should I?"

I sense from the tone in her voice that she does, but I push the envelope a little further anyway.

"Could you tell me what the markings you did on his body mean, please? This is a question that has been keeping me awake at night, yes keeping me awake at night is not an exaggeration, for the last 900 years."

"900 years is not an exaggeration either?"

"900 years. Did I just say 900 years? Well, if I did, that is not an exaggeration. It is litotes. Did you know there is a double time scheme in Othello?"

"Everyone knows that."

"What do they mean?"

"The double time schemes?"

"No, the body markings."

"Everyone so busy searching for meaning." I can see her casting her mind back. "We were on his gap year together. I'm older than him. I just decided to drop out to be with him. We had been hitching around India, the hippy thing. I was quite proficient in yoga, but I wanted to become a true master and study under a proper Guru. 'Guru' is debased as it's used for everything now, but literally the Guru is the supreme master of yoga.

"I did some recreational drugs. Seth wanted to try everything. He's comparatively clean last I heard; but before he got into the bodybuilding super-athlete thing, he experimented a lot. And I guess that's one of the things I liked about him. He was very creative; but with creativity comes curiosity.

"It was in India that it dawned on me that we weren't cut out for one another. He was off his face most of the time, and when he's off his face, he's not very good company. I was searching for knowledge. I found this shaman who was teaching me stuff that took me right out of myself, but the shaman had this head dress of claret and blue feathers. I was experiencing something quite mystical, but you know what Seth said?"

I shook my head.

"West Ham supporter. Like, how to lower the tone in three words."
Now she was shaking her head, remembering it.

"We were in Rajasthan. We were staying in some weird fucking hostel. I could have afforded better in those days; we could have stayed in a palace; but he had his pride, so it was easier for me to go down to his level than for him to try to come up to mine which would have entailed him having to accept money from me.

"I'd tried it a couple of times, but he would get angry and say that he wasn't a fucking ponce, so the only alternative was for me to lower my expectations and we'd both do something he could afford. There were students of every creed and denomination in the godforsaken hostel: some were doing the hippy thing and getting spaced out; others had come to imbibe mysticism; some had come along to buy machine guns.

"In the morning, on wooden sticks, they had these newspapers from every country in the world for all the foreign students to read over their coffees. The papers were scrolled around mahogany poles, and you would pluck a pole down from the tree of poles and read it with your breakfast.

"To this day, we don't know what caused it. Whether it was something he had eaten; whether he had been bitten by something, whether it was some drugs he had taken or needle he had shared, or some kind of allergic reaction. But he went into anaphylactic shock. His whole head swelled up grotesquely like a watermelon. You could see all of the constituent parts of the pigmentation in his skin, like he was pixilated, blotchy. His eyes were white and bulging. Of course, there was no Epi-pen anywhere in sight, so he had to do it cold turkey.

"I remember where we were. Near Ajabgarh in Rajasthan. There was a village of the dead there, where a wizard was supposed to have made the whole town die overnight. And the buildings and the town were perfectly preserved but now inhabited only by monkeys, and I thought maybe one of the monkeys had rabies and had bitten him, but he wouldn't let me fetch a doctor.

"His throat was constricted. He could hardly breathe. But every time I made to go to find a help, he grabbed my wrist to stop me with such insistence, it was painful. I thought that he thought there was something inside him that, if the medics found it, they would send him straight to jail.

"But it was cold turkey literally. I don't remember the weather as being particularly cold, but he was feverish. He was slipping in and out of deliria. One minute he was freezing cold. The next he was covered in perspiration. I remember that, whatever I did, I couldn't keep him warm enough. I was feeling inadequate in the most basic human skills. One second he was so hot he stripped off all his clothes. The next minute he was writhing around naked on the filthy hostel floor covered in clammy sweat and freezing cold.

"I went to the lobby and grabbed all of the mahogany poles. I wrapped him up like a mummy in every newspaper: the *Haaratz* and *Jerusalem Post* of Israel, the *Rajasthan Patrika, the Kantipaur Gazette* of Nepal, the *Pars Times* of Iran, the *Tehran Times,* the *Al Mustaquilla* and *Al-Mashriq* of Iraq. God! I can't remember the names of all the fucking newspapers! Then, I put his track suit tops and bottoms on, then his anorak, and I kept him hydrated in front of a charcoal fire for, I guess a whole week, before he started coming around, and getting back to normal.

"When he was recovering, and we unwrapped him for his first bath, all the papers were stuck to him. It took ages to peel them off without hurting him, because they had become part of his skin. The newspapers didn't have fixative in those days. The printer's ink had leeched off all over the place. It had penetrated into his skin. We couldn't wash it out. He didn't want it washed out. It was like his battle trophy with the grim reaper.

"As he was coming around, and as we couldn't erase the print that was all over him, he told me that he owed his life to whatever was written on those papers, like they were an instruction manual for his survival. No thanks to me for caring for him and cleaning him, and living in that shit hole to humour his working-class hero mentality. He owed it all to the newspapers. And he asked me to cut it into him as a tattoo, so that he'd never forget. He was worried that the print would eventually wear away, that one day he'd wake up and it wouldn't be there anymore.

"I used what was already there as a stencil, and I just traced it into him with a mapping pen. A Joseph Gillott mapping pen to be precise. It took me days. He was shivering all the time. I couldn't stop him shivering. Even when I put the nib in the fire.

"I'm sure it means something, in some Tower of Babel way, all the different languages, alphabets, current affairs, Stock Exchange Prices, sports news, and I signed it with the ∞; or maybe it was just page 8 of the paper. I can't remember.

"He'd asked me to do it. But I didn't realise that he was still flickering in and out of consciousness, so that someone could ask you to do something, so earnestly and with such insistence, seeming to be in full possession of all of his faculties, but moments later have no recollection of having done so; ask you to do something immutable, determinative, so that he'd always remember, and then completely forget the request. Like a guy who has visions and thinks he is doing all sorts of things and going all sorts of places and then when he comes around insists he's been behind his desk all the time, writing up his reports.

"He cajoled me; he begged me to cut him. I hated every minute of it; but it's was the only form of communication he was capable of, so I did it for him, and I disinfected him each time with a swab made from pieces torn off the bottom of my cheesecloth shirt and dipped in that aftershave he wears."

"*Balafre?*"

"Yes, very appropriate. *Balafre* means: slash, scar, slice. I sliced him up. Afterwards, I would puke up at night, at the slicing and the mutilation, the stains wiped down with a copy of *The Jerusalem Post*, then I would resume my work in the morning, longing for the time when there would be none of him left to write on and I could put an end to it.

"I thought he was getting well with all this blood-letting; but then one day he did get well, and it seemed all of this previous time he had been delirious, just functioning on auto pilot, talking shit when he had asked me to cut him. He went crazy the first time he looked in the mirror after he came out of his fever and tried to shave himself. He asked me why I had done this to him. He asked me what it all meant. Well, I couldn't tell him that he had completely fucked up his beautiful body so that he could record the football scores or tin future prices.

"There was a blazing argument. I ran away. I left in a hurry. I didn't take any money, so the British Embassy in New Delhi lent me £90.00 to fly home. Very expensive. Lot of money in those days. I can't remember what class I flew in, and when I got back, they grabbed my passport.

"It had a stamp in it, saying *This passport must be impounded at the*

UK Border, and I couldn't get it back again until my parents had repaid the government the £90.00 with interest. So I guess my mum and dad already thought I was a bad ass girl for running off to Rajasthan with a pauper; then it got worse when they had to pay to repatriate me, and then the Tommy thing was the last straw. I was clearly a reprobate.

"Seth followed me around the world searching for an answer to what it all meant, the stuff I had written on him. If I'd told him the truth it would have killed him, so the fact that I had stupidly glued my eyelids together gave me a rest from having to explain to him that his body beautiful that he used to work so hard to create each day down at the gym, was just football scores and exchange rates shit in foreign languages."

There was a long quiet time when neither of us said anything. Then I said, "But when we put him in the zoetrope and it said The Book of Thoth, what did that mean?"

"It's just wishful thinking and thought transference. What does it mean when people play *Day in the Life* backwards and tell you they've heard some amazing truth, or that John Lennon knows he is going to die because Paul McCartney has bare feet when crossing Abbey Road, symbolising something or other? It's all bollocks."

"So all the stuff written on him…"

"It's just shit."

Like everything else I come into contact with, it's meaningless.

Words, words, words. I should write a fucking book.

A Gentleman's Agreement

"But of course, you're going to be sitting here in Number 11 next term, and I'm going to be out there doing my own thing. Captain of Industry. The after-dinner lecture circuit. We have a gentleman's agreement, don't we?"

It's Ingram reassuring Burt Sully.

"And I'll tell you what; you know, just to make life easier than ever for you, so you don't even have to think up your own policies, I'll transfer the Printer onto your payroll. My spin doctor, Nick Jobs at your beck and call."

"Why would I want that toxic cunt on my team? The middle way!" He sneers. "The sliding scale that slides the wrong way!"

"I know he can be a bit vitriolic when he's under attack, but look at all the crises he's spun the party out of. That has to be worth a knighthood in my resignation honours list."

"You call him the Printer. You know what I call him?"

"I'm sure you're going to tell me."

"Spinocchio."

"Spinocchio?"

"Because he's wooden; he's your puppet and he tells lies."

Ingram has taken his skinny little pencil out of the spine of his Letts diary and is licking the lead. "Burt, I tell you what. I'm going to write that one down."

Hugo

"Nick, meet Hugo."

"Nice to meet you, Hugo." I say, wondering why Ingram is introducing me to this individual. He can't possibly have learned that he shares a name with my girlfriend's favourite cocktail.

"Nice to meet you, sir," says Hugo.

"Hugo is your very own new grace-and-favour bobby. Just like I promised you. He'll be on duty outside your house all night long, keeping a respectable distance so he's not too in your face; but he'll be there. In the shadows, at your beck and call. He's armed to the fucking teeth."

"What was wrong with the previous chap?" I ask.

"Nick, he was a fucking Luddite. Plenty of brawn, but fewer brains. Hugo here is smart."

"I can install a secure App on your smartphone, sir, so that you can summon me that way." Hugo offers.

"And where do you come from, Hugo?" I ask.

"'I'm one of the Lost Boys, sir. I owe my life to you, so it will be an honour to serve,"

"Ingram, why the fuck do you think I need protection from a fucking choir boy?"

"No, no," interjects Ingram. "He's been through the Knights Templar programme. He's licensed to kill. He's radicalised. He made the transformation from choir boy to killing machine as though he was destined for it, as though that's why he was put on—"

"God's earth," finishes the choir boy. "As though I was put on God's earth to kill."

"How do I know he's not going to kill me, Ingram?"

Before Ingram can respond, Hugo answers: "Because we're both singing from the same hymn sheet, sir."

Barcelona Chairs

Calypso and I are sat next to one another on our side-by-side biscuit leather and chrome Barcelona chairs watching the 10-o-clock news on the 100" television, as though we have been married for at least 25 years. We wouldn't normally, but we know that Sky News are screening an interview with me recorded earlier that day, where the expletives that had been bleeped out in the previous version broadcast by the BBC before the watershed, have not been expurgated.

So here we are, curled up in our chairs, Hugos in our hands, taking it all in in its full un-Bowdlerised glory. I'm the spin doctor who coined the term *watershed*, which is another word for 9 pm, after which it's Babylon on the airwaves and anything goes. Nowadays, no-one, apart from some weird geography teachers, even remembers what a watershed really is. I have been so successful in marketing terms that everyone thinks that watershed is another word for nine pm.

"Do you think Ingram's going to be re-elected?" Jeremy Paxman is asking me. I don't remember him asking that or even wearing that tie, so I assume they have put the noddies in later.

On a further even bigger television screen behind Paxman and me, another scene is playing out so that we are like one of those Russian dolls within dolls. On the bigger screen, they are showing CNN footage of the campaign we've been running. Pretty slick, even if I say so myself. I think it would be fair to say that, before I'd come onto the scene, the handling of the media by the politicians had been like a cottage industry; a bunch of well-meaning amateurs. I had made it professional.

The whole country is divided over this War on Islam. No-one talks about anything else. The nation's feckless youths are all taking Ingram's shilling to become Knights Templars, whereby we've bought a whole section of the populace who will vote for Ingram in future because they're on the payroll now; but the policy was not universally welcomed, so Ingram had to move out of Number 10 after the fatwah. He now lives in a bunker surrounded by sycophants, and during a brief interregnum when Burt almost tasted power, the day to day business of running the country was undertaken by Sully from Number 11.

Burt was poised to make his move. Backed by the Momentum movement, he was ready to encash his gentleman's agreement. But would you believe it? Ingram's press secretary, Spinnochio, leaked a story about Burt Sully that turned out for a change to be completely true. Funny how things from the past can come back and hold you to account.

Ever since we ran that story about statutory rape and underage sex with one Bunty Brown, Sully has been shunned by society. He's a busted flush. We've had male prime ministers, female prime ministers, white, black and Jewish prime ministers; straight and gay ones. But a paedophile PM? That was a step too far.

I'll always treasure that last little exchange between Burt Sully, unelected Caretaker PM and me, the unwanted Spin Doctor Ingram had foisted upon him:

"I'm done for, Nick. I'm going to have to go to the country."

"No fucking time to go to the country, Burt. We've got to call an election."

The cameraman has cut back to me to respond to Paxman's question.

"I wouldn't be a very good Director of Communications Strategy if I said No, would I?"

"Oh, slimy Teflon!" exclaims Calypso, poking me in the ribs with her elbow. I love the physical contact.

But I recover my ground: "Look," I say to Paxman, "if he was the CEO of a public company, such as UK PLC, offering himself up for re-election, just examine his track record. We've enjoyed 12 years of burgeoning prosperity, which has been achieved by growth, not by borrowing to fund consumer spending on depreciating white goods and foreign holidays.

"He's kept taxation at the levels he promised in his manifesto, so that the rich didn't all fuck off (This had been bleeped out on the 6 o'clock news but was broadcast in all its rank obscenity after the 9 o'clock watershed.), leaving his Iron Chancellor, Burt Sully, with no economy to manage. He has entertained us with some parochial wars, following the Thatcher example.

"Why shit on your own doorstep when you can bomb the Middle East?"—another detail that had been bleeped out on the earlier broadcast—"I mean to say," I continue, "99% of it's desert already! He's legalised gay marriage. He's made peace with the IRA, so that we can resume having political conventions without having to live under the constant worry that the hotel hosting the conference is about to be blown up and all the delegates smeared in tar and feathers. I would honestly say that if we give him another 4 years, we'll have peace in the Middle East."

"Fuck!" I exclaim.

"What's wrong?" Calypso asks.

"The first thing I say to everybody is *Never say Honestly or To Be Honest*, because it just makes you sound shifty. But listen to me." As the words leave my lips I remember who it was who had taught me this lesson. If I remember correctly, the immediate recipient of the lesson delivered by Calypso had been Ingram, but I'd been an indirect beneficiary.

Calypso: "Do you really believe any of that shit you're talking?"

"Honestly? Me, believe my own bullshit! Do I look like Gerald Ratner to you? I just dish it out to other people. And you know what I give them? I just give them whatever it is they want to hear. Nobody gives a flying fuck about the truth anymore! Let me rephrase that. To be honest, nobody gives a flying fuck about the truth anymore! All they want is self-serving sanctimony served up on a selfie-stick!"

"Wow! Isn't Ingram supposed to hand over power to Burt at some point?"

"Ah! You are referring to the top secret tryst that only 99.9% of the population knows about."

"The gentleman's agreement."

"Well, that's between Burt and Ingram. The problem is that the electorate never wanted Burt, and they certainly don't want him now. If Ingram got himself re-elected and then abnegated in favour of Burt, that would be seen as a betrayal; however I spin it, if Ingram stands down and Burt stands up, the party would lose the election and go back into the wilderness for another 15 years. "

"So Sully's going to be disappointed?"

"He's already bitter and disappointed. And he's growing worse by the day. He can't understand that good kingmakers don't make good kings. If you put a power behind the ceremonial chair, it's usually best to leave it there. But Burt's been decaying beneath the dispatch box for so long, he's become a bad smell behind the throne."

"What do you think Ingram should do next?"

"What should Ingram do? He needs to get divorced and come out as gay. But first of all we've got to do something about the fucking *fatwah*."

We focus back towards the broadcast. Paxman is quizzing me about the gay marriage. Not surprising when half of the people that work in the media are gay. How did it take politicians so long to wake up to that market? And it's a market that is not a drain on society. They haven't pissed their money up against the wall on kids and school fees and divorces.

Two gays living together have a very high net worth. This is a market ripe for political exploitation. Their requirements can be satisfied cheaply in non-monetary terms. You may, as Set pointed out to me, have to outrage moral decency from time to time; but this doesn't necessarily correlate into loss of £sd or votes.

Calypso is more inquisitive than Paxman. Holding her glass out for a refill: "What on earth is all this about gay marriage?"

"It's a vote winner. I'm rolling it out as part of the campaign. I always subliminally drip these messages into the public unconscious ahead of a proper roll-out. It tests the waters and also leaves the public with the perception that actually they've known about these things for a long time and we are simply implementing some earlier consensus that never actually existed. If they think that they thought of it themselves, they are always more receptive to the idea than if we foist it upon them."

"And is this official government policy?"

"Gay marriage? Good heavens, no. I've never even discussed it on the sofa with Ingram. But look, I am working towards an agenda here. We already have civil ceremonies, so logically, the next thing should be full-on marriage—in church."

"But you haven't even discussed this with Ingram?"

"No, nor Sully. I make Ingram's policy; not the other way around. The agenda I am working towards is simple. Ingram's marriage is never going to work, because he bats for the other side and it's just something he endured at the behest of an inferior spin doctor before I came on the scene. One: he is getting a divorce. Two: He is legalising gay marriage. Three: he is going to be the first person to avail himself of this new and venerable institution."

"You mean he's going to marry a fellah?"

"Fulfilling his destiny."

"In church?"

"Well, he could do it in church, but you know it's possible to get married in the Houses of Parliament themselves. They're consecrated. I am toying with the idea of marrying him off either in Parliament or Westminster Abbey."

"Does he know anything at all about this?"

"Like everyone else, he'll read about it in the papers afterwards. Don't you get it? He's just like Winston Churchill's bloke standing in a bucket and trying to pull himself up by the handle. This country's problem is that we have very generous divorce laws. We're the divorce capital of Europe. But we have other laws that prevent a whole section of the community from getting married and thereby reaping the benefits of divorce.

"Directly and indirectly, divorce accounts for 30% of this country's GDP. In the UK, the 5th largest economy in the civilised world, we don't manufacture fuck-all anymore. Everyone's in the service sector—just like you and me. The divorce courts, the lawyers, the financial services sector lending money to people who've just been stripped of all their assets by family court judges impervious to their sufferings: it's our major domestic product.

"We need more people to be able to get married so that two thirds of their marriages can end in divorce, probably more than that, because gays are institutionally unfaithful. It's only through divorce that we can genuinely redistribute wealth under our new socialist ideology at no cost to government. So we need to open the doors to marriage wider."

"So that more people can get divorced?"

"Exactly. It's what makes the financial services sector spin!"

"What's Ingram going to do when you tell him about what you've got in store for him?"

"I should think he'll immediately start wondering what he's going to wear for the big occasion."

"OK, so that's one, two and three. Is there a four?"

"As definitely as there are four horsemen of the Apocalypse."

"I don't know if I'm ready for this, but I guess I have to ask, because, as I believe we said many years ago in Cambridge, the female always undoes herself through curiosity. Tell me, what is four?"

"Four: I'm going to transition Ingram."

"Are you meaning what I think you're meaning?"

"He's going to cross the floor of the House, but not in the usual sense. I'm going to have him change sex, so that in the course of one Parliament, we will have an openly gay PM, a PM who celebrates a same sex marriage in the Palace of Westminster, and a female PM who is in fact the same bloke as the previous incumbent—except he's not a bloke anymore."

"But Nick, in God's name, why?"

"Well, for a start, the *fatwah* against Ingram Frazier. There's no *fatwah* against Ingrid Frazier. So that sorts that problem out. I'll reason with them. I'll say *Look guys, you've got your pound of flesh. We've chopped his dick off for you. Let's call it a day!* Lyca, let's face it, these politicians don't have any power anymore. They haven't had for ages. There isn't enough revenue left for anybody to achieve anything, so we just keep announcing big, subterranean, non-existent infrastructure projects.

"You don't really believe that anybody is actually digging those train tunnels underground, do you? We made it all up, which is why we keep having to make up that they're years behind schedule; because it never started in the first place. Politicians! We put them in there to entertain us. It's all bread and circuses. So let's go the whole hog and transition Ingram Frazier! I believe it's what you used to call a supreme work of self-authorship."

"By the Vanity Press?"

"Sshh! I'm on again."

The Final Brick in the Wall

Whoever the remaining member of Pink Floyd is, the one who isn't dead yet, was performing The Wall at the O2 Arena, and I formed the idea that it would be a great night out for me to take Lyca there by river boat and re-enact some of our depraved youth. I buy tickets for the night she isn't working. The choice was either that or buy tickets for L'Apres Midi d'un Phone. We catch the tide and the Thames Champagne Cutter almost right outside my front door.

The concert is magical. We are on the last Champagne Cutter of the night going back upriver after the performance, and Calypso is spellbound by the lights of Canary Wharf and the jewels of the infinite cranes building London ever skywards.

"None of this was here when I was last in London," she says. "It's like a whole new city has sprung up during the years I've been in Montreal and on tour."

And with your eyes glued shut, I think, but don't say, not wanting to spoil the moment. This is a problem I am encountering more each day. Being the country's greatest spin doctor, my head is constantly filled with brilliant but often hurtful, sometimes terminally vitriolic thoughts. But the language in which my tortured brain expresses those thoughts is just so good, it would be a sin to keep them to myself. So I tend to let them rip.

But if I am in a special relationship, a special relationship such as I am told we have with President Rash, a special relationship such as I am enjoying with Lyca, I must bite my tongue and keep my towering intellect to myself, lest I say something stupid, and lose her. I walk a constant tightrope, because my default setting is to express the vitriolic language that passes for wit, but I know that if I indulge myself in that way, I will probably lose her in exchange for the transitory joy of a cheap jibe.

In this way, she educates me to be a better person without even knowing that she is doing so, and I submit to it in the hope that when I have educated myself, I will be worthy of her love.

She is still so innocent. She is older than me, but she is child-like in her inquisitiveness and her fascination of things. I am beginning to understand that she was the Lost Boys, not us: Tinkerbell. I take her hand in mine as we slip under Tower Bridge and past the Tower of London, past the illuminations of St Paul's, the Shard, the Walkie Talkie, the Cheese Grater, and so to the London Eye and disembarking at Charing Cross Pier. I realise I'm still holding her hand just like I did when we were standing in front of the reproduction of *The Hallucinogenic Toreador*. I don't want to let her go when the circus leaves.

As though we are both thinking the same thought, she says: "They were just a generation of Lost Boys," casting back to our time at Cambridge. "Peter Pan's gang that never grew up. Is it any surprise that kids have no respect for their parents when the parents want to suck up, not grow up? Instead of progressing and accepting the ageing and maturing process, they want to convince their children that they are their mates, not their parents. Rather than inspiring the kids to emulate their parents, the parents are embarked upon a quest to behave like their children themselves.

"How can a parent who refuses to grow up ever be a role model?

"They are in a competitive situation with their kids, trying to prove they are just as cool as them, that they can out-ski them, beat them at tennis, out-fuck them, out-smoke them, everything: it's a generation of parents who only had offspring so they could make them feel fucking useless. It's the exact opposite of the Nazi experiment: the north London experiment is to breed your own fucking useless children so that you can continue to excel over them into old age, and predictably the by-product was a runt crop. It's as though the younger generation was bred as an audience for the older. They're just ambulatory supererogatory selfie sticks!

"And why do you think gays are on the verge of outnumbering straight people? OK, some of it must be in the genes; but the rest of it is the Lost Boys Syndrome, the unwillingness to ever grow up. If you acknowledge offspring, that's the ageing process staring you in the face. If you want to dye your hair and get away with it, don't have any thirty year old children around to call your bluff.

"This is the generation of the Lost Boys. In legal terms, how neat can you get? Normally, legally, a copyright subsists for the life of the author plus 70 years. Then it becomes generic. During the 70 years the author enjoys the royalties. After that, the literary work is in the public domain and anyone can reproduce and publish it for free. But in the case of *Peter Pan*, its author bequeathed the royalties to the Great Ormond Street Hospital for children. Now, wouldn't that be a shame if their income dried up 70 years after the death of J M Barrie? Indeed, so a special Act of Parliament was passed, so that the copyright in that one book alone whose royalties went to Great Ormond Street Hospital for Children, endured forever.

"How symmetrical is that, to think that *Peter Pan* has a copyright that never grows up!"

She had brought some dope home. I knew it was her way of trying to make a contribution, because I wouldn't accept her housekeeping money. I'd seen in the papers that the Cirque du Soleil run had been extended but was ending tomorrow. I was going to have to find my moment, to ask her to stay on. I didn't know how long I'd got, but I was definitely drinking in The Last Chance Saloon.

She fired up the bong. I had to burrow in my cupboards to find an ashtray. I made a mental note to have ashtrays carved into the arms of my armchairs next time around. Last smoke I had had been for old time's sake with Self-Harming Harry on the Blade of Light. Was that the bridge they called the Wobbly Bridge, or did it just feel wobbly after the dope?

"You still smoke dope?" I stated rhetorically.

"Infrequently. Job's too demanding. But, it's just the evening performance tomorrow; no matinee. Plenty of time to get myself together. You?"

"I guess I've been living on my own. Dope was a gregarious pastime for me. Getting smashed solo would probably not be a good idea."

"Quite right! Let's get smashed together then."

After a couple of drags, I felt the old ticking and the tightening in my mouth. I was holding it back. I didn't want to fuck up with Calypso. Nor did I want to reject her dope, because I knew she was just trying to make her contribution. So I poured us some Cava chaser after her Hugo Spritz. We couldn't put the stopper back in the bottle, so the choices were drink it now while it was still bubbly, or pour it down the sink in the morning when it was flat.

What was it Disraeli had said about Palmerston? That he was *only ginger beer and not champagne*. Meaning he still had the old sparkle, but it wasn't for real anymore. An epithet I could have used of Ingram if I'd made it up for myself.

She was reading some free newspaper she had picked up at the Cutter station and suddenly threw it down in disgust.

"That Ingram is such a horse's ass!" she said, passing me the joint. "The arms for hostages shit. A trillion dollars' worth of deadly weapons moving halfway around the world on dodgy EUC's before they end up with the Contranistas. Of course, the Contranistas are a bunch of untrained hairdressers, who were going to retreat at the least provocation from the TerraMoto boys.

"The TerraMoto seized all their abandoned arms, and now a terrorist organisation has a trillion dollars' worth of the highest tech weaponry and President Rash is calling on Ingram to help him defeat them. To defeat them is going to take boots on the ground and dead guys from up north whilst the London bankers sit on their arses, and it's just all so fucking pointless and predictable and unnecessary. And now he's declared War on Islam, as if everyone who reads the Koran is a terrorist."

I am pleased that I have not told her that Ingram is my puppet. I am displeased that the alcohol and the cannabis are taking their toll; and I feel the Ingram in me rising up. This stuff seems 100% more potent than the gear we used to smoke. It will not do anything for our fledgling relationship if she realises that I am operating Ingram Frazier.

To change the subject, I asked her to show me her routine for tomorrow, and she bent herself into some unbelievable positions. Of course, it was incredibly sexy, and she knew it. But it was also vulnerable when she assumed those positions, and all I wanted to do was protect her. But by now I was in no fit state to look after myself.

After a few more puffs on the joint, I tell her it's been a long day and I'd better retire, and I'll clear up in the morning. I want to ask her about staying on, but the moment isn't right. For some reason I go to kiss her on the lips that are inviting me, but I manage to stop myself at the last minute by raising my head a few inches so that I plant a kiss on her lovely forehead instead.

"*Bon soir, bon nuit!*" I say like a true sophisticate, before I withdraw wounded and begin the process of brushing all the smoke out of my teeth. What would Seth have said the inside of my mouth tasted like? It's been a long time. My tongue seems to be on fire and darting around in my mouth like the flailing tail of some serpent. I lie down and close my eyes, but I'm astral projecting.

I am staring down at me prone on the bed. The person I am staring down on is the god Set. And there is nothing I can do about it. I undressed Ingram Frazier and I am wearing the god Set underneath. Nothing else, save the naked god Set and a splash of *Balafre*. Someone else has entered the room.

She just came to my bed and took me. Her belly, smoother than a felucca slipping down the Nile. She climbed on top of me, and the other me is up on the ceiling staring down at my dreams being made true. I couldn't believe this was for real. I was in sensory overload. But part of me thought that she was just bestowing this on me as a thank you, because she was going to walk out on me in the morning. So I said something stupid:

"Is this really you doing this to me, or is Sydney controlling you with his phone?"

Then she cried. Until she stopped crying. Then she hit me in the face. Then she walked out of my life with her wheelie-bag, forever. Forever, that feels like: forever.

This Ingram in me has really fucked up. He's had enough of fucking up other people's lives and now he's started fucking up my own. Controlling things through his medium is a waste of everyone's time. I am going to have to *become* Ingram. I am going to have to *assume* Ingram and move into Downing Street myself. Why send a boy to do man's work?

Calypso has wheeled her wheelie bag as far as the station that is shut for the night, before she realises that walking out on Nick was a stupid, impulsive idea. She had shocked him with too much of herself. He was inexperienced, sexually, probably very much so. He had blurted out some crap in his nervousness. It was as ridiculous as walking out on him for premature ejaculation on his first fuck. She spins on her heels and goes back in the direction she came.

The bag has its own rolling stock. She wheels it through the streets until she gets to the cobbled mews where he lives, and then the wheeling is replaced by clunking as the bag bounces from cobble to cobble. When she arrives, she can't get in, because he's obviously now in the deep, stoned sleep that her joint had induced and he can't hear her pressing the doorbell. She'd left her own set of keys on the radiator cover when she walked out in a huff not intending to return. But it's five o clock in the morning already. He'll have to be getting up and going to work in a couple of hours.

Inside Nick is fitting. He's managed to put a dirty sock in his mouth to stop him biting his own tongue off. He learned that trick off Iago in Laurence Olivier's *Othello* movie.

She knew how to ingratiate herself. He couldn't bear to remain grumpy forever. A playful trick was needed, something to break his scowling face and make him forgive her. How could he continue to hate her if she made his face light up in a smile? She would open up her wheelie bag, dump it on his doorstep, climb naked into it, zip herself up from the inside, and then wait until he came out of his front door in the morning and opened the bag that someone had left there, out of which she would jump, like a naked, erotic jack-in-the box. All would be forgotten and forgiven.

It's still dark now, but it will be getting light in half an hour. She needs the cover of darkness if she is going to take all her clothes off in the street, dump them in the trolley bag and then climb inside after them. When he unzips her, he won't be able to leave her naked in the street outside his house. He'll have to take her in, for decency's sake. Then they will make wonderful love. All will be forgiven.

Off come the bra and pants. Into the bottom of the bag, they go on top of her slacks and tee shirt. She positions the bag bang in the middle of his doorway so he can't possibly miss it, and jumps inside. It's a very tight fit and she has to curl herself into a foetal ball. Doing up the zip from the inside is quite tricky, because she can't rotate her arms far enough; but she uses both hands and then both feet to close it firmly, and then she is snuffling inside the bag snuggled up with her underwear, as though she is a little animal getting ready to hibernate.

Inside the sack, it's pitch dark. Her watch is luminous, but she can't move her arm around to see it. She has no context in which to tell the passing of time, save that she feels first her legs and then each arm go to sleep on her. There won't be any jumping out of the bag like the jack in the box. He is going to have to rub her all over to restore sensation to her limbs before he parts them and has his way with her. All will be forgiven. She lies there motionless whilst the cold penetrates her limbs.

The Book of Thoth

I am sitting on Nick's knee. I used to be Nick, but now he is Nick and I am Set. We are perched on one of my favourite tinpot Dictator thrones; the ermine one with the skull armrests with the built-in ashtrays and matching footstool. This one is known as the Elephant Throne, because the armrests are two huge contraband tusks before they taper off into the skull handles at the ends. It doesn't rest on conventional chair legs; the legs are the cruelly sawn-off feet of an Indian elephant. Spread open upon our thighs is the Great Book of Thoth. I am wearing a waistcoat of endangered species.

We thumb through the Book like an old couple going back through their family album.

"Oh, don't you just love that one!" exclaims Nick.

He is pointing to a very famous montage known as Photo Op. Two political artists, Peter Kennard and Cat Philipps were rifling through old pictures in the Guardian newspaper archives when they came across a selfie taken by Tony Blair during his 2005 election campaign. He had snapped his grinning face on his smart phone in front of a group of naval cadets.

Kennard and Philipps removed the cadets and replaced them with napalm, the billowing black smoke of the shock and awe bombs exploding like the fires of hell. And Blair's delighted self in the foreground. They named it Photo Op and it became a definitive image of the Iraq war and of the maniacal grinning stare of the criminal who helped George Bush get it all started.

We rifle through the pages. Nick keeps licking his claw for extra traction. I might get him one of those finger stools from Rymans. "Ah, the mammoth!" we both exclaim together. We are looking at the photojournalist's piece on how Spud Mullins extracted mammoth's DNA from a perfectly preserved example discovered in the frozen wastes of Siberia, and grew a genuine woolly mammoth, only to find that some evil ivory hunter had hacked off its huge tusks and, and... Nick is tracing the words of the report in the Financial Times with his dampened claw...

"And made them into the Elephant Throne!" we exclaim in unison. We really are getting to be more and more like an old couple, finishing one another's sentences. Of course that's not how the story in the FT ends. It says poachers have removed the tusks and they will be on the black market. It says that it's going to take Spud another thirty years to grow another woolly mammoth in a laboratory. He's going to grow the new one with the DNA of the one he just made. Nothing goes to waste. Perpetual motion.

Little do they know what really became of the tusks.

There are ashtrays in the ends of the armrests. I am flicking the ash off my joint. I really shouldn't do this; but Calypso had left the makings on the table; so why not? Sometimes I think I'm never going to grow up. Sometimes I am Peter Parker. Sometimes I am *Peter Pan*. Sometimes I am Nick Jobs. Sometimes I am Ingram Frazier. Sometimes I am the god Set. The fucking joint is making my head tick.

Curse the bastard who dismantled the Birdwood, the one place I used to be able to find refuge and order when the neurons in my brain were fizzing. Control, control. I need to take back control of my own head. I get up and go to look out of the huge picture windows at my millionaire's riverscape. But all I can see is the giant illuminated bobbin of the London Eye spinning and casting its reflections along the scabrous Thames.

We thumb on through the pages: it's all in there: the tip from the doors of the Birdwood about hanging the luminous watch around your dick; the balled up wax paper with the gold medal inside engraved with *Sequimini me* from the night Sydney tried to summon the god Pan, Seth's black human flag: Isis in a wingsuit. The Senate House leap that crippled Sydney. The photograph of the Crucifixion and the Face of Christ. They're all recorded in here.

The War on Islam.

We turn the pages. There are some reviews of my DNA exhibition: the one that benefited from all the free publicity that flowed from the Prime Minister's wife's failure to get an injunction to close it down. I'd had the sputum she'd hawked on my handkerchief at the Sex Club reunion analysed and we'd produced a diagram of her DNA encoding alongside naked photographs of her taken by me in her mis-spent youth, and they were hung side by side, like the pages of a book, parallel.

On the left were the gorgeous life studies of what she used to look like before she started going haggard. On the right, she was decomposed into endless spirals of double helices. It was a *reductio ad absurdum*, the peeling away of successive layers of the onion, the ultimate striptease. And the wonderful thing was that it was genuinely her DNA. I included some comparable studies of naked men and their DNA blueprints, with the intended result that Olumidé only accounted for about 10% of the content, so as to pre-empt the critics labelling the exhibition misogynistic.

I'd gotten the newly albino'd Harry to wack off into an ignition tube so that we could do a parallel DNA/Life Study of him also for the exhibition. I'd told him he could have any material he required for the purpose of jerking his jism into the tube. You know what he'd chosen? My photos of the Prime Minister's wife. I was surprised, but it seemed a lot of other men and women shared his fantasy.

When someone uploaded the pictures onto the Internet, she got more hits than Percy the Persian Blue who rides around the house on a micro scooter. It seemed that half the nation was tossing itself off to pictures of the PM's wife. Pictures that would have remained private if she hadn't offended me.

The damnedest thing was that Harry's DNA wasn't entirely human. The closest match was Snowflake, the former albino gorilla in Barcelona zoological gardens.

After her lawyers, aided and abetted by her reputation management consultants, conspicuously and publicly failed to obtain an injunction to can the exhibition, having drawn so much attention to it, she then had to spend the ensuing days denying that she'd had an affair with me at Cambridge, something which the media refused to buy given the explicit nature of the photographs. My only comment was *No comment*. The media interpreted that as me being a perfect Gentleman. No-one seemed to notice the glaring disconnect between being a perfect Gentleman and exhibiting naked pictures of your ex-girlfriend.

It was a despicable thing to do, but I'd never have been able to do it if she hadn't gobbed on me.

I don't know if gay Ingram was more furious that half the world had seen his wife naked before he had, or by the fact that the Judge who refused to grant the injunction was his old pupil master, or by the fact that all this nasty publicity was emanating from his own Spin Doctor. But his ratings have been going down since that injudicious

War on Islam business and that pesky *fatwah*. People say he has lost his judgment. I have abandoned him. I am working for myself now.

And it was all my fault. I had been given infinite powers. Despite the fact that they had come from the devil, I had decided to use them for good. I had installed an idealistic young socialist politician, a devout Catholic and family man, a former barrister and champion of human rights, no less, into No 10, Downing Street. What could possibly have gone wrong with that?

Devolution, fragmentation, plebiscites, referenda, pandemic, Brexit, the War on Islam.

"Not long to go now," says Nick. "Only one page left and you'll have filled the book up."

"Then what?"

"Then what? Time to give the book to your successor. You know where to find him?"

"Sure. At the point where the parallel lines meet."

The entire night has passed with the god Set/Nick in a trice. Must be a double time scheme lurking in there someplace. I have to resume control now. I am Ingram Frazier, the Prime Minister. Seeking to trace my destiny through the acts of others has got me nowhere. Everything always goes wrong in the end.

The idea of putting the young, idealistic, devout Ingram Frazier in charge with all his socialist ideals and human rights, aided and abetted by Burt Sully, seemed to tick all the right boxes at the time I made it happen. But it had all gone horribly wrong. No, in the future that I am writing, just as I became the god Set, I am going to have to become Ingram Frazier. I am going to have to roll my sleeves up and do the work myself. When the going gets tough, the tough get going.

I will become Ingram. I will slip into him like a succubus. I will sort out this fucking country. I will put the world to rights.

And I will fuck his wife.

I have work to do. I show Nick to the door. There is a suspicious looking object on my door step. A wheelie-bag about 1 metre long. I need to 'phone for the police. As I walk away from the house, I am ringing Hugo on my cell phone. For fuck's sake get a move on! This is a communication from Nick Jobs, The Prime Minister's Director of Communications. I have my own London bobby on speed dial posted at the end of the road.

Within minutes, the street is evacuated and yellow incident tape blows in the light wind like prayer scrolls on a Tibetan mountainside. Hugo carries out a controlled explosion. It turns out there was no device in the bag, just a load of severed limbs and scorched red hair. Who would play a prank like that on me, I wonder?

I am striding towards the Humber Super Snipe in the basement car park. The car that I concealed from Calypso, because if she knew I had accepted it, and still had it years later, she would think the old control freak was still controlling me, and that's not how it is. I control everyone else.

I wonder if she will ever come back to me. I am suicidal. I want to be dragged out to sea on the riptide and die.

Only a few pages to go.

Sir Nick Jobs

Ingram kept that one very quiet. In the New Year's Honours List, I read that the Prime Minister has knighted me. This is one for the books: someone else surprising me by having me read about me in the papers first before I have put the story out there myself. I double check with MSN news and Google in case this is some post-truth fake news sewn by some new spin doctor that Ingram has retained. But no; it seems to be the truth. I have received a knighthood for services to spin. I've been kicked upstairs. This must be the wackiest, least-deserved elevation since Professor Self-Harming Harry.

I don't want to meet with the Queen. I don't want to go down on one knee. No, no, no. I'll tell Ingram to stick his knighthood where the sun don't shine.

I must go down to the seas again
For the call of the running tides

A nice brisk walk on New Year's Day. Out with the old.

The Meeting of the Parallel Lines

I'd said I wasn't coming back here in a hurry, and it's been more than 10 years.

I park in the usual place, next to a brand smacking new Rolls Royce with a chauffeur in a beaked cap pulled down over his eyes. The Rolls has a weird paint job. More precisely, what is weird is the absence of any paint. It's all chromium. It resembles the silver nitrate of the Face of Christ. I look into its shiny facets to see if a face of Christ is lurking in the back there. But all I can see are multiple reflections of myself in the chrome as in a hall of mirrors. There is nothing else in the car park apart from the fallen leaves blowing around in the dirt.

Usual place I say; it seems like a lifetime since I was last here, but the Humber Super Snipe is still running smoothly, as though it knows its own way. I did not come here. It brought me back to this place itself, like the faithful horse in the children's stories, the tales for the Lost Boys who never grow up. I get the book out of the boot. Fucking things weighs a ton. But, needs must, as they say.

The Rolls looks out of place. The driver's window opens a crack, and a plume of cigarette smoke trickles out. I catch a glimpse of the chauffeur. His hands are hidden in mittens. I think I might recognise his face, but he won't look me in the eye. If I owned a chrome-plated Rolls, I wouldn't let the fucking chauffeur smoke in it.

I lock up the car. Six times I lock up the car. Not because I am paranoid that someone is trying to steal it, but because, in the days these cars were made, you got a whole fistful of keys to drive it out of the showroom with, each one locking or unlocking something different. The proud owner was more like a jailer than a driver.

Having locked all four doors with four different keys; having locked the boot with a fifth key and the locking petrol cap with the sixth, I shove the bunch of keys into my jacket pocket and wander off towards the smell of the sea, the smell of what we used to call ozone, before we discovered the ozone was actually stored in a layer above the troposphere, or such as was left of it, before one had depleted it with the detritus from the tailpipe of one's Super Snipe. There was no ozone. It was just the smell of rotting seaweed.

And then I chuck the keys away. We're not going anyplace else. You can flick forward for yourself and see that we are almost at the end.

They land crossing over each other in the sand: crossed keys: symbol of St Peter.

There is a brisk but pleasant breeze blowing off a hidden ocean. It's been showering, but the late afternoon sun is breaking through the patchy clouds. I glance up at them scudding past the tree tops as I make my progress from the car park, past the decaying hulk that used to be the Cellulite Hotel and Spa, through the pine woodlands in the general direction of the strand, that fugitive low tide that never quite reaches the beach: a margin with no edge.

As we're going for a walk, it seems right to switch on the Walkman in my pocket and shove the buds in my ears. It's *Tubular Bells*. I adjust my stride to the pace.

I am transferring The Book of Thoth from one shoulder to the other. Its sharp pages are giving me a thousand paper cuts; but the smell of the pines is clean and antiseptic, like *Balafre*.

The sun is so bright I have to put my cheetahs on. Bright and low: I cast a long, skinny shadow, like one of Giacometti's walking man statues, or like Mr Fantastic when he is fully extended, or like when I made my ceremonial entrance to this godforsaken planet and descended the cloud staircase with all my pomp and circumstance and army of Setans.

I pause for a rest and unclasp the hasp that closes the volume to view the snaps of that grand occasion, but those images have fallen from the pages of the book, because new ones have replaced them; images of an exploding wheelie-bag have been added to the pages at the end. They're quite disturbing.

I shut the book again and resume my amble as the pine trees grow more scattered in the dappled light and glimpses of the beach begin to shine through the lacy network of tree roots. And there they begin, from the point where the forest gives way to the beach and stretching endlessly towards the invisible crash and blur of the North Sea: the two parallel lines. As far as I can discern, two furrows etched into the sandy mush about one metre apart, slicing both the loam and the lugworm.

I redistribute the weight of the book on my right shoulder and trudge one weary step after another watching my shadow attenuate itself attempting to squeeze between the two ploughed grooves pointing out to sea. The light rain starts falling again. In some of the furrows stagnant water is collecting. The meeting of the parallel lines never seems to come any closer. What else was I expecting?

Then, as I am on the point of calling it a day and taking the millstone of the fucking book back to the publisher, the parallel lines flex and move. They remain parallel, but they begin to trace a radius of 180 degrees to the left, and then, slicing back on themselves like a caduceus. The lines describe a matching radius to the right, before resuming their two continuous ditches towards the sea. It's like a giant figure 8.

Having fruitlessly followed the tramlines of these pointless radii to the left and right, I feel like I am back in the Birdwood reading the runes on the walls and doors: "How to keep an Irishman amused for hours—see other wall".

I turn back, fed up with it all. I turn back to retrace my steps to the car park. But then I see it. Or more to the point, I was seeing it all along, but I needed to stand back from it to see the pattern. Sometimes you see things better when you are not looking at them. The diversion in the straight lines had described a huge ∞, and then the straight lines resume.

Not waving, but drowning!

Not an 8!
Not an 8!
It's a Lemniscate!

He is fooling with me. It's just a pun in the sand, the lowest form of wit. He is playing with my mind. But he is also giving me a signpost to infinity, where the parallel lines meet. Just as I was about to give up and go back, I find new resolution: I am a sturdy Knight Templar. I turn around again, spinning like my little ballerina. The book is leading me to the hidden sea.

And now, a stiff breeze blowing from the invisible ocean is ruffling the leaves of the book and its words and its images are falling from the pages; they are writing themselves in the sand. The two parallel lines are the margins and random words are written in the column of silt between the margins. They stretch into infinity like the credits rolling at the end of a film:

@
SLOB
ANIRELLAB
DNILB
LRIG
OSPYLAC
SULEGNA
TES
ACYL
TSOL
DOOWDRIB

And such like, on and on. The book is becoming lighter as it spills its contents. The calligraphy in the sand is in the same handwriting that first appeared to me in the condensation on the windows, asking to be released, and in the characters on Seth's body. I try to scoop the words up and put them back in the book, but they just run through my fingers like the contents of an hourglass. It is the nonsense writing of a printer's proof. Or optophonetic poetry. But I keep walking, just because I want to read it all. I want to see how it ends. It's crazy, but there has to be some meaning in it all, or what was the point?

As the minutes tick by, the distant soughing of the sea becomes a more pronounced whelp, telling me I am edging nearer. The huge open expanse of this strand seems to go on forever and apart from the insipid clouds brushing across the horizon, everything is always the same, as if I am standing still and an unseen stagehand is revolving the same patch of beach in an endless loop behind me. The only thing that changes are the credits, this constant unspooling of ribbons of nonsensical text. But if we are reading the credits, I tell myself, we must be coming to the end.

After I have been following the grooves for maybe 40 minutes, the breeze has stiffened; there is a distinct dampness in the air, which is beginning to penetrate not just my clothes but the very marrow of my bones; there is no warmth left in the sun. But these are all earnests that I am finally approaching the sea. And then, quite suddenly in the scattered and shimmering light, the blur that lives at the end of the ruts begins to sharpen, as one focuses the lens of a camera.

I am following the tracks of a wheelchair.

By the water's edge, I come face to face with him. He is bald now, save for an outcrop of hair at the back of his skull, secured in the Chinese queue. The palms of his hands that have spun the parallel wheels are smudged with the mud and mica of the beach. He still sports his long, plectrum nail. But the inner skin on his thumbs is worn paper thin and shiny by years of pushing the wheelchair. Just like Harry had said, his famous Shaolin goatee looks like it has been snapped off and glued back on carelessly.

Sidney Syzygy is sitting in his seat regarding the shimmering silver sea. He still has that twinkle in his eye, even if his brows are furrowed as deep as the wheel ruts of his chair. Ginger beer and not champagne.

A light drizzle begins to fall.

"Can I take you for a push anywhere today?" I ask.

He turns his head sideways and looks me up and down, surveying what the years and worse have done to me and the worse still we have done to ourselves, before giving our customary response: "God damn the pusher man!"

Then, seeing I am struggling with the book: "Give it here!"

I pass him the Book of Thoth, leaving my hands free to grasp the two handles of his chair that I turn around 180 degrees so that we are heading back towards the car park, traversing the same tramlines that brought him here. How else? We are in a rut. Looking over his shoulder, I see him turning the book from front to back over and again, searching for the title, but finding only the symbol, ∞.

"Well," he says, considering the tome, "never judge a book by its cover, eh?"

He opens the book up, but it is empty. All the words are spilled out on the beach. I see they are blowing away now, incorporeal, ephemeral, Sybil's leaves. Another hand must begin it.

I push him back, back past the wormholes and the plover's tracks, back towards the piebald beach huts and crabshacks.

"Look at their colours!" he says, waving his parchmental plectrum thumb towards a cluster of seven beach huts with weather-worn wooden ladders leading down from their raised entrances to where the sea must have reached millennia before. I see the sequence from left to right is Violet-Indigo-Blue-Green-Yellow-Orange-Red.

And in the sky above them, fuck me, but there's a double rainbow!

Bols Ballerina

Start-Rite Kids

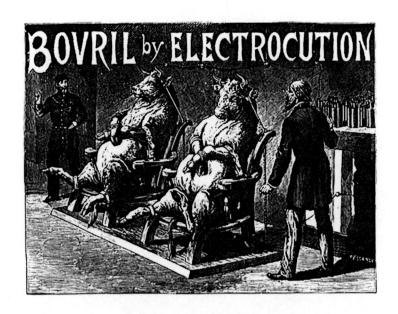

The Ghost of a Flea

Snowflake

Patented alarm clock candle

The author's wife, at their home in Cadaqués standing beside the painting, 'Cadaqués in China' by Ilich Roimeser, which commemorates the cloning of the entire Mediterranean village of Cadaqués at Xiamen Bay, China

Athlete demonstrating the Human Flag

Suggested further reading:
Night Climbing in Cambridge, published under the pseudonym
Whipplesnaith in 1937